SCANDALOUS

Three Daring Charades in the Pursuit of Love

BEVERLEY EIKLI
BEVERLEY OAKLEY

SANI
PUBLISHING

For my mother. A kind and loving person who made everyone she spoke to feel better about their day.
What a wonderful story-teller she was.

And for my father. An intelligent, fascinating man. I know where I got my adventurous spirit from!

LADY OLIVIA'S BUTTERFLY

CHAPTER 1

W iltshire, 1816

'YOUR REPUTATION IS in tatters, Olivia' – Aunt Eunice looked up from adjusting the stirrups of the little grey mare upon which her niece sat nervously – 'and you have lost everything! The time has come to take charge of your life."

Olivia gripped the pommel with whitened knuckles. Opening her mouth to mutter that the truth was of little account when opinion was against her, she gasped instead as the docile animal shifted beneath her.

So much for the studied detachment she'd cultivated during seven years of marriage with Lucien. Her fear was as transparent as that of a frightened schoolgirl's. Now she was on a madcap venture doomed to fail, showing as much backbone in the face of her aunt's determination as she had when her late husband bent her to his will.

Grey storm clouds scudded from the west and the icy wind stung her face.

How was she to succeed in this madcap venture? 'An unfit mother, a faithless wife....' The words Lucien had used to brand her—to damn her forever in his will—were imprinted on her brain. Unable to conquer her terror of the placid beast, she begged one last time, 'Please, Aunt Eunice, *must* I do this?'

'You must fight for justice, Olivia.' The determined 'brook-no-opposition' expression that characterized Eunice Dingley's plain, leathery face brought memory flooding back. Olivia was obedient now but how well she recalled the altercations they'd had when she had been a strong-willed child. How single minded had been her rebellion eight years ago as a headstrong debutante?

She had paid the price; it was why she was here.

Stepping back into soft mud that sucked at her boots, Aunt Eunice regarded her critically. 'Well, child,' she said with grudging admiration, 'you look well enough. Don't tear your riding habit when you fall off.'

Olivia winced as her aunt raised her hand to slap her horse's flank.

'What if he's like Lucien?' she hedged, bringing her mount around. 'Mr Atherton has already refused my request once. He must believe the stories—'

'He is a man.' Aunt Eunice said it as if that fact alone guaranteed Olivia's success. 'For goodness' sake, Olivia, we've already agreed this is your best course, regardless of what Reverend Kirkman thinks.'

The Reverend Kirkman. The knot of fear in Olivia's stomach tightened. The reverend had his own ideas as to how Olivia should win back her son.

This was not one of them.

She closed her eyes. Yet surely this was the best way? If there was any justice in Max Atherton's heart then truth and openness must triumph over the lies which had dogged her during her marriage and cost her the custody of her son?

A great black crow had settled on the dry stone wall in front of her.

Like her aunt, it regarded her with tilted head, eyes bright.

Aunt Eunice laid her hand on Olivia's knee and her tone softened. 'Max Atherton came back from the Peninsular campaign a war hero. That, for a start, distinguishes him from his cousin. I've heard nothing to suggest he bears any resemblance to Lucien. Entrance him, Olivia, as you entranced that good-for-nothing husband of yours.'

'Mr Atherton believes Lucien's version of accounts. You read his reply to my letter.' It was not the cold that now made her tremble.

With a distracted frown Aunt Eunice smoothed Olivia's russet skirts. 'He has no other account to go by. He thinks he's doing what's best for the boy.' Squeezing her knee, she said briskly, 'Go, now! Take that tumble in his barley field so you can set the record straight.'

***

MAX SQUINTED THROUGH THE BLINDING RAIN AS HE TURNED UP THE collar of his greatcoat.

It was hard to be sure from this distance, but the little grey mare sheltering beneath the elm tree at the far end of the paddock appeared to be equipped with a side saddle.

A lady's mount ... but where was the lady?

His gaze raked the sodden field, sensing his stallion's .

'No carrots or bran mash until we find her, Odin,' he murmured into his stallion's ear, sensing its reluctance to proceed in the face of the rising storm.

He'd been returning from his inspection of the new sheep he had been breeding in the northern paddock when his eye had been caught by a flash of scarlet. A female? Curious to make the acquaintance of any woman under forty in these sparsely populated parts, he'd watched the rider canter around the bend that separated his property from his neighbour's, hoping she'd cross his path later. Instead, he'd happened upon her horse.

Lightning split the black sky and Odin snorted. Across the field, eerie in the strange light, the little grey mare gave a frightened whinny as it eyed them balefully.

'Steady, boy,' soothed Max, urging his mount forward, unprepared for the thunder that boomed like cannon fire, seeming to split the sky. Odin reared, forelegs pawing the air and Max strained to keep his seat as he scanned the field desperately for a sight of the woman as her riderless mare bolted.

He glanced down, dread spearing him as he caught a glimpse of russet; heard a faint female cry. Then, muscles knotted and straining, he hauled on the reins as he fought to control his terrified stallion.

Another crack of thunder. Foam sprayed from the mouth of the maddened animal which bucked again.

Before its four legs were on firm ground Max hurled himself from the saddle and ran to kneel at the woman's side as Odin reared again. Pushing back the folds of his multi-tiered coat that whipped his face, he felt for a pulse at the side of her neck.

She had cheated death but he feared the extent of her injuries. A bloody gash streaked the mud which caked her forehead; her body lay twisted. She did not stir as his hands checked the limbs beneath her skirts for breaks or other obvious injury.

Raising his head, he assessed the distance to Elmwood. He could see the battlements above the froth of rain-lashed trees which gave his home its name. In fine weather with no burden it might be a fifteen minute walk. Now, with the ground a marsh and the wind and weight of sodden skirts it would be more than twice that, but he could not leave her to fetch help.

She was still unconscious when he lifted her. Turning his head from the sharp, icy rain that knotted the grass about his legs, he pushed forward, the wind keening like a banshee. His neck and shoulders ached and his breath rasped painfully. The heavens, it seemed, had combined all its force to hinder his efforts.

Once, he'd carried an injured soldier to safety under enemy fire; but there had been no storm and the artillery barrage had left them unscathed.

Now, the going was much harder. Glancing down once more, he was reassured at seeing the young woman's eyelids flutter and wondered, vaguely, if she were beautiful beneath all that mud. Not that it mattered. He'd been struck with a sense of purpose he'd not felt since he'd volunteered to fight for King and country nearly eight years ago.

Gradually the wind calmed and the rain became a gentle shower as the storm moved on. Reaching the tree-lined drive which led from the park to the formal gardens he tried to recall if Amelia had mentioned any newcomers to the neighbourhood. His sister's efforts to find him a wife after he'd returned from the Peninsula too battle-crazed to care suggested she would have.

'Max!' shrieked Amelia as she stood on the top step having sent two footmen to relieve her brother of his burden. 'Who is she? What has happened?' She had seen him from the drawing-room window labouring up the drive amidst the steady rain.

'Take her to my room,' he directed, resting his aching back against the wainscoting in the downstairs entrance hall.

'The blue room,' Amelia countered, adding, 'Don't be ridiculous, Max. What would she think to wake up in a gentleman's bed?'

'If she wakes,' Max said, glowering, because he wanted to have her in his room where he could watch over her, and where he had the tools to dress her wounds and set her bones, if necessary.

'Of course she'll wake,' Amelia said, sharply.

Thick dust sheets were spread upon the large tester in preparation. Amelia had wanted to strip the linen, but Max had decried such inhospitable practicality, reminding her it was not her house.

'And only yours, Max, for a few more years,' his sister muttered, as she made the counter order of dust sheets to Mrs Watkins, the housekeeper.

Ignoring her, Max also asked for a fresh nightgown, and a comb.

'One would think you were in the habit of attending to the needs of a lady, Max,' Amelia said, more archly than unkindly as her heels clicked across the boards to the window embrasure from where she regarded him with amusement.

'And plenty of hot water.' Rubbing his aching arms Max took a seat by the unconscious young woman's side. 'So you have no idea who she might be?' he asked, pushing back his cowlick. 'There's been no talk of visitors to the neighbourhood?'

Amelia shook her head. 'Do you think she's broken anything? Shall I check?'

'Her limbs seem in fine form,' Max replied, with a wry smile as he took up the sponge Mrs Watkins had just placed beside him. 'As for her face, she has a nasty cut.'

Amelia came up beside him. 'She's beautiful,' she remarked, for it was true, and Amelia never minced the truth. Or kept her thoughts to herself. 'But don't get romantic ideas into your head, Max, for she's probably spoken for, or is a widow with no money and six children, and you know very well you can't possibly take a wife to suit you unless she has at least two thousand a year.'

Gently, Max rubbed at a smudge of dirt along their visitor's jawline.

'I shall do whatever I please to suit myself, Amelia,' he murmured, gazing at the perfection of the unknown young woman's features: the gently curving mouth, the wide-set eyes beneath finely arched brows, the high, rounded cheekbones, 'for I answer to no one, and certainly not to you.'

※

THE FIRST SUGGESTION THAT OLIVIA WAS NOWHERE FAMILIAR CAME from the scent of lavender. Without opening her eyes she sniffed appreciatively. Aunt Eunice was not fond of lavender but surely only she would have sprinkled it upon Olivia's pillow in deference to Olivia's partiality for it? Because Olivia was not well. Vaguely she acknowledged this, for the dull throbbing of her ankle and the sharper pain across her brow impinged upon the general comfort she felt nestled into what surely must be the softest mattress she had ever slept upon.

She opened her eyes with a start and struggled on to her elbows, her heart pounding at the confusion of her last memories.

Aunt Eunice had returned to their cottage. Wherever she was, Olivia was to fight this battle, alone.

The day was well advanced. Sunlight slanted into a large and airy room, handsomely decorated in shades of blue. She noticed a book upon the chest beside the bed. A book of poems. Byron? She squinted to make out the author and her head began to ache. Touching her forehead she felt the bandage.

'Good. You're awake,' came a voice from the doorway, and she twisted her head to see a young man advancing, his face obscured by the pile of books he carried. 'I was beginning to grow concerned.'

Bowing slightly after he'd deposited his burden upon a low table, he introduced himself before taking a seat at her bedside and, to her astonishment, picking up her wrist.

'Your pulse is a good deal stronger,' he said. 'You appear to have twisted your ankle quite badly, but only you can assess the extent of that injury. The wound above your eye looks worse than it is. It should heal with no scar. In the meantime I thought you might enjoy some poetry.'

She was too taken aback to utter a word. Perhaps struck dumb with horror would describe it better, she thought, as she stared into eyes the colour of rain-washed slate. The dark, fathomless, unreadable eyes that had belonged to her late husband.

She swallowed. Max Atherton, her late husband Lucien's cousin: the man into whose keeping her son had been placed. With those eyes, confident and inscrutable beneath a high forehead, the straight nose and mouth she had once thought sensitive, it could be none other. He might be smiling but it was an act. Could only be one.

She gathered her wits. He must not see her fear. He would take advantage of it. Make her do things against her will.

Taking a deep breath she fought for control. She could not afford to make mistakes. Lucien was dead while Olivia had survived. She needed only the return of her son to make her happy, and she would fight for Julian to the death. He was the only reason she was here. She and Aunt Eunice had worked out every detail to prove her innocence, to make Max Atherton see the truth. Truth would be her ally, yet she felt the same cornered desperation she had when Lucien had confronted her.

She sucked in another breath. The secret of her survival lay in her ability to act. She could be whoever she needed to be.

'Mr Atherton.' She repeated his name, gaining confidence from the unmasked admiration she saw in his eyes. 'How very kind of you to come to my assistance' – she swallowed again, desperate to keep the fear from her voice – 'when I was so foolish as to take a tumble and thus put me in your debt.'

'On the contrary, you have enlivened what promised to be a very dull week – now that I know you are not mortally wounded.' His smile was open, but his eyes ...

She turned her head away. Any sign of vulnerability would put her in his power, but how could she banter with a man who looked so like Lucien it put the fear of God into her? How could she trust herself not to jeopardize everything for which she had worked so hard?

'When I looked down to see you lying trapped beneath my horse's hoofs, while he was rearing above you, maddened by the storm—' The visions he conjured up were too close to her memories of being trapped beneath Lucien. His description could just as easily have been that of her husband's mad eyes blazing, foam and spittle flying from lips which had just bruised and bitten her.

She tried not to whimper.

'Forgive me, my dear Mrs Templestowe,' Mr Atherton said, his tone remorseful, his expression concerned as he bent over her. 'I have a deplorable habit of not dressing up the truth when it may cause pain. Too long a bachelor, I suppose,' he added with a smile.

'How do you know my name?' whispered Olivia.

'I made investigations around the neighbourhood and learned you were lodging at the White Swan.'

She had offered the publican her maiden name, for how could she present herself as Lady Farquhar in these parts before she had convinced Mr Atherton that the name was not synonymous with sin and vice?

The impulse to correct him died on her lips.

Yet, surely, the pleasantness of Mr Atherton's smile was a calculated ploy to trick her into letting down her reserves?

He was smiling at her, now, the corners of his eyes crinkling into well-worn lines as if good humour were his natural state. But didn't grand manipulators have any number of ploys at their fingertips? Lucien had seemed the most charming of them all, and a man couldn't sink to depths of depravity deeper than those he had gleefully dug using pain and threats, violence and humiliation?

She had come here imagining his cousin was different and that the truth would answer.

Trying to hide her trembling beneath the bedcovers, Olivia forced her mouth into another cool, arch smile. 'Then you know you are harbouring a foolish, helpless widow.'

She was satisfied by the candidness of his look. No veiled, hidden knowledge lurking in those dark depths. Lucien loved to gloat, murmuring his depraved suspicions for which he had already condemned her.

He continued to smile. 'One who is guilty of nothing more than misjudging the weather.'

If only that were true. Shame welled up in her bosom but she kept silent. How could she possibly stare into those slate-grey eyes and tell him she was the shameless widow of his late cousin? Like as not he would punish her so that not even Reverend Kirkman's plan, if that was ever put into play, would restore her son to her keeping.

She closed her eyes and fought the tears.

She'd wanted so much to tell her version of the truth and know the catharsis of exoneration.

Smiling, she replied, 'And I have paid the price.' Her eyelids fluttered closed once more as she murmured, 'My apologies, but I am very tired. Perhaps you could amuse me with Byron's poetry, later.'

SHE SLEPT, WAKING ON THE MORNING OF THE SECOND DAY TO FIND Mr Atherton again at her side. Charming. Attentive. Ready to read Byron to her.

His doctor attended her.

She slept again.

On the third day, she woke to find her lethargy gone, and her senses aroused by the single object which had brought her here: to find Julian.

So far there had been no sign of a child, anywhere. No childish laughter, no nursery-maid, no children's toys. The drawing room where Mr Atherton carried her would be out of bounds to children, but there must be evidence of a two-and-a-half-year-old boy, somewhere.

Olivia thanked Mrs Watkins for the clean, dry clothes with which she supplied her. She was quiet as the housekeeper combed and dried her hair then helped her into the handsome blue velvet gown Max's sister had lent her. The fashions had changed since she had last paid attention to what she wore.

Where *was* Julian? Her heart thundered as she sat at the dressing table, forcing herself to sit still. Since the moment she had entered this house it had taken all her willpower not to leap to her feet and go dashing up and down corridors, like a madwoman, calling his name.

She nodded dismissal to Mrs Watkins and pressed her fingertips to her eyes. Why could Mr Atherton not have simply escorted her back to the White Swan?

If he *were* the antithesis of his cousin, Olivia had not the first idea how to appeal to the instincts of a man who was charming, kind and well meaning and would no doubt be horrified to learn of Olivia's past.

Olivia had learned how to play the devil. Not a man of charm and kindness.

However that was of no account. She would be gone by dinner time. Her mission now was simply to discover what distinguished Max Atherton from his late cousin so she could better craft her next anonymous entreaty to have her son returned to her care.

Dropping her hands she stared, distracted, at her reflection, then rose gnawing her little fingernail.

For so long she'd not made a single important decision on her own. Everything had been decided for her from what she did each day to what she wore.

Leaning toward the mirror she studied herself properly. The simple blue gown flattered her light hair and peaches and cream colouring. She looked young and – frowning – she thought, innocent.

Innocent? She gave a mocking smile as the familiar poisonous misery flooded thickly into her veins.

Carefully she smiled again: the kind of smile she'd practised so many times as a seventeen-year-old debutante determined to rise above the rest and waltz off with the season's most eligible catch.

Then she thought of young Julian, her darling baby, and her whole body throbbed with pain and longing. Choking on a sob she covered her face with her hands while she forced herself to breathe steadily, to slay the demons that mocked her from the darkness so that she could focus on the task at hand. Max *seemed* as unlike Lucien as it was possible to be. What if his kindness wasn't an act? The interest in his eye when he'd looked at her suggested he—

The flare of excitement she felt was quickly extinguished by self disgust.

How she hated the effect she had on men. She turned quickly away from the sight of her reflection, her skirts catching the handle of the silver-backed mirror on the edge of the dressing table.

Sending it spiralling to the ground.

She froze as she heard it shatter, ears attuned to the sound of approaching footsteps heralding a possible witness to her crime. Lucien had been violently superstitious. He'd have beaten her if she'd broken a mirror in his house.

And the servants would have told him. He'd have made sure of it.

The mirror lay at her feet, its back of figured silver uppermost, offering no indication as to whether the glass were shattered. Nor were there any sound of footsteps, and of course it was ridiculous to imagine Mr Atherton or his servants would keep such a vigilant eye upon her. Those days were gone, though it was often hard to believe it.

Slowly she bent. If the mirror were smashed she would leave immediately.

But if it was not ...

Heart racing, not knowing what outcome she wanted, Olivia turned the mirror over.

And stared into her unfragmented reflection.

A strange cocktail of emotions flooded her: hope and despair, excitement and terror, but overall a renewal of courage that perhaps this time she could use her charms to find happiness.

Mr Atherton had read poetry to her. He had remained at her bedside for nearly an hour the previous day, chatting with her as if he enjoyed her company. And all the time she'd had a bandage on her head!

Perhaps she really could entrance Mr Atherton as she had entranced Lucien, and be happy for it. Then she thought of the dangers. Perhaps Mr Atherton's kindness was simply an act, a prelude to the seduction of his unexpected house guest. Lucien would have found such a challenge amusing.

Sickened, she retreated from her simple idea that Mr Atherton's inherent decency was such that he would be so overcome by the emotional reunion between mother and son when he finally produced Julian he'd understand the boy's place was with his mother, with Olivia.

Disconsolately, she picked up the unbroken mirror and returned it to the table. The truth was, she'd demonstrated how poorly she read a man's character—Lucien had proved that—so how could she have any faith in her assessment that Mr Atherton was nothing like Lucien? That he was kind? Lucien had been so very different when he was wooing her.

Still, Mr Atherton was her only hope.

She bit her lips and pinched colour into her cheeks, checking her smile one last time. Yes, she looked pretty and ingenuous. There would be no sultry pout and sinuous sashaying as she made her entrance: the kind of entrance she'd used to captivate Lucien. Stupid, ignorant child that she'd been! Mr Atherton wanted a demure, honest young woman, and that's what she'd give him, though in truth she had no idea what she was, anymore.

Her courage was bolstered when her host turned from where he'd been lounging against the mantelpiece and she saw only kindness and concern in those disturbingly familiar eyes.

Admiration was something she'd had enough of to last a lifetime yet this man's was somehow comforting. She need no longer check over her shoulder in case Lucien was silently observing, interpreting the lust he saw in other men's faces as a deliberate lure she'd set for which he'd punish her in private, later.

The genuine pleasure in Mr Atherton's expression caused an unexpected lurch in the space her heart once occupied.

'Amelia's gown becomes you, my dear Mrs Templestowe. It's the colour of your eyes.' He advanced, his hands outstretched as if he'd known her far longer than the few hours they'd spent in one another's company. 'No limp?' He looked almost disappointed.

Olivia gave a little shrug and smiled. She strove to sound light-hearted, though her heart thundered. How strange that she should feel such an overt attraction to the type of gentleman she had once derided for being tame and unexciting. Well, anyone had fallen into that category when she had been seventeen, simply because he were not the dangerous and alluring Lucien, Viscount Farquhar whom she must have at all costs. She dropped her eyes, her shyness not an act. 'I must have just bruised it. I'm sorry for disrupting whatever plans you might have had, Mr Atherton. You have been very kind but as soon as convenient I will return to the White Swan.'

She saw his disappointment as he led her to the seat closest to the fire, saying, 'It's not often storms around Elmwood result in such charming strays. But look.'

She was still taking in the possibilities as he pointed to the window. He was attracted to her. She should not be so surprised at that. It was not vanity, simply a fact.

Since Lucien's death the previous year, she'd grown weary of the desire and derision she received, in equal parts, as if her beauty were somehow a mask for the corruption within.

She saw that snow was falling fast in flurries of fat, floating flakes, but all she could think of was Lucien's lies. And how readily people had believed them.

'You can't possibly travel in weather like this, Mrs Templestowe.'

Briefly he squeezed her hand before indicating the white, frozen landscape. 'For one thing, you're not dressed for it and, until my sister returns with the carriage, I have no way of conveying you to your lodgings.'

He looked rather pleased at the state of affairs. Nor could Olivia deny she secretly felt the same. Though not in the same, uncomplicated way. Out of the corner of her eye, as she pretended to gaze with dismay upon the thickly falling snow, she realized that acknowledging an attraction to this man would be deeply dangerous.

Impossible, even. She needed to appeal to his obvious kindness, and she believed she could do that. Anything more would end in tears for both of them. She acknowledged the truth with weary resignation. Regardless of the temptations, she could not pander to her heart. Certainly not in *this* instance.

'And here is tea.' On cue the door opened to admit the parlour maid bearing a tray. 'Surely you don't object to a dish of strong hot tea while we wait for Amelia and the boys? They are staying with me while renovations are carried out on their home which is not far from here.'

'The boys?' Olivia knew she'd jumped at the phrase with too much feeling. Her mind had not been in the present. 'There is more than one, Mr Atherton?'

'There are three,' he replied, rolling his eyes with a smile as she settled herself back into her green wing back chair. 'But only one is mine.'

Oh, no, he's not. Somehow, Olivia managed to keep her smile from faltering. 'How old is your little boy?'

'Julian is two-and-a-half. He's been with me the past year since his father, my late cousin Lucien, Lord Farquhar, passed away.'

'The poor child is an orphan?' Anger and mortification threatened to swamp her.

It was small consolation that Max Atherton hedged his reply and obviously took care with his words, as if he were uncomfortable at having to explain the situation further.

'The lad was put into my keeping to avoid contagion when his father succumbed to fever. When Lucien died the following month and the will was read I discovered to my surprise – amazement, really – he'd made me the boy's legal guardian.'

'So his mother also died of fever.' Olivia made it sound a statement. She gave a pitying sigh, masking her anger with an expression of regret, as if it were the only explanation since not even the cruellest husband would exercise his legal rights to deny a mother her child.

'The mother was unfit to rear the Lord Farquhar's heir.'

Yet not unfit to be Lord Farquhar's wife? A terrible rage blackened her vision. She dropped her gaze, unable to give voice to her real feelings, instead murmuring, 'How terrible. I think perhaps I recall having heard something about Lady Farquhar.'

Max sighed and looked even more uncomfortable as he fiddled with his cufflink. 'Alas for the boy, she was a fortune hunter; a vain, showy creature who trapped Lucien into marriage, ran into debt and led an altogether dishonourable life.'

'Yet she was a mother. I cannot believe she behaved so heartlessly towards her son. Did it surprise you, Mr Atherton?'

'I never met her—'

Olivia relaxed with grim satisfaction only to jerk forward in alarm at his next words.

'—though I saw her at a ball, once, two years after the pair eloped.' She waited, breathless.

Mr Atherton indicated to her to pour. With shaking hand she lifted the teapot while he elaborated. 'She was with her husband, my cousin Lucien, but Amelia refused to meet her and as I was accompanying her I didn't make it an issue.'

'What did she look like?' Best to get it over and done with, if an unmasking were inevitable.

Max smiled as he accepted his tea and leaned back in the armchair opposite her. 'Beautiful. Like you, Mrs Templestowe.'

She swallowed; opened her mouth to speak but the words would not come.

He seemed not to notice. 'But obviously not a lady, like you, for her gown was ostentatious and' – he shrugged – 'the way she carried herself I could see the truth in the rumours.'

Lucien had decided what Olivia wore. She had given up selecting her gowns herself, merely waiting and wondering in her dressing room whether he wanted her to flaunt herself like a trollop, or deport herself like a nun. With her husband's moods increasingly erratic towards the end, she had learned to accept his last dictate with the meekness of a child.

Still, it took all her willpower not to slump, defeated, into her chair. The fact that the sight of her, albeit from a distance, only strengthened his belief in the rumours was somehow doubly devastating.

Licking her dry lips she whispered, 'So you never sought her out after ... after Lord Farquhar gave you her child?'

Max raised one eyebrow. The façade of genial, almost overeager host, slipped. Wearing a look of censure he suddenly resembled Lucien once more, and she clasped her hands together to stop them trembling as he added, 'One would expect she would make contact with *me*.' His voice was clipped, and his nostrils flared, as if he were speaking of someone utterly reprehensible. 'I suppose she did,' he eventually conceded, stirring his tea with a frown. 'But not until a good eight months had elapsed. I heard talk she had been gallivanting across the Continent in bad company until then.' He looked up, apology in his eye. 'I should not have spoken like that, Mrs Templestowe, yet I feel such a great anger on behalf of my ward as well as sorrow that he cannot know his mother.' He shrugged. Then his mood lightened and he smiled as if encouraging her to move on to another topic.

Olivia was not ready to let this one die.

'How would you receive Lady Farquhar if she did contact you and ask for the return of her child?' She tried to keep her tone offhand though her breath came in staccato bursts of anticipation as she waited for his answer.

Her host levelled at her a faintly quizzical look. Deliberating over his choice of words he said, 'I am bound to do whatever is in the best interests of the boy and as Lady Farquhar had taken a lover—'

'Surely not!'

Olivia's gasp was thankfully misinterpreted by Mr Atherton. 'I fear it is not as uncommon as you might believe, Mrs Templestowe, however discretion is required. It seems Lady Farquhar had neither discretion nor wit. My cousin was not a man to take such a matter lightly.'

On that they were agreed at least, Olivia thought silently as she racked her brains to think who her imaginary lover might have been. But then, Lucien had always imagined conspiracies when there were none. When death had finally snuffed him out, he'd been raving about that damned elusive treasure that had tormented him throughout their marriage. If he blamed Olivia for enticing him into marrying a penniless jade—as he termed her—he got a grim satisfaction out of punishing her for failing to lead him to it. As if he truly believed she knew its location and was hiding it from him.

She closed her eyes as a wave of fear threatened to swamp her. No! She would not think of it. Lucien could not truly have suspected Julian was not his. Then, upon a deep breath, she quickly dispelled any reflections of what some would consider wrongdoing. If she had ever done wrong, then Lucien's hand was behind it.

Distracted, she registered the chink of silver against china as Mr Atherton stirred his tea. His expression was distant. 'When I heard the boy had been made my ward I sold my commission and took up residence on this estate which I hold in trust for Julian until he comes of age.'

Olivia studied his face, searching for more similarities with Lucien. The physical family resemblance was there, particularly in the eyes, the straight nose and firm chin. Now that he was speaking of serious matters the almost self-conscious banter had gone. He was precise and direct and clearly decided on what he considered right and wrong. Very different from Lucien's arrogance.

Amidst the turmoil of her emotions, she felt a flicker of surprise. 'You gave up your career to look after a little boy?'

'I'd seen enough horror on the Peninsular to last a lifetime; was more than ready to leave the soldiering life and resume my agricultural obligations and' – he smiled – 'find a wife who would love this home and, hopefully, find me not too objectionable.' He cleared his throat.

'The boy needs a mother's love.'

Pointing at the plate of seed cake he exhorted her to try some, adding with sigh, 'Whatever Lady Farquhar's sins, her son's a lovelynatured little chap.'

She could not trust herself to speak. Raising her cup to take a sip her hand was trembling so much that tea spilled on to the Wilton carpet.

'My dear Mrs Templestowe, I think you are still in shock from your fall.' Unexpectedly Mr Atherton moved from the mantelpiece to take a seat on the arm of her chair, relieving her of her tea cup and setting it down upon the table.

Surprised and unsure what she should say as his hands gripped her shoulders, her heart quailed at his expression. There was blatant admiration in those slate-grey eyes and, like a traitor, her heart responded, just as it had with such dreadful results when she had cast in her lot with Lucien all those years ago.

But no, she could only be sceptical of such admiration. She was certainly no longer susceptible though his concern seemed genuine; and in addition to the admiration was something that looked dangerously like tenderness.

Tenderness? To succumb to tenderness would be too rash and much too dangerous. It was a trap!

And yet ...

'I've no idea how long you lay in the mud, soaked to the skin.' His voice was like a caress, full of comfort and reassurance. He leaned across her to pull on the embroidered bell pull, seemingly unembarrassed by their proximity. 'I shall have a warm rug fetched for you. Let me feel your hands. Why, they're as cold as ice. I'll rub them for you.'

Olivia closed her eyes and surrendered to those dangerous, unfamiliar feelings: comfort, safety. Exquisite peacefulness.

Mr Atherton held the key to her future happiness: her son. If he admired her and she could *prove* to him she deserved it, surely happiness might follow?

Then insidious reality intruded and she had to steel herself against her despair, her defeat.

She thought of Reverend Kirkman, imagining his outrage if he learned of the venture on which she had so rashly embarked.

It was he who had cautioned patience. Patience, he had exhorted her, was what she needed when once again her impetuous nature threatened her happiness. Patience would be her salvation, he'd soothed her, when she'd leapt up from her chair at the reading of Lucien's will and later, when he'd physically torn her from her carriage, overruling her determination to drive the horses herself in order to reclaim Julian from this man— this stranger, Max Atherton—who now had her child.

It was too much to take in. Olivia remained in her chair, her eyes still closed as Mr Atherton stopped his ministrations and tucked the blanket around her, making sure her feet were well insulated, bringing the warm wool up around her neck with tender, competent fingers.

'You must be very tired,' she heard him whisper, as he stroked a strand of hair back from her face. 'And quite obviously still in shock from your accident.'

'Yes,' she murmured, her head falling to one side. Vaguely, she realized it was resting against his thigh as he sat on the arm of her chair. She didn't move it. Didn't want to.

Mr Atherton could get her what she wanted.

Her son ... happiness.

If Reverend Kirkman would sanction it. She could be happy. She *could*.

She was in the midst of a dreamless sleep when it happened: the meeting upon which her whole life had been focused for more than a year, the reason she was here.

Jolting awake at the sound of a carriage drawing up before the front door, her ears seemed suddenly acutely sensitive to the crunch of the gravel under what sounded like a dozen little feet, and the joyful chorus of young voices.

Then the drawing-room door was thrown open unceremoniously and three small boys burst into the room.

'Uncle Max! Uncle Max!' they cried, as they leapt upon him.

Olivia opened her eyes. Gripping the side of her chair for support she stared at the three youngsters, all jostling for prime position on their Uncle Max's lap.

Fourteen months. It had been fourteen months since she had last seen Julian. The baby who had been removed from her care when Lucien had fallen ill was now a boisterous and sturdy toddler with a mop of dark curls and a sunny smile. His cousins were both fairhaired, a little older than he, but just as comfortable with their Uncle Max whom they were now pummelling with cushions.

'Boys! Boys!'

The nursery maid clapped her hands for calm. Olivia could only stare. Charlotte, who had accompanied Julian to his new home fourteen months earlier, smiled. She'd been told to expect Olivia but to say nothing. Her pride in her young charge was clear, however the small, thin woman who followed in her wake was less forgiving of the youngsters' unruly behaviour.

'Boys, your manners!' she cried, when she saw Olivia. 'Your uncle Max has a visitor. And Max, you're no better, the way you encourage them.'

Mr Atherton exhaled on a long-suffering sigh as he stood up to greet his sister. 'Afternoon, Amelia. They make me feel young again and I missed them,' he said, his grin half apologetic. 'And Mrs Templestowe doesn't mind. She likes small boys. At least, you gave me to think you do.'

His laconic smile, as he turned back to her, suddenly became one of concern. 'My dear Mrs Templestowe, are you all right?' He took a couple of quick strides across the room and bent to clasp Olivia's hands.

'Amelia!' He swung round. 'Your vinaigrette, or burnt feathers, or whatever it is you ladies use. Mrs Templestowe is still recovering from her nasty fall.'

'I'm all right,' Olivia managed, faintly, as Max with great solicitude, patted her arm and eased her back into her chair.

'I'll send the boys away,' he said. 'Boys! We can play as soon as I've ensured our visitor is—'

'No, please! I'd love the boys to stay.' Olivia was aware of the urgency in her voice, which she hoped would be interpreted as politeness, as she struggled upright in her chair. 'Tell me your names, boys, if you please.'

The exuberance had been knocked out of them. Almost sullenly they ranged before her, fidgeting, anxious no doubt to be out of doors and away from this strange lady. Olivia's heart nearly broke.

Julian didn't recognize her. Even when she took his hand to shake it, solemnly, there was no recollection in his eyes. He was as restless as his cousins, turning his bright gaze upon his Uncle Max as if begging to be reprieved and dismissed from the room.

'So, you're Julian,' she repeated, forcing a tremulous smile. 'I'm very pleased to meet you, Julian.'

'Can I go now, Uncle Max?'

Not two minutes in her company and her darling boy couldn't wait to leave. She meant nothing to him.

She closed her eyes, briefly. Why should she? If his Uncle Max thought it, Julian thought it, too. She had abandoned him. Forsaken him. Without a second thought.

A terrible lump formed in her throat. She couldn't swallow past it. She felt the tingling, swelling in her glands as the tears forced their way up and out.

Releasing Julian's hand, she fell back into her chair. She tried to take a breath, choked on it, then shuddered, burying her face in her hands as she let out a strangled wail.

When rational thought returned, the boys had gone. Amelia, whom she'd barely even greeted with the requisite courtesy, was sitting on the sofa opposite her, regarding her over the top of her tea cup.

At least, she could see part of Amelia. The rest of her was obscured by Mr Atherton.

Dear Lord, she was squeezed up against him, her head upon his chest, her face wet with tears. She supposed she must have been sobbing like a mad creature.

He gave a short laugh when he saw her obvious dismay at the state of his coat sleeve.

'No cause for concern. I'm dressed like a country rustic and it's not as if I'm unused to ruined jackets, Mrs Templestowe, being so often in the company of snotty-nosed little boys,' he said, bracingly. He rose, perhaps realizing their closeness no longer appropriate now that her tears had ceased. 'Wonderful! A smile,' he said, his own warm and sympathetic as he gazed down at her. 'Seems as if a good cry was just what the doctor ordered.' He stooped to place a comforting hand on her shoulder, and his eyes met hers, their expression tender and enquiring. 'Would you care to tell me what that was all about?'

'Max!'

'It's not impertinence.' Mr Atherton sounded defensive as he turned to face his sister. 'If Mrs Templestowe is going to start sobbing in my drawing room for no apparent reason, then I believe it's a fair question to ask what might have upset her. You, Amelia, are wearing a most unbecoming bonnet, which is surprising, for you are generally in the first stare. If that is what upset Mrs Templestowe then I would be relieved to know the fault did not lie with me, for I was up before Frensham was on hand to dress me. Perhaps I've committed some unpardonable crime in the manner in which I've mixed a green and black waistcoat with buff pantaloons. If the fault lies with me, I'd much rather be told.'

'You are entirely blameless, both of you,' protested Olivia with a weak smile, pushing her shoulders back as embarrassment at her emotional outburst washed over her. 'It's just ...'

Her words trailed into expectant silence. Stammering, she tried to come up with a plausible reason for her distress. 'Julian.' Her voice became a whisper. 'I lost my baby a year ago. When I saw Julian—'

She couldn't go on. She took another heaving breath, trying with all her might to resist another embarrassing deluge of sobs. Finally she managed another tremulous smile, blushing at being the focus of attention.

'I'm all right now,' she said, waving away Mr Atherton who looked like he was going to enfold her in his bear-like embrace once again. There was nothing like sympathy to bring on a bout of self indulgent wailing.

Yet hadn't all her efforts been with this portentous meeting in mind?

Success seemed within her grasp.

There was Mr Atherton, the man to whom Lucien had entrusted Julian's future, and who was therefore responsible for Olivia's happiness, looking at her with transparent sympathy and admiration. As if she were the most precious and novel creature ever to have crossed his threshold. She acknowledged the look with a mixture of hope and dread. She was used to men's admiration but it had been a long time since she had courted it. Her beauty was a poisoned chalice. Mr Atherton was kind and decent. If she revealed to him her real identity he would be instantly disgusted. Even if he chose to dismiss the rumours that had blackened her name it wouldn't be long before he discovered the rottenness within. Lucien had tainted her. She knew better than anyone that the beautiful mask she presented to the world concealed a soul that was destined to writhe in the flames of Hell with her late husband.

Hadn't The Reverend Kirkman told her a thousand times?

It only strengthened her quest to regain Julian in this life. At any cost.

'I'll see that Charlotte is preparing the boys for nursery tea,' Amelia excused herself.

'It looks like rain yet again. My sympathies, Mrs Templestowe.' Amelia hesitated in the doorway, looking at Olivia as if she couldn't quite make her out. 'I cannot imagine what it must be to lose a child.'

CHAPTER 2

I F OLIVIA HAD been sleeping, the loud crash of thunder and rattling of the casement would surely have woken her. As Max's new house guest she had retired to bed two hours ago. The soothing pastoral scene upon the wall had proved anything but that. In fact, she'd been staring at it with increasing desperation when the enormous crash rattled the house.

It startled her so much she nearly fell out of bed.

Shivering under the quilt, she wondered if Julian were as afraid of thunderstorms as she. When he'd been a baby she'd taken him into her bed where he'd always slept, contented and oblivious to the wildness without.

Now he seemed barely able to tolerate her. When Charlotte had brought him down to say good night he'd climbed on to his uncle's lap and twined his little arms around his neck for a good night kiss before coming to stand, at Mr Atherton's instruction, dutifully before her. With downcast eyes he'd parroted: 'Say good night to Mrs Templestowe' before being released, with obvious relief, skipping off with Charlotte to join his cousins.

Olivia recalled with pain his tense little smile, just before Charlotte had led him away to bed. Her brief reunion in the corridor earlier with

Julian's nursemaid had reassured her she did not risk an unmasking for the moment. Charlotte's joy was not in doubt, just as her loyalty had never been. But when Charlotte had reassured her that Mr Atherton was 'the most good natured of masters' Olivia had not been ready to relinquish her fear that Mr Atherton's disgust at learning the identity of his unexpected visitor would override his supposed kindness.

Another crack of thunder was followed by what sounded like an eerie, distant cry. More than anything, Olivia wished the flash of lightning could bathe the room permanently in light.

What if Julian was lying in his bed, too afraid to find his nursemaid, Charlotte? Perhaps Mr Atherton had demanded that little boys needed to learn courage, and should not be offered comfort.

These, and similar fears, chased themselves around her head until she thought it would burst, until she had no choice but to force her fear into submission.

Rising reluctantly, she pushed her feet into slippers, threw her shawl around her shoulders, lit a taper and crept into the passage. She knew exactly where the boys were sleeping.

What mother would not?

But a tower room would be more exposed to the elements and if, for some reason, Julian had been placed into a bedchamber apart from his cousins, he would be terrified.

Olivia studiously ignored the probability that the boys would almost certainly be together, and that in this household no two year old would be abandoned to face his childish terrors, alone. It was her duty to ensure her little boy was not sobbing with fear.

Swiftly, she glided along several passageways, found the stairs to the tower, and was soon turning the handle of the room most likely to contain Julian.

No sound of sobbing greeted her. She pushed open the door fully and raised her taper high. The picture that greeted her was one of the deepest domestic bliss. All three boys were cuddled together in one large bed, eyes closed, oblivious apparently to the storm raging outside. An adjoining door was open through which Olivia could hear the gentle snoring of the nursery maid.

She stood for a few moments surveying the scene. Or rather,

studying the face of her little boy. At least now she could gaze upon it to her heart's content.

Long, dark eyelashes swept his chubby, rosy cheeks. His thumb was in his mouth and he wore a half smile, as if he were dreaming of something pleasant.

Olivia drank in the sight that must sustain her until she was able to claim him for her own ... in three months? Two months? When would she finally be granted the legal right to be a mother again? she wondered with a pang.

It all hinged on Mr Atherton. She felt another pang. A very different one.

If only she had confessed her true identity the moment she'd opened her eyes: Mr Atherton was the most charming, good-natured of men.

Yet when honesty was required her courage had failed her.

She tried to dismiss the fear bound up in her lie. When the right moment came, she would tell him. Soon she would leave Elmwood and Mr Atherton – she felt a pang of regret – and from her home with her aunts she would compose a letter that struck the right note, asking for her rights as a loving mother to be respected.

For so long The Reverend Kirkman had convinced her that his plan to reclaim Julian was the only way.

Now that Olivia had broken free to follow her own instincts and had met Mr Atherton, already she felt the reverend's influence over her diminishing. Mr Atherton was open to reason, and weren't truth and reason the source of success and happiness?

A crack of lightning illuminated the room, the accompanying thunder making Olivia gasp with fear and Julian to stir in his sleep. She heard Charlotte's bed creak.

With her hand on the door knob she prepared to tear herself away, acknowledging sadly that the foundation on which her past and, now her future, were built: deception.

She felt the strong, cold fingers of her reality squeezing the chamber of her heart, moulding her mind. However much she liked Mr Atherton he could only ever be the means of restoring Julian to her. For her lie required more than a simple unmasking of her identity. Revealing the full extent of the truth threatened the future of her son.

෧෨

No amount of thunder and lightning and howling wind could wake Max from a deep sleep.

Ghosts and goblins were another matter. Especially if they caused the floorboards in the passage outside his bedchamber to creak.

Someone was tiptoeing about the house in the middle of the storm, he realized, groggily. The thought that it might be a small boy sleep-walking or seeking comfort caused him to drag himself from the cosy comfort of his bed, draw on his thick silk dressing gown, push his feet into slippers and softly open his door. He did not want to alarm the little lad.

There was no point in lighting a taper. He knew this house like the back of his hand, and the glow from his fire reached sufficiently into the passage for him to see clearly enough.

A crack of lightning and roll of thunder was accompanied by a highpitched squeal of fright not two feet from him, and a taper wavered and nearly went out.

With a start, Max found himself staring into the terrified eyes of his new house guest, Mrs Olivia Templestowe.

For a moment he thought it was his sudden entry into her nocturnal path that had nearly frightened the wits out of her. However, when another flash lit up the entire house and the thunder created a din fit to end the world he saw that the young woman's terrors were wholly on account of the storm.

'Let me take that,' he murmured, removing the wavering candle from her grasp. 'What are you doing roaming the house at this time of night? Come, I'll take you back to your room.'

She looked lost and frightened but did not object when he put his hand under her elbow and began to guide her in the direction of her chamber. When another boom of thunder reverberated off the walls she cried out again, and clung to him, burying her head against his chest.

Placing her taper on a low table, he put his arms around her shoulders and held her lightly. More lightly than he wished to but her fear and fragility made him cautious.

When she gave a little sigh, her body nestling against his as if she'd found her safe harbour, Max swallowed and forced his chivalry to override his desire. She was just the right height for him to rest his chin on top of the fine linen nightcap that covered her glossy light hair.

He dared not move though his inaction taxed him as greatly as any exertion under enemy fire ever had. But finally he found himself simply fascinated by the reaction of her body.

Her breathing was completely dominated by the storm: regular when it subsided, fast and shallow when the thunder roared and the lightning flashed.

He could have stayed there for hours, simply holding her, but Max was disappointed when she suddenly tilted up her head, crying out, 'Mr Atherton!' as if she truly had not realised it was he, though she did not step back. 'I thought the boys might be afraid,' she added, dropping her gaze.

'Not nearly as afraid as you, it would appear.' He put his finger beneath her chin to tilt her head up again. They were the most amazing eyes he thought he'd seen: layers of blue disappearing into fathomless depths. And she was the most amazing creature he'd met. He could not make her out, and was looking forward to trying. 'You were very brave to venture out alone.'

'Brave?' she repeated in a whisper. He thought the look she cast him was rueful. 'I only wish I were.'

He realized he still had his arm about her. That she was looking up at him almost as if she didn't know how to phrase a request, and that she had made no effort to pull away. She was so very lovely. Far lovelier even than he'd imagined she'd be before she washed her face. And she certainly did not recoil from his embrace.

When she caught her breath at another roll of thunder he relished the chance to hold her tighter. Acknowledging the potential danger of their situation, he released her with a sigh. 'Come, I'll take you back to your room.'

She clung to his hand, resisting as he drew her along with him. Her face looked ashen in the next flash of light.

'Please don't leave me alone,' she whispered, when they reached her bedchamber. 'I am so terrified of storms.'

Did she not know how easily she could have been misunderstood?

'It'll pass soon enough,' he soothed. Reluctant though he was to say goodnight, he knew he had to leave her. That she couldn't remain freezing in the passage much longer. Well, he wasn't freezing; his blood was fairly up just at the sight of her, but he could feel her shivering.

She closed her eyes, took a deep breath as she put her hand on the door knob, then cried out, 'Don't lock me in!'

'Lock you in your room?' he repeated, trying to understand her. 'Good God, is that what your parents did?'

She frowned, then covered her mouth with her hand. 'I should never have said such a thing. No, my parents were very kind though I lost them when I was quite young.' She leaned against the door as if she were rallying all her fortitude until another crack of thunder sent her lurching back into his arms and as she fixed him with her extraordinary luminous blue eyes he knew he was undone. That he was as enslaved as any man could be when she begged him in a low voice, 'Please don't leave me alone.'

He needed no more encouragement. Feeling like a fearless conqueror Max scooped her up and strode all the way back to his own room. Easing himself into the large, comfortable armchair by his bed, nicely warmed by the fire, he settled her across his lap. Her head, heavy with exhaustion, settled upon his chest and the staccato breaths soon became regular.

He knew it was wrong of him to be alone with her. But her mere presence and the fact she needed him was too much.

In minutes she was asleep.

CHAPTER 3

WHERE HAD SHE fallen asleep? Olivia woke with a guilty start as the maid drew the curtains, relieved to find she was in her own room.

The girl bobbed a curtsy. 'Master said as to leave you to your rest. Sorry, miss, but morning tea is in half an hour an' I thought—'

'Is it that late?' Olivia cut her off, jumping out of bed and drawing her borrowed shawl about her shoulders.

How could she have managed to sleep at all? she wondered, remembering in a flash all that had happened during the storm, and where, exactly, she had fallen asleep. Her hands flew to her flaming cheeks and her heart gave a painful contraction.

'Julian!' she whispered, though her heart threw up a different name. Being reunited with her son was the reason her heart was behaving so oddly, she told herself, as she quickly washed and dressed. It had nothing to do with the boy's uncle who had merely been kind and done what any host would to allay the fears of a nervous guest.

She banished the memory of his warm embrace. It was too dangerous to relive the exquisite sensation of relinquishing her worries in the arms of a man with honourable intentions.

When had she last felt precious? Or deserved to feel so? she thought, choking back her self disgust as she remembered how easily she'd succumbed to the comfort of his caress as he'd held her in his lap, his long sensitive fingers brushing rhythmically across her cheek as if she were a precious child.

With brisk, determined actions, she pulled on her stockings then waited passively while the maid dressed her.

Soon she would see Julian again, and that was all that was important.

But Julian was out walking with his nursemaid and cousins, she was told. The master, added the parlour maid, was in the drawing room, her tone indicating that this was where Olivia should direct her footsteps. Not towards a crowd of unruly little boys.

Arriving at the doorway at the very same moment as Mr Atherton only added to her awkwardness, compounded by his seeming inability to address her coherently. Lord, what must he think of her forwardness last night? she wondered.

'I trust you slept well, Mrs Templestowe,' he began, the colour burning his cheeks as he cast his gaze downwards, stubbed at a mark on the carpet with the toe of his boot and added in a burst of frustration, '*Must* I call you that?'

Dispersing her tension with a small laugh, Olivia replied with a wry smile, 'I think the outrageous manner in which I impinged upon your hospitality last night affords you the right to call me Olivia, if you prefer.'

For a moment their gazes locked, then they both laughed. It cleared the air, Max offering his arm to Olivia to lead her into the room just as Amelia made her entrance.

With the most cursory of greetings for his sister, Mr Atherton's gaze returned to Olivia's face as he took his seat beside her, murmuring, 'Did I tell you, Olivia, that I've made you an appointment to come walking with me after breakfast? There's something I want to ask you.' There was a gentle, teasing note in his voice which made Olivia want to lean towards him and caress his cheek as she entered into the spirit of light-hearted banter.

Instead, she felt dread take root at the look in his eye: a mixture of admiration and affection.

Fatal.

'I think you are a fraud, Olivia, for I can detect no sign of a limp, I'm pleased to note,' he said, casting first his sister, then Olivia, a broad, self-satisfied smile before tucking into a large helping of smoked haddock.

Olivia no longer had an appetite. Oh yes, she was a fraud. But as long as he failed to detect this she and her son had a future together.

THEIR POST-BREAKFAST WALK WAS A GENTLE STROLL AROUND THE rose bushes and the matter which Max wished to broach was Olivia's attendance at a house party he was hosting in three days' time.

'Please, will you continue under my roof in the meantime?'

His look was full of entreaty. She tried to resist it, tell herself it was far safer to leave immediately. She couldn't afford to further her acquaintance with Mr Atherton. She had to invent an excuse which precluded it.

But she could think of no suitable objection, other than to the insistent voice of reason in her head.

Quite simply, she wanted to enjoy his company for as long as she could. When had she last put her head on a pillow – much less a man's chest, God forbid! – and fallen into a sweet and dreamless sleep? When had she last felt so light with happiness at the mere caress or squeeze of a man's hand?

For the moment she ignored the truth of the matter, which was that she had to leave. Soon. Before she was in so deep she was doomed.

'What am I to wear to the ball if I'm not to appear like some little dormouse dragged in by your cat?'

He weighed this up with a frown, turning and clasping both her hands in his. 'Rather, some enchanting little squirrel,' he said, finally. 'At least, that's the impression you gave me when I dragged you out of the mud during the storm. No! That excuse won't wash with me. Amelia can get her girl to come and measure you and work her fingers to the bone so that you may step forth in finery that does your beauty justice.'

'You cannot do that and besides, Amelia's poor girl would never oblige your sister again.'

'Do I really look such a tyrant?' He smiled, leading her along a path through the manicured gardens towards the park. 'I value my reputation amongst my staff and the villagers and was merely trying to impress you with my willingness to ensure all your objections are quashed.'

The smile died on his lips as he halted once more, putting his hands on her shoulders to turn her towards him and asking quietly, 'I really would like you to come, Olivia.'

'Well, yes, I— what are you doing?' For suddenly Max's manner had become quite altered, his expression decisive as he caged her hand which had been lying loosely upon his arm, his footsteps purposeful as he marched her to the copse of trees which bordered the formal garden. Olivia had to run to keep up.

'Taking you deep into the shelter of those trees over there so we will not be observed from the house, or spied upon by my sister who has suddenly decided to prune the roses, by the looks of things.'

'Oh,' said Olivia, faintly, as she found herself shielded from the house by the thick trunk of a large elm tree on one side and Max's solid broad chest on the other.

'Oh!' she said again, as his right hand deftly untied the ribbons of her bonnet. Tossing it aside, his lips curved in a confident, appreciative smile as he drew her against him.

'Oh ...' It was a final murmur of surrender as she melted into him.

She felt her legs give way and her heart seemed to liquefy as his lips brushed hers, his fingers twining in the curls at the nape of her neck.

Need, desire and a growing urgency to deepen what was happening between them skittered over her nerve endings. This was what she'd once enjoyed with a man. Before Lucien had erased all memories of tenderness with his brutality. She'd thought she could never trust again but Mr Atherton— Max—had proved that gentlemen did exist. That desire in a man did not always mean he had to prove his mastery as a consequence.

He was gentle, respectful of her boundaries.

But passionate, too. And she drank in his kiss as if she couldn't get enough.

She was embarrassed when it was he who drew apart, first.

'Lovely Olivia,' he whispered. He held her away from him, observing her with tenderness. She didn't realize she was straining to move back into his embrace until he laughed, cupping her face and bringing his mouth back to hers.

Sighing, Olivia pressed herself against him, revelling in the enjoyment of being with a man who stirred her senses.

It had been so many years since she'd last felt desire, she'd forgotten how much she enjoyed surrendering to a sensuality over which she had no control, of casting away her inhibitions. His chest felt solid and dependable pressed against hers, his arms strong and safe around her, and he smelt good. Of sandalwood soap and horses.

'Darling Olivia,' he murmured, kissing her gently once more for good measure. 'You have a most extraordinary effect on me.' He shook his head as if to clear it.

'Mmm.' Olivia smiled and bit her lip, making no move to pull away. She was disappointed when he released her with a sigh so as to retrieve her discarded bonnet, but she laughed as he fumbled with the ribbons he tried tying beneath her chin.

'All thumbs,' she said, as once again he tucked her hand into the crook of his arm and stood looking down at her with a proprietary air. 'I suppose you're too much the soldier.'

'With a longing for the comforts of hearth and home. My soldiering days are over and I have no desire to dwell on a past I do not mourn.'

She felt a chill and knew the time was nearly upon her that she must leave before she revealed too much of what she truly felt. Much as she might not wish to dwell on a past *she* did not mourn, it was always with her; ready to disrupt her future.

He didn't appear to notice her preoccupation for his tone was light as he added once they'd begun to walk companionably towards the path, 'I no longer call myself a soldier but it's part of who I am. I daresay one can never quite escape one's past, can one?'

'I daresay one can't,' Olivia said softly, as she matched her footsteps to his, her pleasure in the moment gone.

The pine needles were soft and slippery underfoot and at one point Olivia stumbled and fell against him. She quickly righted herself. Max was the kind who would want to protect and cosset her. She recognised that and while it was what she wanted, she knew also that Max's love would always be out of reach. She'd been slow in realising that.

The sloping snow-dusted lawn, now in full sunlight, lay just ahead of them.

Max turned and again took Olivia by the shoulders, his expression pleading. 'You've not yet agreed to stay for my very grand entertainment. Will you?'

Longing gripped her, despite her foreboding. For the first time in months she'd had thoughts other than of Julian. She'd fallen asleep in this man's arms, revelling in the warmth of his embrace as much as the happy knowledge that her son lay sleeping nearby.

And now, once again, she'd surrendered to her instincts rather than reason and allowed her weak, fallible body to enjoy the pleasure of the moment with no thought for the consequences.

When would she learn?

But what could she say? When he was looking at her in a way that made her heart feel near to bursting with happiness and she wanted to hurl herself into his arms and beg him to kiss her again?

She gave a half smile and nodded, expecting to receive one of his open, easy smiles. It was a cruel burden to know that she would soon disappoint him.

Instead of the boyish laugh she'd expected, his expression was grave.

'Good.' He took a deep breath. His eyes glowed and, as she waited for his next words, she felt the warmth of his admiration, ignoring the knowledge, buried for now, that happiness was, as ever, out of reach. For how could she not want to hear the words that conveyed how she had altered his world in such a short time when it merely echoed what was in her own heart?

'I believe you've bewitched me, Olivia.'

She went rigid with shock. She had no response. Shakily, she tied the ribbons beneath her chin more securely, touching the key that hung round her neck – Lucien's key; the key which had driven him mad in its failure to yield him what he believed was his. Shaped like a butterfly, the intricate piece of ironwork had been willed to Lucien by his grandfather with cryptic instructions pertaining to the lock it fitted. And to untold riches. An irony, Lucien had muttered as he lay dying, that his faithless wife should finally gain possession of the unknown treasure when she'd already benefitted from another butterfly—the one on her person the men slavered over.

Olivia closed her eyes as nausea overcame her. Why she continued to wear the key after it had failed to open any lock she could find in the house, she could not tell. It had become a habit and then a talisman. The butterfly-shaped birthmark on her left breast was a reminder of Lucien's poisoning influence that continued beyond the grave. The butterfly key around her neck promised a gilded future.

She continued towards the house.

'Olivia?' His voice was full of concern. He put his hand on her arm to detain her. 'What is it, Olivia? What have I said?'

'It's nothing, a megrim,' she managed faintly, pushing on. Not the truth. *I believe you've bewitched me, Olivia.* The very words Lucien had used to accuse and condemn her.

Of course he would not have let her go and she would have been lying if she'd pretended she wanted him to.

'I've frightened you,' he said, coming to stand before her, not touching her. 'I've rushed headlong, following my heart, thinking only of myself, without even the delicacy to enquire after your bereavement, the true state of your feelings.'

'You've done nothing I haven't welcomed,' Olivia soothed, reaching up to touch his cheek. 'I lost my husband a little over a year ago and it was a blessed relief.' She wondered if he'd recoil. It would be easier if he did.

Yet she could not deny she welcomed his touch when he gripped her arms tightly, his expression full of sympathetic understanding as she added, 'He was a cruel man and I was not sorry when fever took him.' She nestled against his chest when he drew her against him. She would stay there forever, if he'd let her.

When he raised her head with a gentle finger beneath her chin, they were facing the great house in the distance.

'I wish I could offer you all this.' His sweeping gesture took in the sun-kissed landscape, the handsome grey stone house with its battlements harking back to a much earlier age, its later additions making it a home rather than a fortress. 'But it is better to be frank. I only hold it in trust for my ward. When Julian is of age I shall return to my own estate.' He added, softly, 'I'm afraid my own home is a good deal more humble. Nevertheless, it is not the bricks and mortar that gladdens the heart but rather what dwells within. I hope you think the same.'

As he held her lightly, he did not see the spasm of realization that rocked her to her very foundations or the strain in her voice as she ground out, 'I hope you do not resent the efforts you will expend on the boy's behalf, only to be turned out when he turns twenty-one. I must tell you' – it was hard to say the words, looking upon all this that was once her husband's and that she might have held, herself, in trust for her son had Lucien not changed his will – 'I come with nothing, Mr Atherton.'

'What a fine match,' he said, swinging her back into the circle of his arm, his easy smile banishing his former sobriety, as they began to walk again. 'I was hoping I could not be accused of fortune-hunting. However, I was trying only to weasel from you your feelings, not what you had to offer. Promise you'll stay?'

Her feelings. She wanted to wither in his arms with longing before she expired from shame; she wanted to scream at the injustice. Instead, she tried to swallow past the bitterness as she spoke the truth. 'My feelings? That you are the kindest man I've ever met.'

And the lie she was forced to utter. 'Of course I'll stay.'

With an effort she curved her lips into a smile as she gazed upon his strong features, his warm open expression. She wanted to commit them to memory.

For how could she see him again when the child she presented to the world as Lucien's heir denied the man she loved his rightful inheritance?"

'Is it to be the vermilion silk or the Pomona green?' With a decisive snip, another dead-headed rose dropped into Amelia's basket.

Had Olivia known Amelia was on her knees behind the rose arbour she would have chosen another route back to the house. Max had been called away a little earlier by a passing neighbour and Olivia had said she'd like to walk on her own, a little.

Max's sister had not gone out of her way to be friendly. Olivia suspected she considered her a brazen fortune-hunter and, indeed, she could understand Amelia's concern at her charming, good-natured younger brother making no secret of his susceptibility to Olivia's charms.

As Olivia hesitated over her answer, Amelia smiled suddenly. 'Try them both and we'll choose, if you like.' Rising stiffly, she added, 'I'll come to your room directly after luncheon. I don't know if Max told you we're expecting guests for tea.' Taking Olivia's arm she began to walk with her to the house. 'Miss Hepworth and her mother are visiting us from Bath.' She glanced at the sky. 'I hope we shan't have more snow. It's two hours when the roads are good and Miss Hepworth is an indifferent traveller.'

Olivia managed a sweet, responsive smile. Amelia was warning her off; telling her Max had another contender for his affections. Not that it mattered, she tried to convince herself, as Amelia led her away. She had no claim to Max's affections and never would have. But his recent reminder of her greatest—innocent—sin had come to her with such startling clarity that the pain was almost too acute to bear. She wished only she could find her way to her room and cry out her anguish in peace.

Stopping to rearrange a dead rose that was in danger of falling from her cane basket, Amelia said blithely, 'Miss Hepworth is a sweet girl.' There was the tiniest pause. 'With a nature that has not been spoiled by her fortune. I believe Max will see the wisdom of such a match.' The smile she slanted at Olivia was guileless.

But then, women such as this, Olivia thought bitterly as she concentrated on the toes of her boots as they walked towards the house, were always bursting with the stuff when they appeared at their most innocent. The man who had all but told her he loved her had been on the verge of committing himself to another when she had entered his life.

Another who was far richer and undoubtedly more worthy.

'I believe Max told you a little about how he came to have wardship over his cousin's son.' Amelia sniffed. 'It may appear that my brother is well endowed with worldly goods but all this he holds in trust for his ward, Julian.' She indicated the fine house and beautiful grounds with a sweep of her arm.

Olivia was not surprised at the conversational tone. Max's sister was reinforcing her opposition using the subtlest of means.

Without waiting for a reply, Amelia went on, 'Max and his cousin, Lucien, were the sons of twin brothers. Or perhaps he's already told you the sad story?'

Still, Olivia did not answer. Of course she knew, but hearing it from Amelia highlighted the fact that she was acting a charade, being given information as a stranger would. Information calculated to highlight her point: despite her guilt, indignation flowered as Amelia expanded her theme.

'It's not just on Max's personal account that it was a tragedy Lucien's father was the twin born ten minutes earlier' – Amelia made no secret of her bitterness, now – 'since he was destined to become the gamester of the family.'

Olivia's throat grew dry. She understood the direction Amelia's veiled warning was taking, couched as it was in predictable homily: the desperate struggle of a once-great family to survive its past.

With unfocused gaze she stared ahead as they continued along the path. She could not look Amelia in the eye just as she knew she could never look Max in the eye again.

Acid burned her throat. He might forgive her the one deception: but not the other.

If she could keep her tears at bay just two more minutes, she thought, increasing her pace. Lord, she'd become well practised at holding them back when Lucien had been alive.

Max was the innocent, in every way. He would never know how he had been cheated and she could never tell him. Not when it risked the future of —.

'Like father, like son, Lucien followed his own father's dissolute ways just as Max, even-tempered and charming, favoured our father.' Stopping at the base of shallow stone steps that led to the portico she fixed Olivia with her clear, level gaze.

'Now, of course, Julian will inherit Lucien's estates. With Max's guidance we hope he might resist the temptations which were the ruin of his father and grandfather. His father's weakness was gambling, his grandfather's was useless causes.' She gave a bitter laugh, adding, 'Thank God the estate was entailed so neither Lucien nor his grandfather could gamble *that* away. Our grandfather sold everything of value he could lay his hands on to raise funds for the failed Jacobite uprising of '45. Now Max struggles to maintain Elmwood' – With a nod she indicated the house and beautifully manicured gardens, the fields falling away on all sides – 'while he leases out his own much more humble estate. He needs to make a good match.'

She nodded at Olivia, her smile warm again. 'I will be up later to help you select your gown. You would look just as well in either colour. Certainly Max will think so. Your unexpected arrival has been a lovely diversion and I hope we shall be friends. Now, please excuse me, I must speak to Cook.'

She didn't even wait to see how her words registered with Olivia, slipping the basket over her other arm before running lightly up the stairs and through the doors which opened on cue.

Struggling to recover her composure Olivia turned back to the garden. She swept her eyes across the beautifully kept gardens, her vision blurring as she thought of that night a little over two years ago when Lucien had been away hunting and of the terrible storm during which her baby had been delivered.

Dear God, why had she not considered the implications of her actions before she came here? Before she met Max?

'Ma'am?' The housemaid's voice issued down to her. Olivia turned to see that she continued to hold the door open, her expression enquiring.

She dropped her eyes, mumbling, 'I must have lost my handkerchief during my walk.'

Retracing her footsteps she returned to the bench by the rose arbour. She just stood there, thinking, jolted into the present when, in the distance, Charlotte appeared at the foot of the hill. Olivia had not yet approached her, fearful of being overheard and their relationship exposed. Now, her son's faithful nursemaid took a seat beneath a poplar tree while the boys played nearby in the snow with Max's King Charles Spaniel, Pansy.

Julian was trying to knot its ears upon its head but it kept rolling over before scampering in circles around the children.

Olivia stared. It was hard to breathe as she watched his innocent play. He was such a delightful child: dark, like Lucien, but even tempered, sunny-natured.

How she longed to have him back, to be his mother once more, and how it tore at her heart to know he would not thank her for wrenching him from his happy home. She could see he thrived.

She blew her nose loudly, remembering the way the boys had laughed and shrieked with delight as Max had played with them yesterday.

She did not see Max until he was nearly upon her.

'Olivia?' He seated himself beside her.

She kept her head averted though she did not remove her hand when he took it and rested it on the seat between them. She needed to enjoy his touch a little longer.

There was a pause before he said, 'Amelia told you about our guest this afternoon.' It was a statement, not a question.

She nodded. Rather than try to exonerate himself he said, 'I was looking forward to her visit ... until you came along. You have rather complicated matters.' He gave a rueful laugh, adding hastily, 'I mean only to the extent that it would have been more fortuitous if I'd met you before Amelia made preparations for Miss Hepworth's house visit. She returns in a few days for the ball.'

'Amelia intimated you've already fixed your interest with the young lady.' Olivia stared dully ahead, her hand limp in his, her heart like a stone in her chest. 'That she comes with a fortune to match her pretty face.'

It did not seem out of place discussing the matter in such bald terms. She and Max had come a long way in a very short time yet she knew Max's defence made no difference. She had no choice but to leave.

He spoke carefully. 'It is true I paid her particular attention during the week we were in Bath together. Miss Hepworth's mother is ambitious for a match between us and Miss Hepworth, herself, appears not to be averse.' Though Max's voice was matter-of-fact his expression was worried as he looked at her. He added, 'I have never spent any time ... alone ... with Miss Hepworth.'

Olivia felt the heat rise in her cheeks as she brought her head around to face him. 'Do you think I am a fortune-hunter?'

His laugh seemed to drain the tension from him. To her surprise he hugged her against his side. 'If that were the case you would have chosen your target more carefully.'

'Elmwood is a very beautiful property.'

'My pride and joy, though, as I have told you, a property I only hold in trust.' He brought his face close to hers. 'But I bear no resentment at having one day to return to my own lands.' His grip on her hands tightened. 'I have thought a great deal lately about finding a wife whose sentiments were in harmony with my own. One who loves Elmwood but who is not so attached she would not be equally content with my smaller, humbler domain.' He chewed his lip. 'Or a small, humble farmer whose ambition is simply to breed the best wool in the county.' Olivia couldn't let him go on. Not in this direction when her own desires followed his but her guilt tore her asunder. She longed for a quiet life. She yearned for a kind, uncomplicated husband who would love her without making excessive demands, and love her son.

Gently, she withdrew her hand. 'Amelia tells me your cousin gambled away much of the family fortune and that you need to make a good match to maintain Elmwood, and your own estate.'

The words tasted like ashes yet she had to draw from Max his feelings on the subject.

Reclaiming her hand, he stroked her palm with his thumb. 'I know nothing about you or your past, Olivia.' He looked suddenly boyish, almost shy. 'I just find you utterly enchanting. If you are about to tell me you learned since nuncheon that you're about to come into a large fortune, there's no denying I'd be delighted, for you do realize that I wish to court you.' He brought her hand up to his lips. 'The fact that you bring nothing signifies nothing.'

Olivia tugged her hand away. Rising, she looked down at Max.

'Please, don't—'

'Adrian's a bear and I'm a rabbit—'

Careering up the lawn with his cousins in hot pursuit, Julian threw himself at Max's feet.

Max held Olivia's look, then laughing, rose and scooped her son up into the air just as Adrian arrived, roaring at his cousin's heels.

'We will talk about this later, Olivia.' Max reached down to give her shoulder a quick squeeze while tucked in his other arm, Julian shrieked with boyish high spirits. For the moment, though, it was Olivia who had all of Max's attention and the tenderness in his expression made her heart somersault.

Lowering his head to her ear while his nephew squirmed, he said, softly, 'If you have nothing, Olivia, it stands to reason you need someone to look after you. Might I dare hope you could come to care for me? Not just as a gentleman who thinks highly of you but as a... future husband? That you would, at least, permit me to pay you my addresses?'

Olivia gasped as she put her hand to her lips. Then slowly, against her best intentions, she nodded. She had always acted upon instinct but how could she tell him the truth? That she would soon be far away and had no intention of receiving his addresses.

The sweetness in his expression made her heart contract until Adrian lunged, tackling his obliging uncle to the ground.

Reaching down to stroke Julian's curls, Olivia feasted her eyes on him and Max for one long, last look before she turned and walked back to the house.

SHE WAS UNPREPARED FOR THE LOUD AND URGENT KNOCKING ON her bedchamber door before it was thrust open to admit Max. Leaping up from her seat at the dressing table her hand went to her throat.

She had never seen him look like this. For a moment he reminded her of Lucien and she shrank back against the edge of the walnut inlaid table.

'Is it true?' His voice was harsh. He strode across the Chinese carpet and gripped her shoulders. The action was forceful, but the surprisingly gentle caress of his hand across her cheek made her close her eyes and lean into him. She felt the steady race of his heartbeat, heard the suppressed emotion in his voice as he rasped, 'Amelia says you're leaving. Why?'

Olivia winced, stepping back and turning her head so he could not see her own pain and guilt.

'You know why,' she whispered. Trying to inject lightness into her tone as she toyed with the silver-backed hairbrush lying on the dressing table, she asked, 'Did you enjoy your afternoon?'

Olivia had not been present for the tea party. She had pleaded a megrim.

'Miss Hepworth has returned to her home under no illusions as to how matters stand between us.'

When she did not reply he turned back from his contemplation of the garden. 'I told you, I'm not on the look-out for a fortune. It's you I want.' Closing the distance between them, he cupped her cheek and his voice was gentle.

She did not move, though she had to steel herself against the tumultuous beating of her heart and the overwhelming urge to raise her face to be kissed.

She whispered, 'With the right wife you could achieve all your dreams, Max.' She had not meant to but need was making her act against her better judgement. Her hand reached up to twine behind his neck. Closing her eyes she ran her fingers over the rough short hair there. It was torture, knowing this would be the last time, but she could not help herself. 'You have ambitions, you need to make Elmwood prosper. Your agricultural experiments require money. None of that is possible unless you marry well. I am not a good match. I struggle to get by, living in the small cottage my husband left me, and my aunts' charity.' She willed him to understand, and to let her go. 'I have nothing to offer you, Max. When the first flush of euphoria fades you'll quickly resent me.'

'So much for your opinion of my constancy,' he remarked, wryly, stepping back.

With a sigh, he strode towards the window. Leaning against the sill he twisted his neck to look at her. His eyes were dark with longing. Olivia nearly wept. His feelings accorded so well with hers yet was it not the truth that Max would positively despise her if he ever discovered how she had blighted his life, his prospects? Without even realizing it, she had nipped in the bud every ambition he might ever have harboured.

'These things will not bring me the happiness you would, Olivia,' he said simply. When she did not reply he added, frankly, 'We've only just met but I've never felt like this.' He touched his chest. 'Can you truly deny what's here? I can't, and I won't let you either, unless you tell me right now I am nothing to you. I've never met a woman who makes me feel I can do anything, achieve anything; who makes me feel so alive. I felt it from the start. I knew you were the one for me even before you'd even washed the mud off your face.'

Her laugh was cut short by a sob. 'I feel it too, Max, but I also know my fears are not as groundless as you believe. You've never asked about my late husband.' She took a deep breath. At least here was an opportunity to admit part of the truth.

Max said nothing but his look was of patient enquiry. How different from Lucien whose frustration would only escalate into anger.

Carefully, she put down the brush. 'Together we committed a terrible sin for which he never forgave me.' Yes, her words were registering. His brow was furrowed ... but there was no condemnation. She felt a jolt. He looked as if he had already absolved her; as if he could never believe her capable of anything worse than a schoolgirl's misdemeanour. How unlike Lucien. For a moment she contemplated telling him what really stood between them.

Then she thought of The Rev'd Kirkman and her resolve faltered.

Reverend Kirkman, Lucien's long time confessor, Olivia's advocate. The man to whom she owed so much.

He knew too much, too.

And he wanted Olivia. She swallowed painfully. Yes, he wanted Olivia ... for his wife.

She brushed away a tear. The flame that burned so brightly between her and Max was doomed to flicker and die. At least her part truth now would give her an opportunity to leave with dignity.

'He was within days of marrying an earl's daughter. Her dowry was substantial but then ... passion banished reason and he eloped ... with me.' Olivia closed her eyes and drew in a rasping breath.

Would he recognise this as his cousin, Lucien? Olivia was telling Max the truth as much as she dared.

She waited and Max's look of disdain reminded her so much of Lucien she had to look away. Except that Max was looking as if her explanation for denying their love was as waterproof as a leaky sieve.

'So your future husband blamed you for the fact *he* persuaded you to elope.' He gave a short laugh. 'Is *that* why you think there can be nothing between us?'

'There's more,' she whispered.

If only this were the worst of it. If only she had a clean conscience. It was torture standing here before a man worthy of any woman's affections. Eight years on she could finally trust her feelings, but it was too late. She'd sealed her fate when she'd thrown in her lot with Lucien.

She hung her head as she continued, 'I had no dowry. Nothing to bring to the marriage. I was an orphan, my father drank himself to death and my mother died when I was very young, leaving her two older sisters to bring me up. I realized, early, that my beauty would have to count for everything.' She was still telling him the truth, hoping to be revealed so that all would be revealed in its tawdry starkness. Then she could leave the decision as to their future entirely up to Max.

'I was seventeen and, despite my poverty, proud and vain. I enticed my husband with everything I had – except the one thing he really wanted: my virtue. When I wouldn't give him that he married me and, fool that I was, I thought I had won him.'

Desperately she wanted to feel Max's arms around her, in forgiveness, absolution. But she also knew that was too dangerous. If he hadn't realised who she really was; if he hadn't realised that the story she'd told him was of his own cousin's blighted ambitions, then Olivia had no choice but to withdraw with dignity.

At least for now.

Max's voice made her raise her head. 'And he spent the next seven years making your life a misery because his brief lust overcame financial considerations. And as I obviously resemble your late husband you clearly think that if you accede to my wants I, too, will spend the rest of my days punishing you when Elmwood needs repairs, or I find myself without the funds to snap up the local borough in order to satisfy my political ambitions.'

His indignation made Olivia squirm.

Turning towards the looking glass, she couldn't bear to gaze upon her reflection. She hung her head. 'Let me go, Max. At least for long enough to prove this is no youthful infatuation.'

His footsteps pounded across the floorboards and then he was pulling her against him in a fierce embrace. Olivia shuddered at the hard strength of him. Lucien, too, had once had a body of steel.

But there had been no kindness in *his* heart.

'Go, then,' he said, cupping her chin and forcing her to look at him once he'd relaxed his hold on her, 'since it's so important you prove to yourself you're no seductive siren enticing me against my better judgement. But promise to return to Elmwood in a month. I already know that my determination to make you my wife will not have changed.'

She sagged against him. He had let her go. With dignity.

Yet he truly had wanted her for his wife. She nearly wept at the irony.

'Thank you, Max,' she whispered, relief making her light-headed.

He held her upright as he gently stroked her back. 'And you promise you'll return in a month? And that I'll always know where to find you?'

She could only nod while she evaded his eye. Of course she could never return. Of course she could never let him find her?

'There's just one thing more,' she whispered. Her mouth was dry. It was pure stupidity yet she couldn't help herself: she had always been a slave to her body. 'Kiss me.'

CHAPTER 4

'YOU HAVE BEEN punished enough, Olivia.'

With characteristic precision The Rev'd Kirkman replaced the fine, bone-china tea cup upon its saucer. Mesmerized, Olivia watched as he rearranged it until the handle was at perfect right angles to himself. Morning sun streamed through the parlour window, limning the reverend with holy light, so it seemed.

He looked at her, smiling. Expectant. He knew she was well aware of what this portentous meeting was intended to produce.

Aunt Catherine knew, too, and had been an eager conspirator, ensuring his favourite seed cake presided over the beautifully set table in the carefully prepared best room now redolent with the aroma of bees wax polish. She'd fussed over Olivia like a mother hen that morning, producing what she considered the most appropriate gown for receiving a man who, nevertheless, had been a constant visitor for the past year.

The reverend leaned back, his gaze raking Olivia's dark-blue gown with its high-necked lace collar and demure cut. He nodded, approvingly. 'I had wondered what you might choose to replace mourning clothes.'

Olivia felt her face burn. 'You surely could not suppose I'd wear anything from' – she lowered her gaze – 'before.' He knew she had little enough money to keep up with current trends.

'Those days are behind you, Olivia.' He spoke briskly, steepling his fingers and regarding her with mild disapproval. 'Today marks a new chapter. Having made a careful study of Mr Atherton's character, I want to tell you that I have composed a letter that will, I trust, find its mark. Mr Atherton is a man of high moral integrity. He served with great distinction on the Peninsula and has lived an exemplary life since returning to manage Lucien's estates. Lucien's low way of life, I've heard tell, caused him great disgust, although I believe at one time the cousins—Lucien and Max—were often together in Town.'

He was paving the way towards his proposal as Olivia had imagined he would, yet direct mention of Max, especially his upstanding character, made her wince. Mistaking the source of her longing and despair, he said, 'You will, of course, recall the terms in which Lucien couched his wishes with regard to Julian.'

How could she forget? Julian was to remain under the guardianship of his uncle Max until Lady Farquhar could convince Max Atherton she was ready to acquiesce to a rigorous code of moral conduct devised by a husband of exemplary moral character. A pillar of the church who would wash away her sins.

He gave her a few moments. To squirm? Or as final reflection that Nathaniel Kirkman was just that man?

'My dear.' He extended his hand across the table and obediently she placed hers within it. 'The time has come to put an end to your suffering. You know I can return Julian to you, and you know, also, that the strength of my feelings overcomes any aversion to your' — he drew out the pause – 'shame.'

Olivia closed her eyes and shuddered. To what was he referring? The countless humiliations to which Lucien had subjected her, or...? Her throat went dry as she forced her brain to revisit the past. Not for the first time doubt tormented her. Could he suspect, or even know, the truth of Julian's parentage?

As she opened her eyes to face his familiar, inscrutable gaze she realized how important it was to find out. Then the familiar anguish dragged at her soul. What did it matter? Unless she were prepared to publicly declare her child a bastard there could be no future with Max.

'Trust me with your future, Olivia.' His smile over the top of his china cup was sympathetic; as if he understood her suffering and was offering himself to her as a great gift to lessen her mortal trials. 'Marry me, and I will reunite you with Julian.'

Julian.

Julian, not Max, was the cornerstone of her life. Reclaiming her darling baby was all that mattered and only Nathaniel Kirkman could gain him for her, for she had not the courage to travel an alternate path. Nathaniel's will was too powerful. He handed her his lawn, lace-edged handkerchief. She had not known she was crying; and again he mistook its cause.

'Under my tutelage you shall learn to subjugate your wanton impulses. Through me you shall tread a Godly path and find comfort.' His voice grew honeyed. 'I have the power to bring you true happiness, Olivia' – he waited for her to compose herself – 'through your son and humility of spirit. Now my dear, you have not answered me. I have the letter here. Am I to have it delivered to Mr Atherton?'

Olivia gave another sob.

An image of dark, curly-headed little Julian ought to have inspired her to respond in the affirmative. Instead, memories of Max's warm smile and his gentle touch blinded her to reason. His kisses had ignited a need she thought she'd conquered: that wicked, wanton side to her that had been her downfall. She covered her eyes and tried to banish Max's image.

A fortnight, it had been. Two painful weeks since she had left him, and not an hour had passed without her yearning for him, yet she had spent barely two days in his company.

She felt Nathaniel's hand on her shoulder. She thought he might stroke her hair, or otherwise insinuate his touch upon her, but, as ever, he was the model of restraint and propriety.

He indicated for her to pour him another cup of tea. When he spoke again his tone was intimate, collaborative. 'Only you and I know *all* the terrible things you have done in Lucien's name, but there are enough who have been a party to those events which have tarnished your reputation; some would say, forever. I, however, believe you can be redeemed. And I believe it is God's will that I try.'

Another nail in the coffin which housed her hopes and dreams. Max had risked his life for king and country. Honour and valour distinguished him. He could never understand, much less condone, the things Olivia had been forced to do, the wicked, terrible things to which Nathaniel referred.

Still, she could not bend her will to Nathaniel's so easily. Her stubborn spirit which had been the undoing of her in the first place finally came to the fore.

'Your offer does me great honour, Reverend Kirkman,' she said, drying her eyes as she banished her emotion. With dignified calm she gazed at the man who would be her husband; a man to whom she owed a great deal and who had eased some of the pain of her marriage, but whom she had no wish to marry. 'Pray, allow me a day in which to consider it.'

He appeared unfazed and relief washed over her. She hadn't known how Nathaniel would react if she'd thwarted him. 'A very proper request, my dear.' He drained his tea cup, pushed back his chair and rose. Bowing, he said, 'I shall return tomorrow afternoon to receive your answer.'

She found her aunts waiting in the parlour like a couple of impatient schoolroom misses. They greeted her from the window embrasure which afforded an uninterrupted view of the summerhouse.

'Did he ask you, Olivia?' Aunt Catherine looked just like a little pea hen, the fluffy grey hair beneath her lace cap matching her dove-grey gown. Her kind, twinkling blue eyes were full of excited expectation.

'Did you accept?' Aunt Eunice's voice cracked like a whip, her interest completely counter to her sister's.

'Come now, Eunice, why won't you admit that marriage to the reverend is the best future Olivia could hope for?' Catherine appealed to her taller, more formidable sister.

'I said I'd give him his answer tomorrow.' Olivia sank into the chair beside the window and picked up the book lying there, as if her recent assignation was of little account.

'You will, of course, accept, dearest.' Aunt Catherine lay her mittened hand upon Olivia's shoulder briefly, before taking a seat on the sofa, opposite. Her myopic blue eyes blinked rapidly. 'He is quite set upon it, you know.'

'Should Olivia's feelings not take precedence?' Aunt Eunice's tone was dry, as she took a seat beside her sister. 'Let the girl alone, Catherine, and stop trying to force a match if Olivia's feelings are not in accord with the reverend's.'

'Marriage to Mr Kirkman will enable Olivia to be reunited with Julian,' Aunt Catherine argued. 'He is guaranteed success. As a Godly, pious man he has the character required.'

'I'm hardly likely to do better. Certainly not in my current situation.' Olivia put down the book and sighed. The lines of worry etched on her aunts' faces reinforced the pain she had caused them.

She was no longer an impulsive child. It was time to act as an adult, and in everyone's best interests.

If she could only tame her spirit to obey.

Aunt Eunice sounded gloomy. 'Far better to remain alone, Olivia, than subjugate yourself to a man who makes your repentance and submission his mission.'

'Sister!'

'I've considered that.' Olivia cut through Aunt Catherine's predictable admonition. 'Yet if I cannot get Julian back any other way—'

'Mr Kirkman is not the only Godly, pious man on the planet. Have patience, Olivia.' There was an edge to Aunt Eunice's voice. 'Can't you wait until your heart is in accord with one of the many men who fit this broad description? Max Atherton is not the fiend his cousin was. You said so yourself. He'd surely grant you the latitude to find a man you preferred, even one whose Godliness fell a little short of the reverend's.'

'And what else do you know of Max Atherton, Olivia?' Aunt Catherine asked. 'You spent two days with him and his sister. Can you imagine how anxious we were, despite the assurances you wrote us?'

Olivia shrugged. It was too painful to dwell on Max and all that might have been had circumstances been different. She had no doubt Max loved her.

But would he love her if she knew she'd lied to him?

Not just about the fact she was Lucien's wife. That was only the start of it.

'Men of integrity,' she said, 'tend not to find women like me to their taste, Aunt Eunice. I fear that Mr Atherton will need to be doubly satisfied that my husband is a Godly reformer.' She gave a bitter laugh. 'Mr Kirkman undoubtedly fits that description.'

'Good Lord, Olivia, that is not reason enough to marry him.' Aunt Eunice scowled. 'You talk as if you were so sunk in vice no decent man would have you in the same room with their wives.'

'They wouldn't.'

'But if they knew the truth—'

Olivia stopped her Aunt Catherine from continuing. 'Who is going to tell them?' She swallowed, the old bitterness banishing her blitheness. 'Who, in the world, is going to champion me?'

'Well, somebody should! Mr Atherton should, though it sounds as if your appeal fell on deaf ears. Your reputation has been tarnished by nothing but rumours.' Aunt Eunice tried to sound dismissive, but Olivia heard the defensiveness in her tone. She suddenly felt very protective.

'Aunt Eunice,' she said, gently, 'you know as well as I that the moment I'm introduced to anyone remotely respectable they won't see me as Lady Farquhar.' She shuddered as she recalled the shame Lucien had heaped upon her when he'd made her perform at his debauched gatherings. 'They will think only of Lady Farquhar's Butterfly.' She had started her speech defiantly. Now her voice dropped away. 'What man is brave enough to get beyond that stumbling block? I shall answer the reverend's question in the affirmative tomorrow. There can be no other way.'

CHAPTER 5

'MAX, YOU PROMISED you would accompany us to church this morning.' Amelia looked cross as she marshalled her boys, and her husband, into an orderly line before the front door. 'You'll be late! Why, you are still dressed for riding!'

Max hesitated at the top of the sweeping marble staircase and looked down at his sister in the hallway below. Jonathon, Amelia's long-suffering husband, raised his sandy eyebrows heavenward as if mentally and physically preparing himself for another spat between the siblings.

'Sorry, Amelia,' Max responded, carefully, 'but I am not prepared to be seen out with you dressed like that.'

Jonathon and Amelia swept their eyes over her cornflower-blue gown, topped on this chilly spring morning, with a smart white spencer. Jonathon looked startled, Amelia indignant. The two little boys giggled, scuffing their shoes on the marble flagstones.

It was the gown Amelia had lent Olivia.

Max descended a couple of steps and Amelia snapped as realization dawned. 'She was a little trollop trying to insinuate herself into your affections, Max. She thought you would make her gifts of more than simply my gown. Hasn't her continued silence made that clear enough? Though why you felt it necessary to break off your understanding with Miss Hepworth I don't know! She was the ideal consort.'

'She was very pleasing,' Max agreed. 'Ah, Frensham, I wondered where you'd got to with my valise.'

'You are surely not accompanying Julian to his new home?' Amelia stamped her foot. 'You agreed it would be kinder not to.' She closed her eyes as if marshalling patience. When she spoke again her tone was gentler. 'Your investigations regarding Reverend Kirkman's character and your meeting with him satisfy Lucien's idea of an acceptable husband for that scandalous wife of his – you knew you'd have to return the boy, sometime.'

Jonathon cleared his throat. Max waited patiently, watching his brother-in-law's breath mist in the cold air, the profile of his weak chin thrown into relief as the sunlight slanted through a high window and pooled across the flagstones.

'Max,' he said, 'I know it's hard, but it'll be harder on you both if you do your leave-taking under the noses of Julian's mother and her betrothed.'

It was true. He'd thought it himself. 'I know it,' Max agreed, his shoulders slumping as he came down the stairs, 'but the lad hasn't stopped crying since he woke at dawn this morning.'

'Perhaps Charlotte will take his mind off his troubles better than you will, Max.' Jonathon clapped him on the shoulder as he drew level. 'Say your farewells here, as you'd planned. Pretend you're merely sending him off on a grand adventure and that you'll be seeing him again shortly.'

Max shook his head. 'Funny,' he reflected, 'I had no idea what to do with the boy when Lucien saddled me with him.' He cleared his throat. 'Now I've no idea what I'll do without him. Lord knows what I'm sending him to. I do at least owe him that! To find out, I mean. After all, Lady Farquhar was indisposed the day I met Rev'd Kirkman. What do I know of Julian's mother? Considering the stories, it'd be negligent if I did not satisfy myself that her wayward character might benefit from the restraint the reverend promises to exert. What if I consider her irredeemable?' He looked appealingly at Jonathan and his sister who had just directed one of the servants to take their boys to church ahead of them.

The truth was that as much as he truly did need to satisfy himself that Julian was going to a happy home, he needed diversion. It had been a bitter discovery to learn that the woman he loved had lied to him. She had not come back, she had not communicated.

And she had given him a false address.

'I'd share your misgivings if you were returning him to his mother's care, alone. But, Max' – Amelia's voice had lost its sympathetic edge – 'you've established that Rev'd Kirkman is a pillar of the church, a fine upstanding citizen who will lead by example. He has made it his mission to redeem this wretched woman and you've given your sanction. Come along, Max!' she urged. 'You're worse than a clucky mother hen. It'll take you five minutes to change your clothes and we can still make it to church in good time.'

⊗⊛⊗

'I HOPE YOU'VE MADE NO PROMISES TO THE BOY'S NURSEMAID.' Nathaniel tucked Olivia's hand into the crook of his elbow as they strolled across the vast expanse of carpeted floor. All around the edges of the room the furniture was shrouded in dust sheets, lending The Lodge, Olivia's old home, a neglected, shuttered air. Soon new tenants would make themselves at home here, the only means Olivia had of managing the financial upkeep on the nearby small dower house she shared with her aunts and in which Lucien had allowed her to live during her lifetime.

His forehead was puckered with the habitual furrows that appeared whenever he considered a matter of importance. 'We need to decide for ourselves if she is a fit and proper person to keep charge of the lad.'

'Charlotte has cared for Julian since he was born! Her loyalty is beyond question.'

Their gazes locked. Both of them knew this all too well. To Olivia it was a comfort. She swallowed as doubt stirred within. But to Nathaniel, Charlotte's loyalty could represent a threat.

To her relief he conceded, 'It is perhaps best to keep her close.'

They stopped just inside the dining room. Olivia closed her eyes, relief at this small victory welling in her breast.

The smell of dust and damp were different from the beeswax and woodsmoke she remembered, but the draughty remoteness was just the same. She and Lucien had entertained regularly in this room. It had been the setting for countless lively, raucous dinners, charades and games of cards for ridiculous wagers. She shuddered as Nathaniel took her past the long, mahogany table which could seat thirty, and upon which she had regularly been made to dance.

All but naked.

Nathaniel ran his hand over its dust-sheet-covered surface and glanced at her.

The look in his eye told her he remembered, too.

But his tone was bland as he reminded her, 'Mr Charleston will arrive at the end of the month. I thought it appropriate Julian should be given some time, first, in which to settle in.'

Olivia did not say she wondered at the wisdom, even questioned the kindness, of putting a boy so young into the charge of a tutor whom she had not yet met. Years of being Lucien's wife had taught her caution; to think before she spoke. At least she had a little time to assert herself if she were unhappy at Nathaniel's choice of tutor. The most important thing was that Julian would be with her.

She must not think of Max. She squeezed her eyes shut. She would think of anything but Max, though recollections of his charming, easy manner and the kindness of his smile were constant reminders.

They were at the foot of the sweeping staircase about to ascend to the rooms above when they heard the front door open followed by footsteps in the hallway.

A tentative voice called out, 'I was told I'd find you here. Ah, Reverend Kirkman, forgive the intrusion—'

The reverend turned, smiling as he greeted their unexpected visitor. Olivia was slower to respond though the horror had well and truly manifested itself. She'd have known that voice anywhere.

Right now, it was the last voice she wanted to hear.

Ushering Olivia forward, the reverend extended his hand. 'Mr Atherton, delighted you chose to accompany the lad.'

Olivia could not bring herself to raise her eyes. She gripped Nathaniel's forearm, her gaze fixed upon the sweeping stairs as if they provided refuge. Heat and shame flooded her. She was exposed.

Yet was it no more than she deserved?

Beside her, Mr Kirkman was dissembling in his usual obsequious way. 'You do us a great honour. Pray, allow me to introduce my betrothed, Lady Farquhar. Alas, I believe she was indisposed when we met.'

Dignified in the face of what must be Max's inevitable horror and disgust, Olivia slowly raised her head.

'Mr Atherton,' she said quietly, extending her hand, glad it was clad in neat fawn kid so he could not feel its clammy iciness.

She saw his shock, quickly smothered by good manners as he bowed, brushing the back of her hand with his lips, murmuring, 'What a pleasure it is to meet you, *Lady Farquhar*' – she could swear he almost bared his teeth as he added – 'having already met your *betrothed*.'

The turmoil he failed to hide pierced her to the quick, though the reverend seemed oblivious. A month on and she could be in no doubt that he had felt her deception, her disappearance, keenly. A vein throbbed at his temple. The simmering anger in his slate-grey eyes reminded her more of her late husband than the easy-natured Max she loved.

Concentrating on the points of her slippers she whispered, 'I must thank you for providing my son with such excellent care during this past year. Where is he? I have waited a long time for this moment.' It was pointless trying to communicate her feelings through her eyes. It was pointless trying to communicate her feelings through any medium when there could be no future between them.

After being told that Julian had been taken to the dower house where he was being greeted by his great aunts, Nathaniel, with a proprietary air, said smoothly, 'Lady Farquhar is a conscientious mother, Mr Atherton. You will recall from my letter that I have known her for the duration of her marriage and can vouch for her' – he hesitated, as if imbuing the word with meaning – 'softer side.'

Max glanced sharply between the two before focusing his stony gaze upon Olivia. 'It causes me great pain to part with the lad,' he said, adding with heavy irony, 'However only the *cruellest* of men would deny a child his mother's love.'

Focusing on the door at the top of the landing through which she wished she could simply disappear, Olivia nodded.

Max shifted position on the bare floorboards. 'I was more than prepared to lend a sympathetic ear, Lady Farquhar, if you had chosen to petition me personally.' He paused. 'Instead, I see you are acceding, to the letter, the conditions laid out in my cousin's will.'

'I did write some time ago to petition you for Julian's return,' Olivia said faintly. She could not bring herself to look at him. Could not bear his disgust.

'I seem to recall I suggested we meet in person.'

She could hardly say that Nathaniel had decided his course was the better one.

'Lady Farquhar and I shall be married just over the twelve months' mourning period.' Nathaniel's voice sounded overloud and pompous. 'I have known her, did I tell you, since her marriage to the late Lord Farquhar being as I was, in a manner of speaking, his religious adviser. Lord Farquar, though wild in his youth, found God in his final months. A great comfort it was to him, too.'

Max nodded, still looking at Olivia. 'You mentioned it, sir.'

'Marriage is not an institution into which one enters lightly, as Lady Farquhar well knows.' Nathaniel patted Olivia's hand as colour burned her cheeks.

She hated his cloying condescension. Raising her head she saw Max's lips curl into a bleak smile as he muttered, 'You are a fortunate man, Reverend.'

'Indeed, I am, and I wish you similar good luck.'

'I am in no hurry.'

'The marital state has much to recommend it.'

Max transferred his look from Olivia's blushing countenance to offer a nod. 'I'm sure you are right, though smarting after a recent rejection I am in no hurry to pursue it.'

The silence seemed endless. Striving for courage, Olivia interjected, 'You will recover, I am sure, Mr Atherton. Perhaps it is your pride rather than your heart which suffered the injury.' She strove for sympathy and hoped Nathaniel did not notice the trembling of her voice. 'Perhaps the lady had her reasons' – Olivia drew in a breath – 'and they had nothing to do with you. Perhaps she had already promised herself to another.' She forced the emotion from her tone and exchanged a smile with Nathaniel, as if she too felt no more than a distracted, passing interest in Mr Atherton's admission. Turning back to Max she added, 'Having shown such kindness and care towards your ward I cannot believe a disinclination towards your character was behind the lady's rejection.' How could she sound so distant, as if she were indeed consoling a stranger on a matter of the heart? A matter which was of no concern to her?

Max gave an eloquent shrug as he matched his pace with theirs in the direction of the front door. 'It no longer signifies.' This was more painful than anything.

'You must accompany us for lunch,' Nathaniel pressed him. 'The dower house, where Olivia resides with her aunts, is just up the hill.' He smiled. 'Might I offer you accommodation at the manse? I know you've travelled many hours.'

Max inclined his head. 'That is most kind of you, Mr Kirkman, however for the boy's sake I will not linger. Lady Farquhar will be anxious to be reunited with her son and I would hate to' – he transferred his gaze from Kirkman to Olivia as he added, coldly – 'intrude. I have already bespoken a room at The Jolly Miller.'

⚜

OLIVIA ALLOWED HERSELF TO BE HELPED OUT OF THE CARRIAGE IN front of the inn, then stood nervously in the dark for a few moments before venturing inside.

It was madness, not to mention highly improper, even for a widow, to call on an unmarried man, alone, but she owed Max an explanation.

With a nervous glance down the corridor Olivia patted the thick veil for reassurance. Her throat was as dry as sandpaper as she drew back her hand and gave a discreet knock.

While she had no intention of deviating from her course and marrying Nathaniel, she could not bear the thought that Max believed she really was everything he had ever been told about Lady Farquhar. And worse.

'I wondered if you'd come.' He opened the door, standing aside so she could enter. His voice was as cold as his eyes. Nothing in his expression brought to mind the old Max: the untroubled, charming young man with his disarming air of ingenuousness.

'Max, I only came here to apologize,' she said in a rush. She wanted to make this brief. Her mission was to convince him she'd not set out to hurt him; that in fact her actions had little to do with him. She'd charted her course before they'd even met.

'At least do it so I can damned well see you and lift that hideous veil,' he said, closing the door behind them and leading her into the small room with its bed, washstand and chair.

Obediently she removed her bonnet, placing it on the washstand.

She knew herself too well to try and pretend she wasn't waiting for some acknowledgement of longing or admiration. She told herself it would make her task so much easier if there were no sign of it, but when she saw the pain in his expression her own heart answered and her best intentions fled.

Quickly, she turned and went to the window. With her back to him she said tightly, 'Everything I said was true about my motives. I was prepared to do whatever it took to get Julian back. Please understand that I never meant to hurt you.'

'It just pleased you to toy with me.' He made no move to come to her. His voice was strained. 'Pretend, even, you cared for me a little.'

'No!' she swung round. 'There was no pretence and it's the reason I had to explain. Max—' She lowered her voice while she fixed her eyes upon his handsome, beloved face. 'I am not here to persuade you to take me back for I fully intend to marry Nathaniel. I just don't want you thinking my actions constituted any part of some elaborate, prearranged plot.'

He took his time replying. Picking up her bonnet he began stroking the folds of black netting. His tone, when he spoke, was one Olivia had never heard: bitter, ironic and hurt.

'Let me try to understand you,' he said, slowly, transferring his attention to her face. 'You came to Elmwood to try and persuade me to give you back Julian' – he paused – 'but instead of asking me outright you pretended to be someone else while all the time falling madly in love with me.' Tossing the bonnet on to the bed he raked back his hair, his agitation clear though there was no sign of it in his measured tone. 'Then, when I provided you with the perfect solution to all your heart's desires by offering marriage, you skipped back home to marry Mr Kirkman whom you've intimated you do not love, so as to regain Julian as per Lucien's will.' Sparks of anger flashed in his normally calm, grey eyes. 'And yet, you still maintain your feelings for me were genuine. What, Lady Farquhar, do you think that says about you and your motivations? Marriage to me will restore Julian to you. Yet you refuse me?'

Olivia studied him while she struggled to respond. He looked young and vigorous, and so like Lucien it was hard to formulate an answer. So like Lucien might have looked had he been incarnated into a better person. There was the same dark cowlick that almost fell in a curl above his right eye. Lucien had encouraged it to fall. He'd liked its rakish look and the way it enhanced the devilish glint in his eye.

There was no devilish glint in Max's eye. Just raw hurt.

Yet again, she was the cause through her alluring, beguiling, enticing ways. For isn't that what she did? Seduced men for her entertainment? It's what everybody thought.

'Max, I began my...charade... because I was sure you'd believe the rumours and think I was that kind of woman that I did what I did,' she whispered, taking a step closer, holding the back of a chair for support.

He appeared unmoved. Warily, from the centre of the room he watched her. His voice was still cynical though she could hear the emotion he tried to disguise as he replied, 'Actions speak louder than words, Olivia.'

'What would my reception have been, Max, had I announced myself to you as Lady Farquhar?' She looked at him, inquiringly. 'If I'd dressed and deported myself demurely you'd have considered I was acting a part. You'd have waited for me to slip up, reveal myself for the scheming seductress society believes me. You'd not have let me have Julian.'

He ignored this. 'You did not object to my advances, Olivia.

Perhaps you've forgotten that.' A muscle twitched at the corner of his mouth. 'Foolishly I believed at the time you felt something for me.'

'How can you imagine I was pretending?' she cried, bringing her hand to her breast to press against the sudden pain there. 'I assumed my maiden name, but that was all. Everything I said, every action was honest. My only wrongdoing was concealing my identity. Everything I said, every response towards you, was real.'

He gave her a searching look, then, with a sigh, moved to the door.

'Thank you for your apology,' he said, tonelessly, his hand on the door knob. 'I imagine that took some courage.' He inclined his head in dismissal. 'As you pointed out yourself, though, it doesn't exactly alter the fact that you deceived me and are about to marry someone else, despite the fact my offer still stands.'

'You would...still marry me?' She didn't know what to do. Closing her eyes against the roaring in her head, she whispered, 'I can't, Max.'

'You mean you choose not to. And clearly you have your reasons but will not tell me.'

This was not how it was supposed to end with Max calmly showing her the way out. Once the soft click of the latch consigned her to the passageway with Max on the other side of the door the one spark of love that had ever honestly flickered in her breast would be snuffed out and she'd be more alone than she'd ever been.

Yet wasn't that what she'd engineered, herself?

'I gave you my heart,' she whispered, stopping in front of him. 'I'd have given you everything.' *If the Reverend had sanctioned it.* But Rev'd Kirkman knew the truth about Julian and he wanted Olivia for himself. He would destroy them. Marriage to Max, as much as Olivia longed for it, would never be possible.

'I'm sure many men would gladly have accepted, Olivia. I, however, was looking for something more permanent.' He glared at her. 'Something honestly given with no strings attached.' He stepped back as if afraid of coming into contact with her.

Biting back her first response which was to defend her actions she stepped as close to him as she could without actually touching. She'd leave, not because she wanted to, and not before she made one final stand. She could not bear to leave without his forgiveness.

'I responded as I did because you were kind.' Tentatively she rested her hand lightly on his lapel. 'From our first encounter you made my comfort and welfare your concern. I had not experienced such thoughtfulness.'

He looked at her hand with suspicion, turning his head away to stare through the half-drawn curtains. The casement panes were dirty and the room bathed in gloom but his pain was clear.

On her account.

'My husband spent our entire marriage punishing me for' – she made a derisive sound – 'forcing him to the altar when I was a foolish debutante.' How badly she wanted Max to understand. She withdrew her hand. Max brought his head round. His eyes glowed with some emotion she could not recognize. She could not bear to think it was disgust. 'When your feelings for me went beyond mere kindness I responded with every fibre of my being. I wanted you, Max. I wanted you so badly, but I had not the courage to reveal myself as scandalous Lady Farquhar, branded so unfairly by her husband as a harlot, an unfit mother.'

'If you considered me so kind, why not lay bare your scandalous past so you could defend each charge to my satisfaction?' The suspicion returned to his manner. 'Such as the truth behind Lady Farquhar's Butterfly?'

It shouldn't have felt like a slap in the face after all this time. Rage at the long and lingering injustice bubbled up so that she hissed, 'Lady Farquhar's Butterfly paid my husband's gambling debts.' She was so upset she didn't know if she could continue. But she must. She clung to the door knob for her knees had gone weak, the pounding in her brain threatened to obliterate her lucidity. She was so angry even the shock and understanding that registered suddenly in Max's eyes was no catharsis. When he put out a hand to help her she drew back.

'Of course you must wonder. Well, let me tell you, Max, in my own words, of my sins that put me beyond redemption so you'll understand why I deserve Reverend Kirkman though I do not love him.' She sucked in a breath. Each word was an effort. And Max just stared silently down at her as if he were judge and jury and she was digging her own grave. 'One night Lucien lost more heavily than usual.' Her defences were in place. Max would not dare touch her while she glared at him with as much poison in her heart as if he had been his hated cousin.

She went on, 'Perhaps he was more than unusually affected by the drink. He must have made some reference – coarse and ironic, no doubt – about the birthmark on my breast to his gambling partners. A birthmark he fancied was shaped like a butterfly. I was sitting at another table with several of the men who weren't playing Faro. None of the wives was there. It was not a respectable gathering, but Lucien thought I was decorative.' She shrugged as she struggled to control her emotion. She would recount the rest as if it was a sordid moral tale in which she had but a passing interest. It was a trick she'd perfected as Lucien's wife.

'Finally he rose and called me over. I stood by the table, awaiting his pleasure while he and the other men looked me over like a horse. They were leering and sniggering. I was terrified, humiliated, but there was nothing I could do. Then Lord Grimble nodded at Lucien and said he thought sampling Lady Farquhar's butterfly with a kiss would be bargain enough at which point Lucien ordered me to disrobe.' Her voice trembled. 'Right there, in front of them all.' She squeezed shut her eyes. 'I was too afraid to disobey. Lucien was so ingenious at inventing the cruellest tortures. Besides, I thought one of the men in that room would surely protest.' Olivia swallowed as she rested her head against the door. She felt the memories close in on her. Felt her breath start to leave her.

Then she was in Max's arms and he was crushing her tightly against him, kissing her hair, her eyes…and her lips.

CHAPTER 6

S HE RESPONDED LIKE a wilting flower receiving rain. Dare she hope for a future beyond her narrow, dreary existence? For happiness? Past experience had taught her how dangerous it was to imagine she might find either. Still that didn't stop her twining her arms behind his neck and responding to his kiss with all the ardour of their last encounter. She could not deny her passionate nature when it was aroused.

His kisses were incendiary, inflaming her with a desperation to throw all caution to the wind and seal their love upon the four poster in the centre of the room, and she would have had she been able to offer him marriage. She was beyond redemption with no reputation to safeguard but he would expect more. Max was undoubtedly a man of honour.

And therein lay the problem.

There could be no taking it to the next level while she was a woman, betrothed, on a visit intended to explain and reinforce this uncomfortable truth.

When she felt his reluctant but undeniable withdrawal it was like mourning what she'd been unable to mourn before.

'If I told you I believe everything you've told me' – breathless, he chose his words carefully, his dark eyes searching hers as he still held her against him – 'would it be worth my asking you, again, to marry me?'

Olivia covered her face with her hands and stepped out of his arms. This was not supposed to happen.

He looked so desperately, heartbreakingly sincere, his expression so full of yearning she had to force back the tears. And trammel down the desire to throw herself back into his embrace.

She couldn't let him see the answering want in her own eyes. Stumbling towards the light, she again sought the sanctuary of the window. Here she could support herself against the cold glass, stare out into the grey afternoon light and wonder, briefly, why she had been cursed with the kind of beauty that made men want to possess her and punish her in equal measure.

Nathaniel wanted her as badly as Lucien ever had. She was not fooled by his restrained manner. He would fight Max for her using every unsavoury titbit of scandal, every damning piece of character evidence at his disposal.

And he had plenty of it. Nathaniel was a formidable adversary. Max's kindness and honour were no match for Nathaniel's ploys.

Yet hadn't Max just accepted, at face value, everything Olivia had told him in exoneration of her behaviour? Didn't that mean he'd forgive her the rest? All he wanted was the truth. Surely it was worth the risk?

She gripped the window sill as she stared vacantly into the stable yard. All she need do was say: 'I will be yours if you can forgive me the fact that Julian is a bastard who has usurped your position as the rightful Viscount Farquhar.'

She gathered her breath. She could say it.

Then she remembered that not only her happiness hung in the balance. Declaring Julian a bastard meant condemning him to society's scrapheap. He would be entitled to nothing: no social standing, no financial support.

She crumpled against the window pane. She could not do it. She wanted Max above all except the wellbeing of her child. She simply couldn't take the risk.

'Olivia?'

She had to answer him. Soon. Even as she turned, her mouth opening to respond, she hesitated, the truth balancing on the faintest of breaths.

It was as her gaze registered the empathy and compassion in his expression that she knew she'd say no.

Not because of Julian; not because of her fears for him, for Max had honour and decency, she knew that.

But because of her own deficiencies. The tale she'd just told had been cathartic but had also reinforced what she'd begun to doubt.

No, she did not deserve him. Max was good and pure of heart. A gentleman, not a cruel tormentor. It wouldn't be long before those eyes which melted her soul with their gentleness would soon kindle with disappointment.

What did it matter that she had not deserved Lucien's treatment? The fact remained: he had corrupted her. What did it matter that she had wept every night at the seductive, wanton acts she'd been forced to perform with a smile? The fact remained that she'd danced all but naked in a transparent shimmer of gauze on the dining table and men had lined up to kiss her breast with its famous butterfly birthmark.

Regardless of how much she bared her soul to Max now, she did not think she had the fortitude to bear his increasing disappointment, his dawning realization of her unworthiness.

'I'm so sorry, Max,' she whispered. They were the hardest words she'd ever said. A slap in the face for him and the death knell for her own hopes of happiness. She swallowed. 'I cannot renege on my promise to Nathaniel. Please try to understand.' She turned her face a fraction, caught the flare of surprise in his eyes, the blanching of his skin indicating, more than words ever could, his wounding.

She went on, resting the small of her back against the door frame, 'For more years than I care to remember Mr Kirkman has salvaged my dignity in situations too awful to revisit.' She swallowed again, almost elaborated about the table dancing and everything else, but bit back the words at the last moment. He'd need to know if he were to be her husband. Since that wasn't to be, at least let him leave with a less tarnished image of herself.

'I'd like to know what the worthy reverend was doing at Lucien's debauched gatherings in the first place?' Max ground out stepping back.

Olivia gave a helpless gesture. 'Lucien liked to balance vice with piety.' She took a deep breath. 'Nathaniel accepted Lucien's invitations because the only way he could help me was to be in attendance. Usually with a linen sheet on hand to wind around me as the music stopped whereupon he'd whisk me upstairs while I sobbed upon his shoulder. No doubt he disapproved of Lucien's wicked ways, but what could he do?'

It was true and this, if nothing else, should have decided her. After a lifetime of vanity rewarded by her fall from grace she ought to have accepted the time had come to pay her dues to him.

Feeling like an old woman, she drew down her veil as she passed through the doorway. 'I owe Nathaniel so much. An unspoken under-standing has existed between us from the day Lucien died that once my mourning period was over Nathaniel would claim me. He intimated as much as he outlined my best course in reclaiming Julian.' She paused. 'I am only doing my duty.'

In two strides Max had crossed the room and taken her by the shoulders. 'Duty? What has love to do with duty?' he rasped, his face close to hers. 'Nathaniel has no claim on you. He merely did what any decent man was obliged to do.'

Olivia wriggled out of his grasp. Salvation demanded she make her escape now. No matter that it tore her heart in two she had to do this.

'And Julian?'

His voice was thick with a mixture of anger and misery as he let her pull out of his arms. 'If you marry Nathaniel I will not see you again; would not want to, for it would be more than I could bear. But what about Julian?' His voice cracked. 'When Lady Farquhar made no effort to contact me, I, fool that I am, allowed myself to become attached—' He took a breath. 'You read me well enough to know that I would never exercise my authority to keep the boy with me. Am I to lose everything?'

'You may see him whenever you wish,' Olivia whispered, her

wretchedness threatening to consume her. She could not bear to see him like this.

'Provided Kirkman sanctions it,' he muttered.

Olivia gulped, nodding as she stepped out into the corridor. Without turning back, she picked up her skirts and fled.

❦

'I THOUGHT MR ATHERTON WAS LEAVING THIS MORNING.' AUNT Catherine looked anxiously between her niece and her sister. 'Mr Kirkman has just sent a message to say the two of them will be joining us for dinner.'

'Mr Kirkman sent the message?' Olivia put down her sewing and frowned at her aunt who shared the meagre warmth of their little fire from her favourite seat opposite.

'Apparently he's been entertaining Mr Atherton today. They rode to the abbey ruins earlier and—'

'Olivia?'

Olivia jerked her head up at Aunt Eunice's sharp tone and cursed herself for allowing her feelings to be so transparent. She wasn't glad he was coming, and that, clearly, was what had excited her aunt.

'I ... just feel anxious. What if he's decided to renege and take Julian back?' she said, feebly, as she returned to her stitching.

'Mr Atherton appears as unlike his cousin as is possible.' Aunt Eunice regarded her with interest. She had always known how to read her. 'Catherine, why don't you tell the kitchen? One extra place is hardly worthy of all your frowns, Olivia. Mr Atherton seems a very easy-to-please gentleman. I doubt he'd be too concerned if we served him bread and dripping on account of the short notice.'

Olivia said barely a word as her aunts welcomed Max into their fold before ushering everyone through to the drawing room for some Madeira before dinner.

She wished she could simply disappear, taking Julian with her, and never return. She'd leave them all in a heartbeat, she decided, watching Aunt Catherine fawning over Nathaniel, and Aunt Eunice's sharp eye roving over all, as if trying to understand that which Olivia wished heartily to keep from her.

Why had Max come? Why hadn't he just let her get on with her life according to their understanding of yesterday? Despite her long experience in play-acting she did not know how she would manage to behave towards him as if he were a mere stranger she had met the previous day. As for Max, what did he even know of play-acting? He was as transparent as the gossamer gowns her late husband had liked her to wear.

She was terrified.

Smiling faintly, she refused the seat Nathaniel offered her as they congregated in the drawing room before dinner, going instead to the corner of the Wilton carpet to kneel with Julian and Charlotte to play with the tin soldiers Max had bought for his nephew.

The little boy seemed as subdued as she, though perhaps a little more responsive towards her than he had been during the few days she had spent at Max's home. Quietly they lined up the soldiers in a neat row and distractedly Olivia stroked her son's soft dusky curls, listening to the drone of conversation and feeling sick with dread.

Would Max expose her visit to Elmwood in front of Nathaniel? She doubted that was his motive. Wearily she accepted he was making one final bid to win her back.

Misery overlaid all. She couldn't bear it. She'd well and truly accepted her fate.

'—isn't that so, Lady Farquhar?'

She jerked her head up at the sound of her name. All eyes were on her. Max's, most particularly. Without his good-natured smile and the gentle humour that softened his features he looked frighteningly like his cousin.

'I'm sorry, did I alarm you with my sudden question?' Max frowned in polite enquiry.

Olivia's heart pounded like a drum. The tin soldier fell from her grasp. 'You look so much like Lucien,' she whispered.

It took a moment for him to register this. There was shocked silence. She put her hand to her mouth. Mentioning Lucien in her household was akin to mentioning the Devil.

Max smiled and although it was not his usual open, kind smile, his resemblance to Lucien dissolved upon the instant. 'Forgive me, I keep forgetting my cousin was your late husband.'

With a nervous cough, Aunt Catherine said, 'You do indeed bear a striking resemblance to the late Lord Farquhar.'

Max's cool tone was tinged with surprise. 'It is not usually remarked upon.'

'For there is no resemblance when you smile, Mr Atherton, and I think you are generally a good-natured gentleman.' Olivia gave a shaky laugh.

'Please don't stand on ceremony with me.' Max gave a rather thin smile. 'We are surely sufficiently close to call each other by our Christian names.' Was it only Olivia who heard the irony?

She blushed and turned away as an image intruded of Max's hot feverish kisses and her equally feverish response.

'You were away, was it six years, Mr Atherton?' Aunt Eunice intervened, indicating to the servant to bring more Madeira.

'My regiment was sent overseas shortly before Lucien and Olivia were married. I returned to live at Elmwood after Lucien's death.'

Aunt Catherine took an appreciative sip of her aperitif. Entertaining was a rare treat. 'It must have been a shock to have been given the wardship of your nephew though it's apparent you've done a commendable job looking after him.' Grey ringlets bobbing, she beamed at him.

All eyes turned to Olivia at the sound of her stifled sob. Aunt Catherine gasped an apology. Aunt Eunice sounded glacial. 'As you can imagine, it is a sore point with Olivia that her late husband publicly proclaimed her unfit to take charge of her son.' She stared down her autocratic nose at their visitor who sat in the best chair by the piano, facing the ladies. 'A child requires a mother's love above all else.'

'I appreciate that.' Max spoke softly, his eyes roving over Olivia, his mouth a thin line. 'And I can see Julian is in good hands. I would be the last to deny the boy has a very' – the tiny pause was not lost on Olivia – 'loving mother.'

Olivia rose abruptly. 'Please excuse me. I'd like to rest awhile before dinner.'

❧

SHE WAS GLAD TO ESCAPE TO HER BEDCHAMBER. HOPEFULLY SHE'D not see Max again after tomorrow and might even get away without conversing personally with him tonight but clearly Aunt Eunice was not ready to let her off the hook.

Olivia turned from her dressing table, clenching her fists in her lap as the door was thrust open.

'Young lady, I think you've some explaining to do!'

Instead of Max, who had every reason to make such a demand, though his presence in such a manner would have been extraordinary, her aunt swept into the room.

'That'll be all, thank you, Dorcas.' Olivia nodded dismissal at the maid who'd been brushing her hair and waited until the door was closed before she said, defensively, 'You sent me on a mission to reclaim my son. I carried it out successfully.'

'This man, Lucien's cousin, Julian's guardian—' Aunt Eunice shook her head before continuing, 'You led me to believe Max was as unsatisfactory as Lucien and you were only too glad to get away. My eyes tell a different story.'

Olivia turned back to the looking glass, her voice dull. 'I can't imagine what you mean, Aunt Eunice.' She looked stonily at her reflection, unwilling to meet her aunt's eyes. Dorcas had arranged her hair that evening with a tumble of golden curls threaded through with pearls on either side of a centre parting. Her gown of gold and cream satin set off her skin to perfection and around her neck the butterfly key nestled in the hollow between her breasts.

'Don't tell me you've gone to such pains with your appearance on Mr Kirkman's account?' Aunt Eunice ground out. 'The way you've rigged yourself up you'll have the two of them engaged in fisticuffs at the dining-room table.'

Olivia turned, indignant. 'Miss Latimer delivered my new dress this afternoon. I had no idea Max would be accompanying Julian.'

'Just as Max had no idea that the woman who clearly turned his life upside down and with whom he is undoubtedly in love, was Julian's mother. Ah, Olivia, it was ill done of you.' An uncharacteristically sorrowful look replaced Aunt Eunice's anger as she rested her hands on Olivia's shoulders. 'Have you learned nothing since you married Lucien? Not even to trust your instincts?'

Olivia squared her shoulders. 'You think I'd trust Max with my heart? Max is Lucien's cousin. He looks like Lucien; he *glowers* like Lucien. Surely you saw the way he looked at me. No doubt he has a temper every bit as evil as Lucien's. You *hated* Lucien! Yet you would have me wed his cousin in preference to the eminently suitable, well regarded, upright and pious Mr Kirkman?'

'There are many men I'd rather you wed in preference to Mr Kirkman, though your Aunt Catherine begs to differ.'

The dinner gong sounded and Olivia leapt to her feet. 'Nathaniel can't abide unpunctuality,' she said, desperate to escape her aunt's scrutiny. The last thing she needed was Aunt Eunice pressing her to accept Max's suit over Nathaniel's.

At the dining-room door she nearly collided with Max. Bowing, he offered her his arm.

Olivia met his assessing gaze with a distinct lack of composure before turning towards the table where Aunt Eunice was seating herself beside her sister.

Max helped her to her chair. 'You're even lovelier than I remembered, Olivia.' He spoke softly. 'The last month has been a long one.'

Miserably she bent her head in acknowledgement of the compliment. And the gentle reproach.

'I hope Nathaniel deserves you.'

Raising her eyes to his she could discern no malice, nor did his tone or expression hint at sarcasm. 'Max, I'm sorry—'

'Ah, Mr Atherton, Olivia, good evening. My love, you are a vision.'

'She is, indeed.' Mr Kirkman, seating himself beside Olivia, looked smugly at Max who proceeded to his chair opposite.

Olivia turned away from Nathaniel's possessive smile, uncomfortably conscious of his thigh within a hair's breadth of her own. The way he fussed over her comfort seemed calculated to emphasize to Max his exclusive ownership.

'I expect, Mr Atherton – I mean Max,' she amended, with a contrived blush, 'you will be off early in the morning if you've more than three hours' riding ahead of you. Shall you break your journey in Bath?'

'You could, of course, extend your visit.' Aunt Eunice gave Max an expansive smile. 'Nathaniel must attend to business tomorrow. You could help Julian settle in. Isn't that a good idea, Reverend?'

The reverend's nod accompanied a weak smile, as Aunt Eunice went on in answer to Max's appearance of consideration, 'Excellent. Well, there's no need to remain at the inn when there's plenty of spare room, here.'

'That is, if Olivia has no objection to my presence under her roof. I would hate to distress her if I remind her so much of her late husband.'

'Only when you glower, Mr Atherton.'

Max raised his eyebrows. 'Good! In that case any likeness will hardly be remarked upon as I'm renowned for my good temper.'

Aunt Catherine gave a little sigh of happiness as her glass was refilled. 'What a wonderful state of affairs. Julian shall doubly benefit from the tender care of a doting uncle in his earliest years, and the wise instruction of his new stepfather as he grows to be a man.'

Max cleared his throat. 'I trust I might continue to see Julian often in the future.'

'Of course—'

Olivia's prompt agreement was interrupted by Nathaniel. 'Forgive me, Mr Atherton, but I believe it to be in the boy's best interests if there is no contact for some months.' He gave one of his lengthy, considering looks with which Olivia was so familiar, adding, 'Julian needs to settle in to his new life.' He turned at Olivia's stifled protest and patted her arm. 'I want only what is best for the boy, my love. If you can persuade me otherwise, I'll happily accede.'

Olivia refrained from any rejoinder as she acknowledged the devastating effect of Nathaniel's words. Max's affection for Julian was plain and although it would be best that Olivia not see Max again once she was married, she had promised Max continued access to the boy.

THE NEXT MORNING OLIVIA WOKE LATE AFTER A FITFUL NIGHT. HER

eyes felt gritty and her head buzzed with fatigue. Attending to her appearance, she wished she looked the picture of radiance Max had thought her last night, even though she knew it was a shameful wish. Running quickly up the stairs to the nursery, her heart contracted when she discovered the room empty. She hurried along the corridors and into the garden calling for Julian.

Perhaps Max, unable to contain his anger at her deception, had kidnapped him. If he had changed his mind about relinquishing Julian he certainly had enough ammunition to bolster the case against her.

Footsteps in the snow leading through the park gates only increased her fear, but just as she'd convinced herself Max had indeed made off with her son she heard voices.

Advancing slowly, as quietly as she could, she listened.

'Your mother loves you very much and she *is* your mother so it's her turn to look after you.' Max spoke softly. As Olivia could hear nothing from Julian she imagined Max was succeeding in soothing the lad. Raw grief rose up in her breast as she waited on the other side of the holly bush for the right time to announce her presence.

'Not every boy is lucky enough to have such a beautiful and kind mother, Julian. Do you know how many little boys would long to have a mother like yours?'

She heard a little hiccupping sob and was hard pressed not to add her own. Max's bond with Julian was so much stronger than her own. She understood how hard it would be for her son. For both of them. Well, it was further proof Max would be better off without her. It was one thing to make men fall in love with her; quite another to live up to their expectations. Lucien had called her his little cream puff: delectable to look at, he'd said, but without substance.

'And your new stepfather is a very upright and important fellow. At least in these parts,' Olivia heard him add in a none-too-flattering undertone. 'A reverend, no less! A very lucky reverend, young Julian, for he has got himself the most beautiful wife in all England. I daresay your Uncle Max is just an idle wastrel in comparison.'

'What nonsense!' Olivia brushed past the bush and frowned at Max. 'I suspect you wanted me to hear that so I would feel obliged to contradict you.'

Max rose, setting Julian down at his feet. Stooping to put a hand on the boy's shoulder he suggested with wheedling enthusiasm, 'Why don't you collect us some pine cones? Your mother and I have some things we need to say to one another.'

'What a good idea, my darling boy.' Olivia smiled at Julian, trying not to take his sullen rejection too much to heart as she put out her hand to stroke his curls before he ran off. With difficulty she said, 'What do you think needs to be said that hasn't been said already?' She wanted to channel her confusion into anger, but the way he was looking at her, his eyes smiling, a curl to his lip that was more gently challenging than malicious, threw her completely. 'I've said I'm sorry. I've admitted I used you shamelessly to get to Julian and I deeply regret what happened between us.'

Max took a step forward, his smile broadening. With a quick glance at the disappearing Julian, he tucked an errant curl behind her ear.

'What, exactly, do you regret? Falling in love?' He touched her cheek with his forefinger, trailing it slowly down to her collarbone.

Heat rose in her cheeks and her bosom heaved as she strained in a breath. His touch curdled her insides. Damning her susceptibility she said on a shaky breath, 'Lucien made no bones about my deplorable character.' She focused her gaze upon his gently curving mouth, wishing more than she'd ever done to feel the touch of his lips upon hers once more as she whispered, 'He would have said wicked, carnal attraction was between us, nothing more.'

Max chuckled. 'I'm more interested in what *you* would call it, though I have my answer just by the way you are looking at me.' He cupped her face and brought his own closer. 'You are afraid to risk your heart a second time, Olivia, but I am not Lucien,' he whispered. 'Lucien was a jealous madman who did not appreciate the greatest gift he was ever given. You! For I see little evidence of the character flaws Lucien elaborated upon.'

'You'd discover them in good time.' Olivia swayed against Max's steadying arm. 'He lived with me for seven years—'

'And destroyed your self worth. Olivia ...' Max wrapped his arms gently about her shoulders and stroked her hair. The gentle drone of his voice was catharsis, blocking out the awful reality to which she'd soon return. 'I barely slept last night,' he murmured. 'I thought of all I knew about Lucien. He took my initiation into his hands, you see, introducing me to his favourite gaming hells and other dens of vice. I was six years younger and, at eighteen, a willing disciple, though the novelty quickly wore off.'

She heard him take a deep breath before he continued. 'A year before, Lucien had seemed kinder. I suppose because he was in love.' He drew out the pause, adding, 'But something happened. He became the tyrant his father was. I heard he'd made a pact with the Devil; that he believed there was a fortune stored beneath the floorboards. He was insane, I understand that, just as I understand, better than you think, what your marriage must have been like. Lucien respected no one. I can imagine how he treated you.'

Olivia felt dangerously exposed, afraid of revealing more than she could afford. She waited tensely. When he broke the silence his words carried an edge of frustration.

'You say you owe The Reverend Kirkman your hand in marriage. Can you really do that, Olivia, when you know it means sacrificing your life's happiness?'

When still she did not speak, could not, he went on, 'My guess is that Lucien made you feel so worthless you don't believe you deserve happiness.'

She flinched, forcing herself to meet his eye as she stepped back. 'I'm sorry, Max. I've made up my mind.'

With a grunt of irritation he shook her gently. 'You are no longer a wilful debutante or an innocent pushed reluctantly into marriage, Olivia,' he said. 'You are a grown woman with experience of the world and a will of your own.'

Silence stretched between them. When he spoke again, his voice was steady, matter-of-fact. 'You delight me, Olivia.' He smiled as if he truly thought her the most exquisite thing he'd laid eyes upon. 'Every moment I am with you fills me with pleasure. We can make a wonderful future together – you, me and Julian.' He waited, his smile refusing to fade as the silence grew.

She knew she need only nod and it would be enough. She turned her head away, watching Julian in the distance as he played in the late

April snow, her heart knotted with pain and self disgust as Max tried one final gambit, 'If you thought to send me away with tales of your shocking past and your misplaced sense of duty towards a man who did what any decent man would do, Olivia, you've failed.'

How dearly she wanted to accept his offer and step into his arms.

They rested at his sides but she knew she need take only one small step and he'd wrap her up in them, and her life would be just the way she wanted it. Everything she could ever desire would be hers. If only ...

'Oh Max,' she said, at last, brokenly, her misery threatening to crush her. 'If only I could explain.'

'No, my dear.' He stepped back, his look curiously empty as he avoided her outstretched hands. 'If you cannot give me your love, or your honesty, I do not want anything else.' Formally, he offered her his arm. 'Let us fetch Julian and return to the house.'

DINNER WAS A LACKLUSTRE AFFAIR. ONLY NATHANIEL SEEMED TO enjoy himself. He'd imbibed more wine than usual and had taken control of the conversation. Even Aunt Catherine, his greatest admirer, seemed to be losing interest in his learned dissertations.

Halfway through pudding she twisted in her chair to raise the curtain hem so she could look out of the casement.

'Gracious, I do believe it's still snowing.'

'Surely not.' Aunt Eunice pushed back her chair and went to the window. 'The wind has picked up,' she said. Unnoticed above the babble of conversation it could now be heard howling through the treetops.

'It's a veritable storm.' Aunt Catherine's voice was tinged with concern. 'I'm only glad you're not caught up in it during your journey home, Mr Atherton,' she said, before frowning and looking at Nathaniel. 'You'll have to stay until it subsides, Reverend.'

Olivia nearly choked. The idea of being incarcerated with both Max and Nathaniel for any length of time was more than she could endure.

'How wild it is.' Even as Aunt Catherine spoke the keening of the wind seemed to rise in pitch. A dreadful crash sounded in the distance and Olivia jumped.

'Just a tree branch, my dear.' Nathaniel patted her arm and Olivia recoiled. Was it only just now, since she had met Max, that he evinced such a reaction? He had comforted her plenty of times in the aftermath of Lucien's shaming treatment.

The idea that she would soon commit herself to him, body and soul for the rest of her life, made her feel ill.

Perhaps she looked it for Max offered her a bolstering smile. She smiled in return, blushing at the sharp look Nathaniel directed at her.

Carefully she put her knife and fork together and leaned back to allow Dorcas to remove her plate. Her cheeks still felt hot.

'Olivia, surely you still have some of Lucien's clothes packed?' Aunt Catherine asked.

She gave a little gasp. Nathaniel in Lucien's clothes? All eyes were on her and for the second time in as many minutes she felt the heat burning her bosom upwards.

'Of course,' she managed, unable to stop her glance sweeping the man beside her from head to foot.

'Perhaps I can be of assistance,' Max offered. 'I brought several changes of clothing which may help lessen Olivia's distress.'

Olivia cut through the sympathetic tut-tutting. Nathaniel dressed in something belonging to Max was even worse to contemplate. No, she told them, she had a whole trunk of Lucien's nightshirts and other elegant items of apparel. If Nathaniel was happy to be seen wearing shirt points from two seasons ago he could have them all.

'I'll see what I can find, Nathaniel,' she said smoothly, as dinner was cleared away. Rising, she nodded to the gentlemen as she and her aunts left them to enjoy their port.

It was a relief to be out of the room. Clearly the wind was not going to abate. Clearly Nathaniel had no choice but to remain.

In her dressing room she rummaged in one of the large trunks by the window only to realize she had packed all Lucien's things in the attic. She'd never thought to look at them again. Had sworn she never would.

Taking a candle, she followed the corridor which led to the nursery.

At the doorway she stopped to gaze in pained wonderment at Julian's sleeping face. Her beautiful boy. The child she had cradled at her bosom and cared for until Lucien had decided she was no longer fit to rear him. Now he was hers again and Olivia was the guardian of his future. His happiness. She clenched her fists. Well, she would fight for him to the death. She would sacrifice even her greatest happiness if it ensured Julian's future.

At the end of the passageway a narrow staircase – more of a ladder, really – rose steeply to the attic. She felt strangely lighter to climb beyond reach of Aunt Eunice's hectoring, Aunt Catherine's quizzing and Nathaniel's unnerving presence.

And she would be far more composed if Max were not there, either.

In the darkness above she set the candle down on a horizontal beam. If her fears were not so earthly her heart would be leaping about as erratically as the candle flame, she thought, as she settled herself on a large tin trunk and stared at the ghostly shadows that danced by the flickering light.

She drew in a deep breath and tried to smile, even if the darkness were her only audience. She'd never been a nervous girl, but everything whipped up her fears these days, it seemed.

The Miss Templestowe of her youth had never been nervous. Determined and stubborn, yes. And arrogant, with the foolish conviction of a beautiful seventeen-year-old whose head has been turned by admiration that she could get away with anything.

When she'd run off with Lucien it would have taken a hurricane to have pushed her back. No amount of reasoning or threatening from anyone would have had any impact on her decision to go with him. He was London's catch of the season and she, penniless Miss Templestowe, had whisked him from under the noses of every other designing miss competing for his affections.

But she had never enjoyed his affections.

She cupped her chin in her hands and stared at a large painting of Lucien as a child. She'd consigned it to the attic after he'd died. He must have been about three for he was still dressed in petticoats with a pink sash about his middle, his arms wrapped around the neck of a

King Charles Spaniel. How angelic the pair looked posing beneath a cherry tree. She could imagine it was Julian with Max's dog, Pansy. The young Lucien's hair was dark and curling, his eyes blue, like Julian's. It was fortunate Julian had the same colouring, she reflected. The thought caused another pang. Though he was the reason she could never be with Max she could never regret the past when her little boy had given her life's greatest joy – and pain.

She rose, the floorboards creaking beneath her feet, as she bent to open the trunk.

'Make sure the nightcap matches.' The whisper startled her and she leapt back, a scream dying in her throat before she realized it was him.

'Max!'

His head appeared through the gap in the floor, 'You dare not risk his ire if he's not turned out fit to face a congregation.'

'I think Nathaniel is a little less concerned with his appearance than Lucien was.' Olivia was more relieved that Max's good humour had returned than afraid of being alone with him. 'Lucien, as you can imagine, was not best pleased if his valet's taste in matching waistcoats did not accord with his own. I think he went through valets faster than clean shirts.'

Max emerged before her, crossing the small space to lean against a cross beam and watch her as she rummaged through Lucien's clothes.

'And indeed, I do have plenty of nightcaps to match his night-shirts.' Olivia smiled as she scrutinized one of them. 'Lucien would not have dreamed of – or in – anything else.'

'A veritable slave to fashion,' remarked Max, stepping over a pile of old shirts and peering into the trunk. 'Why did you keep so many?'

His nearness sent tremors through her. 'These are just the ones from the year he died. Lucien discarded everything at the end of each season.'

'Good Lord,' remarked Max, looking down at his own blue and gold-figured silk waistcoat while he fingered his shirt points. 'I know I'm up to the mark in this rig-out, but I'm glad I don't need to subject myself to Lucien's scrutiny. The Lodge must have had the best-dressed servants in the village.'

'Lucien didn't believe in charity.'

She pretended to be unaware of the way he was looking at her. She had not meant to sound bitter. She must not play the victim and risk whipping up his chivalry. Good Lord, it was madness even to be alone with him.

He was showing admirable restraint, but she...? She was as weak as dishwater, she knew it.

Cautiously, she straightened. Max had seated himself on another trunk at right angles to her, his attention caught by the painting of Lucien with his parents. In the flickering light he looked devastatingly handsome, irresistibly desirable. Her breasts felt heavy and there was a curious fluttering at the base of her belly. How quickly the comforting feeling she had felt in response to his kindness turned to desire.

Beware, the voice of reason chimed in her head. The ladder beckons. Leave with your dignity intact and the only possible decision open to you, unwavering.

She closed the trunk, topping the pile of garments she had selected to lend to Nathaniel with a blue and white striped nightcap. Moving back, she had to stoop so as not to bump her head on the sloping beam above her.

Max turned back from his study of the painting and smiled. 'Julian looks very like his father,' he remarked.

'With your easier temperament, thank God.'

He put his hand out and touched her wrist, saying, 'Julian is a lovely child. There is nothing in his nature that brings Lucien to mind.'

She felt the charged impulse travel up her arm, through her nerve endings and deliver its powerful jolt to the core of her heart. He felt it too, she could tell, just as she could tell he was equally aware of her answering reaction.

There was a tense breathless pause, lasting less than a second as their silent communication found a mutual answer.

'Oh, Max!' She could not help herself. Couldn't deny the cravings of her body when he tugged her so she landed on his lap; could not stop herself responding with an ardour to match his when he took posses-sion of her mouth, so easily plundering her useless resolve to resist him. His molten kisses consumed every last atom of resistance, sweeping away her fears of discovery, of the secrets between them. They lay in a small, unaffected part of her brain. Forgotten. For now.

She cupped his face as she kissed him back, drinking in all the love and courage he offered, wanting to be everything he desired.

'Lord in Heaven, Olivia,' he gasped, as he branded hot kisses the length of her throat, following the low cut neckline of her dress, his hands roaming over her body while she arched into him. 'I've never wanted anything, anyone, like I want you.'

His words ignited her answering need for a love that was not tainted like Lucien's had been, like Nathaniel's would be.

But reality was a whisper away.

Oh God, Nathaniel.

Then Max's hand stole across the outline of her breast to stroke the sensitive skin at the hollow of her neck and Nathaniel was forgotten beneath the onslaught of Max's redoubled ardour and in her rush of desire for him she forgot herself and whispered the truth.

'I've never wanted anyone like I want you, Max.'

For just an instant he stilled. 'Prove it,' he murmured through his kisses.

Prove it?

Shock banished her pleasure. She gasped and tried to wriggle out of his arms.

As his hands fell away she straightened, her hand going to her throat. Removing the chain from around her neck she handed it to him.

'I give you the key to my heart,' she said. She looked down at her hands, now resting in her lap. 'Lucien gave it to me with those same words — said with irony, I might add, for he believed it was the key to some mysterious treasure he believed was hidden somewhere in the house. I only wish I could offer you something of substance.' She could hear the longing in her own voice, the pained acknowledgement that this was the end of everything between them.

His disconcerted look was quickly replaced by a laugh. His, also, was tinged with irony as he said, 'The key to your heart?' Then, answering his own question, added, 'The key to a chamber which will soon be occupied by someone else, it would seem.'

He set her from him, rising and going to the picture once more.

'Lucien has much to answer for,' she heard him mutter, before she felt his light touch as the pendant was replaced, once more, around her neck.

She glanced down, noticing it felt heavier, that the key was larger.

'The key to Elmwood.' His voice sounded almost distant behind her. 'It is your home if you ever choose to make it so.' He rested his hands upon her shoulders. 'If only I believed you were the scarlet woman Lucien painted you and that you were merely toying with me, I could understand.' His voice grew harsher when she said nothing.

'My God, Olivia, I know this was more than fumbling self gratification for you.' He came round to stand before her, looking down at where she sat. 'Your feelings came from the heart. Like the encounter before. And the one before that.' His face darkened with anger. 'Do you understand how wearisome this is? If it's fear of Nathaniel, for God's sake just tell me. If it's something else, be honest. Surely I'm owed that?'

She could not bear it. Not the anger, nor the thought of losing him. Oh, *why* had she done this? How could she have allowed herself to be so weak?

Because that's what she was. What she always had been. Lucien had said it and so had Nathaniel.

The flickering candlelight accentuated the shadows beneath his eyes. She could conjure him into Lucien if she wished. Pretend he would beat her into submission, violate her – oh, never her face, for what would the guests think? – unless she agreed to what he wanted.

'I...I'll try to explain.' Hunched miserably into herself she noticed his surprised hesitancy as he cocked his head.

She'd explained the myriad brutalities which had resulted in those very actions which stood between them but how could she explain Julian?

'I'm listening,' he prompted after a long silence.

She swallowed, watching the forefinger of his right hand, its silent tapping against the crossbeam the only outward sign of his agitation.

For so long she had acted in *reaction*. Lucien's brutalities had prompted so many self-preserving defences. Now, she felt exposed. Speaking the truth without it being violently torn from her seemed an impossible feat.

All she could do was lay the groundwork and hope that by the time she reached the end he'd have more understanding.

'Lucien was desperate for an heir.' It was feeble, but it was a start.

'I can hardly blame my cousin for that,' Max said, drily. 'Most men want an heir.'

Oh Lord, this was not going well.

'Our first child died within the hour. Lucien blamed me for the fact it was not baptized.' She swallowed, remembering his fury when he came into the bedroom to find her cradling the dead newborn. 'It was a difficult birth,' she went on, blocking out the pain, 'and I' – she turned her head away – 'was not ready for another, but Lucien would not heed the doctor. After that there were two miscarriages. Lucien blamed me.'

Glancing up at him she saw that his expression had lost its censure. Max settled himself beside her on the trunk and took her hands between his.

'Go on,' he said gently.

An owl hooted and Olivia shuddered. The candle flickered as a gentle gust of air caressed it, as if a ghost had waved its hand above it. Olivia focussed her attention on its tiny flame. 'Nathaniel said it was God's punishment on Lucien.' Max's hands felt warm. She always felt comforted in his presence and by God, he was showing the patience of a saint.

Each time he demanded the truth, she found herself able to yield up just a little more. Perhaps...

She sucked in a short, sharp breath. Perhaps she truly could offer up everything that stood in their way. If she had the courage only to do that, then it would be Max who determined their future through his forgiveness.

Not Olivia...through her cowardice.

'I trust he informed Lucien personally of this judgement.'

Olivia nodded. She even managed a smile at his tone. Max wanted the truth. He deserved the truth.

She *could* do it.

'It didn't help. Lucien was even more brutal to me, though he continued to confess all his sins to Nathaniel.'

'An interesting position for your intended.'

Olivia gripped his hand. 'Nathaniel was the only person Lucien allowed to show me any kindness.' Defensiveness made her hoarse. She licked her lips which were dry but took heart from the fact she still had Max's attention. He'd not withdrawn in disgust.

Yet.

'It was like a game to him. He encouraged it. He'd humiliate me in front of his guests, then wait for Nathaniel to cover me up and carry me away.' It was painful just to remember. 'Yet if any member of the company tried secretly to come to my aid, Lucien made sure they regretted it.' She gulped, turning to face Max once more. 'A young man stayed with us for a time. From Bavaria ...'

She couldn't go on. 'Forgive me,' he whispered, wiping her eyes as he stroked her neck.

His touch was soothing, comforting as she remembered. She wanted to enjoy it forever. But of course, her obligation was not yet fulfilled.

'I had recently lost a child and Lucien was very angry. This young man and I spent much time together. Lucien found us reading poetry and took it into his head that we were' – she swallowed convulsively – 'betraying him. He beat Pieter to a pulp before my very eyes, and then ... he punished me.'

Eventually Max asked, gently, 'What happened?'

'Nathaniel appeared and organized everything.' She shuddered.

'Pieter was covered in blood, groaning, the servants too afraid to go to his aid. Nathaniel tended to his wounds and dispatched him.' Olivia couldn't meet his eye. 'I don't know where he went. I never saw him again. When Nathaniel found me I was unconscious on the floor.' She looked at her feet, then held her arm to the candlelight. 'My dress was torn and I was covered in blood for his signet ring had sliced through my wrist. Lucien came back when Nathaniel was bathing me. He stood in the doorway and watched for a long time. Then he laughed and said I was between the Devil and God and whom would I choose? I told him it was a relief to me we didn't have a son because I couldn't bear seeing him turn out like his father. Then I said that while everyone believed I was unconscious I had had a message from our first born who was burning in the fires of Hell. I said little Lucien had informed me the Devil said he'd soon see his father because Lucien, too, was damned. Eternally damned.' Olivia gave a convulsive swallow.

'Lucien was terrified by the prospect of eternal damnation.' Another shiver made her convulse. 'I'd have said anything to stop him laying his hands on me again.'

'My poor Olivia,' murmured Max.

'It worked.' Olivia gulped. 'Lucien kept away from me after that. He held fewer parties.'

'Were you still required to add a ... decorative touch?'

Olivia shook her head. 'I was with child again and quite ill throughout—'

'Olivia! Are you up there?' Aunt Eunice's voice carried up from the base of the ladder. 'Nathaniel has been ready for his bed this past half an hour. Surely you must have found one of Lucien's nightgowns by now?'

Olivia turned to Max as she rose. She felt panicked, her story only half told. 'Perhaps you'd better stay here.'

'Oh no, skulduggery is not part of my repertoire,' he said, as he prepared to follow her down the stairs to greet their reception party: the aunts and Nathaniel Kirkman.

CHAPTER 7

MAX STOOD BEFORE the casement of the little chamber he'd been allotted and stared into the garden. Like ghostly soldiers, the poplars swayed in the pale night and the wind emitted a thin, eerie sound.

Sleep would elude him, he knew. There was no point even trying. Olivia's story appeared like an unfinished tapestry: loose threads everywhere.

She'd been leading up to a confession, but what was her crime? Or the worst of them? She'd been a victim for seven years. Survival would trump morality. Is that what she was telling him? What could she have done that was so shameful she'd chosen to keep silent and lose the man she had, finally, openly, professed to love?

He had no choice but to wait until the morning for answers, but would she be as willing to divulge all after a night in which to consider the consequences?

How would Max, himself, feel when confronted with the truth? For he was beginning to fear the worst.

The storm was building. He must check on Julian as was his habit, but for the first time his thoughts of the boy evinced a shudder.

The nursery was in the west wing, far removed from the rest of the sleeping quarters. Quietly, he made his way along the corridor, pausing at the passage that intercepted it. He raised his candle high to identify the figure which had emerged at the end. Reverend Kirkman. Quickly, he stepped back. Hadn't he been accommodated at the other end of the house? he wondered, waiting for him to pass Olivia's bedchamber. If it were Kirkman's intention also to visit the nursery Max would delay his visit until later.

But he was not going to the nursery. Max heard the faint creak of the door to the only bedchamber along that passageway: Olivia's.

'Heavens, Max! You made my heart nearly stop.'

It was Olivia's Aunt Eunice arriving via another corridor, though it was hard to imagine anything had the power to make Aunt Eunice quake in her boots.

'You're checking on Julian, too, I see.'

Max forced a smile. And forced himself not to brush past Aunt Eunice and into Olivia's chamber on the heels of Kirkman.

'It's a habit,' he said, distractedly, unable to drag his eyes from the glow of candlelight that filtered from beneath Olivia's door. 'Julian isn't fond of storms.'

'Olivia always hated them,' Aunt Eunice remarked, taking Max's arm and steering him towards the nursery.

'I know.' Max glanced down at her, resigned to the fact he could not play sentinel until the other man emerged. 'She used to be locked in her room on such occasions.'

'Olivia slept with me or Catherine during thunderstorms.' Eunice slid accusing eyes across to Max. 'Lucien locked her in her room.'

He should have realized this, of course.

'Once he locked her in for five days on nothing but gruel and water.'

Despite what he'd learnt of Lucien's treatment he was still horrified. Aunt Eunice met his dismay with a hard look. 'Martha, Olivia's maid, told me. She went to The Lodge with Olivia when Olivia married and continued to pass on news even after she married the publican, Mr Mifflin.'

'Five days?' Though after what Olivia had told him he'd believe anything.

'Lucien saw conspiracies in everything she did. If she displeased him, he punished her. I believe on this occasion she'd walked to church with a neighbour, a handsome young man who admired her. The young man got a bloodied nose; Olivia got five days' incarceration. No doubt she learned to choose her companions carefully.' The old woman's voice grew bitter. She slowed her footsteps as they approached the nursery wing. 'He whisked my beautiful niece off her feet, squandered her happiness, sapped her of her spirit and stripped her of her son. And there was nothing I could do for she severed contact when she defied me to be with Lucien.'

She stopped, staring at the door before them. Even in the softening glow of candlelight the woman looked much older than she had earlier this evening. Her grey hair hung in a thin plait over one bony shoulder and her mouth quivered.

'Olivia was the child I never had.' Her voice caught. 'Georgiana, her mother, was the baby of the family. The favourite, for she inherited our Aunt Jane's entire fortune, only to squander it on a fortune-hunter who left her to die alone as she gave birth to Olivia.'

Max patted the woman's arm. 'Olivia's lucky to have had you, then.'

'Perhaps it was a mistake to protect her so much.' There was self doubt in the bleak look she sent him. 'In her childhood we spoiled her, cosseted her, turned her head with compliments.' She sucked in a breath. 'Then she met Lucien.' Max saw her tremble with the force of her hatred. 'Lucien taught her about life's cruelties. He had no mercy, even in death. And now our beautiful Olivia is about to sacrifice herself to that pompous old drone I've had to suffer the past year!'

She fixed Max with a gimlet look. Earlier he would have met it with an equally defiant one, declaring he had no intention of allowing such a thing to happen.

Right now he didn't know what to think.

His lack of conviction must have been apparent. Disappointment kindled in her eyes. 'I know she loves you,' Aunt Eunice said softly as she gripped his wrist with one bony hand. Her look communicated her silent hope that Max would be Olivia's valiant defender.

Max stared at the floor, his resolve to be that man marred by the fear of what he'd discover when Olivia finally confessed the truth. 'She doesn't believe she deserves happiness,' he said, as he wondered how great her crime must be before that became indeed the truth.

৩৯৩

OLIVIA JERKED UPRIGHT AT THE TENTATIVE RAP UPON THE DOOR. A wild rush of anticipation flooded her as she hurried towards it, turning the doorknob with a smile that reflected her burgeoning hope.

Max. He was not a man who'd let suspicions fester. Only the truth would answer and she'd give it to him. Damn the consequences. Yes, in the interval between their discussion in the attic and now she'd become fully resolved. Max's continued affirmation of his love had given her the strength she needed. She'd just needed the opportunity to confess and here it was.

'You'll pardon the intrusion, Olivia.' With his trademark frown and ponderous manner Nathaniel brushed past her, covering her hand with his own as he gently turned the doorknob, closing the door behind them.

'Nathaniel, you can't—'

Ignoring her, he put his hand upon her shoulder and led her away from the door.

She didn't like the way he was smiling at her. The room was small with the bed taking up most of the space. She felt violated already.

Twisting out of his semi-embrace she crossed her hands in front of her chest, knowing the sheer fabric of her night rail left little to the imagination.

'So coy with me, Olivia, when we are soon to be wed?'

'I'm not going to marry you, Nathaniel.'

There. That's all it took. And she had said it. Now what could he do to her? She need only scream once and the entire household would descend upon the room in an instant. A tremendous power was quickly filling her. She felt light and ebullient so that for the first time Nathaniel's darkling look did not cow her.

But he would not surrender her so easily. With both hands now upon her shoulders he steered her backwards. 'So it is as I feared.' There was anger in his eyes though his voice was calm.

'I'll scream.' The power drained out of her as quickly as it had been whipped up. She felt like a rag doll in his unkind grip and she could manage no more than a pathetic whisper. She was trembling so much it was all she could do to remain standing, trapped as she was between the high bed and Nathaniel who was leaning over her.

Wearing Lucien's striped nightshirt.

Nathaniel was short of stature and more thickly set although he was by no means an unattractive man. He could set many a feminine heart aflutter, Olivia knew. More pious ones than hers.

'Don't do this, Nathaniel,' she pleaded. She could feel the hardness of his desire pressing against her thigh through the fabric of her nightgown.

'What? Take you here like a common harlot?' His eyes shone with derision, but at least he kept his feet on the floor. 'Under your own roof with your aunts down the corridor? Credit me with a little more finesse and respect than Lucien. No, Olivia, I mean only to discuss the situation in which we find ourselves. I think that under the circumstances it is quite proper you would entertain your betrothed when he has concerns about your future happiness' – her skin crawled at his heated breath on her neck – 'and the happiness of your son.'

It was hard to control her ragged breathing. She struggled beneath him before giving up, wishing she could manage more conviction as she whispered, 'Did you not hear me? I said I am not going to marry you so we have nothing to discuss.'

'Since this is the first I've heard of this new state of affairs I'd say we had plenty to discuss.'

Looming over her, his expression was difficult to read. Olivia closed her eyes against his anger and wounded pride. She'd not expected intimidation.

'I take it Mr Atherton is behind your change of heart. Clearly you've deceived me. You've met him before.'

Olivia inclined her head a fraction. No point denying it. However it stood to reason Nathaniel would take it badly being superseded by Lucien's cousin.

'I love Max.' It was catharsis to say it though whether or not Max still loved her or *would* still love her was another matter when she'd finished baring her heart. At least telling Nathaniel that the truth was finally out in the open meant he would surely not continue to press his suit.

She was wrong.

He kept her pinioned upon the bed, his body heavy as he angled one knee beside her thigh to gain better purchase. 'I have waited eight long years to make you mine.' His whisper sounded more like a desperate snarl than a reaffirming caress. 'We've had an understanding since before Lucien died.'

Self-preservation battled within. She could not let him dominate her, terrorize her, as Lucien had.

She struggled again, managing to free one arm which she used to push him away, hissing, 'No, we have not!'

'Then we have misunderstood one another for my offer and your acceptance of it so recently seemed to me the only logical outcome of a long and difficult courtship.'

He released her then. She curled up her knees and swung round to gain distance but he sat heavily on the bed, pulling her across his chest and catching her beneath the knees to swing her on to his lap.

Olivia went rigid as he forced her head against his shoulder. The garment he wore was musty from its months consigned to a trunk without air but she could smell the faint essence which reminded her so strongly of Lucien. And beneath it, the animal smell of her suitor, roused by anger and pride.

Nathaniel grasped her by the chin and twisted her face to look at him as he repeated roughly, 'Do not play the coy maiden with me just because another contender for your affections has presented himself. One that you prefer.' He clamped his hand round her neck and pushed her head back on to his shoulder. 'You know you cannot have him,' he hissed, as his hands caressed her throat.

'You can't force me to marry you,' Olivia rasped. She was close to swooning from his smell alone. Unable to struggle to any effect, she lay limply in his arms.

'There are many compelling reasons for a match between us.' The tenseness seemed to drain out of him in response to her passivity. Nathaniel sighed as his fingers explored the contours of her neck and chest. He gazed out of the window. 'Surely, my dear, you gave up fairy stories when you married Lucien.'

Olivia tried to swallow through her fear. 'Nathaniel, I ... I'm very fond of you but—'

'Don't think I'll be satisfied with a sop like that,' he sneered, bringing his face close to hers. 'We were meant to be together. Everything has been orchestrated for this union.'

'I want to be with Max. If—' She tried to be brave. 'If you force me to do anything against my will I *shall* scream, I promise you!'

'I'm not so stupid, Olivia.' Rising abruptly, he pushed her back down upon the bed. 'Look at you!' His voice dripped with scorn.

'Eight years ago you were the toast of the town. A diamond of the first water. Now, you're just a shell. Your reputation is in tatters and the charm and gaiety that captivated society just a memory. Oh, to me you're still lovely to look at. I had hoped to restore to you what you had lost through your own foolishness. I had hoped to redeem you. No doubt Max thinks a vacuous plaything will do very well until he finds the kind of wife he's really after.' His lip curled as he delivered his verdict. 'An innocent, simple creature, pleasing to the eye with no damning past to threaten his manliness.'

She would not let him see he had found his mark. 'Max has honour and he knows his own mind. He wants *me*.'

'I've no doubt he wants you, Olivia,' chuckled Nathaniel as he took a step towards the door. 'Most men want you. *I* want you. But does he want to marry you? And if so, was that after you threw yourself at him ... but before you confessed to him the truth?'

Olivia covered her eyes, twisting away from him. If they'd been empty taunts she could have borne them.

'Ever the slattern, Olivia.' Returning to bend over her, he trailed his forefinger across her collarbone, skimming the tops of her breasts. 'Like satin,' he breathed. He traced the arches of her eyebrows. 'So beautiful yet so stupid,' he added, moving his mouth to her ear. 'So stupid because you cannot let your mind master your body. Unlike me, my darling Olivia, else I'd be walking away, satiated right now. But I shall leave that for another night. Our wedding night.'

Olivia started to cry; short, shallow gasps, tears streaming down her face. His shadow as he leaned over her was as oppressive as the weight of him had been. She hiccupped. 'How can you want me if you despise me so much?'

'Despise you?' He considered the question as he tugged loose the bow of her nightdress then retied it more tightly so that she was respectably covered. 'And love you in equal measure. I shall be your salvation, Olivia.'

'Max knows *everything* about my past,' Olivia whispered, recoiling from his touch, wishing for Max's embrace to wash away the sordidness she felt.

'Everything?' His brow furrowed as he sat. Hunched on the edge of the mattress he reminded her of a calculating toad who has just received a blow. He looked genuinely perplexed and Olivia revelled in her sudden power until he delivered his *coup de grâce*. 'How can he still want you when he knows your dark and dirty little secret?' His astonishment was not feigned and Olivia's self-disgust made her crumple inwardly as he added, 'He honestly forgives you for what you have stolen from him?'

The look on her face must have revealed the truth for suddenly he was standing, his arms around her as he drew her to her feet, supporting her as she swayed. His voice was triumphant as he cried, 'Always the dreamer, Olivia. You say you told him the truth. Ha! You've barely scratched the surface.'

She felt the wetness of her tears on the back of her hand as she wiped her cheek, raising her head from his shoulder where he'd forced it. This time she did not resist as he threw back the covers, lifted her gently on to the mattress and tucked the blankets around her.

'There, there, my love,' he soothed, bending over her, offering her the milk Aunt Catherine had warmed and brought her a short while before. 'Drink this. You've had a nasty shock, discovering your beauty isn't always enough to get you what you want. Soon I will be your husband: friend, not foe. With every weapon at my disposal I shall ensure Julian's future remains secure.' On stockinged feet he padded towards the door, turning when he reached the middle of the carpet.

'Don't worry, Olivia.'

She turned her head from his triumphant sneer.

'You may not love me, but your secret is safe. We both know guarding that little powder keg is essential ... for the happiness of *all* concerned.'

An empty shell.

Is that what she was?

Shivering, curled up in her narrow bed she listened to the mice in the wainscoting and the rattle of the casement.

Hours later the chirping of birds announced the dawn.

How desperately she'd tried to find the words to unburden her soul, to tell Max the truth when they had been in the attic. How close she had been.

And she would have followed through on her promise of the truth in the morning had it not been for Nathaniel's visit.

Max was the light in her life. He made her believe the truth could be overcome.

Nathaniel's visit reminded her it could not.

Quietly, she sobbed, hunched beneath the covers, racked with despair. What should she do? She was torn asunder by her feelings for the three males beneath this roof but Nathaniel held the trump card. It wasn't just his insidious threats of revealing the truth about Julian. Before Nathaniel's visit Olivia had resolved to do just that, herself.

It was his judgement. With time Max would regard her as Lucien had – venality masquerading in a cloak of beauty.

A thwarted Nathaniel would turn her sins into moral outrages and evidence of corruption not even the most besotted suitor could countenance.

Head pounding, she tried to crystallize her thoughts. With the brightening dawn her courage returned.

At the heart of every decision she'd made since Julian had been born was his future.

Marriage to Nathaniel ensured the safety and welfare of her son. But how would Julian judge *her* when he was grown?

A woman too afraid to trust her instincts? Too weak to stand firm against threats and coercion?

Miserably, she reflected on the two men who held her hostage: Max with his love and the fact he deserved an unpalatable truth she was too afraid to risk. And Nathaniel with his threats and his *promises* to hide the truth.

She drew a rasping breath and struggled upright on her pillows, her heart racing.

The truth lay at the heart of everything.

Only the truth would answer. Aunt Eunice had sent her to Elmwood to 'set the record straight' so she could regain her son but from the outset she'd lacked the courage to tell Max the truth.

Yet Max's love had held firm in the face of her shameful deception. Why? Because he believed she was pure of heart.

She was!

She shivered, her mind engaged in a battle between hope and fear. Unless she conquered her fear she'd never realize her dreams.

Nathaniel had made her believe Max represented Julian's greatest threat; that only he, Rev'd Nathaniel Kirkman, had the power to protect Julian's future. He'd used veiled threats to conjure up a future unimaginably perilous for young Julian.

Oh God, she thought, her pulses racing, why had she not seen the truth before?

Max was not Julian's greatest threat: Nathaniel was.

CHAPTER 8

AFIRE WITH ANTICIPATION, Max waited for Olivia at breakfast. After a night in which doubts and fears chased firm resolves to forgive her everything, he now needed simply to see her.

One frank smile and a murmured reinforcement of her feelings for him would be sufficient. He freely admitted he was enslaved.

Olivia had suffered appallingly during her marriage to Lucien. However shocking the truth, she was the victim of forces beyond her control.

With an effort he forced down his smoked haddock – and the impulse to jerk his head round to Aunt Eunice on his left and give her the reassurances she'd wanted last night: that regardless, he would be Olivia's knight in shining armour. He would protect her to the end.

And he would.

He just wished he could reassure Olivia, but her chair remained empty and he was barely able to hide his disappointment when Dorcas appeared with the announcement that Olivia was still sleeping and seemed feverish.

Finally the moment of departure was upon him. He could delay it no longer. Olivia's aunts, Eunice and Catherine, exclaimed their pleasure at his company, pressing him to return soon. Kirkman merely nodded stiffly.

A thick covering of snow whitened the curving driveway that led to the main road. He'd said his farewells at the front step, exhorting everyone to return to the warmth of indoors.

Now, from astride Odin, Max gazed up at Olivia's casement window.

In three seconds he would be out of Olivia's life, but not for long.

Hadn't she avowed her love for him? Surely all she required was affirmation of his understanding and forgiveness. Even if his worst fears were confirmed....

Ignoring his apprehension he held firm, reminding himself of what was at the heart of Olivia's forthcoming admission: she was not to blame.

He lowered his head to whisper encouragement to his horse, twisting in the saddle when he heard the crunch of footsteps upon the gravel. Light, running footsteps.

Wearing nothing warmer than a flimsy Norwich shawl over her dress, Olivia was hastening across the few yards which separated them.

Lord, she was beautiful. With her hair hanging past her shoulders in two plaits she reminded him of one of the Vestal Virgins in a book of illustrations he'd had as a child.

Having been tormented by Olivia's unfinished tale, the myriad possibilities as to why she was unable to commit herself to him – each more lurid than the last – his heart now soared. Her haste and the look in her eye could mean only one thing: she was here to confess and crave his understanding.

And she would have it.

Drinking in those spectacular blue eyes and the full, curved lips he could kiss forever, he would forgive her anything.

'Max! You ask why I believe I cannot marry you.' Her voice came in breathless gasps. 'There is no easy way to say it and no time to dress up the truth but if you will hear me out—'

'Come with me now,' he urged, reason turning him into an impetuous schoolboy as he reached down from the saddle for her. The urge to protect her thundered in his breast. 'If you are frightened of Kirkman, don't be, for I will let nothing harm you. Ever.'

Tears formed on her lashes. It could have been the cold and the exertion but he did not think so.

'Oh Max!' Her voice disappeared on a cry of pain. 'I have wronged you so greatly but Lord knows it was not my intention at the time.'

'Hush.' He dismounted and drew her, unresisting, into his arms.

'Confess your secret, but you already have my absolution. I can see Lucien's lies for what they are.'

'Lucien's lies have nothing to do with this. It is what I have done.'

Brushing his lips across her brow he corrected her. 'What Lucien *made* you do, Olivia. With me you need no longer be afraid.'

She pulled out of his arms, wiping her streaming eyes with the back of her hand. Taking a deep breath she half turned, but her words were clear, misted in the icy air as she gasped, 'Max! Though I have done wrong, things are not as they seem.'

'Ah, Olivia, I am glad to see Mr Atherton is receiving the send-off he deserves.'

They hadn't heard him approach. Flinching, Olivia swung round as Max's shock hardened.

Mr Kirkman placed a proprietary hand upon Olivia's shoulder and confronted Max with obsidian eyes.

'Olivia will miss you very much, Mr Atherton.' It came out a purr. 'She told me so last night.' His hand slid down her arm to clasp her small fist.

She made no move to push him away.

Max stared with confusion at the woman he loved. He wanted to repeat his offer. To take her with him, but her expression was suddenly closed as she half raised her hand in parting.

'God speed, Max,' she murmured. A spasm of fear crossed her face then boldly she took a step forward and placed her hand on his shoulder.

He had to lower his head to hear her.

'I shall write, Max,' she whispered. 'I shall explain everything.'

I SHALL WRITE.

The rebirth of hope gave him new strength. On impulse he halted Odin on a bend of the drive which led to The Lodge.

A gravel path led to the family crypt a few yards away. Dug into the side of the hill, halfway to the dower house, it had been a favourite hiding place during a memorable holiday when he'd been a small boy.

He decided to pay his final respects to his cousin. He'd try to remember Lucien as a boisterous playmate and pleasant companion rather than the violent despot who had tyrannized Olivia for seven years.

But the door to the crypt would not yield. Lichen-encrusted and swollen with age it seemed an impenetrable barrier between the past and the present.

Max stared at it, wondering if his body would be interred within the stone sarcophagus beside his cousin. Imagining Olivia, in black, reclaiming freedom only to lose it to the possessive churchman.

With a surge of angry longing he tugged at the key on its thin chain which he had placed around his neck.

'The key to her heart' she had said, just as the chain snapped and the key fell with a dull jangle to the flagstone upon which he stood. A cruel echo of Lucien's meaningless words.

Bending down he picked it up and, unthinking, inserted it into the lock. It turned smoothly and the door swung open, admitting him to the hallowed precincts of the final resting place for all the Viscounts Farquhar for the past 400 years.

And their faithful dogs, he amended with a wry smile, as he stepped into the gloom.

A high window, just above ground level, admitted the weak spring sunlight and, as his gaze slid from the stately sarcophagus where Lucien was interred to the tiny sarcophagus beside him, he felt a rush of sorrow and sympathy for Olivia.

How terrible it must it have felt to have been consigned to no more than a vessel that must produce the next heir? Derided, abused and worthy of less consideration than the King Charles' Spaniel Lucien showered with affection and which now lay in state in its miniature resting place beside him.

Olivia had been granted life tenure of the dower house with almost nothing to live upon, after being stripped of the one being that gave her life meaning: her child.

'Ah, Lucien, it was ill done of you,' he said, running his hand over his cousin's inscription before turning away.

If only Mr Kirkman had no rightful claim upon Olivia he would stride up the hill and demand that Olivia return to Elmwood with him now. That he forgave her everything and he knew how to make it all right.

He pulled the door shut, blocking out the past but unable to change it.

For Kirkman's involvement altered everything.

NATHANIEL DREW OLIVIA BACK TO THE HOUSE WITH HIM BEFORE Max had disappeared round the bend of the drive. She longed to prolong the moment before his beloved form was no more than a memory but Nathaniel was a force too great to resist, alone.

Pleading a megrim as soon as she was indoors she gathered ink and paper from the drawing room while Aunt Eunice cornered Nathaniel, begging him with uncharacteristic interest to regale her with the details of the sermon he was writing for his forthcoming sermon in Nuningford.

Nuningford. A week from now.

Gazing from the casement window in her bedchamber Olivia watched Max's straight-backed figure disappear round the bend that led to the main road.

She drew in her breath, her nerve ends tingling before setting her writing box on her lap and beginning the hardest letter she had ever written.

Max, her knight in shining armour.

Max, whom she loved more than she'd believed possible, whose love for her gave her strength and purpose.

How would he feel about her when he read her confession?

My dearest Max – she could feel the blood surging through her veins as the pen scratched over the rough surface – *I promised you the truth and you shall have it. There is no easy way to say this—*

The truth.

Dropping her pen, Olivia rose and went to the window.

The truth would change everything: Julian's security, Olivia's future and quite possibly Max's love for her. But the truth was the only way to remove Nathaniel's shackles and to move on with her life.

Looking down at her white knuckles and the ink spots on her fingers, she reaffirmed her resolve. If she continued to evade the truth she would be worse than the creature beyond redemption Lucien had painted her. And if she had any chance of earning Max's continued love and respect she had to take the risk now.

Returning to her writing desk she continued.

The truth is that Julian is not Lucien's legitimate heir. He is not the boy born to me that terrible stormy night when Lucien was away hunting and my physician was delivering a breech birth many miles away....

The pain and horror of that night were engraved upon her mind. Charlotte and Martha had attended her as she had convulsed with birthing pangs upon the four-poster in which Lucien had been born, and his father and grandfather before him.

The raging storm had prevented the message being delivered to the physician for several hours. Charlotte had soothed her after they'd received news that the squire's wife was dying; that with the river swelling, it was doubtful the physician would be able to cross when his painful job was done. Charlotte had tried to reassure Olivia that Martha had delivered six of her mother's babes.

Picking up her pen, Olivia continued.

Our child was born strong and lusty. Charlotte and Martha put him to my breast and we celebrated that at last Lucien had his heir and perhaps I would have my peace.

Olivia forced herself to continue.

But the boy died within the hour. He started to labour in his breathing and in terror I had Martha fetch Rev'd Kirkman. Lucien needed to be reassured that this child would not burn in the fires of Hell.

Unable to continue, Olivia pushed back her chair and took a restless turn about the room. Twisting her hands, she tried to compose herself, formulate her words so that Max might understand the terrible grief that consumed her that night; her fear of Lucien's anger and the maternal cravings which would grasp at any means of giving her the son she and Lucien wanted so desperately.

Even if it meant a terrible deception.

Slowly she lowered herself into her seat and picked up the pen once more. With thundering heart she dipped it into the inkwell.

The moment had come to commit to paper the words that would be the ultimate test of Max's love.

Nathaniel came promptly. In his arms he carried a babe, wrapped in swaddling clothes. Its cry was as lusty as my own child's had been, less than an hour before. But my own child was now silent. Blue and silent and the reverend was too late.

I fought Nathaniel as he removed my beloved infant then watched in wonder as this new child latched on to my breast.

Julian.

Olivia sat back so the tears would not spoil the ink. Wiping them away with the back of her hand, she wrote,

Julian is Lucien's child by his village mistress who delivered the same night. When I saw the eyes and the shape of his jaw I knew Mr Kirkman spoke the truth: that Lucien was his father and that the babe would die unless a wet nurse were found soon.

It took a moment for Olivia to compose herself before she could continue.

Forgive me, Max, for doing what any bereaved mother would surely do.

From the moment I suckled the child, knowing its mother was dead, I could not give him up. A precious gift had been put into my safekeeping and it was my God-given duty to protect him ... to the death.

Julian was not born within the sanctity of marriage but he is Lucien's child, nonetheless. Lucien's fury would have known no bounds if he'd returned to learn his son had died before he was baptized.

I confess that while my love for the child was instant and sincere I was also guilty of cowardice. I did not know how I could survive much more of Lucien's brutality in his determination to father an heir.

Olivia put the pen down and ran the back of her hand across her brow before she was able to finish her task.

Darling Max, I paid no thought to your rights when I acted as I did. Only since I met you have I understood the enormity of my actions which have denied you your birthright. This letter sets out the truth and also begs your forgiveness. I would not hurt you for the world.

You have brought the sun into my life and given me hope where none existed before. I love you like I never believed possible and can only hope your kindness and compassion will temper the disgust you have every reason to feel on account of my continued lies.

The time for lies is past, now, and I offer this full accounting so that you may decide how best to proceed in order for you to reclaim what my actions have wrongfully taken away from you.

Whatever you decide, please know that I shall understand and continue to love you.

Meanwhile I wait in fevered anticipation for a sign indicating your feelings and outlining the course of action you wish me to take in order to redress the wrong I have done.

For now and always, I remain your loving Olivia.

She had to allow herself to hope; to believe that Max's compassion would ensure she would *not* be accompanying Nathaniel to Nuningford the following week.

After sprinkling sand on the parchment she folded and addressed the precious missive just as Dorcas entered to bring her some comfrey tea for her aching head.

'I'll take that with Miss Catherine's letter to her Cousin Mariah, shall I?' asked Dorcas, setting down the mug of steaming tea and picking up the letter.

Olivia turned her head away so as not draw attention to her excitement. 'Thank you, Dorcas.'

'An' what shall I tell your aunts who are worried for your poor head?'

'That I shall be down for luncheon,' she said. 'The rest has done me good, as I'm sure the tea will.'

Dorcas placed the letter in her apron pocket and picked up the breakfast tray she'd brought her mistress earlier that morning. It remained untouched.

At the bottom of the stairs she met Mr Kirkman who had just put on his gloves and greatcoat in preparation for leaving.

'I hope Lady Farquhar recovers her good health soon,' he said, as he reached for Aunt Catherine's letter which lay upon the silver salver on the hall stand.

'She seems better, sir,' Dorcas said, adding as he put his hand on the door knob, 'And if you're going to the post box, I wonder if you'd take this for Miss Olivia."

He turned, raising his eyebrows as he held his hands out for the letter. 'Of course, Dorcas. Why did I not think to ask?' Then, with an uncharacteristically warm smile, 'Thank you, indeed.'

⸙

IT WAS NOON AND MAX WAS HUNGRY WHEN HE DISMOUNTED IN THE stable yard of *The Pelican* less than an hour later, tossing the reins to an ostler.

Olivia's parting had reaffirmed the promise that existed between them. The promise of a future that could withstand the perilous present and the lies of the past.

Olivia was true of heart and her heart belonged to him.

'Regular beauty, ain't he?' The stable-lad's tone was admiring as he stroked the horse's steaming flank. Hopeful, too, as he asked, 'We'll be stabling him for the night?'

'Only an hour or so,' replied Max, nodding as the publican appeared on the back step lacing his hands across his impressive belly as he welcomed him.

Max shrugged off his greatcoat as he entered the low-ceilinged room. He'd expected to find it empty but a returned soldier muffled against the cold sat drinking in the shadows.

The publican seemed disposed to conversation when he learned from where Max had just come. 'Me wife, Mrs Mifflin as she be known now, used to be lady's maid to Lady Farquhar,' he said with pride.

There was a stirring from the settle by the fire in the corner and a slurred voice rang out, 'To the good Lady Farquhar!'

Not happy at the tone, Max turned to see an old ex-solder, muffled up against the cold, raise his tankard.

'Don't mind Dorling over there,' muttered the publican, with a dismissive wave in the soldier's direction as he poured Max an ale. 'Known him since we was lads together afore he joined 'is Majesty's Service.' Raising his voice he addressed the old man. ' Jest keep yer thoughts to yerself tonight, for once, Pat Dorling, or you'll be kissin' Jack Mifflin's great fist.' He wagged a menacing finger in the old soldier's direction. 'Mr Atherton 'ere was a guest of the Misses Dingley.'

A great log in the fireplace shifted noisily in the threatening silence.

Dorling, his rheumy eyes not meeting theirs, jerked his head back down into his ale, his expression sour.

'Never bin the same since his daughter died,' the publican explained in a stage whisper, as he pushed Max's drink across the counter top. 'So,' he added in regular tones, 'How are they at the big house? Mrs Mifflin will want to know."

Before Max could reply, the soldier let out a crack of laughter and interrupted loudly, 'Guest of m' lady, eh? He who is smitten shall be smited.' He shuffled around in his seat and squinted at Max. 'Acquainted with Lady Farquhar already? I's sure you was amply rewarded, a handsome gennelmun such as yourself.'

Max regarded the odorous creature with a cool stare. The tattered scarlet uniform visible beneath his greasy greatcoat and the dirty, unsteady hand that raised his drink to his lips told their own story. The man was drunk and had some grievance against the elderly sisters and their niece. Perhaps he'd been a former employee, dismissed for his fondness for the bottle. Perhaps he'd harboured a *tendre* for Olivia and been given his marching orders.

'I'd thank you to observe the respect due to Lady Farquhar,' he warned softly.

The publican finished up with his own decree as he wiped up a beer spill. 'That's right, Dorling. Else there'll be no more charity from this corner. You'll be out on your ear.'

'Lor', an' you'd do that wivout the good lady Mifflin issuing the

orders?' Dorling fixed Max with a baleful look, adding for Max's benefit, 'I ain't allowed to cross the threshold when Madam Viper's around.'

'Well, it ain't surprising you don't get too much sympathy from that
quarter, mouthing off at them refined ladies at the dower house when
you know my missus'd give 'em 'er last farthing if they'd only say the
word, poor as church mice they all be. Now be off with yer, Dorling,
afore you say summat you really regret.'

'Ah, Jack, that ain't no way to treat a friend of forty years an' more.
Leastaways let me finish me drink wot I paid good money for, then I'll
go, quiet as a lamb.'

The ex-soldier laced his fingers round his mug, settled himself
more comfortably in his corner chair and looked morose. 'I hear The
Lodge is all shut up now.' He sighed. 'The widow Farquhar hain't the
funds to keep it up so 'tis under dust sheets 'til it's leased again, or the
boy comes into his inheritance. There was merry times there afore the
merry widow were a widow, I can tell you.'

He sucked his gums loudly in the silence, his quick darting eyes
showing he knew how to play to an audience.

Max shifted in his seat, his discomfort growing. Of course, he
would have to get used to it. A great deal of Olivia's reluctance to wed
Max was due to the shame she felt at what Lucien had forced her to
do. Of the shame she knew Max would inevitably feel when the locals,
such as this pockmarked old soldier, mouthed off about the past.

He licked his lips that felt suddenly dry and said, 'Lady Farquhar
has mourned her late husband a full twelve months, sir, as is right and
proper.' His voice held a note of warning.

'Oh, aye, she's entitled to find herself a man to her liking, I'll grant
you that,' Dorling conceded readily enough. 'Spoiled for choice, no
doubt, with all them gennulmen who've tasted 'er wares lining up at
her door. Me being one of 'em, but o' course she don't remember me' –
he gave another plaintive sigh and fixed his rheumy eyes on Max –
'when I were just one o' so many.'

'Out!' roared the publican at the same time as Max rose to his feet,
his hand going to his hip where once his scabbard hung; but it was
more than a year since he'd swapped soldiering for farming and he no
longer carried a weapon.

'What would a man like yersel' know of such a lady? You've insulted Lady Farquhar and I'll not have it. Get out!' roared the publican, towering over the little man whose disgusting appearance belied his insinuation.

The soldier made a smacking noise with his lips as he kissed the tips of his fingers in an extravagant gesture. He did not move. 'I's told you afore only seems you were a lot more eager for the details than seems to be the case tonight.'

Draining his mug, he waved it in the air to be refilled. 'No doubt you gazed at the great lady with awe, sir, though I'd challenge you to 'ave said no to a taste of Lady Farquhar's butterfly if it were presented to you on a platter.' In the horrified silence he added with relish, 'Aye, literally.'

Max felt the bile rise up in his throat as the publican yelled, 'Slander!' as he crossed the room and wrapped his large, meaty hands around the little man's neck.

'God's honour, 'tis the truth,' gasped Dorling.

'Let him repeat the story he no doubt tells any who'll listen,' Max said coldly as he finished his ale. 'Then it's my turn to wrap my hands around his neck.'

Reluctantly, the publican released his erstwhile friend. The little man chuckled as he resettled himself, jauntily nodding his thanks as he picked up his newly filled tankard a few minutes later.

'I were invited to the great house on account of my skill wi' the cards and it pleased Lord Farquhar to put on a little entertainment for the assembled company.' He leered at the two men, his beady little eyes greedy for their shock, undeterred by their hostility and contempt. 'Just so happened it was his wife that were the main event. Served up on the most enormous silver platter all covered with fruit. Aye, sirs, fruit and cream with the lady revealed in all 'er splendour when the cover were removed. Then the music started and she did 'er little dance upon the table with the company roarin' an' cheerin' their approval.' He puffed out his chest. 'You think the likes of me ain't fit to lick 'er boots, but let me tell you, I licked a damned sight tastier morsel that night.' He bared his yellow teeth in a parody of a grin as he said with satisfaction: 'Lady Farquhar's Butterfly. Taught 'is Lordship some rare tricks wi' the cards that night and were 'appy not to 'ave to pay for the privilege of rolling that cherry round on me tongue like the others to whom 'is Lordship were indebted—'

The smack as Max's fist connected with his jaw was stifled by his bellow of fury as he threw himself upon the man. Gathering him up by the scruff of his neck he slammed him against the doorframe. Dorling squealed like a rabbit being skinned, but his expression was defiant as he glared at the two men who now hung back, brandishing their fists above his nose.

'You think a lady's above reproach just because she puts a fancy title in front of her name?' Dorling wiped the back of his hand across his mouth, grimacing at the blood. 'Well, me blessed Meg, God rest 'er soul, were a hundred times more of a lady when Lord Farquhar took a fancy to '*er* an' do you think she had any say in the matter? Now she's dead on 'is account while me lady who laughed and danced upon the table like a tuppenny whore sails on to greener pastures.'

With an air of injured dignity he shrugged himself free and hobbled towards the door, rubbing his jaw. 'Anyone'd think you had designs on the lady, yersel',' he muttered, with a narrow-eyed look in Max's direction. 'Reckon you 'as to be mighty plump in the pocket if she'll flutter 'er lashes, or anything else, at you.'

'Lady Farquhar is to become a clergyman's wife,' the publican informed him in a superior tone, brandishing a heavy pewter mug as he waved the man out.

Dorling turned on the threshold. With a guffaw he gripped the doorframe to steady himself.

'Well, don't that beat all!' He shook his head. 'Not that clinging little Reverend Kirkham who sprinkled holy water on 'er ladyship's footsteps before 'e spirited her away after each debauch?'

Sick to the stomach, Max watched as the publican dealt the old soldier a parting kick.

'Reckon it was the clergyman what fathered that child o' hers for I know fer a fact t'weren't that mutton monger of a husband !' Dorling taunted from the passage. 'Ain't no wonder 'e wants to marry her!'

Max steadied himself against the back of a chair as the man continued to hurl his hated abuse.

'Ain't no more than wot the designing trollop deserves! Cursed my Meg, she did, *and* stole the reverend's sister from 'is lordship!' Dorling's eyes were pinpricks of malice. 'Well, 'e's welcome to 'er, 'e is. Lord Farquhar took away her son on account of her loose morals and t'was no more'n she deserved, but my Meg didn't deserve what she got. 'Twas the reverend wot let my Meg die *and* the child she bore, leaving me wi' now't!'

CHAPTER 9

FOR FIVE DAYS Olivia existed in a haze of hope but as the week drew to a close a heavy resignation descended upon her.

She saw the dubious glances her aunts exchanged when Miss Latimer held up the bolt of dun-coloured fabric she'd selected for her wedding gown, and was unmoved.

'That will do nicely.'

If she thought only of the fact that marriage to Nathaniel was still – as it always had been – her only alternative, she could survive.

She clasped her hands at her breast. The spark of hope which had flickered so brightly since she had met Max had died inside her. Her confession had killed his love.

His silence was killing *her*.

Nathaniel had played his trump card and Max had conceded. There could be no more testimony of his change of heart than his silence to the letter of confession she'd written him.

Olivia gazed at her little boy who was playing with some wooden pegs under the table and her heart swelled with love.

Then constricted with fear.

What would happen now?

Perhaps Max would publicly declare Julian a usurper. The repercussions went further than public humiliation and an uncertain future. The small allowance Olivia was paid as custodian of the child would be cut off.

'Do you not think the gown will be a little ... plain?' Aunt Catherine ventured.

'It's not in your usual style.' Eunice touched the drab coloured sarsanet and sighed. 'Though I suppose it's been eight years since I saw you clothed according to your own taste.'

'My own taste?' Olivia's lips twitched. It was a relief for her mind to travel beyond the grief that held her hostage. 'Do you remember the sparks that flew as we fought over the gown in which I was to be presented?' She ran her eyes over the fabric and the sketch which Miss Latimer was holding up. It held no interest or meaning for her. Marriage was a bargain, after all. Few women married for love. What did the reasons for her impending nuptials matter? She and Julian needed a roof over their heads and now that Nathaniel was getting his way he may well be kind to them both. 'I thought you'd be pleased at my new-found sobriety.'

'You're going to be a clergyman's wife, not take holy orders.'

'Is there no pleasing you, Aunt Eunice?' Olivia sighed. Once she'd have flared up and flounced from the room. Now she strove for measured calm and her words contained a note of sorrow rather than recrimination. Indeed, she felt little real emotion. It was as if her heart were contained in a glass box. Now that her future had been determined she told herself she had little further interest in it.

'Let us walk Miss Latimer to the garden gate and then take a turn around the garden,' Aunt Eunice suggested with clearly an ulterior motive.

'So you can try yet again to talk "sense" into me?' Olivia whispered with deceptive sweetness, as Aunt Catherine helped the seamstress roll up the fabric.

She took her aunt's arm and, smiling at Miss Latimer, ushered her to the door.

'So, young lady, Nathaniel is determined to mould you to his own fashion, just as Lucien did. And once again, you're following like a little lamb.'

Olivia's step faltered but she made a quick recover and continued resolutely along the pathway which had been swept clear of snow.

'I can tell you are trying to provoke me into a passion, Aunt Eunice,' she said, calmly, 'therefore I shall not dignify that with an answer.'

'Good Lord, Olivia, if ever there was a girl to try one. I don't know what your mother would have made of you.' She heaved in a breath. 'I expect you'd have been at each other's throats, you're so alike.'

Olivia felt emotion surge through her veins. She did not want to talk of her mother, just as she did not wish to speak of Max.

'Olivia.'

Olivia was surprised at the urgency in her aunt's tone. Even more so when her aunt gripped her shoulders and held her clumsily against her for a brief moment before letting her go.

Resuming her footsteps, head bent, she went on, 'Why do you persist in this madness of atoning for ...' Her words trailed off, though she did not slow her pace. Finally she added, 'For I wish I knew what, exactly.'

'Nathaniel has offered Julian and me a future.' Olivia hurried to catch up with her aunt, still taken aback by the uncharacteristic show of affection as she struggled with the question. 'I thought I was marrying for love when I eloped with Lucien. I do not intend making the same mistake twice.'

'You married Lucien to be perverse because Catherine and I were so opposed to—'

'Are you suggesting I'm marrying Nathaniel simply to be perverse? How little you understand me, Aunt Eunice.'

Her aunt stopped and looked at her sadly. 'Yes, how little I know you, Olivia. How little I knew your mother.' Shaking her head, she went on, 'If it's about money, we can manage. Come with us to Bath, Olivia. Enjoy yourself for a change.'

Olivia bit her lip as she looked past her aunt's old, weary face, now bright with hope, to the fir trees beyond, limned with pink and gold light as the sun faded. Last week it had been a supernatural, ethereally beautiful scene, gilded with promise as she'd walked this path with Max. He made her feel anything were possible. Even happiness.

But happiness had been fleeting. She should have known it.

Bone-jarring shards of pain stabbed at her once more. She had told Max *everything*. Seven days it had been and she had received nothing but silence. What choice did she have but to continue her current course?

To go to Nuningford with Nathaniel? To hear the sermon he had written for her on shame and atonement?

She shuddered as she thought of the man who swore to safeguard Julian's future, Olivia's future and ...

Closing her eyes she sucked in a shaky breath.

... and the secret she had disclosed to Max, but which had been received by cold, stony silence?

The hope in Aunt Eunice's eyes faded at Olivia's lack of response. 'If I thought you loved Nathaniel I'd have no reservations, but you don't.' She gave a grunt of frustration. 'Ask him to release you. I don't know what hold he has over you, but he will never make you happy.' Squeezing her niece's shoulder she tried again. 'Your cousin Mariah and young Lucy would love to see you again. They asked if you would come.'

Olivia shook her head. 'I am twenty-six years old, Aunt Eunice. Old enough to decide that marrying is in the best interests of my son.' A visit to Bath was a far more enticing prospect than going to Nuningford to hear her husband-to-be preach. Yet her choice was clear. She had to ally herself with someone who would provide for her son.

'I'm sorry, Aunt Eunice,' she said with genuine regret, 'but I cannot accompany you and Aunt Catherine.'

They returned to the house to find Julian in tears and an exasperated Nathaniel leaning over him.

'Whatever's the matter?' Olivia hurried over and sank on to the drawing-room carpet so she could take her small son on to her lap.

For the first time he did not push her away, but clung to her, sobbing as he buried his tear-stained face in her shoulder.

Olivia held him tighter. How precious he was. The greatest gift of her life. A huge lump formed in her throat.

'Puppy ...' he gulped. 'I want puppy.'

She turned to where a soft mewling sound came from a cane

basket. A pair of large eyes, as tragic as Julian's, regarded her from over the top.

Nathaniel, frowning, reached across from his chair brandishing a piece of parchment.

Olivia took it, hoping he did not notice her shaking hand.

Max had written.

Barely able to contain her excitement, her eyes skimmed the sparse four lines of text: instructions for Julian on how to care for his new friend and the reassurance Max would see him when his new stepfather deemed fit.

Shocked, her hands dropped to her lap, the parchment fluttering to the floor. There could be no more blunt way for Max to indicate his withdrawal from the contest for Olivia's affections.

Turning her head from Nathaniel's scrutiny, she gave the puppy a distracted stroke. Julian was loving it a little too enthusiastically but she was imprisoned within a cocoon of grief, heedless of all but the pain which shredded her heart.

The extent of her shock made her realize that despite Max's lengthy silence she'd still held out hope. The crisp, business-like tone and reference to her marriage to Nathaniel as a *fait accompli* now made it clear there was no hope.

Forcing herself back to practicalities, she schooled her manner into one of quiet reason. 'Why should Julian not be allowed to keep the dog?'

She must concentrate on the soft warmth of her child and the joy of feeling needed.

The look Nathaniel sent her reminded her she must watch her tone.

With characteristic care he smoothed his coat tails as he rose. Standing, he regarded her, steadily.

'My dear Olivia, while I have nothing, personally, against Mr Atherton and can understand his gift was well intentioned I do not believe it is in Julian's best interests to have such a potent reminder of his life with his uncle.'

Olivia opened her mouth to protest. Her impulse was to flare up at him, tell him that of course Julian could keep the dog. She was his mother!

Nathaniel's expression changed her mind. A tight, warning smile turned up the corners of his mouth while the expression in his hooded dark eyes was implacable. He was not angry. Yet. But she could see this tussle for domestic authority was a litmus test for the future.

She dropped her eyes, hugging Julian closer to her. He was whimpering, but seemed content to be in her arms.

Never had she felt more keenly the responsibility for his future, his security and happiness.

He looked to her to protect him. She felt the pride, the joy, the burden of it churn in her heart. Resting her head upon Julian's she breathed carefully past the panic.

She was Julian's only barrier against a harsh and unpredictable world. Lucien had forsaken him. Now Max had failed to offer his support with the truth clearly an unpalatable burden. While he had given eloquent expression to his change of heart through this gift and letter, Olivia was left in fearful suspense as to what he might do next.

Nathaniel was still looking at her. Waiting. He had assumed the mantle of protector to the wronged and aggrieved Lady Farquhar long ago.

The arbiter of all domestic decisions, too.

Still clutching Julian to her chest she said as evenly as she could, 'Max says in his letter he'd promised Julian a puppy from his dog Pansy's litter when they were parting.' She found she was clenching her hands. She hated to do it, but she was prepared to beg. 'Please let Julian keep the puppy,' she whispered.

Wrenching himself out of Olivia's arms, Julian was like a miniature tornado as he head butted her stomach. 'Puppy, mine! Puppy, mine!' he wept. Holding him at bay, Olivia watched fearfully the play of emotions cross Nathaniel's face.

Would he punish the child for his stubborn resistance to accepting his decree? Nathaniel did not understand not-quite-three-year-olds. He may well consider this a disciplinary matter.

To her relief he elected not to choose this path. Sighing, he turned to leave. 'I shall consider it while I prepare my sermon this afternoon.

In the meantime, see the dog is taken to the kitchen so Julian does not get too attached to it.'

He left her sitting in the middle of the carpet with Julian sobbing in her lap and Max's letter gripped between her fingers.

So Nathaniel had seen nothing untoward in opening the parchment which clearly had not been intended for him?

In a trance she stroked the dark curls of her baby: the fruit of her husband's betrayal, the son whose future only she could protect.

Through the fog of despair came a flicker of hope. Perhaps Max had suspected Nathaniel would intercept any correspondence between them. Perhaps he would communicate privately with her.

Tell her he loved her? That he forgave her everything?

Fear returned.

Perhaps he would coldly demand she announce Max publicly as the new viscount and prostrate herself as the woman who had denied Max his birthright?

Kissing Julian's silky curls she acknowledged Max would not be so cold and that she would do whatever was required for Max to take up his rightful position.

She owed him that.

But without his support she would be a disgraced widow, her reputation even more sullied, struggling for the protection and financial resources needed to ensure the futures of herself and her son.

In such circumstances she had no choice but to marry Nathaniel.

She was not surprised that her downcast spirits reflected Nathaniel's dominance, putting him in a benevolent mood that afternoon.

Setting down his tea cup, he announced with great ceremony during afternoon tea, 'Let the boy have the puppy. He'll forget where it came from soon enough.'

Olivia rewarded him with a teary smile. Just as Max had forgotten all but the treachery he laid at her door.

As soon as tea was over Nathaniel ordered Julian down from the nursery so he could with even greater ceremony present him with his new puppy.

'My sermon for the Nuningford congregation shall focus on

compassion and gratitude,' he said, resting his hands on Olivia's shoulders as he and the aunts watched Julian cavorting around the drawing room with the playful little bitch he'd named Molly. 'You have inspired me.' Guiding her head round so she had no choice but to look at him, he asked, 'You are happy, my dear?'

There was no undertone of malice, no hint of threat. It was as if their conversation in Olivia's bedroom had never taken place. As if Nathaniel were the most genial of men and Olivia the most willing of widows.

'Of course.' She twisted her chin out of his cupped hand so she could watch her son. Whatever she did was to ensure her child's future.

His uncertain future.

'You have certainly made me so.' His voice was a low murmur nearly drowned out by the boisterous shouts from the other side of the room.

'I praise God he set you on the path to righteousness and fulfilment from which Lucien diverted you' – he paused, adding heavily – 'using me as his instrument.'

Olivia shuddered.

'Oh, my dear Nathaniel, just look at them!' gushed Aunt Catherine, beaming as if Nathaniel were the architect of Julian's happiness.

Olivia stepped out of Nathaniel's grasp and went to kneel by her son. 'You must thank Mr Kirkman for his kindness,' she said putting an arm about the child.

Julian shrugged it off and bounded after the puppy. 'Thank Uncle Max,' he lisped, before hurling himself on top of the wriggling animal.

CHAPTER 10

NORMALLY, WHEN THE daffodils first popped their golden yellow heads from the almost frozen ground Olivia would experience a great surge of hope. Spring was here and the hunting season, only a few months hence, would mean she'd see less of Lucien. The world in general looked more promising.

Now, as she watched Nathaniel heedlessly trample those innocent harbingers of hope as he inspected the ropes that tied their trunks to his carriage this chilly April morning she felt nothing but despair.

Not for the first time she wondered at her strength of character in allowing him to trample her dreams and wishes in the same way he was trampling the clumps of daffodils that lined the gravel drive.

Yet what alternative did she have? She was in a perilous situation. Her social isolation was bad enough, but poverty stared her in the face.

With Max offering no guide as to what was in store for Julian, let alone herself, marriage to Nathaniel was the price she must pay.

'Ah, Miss Dingley!' Greeting Aunt Eunice with a self-satisfied smile as she issued out of the house in company with her sister, the clergyman added, 'I have with me my sermon which you recently evinced a desire to hear and with which I shall amuse the congregation at Nuningford. I think Olivia shall find the journey passes in seemingly far less than the two hours the coachman estimates in this fine weather.'

Olivia gulped. Two hours in Nathaniel's presence. Two hours listening to him prosing on about compassion and gratitude.

She could not do it.

Not to herself. Not to Julian. She imagined her boy as a young man forced to submit to Kirkman's uncertain temper. Forced to be humble and grateful.

Nathaniel would trample over him. Trample over any youthful exuberance he might show like he was trampling over her and over the clumps of pretty yellow daffodils.

'Will you get off them!' Starting forward, she gripped his sleeve and tugged.

She heard Aunt Catherine gasp, and the shock in Aunt Eunice's warning, 'Have a care, Olivia!'

Surprisingly, his voice was low and calm as he turned. 'Forgive me, Olivia, for paying such scant regard to your favourite flower.' He raised her palm and kissed it with a smile. 'Are you ready?'

'I'm not going.'

She heard the same mutinous tone she'd used as a seventeen year old when she'd defied her aunts to be with Lucien.

Aunt Catherine stepped forward and put a comforting hand on her shoulder. 'Of course you must go, Olivia.'

Blackness blurred her vision. It was terror. The terror she would lose her nerve before she had shown the courage she might never show again.

'No! I shan't go to Nuningford!'

Aunt Catherine gasped. A spasm crossed the Nathaniel's face as he took her forearm and steered her round to the carriage door. 'Wedding nerves,' he said crisply. 'Perfectly understandable.'

'I'm going to Bath!' Olivia resisted like a nervous filly, flinching at his touch, unable to look him in the eye. 'I'm sure the Nuningford congregation will be as awed by your sermon as I was last night, Nathaniel, but I am going to Bath with my aunts to stay with my cousin Mariah. And I'm taking Julian with me!'

'Julian can come with us if it means so much to you, but you are coming to Nuningford.' Though his voice was smooth it held a nasty undertone, one with which Olivia was becoming increasingly familiar.

'Mrs Snyder is waiting. She is looking forward to accompanying us and does not like to be kept waiting.'

'Puppy! Molly!'

Olivia closed her eyes at the happy shouts of her son and the crunch of gravel as he pursued his new friend. Julian would not take kindly to being incarcerated for the next two hours.

Turning, she saw the puppy bounding towards them, its tongue lolling, its ears flapping in joyful abandonment. It seemed to take as much pleasure from the game as Julian. Glancing back at Nathaniel she could see he was consumed entirely by the need for mastery over her; that he was oblivious to the child and the dog. She winced as his fingers dug into her forearm while he opened the carriage door with the other hand.

She recognized the determination in his angry look. What chance had she against the strength of his will?

'Don't imagine that animal is coming as well,' he snarled.

She saw the boisterous pair careering in their direction, pleasure transcending all. Her heart soared at their innocence. Her son had an ally; the puppy would be a beloved companion.

Turning back to Nathaniel her heart leapt with fear. Oh God, Julian was too young to recognize the malice that dominated his step-fatherto-be.

'Nathaniel, no!' she screamed. He paid no heed.

'No!' she cried again, watching in disbelief his well-aimed kick.

She saw Julian's confusion, heard the muted noise of Nathaniel's boot connecting with the soft underbelly of the small creature. Wincing, horrified, she closed her eyes at the sound of its sharp, truncated yelp.

'Puppy!'

Julian's scream rang out, the aunts turning in unison to see the puppy's little body thrown into the air, a tiny ball of white and brown fur somersaulting against the blue sky before it came to rest limply in a clump of daffodils.

'I will never marry you!'

Anger flowed through her. Perhaps it was courage, too. Nathaniel was evil. He would bend her to his will, just as Lucien had. Olivia must be true to her instincts. Nathaniel would destroy her, as Lucien nearly had.

And he would destroy Julian.

Glaring at Nathaniel, she held her confused, shuddering son against her skirts and hissed, 'Not if you were the last man on earth. I will never marry you and nor will I be your victim as I was Lucien's.'

Nathaniel took a menacing step forward. When she refused to retreat, his look became conciliatory. It had no effect. Her mind was made up. She was her own master, just as she was master of her son's future. She might not be able to safeguard his comfort and security but she could ensure he grew to be a man of conviction who respected her for hers.

Fortunately Julian was too young to understand.

He tried to coax life into the little creature with whom he'd only just become acquainted and cried when it wouldn't play with him. Olivia comforted him as best she could, pulling him on to her lap and rocking him when his realization that he'd lost his playmate for good was too much to bear.

Nathaniel showed no remorse and his anger left Olivia unmoved. Even his reminder that Olivia and Julian faced a future of uncertainty and penury had no effect.

When Olivia remained steadfast in her refusal to accompany him 'so they could at least discuss matters' he finally climbed angrily into his carriage and departed.

Olivia then made plans to despatch the little dog's body, directing Dorcas to dig a hole in the garden, but Julian screamed when he realized the puppy was to be covered with soil.

Struggling to hold the hysterical child, she stopped the maid and together they crouched over the still warm body. Julian quietened then, hopping off her lap and picking up a limp ear.

'Lucien had a dog just like this one,' Olivia said, stroking its silky coat.

'I remember, ma'am,' said Dorcas, wiping her red face with her apron. 'It were called Molly too. How the master did dote on 'er.'

Olivia said nothing. It was no place to remark that Molly held a far greater place in her late husband's affections than she had ever done.

With a sigh she scooped up the little dog's limp body and turned towards the house.

'Take Julian to the nursery and change his clothes,' she directed. 'He'll be coming to Bath with us. I'll take the puppy to the crypt. Molly can rest beside Lucien's beloved Molly.'

'You'll need 'elp down there, Miss Olivia,' said Dorcas. 'I'll run and fetch the key.'

'I know where a spare is hidden,' Olivia called, already heading down the hill. 'You take Julian. It's best he doesn't come with me.'

Hugging the soft bundle in her arms, Olivia went over the decisive parting she had made with Nathaniel. It didn't matter that he had not meant to kill the animal, but it was enough. Enough to throw off the fear and uncertainty he had exercised over her for so long. Enough to forge a new direction. She would go to Bath with her aunts that afternoon and she would never see him again. She was determined upon it. She and Julian would be free.

Resolved, she headed down the hill towards her old home, feeling lighter than she could remember, despite her joyless task. She was a widow. She belonged to no man. It was true she had no money, but somehow she and Julian would manage.

She took the key from its hiding place under a rock and inserted it in the rusty lock. With just a gentle push, the crypt door swung open. Set into the side of a grassy knoll it was a gloomy place a few minutes' walk from The Lodge, though enough light streamed through a window high in the wall for her to see. Lined up like silent sentinels of the past she gazed upon the stone sarcophagi of her husband's ancestors.

And that of her husband.

Gently placing the little dog upon the lid she fingered the inscription. How grand, how noble it made him sound when he had been just a man. A man driven to madness through longing for what he could never find; if indeed it existed at all.

Faithful Molly's tiny sarcophagus was positioned at his feet. Bending, Olivia tried to move the heavy lid but, despite it being so small, it refused to budge. Straightening, she scanned the rows of neat stone caskets. Above Lucien lay his grandfather, the equally infamous 5th Viscount Farquhar. Perhaps the only difference between them was that Lucien's grandfather had tyrannized three wives before his sudden death during the uprising of '45 while Lucien had tormented only one.

Lucky Olivia had outlived *her* tyrannous viscount.

With a wry laugh she bent to move the lid entombing the King Charles' Spaniel whom Lucien's grandfather had no doubt esteemed more than any consort.

This time she encountered no resistance. With only a little effort she was able to shift it sufficiently to make a gap large enough for young Molly's corpse.

She stood up and went to fetch the dog from Lucien's sarcophagus.

'Poor Molly,' she whispered, closing her eyes as she nuzzled its soft coat. 'You had such a short time to enjoy life, and yet I do believe you have given me the freedom I might never have had were it not for your sacrifice. I'm sorry.'

How lonely, she thought, as she lowered the animal on to its bed of dust and old bones. She remembered thinking the same, despite her anger, when Lucien had been interred.

She bent to close the lid, pausing as the cloud which had obscured the sun was suddenly dissolved by its heat, sending its dazzling rays through the grimy window. A flash of something bright caught her eye. Something that was not dust and bones. Cautiously, she put her hand into the sarcophagus, wishing she were wearing gloves as the feel of damp organic matter sent shivers up her spine.

They were not shivers of revulsion for long.

Her fingers, probing through the blanket of dust, encountered something smooth. Smooth and disc-shaped. Cold and flat.

Tingles of excitement tore through her as she closed her fist upon a handful of them. Her breath caught in her throat. A whisper of dust make her cough and she clutched at her chest, doubling over as she gathered herself.

Could it be? She was almost too afraid to dip her hand back into the darkness of the small sarcophagus once the coughing fit had passed. Perhaps she was hallucinating?

But when her fingers found the bottom there was no doubt. She knew exactly what she had unwittingly stumbled upon.

The 5th Viscount's treasure.

With a whoop of joy Olivia plunged both arms into the dark space beside Molly's body and brought up a handful of gold coins.

Too many to hold. Raising her hands to the light she closed her eyes and listened to the dull chinking noise they made as they slipped through her fingers and hit the flagstones. The enormousness of her discovery was difficult to comprehend. Her brain throbbed with wonder, disbelief and finally settled upon reality: the repercussions. It did not matter that the treasure did not belong to her. They would bring her joy, nonetheless.

Dropping the coins upon the lid of Lucien's grandfather's crypt she again plunged her hands into the dust and darkness. Dust comprised only a thin layer. There had been no attempt to hide the coins. The sarcophagus was filled with them.

Dizzy with hope and joy she had to sit down, gazing in wonder at the gold in the flat of her palms.

'Max's birthright,' she murmured. It was hard to breathe through her excitement, to gather her thoughts. Her discovery changed everything.

After a while her thoughts settled. She knew what she must do. This afternoon she would accompany her aunts to Bath. It served as a good halfway point. Refreshed, she would continue the next morning to Elmwood.

Elmwood was two hours' carriage ride beyond Bath. Elmwood – where Max would be waiting.

Hope blossomed once more.

Returning most of the coins to the crypt she closed the lid, keeping five which she would present to Max.

She might have unwittingly denied him his birthright but she was about to atone with more than just a public avowal of the truth.

Her interest on her shame would be ensuring his gilded future.

CHAPTER 11

HUGGING HER NEWFOUND knowledge to herself as the carriage rattled towards Bath and her aunts dozed in each corner, Olivia could barely contain her excitement.

Of course, she was used to keeping secrets. For more than two years she'd kept the greatest secret of all: a secret that would condemn Julian to an uncertain, if not perilous, future.

But this secret offered her salvation. A future with Max.

Sagging against the corner cushion of the carriage with a sleeping Julian across her lap her mind spun with possibilities.

Max would be able to indulge any whim or fancy he chose, whether it was experimenting with wool growing or standing for Parliament.

Even Amelia would welcome her with open arms. Miss Hepworth might come with a fortune to match her pretty face but Olivia had discovered Max's fortune.

And Max loved *her*.

Her instincts told her so, just as she now considered it entirely possible Max had not received the letter she had written him. She *had* to believe this.

The more distance Olivia put between the dower house, especially as they passed the manse where Nathaniel lived, the more she felt her old spirit returning.

It wasn't just the gold. She had done it: she had thrown off the yoke that made her as much Nathaniel's whipping post as she had been Lucien's.

Whatever happened, she and Julian would survive. Her son would survive with his spirit intact because she had shown the strength needed to make it so, albeit thanks to the brutal kick which had killed Molly.

Careful not to disturb the sleeping child in her arms, she leaned forward. Aunt Eunice was stirring, straightening her lace cap as she blinked open her eyes.

'Aunt Eunice,' she whispered, hugging herself tightly, her excitement almost too much to bear, 'I do not intend seeing Nathaniel ever again!'

'But there are just weeks until the wedding!' Aunt Catherine, who had just woken, herself, sounded close to tears. 'What happened was a terrible accident. Think of your reputation, Olivia!'

'What of it?' Olivia managed to keep her voice from wavering though it was true. She would be branded a jilt; more ammunition against her for those who believed Lucien's slurs.

Dabbing at her eyes with a scrap of lace, Aunt Catherine sniffed. 'All we want is your happiness, Olivia, but how can any woman be happy if she is not received in society? Despite this morning's accident Nathaniel has been good to you—'

'Because it profited him!' Aunt Eunice's voice was harsh.

'I shall not marry him and I shall *never* change my mind,' Olivia said firmly, even as visions beset her of a vengeful Nathaniel using every dirty trick at his disposal to wrest from her all that she held dear. But with Max in possession of the truth Nathaniel's power was void.

The boy was stirring. With a yawn he pulled out his thumb and his eyelids fluttered open. Olivia waited tensely for him to recoil when he realized where he was but he did not. Instead, he settled himself more comfortably on her lap, rubbed his eyes with one grimy fist and offered her a smile.

Her heart somersaulted. Love, like molten liquid surged through her veins. She hugged him against her, kissing the top of his head and breathing in his warm, little boy smell.

'Julian, sweetheart,' she whispered, 'Mama's not marrying Reverend Kirkman.'

'Marry Uncle Max?' With his thumb firmly in his mouth the words were indistinct but understandable.

Olivia gave a weak smile as she closed her eyes against the scrutiny of her aunts.

Would it be enough? Fear rubbed at her earlier confidence. Would revealing to Max the whereabouts of his grandfather's lost fortune be enough to restore what had once existed between them? Max regarded principle and morality more highly than material goods.

'A mighty fine sentiment, young man,' Aunt Eunice said approvingly, 'and one I endorse sincerely.'

Olivia held Julian more closely. 'If he will have me.'

'Of course he'll have you!' Aunt Eunice cut in sharply. 'He's as moonstruck as any green boy, that's clear enough!'

Aunt Catherine put her head on one side. 'He is Lucien's cousin, of course, and you do not know him as well as you know the reverend—'

'What does that signify, Sister,' interjected Aunt Eunice, 'when Mr Atherton displays all the heroic qualities needed to set a female's heart aflutter as well as kindness and common sense?' She paused, sending Olivia a narrow look. 'You've not had a falling out on account of something other than Mr Kirkman, have you, Olivia?'

Olivia dropped her eyes. 'I have not heard from Max since last week when I elaborated on' – she drew her breath in through her teeth – 'my sins.' Faintly, she added, 'Nathaniel interrupted and although I wrote Max a full explanation I've heard nothing.'

'Then it's because he never received the letter.' Aunt Eunice's tone was comforting in its conviction. 'Doubtless that conniving, underhand clergyman intercepted it.' She patted Olivia's knee. 'Mark my words, Olivia, Mr Atherton wears his heart on his sleeve and is not the kind of man to let a mere misunderstanding stand in the way of true love. Once he knows you're no longer bound to Mr Kirkman he'll be on the doorstep upon the instant to beg your forgiveness and to make you an offer.'

'DEAREST OLIVIA!' COUSIN MARIAH, RESPLENDENT IN POMONA green and gold, ushered them into the drawing room of her fashionable townhouse in Laura Place. 'I was so hoping you would come. And you've brought the boy!' The peacock feather in her handsome gold toque swayed as she clapped her hands. A servant appeared and, after directing that the sleeping child be spirited away to a nice warm bedchamber, she waved them all to seats, settling herself amidst a noisy rustle of silk skirts. 'Your aunts have told me all about you! Marriage to a pillar of the church, no less! Your wisdom will be of great benefit to a certain younger member of this household.' Her expansive smile was followed by a look of deep concern. Lowering her voice, she added, 'Young Lucy has lost her head to a good-for-nothing so I am counting on you, my dear, to impart the salutary caution required. Your aunts assure me you have learned your lesson.' Barely had she been admitted to the lavishly furnished drawing room than the sense of being welcomed once more into polite society evaporated. Olivia, the temptress, the scheming seductress, would never be allowed to die.

She saw Aunt Eunice and Catherine exchange looks before asking warily as she settled herself on the Egyptian settee, 'What else, pray, have you told Lucy about me?'

'That Lady Farquhar was the most captivating debutante the year she was presented and that she turned down at least a dozen marriage offers before she married Lord Farquhar,' came a breathless voice, as a young girl bounced into the room.

'Meet Lucy,' said her mother, adding in disapproving tones as she plucked at the sleeves of the girl's dress and smoothed a wayward chestnut curl, 'That's no way for a young lady to introduce herself. What must Cousins Eunice and Catherine think of you, not to mention Lady Far—'

'Please, call me Cousin Olivia,' Olivia begged, allowing herself to take comfort in the heavily censored description Lucy had obviously been given; though it appeared Olivia had already been held up as a warning to her lively cousin.

'You're every bit as beautiful as Mama said you were,' Lucy went on, irrepressibly, taking a seat beside her as refreshments were served. 'I'm hoping you can teach me a thing or two, Cousin Olivia, as my first season wasn't a great success, was it, Mother?'

Olivia didn't know how to respond to the embarrassment that crackled through the room. Clearly Olivia was the last person in the room, much less in Bath, who should advise Lucy on how a debutante ought to deport herself. Catching Mariah's eye, though she directed her words to Lucy, she said, 'I think perhaps I could teach you more about what *not* to do.' Her attempt at sounding self-deprecating had the desired result. Mariah sent her an approving look as Olivia added, 'And if you consider a season a failure simply because you didn't find a husband, perhaps the real reason was because there were no suitable suitors for you. One can't simply accept the first offer that presents itself just because the accounting is acceptable.'

'Bravo, Cousin Olivia.' Mariah offered her a plate of seed cake.

'Lucy has got it into her head she must make a spectacular match this year as if to make up for last season.'

'I'm sure I can make a match to please everyone.' The young girl tossed her chestnut curls. Though she wasn't pretty in the fashionable sense, there was a robust and engaging liveliness in her manner Olivia felt sure would appeal to some nice, steady young man. Not the sleek, dangerous rake her husband had been, but wasn't that just as well?

'Besides, I am far more agreeable to look upon now than I was last year,' Lucy went on, daintily picking out the seeds of her cake before her mother hissed at her to mind her manners. Lucy glared at her. 'You said those exact same words, Mama, if you recall—'

Mariah, relaxing her authoritarian bearing, threw her hands up in the air and everyone laughed.

'It seems only yesterday Olivia was Lucy's age,' said Aunt Catherine with a fond look at Olivia.

'I must confess,' said Mariah, 'I did, unwisely, tell Lucy that she'd bloomed in the past year and that—'

'What's wrong with giving a compliment?' Lucy interrupted. 'If it's the truth, I mean. I'm sure it hasn't turned Cousin Olivia's head being told she's beautiful.' She took a mouthful of cake, adding, 'I need compliments to remind me I'm no longer the plump, spotty ape leader I was last season.'

'You have a very well-used looking glass which seems to be constantly reminding you, Lucy,' said her mother. 'Now enough of your chatter. I must press Olivia and her aunts to accompany us to Lady Glenton's midnight masque, tonight.'

As Olivia opened her mouth to demur, Cousin Mariah held up her hand. 'There is plenty of time to rest, for surely Lady Glenton's marvellous annual event was the reason you came early?'

As revelry was the furthest thing from Olivia's mind, she put up strong resistance. She needed rest so she could be at her most radiant when she confronted Max tomorrow. All her senses strained towards this most important, momentous meeting of her life.

'Please, Cousin Olivia!' Lucy begged. 'Mama has a gown for you and now that I've seen you I'm dying to show you off.'

'I'm very tired—' Olivia began but Aunt Eunice cut her off. 'You can sleep a few hours and have plenty of time to prepare yourself for midnight. What you need is gaiety, Olivia, something to take your mind off your ... grief.'

Cousin Mariah leant forward. 'I can think of no finer entertainment to end one's mourning year,' she said, decisively.

Reclining on the bed Lucy watched with avid concentration as Olivia prepared herself for the ball five hours later.

'Poor Cousin Olivia,' she sighed, 'you must miss Lord Farquhar very much. I know Mama disapproved of him, but then, she disapproves of most men.'

Olivia hesitated as she pushed a pin into her curls. Carefully she said, 'One must embrace the future rather than dwell on the past. And of course, your mama is right to be concerned that you meet the right man.' A vision of Max with his kind smile and the cowlick he was forever pushing out of his eyes swam before her and her heart spasmed with excitement. 'There are some wonderful and worthy ones out there. Find a good man to be your husband, not a dashing rake, and you'll not regret it.'

'The worthy ones are so boring.' Lucy grumbled, before brightening.

'I met a woman once who was green with envy when I told her that my cousin was married to Lord Farquhar. She said she was a debutante that same year and all the young ladies swooned over him.' Lucy kissed the tips of her fingers with a flourish as she rolled on to her back and gazed dreamily at the ceiling. 'She said he had the wickedest glint in his eye and was by far and away the most handsome of all the eligibles.' Hesitating, she added, 'But she said that since her mama had warned her against him she was not disposed to court his advances.' Lucy slid her appreciative gaze the length of Olivia's daring dress: a Madame de Pompadour gown Mariah had insisted she wear for the occasion. 'Of course she only said that to save face because he didn't look twice at her.'

'That's as may be,' said Olivia, striving for a note between sounding too censorious, knowing that if Lucy was anything like she had been at her age any warning would be like a red rag to a bull, and too dismissive. 'However, it's one thing if the young ladies consider a gentleman eligible and quite another if their mamas do. The latter,' she added pointedly, 'is all that matters.'

Looking downcast for just a moment Lucy whispered, 'I have a secret, Cousin Olivia.'

Disquieted, Olivia smiled her encouragement. Best to have any confessions out in the open. Lucy was such a fresh innocent it would be in everybody's interests if the girl chose to make Olivia a confidante, particularly if the confession was of an unsuitable nature.

The girl became suddenly coy. Tracing the outline of the fleur-de-lis on the counterpane she mumbled, 'A gentleman has made his especial interest quite clear. I want you to meet him.' With a look of earnest entreaty she added, 'He'll be at the masquerade tonight.'

'I'd love to meet him,' Olivia said. 'What does your mama think of him?'

Swinging her legs over the side of the bed Lucy smiled valiantly. 'I don't really know. He paid his respects so charmingly that I'm sure she was quite overwhelmed only I think she doesn't wish to influence me.' Taking in the mutinous set to Lucy's mouth and the determined fire in her eye, Olivia decided Cousin Mariah had every reason to fear for Lucy.

CHAPTER 12

CLUTCHING JONATHAN'S ARM, Amelia blocked her brother's attempted escape towards the front door. 'You need diversion, Max,' she said, holding her ground at the bottom of the stairs, 'and accompanying us to Bath is just the ticket.'

Halting reluctantly, Max sighed. 'Quite frankly, Amelia,' he said in clipped tones, 'I could think of nothing less diverting.'

'Max!' Releasing Jonathan's arm, Amelia hurried after him as he shrugged on his greatcoat in the hallway. 'It doesn't matter that you won't enjoy it but you need something to take your mind off Julian and …' She didn't say it and nor did Max allude to the fact that the name Lady Farquhar had been about to trip off her tongue.

Forbidden territory.

He stared at Amelia's pursed mouth, her pale, peaked face framed with dark hair, and imagined Olivia's vivid blue gaze and shiny coiffure the colour of newly ripened corn.

Longing ripped through him and he closed his eyes against the vision of the family he'd once believed would be his. But was Olivia an adulteress, a grand deceiver, and Julian, the boy he loved like his own, the result? An innocent usurper, but a usurper, nonetheless?

'You need a wife, Max, and Bath is full of lovely gels who'd be eager to fill the post,' Jonathan corroborated, as he watched Max pull on his riding gloves. 'Why not join us for a few days? It'd do you good.'

'Miss Hepworth is taking the waters with her mother,' Amelia said brightly. 'You were quite charmed by her the first time you met her and clearly she was struck by you.' She fixed Max with an imploring look. 'Whatever you might have said in parting can surely be undone.' Max picked up his riding crop. Olivia's fear of the clergyman was greater than her ability to trust Max with the confession she owed him: that her immoral actions had cost him ... everything! His initial shock and scepticism at Dorling's allegations had turned to contempt for the woman he loved. At first he'd not believed Dorling but everything pointed to the fact that what the man insinuated was true: Julian was Olivia's illegitimate child...by Nathaniel Hawthorne. Why else would she insist on punishing herself, even if it was by marrying the detestable man? She might have succumbed to the reverend's advances in a moment of weakness and through fear of Lucien—and for that Max could have forgiven her—but her failure to trust Max with the truth, too weak to admit the fact she'd denied Max his inheritance, was more than he could bear.

For the past week he'd believed his wounds were mortal.

He was thoughtful as he turned up the collar of his coat. Miss Hepworth was young and pretty *and innocent*. Isn't that, really, all he wanted in a wife?

His thoughts followed this train for but a second, obliterated by the memory of Olivia's lithe body pressed against his and her passionate avowal: 'I've never wanted anyone like I want you, Max'.

A sentiment wholly in accord with his own.

He flexed his fingers, no longer paying attention to Jonathan and Amelia's arguments. Hadn't he accepted that Lucien's cruelty was at the core of everything? The table dancing, the scandalous clothing. He shuddered ... Lady Farquhar's notorious butterfly.

Actions he had long ago forgiven.

Turning at the front door his mind was closer to the dower house in Mortlock than to Bath as he bent to peck Amelia's cheek. 'I'll consider it,' he said.

A cocktail of emotions flooded him as he strode towards the

BEVERLEY EIKLI & BEVERLEY OAKLEY

stables. Olivia had not been married to *him* when she'd committed adultery.

Lucien's cruelty had driven Olivia into the arms of another man.

But she had confessed that all was not as it seemed.

Lord, it had to be the reason she'd held back from committing herself to Max time and again, when her heart and body cried out for him.

Then he thought of Julian, the child who had usurped his birthright, and anger transcended all. For but a moment.

Olivia had promised to write. Perhaps her letter had gone astray. Perhaps she was awaiting his direction at this very moment.

Odin nuzzled him as he adjusted the stirrups. Max patted his flank.

Just as he'd been furious moments before, now he allowed himself hope. It's how he'd been all week. 'Let's not give up on her just yet, eh, feller?' he said softly. 'Perhaps a night amidst vacuous, pleasure-seeking Bath acolytes before we see what the lady has to say for herself *is* just the ticket.'

⁂

WHEN OLIVIA MET THE OBJECT OF LUCY'S INFATUATION IN LADY Glenton's crowded ballroom dressed as a Roman senator, her fears were confirmed.

A Corinthian, to be sure.

'Mr Petersham arrived in Bath a week ago and has already extended his visit.' Lucy blushed prettily and Olivia was acutely aware of the power communicated to the young man in the gesture. His handsome mouth curved in the faintest of smiles, his eyes conveying a subtle subtext Olivia remembered from her youth: collusion; confident of his attractions.

Oh yes, Olivia had jostled for prime position amidst the ranks of rakes like this eight years before. Burnt like a moth at a flame she knew exactly what danger the heart-palpitatingly eager Lucy courted.

She inclined her head graciously, her smile distant. 'Delighted to meet you, Mr Petersham,' she murmured.

'You are a visitor to these parts, Lady Farquhar?' the young man asked, preventing her from making a gracious retreat, which would have obliged Lucy to accompany her.

'My first foray into society following my mourning, Mr Petersham,' she said. Once, the look in his eye would have thrilled her, now she was unnerved. She longed for Max's comforting presence, his straightforward manner and wished, heartily, she had pleaded a megrim and stayed at home, gathering her strength and reining in her excitement for tomorrow's momentous reunion.

'I am an excellent dancer, Lady Farquhar. If you are afraid of being sadly out of practise, it would be an honour to partner you on the dance floor later this evening.'

'Isn't he so kind and thoughtful?' Lucy demanded as they returned to the aunts. She tugged at Olivia's sleeve as if she would force her to concur and sanction Lucy's choice.

'He is' – Olivia searched for the right word – 'a charmer.'

Lucy seemed satisfied. After a pause, she said, softly, with a quick glance to ensure her mother was not listening, 'He told me the other night I was the most beautiful girl in the room. Can you believe that?' Her face shone. 'It was after he danced with Arabella Knight who is coming out this year and who everyone knows will snare a duke, she's so pretty, even if she has no fortune.'

'Unlike you, Lucy, who, I must remind you, is set to come into quite a fortune.' In a quiet corner Olivia stopped and gripped both her cousin's hands. 'Cousin Mariah told me that your Aunt Gwendolyn has made you her beneficiary. It's wonderful you are so well provided for, but if there is one thing I've learnt since I was a debutante it's to be aware of the hidden motive.'

Lucy looked hurt. 'You sound just like Mama,' she accused, pulling away. Her eyes glistened with unshed tears.

With a sigh Olivia followed her as she joined Mariah who was chatting to the aunts. She had barely reached the girl's side before Mr Petersham again presented himself with a bow and after a brief consultation with her mother, led Lucy on to the dance floor where a quadrille was forming.

Olivia nodded after the departing couple. 'Lucy seems taken with Mr Petersham.'

'She's been wearing her heart on her sleeve since he arrived a week ago.' Mariah didn't trouble to hide her disquiet. 'He's the eldest son of a baronet, comes from a respectable though impoverished family, and no one could dispute he's handsome and dashing. I just wonder what he sees in Lucy.'

'Lucy is a pretty girl.' However Olivia knew what Mariah meant. Lucy was not the dazzling swan-like creature one would have envisaged a man like Mr Petersham seeking out when there were in the room that evening a handful of far prettier girls.

Gazing at a couple of brunette beauties she did not fail to notice the flare of interest in Mr Petersham's eye as he passed them, Lucy on his arm. Olivia blinked. Perhaps she had imagined it, for immediately he returned his attention to Lucy, his manner full of gallantry.

'Pretty but penniless.' Following Olivia's look Mariah's tone was dry.

'Like you, my dear, and now I understand you have reneged on the clergyman. Was that wise?'

Taken aback by her bluntness Olivia replied, 'I could not commit myself to him when my heart was engaged elsewhere.'

Cousin Mariah cast her gaze around the crowded ballroom. 'Shall you find the object of your affections here?' she asked. 'Clearly, you have many admirers judging by the glances slanted your way. It is just as well my Lucy has not a jealous nature.'

Eight years ago Olivia's numerous admirers had fed her ego, bolstered her reckless spirit.

She wondered how many in this room knew who she was. The scandalous Lady Farquhar would be an object of prurient interest wherever she went. It was a dampening thought. A reason to conduct herself with the utmost restraint.

'A glass of orgeat?' Mr Petersham, returning to her side, offered her a glass of the sickly refreshment and Mariah drifted away.

Olivia wished she could do the same. Turning, she murmured, 'I only drink champagne.'

Poor naïve little Lucy courted grave danger if she thought this man a worthy contender for her affections and her considerable future fortune.

He chuckled. 'The moment little Lucy's mama left your side I seized my opportunity.' A head taller, he stood slightly closer to her than was decorous. 'I knew it'd not be long before some Johnny Likely came to pay his addresses to the most dazzling creature in the room.'

Olivia stifled the desire to take a step back. Instead she smiled, raising one eyebrow. 'And now he has.'

It took him a split second to digest what he could only interpret as a joke – unless he were to beat a graceful retreat.

'Then I must persuade you otherwise.' He offered her his arm. 'I've told you I'm an excellent dancer. Let me prove it' – he lowered his voice, his breath tickling her ear – 'amongst other things.'

As a debutante she'd revelled in being fêted as if she were a breed apart. As Lucien's wife the interest of other men usually meant sinister designs. She couldn't recall the number of times she'd had to bat away a man's insinuating hand in a dark corner. Lucien encouraged the perception she was a woman of lax morals. He punished her if she appeared too prim. She'd learned to tread a fine line; had in fact developed it to the highest degree.

Tonight she had intended to present herself a model of propriety for the benefit of those who might denigrate her.

Lucy, she now realized, must be her target audience.

Mr Petersham had merely to crook his little finger and Lucy would come running. One unfortunate encounter with the wrong gentleman could ruin the rest of her life.

❦

THE SUN WAS LOW IN THE SKY WHEN MAX SAW THE ELEGANT TOWN in the distance but a pebble in Odin's shoe forced him to stop at a hostelry two miles out.

It was while utilizing the light that spilled from the upper rooms and a knife to scrape out the hoof that a familiar voice made him raise his head.

'Reverend Kirkman?' The words were out before he could think better of it, for the man was disappearing into the inn and, really, Max had no desire to exchange pleasantries – or anything else – with him.

He swung round and Max could have sworn anger crossed his face before he asked with a narrow-eyed look, 'What brings *you* to Bath, sir?'

'Diversion, Reverend.' Clearly, the dislike he felt was mutual. 'And you? Enjoying a few days' gaiety before your nuptials?'

The words created a frisson of excitement. Olivia was *not* going to marry the man. Max would see to that. Two hours of riding like the devil had firmed his resolve.

Kirkman grunted. 'I'm for my bed. Perhaps I'll see you at the Assembly Rooms tomorrow night, Mr Atherton. Good evening to you.'

Max stared after his disappearing back. He'd thought the man had planned to deliver a sermon at Nuningford where he was to spend a few days.

A light rain began to fall as he took the rest of his journey at a leisurely canter for Odin's benefit. Bounding up the stairs to his sister's townhouse he felt full to bursting with renewed enthusiasm for his future.

If Olivia had fallen into an adulterous affair with Kirkman all those years ago, he could forgive her. He knew what a tyrant Lucien had been. As long as Olivia loved only Max, he could forgive her anything.

As he raised his fist to knock, Amelia and Jonathan issued from their front door, resplendent in masquerade.

'What a surprise, Max. Well...we'll see you at Lady Glenton's Midnight Masque, then, Max?' Amelia asked, adjusting her feathers and plucking at her gloves. The look she slanted up at her husband was smug. 'You said you enjoyed it last year and I've told her we're expecting you.'

His notion of pleasure-seeking had ebbed. All he could think of now was a good night's sleep so he could be refreshed for tomorrow's journey to Mortlock.

Amelia wasn't giving up. 'Lady Glenton's famous for her refreshments.'

Caging Amelia's hand upon his arm, Jonathan sent Max an apologetic look. 'Give poor Max a reprieve for at least this evening before you start playing matchmaker, Amelia.'

Grateful and exhausted, Max stepped across the threshold. Within half an hour he was in bed.

Within three hours he was putting on buckled shoes and accepting that as sleep continued to elude him he might as well pass the time in congenial company rather than tossing and turning in a cold, hard bed.

Swept through the front door of Lady Glenton's by a jostling crowd of young bucks who had just come from a spirited game of faro, Max realized immediately what an error of judgement he had made. The clock chimed two. He was in no mood to mingle with the fabulously garbed crowd when all he could think of was hastening to Mortlock to find Olivia as soon as dawn broke. He felt out of place. The pretty debutantes with their shy, hopeful looks only reinforced how much he preferred Olivia with her experience and understanding of the world, pummelled into her at such cost.

Catching sight of Amelia with Miss Hepworth at the far end of the room, he turned. Far better to make his escape before his sister saw him and pounced.

Sidling towards the door he managed to avoid the attention of Sir John Smales, a near neighbour.

Nearly there, he thought with relief, just as another vision intruded into his peripheral vision. One that was far more appealing than the portly squire and which sent ripples of excitement through him, but confusion, too.

The elegant coiffure of shiny golden hair above a slender pale neck made him breathless with longing.

He'd have recognized her anywhere, though her face was half turned and she was dressed in masquerade.

In a small group beyond, her aunts chatted to a statuesque woman in a gold toque, but, as his gaze was drawn back to the stunning wasp-waisted creature sheathed in blue silk adorned with pink bows and roses, he could think only of crossing the room and leading her into some secluded arbour.

Madame de Pompadour? A daring statement for someone who usually dressed in sober colours, but Olivia was full of surprises.

Mesmerized, he watched as she raised her glass and spoke animatedly to her companion, a gentleman he did not know.

Candlelight reflected off the paste ear-rings that hung from her earlobes. The elegant sweep of her shoulders carried the line of her gown in far more alluring lines, surely even than Madame de Pompadour, the late French king's mistress. He found he could not move as he studied her, curious that her manner seemed different, somehow. How he ached to caress the creamy length of her throat, feel the beat of her heart and murmur the words he had no doubt she longed to hear.

As son as she moved away from the companion she was addressing, he'd make himself known.

Timing had favoured him. How fortuitous he'd not ridden poste haste to Mortlock, the home she shared with her aunts, when Olivia was in this very room, resigned to a future with the clergyman.

Longing for Max's absolution ... his forgiveness....

If he told her he knew everything and still wanted her, she'd melt into his arms and accept his proposal, he was sure of it.

'Why Max, I've been looking everywhere for you!'

Dear God. It was Amelia.

Max feasted his eyes a second longer upon Olivia before turning to his sister and her hopeful-looking companion, Miss Hepworth.

Olivia would have his absolution, his forgiveness, before the night was over.

But it looked as if more domestic matters had to be attended to, first.

CHAPTER 13

'THANK YOU, DARLING Olivia, I don't think I'll ever know how to thank you *properly*.'

Lucy's eyes shone with excitement as she drew Olivia into an alcove.

'I can't imagine what I've done,' said Olivia, feeling at a distinct disadvantage. Was Lucy more cynical than she'd thought? Was she using irony as a precursor for the torrent of vitriol Olivia felt was justified?

Lucy lowered her eyes and her mouth curved into a secretive little smile. Olivia waited while the stirrings of disquiet escalated.

'At one stage this evening I confess I felt like clawing out your eyes or pulling out all your hair.' Lucy looked apologetic as she played with her sash. 'I shouldn't even say such things but there must be so many girls who would feel the same. After all, you're so very beautiful without having to work at it, and you make the rest of us feel like dowdy wallflowers while all the gentlemen clamour to ask you to dance.'

'Including Mr Petersham?' Olivia prompted, wondering where this was leading. It was unpleasant having Lucy put into words what she'd always suspected about her female rivals.

'Yes, and by two o'clock I was so in the dismals that when he passed by and said: "What ails thee, my pretty" I nearly burst into tears upon the spot.' As if galvanized by the reflection she reached up to whisper loudly, 'Then he touched my cheek and said, "Ah, so you do care.' Lucy shivered and hugged herself before she went on, "And *then* he said: "You're jealous over my attentions to your cousin? Well, let me tell you, Lady Farquhar has only your best interests at heart and she is helping our plans to be together by deflecting your mama's attention away from ourselves, for we both know that she disapproves of me".'

Lucy clasped her hands and raised her eyes to the ceiling as if her thoughts were floating heavenward. Olivia stared at her, stricken, and wondered what else the young lovers had discussed in those impassioned few moments. 'Shall you see him tomorrow?' she asked.

Lucy looked at her a long moment as if weighing up whether to speak then said in a rush, 'We're eloping, and I was going to keep it secret because Mr Petersham said not to tell anyone, but as you've proved yourself the most wonderful and loyal of cousins I had to tell you.'

'Eloping?' Olivia knew the disapproval in her voice was not a good idea, but she was so horrified she couldn't help herself.

Checked, Lucy said with a frown, 'I believe you, yourself, eloped.'

'Eloping is a very drastic measure which will scandalize society and bring you much distress, Lucy,' Olivia counselled, sounding to her own ears very like Aunt Eunice. She took Lucy's hands in hers as she drew her further into the alcove. The girl refused to meet her eye, staring with trembling mouth at the carpet.

'Mama will never consent to my marrying him before the end of the season,' she said, in a small voice.

'Then have your season, dazzle society and in six months, if you and Mr Petersham still feel the same way and your mother still disapproves, *then* you can consider eloping with him.' She squeezed Lucy's hands, forcing her to look up at her. 'Promise?'

Reluctantly Lucy nodded. But when Mr Petersham appeared to lead Lucy once more on to the dance floor Olivia felt little consolation from the promise she'd extracted.

Or from the weight of her reticule with the coins that would soon transform her life. Olivia was about to embrace freedom and happiness with a man of forgiveness and compassion whereas Lucy ...

She stared after the departing couple, Lucy blushing, giggling as her companion made some apparently witty remark.

It would take only Mr Petersham's impassioned declaration of eternal love and a request to climb into a waiting carriage and Lucy would be halfway to Gretna Green before anyone knew of it.

As she issued out of the alcove and went in search of her aunts she was waylaid by Mariah.

Her initial pleasure in her cousin's company had evaporated.

Mariah's hospitality did not conceal her real feelings regarding Olivia: that her scandalous past could never entirely be erased.

Her cousin gripped her wrist, turning her in the direction of the dance floor where the young couple were positioning themselves. 'I fear Lucy's lost her heart to Mr Petersham and that any caution from me will do nothing but firm her resolve in his direction.'

'Eighteen can be a difficult age if one is not quiet and modest by nature,' Olivia murmured.

'Quite.' Mariah sent her a narrowed look.

Olivia dropped her eyes. She felt uncomfortable, as if Mariah were both condemning her and needing something from her at the same time.

'Cousin Mariah.' She sighed. 'I have told Lucy there is little happiness to be found by resorting to such impulsiveness. That a kind man makes a much better husband than a flattering buck.' Staring at the young people on the dance floor, at smooth, handsome, Mr Petersham and awkward little Lucy with their heads bent close together, her longing for Max redoubled.

'Such wisdom came to you too late, Olivia. Lucy, I fear, is similarly headstrong.' Mariah appeared not to realize how wounding her words were.

Olivia felt the tears forming and looked up as Mariah touched her arm.

'You've been given a second chance, my dear,' she murmured, 'but only because you are a widow. My Lucy may rue this week in Bath for the rest of her life.'

Olivia refused to be drawn. 'Lucy's good sense will tip the balance,' she hedged. She wanted no more part in this conversation. 'What more can I do? Besides, you know Lucy better than I.'

'I fear an elopement is in the cards.' Taking Olivia's elbow, Mariah drew her into the crowd so they would attract less attention. 'Her aunt Scrivener was here yesterday,' she said, 'roundly haranguing her for every sin in the book: loucheness, frivolity, obstinacy. Just the thing to whip up true rebellion in Lucy's heart.'

Stopping on the edge of the dance floor, Olivia followed her gaze.

She wondered if she had looked that young, like Lucy, barely out of the schoolroom, eyes bright with infatuation as she clung to Mr Petersham's arm.

'It's clear she admires you enormously.' Mariah broke into Olivia's reverie, cool green eyes watching her intently.

In a low voice Olivia defended herself. 'I have counselled Lucy against following my deplorable example.'

'You cannot turn back the clock, Olivia.' There was an edge to Mariah's tone, a hardening of her gaze. '*You* can't and my Lucy can't.' Olivia closed her eyes briefly and a tremor ran through her. Mariah spoke the truth.

Struggling to maintain her composure she replied in measured tones, 'What is done cannot be undone. But Lucy's behaviour cannot be put at my door.'

Mariah grew angry. 'Look at you, Olivia. You are magnificent in any sense of the word. No wonder Lucy holds you up as her model. She cannot see how you have suffered, for Lord knows I have heard it from your aunts. You do not need to pretend for me.' She put her hand to her pearl choker. 'To the ordinary eye you appear quite unscathed. You have a title, beautiful clothes, the freedom to move about at will—'

Olivia gaped. Is this how she appeared? With not a feather to fly with, her few clothes had been so mended and stitched to keep up with current fashions she had wondered if she would be mistaken for a lowly companion or chaperon fallen on hard times.

Apparently not.

'But Cousin Mariah, I have said everything in my power to deflect Lucy from following an undesirable course.' She was shaking. 'I flirted shamelessly with Mr Petersham earlier this evening and Lucy thought I did it merely to avert your scrutiny.'

'You can do more.'

Olivia had only heard such stentorian tones from Aunt Eunice.

'Really, I don't know what—'

Mariah sent her another kindling look.

'You have not even begun to utilize your powers of attraction, Olivia, to prove to Lucy that Mr Petersham is as fickle as we've all been at such pains to tell her he is.' Realizing that the strength of her grip had made marks, Cousin Mariah caressed the bruised white flesh of Olivia's arm above the glove. Her smile was brittle. 'If you believe in honour and atonement, Cousin Olivia, there is something I would ask of you.'

Miserably, Olivia stood by her aunts, her pleasure in the evening's gaiety entirely evaporated.

She didn't have to do this, she told herself. The day Lucien died was the day she should have been able to stop acting against her better judgement.

She managed a smile at some inanity Aunt Catherine directed towards her before the aunts resumed their animated conversation with an old acquaintance.

She had only just freed herself of Nathaniel's yoke. He'd used blackmail to bend her to his will, but she'd proved herself stronger than that. Now Mariah was appealing to Olivia's nobler instincts, pressuring her to perform an act of charity designed to save her impetuous young daughter from falling into the same trap that had all but ruined Olivia's life.

Swamped by her own helplessness, Olivia plucked at the embroidered silk of her reticule and tried to draw strength from the fortune it contained. What should she do?

Mariah's eyes were upon her. At her side, Lucy, pink-cheeked and radiant was gushing, 'Cousin Olivia! Mr Petersham has asked me to stand up with him twice already!'

With a smile for Lucy and ignoring Mariah, Olivia pretended to turn her attention to her aunts' conversation.

Her limbs felt heavy but she would do it. She had no choice if her conscience was to be clear. A clandestine kiss in a dark corner observed by Lucy was all that was required. How many men had kissed her when Lucien had been alive?

Revulsion soured her mood further while the memory of her seven long years as Lucien's wife galvanized her courage. If she refused Mariah's request and Lucy eloped with Mr Petersham, Lucy would be ruined and Olivia would be culpable, in part, through her inaction.

That was how Mariah regarded the matter.

Fingering the key at her neck a burst of excitement outweighed her present trials.

Elmwood. Elmwood where her beloved Max lived was only two hours away.

Surely Max would still want her when she was returning more than she had taken away? Surely tomorrow's reunion would compensate for tonight's trials?

As she scrutinized her reflection in the empty ladies' withdrawing room a little later, she bolstered her flagging confidence with the thought of seeing Max again.

Satisfied by what she saw, she stepped back, smoothing the unaccustomed full skirts of her scandalous costume. Her eyes were bright and her skin still lustrous with none of the blemishes of age one might expect in a woman beyond her first flush of youth. She tilted her chin and fluttered her lashes. Her eyes flashed an invitation.

Tomorrow she could be herself, but tonight she had one final duty to fulfil: hoisting Mr Petersham by his own petard. A duty Cousin Mariah believed would change her daughter's life.

'Cousin Olivia?'

Mariah's voice floated from the passage and Olivia felt cold dread fingering her entrails. She was waiting for her, the noise of the ball filtering through the door at the end. With heavy heart Olivia turned to answer her summons.

'You will not fail me?' Cousin Mariah's mouth was a thin line as she drew Olivia back into the throng. 'In less than three years Lucy will have her entire fortune at her disposal.'

'Rest assured, Cousin Mariah,' she said wearily, 'that I shall persuade Mr Petersham three years is too long to wait when other rewards might be forthcoming faster.'

Mariah's green eyes flashed their gratitude. With a faint smile she laid her hand upon Olivia's arm. 'Deliverance and atonement, my dear,' she said, giving her wrist a squeeze before she left her.

Immediately Olivia was struck by the fear that Mr Petersham would fail *her*. Was she not too confident in her powers of attraction? This reservation was swept away as warm breath tickled her ear and Mr Petersham's voice, low and suggestive, asked, 'How many gentlemen have told you you're far and away the most beautiful woman in the room?'

'Too many to count, Mr Petersham.'

He grinned as they stood for the moment, alone, in an uncrowded corner of the ballroom.

'Your dry humour, Lady Farquhar, sits better with me than the endless chatter of a besotted schoolroom miss.'

Slanting an amused look at him beneath her lashes, Olivia remarked, 'I thought what a handsome couple you made when you addressed Lucy tonight. I hope you will not break her heart.'

Mr Petersham gave a short laugh. 'You have not a reputation for being tender-hearted. Besides, Lucy is a willing participant in the marriage mart. I am curious as to your participation,' he went on, caging her hand upon his arm as they made a leisurely progress. 'A widow surely grows bored and lonely in time.'

'I have too handsome a fortune to grow bored and I can assure you, Mr Petersham, I am never lonely.'

She said the lie as a challenge; recognized that he interpreted the subtext that she made herself available for dalliance on occasion.

And that right now she was contemplating him.

'You are a remarkable woman, Lady Farquhar,' he murmured, drawing her towards the dance floor. 'Very different from your cousin, Lucy, who I fear would make a dull bedfellow. Come! A quadrille?'

She could not deny the intoxication she felt as she preformed her moves though she wished Mr Petersham were not holding her so tightly.

Dancing made her feel alive. She must put aside the horror of what

Mariah required her to do. She was on a mission to save Lucy. A mere kiss when she had been forced to do so much worse in her life? It was nothing.

Dear God, rein in your temper, or you'll snap the stem of your champagne flute, Max exhorted himself as he gazed at the couple upon whom surely all eyes were fixed. By the saints in Heaven, she was dazzling. No wonder Lucien had needed to possess her. For this was the Olivia who had set his dissolute cousin's pulses racing. Not the demure, grieving widow she'd pretended to be when she'd made his acquaintance. Not the sincere, responsive damsel in distress who had avowed her love for him. The trouble was, Max was as susceptible to Olivia the dazzling beauty as he was to the maligned widow and damsel in distress.

He swallowed, uncomfortably conscious of his desire as he surreptitiously stared over Miss Hepworth's shoulder while trying to concentrate on the young lady's chatter about her pony.

Olivia fanned herself and whispered something in the ear of her handsome companion.

He had been on the verge of approaching her, bursting with expectation earlier this evening when his sister had thrust Miss Hepworth upon him.

Somehow a dance had been promised which had been followed by more conversation; it had seemed an eternity before he caught sight once more amidst the several hundred guests of the one woman who could stir his senses.

She was certainly stirring them right now. Breathless hope and anticipation had been replaced by white-hot anger as he observed the flirtation in her manner; the sly, colluding glance she slanted up at her companion beneath thick dark lashes.

What was she playing at?

Olivia's betrothed was tucked up in bed at the Duck on Puddle two miles away. Her behaviour made no sense. This was the false persona Olivia had decried; the coquette Lucien had forced her to be for his entertainment. Her humiliations had torn Max's heart in two yet here she was, behaving just as one would expect the notorious, brazen Lady Farquhar to behave – if one didn't believe her version of the truth.

'But I had to stop giving Misty apples because they gave him colic. And as a carrot isn't nearly such a tasty treat, Mr Atherton, what do you think I should give him, instead?'

He jerked his attention back to Miss Hepworth's earnest, pretty face. 'I beg your pardon.'

'What do you think would be a nice tasty treat?'

He nearly answered that all he could think about were devouring Lady Farquhar's luscious lips after he'd ripped her from the arms of her patently unworthy companion; that certainly fell under the heading of 'tasty treat'; when Miss Hepworth was joined by a companion.

'Look at them!' He recognized the young girl having seen her earlier with Olivia's aunts. In her distress she did not acknowledge him, clutching Miss Hepworth by the wrist and pointing to Olivia and her companion.

'Cecily! You must come! I trusted her, but she has betrayed me!' Miss Hepworth turned to hush the girl, blushing as she slanted a look in Max's direction before introducing her distraught, chestnut haired friend.

'Miss Lucy Snelling and I attended Miss Pinkerton's Seminary for Young Ladies in Highgate,' explained Miss Hepworth.

Max regulated his breathing as he listened to her soothe her friend's injured sensibilities before sending her off in the direction of her mama.

Turning back to Max she coloured prettily as she murmured, 'Mr Petersham has paid particular attention to Lucy during the past fortnight, however the arrival of her cousin, Lady Farquhar, appears to have set the cat among the pigeons.'

He should be admiring Miss Hepworth for her uncommon good sense. She would make an excellent wife. Every encounter with her merely reinforced this.

'I'm sure Lady Farquhar is no competition for your friend, Lucy,' Max soothed her. Yet uncertainty warred within him.

The Lady Farquhar he'd observed tonight accorded much more with the scandalous widow whose reputation preceded her than it did with the tremulous Olivia Templestowe who'd intimated she did not believe herself worthy of Max.

CHAPTER 14

'P ERHAPS, LADY FARQUHAR,' murmured Mr Petersham, 'you'd care to admire the Roman busts Lord Glenton has displayed in the long gallery?'

Olivia was conscious of her fading bravado, felt it wilt her smile, felt the insidious progression of cowardice wrap itself around her vital organs.

She nearly said she would like nothing less, but how could she when Cousin Mariah was depending upon her?

As was Lucy.

She'd seen Lucy's eyes upon them several times this evening: luminous and uncertain, her smile so eager to please when Mr Petersham addressed her. He'd danced with Lucy to keep up appearances, but he'd done nothing but mock the girl to Olivia.

'She'll look just like her mother when she's forty.'

'Mariah is very well looking, if a trifle stout. And she's ten years older than forty.'

'My point exactly,' he'd said, stroking her cheek as the dance dissolved. 'Whereas look at you. Your dewy looks belie your experience.'

Had he thought she'd take it as a compliment and smile?

Certainly she smiled. It was expected, and she'd always done what the occasion demanded. What Lucien demanded.

But fear and trepidation gripped her. Oh! For this evening to be over! She wanted to be in her carriage on her way to Elmwood. She wanted to be telling Max that she had found his family's fortune and beg him to forgive her the deception that had brought about this impasse. If he hadn't received her letter, then she would have to tell him, herself, her terrible secret. She thought he would forgive her for rearing Lucien's bastard in place of their own legitimate son. Denying Max his birthright as a result had been the greatest stumbling block in confessing everything but now she had a fortune with which to compensate him.

The gold changed everything.

First, though, was her distasteful duty for the sake of Lucy's future happiness. Girding her courage she said, 'You have a honeyed tongue, Mr Petersham,' taking his arm so he could lead her back to her aunts.

His eyes twinkled. She recognized his lust. It left her cold. Caressing her hand, he murmured as they turned their footsteps towards Lucy who stood, lost and lonely in the centre of the room, 'I hope I may have an opportunity to prove to you just how accurate your words are. Perhaps in the gallery in ten minutes?'

The gallery in ten minutes. The thought made her ill with fear. She met his eye. Slowly, she inclined her head.

After greeting Lucy with fulsome compliments Mr Petersham departed to procure refreshments. Lucy, quiet and uncommunicative beside her, fidgeted, while Olivia, conscious of her cousin's confusion, tried not to feel so traitorous.

'Perhaps tomorrow we can take a country ramble, Lucy?' she suggested. 'The weather looks set to be fair.'

Lucy jumped. 'Tomorrow?' Biting her lip she added, 'Yes, certainly.' Olivia slid her eyes across to her discomposed cousin. So Mr Petersham's honeyed inducements had carried more weight than Olivia's cautions, she thought. And tomorrow was to be the day.

It was enough to banish the reluctance she felt at her part in Mariah's plan. Wouldn't any mother do all she could to ensure her daughter's happiness was not blighted by a misalliance with a fortune hunter?

Olivia's credentials equipped her perfectly for the part; she knew it, but how she railed against what her experience had cost her.

'You seem much taken with Mr Petersham, but I hope you have taken my cautions to heart.'

Lucy's pale skin took on a fiery hue as she struggled for a guileless smile. She looked too young for this sophisticated throng. 'He has been very civil to me.'

'Civil?' Olivia smiled, as she took Lucy's arm and began a leisurely stroll amongst the knots of exquisitely attired revellers. 'He is handsome but he is penniless, though I'm sure he thinks the title he one day inherits is compensation enough. Certainly he is charming, but I know his type.'

'Then why do you enjoy his company so greatly?' Lucy looked immediately embarrassed that she'd snapped out the words, and dropped her eyes from Olivia's face to gaze once more about her. Olivia saw her lip tremble.

'I enjoy testing my theories.' Olivia patted her forearm and lowered her voice. She hoped Lucy would take heed of her sober tone. 'I eloped when I was seventeen, Lucy. About your age. It was an act of naïve impulsiveness which I regretted every day of my marriage. I still regret it. I would hate you to make the same mistake for Mr Petersham reminds me very much of my late husband.'

'You know nothing about him!' Lucy ground out, her eyes glistening as she glared at Olivia. 'Why, Mr Petersham, thank you,' she added, with an unsteady smile as she accepted the glass of orgeat he handed her. Wiping her eyes she said in answer to his concern, 'Cousin Olivia's feather has just poked me. Otherwise, I'm perfectly well, thank you.'

'How careless of me,' Olivia apologized, skimming the length of the plume with her fingers as she slanted a knowing look up at him. She turned to Lucy, stifling her frustration at the girl's refusal to see sense; her fear at what she had agreed to do to ensure she learned her lesson.

'When you're my age, you can add to your consequence with such fripperies and be just as thoughtless of those around you.'

The words belonged to a woman with no feeling, no conscience.

Had she ever been a woman like that?

156

She tried to remember *what* she'd been like as a seventeen year old. Thoughtless? Self-absorbed? Heartless?

Disgusted, she forced a smile for Cousin Mariah and her aunts who had just joined them.

Like an excited child Aunt Catherine was enquiring of Lucy whether she was enjoying herself.

Olivia put her lips to Cousin Mariah's ear. 'The gallery in ten minutes,' she whispered.

❈

WHEN ALL THINGS WERE CONSIDERED, MISS HEPWORTH HAD THE most charming little nose and a rosebud pair of lips, Max decided, grimly, as he led her in the stately steps of their dance. When he clasped her hands to dance down the centre of the room she gave a little gasp of excitement and her hazel eyes lit up. They were shining at him now as if he were the handsomest, most desirable man in the room.

Foolishly, he had imagined it was how Olivia thought of him. That his feelings were reciprocated with the same intense sincerity.

Now that his shoes had been filled, if only for this evening, it was some consolation to feel Miss Hepworth, with her great fortune, considered him a desirable catch.

His chagrin at Olivia's flirtatious behaviour this evening made him say, perhaps unwisely, 'I am sorry, Miss Hepworth, if your last visit to Elmwood proved a disappointment to you.'

His sense of betrayal was acute. Olivia was not languishing, heartbroken, at the dower house, waiting for him to gallop back into her life and forgive her.

So why was she here?

Trawling for an alternative future to marriage to Kirkman – *even if he was the father of her child*?

No, there *must* be some other reason.

Grimly, he wondered if she knew the clergyman was only two miles away. Or perhaps they had arranged to meet tomorrow and Olivia was making the most of her freedom tonight.

As he listened with half an ear to Miss Hepworth he struggled to comprehend Olivia's behaviour. Was she reverting to her true nature? Was her thirst for gaiety, her need for compliments, behind her incorrigible flirting?

And what of Max? Would she assume the mantle of damsel in distress the moment she set eyes upon him?

Miss Hepworth dropped her eyes, blushing. 'Mama explained matters,' she said, as they returned to the sidelines.

'You have every right to be angry with me.'

Fixing her gaze on the other couples performing their figures she said, 'I would not wish to throw myself at you, Mr Atherton. I ...'

She stammered and blushed some more. 'I am only just out of the schoolroom. There is so much I do not understand.' She raised her chin, proudly. It was such a guileless look; the innocent – uncorrupted – smile of a simple, inexperienced girl who makes no apology for what those more worldly may consider shortcomings, that he was captivated.

For a moment.

'Do you think I offended your mama?'

'I don't think so.' Her smiled broadened as she added with refreshing candour. 'But more to the point, you have not offended me.'

There was no time to dwell on the hopefulness and encouragement in her expression as he led her off the dance floor, for they were again interrupted by Miss Snelling.

'Cecily!' Miss Snelling came to a halt in their midst, her heaving bosom and flushed cheeks betraying her distress. 'Cecily, I beg of you,' she gasped, 'please accompany me to the long gallery.' Her voice held the edge of hysteria.

'But Lucy, I—'

'I cannot go alone and I must ... confront my cousin who has gone there with ...' – she gulped – 'Mr Petersham!'

Mr Petersham and Olivia?

Alone in the gallery? Max's anger blackened. He didn't care if Miss Hepworth obliged or not. He certainly needed to see what Olivia was up to in the gallery with this Mr Petersham.

Clearing his throat, he tried to sound fatherly though he heard the angry censure in his own voice. 'Shall we all take a turn about the long gallery, Miss Snelling? I've heard there are some very fine specimens.'

It was difficult to believe that Olivia was in Bath cuckolding, it would seem, the man she had promised to marry *and* the one she had professed to love.

'Please show us the way, Miss Snelling,' he said, offering Miss Hepworth his arm.

Lucy tucked an escaped chestnut tendril behind her ear and wiped her nose with the back of her hand before Max could procure her a handkerchief.

With a shaky breath she turned and led them towards the door in the panelling.

CHAPTER 15

OLIVIA'S INITIAL RELIEF that another couple was promenading in the long gallery was short lived.

'The library is through here.'

Mr Petersham's voice in her ear, low and intimate, made her stomach curdle. She resisted the squeeze of his hand as he tried to draw her towards a rear door, straining towards a Roman senator with the words, 'Aren't we in good company tonight?'

Did he sense her reluctance? Hear the fear in her slightly shrill tones?

If he did it made no difference for his grasp was firm as he ushered her before him into the library.

The door shut behind them and they were alone in a large book-lined room, unlit save for a fire burning in the grate.

'Aha!'

He must have seen the *chaise-longue* by the window at the same time as she. There was satisfaction in his tone. Olivia felt her knees begin to shake.

She should run. Pull out of his grasp and escape but her fear had translated into mute acquiescence which he interpreted as willingness.

'You drew attention to my honeyed tongue earlier this evening,

LADY OLIVIA'S BUTTERFLY

Lady Farquhar,' he murmured, leading her to the *chaise*. 'And I promised to deliver, I recall.'

'Do you have an arrangement to elope with Lucy?'

She could not believe herself, how baldly she uttered the words. Shocked, he dropped her hand.

'Am I to be censured or applauded for my boldness?' he asked, halting in the centre of the room. The moment of uncertainty was over in an instant as his smile resumed its confidence. Staring into her eyes he raised her left hand, slowly circling the palm with his forefinger. His eyes bored into hers as he murmured, 'If you are jealous, Lady Farquhar, I assure you that I would infinitely prefer to elope with you.'

Stonily, she met his gaze. 'I prefer my widowed status, thank you.'

'As I thought.' He sighed, feigning disappointment. 'You have the freedom to' – he paused, recalling her sentiments of earlier that evening – 'enjoy your fortune as you please, and not be censured for the dalliances in which you choose to indulge.'

With a tug Olivia found herself stumbling the last few feet and then she was across his lap upon the gold and blue-striped *chaise-longue*.

She heard herself shriek, a faint, cut-off sound, for Mr Petersham's mouth was covering hers while his arms had assumed the nature of tentacles. She could feel one of them insinuating itself the length of her thigh.

Was this what he thought of her? A strumpet all too eager for a quick fumble in the shadows?

She struggled but perhaps he mistook her objections for the writhings of passion? Just as she had mistaken speculation for admiration all these years in the hooded gazes of other women's husbands? Now she knew it was speculation. How far might scandalous Lady Farquhar be prepared to go with *them* given the right inducement?

Self-disgust united with her terror. What a fool she was. As much a fool as when she had been seventeen.

She tried to pull her mouth away but blind lust gripped him and even if he registered her resistance he did not heed it.

Horrible blackness clouded up behind her eyes, filling her head as she fought for control.

There was no finesse in his exploration. His groping hands sent shivers of revulsion through her but her protests were stifled by the single-mindedness of his quest for physical fulfilment.

Ineffectually, she tried again to push him away. Nothing was worth this foul indignity, this trampling of her sensibilities. His mouth was like a great sponge clamped over her lips, his arms like a vice caging her to his will. Did he not register her unwillingness? Was his mastery over her his enjoyment?

Like Lucien? Dear God, how could she have been so blind as to walk right into the trap set for her? Mr Petersham saw her as a conquest, nothing more. Just as Lucien had. No spark of feeling for her had ever burned in Lucien's breast other than the need to possess and vanquish.

How well she had read Mr Petersham. And she had gone with him willingly!

She twisted and writhed in her attempts to struggle free, but escape was not an option until Mr Petersham had had his fill.

Panic was overlaid with a desperate yet weary resignation that she had no one but herself to blame. There would be no rescue until Mariah had orchestrated the ghastly finale she'd planned for poor Lucy's edification.

And then a sharp, clear familiar voice cut through her horror. 'What is this, pray tell?'

For a brief instant joy and relief pulsed through her as she registered the beloved voice of her rescuer.

Almost instantly her horror metamorphosed into a new form. Of all the people to witness her latest transgression: Max.

The shock of discovery caused Mr Petersham to release her. She wasn't sure if chivalry or devilry made him drape his arm possessively about her shoulders as he sat up on the *chaise*, pulling Olivia up with him. She felt the smug satisfaction conveyed by his caress as Max, eyes like flint, looked past her, his voice low and terrible as he demanded, 'Unhand that woman!'

'Who are you, sir, to interrupt a tryst between willing—'

He stopped as Lucy stepped out of the shadows and the stricken look she directed first at her erstwhile admirer and then at her cousin made Olivia wonder if any of this had been worthwhile – even had it gone more or less to plan.

Though the girl said nothing, Olivia thought she'd never seen the cruel effects of betrayal etched more poignantly on another's features. With a heartrending wail Lucy buried her face in her friend's shoulder.

Olivia darted a brief, guilty look at Max before she slid her eyes to the floor. The disgust in his tone was echoed by the recrimination in his slate-grey eyes.

He put a hand on the other young woman's shoulder. 'Miss Hepworth, I think you should escort your friend back to the ballroom,' he said, his hard gaze still encompassing the guilty lovers. 'I shall follow in a moment.'

As the weeping Lucy was borne away, Mr Petersham rose. His mouth quirked and he clicked his tongue.

'A disappointed suitor, perhaps? I do not believe we have had the pleasure.'

Max ignored the extended hand.

'Lady Farquhar is to marry Reverend Kirkman at the end of the week.' She had never heard his voice so cold. His gaze swept Olivia briefly. 'I am here to ensure she follows through on her commitment.'

'Max, no, I—'

He cut her off, seizing her hand and pulling her up from the sofa.

'Olivia, if you would kindly come with me.'

Mr Petersham did not even protest. Olivia's last sight of him showed clearly his amusement and his words followed her through the door.

'My pardons for having detained you from your obligation to the good reverend, madam. Do call on me when you are again in the market for dalliance.'

Dazed, Olivia could not even respond. It was only after she was hustled outside and pushed into a hackney that she came to her senses.

'Where are you taking me, Max? No, you do not understand—'

'Did my eyes deceive me?' Fury resonated through him as he thrust her ankle free of the door and leapt in after her, slamming the carriage door behind him.

Cowering into the corner her defences drained from her as he leaned across the small, dark, musty space, the once-kind grey eyes boring into her with revulsion.

'It was a mistake—' She grabbed at the window sill to steady herself as the carriage lurched forward.

'Only because you were discovered, Olivia!'

'I did not want to kiss him!'

As she put out her arms to appeal to him he grabbed her wrists, thrusting his face into hers. His eyes glowed with hurt pride and anger and her heart quailed.

'Do you love him?'

'Of course I don't!'

'Yet you compromised yourself out of – what, exactly? The dictates of your wayward body?' Like a wounded beast he was striking out. She winced as if his anger had taken a physical form. If she could just navigate her way through their current impasse all could be made right between them.

She opened her mouth to speak, but he cut her off once more.

'Perhaps it would *not* be so sickening if you admitted you cared for the gentleman. What was I, Olivia? Another dalliance to pander to your cravings and lusts?'

'I've only ever loved you!' Her voice sounded shrill to her own ears as she struggled to free her wrists, impulses warring between flight and the desire to soothe his injured sensibilities in her embrace.

But she lacked the courage, fear and desperation banishing her ability to use calm reason to explain away his misplaced anger. He crackled with it, his body stiff as he ended their contact with exaggerated revulsion, his eyes bleak and cold.

She made another attempt. 'You're the only man I've ever loved, Max! What you saw tonight was a mistake—'

'A mistake! How easily lies and excuses trip off your tongue,' he sneered, flicking away her renewed attempt to appeal to him as he retreated back against the squabs. 'You lied to me from the moment you saw me and it's been lies ever since. I was nothing but a means to an end: the return of your son.' His voice cracked. 'The son you would parade before the world as Lucien's heir! Well, now I know better!'

'Max!' She implored him. 'My ... my indiscretion with Mr Petersham was part of a plan to save my cousin from the fate I suffered at Lucien's hands.'

There was nothing to signify he was at all mollified, much less believed, this confession. Scepticism dripped from his response.

'Really?' He regarded her from his dim corner. For a moment he looked frighteningly like Lucien but the pain in his eyes highlighted by the breaking dawn almost immediately erased this impression and gave her hope. Lucien had never looked so wounded in his anger.

'A shame your earlier indiscretions carried not the same thought for the future of others.'

The direct reference to Julian's parentage made her mouth dry.

'Please, Max!' she cried, 'I'm not ashamed of what I did, though I deeply regret hurting you. Nor am I marrying Reverend Kirkman. I am resolved upon it.'

Though he avoided her outstretched hands her misery was overlaid by hope. Right was on her side. She clutched convulsively at the reticule that dangled from around her wrist. She could give him so much more than he had ever dreamed. A fortune to go with her love.

Soon his eyes would kindle with a very different emotion from the hurt and fury that roiled there now. Yes, he was sickened at discovering her in another man's arms but there was ample evidence to vindicate her.

'What choice do you have?' The words crackled with contempt.

'You made your bed—'

'But I don't have to lie in it!' Olivia railed. Just because the reverend was prepared to accept her, sin and all, didn't mean another wouldn't.

She heard him let out his breath in a slow whistle while she rested her head against the window. 'I told you the truth, Max.' She strove for measured calm. 'I wrote to you and asked what you would have me do. I have been in torment at your silence.'

'So now the fault is mine.' His voice, disembodied in the shadows, was harsh. 'I never received the letter, but that doesn't change the fact that what you did can never be undone. Julian is a bastard yet you were prepared to parade him to the world as the rightful Viscount Farquhar.'

Wounded, she replied, 'Max, I never meant to hurt you. When I looked into Julian's eyes I didn't consider him a bastard. He was a tiny, defenceless baby ... and Lucien was desperate for an heir.' It was an effort to speak through her tears. 'Do you know how many babies I had lost? And yes, I should have admitted the truth. I realized that the moment I met you' – she dropped her gaze. It was painful just to breathe – 'before I fell in love with you.'

His mocking laugh brought her head up. She stared at him. He truly did not understand. She wondered how she could have misjudged him. There was no forgiveness for replacing the babe she and Lucien had lost with Lucien's motherless bastard.

Gasping she cried out, 'Have you no compassion?'

'Not for scheming deceivers,' he ground out, snatching her hands and moving his face close to hers. 'Look at you, Olivia!' With his palms he contoured her face. 'You are without equal. Exquisite. What I wouldn't sacrifice to have you – if I did not know I would pay twice in pain for the pleasure you gave me.' He fell back against the squabs, wiping his brow with the back of his hand. 'Before you destroyed me, as you destroyed my cousin.'

The empty silence stung her ears.

Shocked, she whispered, 'I had no idea you hated me so much.'

'Not as much as I love you' – he gave a shuddering sigh and his voice trembled as he added, 'But self-preservation prevents me from succumbing to the lust that consumes me as we speak. For it is lust, only, Olivia. Tonight you proved there is nothing in you to love.' Raising himself he glared at her. Never had he looked so like Lucien.

'Besides, you are going to marry Kirkman. You know there is no other path open to you.'

Stung to indignation she wiped her eyes. 'Should I be compelled to atone the rest of my life for compromising myself before him?' Hunching herself into the corner the anger built within her. 'I can't do it. I won't,' she flung at him after a moment's silence.

'And Julian?'

Goaded, she muttered, 'He is Lucien's heir and as long as the world believes *that* he will be fine.'

'Is that a threat?' Max spoke quietly. After a moment he let out a humourless chuckle. 'So you would tell the world the truth only if I had been prepared to wed you and conveniently dismiss what stood between us?'

He was looking at her as if he could not believe it.

'I can manage very well without Mr Kirkman and if you choose to deny me my son on account of it, you are within your rights,' she said coldly.

'And I can manage very well without you!'

The anger drained from her. Sorrow took its place. They had once loved each other. It could have been so wonderful.

'Olivia.' There was so much pain invested in the word she nearly wept. She kept her head averted.

After a silence he shrugged and there was a distance to his tone as he said, 'A boy needs a father.'

'Mr Petersham would have done just as well.'

Max gave a sardonic chuckle. 'You really are trying to live up to your reputation.'

She made her tone deliberately careless. 'Since it was only you I wanted – yet clearly it is impossible for us to live with the uncomfortable truth between us – I no longer care what becomes of me. I shall make a point of enjoying my road to eternal damnation.' She smiled sweetly. 'When your worthy Miss Hepworth becomes too tiresome you can look to *The Tatler* for some diverting scandal about the latest exploits of the brazen Lady Farquhar.'

Clearly he did not share her self-deprecating humour for he said with a narrow look, 'The future Viscount Farquhar will not be brought up in such a manner. If you want to keep Julian, you forget yourself, Olivia.'

She heard his shuddering breath. 'At the end of the week you will marry Reverend Kirkman. He has been ... good ... to you. You deserve each other.'

'Oh God,' she whispered, covering her face with her hands. 'Would you really condemn me to torment by *forcing* me to marry him? Just because he knows the worst of me? I am not *so* far beyond redemption.'

'I have discovered too much, Olivia, to know what alternative you have.'

She nearly choked on her anger. 'You self-righteous beast!' she cried, lunging at him with flailing fists. 'You're no better than Lucien! I hate you!'

Caught by surprise as the glancing blow struck his jaw, he gripped her wrists while pain tore behind his eyes.

'You hate *me*?' he repeated.

HE COULD NOT BELIEVE IT OF HER. WHAT DID SHE EXPECT? TO allow her *carte blanche* to continue her reckless, ill-chosen path, dragging Julian along with her?'

Wincing, he acknowledged his love for the boy. How could he not?

For more than a year they had been as close as father and son.

Her eyes were like blue thunder, her skin flushed and her creamy flesh tantalizingly bared by her sumptuous, scandalous dress. Max was not a man who enjoyed conflict and nor did he lust after temptresses but Olivia had behaved tonight like the temptress her reputation made her out to be; and he'd never wanted her so much.

He closed his eyes briefly. The price was too high. She would forever revel in the power she had over him. He did not think his manhood could sustain a lifetime of it.

She was straining across his lap as he caught her wrists. Holding them above her head caused her body to sag into his. He fought against the desire to place a kiss upon the flesh that swelled above her low cut bodice; fought the raging impulses that rushed through his body as anger faded beneath his yearning. Her hot breath on his cheek as he parried her blows quickly fanned the flames into full blown desire.

For an instant she stilled. He opened his eyes in the startled silence and saw that she felt it, too. She wilted in his embrace, her face inches from his, her eyes dark pools of need.

The thread that connected their two hearts from the moment they'd met tugged tighter. He was devastatingly aware of the soft contours of her body and for a second he almost yielded.

Of all the women he'd known, none had the power to stir his senses as the fascinating, faithless creature before him.

Common sense returned and he jerked back as if stung.

He turned his head away before the hurt and surprise on her face could weave their spell upon his all too susceptible heart.

'We're here,' he said as the horses turned into the stable yard. With enormous effort he kept his voice neutral. 'Kirkman is waiting for you.'

She did not want to go. He knew he forced her against her will; that he was abusing his power in this act of spite and self-righteousness.

He didn't care. If she hated him for it, all the better. He didn't know if he had the fortitude to hold out if it was any other way.

Smoothing her dress she sat back in her seat, glaring at him. 'I had not known such a fine line existed between the affection you've always extended towards me and' – she nearly choked on the words – 'the disgust you clearly feel for me now.'

When he didn't answer she whispered after a silence, 'Could I change your mind?' Then, more desperately, 'I do not wish to marry Reverend Kirkman. Since I have made that plain, perhaps you'd like to know my reasons.'

'I'm not interested in your reasons.' He knew he was being childish and pig-headed but he wanted to hurt her. Humiliate her.

The carriage jerked to a halt and Max rose over her in the small space. It was not a comforting thought that his domination and angry snarl: 'Perhaps confessing tonight's little dalliance might ease your conscience' could only remind her of Lucien. Yet perhaps Lucien's behaviour was not so reprehensible given all he had learned of Olivia. Opening the door and jumping out on to the hay-strewn cobblestones he added, 'If you have one.'

A stable boy ran up to enquire if Max needed fresh horses. Shaking his head he turned back to Olivia who remained seated.

'Please Max, I will go anywhere except back to him. Take me back to my aunts! Please!' Her disembodied, heartrending entreaty did not soften his resolve.

The dawn shouts of the inn servants as they began their work and the creaking of the water pump were reassuring. Cocooned in darkness the intimacy between them during the ride here had nearly undone him. Now daylight provided a welcome barrier. Yet as his gaze raked her magnificent body and lingered on the perfection of her mutinous face he acknowledged it would not take much before her charms overcame his hurt and anger.

If he were to accede to her reasonable request to be conveyed back to her aunts the consequent confinement would be detrimental to his resolve to sever all contact. He would be as enslaved as he ever had.

He dare not risk it. Reaching in he took her wrist. She gripped the door and resisted. 'Take me back to my aunts! I'm not going!'

Releasing her, he glanced round, realizing the dangerous path he trod. He could hardly drag Olivia kicking and screaming through the inn and deliver her to a no-doubt still slumbering Kirkman.

Disgusted by his heavy-handed tactics he slumped against the carriage door. What should he do now? He thought he heard her sobbing until her shrill cry shredded all sympathy.

'Take me back and I will restore your fortune, Max!'

Her tear-stained face emerged from the carriage, her bosom heaving above the enormous pink silk roses that adorned her dress. The dress of a courtesan; and the lies of a woman who would debase herself to the limits if she saw profit in it.

'I know where the gold is! Take me back and I'll prove it!'

'Mr Atherton?'

Relief surged through him at the familiar voice. He doubted he'd have had the fortitude to parry Olivia's latest sensual onslaught had rescue not arrived in the unlikely and unexpected form of The Rev'd Kirkman. He did not for a moment believe her last desperate gambit.

Careful not to look at her he bowed to the soberly clad gentleman whose shock at their unconventional arrival was palpable, and said through gritted teeth, 'Lady Farquhar was anxious to see you.'

CHAPTER 16

NATHANIEL'S ROOM WAS cold and Spartan. No fire had been lit as he'd intended spending the day in Bath searching for Olivia, he told her.

'Only, what a surprise to find there was no need.' He chuckled. 'I wonder what you could have done to so vex Mr Atherton.'

Olivia quailed at the menace in his eyes before returning his hard look.

'You ask what I have done to have so vexed Mr Atherton? Perhaps the truth is best, Nathaniel.' Clasping her satin gloves together she adopted a businesslike manner from the wooden chair on which she sat.

'I would hope the truth is always best, my dear.'

She was not deceived by the silken tone. Nathaniel, she had come to realize, was always at his most dangerous when he spoke like this.

In a few sentences she told him about Mariah's plan and Max's anger at discovering her in the arms of young Lucy's paramour.

Nathaniel's scorn turned quickly to amusement. Pacing the floorboards in front of the empty fireplace, he shook his head as if unable to believe her tale. Finally, to her astonishment he began to laugh.

'By the saints in Heaven, Olivia, I cannot believe that you have been delivered to me, on a platter so to speak. And by Mr Atherton!' He could barely speak for chuckling. 'It reminds me of the lively entertainments Lucien staged in which you were the star attraction.'

She glared at him. 'How dare you speak of those days—?'

Grinning, he cut through her objections. 'You realize Mr Atherton believes I am Julian's father.'

Her lungs deflated as she leapt to her feet, the chair crashing behind her. 'He believes no such thing!' Blackness befuddled her thoughts as she grappled to back up her denial, a thousand truncated exchanges teasing her memory with their potential for misunderstanding. 'He couldn't! I wrote and explained everything surrounding the night I took Julian in.'

He quirked an eyebrow. 'Yet he still deposited you here.'

In a gesture of self protection Olivia's hands went to her throat as he slowly circled her before going to stand in the window embrasure.

'For someone who thinks herself so clever, my dear Olivia, you are remarkably credulous.' He chuckled again: a low, evil, gloating noise that made her insides resonate with fear.

She'd never been this afraid of him, before.

'My dear Olivia, of course that letter did not reach Max Atherton.' From his pocket he pulled an elegant wafer which he slapped upon the table. 'When I suspected a damaging little confession from you was forthcoming I was ever vigilant.'

Olivia's mouth went dry as she stared at the letter she had written to Max. She could feel her self-control slipping but managed to sound cool and imperious as she said, 'Since Max has deposited me here and I have no wish to remain, please be good enough to advance me a small sum so I can return to my aunts.' Pushing her shoulders back, she wished her dress did not expose so much flesh.

He stroked his chin, his expression thoughtful as he took a step towards her. Fear made her glands swell and it was hard to swallow but she couldn't let Nathaniel sense it. She tried to choke it back but it was too strong, too overpowering.

'I'm not going to marry you and you're not going to rear the future Viscount Farquhar,' she whispered, recoiling from the hand he extended to stroke the side of her neck. 'That's what it was all about for you, wasn't it? The power you'd have as Julian's guardian.'

It was suddenly clear. Cursing herself for a fool, she railed at him, 'You wanted me to trust you, yet all you wanted was power over me!'

Nathaniel's smile was pitying. 'Dearest Olivia, what have I done that you suddenly hold me in such aversion? Four days ago you eagerly anticipated being a bride.'

'Not yours, Nathaniel.' She closed her eyes briefly and whispered again, 'Never yours.'

He shook his head as if her words caused him sorrow while his eyes told a different story. They were black with anger. 'After all I've done for you, Olivia. The scandals I've had to deny, the lengths I've gone to protect you from Lucien's ill temper.'

'To shore up your own position.' Strange how the truth revealed itself only now.

His finger hovered in the air just below her breast. 'Lady Olivia's butterfly has brought you notoriety, Olivia. If you continue to refuse me, if you won't accept the respectability I'm offering you, you'll not find it elsewhere.'

'I wouldn't marry you if you were the last man on earth!'

'Your Mr Atherton must have been *very* angry to have deposited you on my doorstep.' He pursed his lips in a parody of sympathy. 'Clearly he has withdrawn from the quest for your affections. Still,' he added, 'I've no doubt there are many other worthy, blameless young women eager to fill the breach.'

His hands caressed her throat, toying with the pendant, the key Max had threaded through the chain around her neck in the attic that night.

The key to Elmwood. The fact Max laboured under the most ghastly of misapprehensions and that she had failed to convey to him so much that was important gave her courage. 'He will think differently when I tell him the truth.'

If she could only stop herself trembling. She wondered if her fear would fuel Nathaniel's malice as it once had her husband's. For the moment his manner was restrained, almost gentle. Lucien had used this tactic as a precursor to violence. She trembled even more as

Nathaniel ignored her last remark, murmuring, 'Here you are, horribly compromised in my chamber, yet still you refuse to marry the only man who's prepared to pave your way back into society. You will be ruined, Olivia.'

'Marrying a man I detest is not worth my return to society – in the unlikely event the truth does not change Max's mind.' She held herself proudly. 'Regardless, my greatest comfort is knowing Julian will be well looked after by Max who loves him as his own son. For you surely never did, Nathaniel.'

He chuckled again, staring out through the dirty windows. With his dark, oiled hair combed back from his high, greasy forehead and his full, gloating lips, he looked more like a repulsive toad than ever.

She seized her moment. Leaping out of the chair she ran towards the door, gripping the knob as Nathaniel's voice floated from the window embrasure.

'You really have lost your wits, Olivia, if you think you can simply step out of this room and find your way home.'

'I shall walk if I have to!' she cried, as she tried to make the door yield.

'An attractive proposition for the first drunken rider passing,' he chuckled.

She must not buckle now, though she realized the door had been locked. The key, however, still protruded, though it was stiff. To her relief it clicked as it ground its rotation. 'Goodbye, Nathaniel.'

'Not so fast, Olivia!'

How quickly he moved for such a heavy man, she thought as he gripped her elbow.

'Not when you've failed to give satisfaction.'

His words were ominous, but when he saw the revulsion in her face his lip curled. 'I admit I am disappointed to be denied your charms in the marriage bed, but the idea of forcing myself on you is even more repugnant.'

She twisted in his grip once more, and her reticule spun, whipping him across the cheek before landing upon the flood with a dull thud.

'Nathaniel, I beg you, let me go,' she whispered, looking at his fingers curled around her forearm.

But Nathaniel wasn't following her gaze to where his fingers encircled her wrist.

He was looking at the floor where one gold coin had spilled from
the delicate silk and embroidered bag she carried.

He shook his head, his grip tightening, the silence that followed
nearly deafening. Until he said in a tone that was low with controlled
excitement, 'Not until you show me what's in your reticule.'

꧁꧂

No sooner had Max closed the door of the drawing room of
Amelia's elegant London townhouse than he found himself facing
down a veritable regiment of women.

So much for a quiet sanctuary followed by the catharsis of sleep to
calm his disordered wits, thought Max, as he was confronted by
Olivia's aunts, flanked by a formidable-looking woman in a gold toque.

Where had everyone come from all of a sudden?

Oh Lord, and there was Olivia's cousin, Miss Lucy, too! She looked
highly aggrieved, as well she might, but the censure on everyone else's
faces was hard to stomach.

He couldn't fathom why all these women were here when the
owners of the townhouse, Amelia and Jonathan, had gone to bed. Or
so he'd been told by the weary parlour maid who admitted him.

'Where's Olivia?' Aunt Eunice's voice was strained as she gripped
the arm of the green sofa and peered past his shoulder, as if hoping to
see her niece materialise.

On the sofa beside her, the young chestnut-haired Lucy raised a
pale, blotched face, her mouth trembling as she wailed, 'So you were
too late, Mr Atherton! They've eloped, haven't they?' Before he could
reply she dissolved into tears against her mother.

Max ran the back of his hand across his forehead and prayed for
forbearance. Tonight ranked as one of the most dreadful and disap-
pointing of his life and all he wanted was his bed.

Grimly, he said, 'There has been no elopement, Miss Lucy. I have
just returned Lady Farquhar to Reverend Kirkman whom she is to
marry at the end of the week.' He doubted he had the fortitude to field

any more questions. Especially ones that brought back the uncomfortably draconian manner in which he had handed Olivia over. He shouldn't have forced her but she'd made her bed and clearly she intended to lie in it. With the reverend. Or with that Petersham fellow.

A shudder wracked his body at that thought. How credulous he'd been. Olivia had offered him nothing but lies since the moment he'd met her.

'You've done what, Mr Atherton? You've surely not delivered Olivia to that man!' cried Miss Dingley.

He was surprised that her outraged reaction to his perfectly reasonable announcement seemed to be echoed by the others. Surely marriage between Olivia and Reverend Kirkman was the outcome everyone had expected; desired, even?

'The reverend!' gasped Aunt Catherine, springing up and clutching her bosom as if he'd just told her he'd returned her to Bluebeard himself. 'Oh dear me, no! Surely she did not request it?'

His discomfort grew. He looked longingly at the door before replying. 'It would appear Olivia does not know her own mind, yet it is too late for her to withdraw without great damage to her reputation.' He took a few steps towards the fire and picked up Jonathan's snuff box which lay on the mantelpiece. Distractedly, he added, 'Do you not think it better than facing the accusing stares of all of you in this room? It was a kindness.'

'A kindness?' repeated Aunt Eunice. Her thin frame trembled as she also rose. 'Olivia holds that man in great aversion. She ended matters between them quite decisively before she accompanied us to Bath.'

Aunt Catherine dabbed at her eyes with a scrap of lace. 'She did not deserve it, Mr Atherton. Not after what she did for Lucy.'

Silently, Max prayed for fortitude. Lucy?

'She ruined my life!' Lucy cried on a choking sob.

Aunt Eunice sank back upon the sofa. 'I really don't understand all this talk of betrayal, Lucy,' she muttered with a reproving look at the girl. 'And if Olivia has returned to Mr Kirkman, surely it proves she is blameless and not deserving of your accusations?'

Aunt Catherine lent her argument to the cause. 'Why would Olivia steal away your admirer, Lucy, when her heart clearly belongs elsewhere?' She levelled an accusing look at Max as she resettled herself beside her sister. 'Besides, she only met Mr Petersham this evening and your mama has tried countless times to tell you Olivia is blameless in the whole matter.'

'Lady Farquhar has shown Mr Petersham up for what he is, Lucy!' said Aunt Eunice. 'It was very kind of her when she told your mama so many times she did not want to do it.'

Did not want to do it?

'She was *not* unwilling!' Lucy cried, close to tears. 'I saw them!'

Max had seen them, too. With distaste he recalled the vision:

Olivia's body pliant beneath the onslaught of that ... villain's ... ardour.

Though, on reflection, it was difficult to gauge how pliant she had been. Yet he had jumped to the only conclusion possible, he defended himself, silently.

'No respectable woman would compromise herself like that if she did not want to!' Lucy persisted. 'I hate her! I never want to see her again!'

Aunt Eunice gave Lucy a gentle shake. 'You should never want to see *Mr Petersham* again, for your cousin has shown him up for exactly what he is.'

The lady in the gold toque leant forward. 'A fortune-hunter, Lucy, and it was only because I prevailed upon your Cousin Olivia to ... to compromise herself – though that is too strong a word for I ensured the assignation was in private so there was no risk to her reputation—'

Aunt Eunice turned on her. 'Cousin Mariah, I believe you were quite specific in your instructions to Olivia.' She glared, first at her cousin, then at Max. 'Atonement and honour, I believe were the words Cousin Mariah used to shame Olivia into helping her with her plan to ensure Lucy was under no illusions that her admirer was a philanderer.'

'How dare you accuse me—'

Aunt Eunice cut her off, her accusing glare still turned upon Max.

'Now my poor Olivia has been returned to Nathaniel Kirkman! Against her wishes, for I suspect your anger overruled your judgement, Mr Atherton, did it not?'

CHAPTER 17

LINED UP SIDE by side on the wooden table in Nathaniel's room the two gold coins looked surprisingly dull. Worthless, unless she had known otherwise.

They were to have been Olivia's passport to happiness; atonement to Max, they were to have won back his love.

'You're cleverer than I thought, Olivia,' Nathaniel murmured, tearing his gaze from the coins. 'After all these years you've found the fortune which sent Lucien mad.'

'But *only* I know where it is, Nathaniel,' she reminded him, huddled in a chair with her elbows on the table.

Nathaniel chuckled. 'It's a wonder we never bumped into one another, my dear, during our mutual nocturnal quest. For years I've searched every priest hole, nook and cranny I could think of.'

'I never believed the stories,' Olivia said stonily, fingering the key about her neck. 'I stumbled upon it by accident.'

His eyes followed her gestures and he frowned before a look of enlightenment transformed his features. 'The key Lucien gave to you? Was that it, after all? It finally yielded what he was looking for?'

Olivia gave a mirthless laugh. 'No, it's the key to Elmwood where I shall soon return. Max gave it to me.'

Nathaniel came round and clapped her on the shoulder, his gaze returning to the gold. 'Ever the dreamer, Olivia. You think Max will have a change of heart? Even if he does, it'll be too late. I will have what I want. You and the gold. Both, indisputably claimed by me. for if what you have around your neck is *not* the key to the treasure, you will now lead me to it.' He pocketed the coins. 'Time to order a carriage.'

'I have no intention of meekly leading you to the gold.'

'There is nothing meek about you, Olivia, when your blood is up.' He pinched her cheek. 'It's one of the things I've always liked about you. *Of course* you have no intention of leading me to the gold, just as I have no intention of leaving open the possibility of your escape, since leading me to the gold is *exactly* what you will do.' He put his hand on the door knob. 'Perhaps Julian will help persuade you. Your late husband was very accommodating on his deathbed when signing his name to a list of desires and stipulations I felt appropriate to a man in his position.'

Olivia stared. She felt paralysed. Helpless. Just as she had when Lucien rode roughshod over her desires. Or rather, her objections. Lucien's desires were usually whipped up by Olivia's objections.

'Patience, Olivia. I will return. And save your breath if you've any plans of shrieking for help. I shall tell the publican you're a lightskirt who has stolen from me and that I'm off to fetch the magistrate.' His gaze travelled the length of her costume, so revealing and inappropriate in the light of day. With another chuckle he added, 'The way you're dressed they'll not disbelieve me.'

Olivia sank on to the bed and buried her head in her hands when Nathaniel had gone. Once, she had believed he had her interests at heart; that he had cared when Lucien had beaten or humiliated her. What a fool she had been.

Graft and gain had been his motive the entire time.

No, she would not cry for all that her life seemed to have fallen into shreds about her feet when not so long ago she truly believed happiness was within a grasp.

And yet tears were a catharsis. At last she sat up with the question ringing in her head: What could Nathaniel do to her that her espousal of the truth to the world could not?

She sucked in a breath. Since the moment she'd eloped with Lucien, she'd waited for others to tell her what to do. Just now, she'd been waiting for direction from Max.

Aunt Eunice had forced her to action in order to seek Julian's return but since then Olivia had only proved her cowardice by offering half truths and making assumptions regarding how others perceived the situation.

When in reality, Olivia needed to be strong and to forge ahead on her own—offering the full truth.

Please, let there be time! she thought, as she ran to the desk where Nathaniel had been in the midst of writing a sermon when she'd arrived. How she wished she had done this the moment he'd left the room. She had no idea how long she'd been weeping.

She was scribbling upon the second page when Nathaniel returned.

As she tried to hide the parchment, his gaze from the doorway took in her stricken, guilty look before it travelled towards the hand she concealed behind her back.

'You've shown admirable restraint,' he remarked, crossing the room towards her. 'The servants haven't heard a peep from you. Now, let's see what this drama-filled tale of imprisonment contains.' He put out his hand for the paper.

When she refused to give it to him he snatched it from her, reading it with interest and chuckling several times.

'You don't believe in half measures, do you?' His tone was admiring. 'A full and frank baring of the truth, no less.'

'It is not finished—'

'Yes, there is a little editing to be done.' Nathaniel continued to pace before the grate, still studying the parchment. 'If we dispense with the first paragraph in which you claim to be held prisoner against your will, I think it will do very well.' He smiled at her. 'Had you planned to throw this out of the window, my dear, in the hopes of being rescued? Foolish of me not to have thought of it, yet I am pleased you have so conveniently orchestrated an alternative future for yourself. I had not decided what was to be done with you once you'd furnished me with the gold.'

His cryptic words filled her with panic. She tried to snatch the parchment from him but he held it above his head, gripping her shoulder with his other hand.

'It's not finished, Nathaniel!' Olivia cried again, her hands tearing the air in her desperation to reclaim the document, so damning in its truncated state.

'But *you* are, Lady Farquhar!' he responded grimly, 'and so are your dreams of cosy domesticity with your heroic Mr Atherton.' He pushed her away from him as he made for the door. 'Where is he now?' he sneered. 'Where is the *hero* who delivered you into my very hands?' He tapped the paper before turning the door knob. 'You are confessing to the very crime of which he believes you guilty. He'll not disbelieve it when he hears your burdened conscience has prompted your flight far, far away where nobody will ever find you.'

She felt the knot of fear and hope pull tighter when he said cheerfully, 'It would however appear Mr Atherton's conscience is pricked by his shabby treatment. He was asking for you a short while ago.'

Olivia stopped her pacing and gripped the bedpost for support.

Max was *here*? He had returned?

Surely it could mean only one thing? That he had realized the error he'd made and had come to take her home.

She could not believe Nathaniel would resort to violence, like Lucien. Yet his insidious character had begun to frighten her more than Lucien ever had. Lucien's anger found its outlet upon the instant. He was not a man who would patiently plot his revenge.

She realized Nathaniel had told her so he could enjoy her suffering. He was waiting now for her to beg him for answers. At last she asked, 'What lies was Max told?'

Nathaniel shrugged. 'I informed the publican that you were, on account of your nervous disposition, on your way home to Mortlock. Your outrageous rig-out helped persuade him you were not quite right in the top loft.' He chuckled. 'If you made no noise he may well have presumed you'd already left. Now!' Striding to the table he pulled out more paper and dipped his quill in the ink. 'To business, my dear. There are several letters for you to write in addition to putting your signature to the bottom of this delightfully damning little document.'

'Max will find me!' Olivia declared, firming her grip on the back of the chair by the still unlit grate, refusing his offer of a seat at the desk. 'Once he learns that infidelity is not amongst my crimes he will pursue me to the ends of the earth! And then *you!*'

'He'll have to be persistent to get that far!' Impatiently, Nathaniel tapped the paper. 'Come over here, Olivia and take up your pen. Mr Atherton is on horseback so I'd give him an hour before he turns back after failing to pass us on the road. As soon as we've done this' – he pushed the quill into her hand as he dragged her over – 'we shall leave, taking a more circuitous route. We should reach The Lodge by early afternoon.' He rubbed his hands together after pushing her down upon the seat. 'By this afternoon I shall be a rich man.'

Olivia let out a bold laugh as she shrugged out of his grasp. 'You think the gold is hidden *there?* Why, you have no idea where it is and nor shall you.'

He shrugged, as if her intransigence was of no account. 'You misjudge me, Olivia, if you think I had not considered I might have to resort to extraordinary measures to overcome your reluctance. Mary!' In response to his shout the door opened and across the threshold stepped one of the inn servants, a dirty, dishevelled girl bearing a squirming toddler in her arms.

The child had been crying and although it didn't look instantly delighted to see Olivia, he certainly looked relieved as he was deposited to the ground. Making his way unsteadily across the floor-boards, Julian wrapped his arms around Olivia's knees. 'Mama,' he whimpered.

Tears stung her eyes as she held him on her lap and Julian put his plump rosy cheek against hers in a rare burst of affection.

'When your touching reunion is over you can write the first letter to your aunts, reassuring them that you will be waiting for them at the dower house tomorrow. He held up his hand to stay her objection, his plump oily face twisted with malice. 'If you do not, Olivia my dear, this is the last time you will see your little bastard alive.'

MAX WAS BACK IN BATH BY MID MORNING BUT WITH NO STOMACH for the eggs and haddock with which his sister and her husband were no doubt sustaining themselves, judging by the aromas which wafted out of the front door.

Wearily, he entered the house. He needed to take stock and decide what to do next before he walked the few streets to Laura Place to inform Olivia's aunts of his failed mission.

Since he'd been informed of his terrible misjudgement, he'd returned to the inn where he'd left Olivia with Max.

But they'd gone. He'd been looking for her ever since.

'Max! You look like the devil!' Jonathan greeted him cheerfully, looking up from his laden breakfast plate.

'Like you haven't been to bed,' Amelia added, dabbing her mouth daintily with her napkin.

'I haven't!' Max snapped, sinking into a chair, accepting the cup of coffee his sister poured for him.

'Surely you haven't spent all this time looking for Lady Farquhar?' Amelia grunted her disapproval. 'Miss Dingley was asking after you. Apparently her niece took it into her head to return to Mortlock without informing anyone. Well, she wrote after the face.'

Gulping down his coffee, Max leapt to his feet. 'When was this? Did she' – he hesitated, reluctant to speak the reverend's name – 'travel alone?'

Amelia shrugged, leaning back in her chair. 'Really, I've no idea. Miss Dingley merely said she was here to reassure you that Lady Farquhar is quite well and had written.'

'Olivia has written? What did she say?' Max strode forward and put his hands on the table, leaning in towards his sister, unable to contain his impatience.

Amelia laughed. 'Really, Max, you are too much, sometimes! She's not going to marry you, you know. And she's not going to marry the reverend, if that's what you're worried about. Miss Dingley said the matter had been adequately resolved.'

Raising her eyebrows, Amelia asked, curiously, 'Was there some... incident that occurred at Lady Glenton's masque? I heard that Lady Farquhar's behaviour had been somewhat scandalous but the whispers were that it was only to be expected. Is that what's upset you, Max?'

When he didn't reply, she went on, 'Do you think Miss Hepworth enjoyed herself?'

Max grunted as he made for the door. 'Capitally, I'm sure.'

'Where are you going, Max?' Amelia called after him as he turned his footsteps towards the front door once again. 'Not to see Miss Dingley, I hope. She said she was retiring to sleep for a few hours. And so must you, Max. You look terrible!'

◈

OLIVIA FELT SHE WAS GOING THROUGH THE MOTIONS, ONLY THIS time instead of Lucien's fingers digging into her forearm as he led her through the inn, it was Nathaniel's.

'Your best behaviour, now, Lady Farquhar. 'You don't want to parade your insanity on top of your notoriety,' Nathaniel cautioned, as he led her past a couple entering the premises. He tipped his hat to them on the stairs and they responded with a nod and a smile.

Olivia said nothing but she winced as a gust of cold wind hit her cheek.

'By the way, Julian was asking after you.' Nathaniel's tone was conversational as they headed towards the stables.

Olivia exhaled on a sob, squinting at the grey sky. 'By God, Nathaniel, you had better keep your promise,' she whispered. 'If you won't tell me where you've sent Julian, at least swear to me he'll come to no harm.'

'He's perfectly safe and happy with Charlotte enjoying the hospitality of an old acquaintance of mine,' Nathaniel said, opening the door of the waiting carriage he had ordered. 'Someone who owes me a favour and will be too afraid not to follow instructions.'

Olivia bit her lip. She had not the fortitude to dwell on this cryptic reassurance. Better to concentrate on keeping her eyes open for an opportunity to escape. 'As for notoriety,' she added venomously, slipping on the wet cobblestones in her flimsy dancing slippers, 'that was not something *I* brought upon myself.'

'You thrust your charms at Lucien and he reacted with the predictability of a trained puppy, bless him.' Nathaniel assisted her into the carriage, climbing in after her. It seemed the coachman already had his instructions for with a straining and creaking of harness the carriage lurched forward and began its lumbering progress along the rutted road that led from town.

'Were you never seventeen, Nathaniel? Were you never headstrong at that age? Or did no one notice you like they noticed me? Yes, suddenly I was a woman, no longer a child, and the power of my attractions went to my head. Lucien succumbed. But I was a child wrapped up in foolish fancies.' Olivia glared at him. 'Am I to have that forever thrown in my face, Nathaniel?'

'You sealed your fate with the flutter of your eyelashes, my dear. Lucien could not resist you and I sanctioned it. *I* made you Lady Farquhar.'

In the dim, grey interior, she saw him close his eyes and shudder. Revulsion? When he raised his eyes to hers they glowed as if lit from within by some secret knowledge.

She felt her skin crawl with the caress of a thousand spiders' legs. It was her turn to shudder.

Why had she not seen the truth eight years ago?

Nathaniel had *sanctioned* her as Lucien's choice? What was that supposed to mean?

'Lucien wanted me above all others,' she whispered. She had to believe at least this. It had been her undoing, but it upheld her powers of attraction. Without those, she truly was the empty shell Nathaniel derided.

'Lucien wanted a lot of things, my sister among them.' Though Nathaniel's voice was soft it contained a note of savage hatred she'd never heard before.

Convulsively, her hand went to the key around her neck. She could have been living at Elmwood had it not been for the monster before her.

'You have a sister?' she asked peering at him through the gloom as the dull countryside passed them by. So the philandering had been going on long before she'd even suspected. When he nodded she said with dignity, 'I did not take Lucien from another woman.'

Nathaniel's look was shuttered. 'Dorothy was a sweet, virtuous child.' He tore his eyes from her, as if the sight disgusted him. His nostrils flared. 'So different from you, Olivia. I would not want to make comparisons with the woman who *won* Lucien's heart and the one who *stole* it.'

His voice dropped to a snarl. 'Had she lived, Dorothy's piety would have redeemed the monster Lucien became. The monster you turned him into, Olivia, with your vanity and pleasure-seeking and need to be admired.'

'You lie!' Shocked, she went on, 'Lucien never mentioned Dorothy during our entire marriage. Nor did you. *No one* did.'

'No one did because their love blossomed before Lucien went to London where he was corrupted by the society in which you thrived.' Nathaniel's voice rose. 'No one mentioned Dorothy because she died a miserable, unworthy death. But Lucien admired her. He loved her. He would have made her his wife.'

'Is there no end to what you will blame me for?' Olivia whispered, turning her head.

'My sister was among the most virtuous women who ever lived. Lucien broke her heart. She poisoned herself, Olivia, because she could not bear his betrayal. The tragedy was that Lucien was coming back for her. And then he met you. He never got over the guilt, the grief.'

'I am very sorry to hear about your sister' – she spat out the words – 'but I did not steal Lucien from the arms of another woman. Certainly not a worthier one.' Who knew what women from the lower ranks her late husband had consorted with? It was something she'd not considered as a seventeen year old.

'Dorothy was already dead when Lucien saw you for the first time,' Nathaniel conceded. 'But his soul was black. Blackened beyond redemption for what he had done.' He pushed aside the curtain, his breath clouding the dirty windows. 'When I accompanied him to London he knew it belonged to the Devil, but he was not yet ready to go there. He turned to me for his salvation.'

She felt a terrible gnawing in the pit of her stomach. He had not been in jest, earlier? 'You *advised* Lucien to marry me?'

Nathaniel nodded. 'He needed an heir, and I knew what kind of wife would be best. Someone with a face and figure that would instantly appeal to him, but with a character that was' – his smile was so transparently gloating she felt ill – 'unformed. Someone who was so bound up in their own powers of attraction they could not see the danger they courted in a man like Lucien: a man who had lost all compassion.'

'Lucien wanted me!'

'Oh, yes, he wanted you. He was enslaved by lust' – Nathaniel grimaced – '*if* that's so important to you. And yes, Olivia, you were the season's most dazzling debutante. Why, I even wanted you myself.'

'I'd have turned up my nose at a low creature like you.' How could she not have recognized the evil in him before? Because she had been so bound up in her powers of attraction? 'You'd never have had me willingly,' she whispered.

'I'd have been a delusional fool if I'd thought I could.' Her barbs had no effect. 'As delusional as you, my dear, when you thought you could make something of your spectacular union with Viscount Farquhar. No, Olivia, I realized you would never have me willingly, but I sanctioned Lucien's union with you, nay, encouraged it, for I knew if I bided my time, I would be rewarded for my good advice.'

'But I'm no longer going to marry you.' For a brief moment she felt almost triumphant. As if she wielded the power. How pitiful she was.

'No,' he agreed, sadly. 'I must content myself with memories of enfolding you in my arms as I lifted you, all but naked, from the dining table after your titillating little performances for Lucien and his friends.' He reached forward and squeezed her hand. 'You needed me then, my dear. For most of your marriage, in fact, you turned to me for comfort. At the time it was enough, though I should have seen my dream would never be realized. Still' – he gazed once more through the window and sighed – 'I wanted the lost fortune more than I wanted you, so in that respect I have triumphed.'

'Through coercion and blackmail.' She had persuaded Julian to unclasp his arms from around her neck and go with the servant who would transfer him to Charlotte waiting in the carriage. She'd had no choice, but to what fate had she sent him? 'How can I believe you'll ensure Julian's safety? What will happen once you've got what you want?'

She had to give voice to her greatest fears, if only for the meaningless reassurance he would be forced to give.

'I am not a cold-blooded murderer, Olivia. No harm shall come to either of you unless something interferes with the careful strategy I've laid out.' He was thoughtful. 'Together we've laid the groundwork. Your aunts will not grow concerned for a couple of days; no one will look for you until at least tomorrow afternoon, giving me plenty of time to slip across the Channel, never to be heard of again.'

'What about Julian?' she asked again, though she knew her desperation bolstered his enjoyment in tormenting her.

'Julian's fate' – he leaned forward, putting his face close to hers – 'and yours will be revealed in good time.' She recoiled. 'Max will find me, and you!'

Nathaniel regarded her through hooded eyes. 'Mr Atherton will play the hero because it will be required of him,' he agreed. His fingers beat a tattoo upon his thigh as the corners of his mouth turned up.

'But *if* he finds you, will he still want you, Olivia? That is the question. Poor Mr Atherton is so confused over you and your lies I wonder if self-preservation is not more important to him than the transient pleasures of your fading charms. Once he's nobly deposited you with your aunts I suspect he'll attach himself to the first innocent, uncomplicated debutante who flutters her eyelashes at him.'

Miss Hepworth? If Nathaniel were not watching her so closely she'd give into the tears that pricked her eyelids. Instead, calmly and quietly, she asked, 'Why did you bring me Julian?'

He answered as if he knew she referred to the night of Julian's birth.

'For the same reason I brought him to you just now.' He smiled. 'The power it gave me over you.'

'You never loved the child and yet you would have me believe that only you could safeguard his future.'

'I never *dis*liked him. He was simply a child.' Nathaniel shrugged.

'Puling, puking and sniffling like most children his age.' Reflectively, he added, 'When I lifted him from Meg Dorling's cold dead chest I wondered how long it would be before he followed his mother into the grave. No one wanted him. And then I thought of you,

Olivia.' He touched her cheek. 'I thought of all your suffering and feared, from what Charlotte told me, that it was about to be compounded. That's when it occurred to me I could give you the greatest gift possible: a living child.' He glanced out of the window as the carriage turned into the avenue which led to Olivia's old home. He turned back to her with glowing eyes. 'So you would spend the rest of your life in my debt.'

The carriage ground slowly over the gravel and would have pulled up before the front door had Olivia not given the instruction to halt a few hundred yards away, near a grassy knoll.

The crypt.

What choice did she have? Nathaniel held her son hostage. Had just her life been in danger perhaps she'd have had the strength to resist. Max's respect was vital to her fragile sense of self, but the safety of her son was paramount.

They climbed out, Nathaniel craning his neck to ensure they were alone and well hidden from passers-by. The Lodge was unoccupied and there was no view directly from the dower house.

'The only place I never looked,' Nathaniel remarked as he outpaced Olivia in his quest to reach the iron door. 'Why, it's unlocked!' He gave a delighted laugh. 'Lucien's grandfather gave him the key as a clue only your poor husband had no idea what to do with it. He obviously wasn't in the habit of paying his respects to the departed.' He was speaking to Olivia as a co-conspirator. 'Now then! Show me the treasure! I have waited many years for this.'

Olivia hesitated halfway along the path which led from the gravel drive and cut across lawn to the family tomb. Where was the gardener who tended the hedges once a week? Or the milkmaid who took the common lane to the village?

Hidden from all directions, even the carriage would not be seen from either The Lodge or the dower house.

Nathaniel turned back and gripped her arm to hurry her last few yards. Olivia didn't try to resist. What was the point?

On creaking hinges the door ground open and Nathaniel pushed her ahead of him. Turning, shivering, she saw his breath misting in fast, shallow bursts. The crypt was dark, the air close and clammy. It smelled of death and damp and once they were deep within the cavern there was very little light.

'Where is it?' The urgency of Nathaniel's demands cut into reflections of her treachery. She was about to sacrifice Max's fortune to a villain in order to preserve her own dreams.

Her entire life had centred around reclaiming Julian. When the unexpected love she'd found with Max had foundered, the gold was to have shored up the intense, transient happiness that had gilded her life with hope.

Dashing away a tear she forced herself to attend to Nathaniel. She'd still have Julian, wouldn't she? Shouldn't that be all that mattered?

'You can see the hiding place,' she said, dully, her hands hanging limply at her sides. She did not bother to point; just watched as his greedy eyes darted around the gloomy cavern until they alighted upon the tiny disturbed crypt, its heavy stone lid awry.

With another burst of laughter Nathaniel ran towards it. He looked like a lumbering baby bear, she though fancifully. Yet with far less innocent intent.

'Dear Lord, I mustn't forget to thank Mr Atherton for this!' he cried, thrusting his hand inside to withdraw a fistful of coins, some of which scattered upon the floor. The weak sunlight from the high window illuminated his joy, a manic grin twisting his mouth. He looked up and caught her eye. 'You found it when you interred that cur I kicked to death – though if it's any consolation I never meant to kill it.'

'It's no consolation at all,' Olivia murmured, shivering as the damp seeped into her bones. Wrapping her arms about her, she hoped her ordeal would be over soon. She thought of Julian. Her child though not of her flesh and blood. The child of a village slattern and her cruel husband. Olivia would rear him to be a good man. A man like Max whom she now had little expectation of seeing again.

Nathaniel forced the lid open a few more inches and burrowed into the darkness. Transferring the entire cache of gold he filled the bag he had brought for the purpose, straining under the weight as he headed for the door, his footsteps lengthening as he hurried towards the light.

'How fortuitous you considered the animal worthy of a Christian burial, my love,' he said over his shoulder as Olivia tried to keep pace.

'Where are you going?' She heard the panic in her tone as she reached for his arm but already he was on the other side of the metal grated door, slamming it in her face.

He grinned as he turned the key in the lock. 'To fetch blankets and sustenance for five days. Time enough for me to make good my escape.'

'Nathaniel, don't leave me here!' No more than a square foot of iron grating in the centre of the door admitted light.

'You were shivering, Olivia,' she heard him call. 'I will not have your death on my conscience after all you've done for me. Have patience. I'll be back soon to load up the carriage.'

'I don't believe you! You'll let me die here, won't you?' she cried between panicked sobs.

He brought his face close to the bars, sliding his hands between them to cup her face.

'I'm too fond of you to do that, Olivia' he soothed, as if he meant it, 'and I owe you too much.' Kissing the tears which spattered the backs of his hands he said softly, 'This is a bittersweet moment. It reminds me of all those occasions you turned to me for comfort. Once, I had hoped we might share this discovery. That our joy would be mutual.'

'Five days! Nathaniel, I'll never survive it! I need to be with Julian!'

'Four days should give me ample time to disappear,' he conceded. 'And have no fears over Julian. I have given instructions for him and Charlotte to be released once I have secured a passage across the Channel.'

CHAPTER 18

'BEAUTIFUL MORNING, SIR!'

Max groaned and turned his head from the sight of sunlight bursting through clear blue skies as Frensham drew the curtains. Anything remotely cheerful was a reproach. Since the events of twenty-four hours ago he seemed to have existed in some dark eternity.

Olivia had been delivered into Nathaniel's arms—by him. Max.

He'd believed the worst of her. Why? Because of the rumours. The *rumours* that she was a faithless wife, a conniving schemer.

Wearily, Max performed the necessary ablutions before presenting himself in the breakfast parlour.

He was chewing on a mouthful of haddock and thinking he needed to speak to Amelia about the quality of the food which tasted like sawdust when Jonathan burst into the room, waving the morning's news sheet.

'You haven't finished telling me, Jonathan!' Amelia's shrill voice punctuated the quiet of the early morning household. To Max's surprise she appeared in her husband's wake, her hair hanging undressed down her back, clutching a shawl over her nightdress.

'Lady Farquhar has left the country!' announced Jonathan, breathlessly, slapping the paper upon the table beside Max's plate and taking the seat next to him. Stabbing his finger upon the revealing paragraph he shook his head in astonishment. 'Gone to the Continent to begin a new life on account of her shame, so it says here in black and white.'

Max's mouth went dry. He managed to swallow the remains of his haddock without choking.

Amelia sank into the seat opposite and snatched the news sheet from her brother's grasp, reading quickly before fixing Max with a beady look. 'Lady Farquhar has finally abandoned you, Max! Now you can ask Miss Hepworth for her hand!'

Max knew he was staring like an idiot; that he sounded even more like one when he repeated, stupidly, 'She's gone?'

Amelia's excitement grew as she looked from the news sheet then back at her brother. 'I've never understood the hold that woman's had over you, but it doesn't surprise me that some great shame has finally forced her from the country. Max, Miss Hepworth would make the perfect wife.'

He wouldn't argue that point, but the fact was he loved Olivia. He'd been on his way to tell her. He'd never considered jealousy one of his faults, but seeing her in the arms of another man had turned him into an irrational monster.

Ignoring his sister, he pretended to be interested in his breakfast but jerked his head up at the sound of his sister's gasp. Amelia's eyes were wide with shock.

'What is it?' He seized the news sheet she was devouring, fighting her for it as she tried to take it back.

'Why, there's more! Read it!' Conceding defeat, Amelia leaned across the table to point to the revealing article. 'It's a confession ... for the whole world to see.' She rose and went towards the window, turning with a self-satisfied look.

'So Lady Farquhar has admitted her adultery to the whole world. Oh my Lord, Max, can you believe it? She has deprived you of your inheritance and now the world knows it. Her boy is a bastard!' She shook her head in wonder. '*You* are the rightful Viscount Farquhar! Oh Max, isn't it all so splendid? I shall invite Miss Hepworth and her mother to our house party at the end of the month. If the weather is fine there will be plenty of entertainment to be had outdoors. Perhaps, Max, we should organize a picnic.'

'Are you quite out of your mind, Amelia.' Max spoke carefully, his mind reeling at his altered situation. There was too much too absorb. Miss Hepworth was the least of his worries, but Amelia had the capacity to cause a lot of trouble. 'My matrimonial affairs are *my* concern,

He pressed his lips together, trying to make sense of it: Olivia's motives, the implications. Why had she confessed her adultery to the whole world before she'd confessed privately, in full, to him?

Amelia swept across the room and laid a hand upon his arm.

'Amelia is right,' said Jonathan, tightly, though it was clear he was trying to contain his excitement. 'You must think of your matrimonial duties, Max. Now that you are the new Viscount Farquhar.'

'Yes, Max.' Amelia's voice was urgent with excitement. 'The world now knows Lady Farquhar for the adulteress she is and that I stand beside Lucien's true heir. It is a fitting end.'

End? Or a new beginning? Whatever it was, it seemed Max could not enjoy it with Olivia by his side. He finished his breakfast in silence while Amelia speculated upon the possible candidates who had participated in Olivia's misdemeanours. To extirpate any vestige of feeling he might still harbour?

Oh, he harboured plenty of feelings! He just wasn't sure what they were. Guilt. Desire. And fear for her safety.

'She danced upon her dinner table for the entertainment of her husband's guests!' Amelia's voice rang out with delighted horror before she whispered with exaggerated outrage, 'I'm told she has a birthmark on a very private part of her person which the men used to line up to kiss! Lady Olivia's Butterfly, they called it!'

Studiously Max maintained his silence, even as his sister went on, taking no account of his feelings – or perhaps *because* she knew it would wound him. 'Can you imagine, Jonathan, how many men have seen it?' Was it anger at hearing Olivia maligned, or simply that he must be one of the few men who *hadn't* sampled Lady Olivia's Butterfly, Max wondered, as he fought the urge to hurl his plate across the table like a moonstruck calf and stamp out of the room. Let Amelia prattle on, he knew he could not be held accountable for his actions if he said anything.

Amelia had no idea of how much more there was to the story. Max would find out, even if it meant taking the next packet to Calais and hunting Olivia down. But for the moment, all he could do was stare grimly down at his food as he pretended to eat.

'Visitor downstairs wishes to see Mr Atherton.'

The parlour maid who put her head around the door bobbed a curtsy.

'Who is it, Ellen?' Amelia asked with an almost imperious tilt to her head, as if she were truly the lady of the manor. Max reigned in his anger.

'The lady wouldn't give her name, ma'am.'

'You didn't recognize her?'

'She were heavily veiled, ma'am.'

'You can stay here, Amelia,' Max told his sister curtly when she made to accompany him.

Downstairs in the drawing room a small figure dressed in black wearing stout boots and an enormous bonnet festooned with black netting turned at Max's entrance before hurrying forward.

'Miss Dingley!'

'I came as soon as I read the lies, Mr Atherton!' she cried. 'Though Catherine would have dressed like this to hide her *shame* I have done so merely to conceal my identity.' Her eyes, when she raised the veil, were full of entreaty. 'Please, Mr Atherton, find Olivia and bring her back. She was forced to write this confession. That man made her, though I've no idea how or why. And now Olivia is gone without a word.'

Max was reminded of the night Olivia's aunt had begged him in the corridor to champion Olivia. The night he'd seen Kirkman go into her bedchamber.

The night his faith in Olivia had been eroded. Yet he still loved her —and would love her, regardless of what she'd done, Max thought, wryly as he ushered Miss Dingley to a seat, saying, 'Olivia has gone to the Continent. The newspapers have printed her confession.'

'Confession!' Miss Dingley heaved in a breath and put a hand to

her breast. 'Then why has she taken none of her personal possessions? She never returned to us after you delivered her to the
reverend,' she added pointedly. 'He was the last person to see her and
she certainly did not want to spend a moment in his company *if she'd
had any choice.*'

Max couldn't meet her look. His head was throbbing but there was
something just a little bit hopeful about the fact Miss Dingley questioned what the papers had printed. Then he reminded himself that
Olivia had lied to him from the moment she'd met him and the confession printed in the newspaper had been signed by her. He drew himself
up straight as if it might ease the ache in his body. 'She must have
taken a packet, earlier, and...arranged to have this printed today.' He
paused, frowning. 'Perhaps so she'd not be detained.'

Miss Dingley looked at him as if she believed he'd lost his wits.
'You surely don't believe she wrote this, do you, Mr Atherton? Just as
you surely don't believe she has left the country? Please try and
remember. I once hoped you had a fondness for her. But if that is not
the case, then take pity of me who does. You were the last to see her...
before you delivered her to the reverend.'

'I want to help, Miss Dingley, believe me.' Max tried to sound
calmer than he felt in the face of the woman's accusing look and
despite the fact his heart was thundering in his chest. Olivia had quite
likely written that confession to put a line under her life in England.
She was weighed down by the past and she was *not* the wife for him, he
must remind himself.

He swallowed. '*The Times* states she has taken' – it was hard to say
Julian's name without wincing – 'the child with her to the Continent.
No doubt you'll be reassured in good time as to her whereabouts and
safety. I'm sorry, Miss Dingley. I can't tell you any more than that for
regardless of my feelings for your niece, she chose not to confide
in me.'

Was that why he felt like a limb had been lopped off? Olivia's lack
of faith in Max was worse than having his suspicions about the boy's
parentage confirmed by Olivia in the most public and brazen manner
possible?

He turned towards the mantelpiece, his tone and manner signifying that he considered he had nothing more to contribute. 'If I hear anything more, I will ensure you are the first to know.'

He heard the rustle of skirts as Mrs Dingley rose; her sigh of disappointment and her hesitation before her voice, thin and hopeful, 'This morning on her dressing table I found this.'

Would she never let up? Reluctantly he looked at what she proffered. Blinking to clear his vision, he looked again as Miss Dingley stood before him, a shaft of pale sunlight emphasising the shabbiness of her black bombazine gown.

'Three gold coins, Miss Dingley? Worth a sum, but what of it?'

'Where did she get them, Mr Atherton, when they would finance more than just a new wardrobe? Olivia has lived in poverty since Lucien died. Recently she discussed with us the idea of taking a job as a companion.'

This was a shock. Max took the coins as he rose and held them to the light. He weighed them in his hands and tentatively tested the edge with his teeth. They were real enough.

Miss Dingley's agitation grew and the purple ribbons beneath her chin swayed in agitation. 'Why would Olivia leave a...a *fortune*...on her dressing table if she were fleeing to the Continent and would be in need of immediate funds?'

Turning them over once again, Max felt the flutter of excitement in his gut tempered by a wisp of memory: her last words which she had flung at him before he'd all but torn her from the carriage and thrust her at Reverend Kirkman.

I've found the gold!

He did not tell Miss Dingley this. Not when she would immediately have pounced and formed conclusions that needed more thoughtful deliberation.

Had she found Lucien's grandfather's lost fortune?

Dismay lodged like a heavy stone in the pit of his stomach. Olivia had tried to make him believe her but not only had he dismissed her words as more desperate lies, he'd handed her over to a cruel, abusive man because ... Why? Because he was angry at what he'd just witnessed with his own eyes. He'd believed the worst of her yet he hadn't allowed her to explain. Had that been the moment she intended to reveal all?

Yet pique and jealousy had overridden Max's usual calm and measured approach. Didn't that make him as bad as the reverend?

Silently, he handed back the coins, just as the door was flung open and Miss Catherine and a dirty, dishevelled young woman he did not immediately recognize stumbled across the threshold.

'Mr Atherton! Charlotte and the boy have just arrived!' Miss Catherine collapsed on to the settee while she caught her breath, her face flushed and her ringlets in disarray. She looked wild-eyed between her sister and Max. 'I've brought them directly from Laura Place.'

Max stared. This was Julian's nursemaid and he'd not recognised her. The girl's hair was a tangled mess and her hands and face were dirty and scratched, as if she had crawled through blackberry bushes. She looked terrified.

And there was Julian, cowering behind her as she held the boy close and tried to gather her wits.

Max went down on his knees, opening his arms wide, and the little boy threw himself into them, sobbing loudly as Max held him tightly. Emotion engulfed him. There was relief that whatever terrors that had beset the boy, he was now safe, but now a terrible fear that matters beyond his control—which, quite possibly, he had put in train—threatened the woman he loved.

'Hush, Julian, my boy. No one is going to hurt you,' he soothed. He'd missed the lad more than he could say, or would admit. The boy had become like his own. It was hardly surprising Olivia had gone to the lengths she had to have him restored to her.

'Charlotte!'

Max turned as Eunice Dingley rushed forward for the girl had been swaying in the centre of the room and now her legs buckled. He broke her fall in time and together they supported her to the sofa before Max went in pursuit of some reviving brandy, the obvious question hovering in the air.

He caught Miss Dingley's accusing look but it wasn't remorse that flooded him, it was fear. Olivia would never allow herself to be separated from her child. Where was she?

After the girl had spluttered on the amber liquid, he could contain himself no longer. 'What happened? We thought you'd gone with Miss

Olivia.' He bent over her, burning for answers and chafing at the need for patience for the moment the girl had tried to speak she'd become hysterical.

He poured her another tumbler of brandy and after she'd choked it down she calmed, collapsing against the back of the sofa with her eyes closed.

'I was taking Julian for a walk yesterday morning when the reverend stopped and told us to get into his carriage as the mistress were asking for us.' Her sat up a little and looked at them, trying obviously to stop her voice from quavering. 'We drove a short while to an inn just out of the town. He told me to wait in the carriage and he took Julian inside.'

Max gripped the arm of the sofa. He was kneeling on the ground, finding it almost impossible to curb his impatience. 'What about Olivia? Have you seen her? The paper says she's gone to the Continent.' The litany of fear kept repeating itself, over and over, in his mind. If Julian had been taken hostage, what about Olivia?

Miss Dingley grasped his arm and drew him back. 'You'll frighten the girl, Max,' she warned. 'Let her tell her story.'

Max rose and went to lean against the mantelpiece while he tried to quell the ferment in his heart and mind.

Dear God, what had he done? What danger had he put Olivia in?

Charlotte sniffed before resuming in a querulous voice. 'One of the inn servants brought Julian back to the carriage. She didn't tell us nothing though I heard her talk to the coachman about a grand lady inside. Then the coachman just whipped up the horses and drove us what seemed like hours to a village I'd never seen.' She wiped her nose on her apron and hunched forward.

'Go on, Charlotte,' Miss Dingley prompted.

'When we stopped I asked the coachman where we were and where Miss Olivia was, but he ignored me. Then a man came out and took us inside his house though it were a hovel, really. He started to speak nice, but as soon as we were upstairs and in a room where he said we could rest, he snarled at us that we were his prisoners now and we better behave ourselves else great harm would befall us and our mistress. Then he locked the door.' Charlotte's small bedraggled form shook with sobs. 'I don't know where Miss Olivia is!' she wailed.

'When I took Julian to the privy we were alone after the man went inside, so I grabbed Julian and ran. There were a passing cart and we jumped in the back.' She turned to Max, her face reflecting the same hopefulness as Miss Dingley's that he would be the architect of Olivia's salvation. 'I don't know where Miss Olivia is but you'll find her, won't you, Mr Atherton? And make sure she's safe?'

Make sure she's safe.

Max cut short the suggestion she'd gone to the Continent. That seemed ridiculous now; a ruse to fool the world; a lie that had been perpetrated by her enemies.

It was clear that Olivia was in grave danger and that she needed someone to rescue her. God knew how he'd do it or where he'd start, but Max could not remain here a moment longer.

He stepped into the centre of the room, his mind running over various possibilities as he raked a hand through his hair. 'I'll find Olivia and I'll see she receives justice,' he muttered.

He just wished he knew where to start. A double measure of the brandy which had revived Charlotte didn't seem such a bad idea.

As he paced, he turned the possibilities over in his mind. 'Why would Mr Kirkman do this?'

'Revenge, Mr Atherton!' cried Miss Dingley. 'I'm glad you see the truth now! Olivia wouldn't marry him so he made her write a false confession and kidnapped her son. He wanted to destroy what was left of her reputation and take away that which meant the most to her.'

Still puzzling over events, Max shook his head. 'But why would he kidnap his own son?'

Miss leapt to her feet, eyes blazing as she gasped, 'Is that what you inferred from Olivia's confession? The Reverend? She never could stand the man nor understand his hold over Lucien. Maybe he was kind to her in the early days but she saw what he was at the end. And how could you believe Olivia would *ever* betray her own husband?'

'What confession, please, ma'am?' Charlotte's voice came out a strangled thread, but with enough intensity to cut through the mayhem.

Forcing himself to remain calm, Max said turned from the hatchet-faced expression of Miss Dingley before him to Julian's nursemaid. 'Today's newspaper reported that Lady Farquhar confessed that Julian is the result of adultery and not Lord Farquhar's rightful heir.'

'Oh, Lordy!' Charlotte clasped her hands to her bosom and the colour leeched from her face. She looked close to tears. 'He finally used it against her.' Her whisper was not directed at the others but as if she was speaking to herself.

She jerked with surprise when Max snapped, 'What do you mean?' Immediately he felt ashamed of himself. Charlotte's lip trembled and she exhaled on a sob, covering her face with her apron as she whimpered, 'I can't tell you.'

Max covered the distance between the mantelpiece and the arm of the settee in less than a heartbeat. 'Charlotte!' He crouched before her. 'Tell us what you know about Julian and your mistress!'

The girl shook her head, refusing to drop her apron and pulling her arm free of his grip. 'I swore I'd never speak of a word of it and I never have. I never will!'

'Charlotte, please, you don't know how important this is!' He tried to sound soothing but heard the croak of desperation in his own voice. 'For Miss Olivia's sake, you must tell us. What secret did you promise your mistress you'd always keep?'

'It weren't a promise to Miss Olivia 'cos Martha and I never knew if she knew that we knew her secret.'

Max shook his head at this convoluted logic and tried again. Charlotte was a good girl with a deep loyalty to her mistress but right now she needed to know that her revelation could only be in Olivia's favour. After all, the world couldn't regard Lady Farquhar in a poorer light in view of recent revelations. 'What secret? And who is Martha?' Exasperation threatened to get the better of him but he kept his tone calm.

Charlotte rubbed her swollen eyes. 'Martha were Miss Olivia's lady's maid before she married the publican of The Pelican and became Mrs Mifflin.' Her tone remained mutinous as she added, 'We promised each other we'd never say a word to *anyone*.'

Max rose and went to the fireplace, kicking a log that threatened to dislodge itself. Turning, he told Charlotte, 'Lady Farquhar confessed her adultery in this morning's new sheet. Everyone now knows Julian is not her late husband's legitimate heir. There is no point in keeping your secret any longer, Charlotte.'

The apron dropped. The girl's white face appeared above it like a frightened rabbit's just as Amelia bustled into the room, adding her contribution, 'Yes, Charlotte! Lady Farquhar's sins were made public this morning—'

She stopped short and looked uncomfortable when she saw Olivia's aunt to whom she'd been introduced so recently at Lady Glenton's, before exclaiming, 'Good gracious, Charlotte! What have you been doing?'

'Charlotte has come through quite an ordeal, Amelia.' Max spoke crisply. 'Please! It would be better if you left us alone.'

'No!'

Max turned back to Charlotte. 'If you wish her to stay then—'

'That's not the truth!' The girl started to her feet, her hands cupping her cheeks. 'Why would Miss Olivia say such a terrible thing when Julian is Lord Farquhar's son what she's brought up as her own? Her own husband's child what she's fought for so hard. It don't make sense!' The log in he fireplace thudded from the grate with a hiss; the only sound in the confused silence. Max ignored it, concentrating on Charlotte's horrified expression.

There was no suggestion of play acting. Shock, outrage and confusion were etched into every soft, dirty feature.

Miss Dingley sounded querulous, 'I don't understand. If Julian is Lucien's son there is no secret, no sin—' A flash of inspiration crossed her face. 'Of course! It would only be a secret if Julian were not Lucien's *legitimate* son.' Turning, she addressed Charlotte, 'This is no time for keeping confidences, however honourable your intentions, Charlotte. Only the truth will help us find Olivia.'

Staring into the fire, Max prepared himself for what Charlotte was about to reveal while he cursed himself for the arrogant fool he was.

'I were with my mistress the night the babe was born,' Charlotte began in a soft voice. 'I were to be the child's nursemaid, Miss Olivia said. My reward as I'd been with her since I first went into service.'

'Yes, yes! But what happened that night?' Miss Dingley asked impatiently. 'Where was Lord Farquhar?'

Surprisingly, Amelia intervened as the voice of restraint. 'With due respect, Miss Dingley, I think the girl needs to tell her story in her own words.'

Max cast his sister a grateful look as he took the fire irons and crouched to tend the fire, listening as Charlotte went on.

'Lord Farquhar had never been good to my lady and she'd lost so many babes. Her first went full term but died within the hour and he beat her for it.'

Miss Catherine let out a wail of distress. Turning, Max caught the dismay in his sister's eyes. He knew the story of Olivia's sorry treatment at the hands of her husband. It did not help hearing these abuses reinforced by Charlotte, but it might not be too bad a thing for Amelia to hear the truth.

'Miss Olivia was happy Lord Farquhar was on a hunting trip because she was afraid of what would happen if she gave birth to a girl, or if the babe died.' Charlotte blushed. 'Lord Farquhar was determined to have an heir. My mistress told it to me a hundred times the week before the babe was born. She were terrified something would go wrong.'

'And something did?' Amelia put her hand on the back of the sofa and looked at Max. 'I've heard such terrible things about our cousin—'

'Your sympathies didn't exactly extend towards his wife,' Max responded drily.

'She was the season's most outrageous debutante. They eloped, Max!'

'She was seventeen, Amelia! A child! Lucien was a dashing rake! Perhaps you've forgotten how smitten you were with Lord Sylvester when you were an impressionable debutante. If he'd crooked his little finger—'

'With due respect,' Miss Dingley cut in, as Amelia, embarrassed and outraged, turned away, and Max, ashamed, ceased his defence of Olivia at the expense of his sister.

'What happened to the child, Charlotte?' asked Aunt Catherine. 'The baby to which Miss Olivia gave birth?'

Charlotte smiled, dreamily. 'It were such a beautiful little thing. Perfectly formed with dark hair and eyes nearly black, just like his father. And it seemed so healthy. Miss Olivia were entranced.'

'But it died?' Max could barely contain himself, now, despite his earlier deviation. Here was the crux of Olivia's great secret upon which she would be condemned or otherwise. 'And where was Miss Olivia's physician during all this?'

'Attending a breech birth an hour away.'

'You delivered Miss Olivia's child, yourself?'

'Mrs Flannigan, the village midwife came. We sent one of the stable boys to fetch her but she were already overcome with the gin by the time she got here and soon sleeping in a corner so Martha and me did it. Martha had delivered her mother's last six so she knew what to do and I just followed orders.'

'When did the baby die?' Max asked.

Charlotte sniffed and wiped her nose with the corner of her apron.

'Within the hour. Martha and me were bawling our eyes out. The mistress were in shock. She kept saying, "My beautiful baby's dead. Another one gone to Heaven." She kept saying over and over, "He *has* gone to Heaven, Martha! He *has*! ".' Charlotte choked on the words, adding in a whisper, 'Then she said, "Lucien will tell me it's not true. He'll say if the baby was not baptized it'll be writhing in the flames of Hell and that it's my fault. Martha! Charlotte! One of you must fetch Reverend Kirkman to baptize him. We must beg him not to tell Lucien the baby died before he came".'

She took a shaking breath. 'Mr Kirkman arrived later the same night bringing with him another baby boy. It were Meg Dorling's from the village, 'is lordship's mistress who'd died birthing the babe. Everyone thinks her babe died as well, 'cept for the reverend, Martha and myself – and Miss Olivia, o' course – who only did what any good wife and mam would a' done – looking after the little one like her own.'

Still staring into the fire, he shook his head at his sister's gasp. Finally she understood, too. That Julian was Lucien's illegitimate son.

A weight like an iron bar rested across Max's shoulders. Why had he never considered this? Olivia had intimated Julian was illegitimate. Not for one moment had he imagined the boy was not *her* natural child. He had drawn the only conclusion that seemed to offer itself in view of her insistence upon marrying Kirkman.

Charlotte looked down at her hands in her lap. 'The reverend was Lord Farquhar's confessor and his lordship paid him well for telling tales on my mistress.' Her lip curled. 'Although he kept Miss Olivia's secret I knew he would one day use it to his advantage. I knew I should never have trusted him when he told us to get into the carriage yesterday. Oh, Mr Atherton, we must find Miss Olivia!'

'Yes, we must!' Max agreed, straightening, his mind racing to answer the call to action. 'Finish your story, quickly, Charlotte,' he said, striding to the door. 'If there is something which casts light on the man's motives for forcing Olivia to make that confession and for taking Julian—'

'Oh, I know *that*, sir, because the man what was keeping us prisoner told us,' said Charlotte, blinking at Max. 'It's because Miss Olivia discovered Lord Farquhar's grandfather's fortune and he used Julian to blackmail her into telling her where it was. Reverend Kirkman spent years trying to find it himself, especially after my lord died.' Glowering, she muttered, 'If you ask me, that's why he wanted to marry Miss Olivia. So he'd have a better chance of finding it if he were living at The Lodge.'

CHAPTER 19

DESPITE MAX'S URGENCY to reach The Lodge, he saw the merit in his sister's argument that local knowledge was always the best source of information. He also needed to speak to the publican's wife. If Mrs Mifflin could provide independent testimony of Charlotte's claims with regard to Julian's origins it would cast new light upon Olivia in the eyes of the world.

In the shadows of the tap room, Pat Dorling grinned a welcome from the settle as Max bent his head to step beneath the lintel.

'I 'ear the Merry Widow took to 'er pretty feet and scarpered leaving both you and the good reverend in the lurch, *my lord.*' He guffawed into his drink, as the publican handed Max his ale.

'Out with you, Dorling, if yer plan on speaking disrespectful!' The publican gripped the old man by the scruff of his neck and hauled him to his feet.

'Let him be,' Max protested.

Raking the old soldier with a scornful glance, he asked, 'If you're such a fount of knowledge perhaps you can tell us where the reverend and Lady Farquhar have disappeared to.'

Dorling shrugged and took another swig as if the matter was of no interest to him. 'Only 'eard the news this morning, didn't I? Whipped the village into a frenzy it 'as.' He looked thoughtfully into his ale. 'So the reverend's gone, too, 'as he?' He sniggered. 'And you're here to bring wicked Lady Farquhar to justice, are ye?'

'Any ideas you might have regarding her whereabouts would be much appreciated.'

Despite the old man's sour look Max could tell Dorling enjoyed being solicited for his thoughts. The old soldier tapped his nose, waving his mug to be refilled.

Max tossed the publican a coin and Dorling acknowledged Max's largesse with a nod. 'Reckon there's *more'n* a thing or two I could tell you about the reverend,' he said. 'Mean feller. Wouldn't like to get on the wrong side of him, but he's canny. Knows how to make things go his way.'

Max gave a short laugh as he shifted position on the hard wooden bench opposite the old man. 'Intimates, were you?'

Dorling grinned. 'Like I told you afore, I teached 'is late lordship how to hide a couple of aces up their sleeves and were well rewarded for it.'

In the dancing firelight he looked like an elf creature who had been admitted to the inner sanctum. 'Reckon he finally found the fourth viscount's fortune. Lady Farquhar led him to it and they've skipped to the Continent to enjoy the fruits of their greed.'

'Slandering my good mistress, Dorling? So you's heard all them lies today, too?'

The three men turned their heads. With hands on hips an enormous, ferocious-looking woman blocked the doorway: Mr Mifflin's wife, judging by the publican's cowed smile.

Thrusting out her impressive lilac-upholstered bosom, she sailed majestically into the centre of the room. 'If you're going to get gleeful about a good woman's fall from grace you can get out of this 'stablishment, *Mr* Dorling' – the woman pointed to the door, knitting beetling brows – 'or I'll get my Jeremiah to throw you out!'

Max intervened. He needed to keep the peace if he were to learn anything further. 'You'll find no more ardent champion of your mistress than me, Mrs Mifflin.' Bowing, he introduced himself before assisting her into a shabbily upholstered chair by the fire.

'Lordy! His lordship's cousin! Why, I can see it in yer face!'

Mrs Mifflin's mouth dropped open before she jerked her head in Dorling's direction. The fruit display which adorned the top of her bonnet trembled perilously. 'Pay no mind to the lies others would have you believe. Miss Olivia were the kindest, gentlest lady and what that husband of hers did to her would make a grave robber cry.'

'That's as may be,' muttered Dorling with a baleful look, 'but she danced to her husband's tune! On the dining-room table all covered in cream before the men lined up to—'

'Get out!' screeched Mrs Mifflin, leaning forward and stabbing a stubby, beringed finger in the direction of the door. '*Your* Meg was a harlot, enticing his lordship into her bed. Well, she got her just deserts, didn't she?' She shook her head, adding sorrowfully, 'If you only knew how good her ladyship was to your Meg.'

'She slapped her face!' Trembling from outrage and too many ales, the old man rose to his feet. 'Lady High and Mighty slapped my Meg's face because she were jealous that my Meg knew how to please 'is lordship when *she* didn't!' His thin voice quavered while his ale splashed upon his boots. 'Not five minutes after she called my Meg a harlot Lady Farquhar were dancing naked on the table—'

'Because her husband ordered her!' Max championed, also leaping to his feet.

'Because the *reverend* ordered it!'

Surprised into silence, they stared at the old man. Shaking like he had the ague he dropped his eyes, muttering almost sheepishly, 'He were behind all the humiliations,' as he sank back on to the wooden bench.

They absorbed this in silence as the wind rattled the windows and the fire crackled.

'And did anyone think to have pity on her?' Mrs Mifflin exhaled on a sob. 'My beautiful mistress were forced to perform like a high-class whore so the reverend could wrap her up and whisk her away.' She turned an appealing gaze upon Max. 'Weren't no use telling her the reverend didn't deserve her gratitude. Not when he were so clever at making himself out to be her hero.'

Max recognized the passion that would see Mrs Mifflin defend her mistress to the death. If Charlotte spoke the truth there'd be no trouble getting the publican's wife to add her testimony to the evidence that would vindicate Olivia. Olivia's deceit with regard to Julian would be condoned; so would the behaviour that had branded her the notorious viscountess.

'Why?' Max waited tensely. It was the question behind everything.

'Why would he want to humiliate a married woman? The wife of his benefactor?'

The old soldier hunched into his seat. 'Why does it matter?' he asked, sourly. 'She were the one what danced naked on the table. Not the reverend. Not my Meg. *Oi!*'

With a squeal the old man dodged Max's fist. 'All right! All right!' Recovering his bravado he grinned at their shock, chewing his gums a few seconds before adding self-importantly, 'Meg said it.' He lowered his voice. 'Said Lord Farquhar had sold his soul to the Devil and the reverend was paying his dues on his behalf. That 'is lordship could do whatever he chose so long as he did what the reverend said in return 'cos he were doing all the bargaining on 'is lordship's account with regard to the hereafter.'

The publican shifted his gaze from Dorling to Max. 'There's others what's made claims like this.'

'That my cousin was mad?' Max gave a hard laugh. 'I admired him when I was very young though he fell into bad company shortly afterwards—'

'After Miss Kirkman passed away.' The publican nodded his head sagely. 'A beauty she were, in a ghostlike kind o' way with her pale skin and staring eyes, though she were right queer in the attic. It were ever a surprise to hear 'is lordship's fancy had fell upon her.'

'Farquhar, the old devil, sent her to her Maker, just like he did my Meg and the child she bore 'is lordship,' Dorling said gloomily. 'Same night the young viscount were born.'

Mrs Mifflin clicked her tongue. 'The girl was introduced to society after convincing everyone she were better, but it were a big mistake.' Glowering at Dorling she added, 'Regardless of what we think of Mr Kirkman, his mother was a good soul. Let's not rake up the past. Miss Dorothy's in hallowed ground and that's all that matters.'

But Max was not so interested in Miss Dorothy or the efforts to give her a Christian burial despite the fact she'd taken her own life.

It was disconcerting to realise he sat opposite Julian's natural grandfather. The old man didn't even know it himself, thinking Meg's baby had been stillborn the night his daughter had died in childbirth. An irony that Dorling insinuated Kirkman was the boy's natural father, though he was now still talking of Miss Dorothy.

Max had a flash of inspiration: *Kirkman blamed Lucien for his sister's death.*

And Lucien accepted his guilt giving the reverend leverage over him. When his manipulation of Lucien proved so successful the clergyman made Olivia his next victim.

His veins seemed to ice up. Nathaniel Kirkman had brought Julian directly from Meg Dorling to Olivia. He'd brought her a living child, the fruit of her husband's infidelity, but a living child and an heir. *Olivia would be forever in his debt.*

'I can understand the benefits of having such a hold over my cousin,' he said, slowly, 'but why Lady Farquhar? Why would he orchestrate her humiliation?'

Mrs Mifflin drew herself up until she resembled a mighty galleon about to brave rough seas.

'Why, it were so Lady Farquhar's gratitude would know no bounds when he spirited her away after each debauch and she'd marry him after his lordship had drunk himself into his grave.'

She sniffed, adding, 'But it weren't Lady Farquhar the reverend wanted: it were the power e'd 'ave over the young viscount.'

Dorling cleared his throat. 'That is, what we all thought were the rightful viscount until Lady Farquhar admitted her crimes to the whole world.' Waving his tankard in the air to be refilled, he regarded Max. 'Like I told you afore, I reckon that lad you's looking after be the reverend's son. Stands to reason, don't you think?'

Mrs Mifflin gasped.

'How dare you charge my dear lady with such wickedness? I were with her during her entire marriage *and* the birth. The only reason I didn't stay after his lordship's death was because there was no money for me wages, which is why I finally said yes to Jeremiah, here.' She nodded at her husband who contrived a suitably grateful smile as she went on, 'Miss Olivia were the truest wife ever, and that boy is his lordship's son, I'll swear it on me grave.'

Dorling looked morose. 'The reverend wanted the boy, too. As much as he wanted Lady Farquhar, I reckon, though I dunno why he'd want to be leg-shackled to 'er when no doubt he could tup her anytime 'e liked, and I reckon he did.'

Max breathed through his fury but let the old soldier go on. 'That's why he got his lordship to change his will. So he could get power and influence over the new young viscount, have the beautiful Lady Farquar for his wife, and live in the house where the gold were hid.' Raising his head, he sent Max a challenging look through rheumy old eyes.

Like a fire-tipped arrow this information found its mark.

The Reverend Kirkman influenced Lucien to change his will, too?

'Like you'd know, Pat me old friend,' challenged the publican. 'His lordship died long after your Meg. Reckon yer makin' up what you think 'ud impress us.'

'It's true!' protested Dorling. 'Reverend Kirkman wanted Lady Farquhar that bad—'

'I didn't know you were such a confidante of my cousin,' Max remarked, drily, while his mind turned over the possibilities.

''Twere one of the housemaids what told me wife,' Dorling muttered. 'Daisy, what were a witness at the end.'

'Daisy's a good girl,' affirmed Mrs Mifflin. 'She'd not tell lies.'

'Did Daisy see it written down?' Max asked.

Dorling chewed on his gums. 'The girl couldn't understand what were writ, but she heard them talking when 'is lordship were on 'is deathbed and the reverend saying as how 'e'd be just the man as would look after the boy right and proper.' He sighed. 'If my Meg hadn't a' died she'd bin the next Lady Farquhar with the key to the hidden gold and I wouldn't be sitting here with you lot.'

The publican sniggered and Max leaned forward. 'So what *is* this great treasure?' he asked.

Dorling's eyes shone. 'A great cache of gold the late lordship's grandfather put together to fund the Jacobite uprising after hocking everything of value that he had. That's what the reverend were after – the key Lady Farquhar wore round her neck after 'is lordship passed away – and if he's found it, it's him you want to vent your spleen on, not me!'

The key.

Convulsively Max closed his hand around the key in his pocket he'd used to open the door of the crypt when he'd paid his respects to Lucien after leaving Olivia. The key with which he had replaced the key to Elmwood. The key he'd taken from around Olivia's neck when he'd asked her to marry him in the attic at the dower house.

Leaping to his feet he strained to see how much daylight remained.

'I know where Kirkman is – or has been!' he cried. He was, perhaps, half-an-hour's hard ride from The Lodge, from the crypt. For seventy years the cold, damp cavern dug into the side of the hill between The Lodge and the dower house had hidden the fourth viscount's secret treasure.

Perhaps it was about to yield another hidden secret. One much more important.

CHAPTER 20

HER BONES ACHED. Ached from the cold which seeped through her body despite the three blankets Nathaniel had brought and from the hard, cold stone of her bed: Lucien's sarcophagus. She'd have chosen any other except that his was closest to the light. After so many long hours, including the endless night, she craved daylight.

Her teeth chattered as she rubbed her hands together, trying to find rest and comfort beneath the insubstantial layers of warmth.

Dear God, Nathaniel would surely not leave the country with no clue as to her whereabouts? He couldn't hate her enough to let her die.

No ... She shivered even more.

His revenge would be to orchestrate how she would be judged based on his lies and twisted truths.

Staring up at the ceiling she imagined all England gasping over her damning confession. Nathaniel had had it delivered to the printing press the night before.

Stiffly, she sat up and stared around the dim chamber. Her back ached; her stupidity mocked her. Nathaniel had orchestrated her fate since he had cast eyes on her eight years before.

What chance had she of convincing Max she spoke the truth, even if he did come for her?

The afternoon was closing in on her. Sobs rose up in her throat. Another night alone? How could she bear it?

She froze at the sound of a carriage. The slam of a door. Every sense moved to high alert, relief and desperation making her light-headed as she swung her feet to the ground.

'Help me!' she screamed, the echo of her thin slippers resounding through the chamber as she ran across the flagstones and pushed her face against the bars. 'I'm here! In the crypt!'

The sound of purposeful footsteps followed the gravel path that curved beside the high grassy knoll. Her rescuer was out of sight but surely he could hear her?

'Help me!' she cried again, so hard her lungs hurt, while she rattled the bars.

She saw the black hat before the rest of him came into view. The black coat and breeches and, as he raised his head to look at her, the smug, smiling, satisfied countenance of Nathaniel.

Terrified, she leapt back.

'I was worried about you, Olivia.' His voice was soothing as he unlocked the door.

Horrified she saw his smile of satisfaction, heard the whine of rusty hinges as he closed, then locked, the door behind him, stepping into the crypt.

'I left clues enough for Mr Atherton to have found you by now, Olivia, but perhaps he thinks you haven't yet learned your lesson and no longer cares.'

'Get away from me!' she shrieked, backing towards the far wall of the chamber.

Putting his head on one side, he studied her from near the entrance, his heavy body thrown into relief by the fading sun behind him.

'But *I* care, Olivia.' He advanced slowly, his voice heavy with intent as he murmured, 'That's why I came back.'

With her heart in her mouth, like a mouse staring into the jaws of a serpent, Olivia watched his approach. She was his prey, just as she'd always been.

'You left no clues, did you?' she whispered. 'You never intended Max to find me.' Tears trickled down her cheeks. She was the reverend's puppet, just as she'd always been.

He halted a foot away, close enough for her to see the parody of concern that twisted his features.

'Tears of joy?' His hand reached out, a finger extended to taste the salty evidence of her terror, her submission, before...

Before what? Before he led her to Lucien's sarcophagus to dominate and possess her?

'You bitch!' With a shriek of pain Nathaniel whipped back his hand, choking on another expletive as he sucked the damaged digit.

'You'd bite the hand that feeds you? Where's your gratitude?'

He lunged at her, cursing as she slipped out of reach to hurl herself against the grating.

'Get away from me!' she shrieked, rattling the bars, cringing as his large meaty hands snatched her elbows, whimpering as he pulled her against him.

'What do you want, Nathaniel?' she screamed, struggling. 'You have the gold. You've achieved my complete subjugation. You have damned me in the eyes of the world. Is that not enough?'

Gripping her chin roughly, he forced her to look at him as his other hand seized her round the middle.

'I want *you*! I want you to understand how much you need me!' he muttered, shoving his angry face close to hers as she convulsed with disgust.

She twisted her head out of his grip, clawing at his arms and cheeks with flailing hands, stumbling free only to fall upon the sarcophagi, exhaling on one violent gasp as the air was forced from her lungs.

'Just say it and you shall be free!' he promised. 'The gold is in the carriage. Just say that you want me, Olivia, and together we shall enjoy riches greater than in our wildest dreams!'

'Never!' Her voice broke on a sob. Her spirit was nearly broken, too, but she had to resist with all her might, or her mind would splinter into a million shards.

Then how could she be a mother to Julian?

Once again, Nathaniel's large body filled her vision.

Eyes wide with horror, senses screaming with revulsion, breath and vitality returned in time for her to thrust herself off the coffin and on to the floor.

Immediately she was upon her feet, but her slippers caught in the lavish trimmings of her hem, tripping her up so that she was flung forwards, arms upthrust to break the force of her fall as the flagstones rose to meet her.

Nathaniel was upon her before she could rise. Knees pinned against her sides, one hand forcing her face down upon the floor, he grasped her wrists behind her back and jerked her body upwards. She cried out with pain, tears blinding her as he rolled her over then scooped her up, before dumping her unceremoniously upon Lucien's sarcophagus.

Like a fly paralysed by the venom of a wasp, she felt his hands upon her collarbones, sweeping across the exposed skin to cup her now bared shoulders.

She could smell his excitement: the oil from his hair combining with the familiar smell of animal lust and the arousal of power.

'I have your son!' Pushing his thumbs beneath the lining of her bodice he gripped the fabric and ripped, his eyes feasting greedily upon the sight of exposed flesh above her stays. 'You are in my power.'

'Foul murderer!' she screamed, twisting uselessly beneath him. 'Damn you to the ends of the earth!' She struck out at him with her right hand, but he caught it, pinioning both her wrists to the lid of the sarcophagus while he straddled her, his body threatening to crush hers.

The fingers of his right hand dug into her shoulders painfully. 'Take what I'm offering you!' he shouted, as he pushed his face into hers. 'My love and the gold! Freedom! Do you *want* me to take you by force?'

'Let me go!' she wept, twisting her head away. 'It's Max's gold!'

Wincing at the pressure of his grip she sobbed, 'You damned me in the eyes of the world, but you will never get your final satisfaction for I love Max!'

His violence filled her with defiance. She would not give him the satisfaction of her submission yet again. 'I hate you, Nathaniel! You are cruel and evil and your power comes from threats!'

He laughed at her struggles, his lip curling as she spat out the words, 'Max is a thousand times the man you are and I will always love him for he is good and kind and he believes the best of people—'

Nathaniel drew in a venomous breath. She could feel the heavy beat of his heart and the oppressive hardness of his desire for her through her gown; the ultimate expression of his domination.

'He doesn't believe the best of you now, my love!'

She felt his hand fumbling beneath her skirts, his hot, foetid breath upon her neck as he panted above her.

With a scream, she freed one of her hands and tried to push him away but he was too strong for her and his voice was triumphant as he delivered his verdict. 'The sight of you ... the mere mention of your name—'

'Inspires me with love, respect and deep remorse! Get off her, God damn you, Kirkman!'

Sobbing, Olivia wriggled out from beneath her oppressor whose sweaty labours had been arrested by his shock.

'Oh, Max!' Tripping upon her torn skirts Olivia fell to her knees as she tried desperately to reach him on the other side of the iron door.

Max had come for her.

Not only to rescue her from danger but to take her away ... with *him*. Surely that was what his impassioned tone implied for his face had been in shadow and now she was on hands and knees like a cornered animal.

'She led me to the gold, Atherton!' Nathaniel crowed triumphantly as he whisked her up from the ground, her arms and legs flailing as uselessly as a cloth doll's. 'And now she's mine and you can't do a damned thing about it.'

'More lies, Reverend?' Max's tone was strained as he worked the key in the lock. 'Yes, I have the key. The key to the crypt and the key to the truth.'

The truth. She tried to wriggle free but Nathaniel was too strong. Struggling to breathe, unable to move, she wondered how she was painted in the version of the truth Max claimed to know and if that was why he didn't close the distance between them now he'd gained access to the crypt.

Her answer came as she felt the cold press of steel against her breast; looked down to see the small silver barrel of a pistol digging into her flesh below where her bodice gaped open.

'No!' she gasped. Swallowing down her terror she strained towards Max, wishing she could see the look on his face, to be reassured by the concern for her wellbeing endorsing the tension in his voice.

Had he come to rescue her *despite* what he believed? Or did his love for her transcend lies and half truths?

'I shall kill her!'

She forced herself not to react. Fear motivated Nathaniel. It shored up his power; his belief in his invincibility.

'I wanted her since Lucien made her his,' Nathaniel snarled. 'For eight years I have worked towards this moment. I shall not let her go so easily.' He gave a humourless laugh. 'If I can't have her, you certainly shan't!'

Max did not move. 'You're vanquished, Reverend, and you know it.' His voice carried across the three yards that separated them, a low and controlled murmur. 'Drop the pistol and let her go.'

Nathaniel's left arm squeezed Olivia tighter; the other pressed the pistol harder into her flesh just below her breast. Her neck was clammy from his foul, hot breath. She could smell his desperation and knew he would never relinquish her willingly.

'Right through the heart, Atherton. Or should I say, "my lord"?' Nathaniel sneered. 'You have me to thank for that! Where is your gratitude?'

'It is my birthright.'

Olivia trained her gaze on Max's beloved face. Anything to block out the fear engendered by the barrel of the pistol which stabbed into her.

The tone of his voice continued to reassure her. 'Olivia tried to tell me that a long time ago, but I was too obtuse to understand her.'

A ray of sunshine burned through the heavy cloud and slanted across Max's face. To her relief she saw concern for her in his expression, not condemnation. He was speaking from the heart; here to save her and exonerate her in the process. Her fear of Nathaniel dissipated, despite the noxious smell of him that burned her nostrils and the painful, threatening hold he had upon her.

Not ten feet away Max represented her salvation. His expression confirmed her greatest longing: that in his arms she would bask in the loving warmth of his embrace, revel in the urgency of his kisses and glory in the knowledge that he was her future.

But Nathaniel held the upper hand and he was unpredictable.

'She considered her son more important than either you or the truth!' Nathaniel spat.

Max raised one eyebrow but said nothing.

'Max, I wrote to tell you ...' she said, brokenly. How wicked, how venal the truth sounded when distilled. How calculating it made her when presented in its essence.

'Hush, sweetheart,' he soothed with a smile for her. 'I've no doubt that man intercepted it.' He took a step forward. 'Despite your lies, Reverend, and the lies you forced Olivia to publish to the world, I know what kind of woman Olivia is—'

'The kind who will dance naked on the table, who will let the men line up to lick the cream from her!' Edgily, Nathaniel jabbed the barrel of the pistol harder into Olivia's flesh. 'Tell me, Mr Atherton, have you ever kissed Lady Olivia's Butterfly?'

With a cry of shame, Olivia brought her hands up to her face.

'I look forward to doing so when it is not a sin,' said Max with a wry smile. 'I daresay you have not, either, Reverend.'

'Do you *want* me to kill her?' Kirkman screamed, pushing her so hard that her upper body snapped back over his supporting arm. 'Are you so arrogant you believe you can arrive like an avenging hero and everything will go your way?'

Ignoring him, Max's voice continued, low and mesmeric. 'At every opportunity you prevented Olivia from telling me the truth when she was desperate to unburden herself.'

Nathaniel laughed. 'The truth? You don't know what to believe! That's your eternal problem. Look at her!' Roughly he gripped Olivia's chin and turned her face upwards. 'Beneath this perfection lies a heart and soul more corrupted than mine! Olivia and I are soulmates, Atherton. I will *never* give her up!'

Olivia wrenched her face free. 'I would rather die knowing Max loves me and believes in me than suffer a lifetime with you, Nathaniel!' she cried, as she tore herself from his grasp.

'Olivia! No!'

She heard a dull thud, realized it was her head striking the edge of the sarcophagus and Max's cry, echoing through the chamber.

She heard the scuffle of feet; the heavy toe of a boot that clipped her ear before it was swallowed up by the darkness. A body thudded to the ground before hauling itself upright, disappearing into the gloom amidst shouts and scuffles.

She felt ... Nothing.

Certainly she felt no pain, but when she tried to raise herself she could not move.

Closing her eyes she listened to the muffled cries of fighting men: a wail of pain, a shout of anger.

A muttered curse. Max's voice, tight and desperate: 'Oh God! Olivia! You're bleeding!' followed by a cry, a snarl, low and heartfelt, 'I will never forgive you if she is harmed.'

Fearfully, she blinked open her eyes, orienting herself towards the fading daylight, the entrance to the crypt where she could see Max and Nathaniel locked in a violent dance of mastery over her.

Her life lay in the balance. She would belong to the victor. Nathaniel had a gun and if it found its mark and Max was vanquished Olivia would forever remain in Nathaniel's power.

She put her hand to the sting at her forehead. In horror she stared at her bloodied fingers. As she struggled on to her elbows she wondered how deep was her wound. If Nathaniel was to claim her she did not care. She'd rather die.

But while they fought hope remained. The possibility of a future with Max, lies and twisted truths untangled, confessed, accepted, forgiven and condoned was her greatest hope. As it always had been.

The cacophony of grunts and groans was pierced by a single cry. Something stung her knee. Her swimming vision came into focus. Upon Lucien's sarcophagus she saw Nathaniel stretched over Max who struggled beneath him, hands reaching up to clasp the other man's throat. Against the noise of labouring breaths and muttered curses Olivia could hear the rapid beat of her own heart, or so it seemed.

She struggled to her knees and nearly swooned. Blood dripped from her head wound on to her dress. Her life blood. Draining away before her very eyes. She had seen the same thing when her first baby had died. In her pain she had cried out that she wanted to die, too. Now, never had the need to live battled so strongly within her.

She had responsibilities she could not forsake: a child whose tenuous future only she could safeguard. A man she loved whose respect she would fight for to the death.

Trembling, she gripped the side of the sarcophagus and closed her eyes.

She heard Nathaniel's gloating snarl, 'Too bad you were so ready to jump to the worst conclusions, ye of little faith, *my lord!*' She opened her eyes and saw Nathaniel had the upper hand. Olivia could see Max struggling for air. She tried to stand, but pain shot across her vision and she slumped into a pool of weak, ineffective passivity.

The woman of strength and conviction was dying within the empty husk Nathaniel derided. The woman she so wanted to be would not be heard.

Her heart screamed out in pain. In the echoing cavern it came out a muted whimper.

Dear God, please give me one more chance, the fading, flickering voice of hope cried out within her. Let Julian and Max know the kind of woman I really am. The kind of woman I could have been all these years if Lucien hadn't stepped in to corrupt me. If Nathaniel hadn't manipulated and intimidated me.

'Olivia!'

She jerked her head up at the sound of Max's croak. In the dim light it was hard to see him. Already he was fading, though perhaps it was she who was fading. The dark stain on her skirt was growing. She no longer felt any pain but that's how it was when one bled to death. She knew that.

'The pistol!'

The pistol? she thought stupidly, straining to sharpen what reason was left to her, panic at her ineptitude surging through her as she continued to support herself against the sarcophagus. She winced at the pain in her knee and looked down.

She was kneeling on the pistol.

The pistol!

With trembling fingers she picked it up. Elation shimmered through her, despite the dulling of her senses. She stared at it. For the first time in her life she held the balance of power. Cognisance of the danger snapped her senses to alert. Raising the barrel, she pointed it in Nathaniel's direction.

'Release Max or I'll kill you.' Her threat sounded like a parody. Nathaniel's mocking laugh echoed round the chamber. 'The roof is in greater danger, Olivia, you're shaking so much.'

Struggling to see clearly she cried out, 'I *will* shoot straight, Nathaniel and I swear I shall get you through your rotten black heart.'

'Max or me. It'll be a lottery, my dear.'

His gloating confidence frightened her. 'Your life blood is draining from you until you staunch that wound.' With a grunt he forced his thumbs deeper into Max's windpipe. Olivia winced at Max's gasp, the struggle she saw in his eyes. Nathaniel was a much heavier man. Luck had favoured him when he'd hurled himself upon Max, the lighter-framed man buckling over the lid of Lucien's coffin beneath his adversary.

Dear God, she had to help him.

'I have the upper hand, as I always have.' Nathaniel sneered. 'Realize that fact, my love, and I'll realize your wildest dreams.'

'I wouldn't go with you if you were the last man on earth. If I can't be with Max I'd rather die.' Carefully she brought her other hand up for greater support, her eyes trained on her trembling grip on the pistol as she heard a grunt of effort and a bellow of pain. Jerking her chin up she saw Nathaniel sprawled across the floor of the chamber in the gloom some yards away. Max was struggling to his feet having brought his knee up to deliver a kick of sufficient strength to release him from Nathaniel's grip.

'Don't go to him!' Olivia cried. 'Let his blood be on *my* hands.'

Max halted his progress across the floor and Nathaniel rose slowly to his feet, a crooked smile twisting his mouth as he faced Olivia.

'What? Shoot me in cold blood?' He extended his arms wide before tapping his chest. 'Through the heart? Here it is, Olivia. I offer myself up as a sacrifice.'

'You think I jest—'

'There's no need, Olivia.' Max's voice, low and soothing, carried across the chamber. 'Give the pistol to me.'

She did not look at him. Could not. Her hands were shaking so much she felt a fool.

Nathaniel laughed.

'Not your heart, Nathaniel,' she said through clenched teeth, 'for I don't want your death on my hands. I just want to see you suffer a little for the misery you've caused.'

She lowered her hands, training the barrel of the pistol upon his groin. She was rewarded by the blanching of Nathaniel's face when he saw her determination, the absence of mockery as he muttered, 'Think how you'd be judged, Olivia.'

'You've orchestrated how I shall be judged, Nathaniel.' She gulped, sweat and blood blinding her. 'And you've ensured I have nothing to lose.'

She swallowed and closed her eyes as she dropped her hands.

Nathaniel's mocking laughter rang out. 'A coward to the end, Olivia!' he cried. "You'll never pull the trigger.'

Once again, she raised the pistol but her hand was shaking so much she nearly dropped it.

Turning to Max she saw he was smiling at her, bolstering her courage with further affirmation of his love. Of course he knew she could not do it. Forcing herself not to sob, she took a step towards him. Towards the man she loved; the man who was at last offering her the future she'd always wanted. She knew it from the expression in his eyes. Three more steps and she'd be in his arms. Nathaniel was vanquished. As long as she had the pistol, Nathaniel was powerless.

She was nearly there when alerted by movement in her peripheral vision. 'Max! Be careful!' she shrieked, jumping back as Nathaniel swung high the lid of Molly's sarcophagus to bring down upon Max's head.

The crash of splintering masonry, of Max's angry triumphant shout as he leapt clear, was drowned by the explosion of the firing pistol and Nathaniel's ghastly scream.

Dropping the weapon, Olivia collapsed to the ground.

Nathaniel's taunts echoed in her head. 'You'll never pull the trigger.' Well, she had, and now she was drifting into blissful oblivion, reassured by Nathaniel's moans and the shouting of her name – it seemed a league away – confirming that Max was safe.

Boots rang out upon the flagstones. She heard a sigh, an urgent hiss of breath as strong arms slipped under her knees and shoulders, raising her from the cold stone floor. Max's voice, unsteady for the first time.

'Olivia! Open your eyes!'

She blinked them open, breathing in the wonderful smell of him; revelling in the hard strength of his youthful, vigorous body as he cradled her against his chest.

'We must get you out of here. Quickly! You're losing blood! We must attend to your wound!'

The concern in his slate-grey eyes nearly undid her. Chocking back a sob she whispered, 'Julian?'

'Julian is safe with Charlotte and your aunts.'

She exhaled on a sigh of relief. Settling himself on the lid of the sarcophagus he rocked her, dropping feather light kisses upon her brow as he staunched her wound with a wad of linen. His torn shirt-sleeve, she realized as she blindly kissed the warm flesh of his arm.

At last he rose, still cradling her.

She whispered, 'Is Nathaniel going to die?'

'Exquisite aim, my angel. Maximum pain and humiliation but I doubt you'll have his blood on your conscience.' She heard the grinding of rusty hinges and winced at the light, almost blinding although it was dusk. 'I'll assume responsibility if luck goes against you.'

She curled her arm around his neck, basking in the warmth of his strong, hard chest. 'Why would you do that?'

He stopped on the gravel path. Odin was tethered to Nathaniel's carriage. The horse raised his head and whinnied, pleased to see its master.

'Atonement.' His face above hers radiated warmth and good humour. As if the battle over life and death just minutes before had never taken place though she could feel the urgent need for him pulsing through her body and felt his answering response. 'It's a good time to start affirming my faith in you.'

'Max,' she began through dry lips, 'the gold—'

'It doesn't matter, sweetheart,' he soothed, kissing her lips lightly as if to allay her fears. 'If Kirkman has taken it we may still find it. And if we don't, we're better off than we were before, aren't we?'

'No, it's—'

'Yes, we are, because everything's out in the open – the lies and the truth – and we still have each other.'

'The gold is in the carriage because he told me so.'

Checked, as he settled her carefully on to the carriage seat, his expression was thoughtful. A slow grin spread across his face. 'Then I may buy you diamond ear-rings and gowns worthy of a duchess sooner rather than later.'

'I don't want to be a duchess.'

Tenderly he brushed a strand of hair from the wound on her temple.

'A mere viscountess will do?'

She nodded, not trusting herself to speak.

He reached up and kissed her properly then, nuzzling her throat as he stood on the path by the crypt against the setting sun, Nathaniel's cries, more of anger than of pain, issuing from within.

Reluctantly he raised his head. 'It's time to take you to Julian. And then we'll all go home.'

She heard the catch in his voice. Gazing up at him, she drank in his look of love, and the hope he radiated for their shared future, knowing it would sustain her through all the trials she would face on her journey to acceptance.

'Home, my beloved Olivia,' he whispered as he climbed into the carriage beside her, closing the door against Nathaniel's threats. 'Home,' he added, softly 'to Elmwood.'

THE END

LADY SARAH'S REDEMPTION

CHAPTER 1

E ngland, 1819

"DO YOU SUPPOSE SHE'S A DANGEROUS SIREN COME TO BEWITCH US all, Cosmo?" Brushing aside a beech tree branch, Roland reined in his mount beside his nephew's. "Or have I acted properly in taking her in?"

"I wasn't spying, sir!" Blushing, Cosmo turned in the saddle. "When I saw the new governess had arrived, naturally I was curious—" He broke off. "If indeed it is the new governess."

Roland followed Cosmo's gaze through the screen of trees, across the manicured lawns to the gravel drive where a carriage had just drawn up in front of the house. The slender young woman standing on the bottom step overseeing the removal of her trunk could have passed for any governess, anywhere in the country, she was so unremarkable.

Which was, of course, why Cosmo had sounded doubting and, understandably, disappointed. Miss Morecroft's appointment had been so vehemently opposed by Roland's sister-in-law, Cecily, that Cosmo had probably conjured up an image similar to the provocative siren suggested by his uncle.

Perversely, and despite his drollery, Roland, too, was disappointed by this vision of ordinariness.

The young woman glanced briefly in their direction, before mounting the steps to the house. Her old-fashioned poke bonnet concealed her features at this distance but her outmoded, ill-fitting gown of faded puce lent her a homely air.

Cosmo stroked his chin, a new habit developed since he'd started shaving only recently, and asked, "Will she be here long? Aunt Cecily says it's only until we find her another position. Caro says she's too old for a governess and Miss Morecroft won't last." He shifted in the saddle then slid his eyes across to his uncle's face. "You know what Caro's like, sir."

Roland nodded absently, still trying to reconcile the image of the dowdy governess with his memories of the young woman's father. Any daughter of Godby's should be brimming with exuberance, flashing her ill-afforded finery with the same devil-may-care defiance as her ill-fated Pater. Now Godby, his foster brother was dead, snuffed out in a far distant land, forever denying Roland the catharsis of reconciliation.

"I know, Cosmo." He sighed. He had as much desire to dwell on his obstinate daughter as he had on the new governess. "I hope Caro and your Aunt Cecily will be kind to Miss Morecroft. First the death of the young woman's family, now this terrible accident—" With a sigh he took up the reins. "Go and pay your respects to your foster cousin, Cosmo. She is to be treated with respect and not judged on account of her father's actions."

How, he wondered, as his mount picked its way over the stony ground to the rise at the far end of the Western paddock, should he deal with Miss Morecroft? Any hint of kindness would be sure to invoke Cecily's wrath.

From the top of the hill he looked down upon Larchfield, the lovely home he'd never expected to inherit. Its honey-coloured stone glowed, mullioned windows twinkled in the sunlight. It looked a fairytale castle. Once Roland had believed it was, until thieving passions had destroyed all that was good within its walls.

Until Godby, newly returned from war, had burst in upon their tranquillity. A boy no longer, he had changed the delicate balance, setting Roland against his brother, Hector. Three young men and only two women yet - despite her fortune -poor, ugly Cecily, Hector's wife, had still been discarded. Now she seemed to forget that Roland had lost a wife: his exquisite Venetia. So beautiful. So beguiling.

So faithless.

Strange, reflected Roland, as he turned his mount for home, how the pain still lingered, long after her image had blurred.

Now Godby's daughter was here and, in truth, Roland felt as much enthusiasm as his sister-in-law for having her at Larchfield.

The image of Miss Morecroft's quiet dowdiness was suddenly immensely reassuring. He felt confident Godby's daughter posed no threat to the peace at Larchfield, after all.

◦৵৩

CECILY HAWTHORNE'S CRITICAL GAZE TRAVELLED FROM THE TOP OF Sarah's dowdy straw bonnet to the tips of her worn leather boots which peeked beneath her gown.

She sighed, tapping her fingers on the arm of the sofa. "The truth is, Miss Morecroft, you're not what I expected and, to be blunt, nor am I convinced you will suit. Mr Hawthorne, however, was most insistent."

"Then I am greatly obliged at being given an opportunity to prove myself." Sarah had not considered a hostile reception when she'd embarked upon her rash charade. She'd thought it bad enough wearing the second-hand boots which pinched horribly and which the nuns had retrieved from the waterlogged trunk they'd believed was hers when she'd been saved from the wreck of the *Mary Jane*. She'd nearly wept with shame at having to appear in public wearing such an abominable gown. Now anxiety gripped her as she tried for a suitably grateful smile. She'd have to summon up all the humility she'd rarely had to use in her cosseted life to temper the threat to her plans that Mrs Hawthorne's hostility posed. Rarely, in her twenty-four years, had she felt at such a disadvantage.

The springs of the faux bamboo sofa creaked as Mrs Hawthorne shifted position, and the ormolu clock on the mantelpiece ticked loudly. They were the only sounds in this silent, oppressive house that was supposed to contain a brood of children.

Mrs Hawthorne sniffed. "I'm told your French is flawless and you can play the pianoforte, but can you waltz? Have they even heard of the waltz in India?" Looking quite fierce, she added, "A most inelegant dance, but Mr Hawthorne considers it an essential accomplishment. Caro is coming out next year."

"I am an accomplished dancer, ma'am," Sarah assented, trying to restrain her curiosity with regard to the novel hairpiece her employer had used to supplement her sparse ginger curls. She was sure the furry appendage peeping beneath the lappets of Mrs Hawthorne's white lace cap had once adorned a squirrel's behind.

"It's not a question of how accomplished *you* are, Miss Morecroft, but how accomplished you are at imparting these graces to Caro and the girls." Mrs Hawthorne reached over the arm of the settee and tugged on the embroidered bell pull. "No doubt you're anxious to meet your new charges."

"Lovely." Sarah smiled weakly, wondering how she'd survive the two or three weeks she needed to remain at Larchfield. She didn't like Mrs Hawthorne and, clearly, Mrs Hawthorne didn't like her.

"Girls, meet Miss Morecroft, your new governess."

Sarah watched them weave their way amongst the clutter of occasional tables and spindly chairs to curtsy before her. The youngest gave her a shy, gap-toothed smile, the redheaded ten-year-old, a cheeky grin. In their wake came a tall, ungainly black-haired girl with hunched shoulders and dark eyes burnt into a sallow face.

"Caro!" Mrs Hawthorne squawked and her hands flew to her cheeks.

"Sorry!" wailed the future debutante, struggling to right the brass Argand lamp in danger of toppling and singeing the fringed damask tablecloth.

The little girls sniggered and Sarah felt a rush of sympathy for the girl quailing beneath Mrs Hawthorne's withering scorn. Poor Caro was the most unprepossessing debutante Sarah had ever laid eyes upon.

"Never mind, Caro," she said, "it's in such an awkward position, I nearly did the same."

This, of course, did nothing to endear her to Mrs Hawthorne. Nor did it appear to gain her any advantage for Caro lanced her with look of suspicion as she took her place beside the other girls.

Sarah had rarely encountered hostility in her life. It was an uncomfortable sensation. Swallowing, she managed to retain her smile. "I'm sure we'll all deal together, famously," she said bracingly. For weren't little girls easy to win over? As for Caro, Sarah could well remember being a rebellious adolescent herself, the despair of her beloved Papa.

Her beloved Papa.

She cut the thought off at the root. A little pain now while she saw through this vital element of her plan ensured she could soon resume her valuable role at his side.

All heads turned at the sound of footsteps in the passage before a tall youth with a mop of sandy curls above immensely high collar points put his head around the door.

"Aunt Cecily, forgive the intrusion," said this eager young slave to fashion. "I'd forgotten you were receiving the girls' new governess."

His assessing eye as it roamed over Sarah gave the lie to his erring memory, though she would have expected more of an appreciative gleam. Smiling up at him, she consoled herself that one hardly looked one's best in someone else's cast-offs, and puce, which always reminded her of coagulating blood, was definitely not her colour.

"Master Cosmo is unaccustomed to the company of young ladies," said Mrs Hawthorne after dismissing her nephew. "He'll be returning home soon." She rose. "Let me show you your quarters."

Sarah followed her new employer, listening to her strictures regarding the girls' education.

"—And you'll have to curb Caro's preoccupation with knowledge. The girl is likely to turn into a blue-stocking." Halting at the end of a long passage she threw open the door to a tiny chamber. "You've just enough time to put away your things and change, Miss Morecroft. The girls have their supper at five." Mrs Hawthorne turned on her heel. "I shall see you in the nursery when you're ready."

Sarah was too dispirited to take consolation from the sight of the squirrel's tail now dangling at a rakish angle over her employer's left eye.

"Yes, ma'am," she managed, disappointed nevertheless that the hairpiece retained its tenuous grip.

With dismay she took in her sparse surroundings. Apart from the bed, wash stand and chair, the garish rag rug provided the only splash of colour. On top of it rested her trunk — or rather, the other Sarah's trunk. After all the trauma she'd endured lately, she was visited by such a wave of loneliness and longing for home that she sank against the door frame and covered her face with her hands. Could she really endure a ticking mattress and coarse woollen blanket when duckdown and fine linen and all the other comforts she'd taken for granted were just a five-hour carriage ride away?

She'd have to, wouldn't she? she told herself as she sank to her knees and struggled with the corroded buckles. She might not have actively chosen this course, but she had endorsed it with her silence, thinking at the time it solved all her troubles. Just a couple of weeks was all she needed and then her darling papa would welcome her home like the prodigal daughter. Never again would he ride roughshod over her happiness.

Though her hands were still tender from their long immersion in icy sea water, making the chore more painful than difficult, she forced herself to count her blessings. Her maid was dead and poor Sarah Morecroft, the governess whose place she'd taken, was at the bottom of the North Sea.

The clattering of hooves on the cobblestones outside was a welcome diversion. Throwing open the casement Sarah looked down into the stable yard, wondering what other diversions Larchfield offered.

The horseman who'd just arrived raised his head at the sound and doffed his hat with a cursory glance at Sarah, before dismounting.

Sarah retreated a little.

From this distance, he appeared to be in his late thirties. Mrs Hawthorne's husband? At a pinch their ages might make it possible, but surely not even a vast fortune could entice a man as elegant as this one to throw in his lot with Sarah's demanding employer.

His expression was serious, distracted, as he threw the reins to a stable boy and strode towards the kitchen steps.

Thick dark hair swept back from a high forehead and framed a pair of well-chiselled cheek bones. His manner was decisive. She noticed the way the servants bowed and scraped. The head groom tugged his forelock and the kitchen maid, scurrying across the cobbles with an apron overflowing with vegetables, curtsied and dimpled at his brief greeting.

Sarah strained forward to observe him better before he disappeared. This was no country bumpkin. Highly polished top boots reached the knees of a pair of buckskins that covered shapely, muscled legs. The immaculately cut coat of navy superfine that stretched across his broad shoulders was surely Savile Row.

Unlike Master Cosmo, there was nothing of the fop about him, although his attention to detail was apparent in his attire. A nonpareil, decided Sarah with satisfaction. And a particularly dashing one.

Dashing, just like James – Captain James Fleming.

She sighed. No point reflecting on the past. And she mustn't hold dear James entirely accountable for her predicament despite his volte-face regarding a marriage between them.

Sarah listened to the ring of his boots upon the stairs, two floors below as she crossed to the tarnished looking glass. A critical perusal of her reflection hardly bolstered her spirits. However, she reassured herself, with her chestnut tresses shining and her normally flawless complexion glowing, the lowly governess Sarah Morecroft would soon receive the same admiration to which she, the feted beauty, Lady Sarah Miles, was accustomed.

Feeling almost reconciled to her new life at the thought she returned to her unpacking, only to gasp with horror as she pulled out the first garment that came to hand.

Dropping the drab, high-necked grey merino gown, she put her hands to her flaming cheeks. How could she possibly hold up her head in public wearing such a repulsive object? It would be more mortifying than anything she'd ever done in her entire life.

Swallowing convulsively, she reassured herself this must be the worst of the garments Miss Morecroft had packed. She'd probably tossed it into her trunk at the last minute.

But as Sarah began laying out the gowns, petticoats, chemises and other items in an orderly pile, her dismay grew. By the time she'd pulled loose a beige fustian gown adorned with two rows of badly sewn flounces that might just pass muster for eating nursery tea she was close to tears. What was she to wear for family dinner in the formal dining room? Regardless of what Mrs Hawthorne said there was no way Sarah was going to subsist on a diet of endless bread and butter, disgusting lumpy suet puddings and — she swallowed — no Madeira for more than a week.

What, then, could she deck herself out in? She had no money. Her reticule had gone down with the boat. She fingered the gold cross at her throat. She'd have to pawn that, she supposed.

A cursory rap on the door heralded the entrance of a young personage who bustled into the centre of the room as if she owned it. Judging by her starched cap and apron, Sarah assumed she must be the nursery maid.

"Miss, you're not even dressed!" The stout, ruddy-faced creature, who looked as if she was in the habit of gobbling up all the nursery leftovers, scowled, hands on hips. "And there's the little girls waiting for their tea!"

"They're hardly going to starve if I'm five minutes late." Enraged at the maid's impertinence, Sarah pretended to examine the beige dress. Tossing it over the iron bedstead, she sank back onto the threadbare grey blanket and covered her face with her hands. "I declare, the sea water's ruined my entire wardrobe. Isn't that a greater calamity than keeping a couple of children waiting for nursery tea?"

"Yes, Miss." Sarah's lofty tone appeared to have put the girl in her place. She shifted position, scuffing the oilskin floor covering with her toe as Sarah dragged herself into a sitting position. "Right sorry we all were to hear of the accident, miss. First losing your family to fever in India and then nearly going yerself, afore yer time. Beg pardon, too, for me lack of manners only the mistress gets on her high ropes when it comes to punctuality. I'm Ellen, by the way. And Mrs Hawthorne'll be bound to forgive you considerin' yer terrible ordeal, Miss."

"That's encouraging," replied Sarah, getting wearily to her feet, her irony clearly lost on Ellen. "I shall be down shortly."

Struggling into the beige dress was an effort and the response she received from Mrs Hawthorne, who was waiting for her in the nursery, made no secret of the other's disparagement. But when Sarah cunningly and plaintively said, "Oh, ma'am, two days floating in the ocean has done my wardrobe no favours," a look of guilt immediately crossed her mistress's face.

"Of course not, my dear. I daresay there are a few of my things I no longer wear that can be altered. They may not be in the first stare, but that hardly signifies in your situation."

No doubt they'd be simply hideous, thought Sarah, but at least they'd be of finer quality than Miss Morecroft's coarse cottons and serviceable woollens.

The nursery was as Spartan as she had feared, the expressions of her charges hardly compensation. Not one to be daunted by a trio of little girls, Sarah swept past them to the window.

"First lesson, girls! There's a difference between staring, and paying attention," she said, softening her stern tone with a smile as she turned. Despite the appalling deprivations she'd have to endure, there were compensations, she decided, her optimistic nature rising above the gloom. It could even be fun: the erudition of three sponge-like little girls. It gave her a sense of power she was unused to at home, despite her privileges.

"Yes, miss." Their blank looks were replaced with curiosity. Even Caro did not look quite so hostile.

"And while we're waiting for the sumptuous fare about to be laid before us, you can tell me what you'd like me to teach you. I've no doubt I'll be the best governess you've ever had." She warmed to her task. She loved to learn. Now she'd find out if she were as gifted in imparting her knowledge. "I'm an authority on all the graces, with a special passion for the classics and, believe it or not, Caro, the sciences."

Harriet looked down at her exercise book where she'd drawn a stern-faced insect wearing a monocle and lisped, "I want to learn about worms, and Mama says Caro's going to need a lot of help if she's to catch a husband."

"Worms? We'll make a worm farm, then." Sarah spoke above Caro's protests. "As for Caro-" Her tone was thoughtful. Caro glowered and mumbled something incoherent as she stared down at her empty place setting.

"Enunciate, Caro." Sarah spoke crisply. "All I caught was the word ridiculous, and I do concur, it's a ridiculous notion you'll never catch a husband. Certainly you're no beauty but that's sure to change. I was at my most unprepossessing at sixteen, and I remember girls far worse off who turned into veritable swans and waltzed off with nabobs and dukes."

"You didn't hear, Miss Morecroft," Harriet piped up as nursery tea — predictably, egg and toast — was served. "Caro doesn't want a husband, but nobody ever listens."

"Not want a husband?" Sarah frowned as she took her seat at the table.

"Finding a husband is not life's most noble pursuit," mumbled Caro.

"Noble? There's nothing noble about securing a husband but unless one intends to be a nun it's a young woman's most important enterprise. A girl must use all her wits and wiles to ensure she is as well-placed as possible."

"Caro wants to be a blue-stocking," said Augusta.

"Will you be of independent means some day?"

"What?" Caro was clearly affronted.

"Unless you are," said Sarah patiently, "an indulgent husband who will grant you the latitude to pursue your intellectual leanings is a far more desirable proposition to playing unpaid servant to those in the household who feel they have a legitimate claim upon your time."

"You're not married," Harriet pointed out, "and you're much older than Caro."

Caro sounded triumphant. "So if there aren't enough of the good ones to go around—"

"There are," Sarah interrupted. "In fact, during my first Season out

I found the perfect husband after turning down half a dozen manageable suitors."

"But you didn't marry him, did you?" Despite herself Caro looked interested.

"He died on the Peninsula two weeks before our wedding day." Sarah toyed with her food. She was dismayed to have experienced only the slightest pang recounting this distant chapter in her life. Not so long ago she'd believed she'd never get over it. Could she really have lost her heart? Certainly, she'd lost it to Captain Danvers, seven years ago. But was she now so old she was immune to the heady sensations that accompanied being in love?

When the girls pressed her she was tight-lipped. For one thing, she was not sure what the Hawthornes knew of Miss Morecroft's history. For another, she hadn't the heart to pursue the topic. Her first love had ended in tragedy, her second in disappointment. James, her distant cousin whom she loved like a brother, had betrayed her by supporting her father's cork-brained quest to marry the two of them off to each other, simply because James was next to inherit Lord Miles's title and estate.

"Not another word on the subject!" Sarah rapped upon the table for silence. "Life contains many disappointments."

"You must be very brave, Miss Morecroft." Admiration shone from Augusta's serious dark eyes. "You're not scared of spiders, are you? You wouldn't even be scared of Master."

"Your dog?" asked Sarah, and Caro giggled.

"My father," she said. "Everyone's scared of him."

"Goodness." Sarah frowned. "Nobody should be scared of their father. Why, mine's the world's most terrible ogre but I'm not scared of him. Or rather, I wasn't," she amended, hastily.

"You defied him?" whispered Caro, round-eyed as she fidgeted with her lilac sash, her food untouched before her.

Lilac! Shuddered Sarah. Only the most unfeeling guardian would dress a girl of Caro's colouring in such a shade. Transferring her attention to the girl's intense expression, Sarah said, "Not outright. That would have been to no purpose."

"Then how did you manage such a thing?" Caro strained forward as if the question were of the greatest importance.

Sarah chose her words, carefully. Caro might not be such a lost cause, after all. "You have to work out how a person thinks." She smiled. "Learn cunning, while all the time appearing ever so meek and obedient. They think they're getting their way when, really, you're getting yours. Or, at least, you're not completely giving into them. Take these eggs, for example," she added, gaining inspiration from the soft-boiled eggs that were growing cold in front of them. "Pass the charcoal, please, Harriet."

Perplexed, the girls watched as Sarah drew a face on her egg. She pushed it towards Caro, together with the charcoal.

"Now draw the face of whoever frightens you most in the world."

With great deliberation Caro pencilled in sideburns, a head of wavy hair, adding a smart cravat before touching up Sarah's attempts at a face.

"You're quite an artist." Sarah's tone was admiring. "Obviously this is a man of consequence. Now, face him squarely and tell him what you feel. Then chop off his head!"

The girls looked at Sarah, horrified.

"I couldn't possibly," gasped Caro.

"If you can't even tell it to an egg, small wonder the man himself reduces you to a quivering jelly. You're hardly going to get your own way if you lose your nerve every time he looks at you. So go on, face your egg sternly and tell it what you really think. Come now, Caro. Say: "I despise the way you ...""

Caro hesitated. Then taking a deep breath she hissed, "I hate knowing you're ashamed of me, that you're so concerned at the impression I make upon people who in your opinion matter but who I don't ever want to see again. I hate the way you ignore me, think I'm ugly and stupid-"

"Right! Well, I'd be surprised if your egg hadn't got the message-" Sarah cut in. Caro's voice had risen alarmingly. "Perhaps now is a good time to cut off its head."

"So I cut off your head! Like this! So I don't ever suffer the agonies of your ill opinion again!"

Seizing the bread knife, Caro sliced it through the air, wielding it with as much enthusiasm as any London executioner.

In shocked silence they all watched as the egg shot out of its cradle and hurtled through the air towards the door, levelling off at chest height ... at the precise moment the door opened.

And as nursery dinner made contact with the immaculately clad torso of the handsome gentleman Sarah had made eyes at earlier that day, Caro cried out in anguish, "Father!"

CHAPTER 2

SILENTLY, THE OBJECT of Sarah's earlier admiration – no longer so immaculately attired – stared at the mess of yolk that now adorned his striped waistcoat.

"Such dreadful timing, sir!" muttered Sarah, seizing a napkin and dabbing at the sticky yellow patch. Conscious of the hard muscle beneath the two thin layers of clothing, and the fact that her enthusiasm in righting the damage was compounding the awkwardness, she stopped.

He removed the napkin from her grasp. "Miss Morecroft, I presume?" Studying her through cool grey eyes, the gentleman tossed the linen upon the table.

Sarah was stunned into silence. No man had ever spoken to her like this. Like some erring minion. She could feel her cheeks burning. "My apologies for the egg upon your waistcoat, sir, but it is decidedly me who has it upon her face, since I put Caro up to it."

To her dismay the joke fell flat. Obviously the gentleman had no sense of humour. None of the sensual merriment she was accustomed to in her usual dealings with the opposite sex shone from his handsome, ascetic face. And indeed, it was a particularly fine face.

"Surely playing cricket with eggs falls within the domain of high-spirited young scamps, not gently nurtured young ladies?" He continued to frown at her, almost as if he couldn't make her out. "I hope your curriculum, Miss Morecroft, takes account of the station in life to which these young ladies aspire."

Sarah hung her head. "Yes... Mr Hawthorne."

"I came to welcome you into the household that was once your father's home." Again, no smile to soften the effect of his earlier rebuke. "I was sorry to hear of your misfortunes, Miss Morecroft."

"Thank you." She could not raise her voice above a whisper. Guilt stabbed at her once again. She was wicked. She would get her come-uppance, though at least she need not fear exposure from this quarter. The real Sarah Morecroft had been a child when her father had taken the family to India.

"And, while I appreciate your honesty in acknowledging your influence behind my daughter's uncharacteristically hoydenish behaviour, I suppose I should be glad your recent traumatic experiences have not sapped you of all spirit."

Sarah's gratification at what she'd interpreted as reluctant admiration was short-lived. There was not a jot of appreciation in his look as he scrutinized her. How dare he sweep his eyes over her with such scant regard, as if she were simply the - well, the mousy governess?

Glancing at a clearly mortified Caro, she felt a surge of anger replace her guilt. Yes, her own father might shout and try to cow her, but he peppered his fiery words with reluctant praise for her beauty, wit and intellect, damning her at the same time for not having been born a son.

Mr Hawthorne's tone still carried a warning as he put his hand on the door knob to leave. "Caro will have her come-out next year. Your father presented a very persuasive case for my employing you, Miss Morecroft. I trust you'll not disappoint his memory."

"Sir— " Desperate to detain him so as not to be abandoned to the girls in such a humiliating manner, Sarah strove for a disarming combination of entreaty and contrition. "I realize what a great debt I owe you for the opportunity to prove myself as tutor to your children, especially Caro whom I consider has great potential—"

"—For improvement, yes," Mr Hawthorne cut in. "Now, if you'll excuse me, my dinner guests are waiting. I merely put my head in to welcome you to Larchfield. I, too, have every confidence Caro will make a shining debut in another six months-" he levelled a meaningful look at Sarah – "provided her new governess can impart the many accomplishments with which I was assured she was endowed."

The door closed. Three seconds of shocked silence was broken by Caro's plaintive wail, "He despises me!" as she plunged out of the room.

Harriet and Augusta exchanged looks, the latter remarking, dryly, "Uncle Roland wasn't very nice, was he?"

Nice? Sarah was furious. What callous brute would dismiss his daughter in such a manner? But diplomacy was her ally in desperate circumstances and she managed a dismissive, "Your uncle is probably not feeling quite himself," before she went in search of the distressed Caro.

Sarah's indignation had assumed monumental proportions by the time she finally retired to her poky little bedchamber, after trying to soothe Caro. She'd made some headway, but of course, what gains could she make when they'd barely met?

Mr Hawthorne was a monster. A cold, emotionless brute, completely derelict in the discharge of his paternal responsibilities. The way he'd treated the new governess was little better.

She tore out the pins securing her unflattering topknot with a serious of vicious tugs in line with her righteous anger, then shook out her hair. Mr Hawthorne would change his tune when she was done. In three weeks, as he acknowledged Caro and the miracles his new governess had wrought, he'd be begging her to stay.

Then her anger drained away. Covering her face with her hands, she slumped over the dressing table. It was a terrible thing to impersonate a young woman who'd died. And she was being justly punished.

The candle guttered, sending lonely shadows dancing upon the walls. Everything was hideous, alien. No elegant Argand lamp by which to read the classics or a thrilling romantic novel. No witty conversation, Madeira or tempting delicacy to round off the evening.

Yet this was the way governesses lived and it was her choice to have joined their ranks. Though, frowning, she thought that surely her own series of governesses had been pampered and spoiled. Then she recalled that they had had rooms just like this one and she'd not given a thought as to whether they might wish for surroundings less austere.

No point thinking about what could not be changed, she decided, as she returned to the trunk. There was no maid to tidy up after her and she needed to find a home for the last of the garments littering the floor. Perhaps that impertinent nursery maid had a brood of brothers and sisters and would be glad of them, she thought. She'd rather go naked in a blizzard than suffer the feel of such coarse, ugly material against her skin.

As Sarah pushed the threadbare garments to the bottom of the trunk her hand came into contact with a hard object. A book, by the feel of it. Intrigue quickly turned to scepticism. No point in pulling it out if Sarah Morecroft's taste in reading matter was as deplorable as her style.

But of course curiosity got the better of her and, taking a seat on the bed once more she flipped to the flyleaf and studied the neat, heavily looped writing. Miss Morecroft's diary.

"So how do you find everything?" Once again, there was Ellen's inquisitive little nose poking around the door after the most cursory of knocks. Without waiting for a reply she bustled across the room and settled herself upon the spindly chair beneath the window. Clearly she expected all sorts of confidences Sarah had no intention of sharing, though Sarah conceded in the next moment she might at least learn something of this strange household and her odd employers. Straightening up to sit on the bed and tucking the diary she now couldn't wait to read under her pillow she asked, "When I met Mrs Hawthorne I assumed she was married to the master."

Ellen giggled. "Lord, no! He thinks her the silliest thing under the sun, not but what he's always ever so civil." She grinned, clearly delighted to find herself custodian of knowledge Sarah would want, and need, to know. Tucking a strand of lank brown hair back into her starched white cap, she went on, "Mrs Hawthorne married Mr Hawthorne's older brother, Mr Hector, only he died seven years ago just afore Augusta was born."

"What happened to Mr Hawthorne's wife?"

A cunning look crossed the nursery maid's face. "Died in the same accident as Mr Hector. Mrs Hawthorne's kept house for the master ever since."

Sarah, still discomforted by her meeting with her employer, was intrigued. "So Caro is Mr Hawthorne's only daughter. He seems very hard on her."

"That's because Caro's mother was a trollop!" Clearly, Ellen enjoyed a bit of gossip. "She were running off with dashing Mr Hector when the carriage went off the bridge and they both was drowned. Not that it were the first gentleman she ran off with what wasn't her husband. Anyway, the poor master's terrified Caro might have inherited her mother's loose morals. She didn't inherit her beauty, that's for sure."

Good Lord, poor Mr Hawthorne. Sarah frowned, calculating as she surmised, "He must have married very young."

"Just come into his majority." Hugging herself, Ellen leaned forward. "You ready to hear a tale of dastardly doings?"

Sarah decided not to dignify this with an answer, although she managed an expression that was mildly interested. Fortunately, it did not take much encouragement to set loose the nursery maid's tongue.

"When Caro's mother — Lady Venetia as she was called then — met Mr Hector he were affianced to Mrs Hawthorne. As you can imagine, the mistress were as much a beauty then as she is now." She sniggered. "But she came with a great fortune whereas Lady Venetia was penniless. But so beautiful! You can see her portrait in the gallery."

She sighed, then added matter-of-factly, "Only good thing to say about 'er, really. Anyway, she begged Mr Hector to choose her, instead. Oh, he was tempted, but the money talked louder and he and Mrs Hawthorne were married." Ellen made a moue, parodying the late Lady Venetia's apparent disappointment before continuing, "So poor, spurned Lady Venetia turned her attentions to Mr. Hawthorne, the master, as is, now." Her eyes darted to the door and she lowered her voice. "Word was that Lady Venetia's reputation was ruined with all her carryings-on. And that young Mr Hawthorne's honour — which was a great deal stronger than his brother's — was prevailed upon. Anyway, the poor man was smitten so it didn't matter what she'd done, and besides, he had money enough. A rich inheritance from a doting aunt. So he married her ... to his eternal regret for there never was a less loving or grateful wife."

Sarah hoped she did not appear as intrigued as she was. What a delicious scandal. It was hard to imagine the austere man who'd presented himself just now in the nursery smouldering with passion for a heartless beauty.

"What was she like?"

"She were the vainest creature what ever lived. She ate men for breakfast - leastaways, she did until she met 'er match in the villainous Sir Richard Byrd, only that's another whole story." She sighed, as if hankering after this bygone era. "I could tell you a thing or two about Lady Venetia and this household that would make yer hair stand on end. It were a lot livelier then!"

The magnificent oil painting of the late Lady Venetia, commissioned by Mr Hawthorne as a wedding present, hung near the mullioned windows at the end of the parquet-floored gallery.

Poor Caro, thought Sarah, as she stared up at the proud, fiery eyes that gazed out beneath disdainfully arched brows. Although her eldest charge possessed her mother's fine dark eyes and coal black hair all similarities ended there. The slight upturn of the late mistress's full and sensuous mouth hinted at some private satisfaction while her sumptuous gown and rich jewels indicated a love of finery.

She wondered if Caro's refusal to make any attempt at improving her appearance was simply rebelliousness. Well, she'd soon set the girl straight.

She also wondered if the swell of Lady Venetia's creamy white breasts above her daringly cut evening gown still had the power to move the master when he stopped to admire the likeness of his late wife.

Sarah glanced down at her own awful gown. Last night she had borrowed needle and thread in order to launch a serious attack upon her wardrobe. Instead of dropping hemlines she'd worked hard to increase the deleterious effects of shrinkage and staining. Surely Mrs Hawthorne would remember her offer of cast-off clothes.

"My mother was the most beautiful woman in Dorset," came a cool voice beside her, and Sarah turned to see Caro at her left shoulder staring dispassionately at the portrait. "Hard to believe when you look at me."

Sarah hesitated, sensitive to her adolescent charge's vulnerability. Though she'd always been confident of her own beauty, she still remembered the uncertainties of her adolescent friends and cousins. "There's little resemblance but your eyes are finer."

Caro arched her brows. "False flattery, Miss Morecroft."

"What would you say if I told you I was considered a great beauty where I come from?" countered Sarah. Laughing, she added, "Your silence wounds me. But what if I told you that clothes, the artful application of my favourite Liquid Bloom of Roses and my hair styled *à la Greque*, instead of this unflattering topknot, would make me the toast of the town?"

At Caro's sceptical look Sarah's amusement grew. "Just wait, Miss Hawthorne. When I'm done you'll see that you can be both a beauty and a bluestocking."

Sure enough, Sarah's ploy with a needle and thread worked upon Mrs Hawthorne's conscience, for several days later Sarah returned to her room to find three day dresses and an evening gown upon her bed. Their flounces and furbelows screamed their decrepitude (three seasons ago!) but Sarah was as gifted with a needle in creating wonders as she was in wreaking havoc.

She was gratified by the admiration in young master Cosmo's eyes as he greeted her on the stair the following day.

"Oh, miss, you look lovely," breathed Harriet when Sarah entered the schoolroom; and although Caro said nothing, Sarah, who was watching her closely, registered the surprised widening of her eyes.

"All it needs is the right bonnet," Sarah announced, stooping for the copy of *The Iliad* which lay upon the table. "I thought you girls might like to go into town and help me choose one."

Harriet and Augusta regarded her as if she were mad while Caro actually choked.

"Did your previous governess never take you on shopping expeditions?" Sarah looked up from her task of selecting a passage from the text. She had surprised herself at her desire to devise a curriculum for the girls that was both instructive and entertaining.

"Oh miss, do we have to read that?" groaned Harriet.

Sarah snapped the book shut. "If society decrees that your social success depends upon your being a beauty, my job is to ensure you are at least a well-read one."

"Governesses have not the means to go shopping," Caro pointed out virtuously, raising her head from *The Revd Huckerby's Treatise Against Sin,* ignoring Sarah's last remark. "And Papa would never countenance such frivolity."

"But he *has* countenanced a visit to the circulating library. The carriage is being brought round as we speak. Naturally we'll need refreshment, also. And it would be foolish to walk right by a milliner's if one happened to get in our way - don't you think?"

The younger girls were vociferous in their agreement. And although Caro said nothing, at least she didn't object when Sarah ushered her out of the schoolroom and down the stairs.

FOR THE FIRST TIME SINCE SHE'D SURVIVED THE SHIPWRECK, SARAH was enjoying herself. The fresh spring air, the warmth of the sun on her face as they sauntered through the prosperous little town, was balm to her soul. The visit to the circulating library, however, was cursory as she chivvied Caro to make her selection so they'd have time to do the important chores – such as visit the milliners where Sarah had noticed a very pretty chip bonnet in the window.

"You can't possibly mean to buy that?" Caro gasped when she saw the price.

"Indeed I do," Sarah assured her. "Only I have one more errand. Caro, here's money for currant buns your aunt was generous enough to donate to the occasion. Now I want you to look after your cousins and I'll meet you here in ten minutes. No, you can't come with me."

Shameless she might be, but little girls had a habit of innocently revealing all, and Sarah's visit to the pawnbroker's was not something she wanted Augusta happily divulging to her mother or uncle.

With no regret she handed over her necklace in return for a sum that would keep herself in the luxuries necessary to make the following couple of weeks tolerable.

The next visit was to the apothecary's. Caro might disapprove of her purchases: Royal Tincture of Peach Kernels, Olympian Dew and, of course, the essential Liquid Bloom of Roses. Mr and Mrs Hawthorne *certainly* would.

With these items carefully concealed in brown paper, Sarah gave a sigh of satisfaction and stepped out onto the pavement.

Right into the path of Mr Hawthorne.

"Good morning, sir," she said, endeavouring to maintain her composure and wishing heartily the three girls were in tow. She was upon the point of calling them, pretending they'd disappeared round a corner, and then excusing herself and supposedly dashing after them, when he remarked dryly, "While I am glad you had delicacy enough to shield your charges from a pawnbroker's, might I ask what supervision they currently enjoy?"

"Caro is buying the girls currant buns—" Sarah tried to sound as nonchalant as she could. "I considered ten minutes' absence in the care of their cousin, who, after all, might be married within the twelve-month, safe enough. And of course, as you yourself remarked, I couldn't take them to a pawnbroker's."

"Not a pawnbroker's ... no." He waited, expectantly, the sun at his back throwing his lean, athletic body into relief.

Sarah sighed. "Sir, my clothes have been ruined by salt water. As I had a necklace I was able to pawn I did so in order to make those additions to my wardrobe necessary to do honour to the family which employs me."

Mr Hawthorne looked unimpressed. "Mrs Hawthorne, I believe, generously donated four fine gowns and shawls of her own."

"From three seasons ago," objected Sarah before she could stop herself.

His disapproval was palpable.

Quickly, Sarah continued, "Of course, she *was* very generous but—" she put out her hands, as if exhorting him to concur- "there were the other necessary additions ... like a new bonnet, and slippers. And of course, gloves."

Her defence was not having the desired effect. Mr Hawthorne was positively glowering.

"Miss Morecroft, such frivolity is not countenanced in my household. Your father assured me of your sober temperament. I paid your passage and offered you a home upon the death of your late mother—"

"Oh, Sir!" Sarah caught her breath in what she considered a heartrending manner. Running the back of her hand across her eyes, she darted a surreptitious look from between her fingers. Yes, this was proving a most effective way of quelling his diatribe. She could see his immediate self recrimination was genuine. "You have been kindness itself!" She hiccupped, unable to continue, for her tears were suddenly no longer feigned. She thought of her darling Papa who must be mad with grief. Guilt bubbled up inside her. Nor had she any right to deceive the decent, if somewhat grim, gentleman before her.

But how to extricate herself?

Mr Hawthorne's frown was now one of deep concern. Taking her by the elbow he led her into a narrow alley, away from the curious looks of passers-by.

Sarah stared at her feet, encased in their ugly, serviceable second-hand boots, bit her lip and gave another hiccupping sob.

"Miss Morecroft, I apologize."

Raising her head she was struck anew by his fine grey eyes regarding her with ... compassion? She was even more surprised when he put his hand on her shoulder and said with genuine feeling, "My behaviour was unsympathetic and ungentlemanly."

Her heart gave an unexpected lurch. To cover her awkwardness she managed a brave smile as she said briskly, "You had every right. Please, sir, if I promise never to set foot in another pawnbroker's, may I be forgiven and fetch the girls? I must get them ready for nursery tea."

His normally severe expression softened. The extraordinary transformation only increased Sarah's loss of composure.

"I hope you did not pawn something that was precious to you, Miss Morecroft. I will gladly redeem it. That is, if you do in fact promise to approach me before you consider setting foot in such a place again."

"It was nothing precious, sir." Though her heart was beating quickly Sarah ventured a wicked grin. "Merely a trinket I happened upon during my brief visit to the ocean floor."

· · ·

"THE GIRL IS QUITE UNLIKE GODBY'S DESCRIPTION OF HER." ROLAND scowled at Mrs Hawthorne who was stitching an elaborate pastoral scene that consumed most of her daily hours.

With speed and deftness she worked the needle and coloured threads. Roland often wondered how she could spend so many hours by the fire — in all weathers — when the garden beckoned, beyond.

She picked up a skein of gold and glanced at him. "I believe excessive sea water in the system can unhinge the mind. Her manners are lax. I did warn you, Roland, but hopefully time will reveal a more sober nature."

Roland raked his fingers through his hair as he kicked a burning log further into the fire. "I'm not about to turn her out." He sighed. "I owe her father too much. But when all's said and done I must act in Caro's best interests. I cannot risk her being corrupted by a frivolous and hoydenish young woman."

His scowl deepened as he reflected on their encounter the previous afternoon. Yes, the girl was quite unlike Godby's description of her and Roland was dangerously discomposed. Both by Miss Morecroft, and his response to her.

Mrs Hawthorne clicked her tongue before adding, "Indeed, Caro is in the greatest moral danger ... through no fault of her own." She bent once more over her work and shook her head to emphasize her point.

Not for the first time Roland looked dispassionately at the bobbing ginger corkscrew curls which his brother had so cruelly derided before he'd married Cecily for her money, and wished his sister-in-law could bring herself to feel a little more kindness for his daughter.

"Caro is old enough to eat with us at table," he said abruptly, ignoring Cecily's dire prediction. He didn't want to risk her dredging up the past, yet again. "With her governess. That way we might better observe Miss Morecroft's manners." Picking up a small plaster bust of a cupid wearing a seraphic smile, his frown became even more pained. "If she proves unsuitable we will have to find her another post."

"SIT AT TABLE WITH MY AUNT AND FATHER!" WITH A SHRIEK, CARO

leapt up from the nursery table and threw herself against the window sill, her hands to her face. "Oh, that's worse than anything!"

Sarah's smile faded. "But you'll do them such credit." She stepped forward and put a reassuring hand on the girl's unresponsive shoulder. "I'll teach you how to deport yourself with confidence. We'll turn you into the toast of the town."

"I don't want to be the toast of the town!" Caro sobbed. "I want to be left alone to read my books."

It took two days before Sarah finally persuaded Caro to submit to her cache of beauty aids. Afterwards she cajoled Ellen into helping them both with their hair using tongs, a jug of water laid before the fire, and sugar to set the curls.

Sarah had again been busy with her needle and thread. The little girls had been her willing assistants, happily parroting French conjugations as they handed her the various coloured threads and other tools she needed.

Now it was the day of reckoning and she was ready. As the dinner gong reverberated through the house Sarah allowed herself a moment of self-congratulation. Then she hastened Caro to her own room to look in the tarnished mirror which rested on the chest of drawers.

"A credit to your father, don't you think?" Her eyes raked her young protégé with pride.

Caro's dull cheeks had been enlivened with a discreet touch of Liquid Bloom of Roses. Her best dress, once a utilitarian and modest gown of Pomona Green velvet, had been remodelled to resemble something in the first stare.

Sarah's heart leapt with anticipation. She could not wait to present her handiwork and earn her employers' admiration.

"Are you ready, Caro?" she asked, and was gratified by the spark of wonder in the young girl's eyes as she continued to stare at her reflection.

"I don't look anything like myself," she whispered, her tone indicating this was a good thing.

"You look beautiful," Sarah said, and meant it. "Just don't spoil it with poor posture. You need to make your entrance with pride and dignity." She gave the girl's arm a quick squeeze. "Just you wait, your father will be overcome!"

As Sarah had anticipated, amazed silence greeted their entrance. She smiled demurely at her employers as she sank into her seat. Lowering her eyes to her plate she waited for the praise.

Silence.

Clearly, they were lost for words. She had obviously excelled at her self-appointed task of transforming Caro into a vision of loveliness.

Only as the silence lengthened did she feel the first stirrings of doubt. She raised her head to glance, first to her left, where Caro was cringing with unconcealed embarrassment, not daring to look at anyone, then to the head of the table where Mr Hawthorne sat.

Her heart missed a beat, then uncertainty turned to anger. What father would look at his daughter with such undisguised recrimination? As if it were a crime for a woman to try and improve herself.

But it was Mrs Hawthorne, clutching her scrawny throat, who shrieked, "Have you been using complexion enhancers, Caro?"

The direct accusation stirred Caro to retaliation. Her cheeks took on a feverish hue. "Do you mean like Mother?" she ground out. "Yes, I found them once in her dressing table drawer and decided to use them tonight." She took an unsteady breath. "I did not realize Mother was considered *such* a harlot!"

Shocked silence greeted her outburst.

Caro gave a choking sob as she added, "Forgive me, Father, for *daring* to remind you of her."

Sarah bit her lip, watching Caro confront her aunt and father. Both looked increasingly concerned as Caro, now in full swing, went on, "Poor Mother, it's a good thing she's not alive to see what a hideous creature she brought into the world. But then, how much easier it will be to eschew the vices and wickedness which brought her down. I recall you saying something along these lines, once, Aunt Cecily."

Mrs Hawthorne turned puce. "Really, Caro, I don't recall ever—"

But it was Sarah who finally took charge, saying brightly — despite having to quell her own trembling — "I read in the news sheet that the Prince Regent's banquet for more than a hundred guests at Carlton House is the talk of the town."

Hopefully that would deflect attention from Caro who appeared on the verge of a breakdown. Caro's fears and insecurities must have been feeding on gossip for years. Sympathy washed over Sarah. Outrage, too.

She took a spoonful of lobster soup. "Delicious," she pronounced.

When there was no response she glanced up again. Why was everyone staring at her as if she had somehow scandalized them as much as Caro had? Caro was glancing at her nervously. Mrs Hawthorne, even more puce now, was looking as if she'd like to turn Sarah into a lobster and then into soup. And Mr Hawthorne was regarding her as if she had already turned into, if not a lobster, then certainly something very much resembling a spiky, hideous crustacean. At least Cosmo was gazing at her with undisguised admiration. That was some solace.

Sarah raised her chin. "Sir, do you not believe Caro's appearance tonight vastly improved? It will increase her confidence and, in turn, her chances."

A succession of emotions seemed to flit across her employer's face. His slate grey eyes, seemingly darker, settled disapprovingly on her bare arms before he fixed her with a cold level stare. "Clearly, Miss Morecroft, you had eyes only for the description of the Gothic Chapel in which the Royal Entourage dined; of the fifty-six haunches of venison, ninety-three brace of pheasant and two dozen turtles that were devoured. You were unmoved, it would appear, by the news sheet's report on what I suspect you'd consider a fairly minor occurrence at St Peter's Fields in Manchester."

Sarah stared at him.

"An orderly meeting of fifty thousand people wished for an audience to hear their grievances. Like the high cost of bread. The average labourer breaks his back so his landlord can dine on *Le jambon à la Broche* and truffles, yet his wage cannot support his family." His expression became thunderous. "Then the cavalry moved in. Eleven people were killed, and more than four hundred injured. Should we countenance such things in civilized society? Are you teaching my daughter respect for worthy values, or filling her head with frivolous nonsense?"

Sarah was lost for words. She had heard her father rant and rave on such topics. Only he came from the opposing side.

Carefully, Mr Hawthorne pushed together his knife and fork. "Miss Morecroft—" his glittering eyes lanced her with scorn - "I would like to see you in my study after dinner."

SARAH'S PREPARED SPEECH, SHE BELIEVED, INCORPORATED A FINE balance of contrition with just a dusting of flirtation. Yes, she took her role as governess seriously but while she sympathized with the families of the dead there was a place for frivolity. She was quite happy to agree that if she knew what the cost of bread was, it was undoubtedly too high.

By the time she had finished Mr Hawthorne would be begging her pardon for having maligned and misjudged her.

But reflecting on the scorn and anger in his turbulent grey eyes unsettled her in a way that was entirely alien.

CHAPTER 3

What was he to do about the girl? Roland paced before the fire which warmed his study. His sanctuary. The only room in the house where he was safe from Cecily and the silly, chattering acquaintances she liked to entertain.

Yet he did not feel at peace.

He drew back the curtains and stared out into the starlit night. As cold and black as his soul.

The girl was not at all what he had been led to believe.

But what was worse than her apparent preoccupation with life's worldly pleasures was her resemblance to her father. To his old schoolboy companion and foster brother, Godby Morecroft. Oh, not in features but certainly in character.

The way her eyes glittered with challenge in that beautiful face of hers when she was gainsaid. The mutinous set of her rosebud mouth when she was waiting to put across her opposing point of view. Why, it was Godby all over again.

He did not turn immediately as he heard her enter. He knew only too well the look she would level at him. He could almost hear Godby's voice: smooth, cajoling with a hint of humour intended to ameliorate his anger.

He would not allow her the chance to speak first in order to defend herself. Somehow Godby had always managed to make him feel a killjoy Puritan when he had as much desire to enjoy life as anyone. Just not as thoughtlessly as Godby.

"My daughter is not to have her head turned by foolish fancies." He came directly to the point, waving Miss Morecroft to a chair while he returned to stand in front of the fire.

If she would just bow her head and show a little contrition it would be a good start, Roland thought. *Don't be like Godby who could never admit he was wrong.*

"Foolish fancies?" Her smile was guileless. She was confident, no doubt, that she was incapable of doing wrong. Just like her father.

His heart hardened.

How different from when she had landed on his doorstep, penniless, orphaned. Nearly a victim of the high seas. At the time it had seemed she'd not even good looks to recommend her.

But then some extraordinary metamorphosis had occurred. Within the space of a few days Miss Morecroft had been transformed; like a water rat she had emerged, sleek and jaunty and ripe for anything.

"Sir, your daughter is in little danger of having her head turned. All she thinks about is improving her mind."

Her gaze was steady, her bearing composed — very different from the way he felt. He tried to retain his dignity as she stared at him from the depths of her leather armchair.

"Caro," he managed to say, evenly, "is not a beauty and you will only make her look a fool by trying to turn her into one."

"With respect, sir, the sad truth is that a woman's face is, more often than not, her fortune."

Until now — well, recently — Roland had not appreciated what a fine face Miss Morecroft possessed. Her eyes were amazing, glowing bright with life and humour; her cheek bones were well defined, her chin slightly pointed so that her face appeared heart-shaped when combined with the effect of her coiffure: a fashionable 'V' parting with cascades of shining ringlets tumbling from the band which secured them at the top of her head. And her dress. He frowned. Cecily's gown, he remembered it, now. A drab, russet confection once adorned with too many frills and furbelows. What a transformation. This girl had obviously worked wonders with her needle and thread. She would have got on famously with Venetia.

Venetia ... and Godby.

His heart turned to stone. However persuasive Miss Morecroft's argument, his armour was back in place.

Oh dear, thought Sarah, this man really was a Puritan. The moment she even mentioned 'worldly pleasures' he seemed to tense. And the way he spoke of his daughter made her blood boil! But she went on blithely, "I have always believed confidence and wit among one's greatest assets. If Caro is to be presented next year she'll be competing with a great many beautiful and accomplished young ladies."

Now why was he looking at her like that? Sarah wondered indignantly. Had she dropped sauce upon her dress?

Instantly she saw him colour and his eyes return to her face where they were now fixed, grimly. She stifled the impulse to smile. Oh ho, so the master did appreciate a pretty face and figure. Only right now he was doing his best to fight it.

The observation gave her confidence.

Yes, Sarah had learned a thing or two about men since storming her way out of the schoolroom as a precocious fifteen-year-old to play hostess at her father's parliamentary dinners after her mother had died.

Mr Hawthorne, however, was unlike any of the men her father entertained. Dangerous radicals like Roland Hawthorne did not receive invitations from Lord Miles.

Yet he hardly looked the threat to law and order, as her father would have maintained. Larchfield, with its exquisite grounds and works or art was a testament to refinement.

Mr Hawthorne, himself, was a fine specimen of civilized manhood, far more to her taste than the pleasure-seeking rakes and popinjays her father entertained and who regularly made up to her. Well, as much as she would allow them. She quickly tired of their vanity and pomposity, although she'd pretended to encourage it. It was, after all, what was expected.

She flashed him another smile and was surprised and gratified by his brief awkwardness.

Clearly, there was more to her employer than met the eye. How intriguing. If this was a man who could smoulder with passion for a heartless beauty seven years ago, thought Sarah, she would be more than interested to find out what excited his passions now that he had apparently adopted a more sober outlook on life.

She bowed her head. "I accept your censure, sir. I will not turn Caro's head with foolish nonsense. And I shall read the news sheets, for I must admit, I had in fact been reading some gossip column whose talk of the Carlton House Set I had thought might divert the girls—" she stopped, adding ingeniously as she interpreted his glowering look — "with examples of deplorable behaviour to be condemned."

Mr Hawthorne seemed to struggle for words.

"Miss Morecroft," he said finally, "you are here to instruct the girls in simple arithmetic, spelling, French and drawing. Not to provide moral guidance. That," he added, crisply, "is something you can leave to me."

He nodded in dismissal.

Sarah hesitated, about to cast one of those seductive lures which came naturally and which had successfully hooked many an admirer in the past.

No. Coquetry was not going to win over Mr. Hawthorne despite experience showing her men liked their women beautiful and vacuous. She paused, turning, her hand on the door knob. He nodded stiffly, his eyes nevertheless lingering upon her.

Her heart gave an unexpected little skip. She couldn't remember when she had last felt such anticipation.

CHAPTER 4

"SHE'S A MEAN old cat and I'm not going down."

"Yes you are." Sarah bared her teeth in what she'd intended to be a saccharine smile. "Now, shoulders back and get rid of that scowl." She took Caro's arm and propelled her to the nursery door. "Whoever conjugates the 'to be' verb first can have my portion of suet pudding," Sarah said to the younger girls. "Just think, Caro," she added, as they descended the stairs in answer to Lady Charlotte's summons, "in six months you'll be dining on caviar and champagne instead of suet and roly poly pudding."

The notion failed to rally Caro. Glumly, she said, "It's Papa's idea I be presented."

"Surely you want to reflect well upon him?" With a sigh that wasn't devoid of affection, Sarah tucked an errant curl behind Caro's ear as they reached the drawing room door.

Lady Charlotte was a fascinating creature whose like Sarah had not met. With an acerbic wit and political leanings in sympathy with Mr Hawthorne's, her view of the world was a revelation. No sooner had Sarah and Caro seated themselves than they were regaled with a scathing oratory on the heavy-handed tactics used to quell the Peterloo Massacre, as Lady Charlotte referred to it. Sarah suspected her father would have advocated that the cavalry move in to break up the 'rabble-rousing crowd', muskets blazing.

Now well into middle age, Lady Charlotte had bone structure and a porcelain complexion that would see her a beauty at eighty. Once she had finished her diatribe she relaxed into her blue chintz seat and, with a sharp look at Sarah, observed, "You favour your father, Miss Morecroft. Do you not think so, Cecily?"

"In manner, there is a strong resemblance," replied Mrs Hawthorne with a disapproving twist to her thin mouth.

"Then we must hope you don't follow the same dangerous path—" Lady Charlotte looked grim as she added - "and that you appreciate gratitude better than your father." She sighed. "How thoughtless of Godby to foist a brood of brats upon your poor mother on nothing more than soldier's pay. Still, he had no one else to blame for losing out on the fine inheritance he'd been expecting." She shook her head at Sarah. "I daresay your father could do no wrong in your eyes."

So that was the story, thought Sarah. Or, at least, part of it. "He was my inspiration," she murmured, determined not to be cowed by Lady Charlotte's bully tactics. Not a page of the first half of Sarah Morecroft's diary was without some glowing reference to the apparently incomparable Godby Morecroft. The diary also did not seem to contain much else of interest, which was why Sarah had left most of it unread.

"Not, I trust, the kind of inspiration that leads to similar disgrace and penury." Mrs Hawthorne's tone was sharp.

Sarah realised her error. Clearly, she needed to learn more about the relationship between the late Godby Morecroft and her employer if she were not to land herself in worse trouble.

When Mrs Hawthorne excused herself to attend to some domestic matter Sarah tried a more subservient approach. She glanced at Caro. The girl seemed immersed in her own thoughts. "Pray, Lady Charlotte, my mother made it clear what a great debt we owe Mr. Hawthorne and yet—" she bit her lip — "how am I to avoid my father's mistakes if I don't know precisely what they are?"

"Good Lord! Your father said *nothing* of his disgrace?"

Sarah shook her head.

Lady Charlotte adjusted her lorgnette. She looked undecided. After a quick glance at Caro, still daydreaming, she said, "You know that your father's advancement was on account of the especial fondness old Mr Hawthorne — Roland's father — had for him. Of course you do. Well, better get it over with before Cecily gets back. If there are two things that require us all dashing for the burnt feathers it's mention of —" she lowered her voice — "Caro's mother." Resuming a more normal tone, she went on, "Your father was the son of old Mr Hawthorne's estate manager and even from the age of eight, which was when old Mr Hawthorne first took an interest in him, he was a charmer. He and Mr Hector were the same age and great friends. Cut from the same cloth, too," she added, disapprovingly, "unlike the present Mr Hawthorne who was born three years later. Your father's destiny was the local dame school and perhaps an apprenticeship had not old Mr Hawthorne decided such a gifted lad ought to be tutored with his own sons and then bought a commission in the 10th Hussars. If you don't know what a pretty price a pair of colours that would have set him back it's not my place to tell you! It was commanded by the Prince himself, for nothing but the best would do for your father, but it was his eye for the ladies that was his undoing."

Sarah was fascinated. What a marvellous story. What could the rakish Godby Morecroft have done to have landed up in apparent ignominy, in India?

"Your mother was a comely lass of seventeen, and your father barely a year older when she ... er... caught his fancy. A publican's daughter! Of course, he could have done a great deal better for himself but honour prevailed, or rather, old Mr Hawthorne's honour did, and your parents were married ... in fairly timely fashion for shortly afterwards you were born."

Sarah blushed. "So that's why my father was disgraced."

"Indeed not!" exclaimed Lady Charlotte. "I can't image to what purpose you've been shielded from all these ... tawdry details, though I suppose Godby left it too late to tell you, as usual," she added, with what Sarah considered great lack of feeling. "Well, old Mr Hawthorne was far more generous to the newlyweds than your father deserved—

Ah, Roland." Lady Charlotte's cornflower blue eyes widened almost coquettishly.

Not so long ago just such a smile would have come naturally to Sarah, but now she was tongue-tied, and her heart was skipping a little too fast for her liking.

"Ladies." Mr Hawthorne acknowledged them with a small incline of his head, standing aside as Cecily re-entered the room.

"Sit down, Roland," commanded Lady Charlotte, "and tell me what else you know about these barbarians. I'm all for one knowing one's place but I do believe in an honest wage for honest toil."

A shadow crossed Mr Hawthorne's face. Glancing at Sarah he hesitated, almost as if he was of a mind to plead his excuses and retire. When he took the only vacant seat just a foot from her she was conscious of his nearness in a way she hadn't been since as a debutante she'd fallen in love with Captain Danvers at first sight.

Unaccountably awkward, Sarah glanced away as Lady Charlotte launched into an animated monologue on the likely outcome facing the ringleaders of the uprising. She hoped her high colour, if noticed, would be attributed to the heat of the fire.

Mr Hawthorne, dark and brooding, was the antithesis of her lost love whose Roman nose and blonde curling hair had fired her adolescent senses.

Within weeks of gushing to James all those years ago that Captain Danvers was the only man she'd consider marrying, she was mourning his death and declaring her intention never to wed. She recalled, with painful affection, James's endless patience during her grief. Poor James. He'd be beside himself, thinking her dead right now. What was worse, he'd be so terribly wounded if the truth came out that she'd actually pretended to have drowned to avoid marrying him. Her plan was simply to turn up on her father's doorstep in a couple of weeks claiming to have been washed up on a beach and cared for by local villagers. Her grief-stricken father would grant her anything, then.

"Isn't that so, Miss Morecroft?"

She jerked her head round at the sound of Mr Hawthorne's mellifluous tones and stammered her apologies.

He regarded her a moment, smiled, then repeated, "I was telling

Lady Charlotte of your admirable approach to teaching Caro values and restraint."

Lady Charlotte, looking dubious, responded, "I'm not sure the gossip sheets are something Caro should even know about, but if you condone it, Roland, I daresay there are moral lessons to be learnt if approached in the right manner." The way she was looking at Sarah suggested a healthy scepticism about Godby's daughter having any handle on morality.

Sarah looked past her and caught the glint of amusement in Mr Hawthorne's eye. Her heart did a little somersault. She smiled back. The air felt suddenly charged between them, despite Lady Charlotte's and Mrs Hawthorne's presence. The darkening of Mr Hawthorne's pupils revealed he felt the same. Sarah had not spent the last six years encouraging or warding off the approaches of potential suitors without learning to recognize the signs of a male's interest.

Then it struck her anew that it was just as likely that, even if Mr Hawthorne was flirting, he believed he was doing so with the mere governess; that likely he was simply making atonement for his harsh words of earlier. It was a dampening thought. Squaring her shoulders Sarah rose to the challenge. When the time was right she'd face Mr Hawthorne on equal ground.

"So there you have it, Caro," she said, as they passed through the nursery on their way to Caro's bedchamber. Ellen was putting the younger girls to bed. "I am the product of vice and sin, the grand-daughter of a lowly publican. No wonder I was only reluctantly elevated to the dining room."

"Don't say such things," Caro muttered. "My father believes people are distinguished by their actions, not by their rank. Lady Charlotte should never have said such things!"

"Your father faces a tough battle if he thinks the baker's apprentice and the fishmonger worthy of a seat in the House of Commons." She lit the candle on the bedside table. A very different code of morality existed in the circles in which she had grown up. Rank was everything. As for morality, Sarah knew many of the aristocratic matrons who visited her home at Thistlewaite were guiltlessly indulging in extramarital affairs having dutifully produced the required male heir.

"My father is not a radical," Caro said angrily, pulling on her night rail. "Nor does he believe in turning rank on its head. He is a good, honourable man who hates the inequities of society. At least he has the courage of his convictions. He fought a duel for them once."

Sarah raised her eyebrows. "Over your mother?" she ventured, ingenuously, helping Caro into bed. She'd like to hear more about the fascinating Venetia.

"My father would *never* fight a duel over a woman." Caro's voice was full of scorn. "He is far too principled to commit murder over something so ... unimportant."

"Yet not too principled to fight a duel over something else." This time it was Sarah's turn to sound scornful.

"Obviously you care nothing for the people to whom Papa has devoted his parliamentary career championing," said Caro through gritted teeth as she reached for her book. "You're lucky you're not a man, Miss Morecroft. It was an argument just like this that Papa had once in the House of Commons. Lord Miles challenged Papa to the duel right there and then."

One minute Sarah was directing an indulgent, slightly mocking smile at Caro, the next she was wincing at the sudden roar in her ears. For a moment she truly thought she was going to faint. She sat heavily upon the bed.

Caro didn't notice. She was too busy thumbing the pages of her book with unusual energy, a snarl upon her face. "Narrow-minded bigot! That's what Papa called him, and said it demeaned him to have to answer his challenge."

Blinking rapidly to clear her head, Sarah murmured, "I never heard about it." She gazed at the brushes and combs lined up on the dressing table.

Her own father! Fighting a duel with Mr Hawthorne. She tried to imagine it. Her red-faced, apoplectic father, trembling with the passion of his convictions, seeing nothing but a dangerous radical as he stared down his opponent.

No doubt Mr Hawthorne coolly stood his ground. Compared with her father he was a *very* controlled man.

"It was lucky they both didn't have to resign from Parliament," said

Caro, "because of course he thought it was ridiculous that honour decreed he must fight."

"What happened?"

"Papa shot wide and Lord Miles missed. Well, he grazed Papa's shoulder but it was only a flesh wound." Caro shuddered. "Why drive a man to murder for pride?" She hugged her book to her chest, rolled over and presented Sarah with her back.

Sarah did not leave, as Caro had clearly indicated was her desire. Instead, she rose and went to the window.

"It's called passion," she murmured, drawing aside the curtain to look into the darkness. "Sixteen-year-old girls are not supposed to know about such dangerous emotions."

Her voice trailed away as she contemplated if she had ever felt passion.

"I'll never fall victim to my passions," mumbled Caro.

Sarah quirked an eyebrow at the huddled bedclothes then returned her gaze to the darkness beyond the gardens. Not even a sliver of moon touched the landscape with light. "Really?" Her tone was droll. She sighed. Such talk made her restless. She wanted to feel desire but it was as if in this household love, desire, passion ... had destroyed the trust of a generation. Passion at Larchfield was the handmaiden of sin and vice. If Caro were lucky enough to experience the same spark of feeling which Sarah found so necessary to sustain her enthusiasm for life, she'd be forced to extinguish it long before it took root and blossomed.

"Do you not wish to fall in love, Caro?" she asked. "Is it not the desire of your aunt and father that you marry a good man? That you marry for love?"

Caro said nothing.

Sarah sighed again, the girl's pubescent virtue suddenly irritating her. Caro would be dried up by nineteen.

She turned back to the window. "Do you not long for the embrace of the man whom you admire beyond all others? The caress of his hand upon your cheek...?" Her voice dropped to a whisper as she added, "The sweet, gentle touch of his lips upon yours."

Turning at the loud thud of the book thrown forcefully upon the floor Sarah realised she'd gone too far.

It was time to apologise and take herself off to bed before she reversed all the gains she'd made with her difficult, but increasingly endearing charge.

CHAPTER 5

As Roland turned into the gallery, he was arrested by the odd sight of his sister-in-law on her toes upon the window seat, peering through the mullioned windows.

She swung round, red-faced — with anger not embarrassment — at the sound of his footstep. "If Harriet's new dress is ruined I want Miss Morecroft dismissed upon the spot."

Roland put out his hand to help Cecily to the ground. "I wonder if their expedition will be as successful as last time?" His tone was mild. "Harriet and August tell me they captured a dozen inmates for their new worm farm."

Cecily glared at him. "I do not share your amusement, Roland. Miss Morecroft is impulsive and wayward and as such, highly unsatisfactory."

Unsatisfactory? With an effort Roland kept his expression neutral as an image of Miss Morecroft's lovely face, eyes dancing with merriment, mouth trembling with barely suppressed laughter, appeared before him.

Steeling himself against the extraordinary and dangerous yearning to possess that which he knew could only bring heartache, he asked through gritted teeth, "How could I refuse Godby's wife?"

Cecily stamped her foot. "What Godby did to you, not to mention to his men in battle can never be forgiven. His daughter is cut from the same cloth, Roland. Do you see the way she courts attention? It's a good thing Cosmo's returning to his own home-"

"Miss Morecroft may not be as docile as her mother led us to believe, but she is capable and the girls are fond of her."

Cecily glanced over Roland's shoulder at Venetia's portrait and her eyes narrowed. "Surely you are not suggesting Caro model herself on Venetia!"

Roland turned away from the venom in her eyes, even though he acknowledged the many good reasons Cecily had to despise his late wife. "I am suggesting nothing of the sort." Though his response was mild he could feel the blood pumping through his veins, under great pressure. Normally he avoided Venetia's name, but now he felt it was pertinent.

Striving to keep his growing anger in check, he went on, "However Venetia was her mother. I believe Caro tries too hard to be everything Venetia was not."

"Of course Caro must endeavour to be everything Venetia was not!" Cecily flared. "And if you think I am responsible for the whispers, you are wrong."

Roland looked at her steadily. Her face was red, knots of anger protruding from her scrawny neck. Anger had been his first impulse, too. Now he merely felt sorry for Cecily. How cruel of his brother to have made no secret of his enduring love for Venetia, while happy to take Cecily's money. Hector and Venetia should have married. They'd have made each other miserable very quickly instead of drawing the rest of them into it ... the survivors who had to keep living with the memories.

"I have always admired your discretion, Cecily. It is the servants who are not so reliable." He seated himself on the window seat and beckoned to his ugly, red-faced, trembling sister-in-law who was not a bad woman by nature, but who had never got over being so ill-used. He sympathised. It was hard to live with the betrayal of the only person one has ever loved. How much worse, though, to be a woman, seeing oneself age with little, if any, prospect of love on the horizon to ameliorate the damage of the past.

She sat, and he took Cecily's clasped hands between his. "I have long suspected that Caro has been aware of the whispers."

Cecily jerked her head up. "You must refute them. Deny everything!"

With a sigh, Roland dropped her hands, and rose. Changing the subject, he said, "You will, of course, launch Caro next season. I trust it's not an imposition for I realize I am sometimes guilty of taking your good offices for granted. Perhaps you might enjoy a little enforced gaiety." He managed a smile.

Cecily was in no mood to respond with similar good humour. "I consider it a duty I am happy to discharge, Roland," she said through pursed lips. "Hardly a pleasure! Ugly old women like me are fools if they deck themselves out in frills and furbelows to seek out pleasure."

"Good," said Roland, ignoring her last remark. "In the meantime I thought a little practice in advance of Caro's come-out would be in order. I plan to hold a small ball at Larchfield for Caro's seventeenth birthday next month. Just twenty or so people from the neighbourhood. Caro will, of course, hate the idea but I think Miss Morecroft might be just the person to bring her round."

Seeing her stiffen, he tried a final approach. "Come now, Cecily," he cajoled. "With your deft touches and skill at organization the evening is sure to be a success."

"IT'LL BE A DISASTER!" WAILED CARO, TWISTING HER HANDKERCHIEF around her fingers and looking at Sarah as if for corroboration.

Unmoved, Sarah bent over Harriet's shoulder to correct her French translation. Caro, opposite her, gripped the back of Augusta's chair as she fixed Sarah with a tragic look.

"The evening will be a disaster, or you will be?" Sarah enquired, gently, not looking up.

With a huff Caro began pacing around the table. "Both," she said, finally. "I will be a disaster and so bring great shame and embarrassment to Papa."

BEVERLEY EIKLI & BEVERLEY OAKLEY

"Oh, so you do recognize the correlation," said Sarah, as if discussing a lesson in logic. "I'm glad, Caro. It's time you learned that how you deport yourself reflects upon those who reared you. If you behave charmingly your father's guests will go home saying, 'How fortunate Mr Hawthorne is to have a daughter with such pleasing manners. What a credit she is to him'."

Caro was not such a fool she could not recognize the sarcasm in her governess's tone. But when Sarah looked up she was taken aback by the anger in the young girl's eyes.

"You understand nothing!" Caro hissed. She thrust herself across the table to glare at her governess. Harriet and Augusta looked up in alarm. "No, nothing!"

Sarah eyed her with concern. "Calm yourself, Caro," she soothed. She did not fancy another hysterical outburst with consequences worse than last time.

"Do you think I'm insensible to every nuance of my voice?" demanded Caro. "Or that I am not afraid every time I smile that I might be creating the wrong impression? If I smile 'charmingly' as you put it, how is that different to the enticing way my mother smiled? She used her 'pretty manners' and enhanced her beauty to enslave men. Do you think I wish to be called a harlot, too?"

Sarah did not interrupt. Her heart went out to the girl.

"This birthday ball of mine-" Caro put a hand to her temple and closed her eyes briefly. "I shall feel like an-an animal in the zoo. Everyone will be watching me, studying me, making comparisons. They won't come with the object of helping Mr Hawthorne celebrate his daughter's birthday. They'll be there to see if his daughter is as beautiful as her mother, as flirtatious as her mother, as gay and lively and ... and likely to be as immoral as her mother."

She sank down upon the paint-chipped nursery chair and covered her face with her hands. Sarah stifled the urge to go to her. A brisker approach, she decided, was safer.

"You've made some interesting observations, Caro, and with your permission I should like to conduct an experiment." She smiled from across the table, her tone matter-of-fact. "I have an aptitude for charades and amateur theatricals, I am told, which will enable me to show you how to create any impression you want."

Caro looked at Sarah as if she were speaking nonsense.

"But the experiment is to be conducted in the evening, when your aunt and father are out visiting. I believe they are to play cards with Colonel Doncaster and his wife tomorrow night?"

"What do you want me to do?" Caro sounded suspicious.

"Oh, *you* don't have to do anything, except observe and" - Sarah crinkled her brow - "supply me with one of your mother's old dresses." She gave a satisfied smile at Caro's look of horror. "One of her most alluring."

DESPITE CARO'S APPARENT RELUCTANCE, THE GIRL'S CURIOSITY clearly overrode her aversion to looking through the scandalous, diaphanous wisps of fabric that had once clothed her mother. A sense of devilry obviously made her select the most scandalous, diaphanous of them all.

Sarah was still wearing her own evening gown when Caro came to her tiny bedchamber while Ellen put the girls to bed. The garment had been bequeathed to her by Mrs Hawthorne but Sarah had transformed it into an eye-catching sheath of peony-red *gros de Naples* with three rows of gold trimming around the hem. She'd noticed Mrs Hawthorne's gimlet eye stray towards the creation throughout the evening. Mr Hawthorne's ill-concealed admiration had, however, been more gratifying, even though he'd addressed her with the same studied coolness.

"Wait for me in the drawing room," instructed Sarah, relieving Caro of her mother's evening gown.

"Why can't we go down together?"

"Because I am the one issuing instructions and it's my desire that you take a seat by the fire and pretend you are simply a guest. I shall come down in one guise, take my seat at the piano, and pretend to entertain my audience. Remember, you are merely to observe. I shall then leave, and return, as another person-"

"You mean my mother."

"It doesn't matter. Perhaps I will pretend I am Lady Venetia, or perhaps I will pretend I am Caro who is pretending to be her mother. You will know, believe me. Just do as I say, Caro."

She leapt into action the moment Caro had closed the door. Out of her trunk she pulled the real Sarah Morecroft's most hideous garment and, with satisfaction, struggled into the drab grey merino gown with its ill-made trimmings. She then rearranged her hair to fall in two unflattering loops over the sides of her face and topped it with a poorly sewn toque adorned with a sadly drooping feather.

Regarding herself with satisfaction she proceeded down the stairs. At the door to the drawing room she turned her attention to her posture. With shoulders slumped, neck thrust out, eyes darting suspiciously from side to side, she made her way to the piano.

Executing a clumsy, self conscious curtsy as if she were about to perform before a small audience, Sarah's voice was a flat monotone as she muttered in Caro's general direction, "I shall play *Hey, Betty Martin*". Placing the music onto the stand, she dropped ungracefully onto the piano seat and began to play, haltingly. The music's lack of feeling was matched by Sarah's unemotional rendering of the words.

Once Caro's dutiful clapping at the end of the piece had died away, Sarah rose. Staring over Caro's shoulder into the middle distance, she collected the music sheets, shuffled them nervously, then muttered an incoherent thank-you before exiting the room.

She took the stairs two at a time. A few minutes would be needed to transform herself though she did not want to take too long about it.

"Ellen," she called in a loud whisper as she passed the nursery, and was glad the girls had obviously gone to sleep so that Ellen was free to assist her.

The nursery maid's face was a picture of horror as she stared at the barely decent dress Sarah held out to her.

"Quickly, help me put it on," Sarah ordered, as she pulled off the grey merino and stood in only her chemise and short stays.

"Lordy, what are you doing?" Ellen squeaked. "You'll lose yer job! That dress don't belong to you!"

"The master's out. This is for Caro's benefit," Sarah explained. "I'm showing her the difference confidence and poise can make. And don't look at me like that. I charged Caro with the task of finding me something suitable of her mother's, and this is what she selected. Now quickly!"

The dress fitted like a glove, once Sarah had removed her chemise in order for it to hang properly. Then, on an impulse of pure wickedness, she dashed water from her pewter jug onto the garment and began to smooth it through the folds. Admiring herself in the full-length cheval mirror she had purloined from Caro she was gratified by the seductive effect created as the diaphanous garment clung to her limbs.

"Dear Lord," whispered Ellen, stepping back after she had hastily worked Sarah's hair into an attractive topknot of tumbling curls, "I'm right glad the master's out. He'd drop dead at the sight of you. Reckon it's the dress m'lady wore the night everything blew up with Sir Richard."

"Who is Sir Richard?" Sarah had heard his name before.

"Another of m'lady's lovers, only he were the worst." Ellen looked more scared than eager to impart gossip. "She met her match, alright. He were a true villain. Gave her a pearl necklace wot cost more 'n diamonds so's she'd run off with him, only she soon came back, she were that scared."

"Good Heavens. How many lovers did Caro's mother have?" Sarah adjusted a curl.

"Well, there were Mr Hector and of course-" Ellen shot Sarah a quick look, hesitated, then added, "and ... Sir Richard. So I s'pose that ain't too bad." She bit her lip. "Just don't let the master see you, for it *were* the dress m'lady wore when she came back a week later and Mr Hawthorne had to fight Sir Richard."

"Mr Hawthorne seems to be in the habit of duelling," Sarah remarked, her tone dry though her heart beat loudly.

"Reckon this was the only one. Only lover, I mean. He's a good shot, the master."

"What happened?"

"He winged Sir Richard. After that, the fellow was exiled for debts."

Sarah hurried down the stairs to the large, lovely drawing room where Caro waited patiently. The longer she spent at Larchfield, the more intrigued she became. Poor Caro. Even running a comb through her hair must fill the girl with doubt as to whether she was doing it to court admiration, or simply to get the knots out.

Well, this was a great lesson in demonstrating the vast middle ground between being a self conscious dormouse and a raging coquette — and it was fun!

Confidently she threw open the door, boldly meeting Caro's eyes above her ivory fan. Oh, she knew how to use her eyes to great effect, and she did so now, playing to her young charge as if Caro were the most handsome, gallant gentleman in a room crowded with them.

"Since you have asked me so charmingly to play for you, sir, how can I refuse?" she asked, inclining her head coquettishly and sweeping Caro a smouldering look from beneath downcast lashes. "*Any* requests from such a handsome gentleman, will be happily acceded to."

Caro's eyes widened at the double entendre though she stammered, obligingly, "Perhaps, Miss, you would regale the company with *Over Yonder Mountain?*"

Sarah affected a show of false modesty. "Oh, but you will think my singing very poor after what you have already heard this evening." With a dazzling smile she took a deep breath so that the swell of her breasts could not fail to be admired above the line of her low cut evening dress. "However, if you insist." Sarah sank gracefully onto the piano stool and began to sing in tune to the emotional music.

Everything this evening had been play acting. But this, her singing, was real, and her voice was exquisite. She knew men found her attractive, but the many sincere compliments she'd received on her voice were even more gratifying. She adored music. Until now, she hadn't realised how much she'd missed it in this sad, songless house.

Soon Caro, who Sarah knew worked hard to maintain a cynical exterior, was dashing tears away.

The strains of the last chord drifted into nothing but Caro did not applaud; just stared at her governess with wonder while Sarah was filled with a sudden sadness for the home she had left behind, and the lovable, tyrannical father who would probably be out of his mind with grief.

Footsteps sounded from beyond the open French doors that led onto the terrace behind her. Alarmed, Sarah half turned, then rose and stepped out from behind the piano stool.

The footsteps stopped. There was silence. Mr Hawthorne stood on the threshold to the garden, his face blanched by moonlight. He looked as if he'd seen a ghost.

Sarah's hand went to her breast, as if to still her thundering heart. Her mouth went dry.

Passionless? Had she once thought this man passionless?

The seconds became an agony of eternity as she waited for him to come to her. She watched the play of emotions roil in the tortured depths of his dark grey eyes. She thought he looked like a man who'd found Nirvana and would risk his life to cross the crocodile-infested raging torrent to lay claim to it.

In three strides he'd closed the distance between them. Then she was in his embrace. Thrown backwards over his arm, helpless and not wanting to be anything else, his mouth came down, swiftly and all-consumingly, upon hers.

She did not struggle. Objection was the last thing on her mind.

Breathing in his familiar smell of sandalwood and leather, she twined her hands behind his neck. She could feel the pounding of his heart beneath his waistcoat of watered silk, his hard chest pressed against her breasts.

It was not a gentle kiss; rather the kiss of a man who fears his chance may not come again and wants to plunder what he can before all is taken away.

Sarah did not need gentleness. With her mind in thrall to her body she surrendered herself wholeheartedly. The redoubling of his passion signalled he'd registered her enthusiasm.

Clearly, he hadn't registered her true identity.

Sarah wilted with want, bent to his will, consumed by a primal determination to take everything this fascinating man could give her before he realized his mistake.

She'd had many admirers but as a young, unmarried woman she'd been kissed by only one man: her fiancé. This was infinitely more exciting.

She arched her back to achieve a more snug fit, and he responded, skimming his hand the length of her body from cheek to thigh while his other arm bore the full weight of her.

Waves of desire hit her with increasing force, coursed hotly through her veins, and pooled in her lower belly.

She gasped with disappointment when his mouth left hers. Compensation was swift as he thrilled her body with a feathered line of kisses down her throat. He trailed them over her collar bones, tracing the contours of her cleavage before returning once more to plunder her mouth.

She never wanted him to stop. Arching deeper against him, she raked her hands through his hair.

Then Caro screamed.

CHAPTER 6

SARAH STUMBLED AS she was released, abruptly. Dear Lord, how could they have forgotten the girl? Endeavouring to master her breathing, she stared across the chasm that separated her from Mr Hawthorne. His expression was inscrutable. He ignored his daughter who whimpered from the settee and Sarah wilted inside as she saw the passion drain from his face.

At Caro's second scream, shock reflected like a flame, quickly extinguished, in his dark eyes. Instead of going to her, he turned on his heel, the doors clicking shut behind him as he disappeared into the moonlit darkness.

"What has father done?" cried Caro, throwing herself at Sarah.

Sarah stumbled backwards and sank upon the piano stool while Caro slid from her shoulder to weep at her feet.

"So wicked! Terrible! Mother's spirit must've been in that dress and bewitched him. Poor Miss Morecroft!" Her muffled voice came in choking gasps.

Still dazed, Sarah realised the need to make Roland appear blameless in his daughter's eyes.

"Perfectly understandable," she said with a briskness she was far from feeling. "I had no right to deceive him like that."

She patted Caro's head, then, seeing the concern still in the girl's raised eyes, reassured her, "Have no fears on my account. I didn't find it horrible."

"Roland!" Cecily's voice drifted, disembodied, from the depths of the house.

ROLAND GRIPPED THE DOOR HANDLE OF THE LIBRARY TO STEADY himself, closed his eyes to ward off the memory of what had just happened, and waited for Cecily.

"Roland, there you are. Have you seen Caro? Ellen says she's not in bed yet. I was just about to retire when I thought I heard her scream!"

Cecily stood at the top of the stairs. The pins and hair pads had been removed and her hair hung lankly and unflatteringly down the sides of her anxious, drawn face.

"I saw her just now."

Turning his back on her, Roland slipped into the library and closed the door firmly behind him. His first priority was to pour himself a fortifying brandy. It was easier said than done. He was shaking so badly he had to steady himself against the mantelpiece as he removed the glass stopper.

Closing his eyes, he took a long swallow of the amber liquid, hoping to burn away all traces of Miss Morecroft's kisses. Kisses, which lingered like rose petals upon his lips.

SARAH WAS STILL TREMBLING AS SHE SAT ON THE EDGE OF HER BED and peeled off her stockings. Ellen had unbuttoned the tiny row of pearl buttons at the back of her dress, but now she was alone.

Haunted by the look in her employer's eye as he'd stood in a shaft of moonlight and gazed at her, believing her to be his dead wife come to life.

She touched her lips. They still burned. The hunger in his eyes was branded on her mind. No one had ever looked at her with such longing and ardour.

She didn't know what to make of him. Nor did she know what to make of her own tumultuous heart. Would she feel the same if just anyone kissed her?

She feared not.

Drawing in a ragged breath, she contemplated the difficulties. Mr Hawthorne had kissed her while conjuring up his dead wife. A great deal of delicacy would be required on her part to counter his mortification upon seeing her again.

And if that that was how Venetia had been revered by her husband, Sarah had her work cut out to compete. For compete she must. The feelings he'd whipped up could not be discarded lightly.

She blew out her candle and climbed into bed.

It would be a long night.

"DANCING!" CARO BLANCHED. "I ALREADY KNOW HOW TO DANCE."

Sarah cocked her eyebrow. "But not to waltz. I don't believe I've ever heard of a debutante who doesn't waltz in this day and age. Excuses like that are the preserve of dried-out spinsters, like me." Sarah held out her hand to Caro. "Come, Lady Charlotte has brought her three nieces to visit. They're in the drawing room and anxious to meet you."

Reluctantly, Caro followed Sarah downstairs.

Sarah entered the room with a smile. "Lady Charlotte, this is just what Caro needs: company, and a spur to learning her dance steps. We are short of gentlemen, however my Mama used to employ a broomstick on occasion when teaching us, and I'm sure there is very little difference."

Lady Charlotte waved an imperious hand from her seat by the fire. "This is young Georgiana and her older sister Philly who will be coming out with Caro next year. I have the dubious pleasure of playing duenna to the young ladies while their mother is indisposed. It hasn't taken me long to discover that young ladies need a great deal of amusement." She looked as if she were already fatigued by her duties.

"My, and don't I know it," exclaimed Cecily, catching her last words as she entered the room. "Certainly, useful recreation is to be recommended, and dancing, while some might reckon it distinctly un-useful, is an indispensible accomplishment." She directed a pointed look at Caro as she seated herself upon the piano stool. "I shall accompany but first we must find Cosmo. Yes! And Mr Hawthorne too for it is intolerable to have no gentlemen with whom to practice when there are two perfectly able-bodied ones in this very house. Mabel," she said to the parlour maid who had just answered her summons, "fetch Master Cosmo and Mr Hawthorne. Tell them to present themselves in the drawing room at their earliest convenience. Also, find Dorrington to arrange for their dancing shoes to be brought down."

Mention of Mr Hawthorne made Sarah's heartbeat do a little dance while heat rose in her cheeks. She pushed Caro into the centre of the room.

"What a treat to have an impromptu dancing lesson, Miss Hawthorne," said Philly, dimpling as she smoothed her sprigged muslin skirts over her ample hips. Her round, ruddy face was flushed with pleasure. "Aunt Charlotte is sponsoring me for the season, you know. She says you're not fond of dancing, but surely it is an accomplishment a girl cannot do without."

"That and never revealing when she feels at a disadvantage," came Lady Charlotte's stentorian tones.

Well, no one was going to know the extent to which the governess felt at a disadvantage, thought Sarah, as the door opened and Mr Hawthorne strode into the room.

It was immediately clear that Mabel had not elaborated on the nature of the summons for it was Mr Hawthorne who looked at a complete disadvantage, greeted as he was by a room full of expectant ladies and his sister-in-law jumping up from the piano stool saying, "How very good of you to come so quickly, Mr Hawthorne. The young ladies are eager to be put through their paces. We are having a dancing lesson, don't you know."

Sarah felt a wave of sympathy as his dancing shoes were thrust in front of him.

"I fear, Cecily," he said, looking pained and studiously ignoring Sarah, "that I am not going to satisfy your demands for excellence.

Surely the young ladies have been doing country dances since they could walk?"

"Oh, not country dances, Roland. No, we mean to perfect the waltz."

His eyes widened, but Sarah was able to say, soothingly, "Here comes Cosmo. Perhaps he would prefer to take a turn with one of the young ladies."

"A waltz." Cosmo beamed at the unexpected but obviously welcome sight of such a large female contingent. "Why, I should love to render my assistance. Who shall go first? I should hate to set the cat amongst the pigeons by favouring one pretty girl above the other."

Clearly gratified by their blushes and giggles, Cosmo glanced up as he changed his shoes. "Miss Morecroft, I daresay waltzing does not fall within the curriculum of most governesses, but since you are a breed apart, is it too much to wonder if you felt up to partnering me?"

"With pleasure." Sarah felt no embarrassment as she stepped forward and placed one hand upon his shoulder while he clasped the other and rested his hand upon the small of her back.

"Ready?" asked Mrs Hawthorne, and began to play.

However Cosmo proved no very great proponent of the dance and was soon relegated to the sidelines by his critical aunt.

"You're all over the place, Cosmo, and half the time upon poor Miss Morecroft's foot. Roland, you're an excellent dancer. Step up and take his place."

Sarah turned, smiling slightly, in time to see Mr Hawthorne's dismay, quickly masked by a look of cool indifference.

But while her own heart was being exercised somewhat more than usual, and not just by the energy required in twirling around a room, she managed, to her surprise, a smile that was not at all tremulous.

"Shall we show the young ladies how it's done, sir?" she said clearly and for the benefit of all, smiling over her shoulder at Caro, for she wanted to reassure the girl she did not consider herself in the evil clutches of some shameless villain.

He could not look at her. "Yes, of course." Fortunately, his dancing was not as stilted as his manner. Roland was, as Mrs Hawthorne claimed, an excellent dancer. Sarah felt herself perfectly matched, light on her feet and expertly led as they twirled around the room.

She adored dancing, and it had been a long time. Trapped in his arms, feeling the heat of his body and moving in time to the music was joy to her senses but after a few moments, she acknowledged Mr Hawthorne's grim expression. Clearly, he had not lost himself in the dance as she had. Her pleasure drained away. Pique turned to indignation. She pushed it back down, murmuring, when they were in the farthest corner of the drawing room, "I fear you are angry with me, sir."

He jerked his head up to look her in the eye for the first time. "Angry with *you?* Obviously Caro put you up to it. The charade, I mean. Giving you Venetia's dress to wear. No, my behaviour last night was reprehensible."

"I'm afraid it was entirely my idea. But if you're not angry with me, perhaps you could look a little less like you are-?" Sarah paused as he raised her a little off the ground to compensate for dancing her too close to a potted palm. He was not just adept on his feet. It was a relief to surrender herself to his skill on the dance floor knowing she could say anything, it appeared, without risk of being tripped up over the rug. His scowl was unsettling but it was his nature and Sarah was determined to reduce the frequency of such signs of unhappiness. When the time was right. For now, his obvious discomfiture gave her the advantage. "At least for the benefit of the others. And for my reputation," she suggested, mildly.

"Forgive me. My manners have deserted me. I'd also understand completely, Miss Morecroft, if you wished to give notice and leave Larchfield directly."

"My notice?" Sarah gasped. Such a thought could not have been further from her thoughts.

His eyes narrowed as if he suspected the turmoil in her heart. "It would be entirely appropriate for you to wish to hand in your notice," he said, carefully, as he set their course for their audience. "As your employer I have behaved unacceptably."

Without giving her a chance to reply he deposited her amidst the others. "And that, Caro, is how your mother and I used to dance when the waltz was still considered quite daring." He smiled at her. "I am sadly rusty, but Miss Morecroft has shown how it can be performed with skill and elegance. Come Caro," he invited. "It would be kinder to all if you tread first upon your father's feet before you are let loose to injure other innocent parties."

Sarah's thoughts were in such disorder it was a relief to have half an hour to herself before putting the children to bed. Snatching her shawl from the hook on her bedroom door she made for the ornamental lake.

Would Mr Hawthorne really let her go so easily when she knew he reciprocated her feelings? Dismay replaced her confidence as she wondered if he considered *she* were the one to have exhibited a certain laxness by not pulling out of his embrace earlier. Surely not? He'd made it clear he regarded himself entirely at fault. He'd also made it clear, whether he later chose to refute it or not, that he found her entirely irresistible.

Yet he'd offered to let her go, as if he cared neither way.

She would not go. She'd been at Larchfield nearly three weeks but her task was not finished. Caro's birthday was coming up and Sarah needed to see her through it. After that it would be time to leave. But she'd return ...

And she'd return as Lady Sarah Miles, Mr Hawthorne's equal, with a thoroughly convincing reason for having done what she'd done.

"Miss Morecroft."

She turned, her heart lurching at the familiar voice.

Burnished by the setting sun, Mr Hawthorne looked like a mythical creature emerged from the waters of the lake. But though Sarah managed a smile of polite enquiry, he exhibited no answering pleasure.

"My apologies for my behaviour in the drawing room this morning," he began. He ran one finger inside his cravat, as if it were tied too tightly. "It was unpardonable that the apology should have been prompted by you when I had every intention of offering my sincerest regrets, in person."

"I had no right to wear your wife's dress," said Sarah, lightly, trying to make it easier for him.

"You must not think that I-"

"Oh, it has occasioned no alarm or dread on my part, sir." Sarah wished his brooding look really did inspire the pique she now strove for, rather than making her want to kiss and stroke the lines of strain away from his face. She went on in the same unconcerned tone, "For I cannot for one moment think that it was desire for a mere governess which prompted your uncharacteristic behaviour."

Frowning, he advanced a few feet. "The 'mere governess' as you term yourself, should feel properly protected. Do not imagine I am in the habit of preying on the vulnerable members of my household."

Her heart thundered but her voice was soft. "Let us walk," she suggested, stepping onto the worn path that led towards the wood. He hesitated, then fell into step beside her.

"You are very like your father, Miss Morecroft," he observed. "You have his fearless spirit."

"Tell me about him."

"Our golden youth?" His tone was ironic. "I'll happily recount those halcyon days if you promise not to press me further, Miss Morecroft. Godby was closer to me than my own brother. But boys become young men, and life becomes complicated."

They halted in a copse shaded by leafy elms. The air was damp and in front of them was a grotto, overhung with ferns. Dominating the small cleared space was a memorial stone dedicated to Venetia and Hector Hawthorne.

"Venetia died seven years ago, yesterday," he said, clearly glad to change the subject as her gaze went to the posy of flowers at its base. "I gather Caro didn't mention it?"

Sarah evaded his look. "She mentioned it."

"Since Caro turned twelve she's refused to accompany me here. She says she hates her mother. Can I ask you what she said to you?"

Weighing up whether to spare him the truth, Sarah stared at the limp dewdrops upon the woodleaf floor. Everyone at Larchfield had remarked upon the anniversary yesterday. Seven years after her death Lady Venetia and her powerful influence over her husband – amongst other men – continued to provide the servants with a rich source of gossip.

When it was clear he intended waiting for her answer, she said, hesitantly, "Caro asked why her father would erect a memorial to a harlot."

To her surprise he looked amused. "Caro has spirit. It's not customary to cultivate the society of our adolescent daughters. They can seem like strangers on occasion."

Sarah thought of her own father. He had not been customary in his approach to her upbringing, throwing at her books she must read, quizzing her, arguing with her. He even took her shooting when only close friends were visiting.

She felt a pang, but as ever her resolve hardened when she thought of his parting words: "Marry James, or my doors are closed to a crotchety spinster who insists on spurning life's bounties."

Well, she'd be going home soon, if only to prepare herself for her return to Mr Hawthorne.

"Yes, she has spirit. Like her mother." Boldly, Sarah moved closer, putting her hand on the mossy surface of the rock face for balance. He did not step back but the gaze he levelled at her was harsh.

"Venetia was a poppy eater. Did the servants tell you that?"

Shocked, she shook her head. It explained so much.

"Her addiction made her moods volatile and unpredictable." His eyes left hers and he gazed over her shoulder. His reflective smile suggested happier memories. "When Venetia needed me she was everything I could have wished for-" He gave a short, wry laugh, adding, almost imperceptibly, "Well, almost. Sarah saw his pain as their gazes locked. "It's one thing to be needed, Miss Morecroft. His voice was now so low she strained to hear him as he finished, "quite another to be loved."

She was not prepared for such a revealing confidence. Nor what he required of her. Sympathy? Understanding? But it was her heart, not her head that dictated her next impulsive move. As if it were the most natural thing in the world Sarah raised herself upon her toes and put her hands on his shoulders. She closed her eyes. An instant later she felt the answering touch of his lips upon hers. His hands cupped her face, and her senses were assailed by sandalwood and leather, yearning and desire as his strong hard body pressed her back against the stone.

She might have been a seasoned flirt, but Sarah had little experience of physical desire. Tingles of sensation rippled through her as she twined her hands in the short hair at the nape of his neck and felt the roughness of his skin against her cheek, the sweet gentleness as his tongue skimmed her upper lip before he deepened the kiss. Her bones became jelly as he rained kisses upon her lips, her eyes, her neck. He kissed her like a drowning man replenishing himself, and Sarah responded like a flower soaking up the sun.

He released her suddenly. Breathless, she steadied herself against the rock behind. The turbulence in his eyes revealed mixed emotions. She could see he wanted her still. Against his will.

The rapid rise and fall of his chest mirrored the turbulence of her own reaction, but she was aware of the need for restraint.

"A gentleman would apologize to you, Miss Morecroft." His voice was strained as he stepped back. "Yet I'm not sure I'm entirely to blame."

She felt stripped bare, from the inside out. Unable to respond, she touched her lips.

"It shan't happen again." He turned, but she could not let him go.

"If I am to blame, then forgive me," she ground out. If he didn't blame her, he was blaming himself, and hating her for it. She couldn't bear it.

"Pretend it never happened." She lurched towards him, stopping herself before she stayed him with a hand upon his sleeve. "Don't let it spoil what was between us."

He turned, his eyes drinking her in. There was more than just regret in his expression, as he responded. "There was, and is, nothing between us, Miss Morecroft." At the devastation in her look his tone gentled. "Nor ever will be." He sighed. "I'm sorry."

He was wrong, but now was not the time to persuade him. Smoothing her skirts as she stepped away from the memorial stone, Sarah managed at last to control her trembling mouth and in a voice that was light and careless, said, "It's getting late. We should return to the house or Caro will wonder what's become of us." With an inviting smile she indicated the path and was relieved when he began to walk with her. "Which brings me to the matter of Caro's Birthday Ball." Her chatter was deliberately inconsequential. "I was hoping you'd do me –

and Caro – the great honour of allowing me to be final arbiter of in the choice of Caro's gown. Mrs Hawthorne, you see, has her heart set on primrose. Caro exhibits great fashion understanding when she declares that in primrose she'll rather resemble Banquo's ghost dressed for a wedding."

CHAPTER 7

GEORGIANA AND PHILLY were constant visitors to Larchfield in the lead-up to Caro's ball. The daily curriculum of dance practice, deportment lessons, drills in how to use a fan to convey a hundred moods and meanings, and how to execute the perfect curtsy had been gruelling. Despite that, the girls' enthusiasm seemed to have rubbed off on Caro.

In another couple of weeks her work here would be done, thought Sarah with a pang. Caro, her 'special mission' had proved far more amenable than expected, which was not surprising. Caro was like any normal young girl. A boost to her self confidence, and a few friends, had made an enormous difference.

Mrs Hawthorne, inferring at the outset that a lowly-born piece of goods like Sarah would know nothing about such matters, had soon entirely discharged to her all duties related to Caro's initiation into the adult world.

Mrs Hawthorne's ill opinion amused Sarah. Mr Hawthorne's feelings were another matter. He ignored her. No amount of persuasion from the young ladies would induce him to partner them in their dance lessons. Sarah knew she was the reason.

She felt hurt. He had confided in her. The connection had not only been physical. Clearly, he feared his attraction for Sarah, the lowly governess.

If it were to be a battle of the wills, she thought, fluttering her fan as she dropped a curtsy in mock deference to Caro at the conclusion of a minuet, practiced in the drawing room with the chairs and tables pushed against the walls, hers would prevail.

But for once, she was not entirely convinced that her powers of persuasion matched her powers of attraction.

ROLAND WATCHED THE SPRAY OF DROPLETS CATCH THE LIGHT AS two birds bathed with rapturous abandon in the birdbath a few yards from his study windows. It seemed a lifetime ago that he and Godby had bathed in the river that ran through Larchfield, splashing water at each other with similar abandon. Venetia had eaten his heart for breakfast the day he'd met her, and made short work of the rest of him. He had nothing left of himself to offer anyone. When Miss Morecroft had made clear she thought otherwise he'd responded with a resurgence of symptoms indicating his dangerous suscepti-bility to her overtures. How nearly he'd become a fool in love yet again.

He groaned inwardly, trying again to turn his mind to the accounts with which his bailiff had presented him. The man was breathing over his shoulder, waiting for him to endorse his monthly summary so Roland could send him on his way.

Roland turned the inked paper over in a useless gesture, while he re-lived his encounter with Miss Morecroft at the grotto. Godby's daughter, charming and as apparently careless and forthcoming with her affections as her father, was never far from his thoughts.

Through the open window his eye caught a flash of white sprigged muslin. So much more interesting than the paper in his hand. His gaze followed Miss Morecroft's graceful figure down the path across the sloping lawn towards the woods. Flanked by the two little girls, the three appeared to be chatting easily. He smiled as he imagined Harriet insisting on another worm expedition.

As if she knew she was being observed Miss Morecroft turned to look over her shoulder. She smiled in his direction then returned her attention to Augusta who was pulling her arm and pointing.

With a final, lingering look at the disappearing figures, he picked up his pen and dipped it in the inkpot. In a moment Cecily would knock on the door to show him the guest list for Caro's ball. Launching Caro in the hopes she'd find a suitably connected and indulgent husband was Roland's immediate priority. He hoped Caro would never suffer the disappointment that had blighted her mother's happiness. But Caro, less beautiful, more practical, had become increasingly grounded in reality since Miss Morecroft had entered her orbit.

CARO ENTERED THE NURSERY, TYING THE RIBBONS OF HER BONNET beneath her chin. "I'm ready, Miss Morecroft?" There was excitement in her voice.

Sarah gazed at her with approval. The girl's simple white muslin gown with its blue sash flattered Caro's slender figure and set off her striking combination of dark hair and pale skin. The ensemble had been selected by Sarah after a battle of wills with her employer. Mrs Hawthorne was reluctant to countenance any expenditure upon her niece, even though Mr Hawthorne paid the bills.

"I'm afraid you younger ones must stay here," Sarah told them from the doorway. "This is Caro's special treat."

"How can you bear them clinging to your skirts, Miss Morecroft?" grumbled Caro as they descended the stairs. "I daresay you're used to it, with so many brothers and sisters." Clapping her hand to her mouth as she remembered her error, she turned on her heel. "I'm so sorry, Miss. They're all gone now. You're alone in the world."

Sarah could not feel personal sorrow for the death of all those Morecroft children she had never known, but she felt a pang at the fact she had no siblings. She enjoyed Augusta and Harriet's happy chatter *and* the way they clung to her skirts. "I don't dwell on what can't be changed," she said briskly. "Now what do we need? Ribbons for you and–"

Caro skipped across the black and white flagged entrance hall.

Turning at the sweep of stone stairs, she said with an impish grin, "And something for a fine gown for *you* to wear for my birthday ball."

Sarah laughed. "How do you suppose I might pay for that out of my wages, Miss Hawthorne? No, I shall refurbish your aunt's cerulean blue velvet. You won't recognize it."

Caro slanted her a secretive look as they made for the bridle path that led over the hill to the village beyond. "Perhaps you'd relish an even greater challenge. Like constructing a garment entirely from new." Her eyes shone as she looked at Sarah. "Of *any* material you choose. I asked father yesterday and he has given his consent."

Before Sarah could respond, Caro rushed on, "I said I couldn't possibly enjoy my birthday ball unless Miss Morecroft, who loves fine clothes far more than I do, had the prettiest gown of her imagination. We're going to the village today to choose a bolt of fabric, and all the trimmings, for you!"

Caro laughed at Sarah's silence and the expression of shock on her face. "You'll enjoy sewing it yourself, won't you? There's plenty of time."

Sarah beamed. "I couldn't think of a nicer surprise," she said, clapping her hands together. "What a capital girl you are, Caro."

In the village shop Caro deliberated over a bolt of Egyptian Brown sarsanet and a silver grey lutestring called Esterhazy.

Sarah felt moved beyond words. There had been more than a few occasions when she'd wondered if her young charge positively *dis*liked her. How curious, she reflected, that this home-sewn gown, conceived by Caro and sanctioned by Mr Hawthorne, filled her with more honest excitement than any extravagant creation she had devised with her seamstress.

"Hardly an appropriate colour for one's foray into the world, Caro."

They turned to see Lady Charlotte, flanked by her nieces, regarding their choices with disapproval.

Sarah sent a swift look at Caro, to indicate she would deal with this, but with a petulant tilt to her chin, Caro announced, "I intend wearing scarlet to honour my mother, Lady Charlotte. This is in fact for Miss Morecroft."

Sarah's heart sank. "Caro should not have spoken like that," she apologised, but Lady Charlotte ignored her.

"Mr Hawthorne must pay you handsome wages to teach his daughter decorum and respect if you can afford such finery, Miss Morecroft. Georgiana, Philly." She put a hand on each girl's shoulder to shepherd them out of the shop. "Your visit to Larchfield this afternoon is cancelled due to Caro's gross incivility."

Caro looked abashed but her eyes flashed defiance when she turned at Sarah's gentle rebuke. "That woman has never said a kind word about either you, or mother," she began. However as Mrs Willow, the shop proprietor, returned to show them a selection of ribbons that would complement each fabric, Sarah decided not to pursue the matter.

Caro had regained her former ebullience by the time they'd left the shop, and when she saw Philly and Georgiana running towards her across the village green, she beamed.

"We're so sorry Aunt Charlotte was such a gorgon."

"How did she agree to you coming out again?" Caro asked.

Georgiana giggled. "We had a harpsichord session, and Philly did lots of very loud singing, until Aunt Charlotte positively begged us to leave her in peace. Oh Caro—" She took her friend's arm and fell into step. "Isn't it exciting to have so many men in red at the ball? What a boon that Hetty Siskin's brother is so well connected. Your father has agreed, hasn't he?"

Caro nodded.

"And is he inviting Mr Hollingsworth?" Philly's tone was urgent. "Please say you've asked him?"

"Who is Mr Hollingsworth?" Sarah's tone was sharp.

The three girls gasped. "Talk of the devil," said Philly. "He's over there. Do you think he could have seen us and come out specially?"

Before anyone could respond, a tall, smiling gentleman strolled up to them.

"Ladies." He removed his low crowned beaver with a bow. "You all look especially lovely this morning."

When the introductions had been performed, Sarah silently observed the newcomer's disquieting effect upon the three girls.

He was, she judged, several years older than herself, with the kind of handsome looks, detail to fashion and personable manner calculated to win him female admirers. Caro, Georgiana and Philly crowded round him, chattering as if they'd known him forever.

"And where do you hail from, if I may be so bold as to cut in?" Sarah asked, eventually. Not only was it growing cold on the damp grass, there were some who'd consider it unseemly for all the world to witness the young ladies feting an unfamiliar gentleman.

His smile was as warm for the governess as it was for the young ladies. A shrewd touch. Sarah wondered for whom he might have a possible interest.

"I've leased Hawthornedene for the season."

Caro took Sarah's arm. Sarah had rarely seen her so animated. "Uncle Hector's house. Well, he owned it though he didn't live there, of course. It's beautiful, Miss Morecroft."

"You must be my guests some time," the young man said. "I shall organise a picnic by the lake."

This was greeted by squeals of enthusiasm. Sarah realised it was hardly fair to criticize him for looking so self-satisfied but when she'd dragged Caro away from the group she demanded, "Since when has Mr Hollingsworth become your latest bosom-bow?"

"I did not think it a crime to speak to a young man." Caro's tone was defensive. "Or that you'd think ill of me, Miss Morecroft. He's a friend of Hetty Siskin's brother. I've met him several times on walks and once when we were at Hetty's house." Caro wrapped her cashmere shawl more closely around her and stuck her nose in the air as they walked across the common.

Wrapping her own, more serviceable woollen shawl around her shoulders, Sarah followed. "Don't be cross with me, Caro. I must be accountable to your father and aunt." She put her hand on Caro's shoulder and was relieved that her conciliatory gesture wasn't rebuffed.

"It seems I'm to be criticised whatever I do," Caro grumbled. "Aunt Cecily harps on at me to be more sociable, but she's such a high stickler that only means being nice to Lady Charlotte and mean old cats like her."

"That would have been a good start." Sarah's tone was dry. "But now we are nearly home, so let's say no more about it. I was not criticising you for talking to Mr Hollingsworth, merely executing my duty as your governess by ensuring he's a nice, suitable young man worthy of your addresses."

Caro halted and fixed her with an intense look. "Oh, he is, Miss Morecroft," she breathed.

CHAPTER 8

"THERE ARE NOT nine pence in a shilling, Augusta," Sarah snapped, tossing the gown she was sewing onto the nursery table.

Remorse was swift as she saw Augusta's trembling lip. She sighed as she acknowledged she was taking her frustration out on the girls as she drilled them, in between sewing straight seams and fine pin tucks. "I'm sorry I was sharp," she said, more kindly. "Tell me the cost of a loaf of bread, and there'll be no more sums for today."

But they could not, and Sarah did not know the answer, herself. She tried to bolster her spirits but it was no use. What was the point of the lovely creation taking shape? Mr Hawthorne would pay her no attention. He'd gone to pains to keep his distance since their encounter at the grotto. He'd hardly seek her out at Caro's birthday ball.

"I have a secret," announced Augusta, from her cushion at Sarah's feet, recovering her spirits.

"If it's about Caro, then I already know it," said Harriet who was sitting beside her. "It's not nice to gossip about people behind their backs."

"I'm only telling Miss Morecroft." Augusta stuck her tongue out at her sister. "She'd not get Caro into trouble."

"And what is this secret?" asked Sarah mildly, hiding her disquiet.

"I saw her with Mr Hollingsworth in the churchyard ... alone," said Augusta in weighty tones.

"The churchyard in the middle of the village?" Augusta's tone was scornful. "Where everyone in the village pays their respects to the dead?"

"Well, I nearly didn't see them," said Harriet. "I was with Ellen and she was hurrying me along. But it *was* Caro *and* she was in the shadow of the yew trees where I'd seen them talking the day before, too."

"I hope you don't mean to gossip like this to your mother," reproved Sarah, biting off a thread.

The girls looked indignant. "We never tell mama anything! Not even when we hear the servants gossip about *her*."

"That is most wise," remarked Sarah, with irony. "Not that your mother is the kind of woman to excite a great deal of gossip, I would imagine."

With her heart — not to mention her dignity — bruised and battered by Mr Hawthorne's rejection, it was difficult to concern herself with much else. She held up a seam for inspection, her eyes blurring as they ran across the stitches while she remembered the finality of his let-down.

Why? When she *knew* he was not insensible to her?

"Mama never does anything scandalous," sighed Augusta, as if this were her greatest failing.

"And never did," said Harriet. "She was never a beauty, like Aunt Venetia. Do you think I will grow up stout and turkey-necked like Mama, Miss Morecroft?"

"And that Caro will stop looking like a long-necked goose?" asked Augusta.

"Girls, girls! Where do you hear such things?" asked Sarah, sounding more shocked than she felt.

"The servants, of course," Harriet replied, as if she were stupid. "They talk about such interesting things."

"Only they think we don't understand because we're children," said Augusta. "You didn't know that Aunt Venetia ran off with my father and it was their sin which killed them, did you?"

Sarah was about to open her mouth and say that, indeed she did, thereby upping her status in the girls' eyes when Harriet said, with a sly roll of her eyes, "But Father wasn't her true love."

"Harriet!" her sister hissed, with a meaningful look at Sarah.

Sarah knew she should nip such gossip in the bud, but she wanted to know how Harriet's version differed from any other. She pretended unconcern as she worked the cloth in her hands, hoping they didn't notice how her fingers trembled. "You're obviously dying to tell us this latest piece of unreliable servants' gossip, unless you're just making it all up."

"I'm not making anything up. Ellen and the other servants say her true love was Uncle Godby," said Harriet.

"It was not!" cried Augusta with another meaningful look at Sarah.

Harriet looked suddenly guilty. Pretending concentration as she stuck pins into her cream sash, she mumbled, "Sorry, Miss Morecroft. I keep forgetting you're Uncle Godby's daughter."

"So do I." Sarah's voice was distant. She hoped her creased brow would be attributed to shock at this bombshell regarding her supposed father. They wouldn't know she was mentally digesting the implications of this altered history.

Hope surged through her. Had she just stumbled upon the real reason for Mr Hawthorne's rejection of her?

"Why are you smiling, Miss Morecroft?" Harriet asked.

"I have an eyelash in my eye." She covered her face with her hands to hide her joy. There was hope, after all.

IN THE SMALL, GLOOMY ANTECHAMBER WHICH ACCOMMODATED Venetia's enormous wealth of sumptuary display, cobwebs hung thickly.

Roland had had to use his pocket handkerchief to wipe the dust from a window pane to let in enough light to see the location of Venetia's fashionable, elegant furniture much less what was contained in the drawers.

He was so absorbed in his examination he did not hear the soft-slippered approach of his sister-in-law. But he nearly dropped the rope of pearls that he held, suspended between two hands, at her screech.

"You're not giving Caro *that?*"

"It would appear you're not in the habit of visiting Venetia's old apartments." Roland wiped a finger through the dust on the windowsill as he raised a disapproving eyebrow.

"I swore I'd never enter these rooms again." Cecily shuddered. "I told the housemaids to stay away, too, but when I saw the door open ..." Her voice trailed away. "Even after all these years these rooms *still* smell of her." Her lower lip trembled as she looked at Roland.

When he offered no sympathetic rejoinder she begged him, "Give them away, throw them away. They're bad luck."

"I note the absence of one or two of Venetia's favourite pieces. No, I don't blame you, Cecily," he added quickly, at her look of outrage. "Hector used your dowry with little regard for you. I'd be the first to sanction your behaviour. But these—" He swung the strand of gleaming pearls closer to her face. "Do you know how much these are worth? A perfect pearl ... rare and priceless. And dozens of them on this one strand. All because Venetia demanded-"

He stopped abruptly as Cecily shrank back, her mouth bared in a rictus of a snarl as she hissed, "They're worth more than a king's ransom which is all the more reason not to give them to Caro." Her bulbous eyes flashed anger. "You surely weren't thinking of it, Roland?" she demanded again. "They're tainted. *You* didn't buy them. They cost you nothing."

"They cost me my wife."

Cecily stamped her foot. "If Sir Richard was prepared to spend that sum on his mistress and bankrupt himself in the process then he was a fool!" She spat out the words with no regard to his feelings. "Though much good it did him. Venetia soon moved on to greener pastures, didn't she?"

"She came back to *me*," Roland observed, dryly.

Cecily put her hand to her stringy neck and her lip curled. Had her look not been not so venomous Roland might have smiled at the sight of a dusty spider's web adorning the finely pleated rows of lace on her fashionable high crowned cap.

"You should have closed your doors to her forever, Roland."

"When Caro was crying for her mother, every night?" Roland put his hand on Cecily's shoulder. "Why can't you put the past behind you? You'd be so much happier."

"Like you, Roland?" Cecily's tone dripped scorn. "You still live in the past, so don't preach to me." She turned on her heel. "You've not forgotten your interview with Miss Morecroft? Don't be soft with her. I fear she's insinuated her way into your affections just as her father did. It was a mistake to take her in."

"We made the decision jointly."

"In a moment of weakness when her poor mother all but swore she'd cut her own throat if we didn't. Now, I'm going to see cook."

She was gone before he could reply.

Venetia. On a whim he withdrew her likeness from his desk drawer, once he had returned to his study.

Proud and confident of her beauty she stared back at him. Dispassionately, he studied her features: the lustrous dark hair, curled at the front and cascading in ringlets from a high crown; the rosebud mouth, so divinely kissable when that was what she had desired.

Oh, she had taught him how to please her. It was just that he, alone, was not enough for one of her ... vanity? He preferred to think that was the reason she'd strayed rather than that the fault lay with him, alone.

Replacing the miniature with the usual disquiet he felt every time he thought of her, he moved to the window. A team of gardeners was clipping the topiary-adorned hedge beyond the rose arbour. He watched them as he prepared himself. It was not Miss Morecroft's position that was at risk in this upcoming interview, it was Roland's heart and integrity.

At the gentle tap on the door Roland turned, unprepared for the sudden drumming of blood in his ears, although his voice was steady and cool as he said, "Please sit down, Miss Morecroft."

So that she was under no illusions as to the nature of his request for her company, he said without preamble, "I hope I've not inter-rupted any plans you may otherwise have had for the engagement of the girls. However, I have promised Mrs Hawthorne to investigate a matter which is of concern to her."

The young woman looked at him enquiringly while she settled herself in one of his large armchairs with that peculiar grace of hers.

Roland tried not to be distracted by the tendrils of chestnut hair which brushed the high planes of her cheeks in such an artless fashion. He cleared his voice and frowned but this did not have the desired effect for she merely deepened her smile as she waited for him to elaborate. The smile insinuated its way like warm honey through the cracks of his heart, thawing the ice which sheathed it. He fought to remain impervious.

"Yesterday," he went on, feeling at a distinct disadvantage, "Mrs Hawthorne brought to my attention a matter which she considered betokened negligence on your part. Apparently Lady Charlotte observed my daughter conversing with an unknown gentleman, in the street in front of the haberdasherers." He paused, waiting for her to colour at the recollection. When she did not — in fact her smile broadened — he continued in more sonorous tones, "Caro was alone and unchaperoned."

"Scurrilous gossipmongers!" Miss Morecroft shook her head. "To report such tales reflects badly on *all* parties and is deeply insulting to Caro. It so happens that as we stepped into the haberdasherer's yesterday afternoon to purchase some last-minute trimming for Caro's gown, Caro was greeted by Mr Hollingsworth who, I'm pleased, you saw fit to invite to her birthday. Not wishing to interfere directly, I remained just within the building and listened to Caro and Mr Hollingsworth discuss the weather and his pleasure at having been included on the guest list for Friday's entertainment. Shortly afterwards the young gentleman bade her good day and moved on again. I would say the exchange lasted about one and a half minutes."

Despite her smile her fine hazel eyes were alight with challenge. "If you wish to verify my story, Mrs Willow, who works in the shop, will corroborate everything."

"That will not be necessary," Roland said, hastily. "It was merely incumbent upon me to investigate the matter at Mrs Hawthorne's request. Please be assured that I, personally, have no concerns regarding your care of my daughter."

He should have left it there. Should have nodded, politely, risen, and shown her the door. But he couldn't help adding, "Caro's confidence has increased under your tutelage. I would not want to disappoint her."

The last was a thinly veiled warning. He did not need to elaborate. Miss Morecroft must be fully aware of her danger in making an enemy of the mistress of the house.

Expecting her to thank him and take her leave, Roland nodded in dismissal.

She rose.

"So I am in danger, then, of losing my position, Mr Hawthorne?" she asked, bluntly. "Once people like Mrs Hawthorne decide menials such as myself no longer give satisfaction it is usually not long before we are given our marching orders."

He regarded her with a level look. "I have said I will protect you, Miss Morecroft." He nodded in the direction of the door. She had to go, now. He wasn't sure how much longer he could trust himself to refrain from reassuring her, in the most unseemly fashion, of her security. The knowledge made his expression sterner, his stance more rigid.

She took a step towards him. "You are to leave for London this afternoon for several days."

He registered the rise and fall of her chest, the concern in her eyes. "That's all the opportunity Mrs Hawthorne needs. After all, I am in charge of her girls, as well as Caro. What then, sir? Remember, I have nowhere else to go."

Retreating, he turned to stare out of the window. "I am not one to tolerate injustice, Miss Morecroft." He could feel his breath quickening and the blood surging to his extremities. This was madness. She had to go. Now!

"Yes, you are a fair man," she said, angling herself so that she was within his vision.

He ignored the rustle of her gown but the scent of orange flower water made him turn his head.

"And that," she said, the shadow of a smile upon her beautiful face, "is why I want to stay. That, and my sincere affection for the girls. Your warning suggests it would be wise to explore alternative avenues of employment." Her eyes were dark with entreaty. "I do not know whether the fault is mine alone, or whether my father's wrongs have sealed my fate, but I do know that I love it here, Mr Hawthorne — working for you — and that I don't want to leave."

"Yes, yes," he said, suddenly finding himself in possession of her hand. He had no idea whether he'd taken it in response to her distress, or whether she might have offered it to him. "You have, I assure you, given every satisfaction." He stopped, colouring at his choice of words, and did not like the fact that she smiled back, rather like a cat, her face tilted to one side, her eyes bright with mischief beneath demurely lowered lashes.

What might have happened next, had footsteps not sounded in the passageway, he did not care to dwell upon, for his actions were not about to be dictated by his head — he was uncomfortably aware of that. But the sound of Cecily's voice was like cold water upon him and the next he could remember, he was leading Miss Morecroft to the door and bowing to her in polite dismissal.

The turmoil in his breast did not abate at her departure.

He stared at the papers on his desk and knew he'd be unable to concentrate. Then he headed for the door. Perhaps a bracing ride would help cast out the madness that was beginning to consume him.

CHAPTER 9

"PAPA, YOU SHOULD see the ballroom." Caro was barely able to contain her excitement. Sarah knew she could claim some of the credit for the girl's recent transformation, but not all. Love was in the air.

Caro's eyes shone. "Bows and flowers everywhere. People will talk about my birthday for months to come."

She smiled at her father in happy expectation. The house had been a hive of activity and the air was thick with the anticipation of tomorrow night's ball.

Sarah watched Mr Hawthorne finish the carp on his plate. If this couldn't wipe the scowl from her employer's face, she thought, nothing could. He'd not addressed a single word to his daughter or sister-in-law the entire meal. That he'd said nothing to Sarah hardly signified. Two afternoons ago, though, before he'd rushed off to London ... She tried not to think about it. If Mrs Hawthorne hadn't trumpeted her orders to the housemaid right outside the study door, who knew what might have happened.

With careful precision Mr Hawthorne put together his knife and fork and directed a reproving look at his daughter. "Just remember you are of the privileged minority, Caro. Few people in this country, much less the world, are as fortunate." His voice was chilly.

Indignation on Caro's behalf replaced Sarah's romantic ruminations on what might have been. She bit her tongue to prevent herself from voicing a tart reminder that Caro was the last young lady who put her own pleasure above the needs and suffering of others.

Only the click of the ormolu clock on the mantelpiece broke the tense silence.

"Tonight we dine in luxury while a large majority of Englishmen and their families will barely fill their stomachs. Tonight a dozen wives are weeping for husbands condemned to death for challenging a society which denies them a fair wage for an honest day's work." Mr Hawthorne glared at Caro, impervious to her quivering lip.

Sarah couldn't help herself. "I do not think Caro's enthusiasm is a reflection of her indifference towards those less fortunate than herself."

Mrs Hawthorne snapped her head around and looked at Sarah as if she had suggested they open their doors to the starving masses, and serve them, personally. "I do not believe, Miss Morecroft," she said in clipped tones, "that your opinion was solicited."

This had the opposite effect of dampening Sarah's defence. "I deplore injustice as strongly as you," she bit back. "Caro said nothing to warrant her father's criticism. It was unjust to accuse her of selfishness when she is naturally excited about her ball tomorrow night."

"Injustice!" Mrs. Hawthorne cried. "You accuse my brother-in-law of injustice when I can think of no other man who has expended more time and energy fighting for the rights of the working man. With an agitated hand she repositioned her vermilion toque which was favouring one ear, and nearly dislodged the squirrel's tail hair piece. For once, Sarah was in no danger of succumbing to unwise giggles. Caro had started to cry. Though no tears came Sarah could see the trembling of her thin, white muslin-clad shoulders. She turned to Mr Hawthorne. Surely he knew he was in the wrong?

He was staring at the silver epergne centre piece, clearly resolved to have no part of the argument. Anger seared through her.

"How dare you answer back to your betters!" cried Mrs Hawthorne. "Leave the table at once, Miss Morecroft."

With a cold, hard stare at her employers, Sarah rose. "I am sorry if the truth offends you," she said with quiet dignity. Passing close to the back of Mr Hawthorne's chair as she made her regal exit she hoped he could feel her anger.

He had been vastly unjust. Surely he must realize it.

Then she heard his voice, music to her ears, despite its arctic tone. "Wait for me in my study, Miss Morecroft. I will see you there when I've finished my dinner."

FIVE MINUTES WAITING FOR HIM HAD FANNED THE FLAMES OF Sarah's fury to a blaze. Swinging round from the fireplace, she seized the initiative.

"I've not had time to pack my bags, sir. No doubt Mrs Hawthorne has instructed I be dismissed on the spot."

Wearily he waved her to a chair. "Be seated, Miss Morecroft." He took her place in front of the fireplace. Standing a little to one side so he didn't block the heat, he removed a gold enamelled snuff box from his coat pocket and toyed with the lid. Finally his eyes travelled from the apparently fascinating object to meet hers.

The hunted look in their intense depths shocked her. He ran a distracted hand through his dark hair and said, "Contrary to what happened at dinner, Mrs Hawthorne does not override my authority. The irony is that my reaction to the terrible injustice meted out to the men charged in relation to the Peterloo uprising blinded me to the injustices perpetrated at my own dinner table. I apologise."

She was caught off-guard by the plea for forgiveness in his smile. Then she realised his apology was meant as a dismissal.

She would not be that easy to be rid of. She smiled back. "You fight your battle on many fronts, Mr Hawthorne." They were not the words of a governess, but then, theirs was not a conventional relationship. She eased herself from the depths of the armchair and moved towards him.

He stood his ground. The wary look in his eyes amused and angered her. He had every right not to trust her.

She stopped inches from him, forcing him to lower his head to look at her. "I admire a man who holds to principle with such passion." Her voice was low. "My father was more interested in passion than principle, it would seem. I've heard whispers that connect him with your late wife and I can only say how sorry I am for the damage caused."

She had to stop herself from reaching up to caress the vein that throbbed at his temple. Anticipation crackled between them but he made no move to touch her.

Unsteadily, she went on, "I apologise if my frankness offends, but as my days are numbered I want the satisfaction of giving voice to my feelings."

He said, tightly, "I have already assured you, Miss Morecroft, your position is safe." He deposited the snuff box on the mantelpiece and clasped his hands behind him. "At Larchfield the principles of fairness I hold dear are enshrined. Last night, Lord Miles's calls for bloodletting drowned out my entreaties for reason but at least I am master of my own home. I repeat, your position is safe."

He would have gone on. Perhaps he did. Sarah had no recollection of what happened next. She could only register deep, stultifying shock.

"Miles? Lord Miles?" The words forced their way through her constricted throat. She covered her face with her hands.

Lord Miles, her own father. She couldn't bear it. Blinking, she dropped her hands to stare at her employer. Then, unable to bear her agitation, she took a few steps towards the window, gripping the heavy gold curtain as she turned. Anguish for her darling father swamped her, replaced by the realisation her position was hopeless. Her feelings for Mr Hawthorne had just been consigned to a dusty grave. She really was the daughter of his nemesis, only this time, it was no lie.

"Yes, Lord Miles." Mr Hawthorne ground out, staring into the flames. "Crusader for the status quo. God knows how he can harden his heart to such suffering." He became silent, his frown deepening. "But grief changes a man." He turned slightly, but did not meet her eye. There was hesitancy in his voice as he went on, "It can open his heart to compassion, or harden his heart through fear."

Helplessly, Sarah watched him. She was losing him. With every word, their distance increased.

"The fear of being hurt, twice, Miss Morecroft, will drain the courage of most men. Slice away at our legs and our arms, but don't tamper with our susceptible hearts."

She searched vainly for an appropriate response. But what could she say? 'I am not the daughter of the foster brother who betrayed you? I'm the daughter of your sworn political enemy.' The silence lengthened and she lost her opportunity. He turned and when he addressed her directly the passionate undertone had left his voice. "Lord Miles, pity the man, is deranged with grief at the loss of his daughter but he hardens his heart when it comes to the loss of others."

Sarah closed her eyes as she continued to grip the curtain with both hands. She was in orbit, her world was spinning. Mr Hawthorne's words taunted her. Shame, remorse and fear at her deception swamped her. The curtain, worn with age, tore and she stumbled forwards. Unable to focus through her tears, she started blindly towards a chair. Had he realized? Was disgust about to replace his earlier grudging admiration?

"Miss Morecroft!"

Before the ground met her, strong arms swept her into the air and against his chest. She squeezed shut her eyes, drinking in the heat from his strong, hard body, breathing in his comforting, familiar smell. Exhaling on a sigh of disappointment as he lay her on the leather sofa, her senses snapped back to life as he knelt, his face inches from hers.

"You are ill. Shall I send for a doctor?"

She reached for his hand, unable to open her eyes. Or unwilling? His anxiety would only be further reproach.

With a small shake of her head she whispered, "It's nothing. I shall be myself in a moment."

Unconvinced, he raised her head with gentle hands to push a cushion beneath.

"So weak and foolish of me." She turned away and covered her face with her hands. Tears threatened and her voice wavered. "I've never succumbed to the vapours, yet your talk of injustice fuelled my fears for my precarious situation."

It was true enough. No artifice required here. Without a shadow of a doubt she'd be punished for a situation entirely of her making. She had no one to blame but herself. Once the truth were known her father would hate her ... and Mr Hawthorne would hate her even more. It was enough to reduce the strongest of women to heart-wrenching sobs.

Sarah could not hold them at bay. Here was Mr Hawthorne at her side, on his knees in fact, yet her life lay in tatters. Her selfishness had resulted in this terrible situation of her own making. He'd never forgive her.

"Please, don't cry."

The depth of feeling in his whispered entreaty sounded a breath of hope. This was her moment. She must tell him now. But as his arms encircled her and she was pulled against his chest and set across his lap, and she knew he was about to kiss her, her resolve melted. This was the clearest and most passionate declaration she'd had yet of his feelings. She had not the courage to test them to such an extent.

"Forgive me," he murmured. He cupped her cheek and with his thumb, gently traced her lower lip. "I've unfairly attributed to you Godby's disregard for the feelings for others."

Sarah closed her eyes against the heartbreaking concern in his eyes. In a moment the tables would be turned. She'd be the one uttering the apology and she felt sick with apprehension. She chose her moment before he could kiss her again, knowing she'd never have the strength to utter her confession afterwards. "I'm not Godby's daughter." She took a quavering breath, tensing for his response, but he misunderstood. Brushing an escaped tendril of hair from her brow he said, hoarsely, "No, Godby has no part in all this. You are a woman, whom I must judge in your own right."

His breath tickled her ear and sent shivers down her spine. She cried even louder, and fearing he was holding her for the last time, sobbed into his neck, "I don't ever want to leave you." He'd certainly set her away after that admission.

He did not. In the heartbeat and a half it took him to digest the enormity of her confession, she felt him stiffen. She opened her eyes and stared into the depths of his tortured soul before their hearts collided. With one hand supporting her head, the other cupping her cheek, his mouth claimed hers.

It was a kiss that demanded surrender.

And she surrendered everything, except the truth, for she knew now that would be the death knell of all the hopes and dreams that were at last being satisfied here, on the Chesterfield in his library.

She met him at every level. The initial urgency of his hunger became the rapture of discovery as he trailed kisses along her jawline, her throat, her collar bone and she responded, leaving him in no doubt as to the intensity of her feelings.

"Father!"

They heard Caro's cry in the passage before she threw open the door and burst into the room leaving them just enough time to rise to their feet.

"Father, you can't let Miss Morecroft go!" Breathless, Caro gripped his coat sleeve. "Aunt Cecily says she won't tolerate any more impertinence, but Miss Morecroft was only defending me. She is the most wonderful governess I've ever had - and I love her!"

Mr Hawthorne cleared his throat. Above his daughter's dark head he gazed into Sarah's face, as if he were seeing it for the first time. She saw the softening in the depths of his intense dark grey eyes.

With a rare, sweet smile, he said, "Miss Morecroft is going nowhere. She will be very busy making sure tomorrow is everything you could have wished for. After that" — the look he sent Sarah made her tremble — "I think it's time to review the current arrangements."

CARO AND SARAH STOOD IN THE CENTRE OF THE BALLROOM VENETIA had had built and gazed with satisfaction at the huge vases of flowers placed on plinths in each corner. Swathes of pink muslin tied in bows — Sarah's idea — adorned the gilt chairs arranged around the walls.

"I hope I don't spend my evening occupying one of those," sighed Caro.

"You'll be so sought after you'll want nothing more than to rest your tired feet sitting in one of those," Sarah prophesied. "I'll wager there are more than a couple of eligible gentlemen, as we speak, who'd like to engage you for *every* waltz." She squeezed Caro's shoulder as they turned their attention to the refreshments table, before adding slyly, "Perhaps that nice Mr Hollingsworth is one of them."

Caro blushed. "Philly is much prettier than I am," she mumbled, pretending concentration on a silver urn filled with Lilies of the Valley.

"Only if one prefers plump, giggling girls." When she saw Caro was staring at her, eyes wide with expectation, she added, "In my opinion Mr Hollingsworth appears far more interested in tall, dark, serious young ladies."

Caro put down the urn with a clatter and clasped her hands together in a semblance of entreaty. "I don't suppose I could borrow a touch of your Olympian Dew?" she asked.

"I thought blue-stockings didn't approve of such artifice." Sarah pretended to sound prim as she took Caro's hand and led her to the stairs. "Only three hours until the guests arrive. We might as well start preparing ourselves now."

When they reached her tiny room, Caro sat on her lumpy bed while Sarah rummaged in her drawers for the pot of magic ointment.

"Didn't you say it was possible to be both a blue-stocking and a beauty?" Caro asked.

"I did." Sarah unscrewed the lid and dipped in her finger. "Aren't I just such a manifestation? Now you shall have just the merest suggestion of a blush of roses upon your cheeks, if you will allow me to do it. Exercising restraint is the secret. With your lustrous dark curls to set off your perfect pale skin, a tinge of colour will instantly transform you."

Caro returned to her own room to finish dressing with the help of Aunt Cecily's maid, Betty, but was soon back so that Sarah could complete her toilette. Betty could not be trusted with tales of Caro's use of complexion enhancers.

"What a couple of beauties," declared Sarah as they stood side by side in front of the small tarnished mirror which balanced on her chest of drawers. "Your father will be so proud of you tonight."

"And of you," replied Caro. But when Sarah glanced suspiciously at her she was met by Caro's ingenuous smile. She swallowed down her nervousness as she recalled Mr Hawthorne's expression when he'd vowed she'd remain. Dear Lord, dare she hope it would all end well?

"Let me help you into your dress, Miss Morecroft. I haven't seen it yet in all its glory."

"Only because I sewed the last stitch at four o' clock this afternoon." Sarah was pleased with the finished work. The esterhazy lutestring, the colour of rain-darkened sky, was cut low and fell in shimmering folds from just beneath the bust. A sense of devilry had inspired her to use the silver grey netting from one of Mrs Hawthorne's cast-off gowns for the puffed sleeves and a decoration of leaves around the hem which ended at Sarah's ankles. She still had the unusual silver and green dancing slippers beneath her bed which Caro had given her the night she'd supplied her with Venetia's clothing for her demonstration.

Caro gasped. "I cannot believe that with just a simple bolt of silver fabric you have made ... this! You should be a modiste."

Sarah preened at the compliment. "Your aunt helped," she said, smiling at Caro's open-mouthed amazement. "You remember her grey round dress from last season which she gave me? The one with the ugly, bulky rouleau just above the hem? I unpicked the rouleau, smoothed it out and cut from it the sleeves and leaf decoration."

Caro giggled. "I can't wait to draw her attention to it. She'll look like a boiled chicken."

"Now, now, Caro," Sarah admonished mildly. "Life has dealt your aunt a poor hand whereas you can look forward to a glittering future. As to becoming a modiste, it is a hard way to make a living but more than that, I'd miss you too much."

Caro stared at her for a long moment. "You won't ever leave Larchfield, will you?"

Studying the silver-backed brush in her hand, Sarah weighed up her response. The lie she was living had turned into a nightmare. She longed to unburden herself, but how could she under present circumstances?

"Not willingly," she said, unable to predict Mr Hawthorne's response to her deception? So much depended on how she conveyed to him the truth.

She gave Caro a quick hug and pushed her towards the door. "Your aunt and father will be looking for you. It's nearly time to start receiving guests downstairs."

Apparently satisfied, Caro turned the door knob then hesitated, her thoughts now focussed on herself. She looked suddenly stricken. "What if I'm not good enough?"

"Good enough?" Marching over to her, Sarah grasped her shoulders and looked into her face. "You, my dear," she said, severely, "will be the toast of the town."

Caro's frown vanished. Smiling, she stepped across the threshold, "My mother would have been proud of me, I think."

Sarah watched her disappear down the stairs, her fondness for the girl suddenly replaced with terror at her own imminent entrance. It was ridiculous. She'd been to dozens, if not hundreds of balls, all far grander than this small, country birthday celebration for Caro.

But Mr Hawthorne would be there, and that changed everything. She swallowed nervously as she smoothed her hair which she had dressed with ribbons to match her dress.

When it was time, she took the stairs from her bedchamber to the ground level. Servants scurried about, making last minute preparations, replacing the occasional wax candle that would not sit straight, glancing anxiously out of the window as the crunch of gravel heralded the first arrivals.

From half way down the stairs Sarah watched Mr Hawthorne greet his daughter as she was about to progress into the ballroom.

"I have never seen you in greater beauty, Caro," he declared, as she curtsied.

His gaze moved on to Sarah. She saw admiration flare into astonishment and her heart pulsed into renewed life. In a state of self conscious turmoil, she took the last few steps to the bottom.

"Miss Morecroft," he murmured, the touch of his lips sending shivers of excitement fizzing through her veins as he bowed over her hand, "you are without equal."

"Roland, there you are—" Mrs Hawthorne stopped abruptly as she rounded the corner. She frowned at the trio, her eyes drawn to Sarah's dress. "I had no idea you possessed such a fine gown, Miss Morecroft?" She slanted a suspicious look at her brother-in-law.

"Miss Morecroft has done a magnificent job making up the fabric we gave her, hasn't she, Papa?" Caro burst out. "It's a pity you didn't ask her to make your gown, Aunt Cecily."

Bridling as she glanced at her own gown of ruby velvet, adorned with every embellishment, Mrs Hawthorne presented Sarah with her back as she took Caro's arm. "Lavery is admitting the first arrivals. It's time you and your father did your duty."

Mr Hawthorne ignored the departing pair. His gaze locked with Sarah's. Laugher pealed in the hallway. Sarah recognised it as Philly's. She heard the click of the front door closing, the approach of voices, the rustle of silk. The lengthening silence was heavy with a thousand unsaid words, but Mr Hawthorne's eyes reflected everything she longed to hear. With a final lingering look at Sarah, he stepped back, ready to do his duty by his daughter but not before he'd asked in a voice hoarse with longing, "Promise the first waltz to me?"

Unable to speak, she nodded, admiring the way his evening clothes hung on his strong, athletic body and the confident way he carried himself as he strode into the saloon after Caro. Like a schoolroom miss, she shrank against the wall and covered her eyes with her hands, shivering with excitement.

He loved her! She'd known in from the start. And Caro endorsed their union. Arriving at the entrance to the ballroom she was still shaking, though now fear outweighed her excitement. She was going to have to exercise every piece of cunning and understanding of Mr Hawthorne's character if her heart's desire were to be realised.

Chattering and giggling, Philly and Georgiana entered the ballroom by the door opposite, accompanied by their dignified aunt. Sarah watched as the girls crowded around Caro, marvelling at her fine dress and improved looks. Some time later, their entrance was followed by a group of officers, dashing in scarlet, who stood, rather awkwardly in the centre of the room, casting surreptitious glances at the young ladies.

Sarah's mouth curved into a smile which took on the added joy of being collaborative as Mr Hawthorne joined her, observing, "The boys admire the girls when they think they're not looking, and the girls pretend ignorance, ogling the boys the moment their backs are turned." Leading her towards a corner, he plucked a glass of orgeat from the tray of a passing footman.

She accepted it with a grimace. "I trust you'll serve something a little more fortifying, later this evening."

"You perplex me, Miss Morecroft." He looked puzzled. Unconsciously, it seemed, he'd led her into semi seclusion behind the luxuriant fronds of a lush indoor fern. "When has champagne been the diet of a poor governess?" His hand moved to a small, faded scar above her wrist. Tracing it with the forefinger of his gloved hand, he smiled up at her as she trembled. "There is so much more I want to know about you."

Not yet! a voice screamed inside her head. *When the time is right ...* She swallowed and put her hand to her bosom to control her erratic breathing. Light strains of music drifted from the annexe where the orchestra was tuning up. The room filled with guests, but here they were alone. In a cocoon of intimacy.

"How can you possibly have escaped marriage" — his smile faded and his gaze grew more intense — "when you are so very lovely?"

Still she could not reply. He went on. "Or did you always wish to be a governess?"

Sarah tore her eyes away. Carefully, she said, "I became a governess because my father wished me to marry someone I could not care for. Not as a husband, anyway."

Clearly, her response astonished him. "Godby-?"

She cut him off, quickly. "My father wanted me to marry my cousin. We were more like brother and sister. My cousin didn't want to marry me, either, but when a parent believes he knows best" — she shrugged — "drastic action is sometimes called for."

"I would not have thought it of your father," he murmured.

"I nearly married—" She nearly said in her first season but stopped herself. She was treading a tenuous line between giving the truth and a reason for her actions. She could not risk being caught out, yet.

"Was it a match of your choosing?"

"We were mad for each other." Over Mr Hawthorne's shoulder,

Sarah regarded the group of young men in the centre of the room chatting amongst themselves. What callow youths they appeared compared with Mr Hawthorne. She slanted a glance at him. He regarded her soberly, the flirtation gone from his manner. He understood she wanted to give an account of her past as straightforwardly as she could before she was ready to embrace the next phase.

If her courage didn't fail her. "Two weeks before our wedding his regiment was called to fight. He did not return."

"I'm sorry."

"Yes, but that is nearly six years ago now." She met and held his eye. "Nearly as long ago as your wife died. At the time I believed I'd never get over it, but one can't forever mourn for what one cannot have."

"One can mourn for what might have been."

"Only hopeless dreamers do that. And not forever."

Mr Hawthorne's smile held admiration. "Your presence at Larchfield has been good for us all," he said. "The change in Caro has been remarkable. See, a young gentleman has just engaged her in conversation and she doesn't look as if she's about to sink through the floor."

"That's Mr Hollingsworth, whose innocent addresses to Caro nearly cost me my job." She gave him a wry look. "He's renting Hawthorndene until the end of the hunting season and appears a personable fellow. Certainly, he's charmed Lady Charlotte who seems to want to push Philly his way."

A group of young ladies brushed past Mr Hawthorne. When he stumbled against Sarah he did not move away. Sensation charged through her. She could tell he felt it, too. His breath stirred the tendrils that curled about her ears. "I need you about the place, Miss Morecroft" — his smile was self deprecating — "to keep me from descending into a crotchety dotage."

She could have adopted the light, bantering tone he'd employed, perhaps to put her at ease. Could have said such a thing was a long way off.

"I am not the governess you think me," she blurted. There! She'd exposed herself, at last. The truth had to be in the open before they could proceed. She tensed for his horror, his outrage.

Instead, he transferred her glass from her trembling fingers to the depths of the urn so he could grip both her hands.

"No, for I misjudged you. You are *so* much more yet I've been blind to the truth and for that I offer my humblest apologies." He lowered his head to gaze into her eyes.

"What?" Confusion swamped her.

"I believed any daughter of Godby's must share his disregard for the feelings of others. You have proved a true and loyal friend to my daughter. You have the courage of your convictions. You have earned my esteem and admiration—"

Oh, dear Lord, I must *tell him the truth.* She stepped backwards, drawing her hands from his grasp. Sick with fear, she struggled for the right approach. How could she not be tarnished, however artfully she offered her excuses? She had embarked upon her charade as a spoilt and thoughtless young woman. *But I am no longer that young woman*, she screamed inside. *I was once as careless as you believed, but you have shown me how to view the world with a new understanding.* She lay the palm of her hand upon his heart and fixed him with an intensity she had never felt before now. "Whatever happens, I hope I will always be worthy of your regard—"

"Father, Miss Morecroft, allow me to introduce to you Mr Hollingsworth."

Dropping her hand, Sarah turned, forcing herself to smile. Clever green eyes set into a handsome, chiselled face, smiled back. He had the kind of looks that would make the heart of many a young girl beat more quickly, thought Sarah, forcing her mind into the present. Dark brown curls swept back from a high forehead and pronounced side-burns followed high cheekbones above a strong chin and stylishly high pointed collar. In the final decider, his cravat could not have been more dextrously tied.

A quick glance at Caro confirmed that she was far from immune to his charm. Mr Hollingsworth, though of similar age to many of the young men here tonight, had an air of assurance which set him apart.

After he'd brushed his lips across the back of Sarah's hand and complimented her, Sarah excused herself. This was Caro's moment. She needed to win her father's approval of her new beau. And, Sarah

LADY SARAH'S REDEMPTION

needed time to rally her defences and embark upon a fresh approach before she was completely undone.

En route to the supper table she was waylaid by Mrs Hawthorne and Lady Charlotte. The latter peered at her through her lorgnette. "The silver lutestring I had thought so unsuitable for Caro makes splendid finery for yourself, Miss Morecroft." Her tone was cool. With a start she added, "Is that not the grey net from your old dress, Cecily? Why, Miss Morecroft, if you should unexpectedly find yourself without employment here, perhaps I shall take you on as my dressmaker."

Sarah inclined her head while anger bubbled up inside. "Mr Hawthorne reassures me that he and Caro have become far too attached to me to let me go" — she forced a thin smile — "and nor shall I be tempted to leave, no matter how great the inducement." With a haughty nod she left them.

The refreshments table was not far from the dancing but was afforded some privacy by its separation through open double doors. Sarah began making her selection as she watched Mr Hollingsworth lead Caro onto the dance floor to join a set for a country dance.

"It was not an auspicious moment to be interrupted, but nor was it the ideal place for such a conversation, Miss Morecroft."

Sarah started. She'd been unaware of Mr Hawthorne's approach.

His smile was artless and her heart somersaulted as he said, "We shall enjoy more privacy on the dance floor."

Retrieving the slice of ham Sarah had dropped upon the tablecloth with a fork and placing it on to her plate, he added, "Although I think perhaps one dance may not be enough to say all that needs to be said."

She hesitated. "I think it might be unseemly to engage the governess in even one dance." She'd been weightless with joy, earlier, but the truth of her situation could not be ignored. She was in an impossible situation and had not the least idea how to extricate herself.

He laughed and Sarah was struck by the transformation. The warmth of his expression erased the deep lines etched from nose to mouth, and his eyes glowed with humour and affection.

"I am master of Larchfield and tonight's host. You would do me a great honour if you reserved for me each of the three waltzes on

319

tonight's programme, Miss Morecroft. I think it would send rather an unequivocal message to the rest of the company as to how matters stand between us, don't you?" he murmured.

Sarah swayed towards him.

"May I take it you'll grant my request?"

What could she say? Her whole being screamed to be enfolded in his arms, the truth no longer a barrier as he rained kisses upon her face and lips. Well, perhaps he'd reserve that for once they'd left the dance floor.

Her longing must have been plain for briefly he cupped her cheek, his expression tender. "I hope I'm not being too presumptuous in taking that for a yes," he murmured, before he left her.

The 'Sir Richard de Coverly' was in progress. A dozen couples participated, performing their steps with endless repetition.

In the meantime there were more arrivals: a group of noisy young men in regimentals, causing the half a dozen wall flowers to raise hopeful heads in their direction.

Sarah stood near a group of neighbourhood matrons, pointedly ignored by Mrs Hawthorne. She tried to calm the turbulence of her emotions, tried to whip up the sense of delicious empowerment she'd have felt not so long ago at the prospect of Mrs Hawthorne's reaction when Mr Hawthorne led Sarah off the dance floor at the conclusion of the third waltz. But she knew she'd not be released from the grip of her overpowering dread and apprehension until her conscience was clear.

She returned Mr Hollingsworth's smile as he passed by with Caro on his arm. There was no point making some trite enquiry as to whether Caro were enjoying herself. Sarah had never seen her look so happy, nor so poised and beautiful.

Had Caro just discovered the antidote that would banish her demons forever? Sarah had no doubt that Mr Hawthorne had invested in herself the care of his damaged, passionate heart. It was a weighty responsibility. She prayed she would not fail him.

She shivered at the chill gusting in with the arrival of some late-comers. More young men, self consciously adjusting their high pointed collars after they'd been relieved of their outerwear by Lavery. She smiled at the stir of feminine interest.

A smile soon replaced by dismay as the assembled group broke up revealing a young man whose sheer height and breadth and thick red hair set him apart. Only that was not what drew Sarah's attention, and soon all those nearby.

Run! screamed the voice of salvation in her head. *It's all over for you. You've lost your chance and you can never be redeemed.* But horror curdled into sick inaction, rooting her to the spot.

The ringleader, a blonde, tousle-headed young captain, rose from his bow with an engaging smile, and glanced about the room. "Mrs Hawthorne, ladies. "Forgive us for being so late. Is Aunt Charlotte here? I daresay I deserve the earful she'll no doubt dish out, but we are here at last and-"

"Sarah!"

She hadn't realised how tensely she'd waited for it.

"Sarah?" the red-haired man asked again, his voice now low, questioning. He advanced a few steps. Sarah retreated in the face of his stricken look. Pale-complexioned with a dusting of freckles across his nose, and hugely broad shoulders, his presence filled her with as much affection as alarm. She hadn't realised she'd missed James so much. Her heart pounded. She wanted to throw herself into his arms then drag him from the room and tell him everything. She could not with so many eyes upon her. Her future happiness hinged on how she dealt with the next few moments.

She was aware of Lady Charlotte's gimlet eye trained upon her. She forced herself to give a little laugh as James approached. *Be calm*, she exhorted herself. *If you lose your composure now, it could be all over for you.*

"Hello, James." She grasped his wrist. How she kept her voice steady, she did not know. Smiling, keenly aware of the interest still trained upon her, she pulled him a few feet away. She realised she could not bask in admiration all evening without exciting the glare of publicity at such an interesting change of tone. "Goodness, you look as if you've seen a ghost. Had you not heard I'd taken a position as governess for Mr and Mrs Hawthorne? No?" *Please*, she prayed. *Not here. Don't let him unmask me in front of everyone.* Taking advantage of James's confusion, she went on, quickly, "It's a long story and I can't wait to catch up with all you've been doing. Only you'll have to excuse me as I've promised the next dance." In a low hiss she added, "Meet me at the supper table in two minutes."

Shaking, she made her escape. She soon gave up trying to load up her supper plate, instead watching beadily as Mrs Hawthorne quizzed the red-headed newcomer across the room.

A few minutes later James was by her side. Gripping her arm he exhorted her, "Dear God, Sarah, you know we all thought you were dead? How could you—?"

"Please, James!" she entreated under her breath, for another couple was now helping themselves to food, nearby. "There's a terrace just outside. I'll be there as soon as I can get away. I promise I'll explain everything! Just don't tell anyone who I am."

She pulled away, leaving her plate upon the sideboard. Her breath came in short, sharp bursts as she hurried towards the double doors. Caro smiled at her over her shoulder as she waited in line to perform her dance steps. Lady Charlotte cast her a narrow-eyed look as she slipped from the room.

Sarah steeled herself as she stepped from the passage out onto the terrace, heedless of the chill upon her bare shoulders.

In just a moment she'd be calling on all her reserves of remorse and tact to soothe the feelings of a kind and honourable man who had every reason to feel hurt and betrayed.

Poor James, she thought as she prepared to sink her pride. Her spirits sank even lower as she reflected that her ordeal with James was just the prelude to her mortification.

CHAPTER 10

TREMBLING, SARAH PACED the gravel terrace just around the corner from where the doors opened wide upon the garden outside.

The final chords of the 'Sir Richard de Coverley' were followed by a smatter of clapping. Sarah chewed her knuckles. After a short interval the orchestra would break into the exciting, romantic strains of the waltz. She stifled a sob of disappointment. If she could tell James the truth, quickly, she might be back in time. The fear of James revealing her true identity battled with her fear that Mr Hawthorne would come looking for her.

She continued to pace, her mind in a panic, oblivious to the soft tread upon the gravel until she virtually collided with him.

"James!"

"Sarah!"

Seizing his arm, she pulled him into the seclusion of the shrubbery.

"Do you realize your father is half mad with grief?" he demanded, angrily. "Not to mention the agonies *I've* suffered on your account. I can't believe you've done this!"

His words were like barbs in her already battle-scarred conscience.

She couldn't bear to see the pain and anger that roiled in his hurt, angry green eyes.

"You don't understand, James. I had to leave."

His chest heaved but he said nothing, though he quirked an eyebrow in invitation to go on.

"It was because of you—"

"*Me?*"

She reached up to put her hands on his shoulders. "Papa was pressuring me to accept your offer. I knew you didn't really want to marry me—"

"That's not true!" he interjected, but his voice lacked conviction.

"Oh James," Sarah sighed, hooking her hands behind his neck and wilting against him. She wanted him to forgive her but she didn't want to be forced into revealing the full truth. Not now.

"It *is* true. And as I wanted to marry you as much as you wished to marry me—" she shrugged, nestling her cheek against his chest — "I thought that disappearing would be the best way of winning Papa round."

James grunted as he stroked her hair, the sounds of the next waltz drifting through the open windows. "Lord Miles would hardly have forced you to the altar against your wishes. Sarah, come back!" He made a lunge for her as she disengaged herself and ran towards the house.

"I'm promised for this dance." Frantic, she skirted the bushes which separated the terrace from the French doors leading into the house. "Say nothing. *Please*," she begged over her shoulder. "My entire life's happiness depends on this waltz."

She was reassured more by his expression of dawning understanding than his attitude of resignation. But she'd known James her whole life. He'd often looked at her like this. And he'd never yet let her down.

SMILING, ROLAND WATCHED MISS MORECROFT WEAVE HER WAY over to the supper table. For such a slender young woman she had a hearty appetite. It was the second time this evening she had piled her plate so high. A frisson of excitement ran through him as he antici-pated their forthcoming encounter on the dance floor.

"Know you'd have me whipped for the sentiment if you could, Hawthorne, but I wasn't sorry to see those trouble-makers swing."

Roland turned with a resigned smile. He'd known it wouldn't be long before Colonel Doncaster espoused such sentiments. Wrinkling his claret nose, his oldest friend and neighbour went on, "They'd turn England on her head if they could."

Now was not the time to enter into a spirited debate on politics, justice and the social system, though Roland knew this was what the colonel was angling for.

"Colonel, we are celebrating my daughter's come-out." He smiled a warning before greeting Mrs Doncaster with genuine pleasure. A sensi-ble, good looking strawberry blonde in her early forties, she knew how to keep her husband in check.

"You've picked up a pistol for less, Roland," the colonel reminded him.

It struck a nerve. "I was a callow youth."

Mrs Doncaster put a gentle hand on her red-faced husband's sleeve. "Roland has more sense now. It's time you married again, Roland," she told him. "The days of Venetia and duelling and risking your life for your beliefs is over." There was a glint in her eye. "I know several young ladies who would suit you very well if you'd let me introduce them."

"Frances prides herself on being the canny one in matters of the heart," her husband said, putting an arm about her waist, "but I'd wager something's already in the wind if Roland won't talk politics with me."

Roland gave a good-natured laugh. He'd lost sight of Sarah though he'd scanned the room several times for her. The 'Sir Richard de Coverly' was winding down and he was aching for the promised waltz.

Unconsciously he shifted position to ease his growing anticipation, and was whisked into the present by Frances remarking slyly, "I believe you're right, Seb! Tell us, Roland, is Cecily's position as mistress of Larchfield about to be usurped?"

Roland blinked. Was he that transparent?

Laughing, she observed, "You always were one to wear your heart on your sleeve, which is why I know there's been no one since Venetia."

"Frances, you're embarrassing the poor man." The colonel's tone was full of disgust. "Men of sound mind do not wear their hearts on their sleeves like namby pamby boys or swooning maidens."

"But my dear, I well remember Roland doing just that when you brought me here as a new bride," she objected, undaunted. "He was captivated by Venetia, just as you were captivated by *your* new bride." She patted the colonel's arm as his complexion took on the deep ruby hue of her gown.

"Excuse me." Roland left them with a bow and a smile. "I am under an obligation to claim the next dance." Full of expectation he left their good-natured circle in search of Miss Morecroft.

"Caro, you haven't seen Miss Morecroft?" he asked his daughter, who was being escorted onto the dance floor yet again by Mr Hollingsworth.

"No, Papa. Aunt Cecily, have you seen Miss Morecroft?"

"Miss Morecroft?" Her aunt sniffed while Lady Charlotte indicated the doorway. "Left a couple of minutes ago. Seemed quite discomposed by some fellow who'd just arrived."

With a final, worried glance around the room Roland turned into the passage as the orchestra tuned their instruments. Waltzing with Godby's daughter would cause far more of a stir than dancing with a mere governess. Had Miss Morecroft taken it upon herself to *spare* him?

Impatiently, he waited outside the mending room set up for minor repairs to the ladies' gowns. He could think of nowhere else she'd be. She wasn't downstairs, Augusta and Harriet were in Ellen's care, and Miss Morecroft would hardly be out in the chill night air.

He willed her to issue through the doorway; to look him up and down in that assessing way of hers which always reassured him she didn't find him wanting.

Pacing impatiently, he pictured her in his mind's eye. Like Venetia, she was beautiful and proud. But Venetia had been venal and calculating. Venetia had taught him how to reap the rewards of desire: how to pleasure a woman and what unexpected pleasures a man might likewise enjoy at the hands of a woman. He'd been a willing pupil, hurling himself headlong into a surfeit of lust. And when he had totally surrendered to her all he had to give – his heart, his body, his every waking thought, almost his own sense of self – he had realized her pleasure had been largely in his surrender, in her ability to conquer.

Then she had moved on, like a predatory shark, to fish other waters.

But Miss Morecroft was not like that. Miss Morecroft had kindness and sincerity to compensate for the traits she shared with Venetia.

"Mary, have you seen Miss Morecroft?" he asked the maid who opened the door of the mending room. Hearing the urgency in his voice, he added, "Caro is looking for her."

Instantly he was ashamed of himself. Was it necessary to conceal from one of his employees that it was he, himself, who wished to find the governess?

No, he didn't care what Mary, or Cecily, or anyone thought. Miss Morecroft was the most divine, spirited, engaging woman he'd ever met. He'd thought keeping her at Larchfield as the girls' governess would be enough. Now he knew he had to marry her.

Instead of being dismayed, he exulted. For the first time in his life he was about to yield to his desires with supreme confidence in the outcome. They would make each other happy. He was certain of it.

His frustration increased as the orchestra launched into the waltz he had looked forward to with such anticipation.

"I saw her running outside just a few minutes ago, sir." The maid looked disapproving as she rose from her curtsy. "Not even a cloak or shawl to keep her poor bare shoulders warm this freezing night."

Thanking Mary, he stepped through the French doors. He was worried now. The sharp air stung his face and he stamped his feet and rubbed his hands together to warm them. Why on earth would Miss Morecroft rush outside into the freezing night when she was supposed to be enjoying the warmth of his embrace? He thought of a dozen reasons to reassure himself as he crunched his way along the terrace. Perhaps she'd fallen ill, or felt faint, then re-entered the house by another door.

He scanned the immediate area as far as the light from the windows penetrated, then continued along the side of the house to where the terrace disappeared around the corner, half shrouded by shrubbery.

Hearing voices, he moved closer.

"Oh, James ..." There was anguish in the young lady's voice. He could not see her, obscured as she was by the shrubbery, but it was clear by the sigh and tone of her voice as she continued, that she was in company with someone familiar to her.

Caught between making his presence known, and the natural impulse to eavesdrop, Roland was on the point of retracing his footsteps to the house when the urgency in what only now he realised was Morecroft's voice arrested him.

"I wanted to marry you as much as you wished to marry me."

Disgust infected Roland's veins with cold, sluggish blood as he heard her next words. "I thought that disappearing would be the best way of winning Papa round."

Then the young man answered. "Lord Miles would hardly have forced you to the altar against your wishes. Sarah, come back!"

Roland stepped back against the bushes as she ran past him. He heard the doors slam shut behind her. The low groan of the now deserted young man was followed by the sound of his footsteps disappearing in the opposite direction.

Roland's breath rasped on the icy air as he stumbled towards the house.

SARAH SCANNED THE ROOM FROM HER SECLUDED CORNER VANTAGE point while she regulated her uneven breathing. There he was, talking to Colonel Doncaster on the far side of the room.

Surely, she thought, Mr Hawthorne could not be thinking her a flirt or a jilt for missing their appointed waltz? A sudden call upon her time by one of the girls, a torn skirt, or twisted ankle was far more likely.

He appeared not to be aware of her as she brushed past him and the colonel. Glancing over her shoulder, she tried to catch his eye as she wove her way through the crowd. Her ploy was not successful.

For a few moments she stood alone by the double doors which separated the card room from the dance floor. Her glass replenished, but not her spirits, she frowned at him as he disengaged himself from the colonel. If she didn't know better she'd think he was ignoring her.

Out of pique?

She felt sick. Mr Hawthorne couldn't imagine she was playing games with him — could he?

James had engaged Caro for the next set. Caro smiled, acknowledging her governess with a wave as they passed nearby. To Sarah's relief, James pretended ignorance of who she was.

Growing fear twisted her gut. Miserably, she watched as Mr Hawthorne stood, grim and woodenly, conversing with Lords Digby and Denning, ancient acquaintances of her father. It felt as if the evening were closing in on her.

Sarah positioned herself a little away from Philly and Georgiana so as not to bring attention to her solitary state while she waited for an opportunity to waylay him. He must know she was here. All evening she'd been thrillingly aware of his eyes following her around the room.

Watching him discuss a matter that was apparently of weighty concern, she was gripped with longing as he raked his hand through his hair in that familiar gesture of his.

Was he talking of universal access to education and male suffrage? Such notions would send her father into paroxysms. He'd certainly have paroxysms if she informed him she intended marrying Roland Hawthorne.

With a determined tilt to her chin she pushed her shoulders back. Marrying Mr Hawthorne was exactly what she intended doing.

Lord Denning shook his head with sudden vehemence and Lord Digby scowled. She wondered what Mr Hawthorne could have said. Both men were her father's age, with a propensity towards apoplexy – on little provocation. Just like her father. She felt a pang, then rallied. Soon, this whole charade would be at an end.

As he extricated himself from the group Sarah seized her moment and glided into his path.

"Forgive me, Mr Hawthorne, for missing the waltz I promised you. I was called away, suddenly." When her apology was not greeted with the immediate pardon she'd expected, she stammered, "Calls on my time come from all quarters and the little girls required me for a moment. I am merely the governess, after all."

He frowned down at her. "Ah, yes, merely the governess."

Discomposed, she suggested, "Perhaps the next waltz?"

"There will be no more waltzes for me tonight," he said. "Forgive me." He bowed and was about to pass on but she stopped him, alarmed.

"Mr Hawthorne, I have angered you? Surely you understand-"

"Indeed I do, Miss Morecroft. If you will excuse me, there has been distressing news this evening. I am poor company in my current mood."

With another cursory bow, he was gone.

Sarah stared after him, fear and disappointment wrestling one another.

Think! It was perfectly reasonable, she told herself, that a man with such a powerful social conscience would need to mull over events in private. She'd do herself no favours badgering him for the cause of his distress.

Ignoring Mrs Hawthorne's beady-eyed stare, she rested against the large urn where he'd caressed her arm. Longing tore through her. And uncertainty. Perhaps he'd call her into the library to apologise, later.

"I've been trying to put my finger on it all evening, Miss Morecroft, and at last it's come to me."

Sarah met Mrs Hawthorne's gloating smile across the top of the plinth. She didn't intend straightening out of deference.

"Those dancing slippers belonged to Lady Venetia. I recognise them."

"You don't think I—"

"I'm not accusing you of theft, Miss Morecroft, merely recalling the last time they graced her ladyship's dainty feet."

Sarah said nothing. Mrs Hawthorne clearly would enjoy telling her.

"When the men brought her into the house from the river I asked my brother-in-law if he should like her buried in them." Mrs Hawthorne touched her necklace with bony fingers, feigned wistfulness twisting her features as she gazed at the couples on the dance floor. "Poor Venetia looked so lovely in death, her white gown clinging to her, her dark hair loose around her face." She fixed Sarah with a hard look. "In that moment I felt closer to her than I ever had." With a nod at the offending dancing slippers, she added, "I even felt sorry for her when Roland said he hoped they'd carry their deceiving baggage to hell."

CHAPTER 11

"MASTER WISHES TO see you, Miss Morecroft." Ellen put her head around the bedroom door and eyed Sarah, speculatively.

"When? Now?"

"At your convenience, miss."

It was, after all, still early. The household had retired late to bed.

But the few intervening hours had yielded little sleep. Sarah had not yet finished dressing, and as she bent over the small chest of drawers to peer into the mirror she was dismayed at the haggard face that stared, hollow-eyed, back at her.

"Have you done summat you oughtn't?" Ellen was nothing, if not blunt.

Sarah's heart lurched with the fear that had kept her awake half the night. He couldn't have seen her with James, surely. They were well hidden in the shrubbery. Perhaps Mrs Hawthorne, or someone else, had said something which reflected badly upon her? She tried to bolster her courage at the prospect that Mr Hawthorne might end the interview championing her, rather than chastising her.

Sounding as jaunty as she could, she replied, "Mr Hawthorne

received distressing news last night but he wants to talk to me about Caro."

Ellen nodded, apparently satisfied. "I'll send a message you'll be down directly," she said, disappearing.

Sarah set to work, remedying the damage of a sleepless night and low spirits with all the artifice at her fingertips. Fear and trepidation soon turned to anticipation. Perhaps his disappointment at matters beyond his control would lead him to seek solace in the arms of a woman he desired.

No longer sallow and hollow-eyed, Sarah appeared before him, roses blooming in her cheeks.

"You wished to see me, sir." She smiled as she bobbed a curtsy. She had exorcised her fear. She was filled with vigour and expectation.

He pushed back his chair and rose from his writing desk. There was no answering smile as he waved her to a chair. Yet his eyes appeared to drink in every detail, from the curls she'd arranged with such care to tumble from her Greek knot, before travelling the length of her best sprigged muslin.

Finally they returned to her face as she settled herself in a chair. Her heart beat wildly, in confusion. He looked as if what he saw pleased him not at all.

"That is correct, Lady Sarah." His tone was cold and formal.

She felt a moment's sense of disembodiment; as if she were looking at him through a waterfall. She blinked. He appeared to grow indistinct while the thundering torrent filled her head with noise.

She closed her eyes, gripped the sides of her chair and whispered through her dry throat, "How did you find out?"

"From your own lips."

When she opened her eyes it was to see his trained on her as if she were a spy who had infiltrated his household. "I overheard you and your ... lover ... out on the terrace last night." His disgust was evident.

"My lover?" She swallowed. "James is my friend. My childhood friend. You misunderstood—"

"Have I misunderstood that you are here on false pretences, impersonating a dead woman? Have I misunderstood that you are not, in fact, the daughter of my late foster-brother but the daughter of the man against whom I have fought tirelessly in the parliament for so many years?"

Shame burned her cheeks. How underhand and wicked he made her actions seem.

"I did not set out, intentionally, to deceive anyone," she murmured, plucking at her sleeve. "I was misidentified after the ship went down. And ... I had my reasons for not wishing to return to my father immediately."

"Well, your father's on his way here to collect you, madam. So you had better prepare yourself."

Sarah gasped. "No! Please, Mr Hawthorne. You don't understand—"

"There is no deficiency in my cognitive powers." His voice was chilling. He began to pace before the fireplace. "I understand perfectly that you have been acting out a charade, in my household, taking us all for fools. Having been deceived once before, Miss Morecroft — I beg your pardon, Lady Sarah — I am in no hurry to be taken advantage of again."

"But ... but I don't want to go. Please Mr Hawthorne—"

"Having crossed swords with your father, myself, so to speak, I am not surprised you don't want to go." He finished on a snarl. "But go you will."

There was no hesitation or wavering that could give Sarah encouragement.

"His anger's not the reason—"

"I do not care for your reasons, Lady Sarah. Your deception is enough." Already he was turning back to his desk, dismissing her. He waved his hand towards the door. "Please, go."

She rose. Clenching her hands into fists at her sides for strength, she made one more appeal.

"It was because of *you*, sir, I continued the charade. No other reason." She took a step towards him, widening her eyes in entreaty, although his back remained towards her. "Don't send me away, I beg of you. I cannot bear to leave you!"

Slowly he turned. Hope reignited in Sarah's breast. She had never spoken the truth more sincerely. If he would just forgive her and let her stay she would gladly spend the rest of her life doing penance.

"I have heard enough impassioned promises of reform to last me a lifetime, Lady Sarah." His voice was impassive. "Good day to you."

Blindly, Sarah rushed towards her room. Someone addressed her in the corridor. She ignored them, hurrying on until she had gained the privacy of her tiny chamber where she threw herself, face down upon the bed.

Oh, dear Lord, she exhorted silently. Make Mr Hawthorne accept her charade for what it was. He was drawing parallels between her behaviour and Venetia's. As bad, he suspected she was a spy. Clearly, he'd not considered her real reasons to be the truth.

After some time Sarah became conscious of a tapping on her door. A small dark head appeared, followed by a taller, red-haired one. Two pairs of eyes regarded her anxiously.

"Are you all right, Miss Morecroft?" Harriet asked, pushing open the door and padding into the room.

"Of course," said Sarah, as brightly as she could. She sat up, forcing herself to smile, then caressed Augusta's dark curls as the little girl rested her head against her arm. Harriet snuggled up close on her other side.

Sarah's contrived cheerfulness seemed not to assuage their concerns. They continued to eye her fearfully.

"Why would you think I am not? Caro's ball was perfectly delightful," she babbled. "Your sister was a credit to you all; and I am as hale and hearty as I ever was. Perhaps you are here to pester me to give you more French verbs to conjugate?"

They ignored her attempt at levity. "Ellen was being strange this morning," said Augusta. "And then she just left us in the nursery ... alone."

"She never does that," said Harriet. Her dark eyes were luminous with worry. "And she said you weren't coming to teach us this morning. That something had happened and that you weren't our governess any more."

"But if you're not our governess any more," said Augusta, her bottom lip quivering, "I swear I'll not conjugate French verbs for any other governess, ever again."

"Come now." Sarah hugged the little girl who had started to sniffle. "Ellen has made all this seem like the end of the world. I'll never leave you completely. I'll always be there for you in spirit. And even if I have to go away for a little while, I ... I'll do my best to come back."

It was hard to keep her voice from breaking. The thought of leaving her young charges, she now realized, was almost as heart-breaking as being wrenched from Roland.

"I knew it!" cried Caro, bursting into the room and confronting Sarah, hands on hips. "I knew you didn't *want* to leave. And we won't let you! Whatever father says ... well, I don't know what all this is about, but he's *wrong*!" With a hiccupping sob, she began to pace.

It was all too much for Sarah. Unable to check the tears that rolled down her cheeks she tried to comfort the girls who were all crying loudly.

The door opened once more. This time it was Ellen, standing stony-faced in the passage.

"Lady Sarah, Mrs Hawthorne says your new bedchamber is ready for you."

"What?" Sarah frowned.

"Bein' a lady an' all, miss, you can't be expected to sleep rough like a servant," said Ellen, bobbing a respectful curtsy, although her expression remained cold. "Mrs Hawthorne has had one of the guest rooms prepared until such time as 'is Lordship arrives to take you 'ome."

"So, it's true," said Caro, slowly, drying her tears with her cuff, and frowning at her when Ellen had gone. "You really are the daughter of Lord Miles. Papa said ... you had deceived us all."

Sarah found it hard to meet her eye. Taking a deep breath for courage she said, quietly, "If you would allow me to tell you the whole story, I would greatly appreciate it."

She left nothing out. The spoilt, pleasure-loving society darling had learned some hard lessons, and she was prepared to put herself forward as an example of what not to do when faced with an obdurate papa. At the same time, she needed the girls to know her affection for them, and her employer, was deep and sincere.

At last she rose, with a sigh. "I'd better prepare myself for my father's arrival."

"What will your father do?" whispered Harriet.

Sarah considered a moment. "Well, he will probably be very courteous and correct and polite because he will be a guest in your house. But later he will shout and stamp around, probably throw a good many things."

"At you?" Caro asked, horrified.

"No, at the wall. And then he will hug me so hard I'll hardly be able to breathe, and then he'll cry a great deal."

The girls blinked in surprise. "Men don't cry," said Augusta. "At least, Uncle Roland doesn't."

"He does," said Caro. Colouring, she mumbled, "At least, he did."

"When Aunt Venetia died, I suppose," said Augusta. "Well, that's allowed. Even men can cry when people die."

"Oh, Papa never cried *after* mama died," said Caro. She glared at Sarah before her face crumpled. "But I'd wager he will, now," she said on a sob.

The door opened and Ellen reappeared.

"I shall take the girls now, m'lady," she said, briskly.

Sarah stared with longing at the young charges she might never see again, and the funny little nursery maid whose trust and dignity she'd so injured. "Please Ellen, I-"

Ellen cut her off. "Lizzie will be here shortly to pack for you." The girl refused to look Sarah in the eye. "Mrs Hawthorne says tea is in the drawing room whenever you wish to present yourself."

ROLAND'S HAND TREMBLED AS HE REPLACED THE DECANTER, THE sharp brandy fumes burning before he had taken the first sip. He hadn't felt like this since Venetia had left him the first time.

Or had the familiar loneliness that now consumed him been more a feature of his life *with* Venetia while her departure had occasioned relief?

Roland was not given to detailed analyses on the state of his heart. He had lost it when he was twenty, and the mauling it had received over the next ten years of marriage had convinced him that hearts were best left to the domain of women.

To banish the thought of Miss Morecroft – Lady Sarah - he thought of his election campaign just around the corner. He was for the abolition of rotten boroughs.

He smiled grimly. Not an idea Lord Miles favoured. And why would he when he could exploit his position and be re-elected time after time with little inducement – just the threat of increased rents for his tenants.

Taking another sip, he stared down the gravel drive that wound through the gardens, disappearing into the darkness of the park beyond.

Soon Lord Miles's carriage would lumber up that driveway. He wondered at the nature of the inevitable exchange between them before it lumbered back down the drive again, Lord Miles's daughter ensconced, inside, in padded comfort.

It would be the last he would see of Lady Sarah.

As it should be.

He sighed deeply, wishing the exhalation and the refilling of his lungs occasioned some relief. But there was pain in every breath.

He was replenishing his tumbler when there came a knock upon his door.

Caro? He hoped not. He hadn't the stomach for more of her tears and passionate entreaties. She'd left him half an hour before, weeping and vengeful. He was still shaken by the encounter.

"Your harsh judgment of me is ill deserved, Mr Hawthorne, for all I admit I am guilty of deceit," came a cool, formal voice.

Unannounced and uninvited, she entered the room, moving with her peculiar grace until she stood squarely before him.

Lord, she was beautiful. The light seemed to have laid a rosy cast upon her perfect skin, set off by her gleaming hair which seemed tinged more with russet in this light. She had always been confident but standing here before him, as Lady Sarah, she seemed like an unobtainable goddess.

Unobtainable, like Venetia had once seemed. And little joy he had got from attaining what he had once believed was his heart's desire.

Silently, he digested the young woman's impertinence while he drank in the perfection of her form: full breasted and wasp-waisted with the most kissable lips he'd ever encountered.

He glanced away, pretending to note the hands of the clock, so as to hide his aching desire. Longing tore at him, devastatingly familiar. He clenched his fists at his sides. Succumbing to his heart would be his undoing.

"I believe Mrs Hawthorne is expecting you in the drawing room." He ignored her words, his expression impassive as he turned back to face her.

"Why are you doing this?" She took a quick step forward, her voice barely above a whisper.

He noted the effort it took her to keep it under control. Well, it was hardly surprising she was upset. She had been unmasked; her whole story was a fabrication. She had taken them all for fools, to suit her own ends. Whether it was for a lark, or because she was acting the spoiled child who wanted to teach her father a lesson, or even if she was a spy, which he naturally no longer believed. Of course she would feel the need to justify herself. Her pride required that he forgive her and farewell her as his friend when she left on the arm of her father, rather than ejected in ignominy.

"I'm sorry?" He raised an eyebrow, his tone as disparaging as he could manage when sorrow and disappointment were equally in the ascendant. "Why do I do what, Lady Sarah?"

He could see her barely contained anger in the rise and fall of her bosom as she stared at him through those exquisite, heavily lashed hazel eyes.

He answered his own question. "Why do I expel an imposter from my household? A woman whose motives can only be under suspicion for failing to reveal herself?" He had not meant to insult her so directly. But his instincts for self preservation were honed to the highest degree.

"I have explained that my reasons were entirely prompted by a spontaneous act of ... desperation," she said, tightly.

He turned his head away from the sight of her eyes bright with unshed tears. Silently he willed her to give up the fight and just leave.

He did not have the fortitude to cope with another emotional female right now. Hadn't he spent the last few years ensuring that emotion — certainly that of a romantic nature — did not become the architect of his destruction? Ten years of Venetia was more than a lifetime of tears and tantrums. And one glance at Lady Sarah's damp, glistening lashes was a frightening prospect. What if she should cry ... throw herself at him?

Good God! He would be undone. Under such heavy fire he didn't trust himself not to reveal what was in his heart and do something unutterably stupid. Like tell her he loved her. Then she'd never give up her fight.

She took a steadying breath. "If you choose to put a more sinister slant upon it ..." Her voice was controlled, cold, even.

He didn't like to admit he was disappointed that she refrained from continuing in a more emotional vein. The heat had gone from the exchange. Reason had returned.

"Clearly, Lady Sarah, you cannot remain as governess to my girls," he said. He tilted his head, awaiting her corroboration.

She bowed her own, her rich reddish gold locks gleaming in the slanting sunlight. It took the greatest self control not to brush his hand over her silken tresses and tangle his fingers in the soft curls that fell from her top knot. A tantalizing expanse of white, flawless skin extended from the nape of her neck to the back of her gown where a row of tiny pearl buttons began, and ended somewhere – he swallowed – below her waist.

Roland closed his eyes as he fought to retain his distance. When she raised her head to fix him with her hurt, angry eyes, he had put the sofa between them.

She whispered, "I shall miss them."

Was the regret just part of the act? he wondered. They did seem fond of her, but an accomplished imposter surely did not form dangerous personal attachments?

"Then I'm sorry you set yourself up for such disappointment." Though his tone was dismissive he longed to continue the exchange. He realized with a wave of overpowering disappointment it may well be their last. "Please don't paint me the villain for acting differently from any other responsible employer, or gentleman."

At her look of entreaty, he added, "What else would you have me do? Keep you on indefinitely as a most attractive houseguest?"

He wished he had not said that, just as he would have regretted anything else said to cause the rise and fall, the delectable swell of lily white flesh above the low, lace-lined cut of her bodice. It was a direct assault upon his senses, upon his ability to utter words of reason. For indeed, his words were reasonable. What else could he do but send for her father to fetch her?

"Is that all?" She swallowed and bit her lip. There was a dangerous gleam in her eye. "Do you mean to tell me that ... before ... you were simply taking advantage of an attractive... governess? If there was nothing else ...?"

She could not finish and he immediately felt put in the wrong. "I am not that kind of man," he muttered. "I told you before."

"Then if there were some ... feeling behind your past words and actions, how can you dismiss me so coldly? Why are you unable to acknowledge-"

No, this was too dangerous. He cut her off, running the back of his hand across his eyes to ease the pressure pounding in his head. "We are getting nowhere, madam." He took several decisive steps to his desk. Pulling out his chair, he turned with a look of cool enquiry, as if daring her to detain him further. "Thank you for your services. If you have any further requests, I suggest you direct them to Mrs Hawthorne. Good day."

From the casement Sarah watched the crested carriage roll up the driveway and halt before the front steps. She felt a surge of guilt, fear and, yes, above all, joy at seeing her father's mane of grizzled white hair as he removed his top hat for a moment to give his scalp a good scratch, frowning up at the house as he did so.

Then she saw the hunted look in his tawny eyes replaced by echoing joy as he recognized her through the glass window.

Within moments he was indoors, thrusting his outerwear at Lavery, while Sarah was running down the curved staircase, throwing herself into his arms at the bottom.

Unashamedly, they both wept. Then Lord Miles raised his head and caught sight of Roland over Sarah's shoulder.

For an instant he froze. Sarah, still gripped in a fierce bear hug, felt the strange cocktail of emotions replaced by one dominant feeling: fear. What would her father do now?

He appeared to falter. For one ghastly moment she thought he was about to break down and would have to be led to a chair and revived.

That, she decided a moment later, would have been preferable to his finding solace in anger, his habitual refuge. It would be over in an instant, but she cringed as he directed his obviously confused emotions upon Roland.

"How dare you contain my daughter, a vulnerable unmarried female, under your roof for nearly two months while I am left with the unspeakable devastation of believing her dead?" he thundered.

Shaking his fist, Lord Miles took a threatening step towards Roland. Sarah wondered if Roland, too, would defend himself using his most comfortable defence: irony. She was surprised when he advanced towards Lord Miles, hand outstretched, a tight half smile upon his face. Surprised, and touched, that when her father refused to grasp it, Roland placed it instead, in a most conciliatory manner, upon the old man's shoulder.

"Lord Miles, may I offer you some refreshment — brandy — perhaps, after your tiring journey?" he suggested. Already he was motioning to Lavery to expedite this request.

"Do you think I would accept refreshment from my enemy?" thundered Lord Miles.

Sarah held her breath and watched as Roland gently propelled Lord Miles through the hallway. Her father moved slowly, like an old man. Remorse cut through her like a knife.

"Our opposing political views and previous history," said Roland, carefully, "do not necessarily make us enemies."

"An enemy milks his advantage. For the past two months you have detained the one treasure I hold dearer to my heart than any other."

He stumbled as he turned to look at Sarah, who was bringing up the rear. How feeble he appeared, she thought with horror. Surely he had not lost his mind? Dear Lord, she prayed, do not let her be the cause of that.

"My lord," said Roland, taking a seat opposite Lord Miles once they'd gained the library, "make what charges you will once you have spoken to your daughter. She's been recovering after a terrible ordeal at sea and, I fear, has not known, herself, who she really is. Had the truth been apparent, your Lordship would have been informed upon the instant."

Sarah wished Roland had given *her* the benefit of such a plausible pretext.

The brandy revived Lord Miles. He sat up straighter and fixed a pair of small but intense eyes on Sarah. How well she remembered that look, terrifying beneath his beetling white brows. He'd often used it to great effect, quelling her when her opinion ran counter to his.

But now there was no firm conviction to defend. Only his grief and pain to assuage.

Seated opposite her father, Sarah clasped her hands in her lap and hung her head. "Forgive me, father," she murmured. "I accept all blame. I've taken advantage of Mr Hawthorne and his family who have looked after me so kindly, ignorant of the truth. And I have given you more pain than any father ought to bear."

"Why, Sarah?" Lord Miles's confusion was pitiful.

Mr Hawthorne rose. "I shall leave you for a few minutes."

Sarah nearly wept at the regret on his face as he looked at her en route to the door. She wanted to leap up and throw her arms around his neck, delivering a different and far more passionate apology for her behaviour than the one she was making her father.

So this was it. She would not be granted a reprieve.

He was nearly at the door when Mrs Hawthorne's raised voice issued from down the corridor.

"Roland!" she cried, sweeping into the room and wringing her hands. Without acknowledging her guest, she added, breathlessly, "Caro's gone! It's true, I found this upon your bed!" She waved a piece of parchment, its seal broken.

He took it, scanning it quickly. "This letter is for me."

"The door to your chamber was open, Roland, and when I saw it I thought ..." Her voice trailed off as she looked with unmistakable loathing at Sarah.

So, thought Sarah, she would have had no compunction in intercepting and keeping secret from Roland any communication Sarah might have attempted.

"You must act quickly, Roland! Oh, my dear Lord, what will we do?" Crumpling onto the nearest chair in a heap of lavender stripes she began to wail.

Dry-throated, Sarah asked, "Does she say where?"

Not looking at her, Mr Hawthorne carefully refolded the paper. "She has gone to London," he said in clipped tones, "with Mr Hollingsworth."

Sarah gasped. "Does she say why?"

Mr Hawthorne ran a hand across his brow, while Mrs Hawthorne shrieked as she rose to her feet, "She has learnt the truth, Roland. I don't know how she could have discovered-"

"There is no proof to be discovered!" snapped Roland. "There has always been servant's gossip. It's not a plausible reason."

Sarah caught her breath and wondered why it hadn't occurred to her before that Caro's parentage would inevitably be called into question given Venetia's faithlessness.

"Caro is highly emotional, particularly now. He directed a pointed look at Sarah. "If she has overheard something which threatens her sense of security in this household I've no doubt her vulnerability has been compounded by feeling deceived by those she once trusted."

Anger replaced Sarah's lovelorn passion of earlier and she trembled with it as she rose. "I cannot leave unchallenged the insinuation that I bear some guilt for Caro's desertion."

"There's nothing you can do," he said, roughly. Addressing Lord Miles in more civil tones, he said, "Forgive my rudeness, sir, but I must leave, urgently. Please consider yourself a welcome guest in my home for as long as you choose. Arrangements have been made for you to stay the night rather than oblige you to repeat your long and tedious journey, in the darkness. Cecily." He turned to his trembling sister-in-law. "If you need me I shall be at my club."

"You cannot stay there if you find Caro," Sarah pointed out. Clubs did not admit women.

"At the Crown and Anchor, then," he said, tersely, his hand upon the door knob.

"Please, Mr Hawthorne," Sarah begged, "let me come with you. Caro trusts me ... "

Her voice trailed off at his withering look. She saw him close his eyes briefly, as if in pain, and run his hand over his face. "Caro," he said, "trusts no one anymore, it would appear."

CHAPTER 12

THEY BROKE THEIR journey at the White Swan after four hours of bad roads and inclement weather.

Lord Miles had managed to doze over the deepest of ruts and fords. Now that he had been reunited with his beloved daughter, Sarah supposed he probably had a few sleepless nights to catch up on.

As they waited in the parlour for the sumptuous feast Lord Miles had considered necessary Sarah felt at a distinct disadvantage. Fatigue sapped her, as if she had not slept a wink in two days.

"A bottle of claret, a saddle of beef and a blazing fire will make words between us easier," said her father.

Sarah nodded as she thought of Roland, galloping towards London to try and find his daughter, yet having no clue as to where she might be, and her heart convulsed. Vulnerable, overwrought Caro could not be in her right mind to have accepted an invitation to run away with Mr Hollingsworth. It was not even as if they were eloping. If they'd been heading north towards the border there was at least the consolation of assuming a hasty marriage was their intention. But London? Alone with Mr Hollingsworth? Surely she must know she could only be ruined by such folly?

Having polished off a bottle of claret her father's mood was much more sanguine.

"So you were punishing me for meddling in the affairs of your heart, my girl," he remarked, chewing on his beef and looking at her over the rim of his glass. "Well, you couldn't have devised a better way." Recrimination had been replaced by a soldier's acceptance of being bested in battle. "I'll not interfere in your matrimonial affairs again. James is courting a young lass, I hear. Well, perhaps that's premature, but it was only this last week that he has resumed pleasure-seeking. Nevertheless, he'll be overjoyed to hear you're safe and well. But if he comes courting–"

"He won't, father," Sarah told him with conviction. "We were never more than friends. Too much like brother and sister."

"I've been blind to a good many things, Sarah. With you gone I realized how much I relied on your cool judgment to temper my occasional outbursts."

"When have you ever lost your temper, Papa?" Sarah's mouth quirked before they both laughed. Lord Miles reached across the table and placed his hand on Sarah's. "Never leave me again, Sarah ... unless it's to be worthily wed. I've always wanted that but it appears you truly are determined to remain unfettered by the bonds of matrimony."

"No, Papa," Sarah said steadily. "I have no aversion to becoming a wife ... to a man worthy of me. Until that time I am quite content to pander to your vagaries of mood. I shall *try* and keep sufficient staff for our needs with the usual reassurances that the silver salver was aimed at the wall and not at their heads. It is a great relief," she added, pointedly, "that you are prepared to sanction my ultimate choice of husband."

"Looked to me like that young pup Hawthorne had a gleam in his eye when he turned it on you," Lord Miles said, reflectively, taking another sip of claret, apparently oblivious to the sudden flaming in his daughter's cheek. "Not but that he didn't try to hide it behind his stern words. Had he gone on trying to point the blame at you I'd have called him out!"

"I believe you called him out once before, Papa."

"Lily-livered girl didn't want to fight me. Had to, though, else it'd have been the end of that precious parliamentary career of his. Not but that we'd all be better off without his ilk – dangerous radical!" Lord Miles snarled. "It's the quiet ones with their bottled up passion you'd best be wary of, Sarah."

"Your passionate outbursts can be spectacularly frightening on occasion, Papa."

"Look at me and what you see is what you get. You'll have a much easier life with someone in my mould than a buttoned-up Puritan simmering with passion."

By dinner's end Sarah had managed to keep exhaustion at bay by sheer effort.

Theirs was a discussion long overdue. She needed to explain the desperation and helplessness that had driven her to flight. She needed, also, to reassure him of her love and remorse. She did not lie by citing amnesia as a reason for her deception, however she was guilty of omission as to why she had maintained her charade. She could not reveal her feelings for Mr Hawthorne. Instead she told Lord Miles it was her sense of responsibility towards the girls, Caro in particular, which had decided her to stay.

Finally she crawled into bed and slept, her reconciliation with her father at least some consolation. Lord Miles had been more angry that Sarah believed he'd force an unpalatable marriage upon her, than he was at her deception.

Sleep claimed her the moment she put her head on the pillow after their early dinner. Less than an hour later, she was wide awake. But of course how could she sleep when Caro was still missing and she and Mr Hawthorne remained estranged?

Wrapping herself in the counterpane to keep out the biting cold, she took herself off to the window seat.

The moonlight was blinding. Sarah dug the palms of her hands into her eye sockets, shivering. Her sleep-fogged brain whirled over the same points, without solution. If Caro's reputation were destroyed, she would never forgive herself. Was Mr Hollingsworth no more than a fortune hunter? Had he deceived them all? Or did he have a parson with a special marriage license waiting in London?

Her frozen feet throbbed from the cold. Stiffly, she padded over to the old trunk at the foot of her bed to look for something in which to wrap them. No longer did it contain the shabby garments belonging to the poor late Sarah Morecroft. Through industry, energy and cunning Sarah had managed in a short time to invent a wardrobe worthy of the lady she was. Minus, of course, those little extras. Like a rainbow-hued selection of dancing slippers and a fur wrap or ermine-lined mantle or pelisse, which would have been so useful at a time like this.

Her seeking fingers found the coarse woollen shawl Mrs Hawthorne had given her. In it, Sarah had wrapped Miss Morecroft's diary, but it held little interest. Poor Sarah Morecroft's life, despite her glamorous, dissolute father and exotic background, had been rather dull. Only her reverence for the rakish Godby had infused it with life.

Guiltily, Sarah fingered the soft, tooled leather cover as she resumed her seat. How amazing that it should have survived what its mistress could not. Only a few pages were rendered unintelligible by water damage, due to its thorough wrapping in oilskin.

She thought of the young woman whose life she had effectively commandeered for the past six weeks. They'd been friends during the few days Sarah had been aboard the ship which had carried Miss Morecroft from India.

Perhaps Mr Hawthorne's anger at her was born of his disappointment that Sarah was not the last link with his foster brother, after all. Perhaps he had believed a sense of kinship existed between them. Instead, he had decided she was nothing more than a pleasure-seeking society miss, out for a lark at his expense.

She flicked through the thick, parchment pages until she was close to the end. The diary had been started long before the young woman had known her family would soon be dead and that she would be setting sail for England to work for her father's foster brother.

Five pages from the end the ink had run and the smudged handwriting became difficult to read. Nevertheless, Sarah was soon absorbed by the young governess's thoughts regarding her impending journey.

She smiled, wryly. So her namesake hadn't had a high opinion of the dreary gowns her mother had mended and stitched for her, either. Pity

Miss Morecroft hadn't been blessed with Sarah's imagination and skill with a needle.

It was almost impossible to make out the final page. Sarah was on the point of giving up when three syllables in careful, looped writing caught her eye: Hollingsworth.

Her smile faded. With growing foreboding she bent her head, straining to read the context. It took several minutes to make sense of it and by then her heart was hammering. She no longer felt the cold as she cast off the counterpane. Only dread as she threw down the book and looked desperately for the clothes she'd worn last night. There was no time to lose.

Although the last sentence remained unfinished its ramifications were clear enough. Miss Morecroft's final diary entry had been a girlish eulogy of the handsome and charming Mr Hollingsworth.

"OI! WATCH IT!"

Roland sidestepped, just avoiding the wheels of the heavily-laden cart rounding the corner. Heart pounding, he leant back against the wall and closed his eyes.

Time was running out. For hours he'd called on friends and acquaintances, and scanned crowds in his attempts to find his daughter.

His initial inquiries around Larchfield had turned up nothing. Clearly, Mr Hollingsworth had invented himself; had arrived in the local area with no intention of ever being traced.

The noise of shouting and rumbling traffic echoed painfully in his ears. He knew he should keep moving but had not the energy. Eyes still closed, he surrendered to the dreamlike state that had begun closing in on him since he'd arrived in the capital. He thought of lovely Miss Morecroft — Lady Sarah — and conceded for the first time since banishing her that her motives may not have been all bad.

It was too late, of course. The damage had been done. He'd refused to give her a hearing. Whether she was now a prisoner of her tyrannical father or just her own guilt, he'd not see her again. She'd made clear her affection for him was deep and sincere but he wondered how long under her own roof, feted by admirers, it would be before she forgot him.

Despair and self recrimination curdled in his belly. How nearly he had become a fool in love, yet again. Lady Sarah wielded the same power over him Venetia had once had. If he gave her another chance, wasn't it likely she'd use it, like Venetia, to test his affections? Venetia had regarded the suffering her every betrayal caused as confirmation of her supremacy over him. He did not think his masculinity could withstand it happening again.

A tremor ran through him. He was not thinking clearly if he allowed his loss of Lady Sarah to override his concern for Caro.

Pushing himself away from the wall, he followed the pavement with unsteady footsteps. Dusk blanketed his long distance vision with a grey haze. Or was it weariness? His mind was not as sharp as he needed it to be. The hand he raised to his brow seemed made of lead. It was time to return to the inn and sleep. Sleep would be the restorative he needed so he could look at the problem with fresh eyes.

ROLAND AWOKE WITH A START. ALL WAS BLACK. HE HAD NO IDEA what time it was, or what had wakened him. He thought he heard a tapping. Had he asked for a light supper to be sent to his room? He closed his eyes. Perhaps he'd imagined it. Sleep beckoned once more. The comfort of its soothing embrace competed with the insistent tapping.

With a growl of irritation he hauled himself off his bed. He noticed he was still dressed, even had his boots on. Rubbing his eyes, he stumbled to the door and opened it a crack.

"I do not wish to be disturbed—"

Quick as lightning a small hand darted through the crack and gripped his arm. "Mr Hawthorne, it's me!"

"Caro!" Surprise and delight jolted him out of his foggy state but before he could respond in a more adequate fashion he was subjected to a fresh assault of shock waves.

"No, it's ... it's your wife."

His wife? What dream was this?

Blinking as the thickly veiled figure tried to push open the door, his brain ached with the effort of seeking reality.

The woman was unrecognizable beneath the black hat; the sweet, husky voice, however, clearly belonged to that of his nemesis.

Lady Sarah Miles.

"Sorry to disturb you at this late hour, darling." Her musical tone sounded over loud. "I was delayed but certainly hadn't expected you to have retired so early. Mr Hawthorne, I need to talk to you!" Dropping her voice to an urgent hiss, she made another attempt to force an entrance.

He stared at her, his boot firmly wedging the door against opening further. What was she playing at? She couldn't possibly come into his chamber.

He saw the publican in the crack of light taking the corridor to the west, and called to him. "My wife has arrived unexpectedly and requires her own bedchamber."

There were none to be had, the publican told him, pausing briefly. There was one room of ladies but the bed was already sleeping three. He could organize a truckle bed if m'lady desired that.

"No, no, I'll suffer my husband's snoring for just this one night," Sarah said with a sigh, elbowing herself finally into Roland's room, and closing the door behind her.

"What the devil are you doing here?" Roland hissed. Of course she could not stay. And he could show no weakness. For both their sakes. Her actions were tantamount to social ruin. Her father would put a bullet through his head.

"I have news." When she lit a candle he saw her eyes were wide with urgency rather than shining with the seductive gleam he had been expecting. She cast her hat upon the bed and said, as she raked her fingers through her hair, "I think I know where to find Caro–"

"Why did you not tell me, before?" he exploded, gripping her shoulders. He was aware his overwrought nerves sought refuge in a suspicion that was unjustified. But suspicion was so much easier at this moment than trying to make sense of the other confusing emotions besetting him in equal measure.

She looked at him, hurt. "Do you think I, who care as much for

Caro as you, would have kept from you *anything* that may have assisted in finding her. Listen-"

She stopped. Frowning, she tilted her head. "Roland?" It was the first time she'd used his Christian name. Music to his ears. Gently, she shrugged herself out of his grasp then helped ease him down into the comforting depths of the cracked leather armchair by the bed.

He opened his eyes to see her holding out a tumbler full of brandy. "I don't know if this will do you any good, or is the last thing you should be drinking in your exhausted, muddled, state," she said, with a small smile. "Do you mind if I help myself?"

Without waiting for an answer she poured another measure from the cut glass decanter on the mantelpiece before settling herself on the edge of the bed opposite him.

"I believe Caro's disappearance is connected with Sarah Morecroft."

Lord, but she was a sight to behold. Liquid fire burned his throat as desire pumped through his veins. Miss Morecroft was in the past. All that mattered was the young woman sitting before him. He could drink her in forever, watching her recount her fairytale, admiring her burnished hair while her melodic voice provided the pleasant background.

"Miss Morecroft's diary was in the trunk that was rescued."

He smiled. He liked the way her eyes fixed him with such intensity.

"When we broke our journey I could not sleep so I read the last few pages which I had not read before."

She stopped. Roland blinked.

"Are you listening to me?" Her tone was suspicious.

He frowned. "Of course."

He was trying. But the sleep he had snatched had done him more harm than good. Jolted into wakefulness by the very woman who occupied so many of his daydreams and nightmares, he now existed in a pleasant state of unreality.

Struggling to regain the urgency he knew was required, he leant forward. "Go on." He rubbed his chin and was uncomfortably aware of his dishevelment. Glancing down at his muddied topboots and limp neck cloth he couldn't even remember when he had last shaved. The

BEVERLEY EIKLI & BEVERLEY OAKLEY

hours he had spent thundering through the countryside must have exhausted him more than he realized.

"Sarah Morecroft helped Mr Hollingsworth with Caro's kidnapping!"

Roland smiled at her preposterous words. "You're saying my foster brother's daughter plotted—" he waved vaguely — "all this ... several months after her death."

"Sarah Morecroft intended revenge when she set out from India. When she met Mr Hollingsworth on board the *Mary Jane* they hatched a plan—"

Judging by her exasperation and sudden sharpness she had taken exception to something. Yet Roland had said nothing beyond "Oh really", and nodded his head. Perhaps it was his tone — some people took exception to his tendency to sarcasm. Miss Morecroft certainly seemed to, for she slid from the bed. Appreciatively, he sniffed her scent of Orange Flower water, and opened his eyes to find her standing over him. Her little white fingers dug into his shoulders as she tried to haul him to his feet. She looked angry and when she opened her mouth he expected her words to convey this.

Instead she froze. Slowly, her right hand travelled up his arm and then down, across his chest. He held his breath, a strange sensation pooling in the pit of his stomach.

"Roland, you're soaked right through." Her voice was low, almost accusing. The dainty white hand continued its exploration. It was a pleasant sensation. He made no rejoinder, simply closed his eyes and enjoyed her touch.

"No wonder you've taken in nothing!"

Oh, he was taking it all in. Revelling in it. He blinked at the insistent tugging at his waistcoat. She was undoing the buttons!

"Take it off," she said through gritted teeth when she was finished.

Weakly, he gripped her wrist to stay her, his sense of honour finally roused.

"Madam, I don't think you—"

"And your shirt."

Before he could object she'd rested her cheek against his chest.

"Lord, but you're chilled to the bone!" she exclaimed. "You'll catch your death unless I can get you warm."

He had not the energy to help her as she stripped off his shirt and bundled the counterpane round his shoulders. It was an effort for her to remove his boots but she succeeded. He suspected Lady Sarah achieved most things she set out to do.

Standing back, she raked him with a critical eye. "Now get into that bed and warm yourself." Her voice was sharp. "I think it's probably time for me to go. I'm not going to have you accuse me of taking advantage so I can demand satisfaction at the altar." Her voice was low and grim as she resumed her task of trying to haul him out of the chair and transfer him to the bed. "Despite the fact that would be eminently pleasing to me."

No, she had not said that. He had imagined it to complete his beautiful dream. He must not let his mind and body betray him into believing what he only wanted to hear. She'd betrayed him once. She had not the purity of heart he'd attributed to her before she'd shattered his trust.

With a final effort she had him on the bed, rolling him onto his back so that he looked right up into her eyes. Her beautiful, clear hazel eyes. She didn't step back. He swallowed, overcome by sensation. Lord, she was inviting him to take her into his arms. He closed his eyes, his honour engaged in a bloody battle with the exquisite sensations engulfing him.

"Roland."

"Darling Sarah," he whispered, opening his eyes. Gently he traced a finger down the side of her cheek and tucked a tendril of gleaming hair behind her ear. If the parson now came knocking with a special licence, he'd be the happiest man alive. He was almost the happiest man alive for the fact that her desire for him overrode the terrible risks. But she was as impulsive as she was beautiful. It was up to him to persuade her to wait. It took all his willpower. "Flattered though I am, my love—"

"You're lying on my arm ..."

"Oh, Lord," he muttered, shame and disappointment colliding as she tugged at her arm trapped beneath the weight of his body. He heard the urgency in her voice, but it was the fear in her eyes that went some way to clearing the mists swirling in his mind.

With an effort he rolled to one side and she stepped back, rubbing at her wrist.

"Roland, I think I may know where we can find Caro."

Caro. He groaned, covering his throbbing eyes with his hands. "What must you think of me?"

Amidst the rustling, he heard a chink of glass, another waft of the heady scent of orange flower water and the heart-stopping words, "That you are the most wonderful and honourable man I've met but that you are also very ill. Drink this."

His prayers were answered as she supported him behind the shoulders then held a tumbler of sweet water to his lips. He fell back when he'd finished, but not before he'd planted a kiss on the soft white skin below her collar bone.

"Sarah, you are a gift from the angels," he murmured.

Her soft, ironic laugh as she gently sponged his forehead filled him with longing. "Tell me that when you're in your right mind. I'm going now, Roland. I have to find Caro but I'll be back as soon as I can."

He wished he could open his eyes, but they hurt too much. Vaguely he held out his hand in her direction and she gripped it.

"Must you go, alone? Perhaps—"

"There's no time to waste and you've not the strength to pick up a kitten." He felt her lips upon his brow, heard her tremulous whisper. "If anything happened to Caro, I'd never forgive myself. I need you to know that."

CHAPTER 13

"**W**RITING IMPLEMENTS AND parchment in the private parlour," she demanded of the publican, searching in her reticule for a coin. "And a hackney."

Fear churned in her breast, but excitement, too, as Sarah scratched her note to Roland a few minutes later. She would find Caro. She would save the girl's reputation and Roland would give her the reward she craved.

The rest of her life in his company!

Hearing voices in the passage outside the door she put her hand to her bonnet to pull down her veil while she hastily sprinkled sand upon the parchment.

The veil was no longer there. As the voices stopped outside the door she heard the stentorian tones of a formidable matron apparently admonishing an errant daughter. She shrank into the shadows, clutching the folded parchment as a stout middle-aged woman wearing a green velvet round dress with matching turban entered the room.

"What were you thinking, Millicent? You danced three times with him. A young lady's reputation is her most precious commodity."

Horrified, Sarah realised the formidable Lady Bassingthwaite stood not three metres from her in the private parlour she'd been on the verge of departing. A stickler for observing the rules, she had in tow her plain and clumsy daughter. Although Lady Bassingthwaite was always scrupulously polite Sarah knew she disapproved of her. She guiltily wondered if that was because word had filtered through to her ears of Sarah's charade impersonating the venerable lady. She'd poked gentle fun at the lofty ideals of propriety for which Lady Bassingthwaite was known when she had pretended that accepting a handkerchief from a gentleman was tantamount to accepting his marriage proposal. Sarah winced. How foolish she had once been.

Fortunately Millicent's tears provided the diversion Sarah needed. As the two women made for the fireplace, she sidled towards the door.

"I beg your pardon, madam. I did not mean to intrude." Lady Bassingthwaite cast a distracted glance in Sarah's direction, but Sarah was not about to respond.

With thundering heart she dashed into the passage and thrust the parchment at the publican with instructions that it find its way to Mr Hawthorne.

To her relief a hackney carriage was waiting by the front entrance and she plunged inside. The excitement of her near discovery had sharpened the edge of tonight's whole drama, limned by the fact that Mr Hawthorne loved her. After tonight's dealings with him she needed no further proof.

Sinking back against the squabs as the carriage lurched forward, relief enveloped her.

Mr Hawthorne had called her his angel. He'd made clear that despite banishing her his feelings remained as strong as ever. How Sarah had struggled to beat her impulses into submission when the truth became clear in that close, dimly lit bed chamber, she'd never know.

Lady Bassingthwaite's stern reminder to her erring daughter was a timely reminder. A girl's reputation was her most precious commodity and to lose it was worse than death. Roland had admitted that he cared too much for Sarah to jeopardise hers. Now Sarah lay back against the squabs in the happy confidence that once she delivered Caro to Roland, she would have her 'happy ever after' ending.

Travelling through the Haymarket at this time of night was a new experience. With fascinated horror, she watched street urchins beg for pennies, and streetwalkers in tawdry, gaudy gowns accost gentleman passers-by. She'd been shielded from the seamier side of life on the occasions her father had escorted her back from the theatre.

Soon, though, her bravado fell away, eroded by the frightening unfamiliarity of the environment once they'd left the entertainment district. Shouts, hisses and catcalls punctuated the night. She snapped the curtain closed when a glimpse of her face attracted a half admiring, half jeering response from a young man with a dirty face and blackened teeth. And when the hackney turned down a narrow side street and slowed to a stop, her courage nearly failed her.

Sarah Morecroft's diary identified the street in Marylebone where the widow Hollingsworth kept a girl's school, but not its number. Rapping on the roof, she put her head out of the window to quiz the jarvey.

"School for young ladies?" The jarvey had smelled of beer when he'd handed her in, and now he gave a scornful laugh as he mimicked her refined accent. "'Ere? Not 'less you mean Sally Hollingsworth's nunnery wot we're standing a'front of. Guess yer could call that a school of sorts."

"Nunnery?" There was little to suggest the ecclesiastical.

"Bawdy 'ouse, ma'am."

Terror ripped through her. But no, the man was leering at her, drunkenly. If Sarah believed him, she was lost. She was calling on a respectable widow. One who'd be as shocked and upset as Sarah to learn her son had enticed a gently reared young woman away from her loving home.

The house looked respectable enough, and no different from the other four square buildings with neat iron railings in front. Its blinds were drawn and lights burned in the upper rooms.

But as the jarvey set down the steps she was beset by indecision. If this *were* a house of ill repute, she'd be a fool to venture out of the carriage. She should contain her desperate impatience and return with Roland, later.

"So wot yer plannin' on doin' then, miss?" asked the jarvey, holding open the door. "If you've the blunt I can stay 'ere all night."

She glanced the length of the dim street. Caro was inside, she was almost certain. What choice did she have? Roland was gripped by fever and quite beyond moving further than the posting inn.

"I'll pay you half a crown if you'll come with me, now. Double that amount when you return me to the Crown and Anchor."

He responded with alacrity, though Sarah's relief was tempered by his difficulty in keeping his balance. Still, his intimidating size kept her fear in check as she waited for an answer to her knock.

The door opened and a young woman of about twenty regarded her, suspiciously.

"What yer after?" she asked.

She did not look like a servant girl. Instead of cotton print she wore a flashy gown of mauve and yellow satin. Nor did she look — much less talk — like Mr Hollingsworth's sister and, in fact, laughed uproariously at that suggestion.

"Me name's Kitty," she told her. "If you's come looking fer him yer outta luck. He ain't in."

"What about Mrs Hollingsworth?"

"D'yer mean his wife or his muvver?"

Sarah gasped. His wife? Could that mean Caro? Or did he already have a wife?

Whatever this place was, Sarah had come too far to turn back, now.

"Well, mightn't be no matter to you as to which one," said her informant in answer to her question, "fer old Mrs Hollingsworth is out, too, and the young one won't see no one. But if yer that anxious then you might as well come through and wait."

Sarah turned to the jarvey. "Stay with me," she whispered and, though grumbling that he 'ought to see she had the blunt to pay 'im first' he stumbled after her down a dimly lit corridor and through green velvet curtains into a well lit room beyond.

"More privacy here where you and your ... gennelmun friend can wait. They shouldn't be too long. Just a-visiting, and things don't get busy for a little while yet."

Sarah glanced around at her surroundings, her eyes dropping quickly from the Bacchanalian oil painting above the fire place.

Trying to retain a dignified composure, she said, "Please tell the young lady upstairs that her old governess is here. She'll see me, I know it."

Kitty looked Sarah in the eye and sighed. "Tain't worth it to me, miss. Girl's not allowed to leave the 'ouse."

Her words occasioned both relief and alarm. At least she'd come to the right place.

Sarah fished in her reticule and brandished a half crown at her. For a second Kitty stared at it longingly, but at the sound of new arrivals she dashed Sarah's hand away.

"Hide it!" she hissed, nodding at the coin and looking furtively at the curtained doorway. "And don't go offering 'ticements like that to the madam. It won't go down well."

"Ah, Kitty. Visitors so early?" chirped a female voice. The curtain was drawn aside and an enormously fat woman entered. Although well past her prime she wore her hair in girlish ringlets, their golden hue contrasting strangely with the grey pallor of her skin. Her dress of red silk, too, looked as if it had been designed for a sylph. Cut indecently low, it clung to her rolls of fat, leaving nothing to the imagination.

But it was the man next to her who chilled Sarah's blood.

Like the woman he appeared surprised, before his face split in a sly grin. Not this time the charming boyish smile for the ingenuous governess as he regarded Sarah, speculatively.

"What a deliciously unexpected surprise," he purred, brushing aside the lock of brown, curling hair that flopped over his forehead. "Alone? Or is this ... er ... gentleman your companion? An unlikely coupling, I must say."

"My friend has agreed to bear me company while I make enquiries about Caro. I believe I have come to the right place." Sarah's tone was far bolder than she felt, but she had to take the risk. Although the bull-like jarvey was the worse for drink, he looked as if he could fell Mr Hollingsworth with an idle flick of the wrist.

"Caro?" frowned the young man, pretending to search his memory while ushering Sarah to a chair with unctuous care. "Refreshment, Lady Sarah? Kitty, if you please-?

"Kitty, love," his mother cut in, "you do realize the time, and that you're not yet painted?" With a thoughtful frown followed by a saccharine smile, she added, "*I'll* fetch our esteemed guests some refreshment."

"And please tell my dear wife she has a visitor," added Mr Hollingsworth.

Settling himself in a delicate gilt chair opposite Sarah, Mr Hollingsworth regarded her, quizzically. "Lady Sarah, I confess to astonishment. Both to seeing you here, and at the very ungallant behaviour of Mr Hawthorne." He shook his head. "Leaving you with the responsibility of tracking down his errant daughter. I can't imagine how he knew where to send you since I had not yet made contact with him regarding ... ah ... terms."

Mrs Hollingsworth soon returned, followed by a child carrying a tray. Sarah accepted the wine she was offered, which she had no intention of drinking, and watched with dismay as the jarvey downed his ale greedily.

Mrs Hawthorne settled her formidable bulk upon a gilded Egyptian sofa. "Now, dearie, what's this all about?" she asked. But despite her smile and the fact her tone was designed to put Sarah at ease, there was the glint of steel in her small, pig-like eyes.

"Mr Hawthorne will be here to fetch Caro, shortly," Sarah said, bravely, hoping the threat of reinforcements would help her cause. Burying her clammy hands in the folds of her primrose skirts to hide their trembling, she went on, "I came ahead to this address, believing that you, Mrs Hollingsworth, would be horrified to learn of Caro's disappearance in company with your son. However, as Mr Hollingsworth is already married, I see we misread the situation and should be grateful to you both for providing Caro with a refuge. If she was running away, please tell her she is forgiven. It would be best for everyone if we took her home, now."

Unfortunately, the Hollingsworths were not inclined to take the avenue with which Sarah had provided them.

"Best leave the negotiations to Mr Hawthorne, dear," said Mrs Hollingsworth with exaggerated condescension. She was about to go on when soft-slippered footsteps sounded in the passage.

"I'm glad to see you in such good health, Lady Sarah." The familiar brown-haired young woman framed in the doorway acknowledged Sarah with a thin smile. "It has been a while." The voice, soft and slightly breathless, was as Sarah remembered, but the lively Miss Morecroft she'd known on board ship was now a dispirited creature. Although she no longer wore homespun, the tawdry green satin gown looked out of place against her sallow complexion and plainly dressed hair.

Conscious that her own behaviour was not unblemished, Sarah nodded warily at the woman whose identity she had assumed these past six weeks. When Caro failed to appear in her wake, she took the offensive. Sarah might have acted the opportunist in upholding the assumption she was Miss Morecroft, but Miss Morecroft's actions had been far more calculated and wicked. She levelled an accusingly look at her. "I believe I can thank you for leading Caro to this place."

"You attribute too much to me," the young woman protested softly, looking away, but Mr Hollingsworth, who had risen at her entrance, took her elbow and drew her to the seat beside him, declaring, "Such modesty, my angel, for I could have achieved nothing without you. Let us toast Divine Providence for joining our fates upon the slippery deck of that doomed ship."

Sarah seized her opportunity while their attention was for the moment elsewhere. She was halfway to the door when Mrs Hollingsworth purred, "You're surely not leaving us, my dear?"

Sarah swallowed. She had to get out of here. The cloying atmosphere of cheap perfume and the smoke from the coal fire was nauseating. "If Caro is sleeping I would not have her disturbed. Mr Hawthorne will be here shortly."

Mr Hollingsworth smiled. "Where *could* Mr Hawthorne be?" Rising, he cast a quizzical look at Sarah. "Somehow I fancied a lady of your determination preferred the more forceful type."

Sarah glared, silently ordering the jarvey to his feet with an imperious look. Rubbing his drink-sodden eyes, he followed her to the door. With her hand finally on the knob, Sarah gave them her haughtiest look. "Mr Hawthorne is the consummate gentleman – something you will never be!"

"Dearie me!" said Mrs Hollingsworth, her brassy ringlets bobbing as she leant forward. "It seems you're uncommonly taken with our esteemed friend—" A great crash drowned her words.

With dismay Sarah watched the skittering shards of the porcelain urn which the jarvey's head had collected on his way to the ground roll across the floor.

"Can't hold his liquor, poor feller," sighed Mrs Hollingsworth, looking sadly at the body slumped against the wall. "Thank you, Barnabus! Take the gentleman out. Lady Sarah, you mustn't worry about your friend. Barnabus'll take care of him. Now sit down and drink up. I'm enjoying our little chat."

"No." The walls were closing in on her. The Hollingsworths with their speculative smiles and Miss Morecroft in her trance-like state threatened all she held dear. They would keep her here against her will. They would take Mr Hawthorne, too, and then she had no idea what they planned. They were evil.

She tried to force her way past the door and into the passageway where she hoped for a clear run but Mr Hollingsworth's hand was upon her elbow.

"Lady Sarah, you can't possibly rush into the darkness, in a neighbourhood like this. Mr Hawthorne would never forgive us. Ah, good evening, Caro." His smile was very different from the one he'd reserved for Caro's birthday, as he ushered the terrified girl into the room.

Caro's wan, pale face lit up when she saw Sarah. With a sob she threw herself into her arms.

"Very touching," observed Mr Hollingsworth, closing the door firmly behind them and leading them to a green settee. "Now, I must dispatch one more note. There is a gentleman who has, for the past six weeks, been all eagerness to meet the lovely Miss Caro. The fact that a lovely imposter" - he looked pointedly at Sarah – "has sweetened the dish is sure to garnish my reward. Now, let us have another drink while we wait for our happy little gathering to be complete."

CHAPTER 14

ROLAND WOKE WITH a raging thirst.

He needed water, or he would die. Swinging his legs over the side of the bed he attempted to rise. But his legs buckled and he landed on his face upon the floor.

It took him all his energy to struggle back onto the mattress where he sat a few minutes, his head reeling, as he tried to recollect what had brought him to this indifferent London posting inn. If he was in London, as he believed he was, he ought to be enjoying the rarefied atmosphere of his club. This place smelled of musty linen and cheap candles.

He noticed his boots were off and he was shirtless. But there was a basin of water and a sponge still damp on the washstand. His valet had not accompanied him on this apparently hasty, clandestine trip and yet he had been attended to.

A vision of Lady Sarah swam before him, though he couldn't imagine why. While he searched in the gloom for the water jug, wisps of memory drifted through his muddled brain. The image of her was so very strong.

When he lit a candle and saw her veil upon the bed, he put his hands to his head and groaned.

Dear Lord, if she'd been with him last night what atrocities might he have committed? If – as clearly had been the case – he was not in full charge of his mental faculties, the beast within would have taken over. He'd have given free reign to the lustful desires she inspired and which had consumed him during the past six weeks.

He groaned again. If she had been here last night, where was she, now?

Caro!

Guilty fear galvanised him into action, but as he reached for his shirt, nausea gripped him and he fell to his knees on the wooden boards.

First Caro had disappeared. Now Sarah was gone. It was starting to come back to him. Sarah's tender ministrations, but there had been an urgency about her, too. Yes, something about Caro. What *was* it she had said? Something about knowing Caro's whereabouts? Surely he hadn't dreamed that?

If she really had been here at all? Surely Lord Miles would never have released her to travel, unescorted, to London? Surely Sarah would never have been so reckless as to have come, alone and unchaperoned, to his bed chamber?

Never! he reaffirmed, nodding decisively in part to shake his disappointment. The veil belonged to someone else and had inadvertently appeared on his bed. It was as simple as that.

He pulled his shirt over his head. He was feeling a little better, though he had no idea where he'd start his search. It was all so hopeless.

Then he saw the note pushed under the door with his name written clearly on the outside. Thank the Lord, he thought as he struggled to cross the room and pick it up. It must contain news regarding Caro's whereabouts. Perhaps, even, that she'd been found safe.

But all it contained was a single address.

TWENTY MINUTES LATER HE STARED WITH REVULSION AT THE TWO-storied residence. No gentleman of fashion could be ignorant of the notorious Sally Hollingsworth's nunnery. That his daughter — and Sarah — might be inside was almost more than he could bear.

He shuddered, stepping up to grip the brass door knocker. What would he say? He'd never been in a bawdy house before. When he'd told Venetia something to this effect, she'd laughed and said, well then, wasn't he the lucky one since out of the goodness of her heart she'd show him all the things girls in bawdy houses did. He didn't want to dwell, right now, on what she'd taught him.

He was still hesitating as to whether this direct approach was even advisable when a metal grill slid open.

"What's yer business, then?" asked the owner of a pair of eyes that regarded him with suspicion.

"That which brings most gentlemen to a house like this," he said, in bored, clipped tones.

The door opened a crack and stepping inside Roland found himself in a dimly lit vestibule.

"Yer won't find better'n this, then. Come," said an old man with lank, shoulder-length grey hair. Holding aloft a tallow candle, he led the way down a narrow passageway, dragging his club foot.

It was the early hours of the morning. A pretty girl in yellow and mauve was descending a flight of stairs, yawning. She caught herself up when she saw Roland, and smiled. She had nice teeth, he noticed. Like Sarah, he thought, and his heart contracted with fear and longing.

"Don't tell the missus," she said in a collaborative whisper as she lounged against the newel post and waited for Roland to draw level, "but would the fine gennelmun like a glass of sommat?"

Roland did not answer – he guessed he looked as dazed as he felt.

"Now my 'andsome," she said, taking his arm. "You don't look at all the thing. Just come from a ruckus with the missus? Needin' someone to love yer? Well, Kitty's yer girl. A nice drink to start us orf? No? So it's right down to business, is it? Well, ain't so often I'm lucky enough to snag such a 'andsome fella, and I don't say that lightly. Come along a' me and Kitty'll look after yer."

Roland's first instinct was to recoil, just as he did regularly from the lightskirts who plied their trade in the haymarket and the streets near his club. But a combination of his reeling head and the sudden hazy thought that perhaps he could pry information more easily from this young woman than he could from the brothel madam – and that the truth was more likely to be reliable – made him surrender his arm and allow himself to be led up the stairs to her room.

"There now, if you'd like to make yerself comfortable and tell us yer fancy," she said.

Dazedly, he watched her preen in front of a small tarnished looking glass. The room was comfortably furnished, dominated by a large bed with a thick pink feather bolster.

He must have been frowning unconsciously and fingering the satin cover with unusual concentration for she said in her pert, friendly voice, "Like it, then? Stitched it meself. Makes things a bit more homely, like. Not that 'ome's a place I'm likely to visit ever agin."

"Why?" he asked, distracted.

"Well, now ..." Kitty looked at him, startled. "Daren't darken the doorstep now, do I? Not now I've taken to a life of ... of bringing pleasure to gennelmun what can do with a mite cheering up."

The next moment she was on his lap, coiling her arms around his neck and nuzzling his cheek, easing his coat from his shoulders and marvelling in a low, intimate murmur at his muscles, his fine and handsome physique.

It was not until she took his hand and guided it under her chemise, that he jerked into awareness.

Rising abruptly, he was unable to prevent the girl from falling to the floor with a thud. She looked up from where she lay amid a tangle of skirts, her face full of fear.

"Now sir, playing rough ain't my game," she said. "I'm 'appy to pleasure you any way you want, sir, but I don't like playin' rough."

"Forgive me," he said, helping her up. "I ... I ... you've got to help me."

She must have seen the genuine anguish in his eyes for her fear appeared to abate. Smoothing her dress and putting a hand to her hair she curved her small body against his and nuzzled his neck. "Course I'll 'elp yer, sir," she purred, leading him to the bed and gently pushing him down.

"No, no, not like that," protested Roland as she began undoing the buttons of his waistcoat.

"Oh, I'll give no cause for complaint, sir, if yer just bide yer time a wee bit," she said.

Taking a steadying breath Roland gripped her wrists and put her away.

"Well, if yer want to do all the work, that's fine by me," she said, lying back and starting to pull up her skirts.

Averting his eyes Roland blurted out, "I'm looking for my daughter. Please ... I need to know if she's here. I'll pay you handsomely."

He was conscious of her sudden stillness. When he turned, her eyes were black with terror. "Lower yer voice, sir." Her own was thick with fear as she sat up and smoothed her gown. "You don't know what yer askin'."

"I believe my daughter has been tricked by a scoundrel who gained her trust and—"

"You mean 'ticed?" Kitty asked, rising. "But a girl what's been 'ticed ain't got no respectability left and can't *possibly* go 'ome. 'Oo'll 'ave a girl like that? I suggest you just leave 'er be. Might even take to the life ... like me." Regaining her composure, Kitty draped herself over his shoulders.

He shuddered as he felt her small tongue dart into his ear and was about to shake her off when he realized she was whispering. "There's spies everywhere," she hissed. "Every word is listened to and there's eyeholes in the walls and door. I suggest you let me tend to you like you was any gennulman takin' yer pleasure and we'll 'ope your words of just now weren't overheard."

"Please, I don't want—" he started to protest as she pushed him back down.

"S'orright, sir," she soothed, loud enough for any listeners to overhear. And then, lowering her head she again whispered, "Pity, cos yer just the kind of genulman a girl like me could fancy." Then more loudly, "Oooh, yes, sir, very nice," before adding in another undertone, "Tell me her name. Madam's got all sorts of gals, and we're not all common like me."

The situation was surreal. Good God, it had been so long since he

had had a woman, and to have one so willing, squirming on top of him
...

But she was not Sarah.

"Sure you don't want what yer paid for, since yer goin' to 'ave to pay
for it anyway?" Her breath tickled his ear but it was not hard to
decline. Only Sarah had the power to make him feel like a man.

"I'm looking for two women," he whispered against her neck,
pretending to embrace her. "Caro, my daughter and her governess,
Lady Sarah, or perhaps she might go by the name of Miss Morecroft.
She came here about two hours ago."

He felt the girl go rigid.

"*You're* the gennulman, then, they's bin waitin' fer," she whispered.
He had to pinion her with both arms to keep her on top of him for if
there should be spies to interpret her terror ...

"I'll pay you well for your information," he managed, hoarsely.
"Obviously you know something–"

"Yeah? I know a lot, but I ain't spilling nothin', for it ain't worth me
pretty neck. And money won't buy me, fer I get searched, and so does
this room. Ain't *nuffink* I can keep from the missus." She seemed more
angry now, than frightened.

"Just ask what it is you want, then?"

"I want to get out of 'ere, but you certainly ain't goin' to be able to
'elp me do that!"

"Of course I could–"

"No, I signed a piece of paper wot gives madam and Mr
Hollingsworth 'normous power over me," she whispered. "And I'd
rather be here than Newgate, for that's where I'll go if I don't do what
I agrees to in that there piece of paper."

Relief mingled with horror. "So, Mr Hollingsworth is part of all
this?"

"Mr Hollingsworth is madam's son and they's downstairs waitin' fer
ya. There'll be hell to pay when they realize you're up here with me an'
all, 'stead of frontin' up to them direct."

"Stop! Please don't go." Roland struggled to hold her in his
embrace. "I *must* find Caro and Sarah. Tell me where they are and I'll
do all within my power to help you."

"I's well past savin', sir, and 'sides, t'ain't no good since your precious Caro and that other gal's wiv 'em as we speak. So you got no choice." She paused as she buttoned her dress, then followed up a rather assessing look with a coy smile. "Sure you don't want to get yer money's worth, now?" Frowning, she added in a more concerned tone, "You orright, sir?"

Ignoring her, Roland tried to ignore the reeling of his brain as he steadied himself with his hand on the door knob. "I presume I'll find the people I'm after if I continue down the passage and through to the back?"

"S'right. And thank yer, sir," she said, pocketing the money he placed on her dresser. "You bin most generous." Kitty's words filtered through the open doorway as he hastened towards the stairs.

CHAPTER 15

BLINKING AT THE sudden brightness of the gaudily decorated room, Roland found himself the focus of a small party seated around a cosy fire.

An enormously fat woman was seated on an Egyptian sofa decorated with gilt winged sphinxes. Her garb screamed her calling. Dear God, Caro didn't even know of such practices! Or, she hadn't two days before.

But it was the man next to her who caused the bile to rise up in his throat and his weakened frame to almost buckle. This time he was not taken in by the charm of his boyish smile as he had been when the personable Mr Hollingsworth had requested permission to lead his daughter into the next dance.

"Mr Hawthorne, so delighted you could join us. We are quite a crowd," Mr Hollingsworth's caramel tones penetrated. "Pray, allow me to introduce to you my wife, the fair Mrs Hollingsworth ..."

Relief that the lady in question was not his daughter was short-lived. For when he opened his eyes again, there was Caro, in the gloom where the light cast by the oil lamp barely penetrated, huddled on a green velvet-upholstered settee.

She did not greet him but stared, unfocussed, like a frightened animal, her hand clasped in Sarah's. Beautiful Sarah who regarded him calmly through liquid hazel eyes, which clearly conveyed her relief.

Dear Lord, the two of them looked to him to save them from this hellish situation, yet he could barely keep them in focus. He found the back of a chair for support and his gaze returned to the young woman introduced as Mrs Hollingsworth.

"Good evening, Mr Hawthorne, it's been a long time," she murmured.

At first he did not recognize her; he had not seen her since she was a child, after all. Then Sarah's words drifted into his consciousness. Miss Morecroft. Godby's daughter, for it could be none other. His heart turned to stone. She was behind all this. Back to haunt the next Hawthorne generation as her father had bedevilled his. He held her gaze before she looked away, her face an impassive mask.

She had her father's grey eyes fringed with jet black lashes, and his mouth set in a pretty, round face framed by light brown hair. But she looked a pale, irresolute imitation of the Godby he remembered, and he felt a pang of disappointment. For her father? For what this had all come to?

Disappointment, however, was an insubstantial word for the way he felt as he returned his gaze to Caro and Sarah. Motivated by the determination to fight to the death to save them both, he was almost felled the next minute by another wave of dizziness.

Using the manner of one gentleman to another, the effete, self-assured Mr Hollingsworth introduced his mother, the fat evil woman who regarded him speculatively, her eyes tiny pinpricks of steel in their folds of fat.

The sight of her made his skin crawl. She had grown fat on the profits of the flesh trade, on human misery. How many fallen women like Kitty upstairs would willingly have embraced lives of bondage, slaves to the lusts of men and the greed of people like the Hollingsworths?

"How much do you want for the girls?" Roland did not trouble to hide his disgust.

Mrs Hollingsworth's hand fluttered to her throat. "Why, the language of common bartering sits ill with the likes 'o us," she said.

"We was just protectin' your dear 'uns, now, weren't we, Mr Hollingsworth? Til you got 'ere, though I must say you've taken yer time about it."

"I'm not in the mood for games. Name your sum," muttered Roland. The relief in Sarah's eyes only made him more wretched.

"Is pecuniary reimbursement for the care of your daughter? Or for the governess, also?" asked Mr Hollingsworth. "Leaving Lady Sarah out of the transaction I'm sure we'd soon come to some mutually agreeable negotiation. But you see, Lady Sarah's style of beauty is particularly sought after at the moment." He smiled. "She is beyond any price."

"Don't insult Lady Sarah unless you wish to earn more than my anger." Though he spoke through gritted teeth, Roland feared his anger was something that would be difficult to translate into overt action in his current state.

"Ah, now, isn't it wonderful when a real gentleman champions his lady-love in our establishment?" crowed the fat old crone. "If I were ten years younger-"

Her son cut in. "The problem, my dear fellow, is this-"

"I don't care how much," Roland snarled, closing his eyes as he swayed.

"Well, money's one thing, but it ain't goin' to please our esteemed guest whose company we presently await," purred Mrs Hollingsworth. "Ah, Sir Richard!" She simpered up at a new arrival whom the clubfoot ushered into the room with a great deal of supercilious care. "Mr Hawthorne has been ever so impatient to get down to business. We thought you'd never get here."

"A street urchin delivered your message when I was up to my wrists in gold coin at The Hellraker." The newcomer rose from kissing the back of Mrs Hollingsworth's hand, a sardonic smile curling his thin lips as he surveyed the company.

Roland blinked at the man who'd inhabited so many of his nightmares.

Sir Richard Byrd.

Trickie Dickie, as he was commonly known.

Back from exile.

About five years older than Roland, tall but powerfully built, he was still a handsome man, although dissolute living had made its inroads.

"Not even a run of good luck could have enticed me to stay, knowing what other ... enticements ... were on offer, here."

His gaze slid over Caro, his velvet tones at odds with the lack of empathy in his cold, hard eyes, though he smiled as he bit his lip in apparent contemplation. "This frightened looking damsel must be Miss Hawthorne. Venetia's child without the fire and ice." His eyes travelled to Sarah. "And this lush little morsel must be the governess, yes?"

"How dare you!"

With a laugh at Roland's ineffectual outburst, Sir Richard went on, "Mrs Hollingsworth and her son have been maintaining these two young women at their own considerable expense. Knowing my interest in the welfare of any Hawthorne family member, they kindly requested my presence to help resolve an adequate means of recompense ..."

Roland waited. A weary acceptance that matters were about to become very complicated settled upon him.

Sir Richard moved to the fire to warm his back. He looked at home, an image he upheld as he said, "Being a regular patron of Mrs Hollingsworth's esteemed establishment-"

At Roland's look of derision, Sir Richard laughed. "Do not make the mistake of calling me inconstant. Venetia did that. No, my dear Hawthorne, I have but one fair and faithful creature whom I visit here regularly; the magnificently endowed Queenie. So it was an unexpected and delightful surprise when Mrs Hollingsworth sent me the message this evening informing me that Lady Sarah's quest to find your daughter had led her here."

"The last person we'd expected to see!" exclaimed Mrs Hollingsworth, clapping her hands and leaning forward.

"Certainly a lucky chance I'd never thought would fall into my lap," murmured Sir Richard.

Moving stealthily around the back of the small sofa upon which Sarah and Caro were huddled, Sir Richard took up one of Caro's smoky ringlets between two fingers. Lowering his face, he brushed the curl across his face, breathing deeply before he released it with a kiss.

Roland's fury ignited at Caro's frightened intake of breath. He took a step forward but the menacing effect for which he was striving was marred by his unsteadiness.

Sir Richard gave a bark of laughter. "So you intend defending the girl's honour as you never did her mother's?" He caressed Caro's neck and his lip curled. "Though it would appear Venetia's daughter is not as willing with her favours as her mother. Darling Venetia was ... so very accommodating." With an assessing look, he added, "Nor does she have her mother's ripe sensuality but she is very young and that may come." Leaning further over the sofa he reached towards Caro's bodice.

"How dare you?" Sarah hissed, batting away his hand. Sobbing, Caro sank against her shoulder.

"If you're after vengeance, not money, then pistols at dawn," Roland managed, hoarsely. "You'll not find me hard to negotiate with when the safety of Caro and Lady Sarah hang in the balance."

It was an exhausting speech. Dear Lord, just give him the strength to endure what he must in order to rescue the women.

"I don't think Sir Richard was entertaining thoughts of duelling, but rather had in mind some other kind of challenge." A tremor of excitement rippled through Mrs Hollingworth, like a gentle blow to a blancmange. Widening her eyes and biting her lip like a child barely able to keep a secret, she turned to Sir Richard. "Are we to play our favourite parlour game, Sir Richard? Do you wish all of our large, happy company to participate, or just you and Mr Hawthorne and the two young ladies?"

"No one will play any parlour games!" Roland was surprised at the energy he managed to inject into his voice. He slid his gaze across to Sarah and she smiled. To his amazement she raked her eyes upwards, the length of his body in that lazy, maddeningly sensual manner she had, and then pursed her lips slightly.

He could barely believe it. There they were, in the direst danger, and she was flirting with him.

Yet was that not her way of bolstering him? Her feelings were reflected clearly in her gaze. Despite the depths to which Roland was now reduced, she was reaffirming her desire, sustaining him at this moment when his manhood had never been more vulnerable. He felt a surge of love and appreciation for the woman he had banished from his household so recently.

"I am taking my daughter and Lady Sarah home now," he told Sir Richard, quietly. "If neither money nor satisfaction at the end of a sword are what you want-"

Sir Richard began to clap his hands in a desultory fashion. "Heroic words! And yes, satisfaction is what I'm after, but not at the end of a sword. Rather, upon the roll of the dice."

Roland closed his eyes.

"Yes! I've in mind a very diverting parlour game which I think we'll all enjoy. I can see you're not up to much, Hawthorne. I'm surprised, and disappointed, I must say, to find you in your cups but as it's not a game of skill it hardly signifies."

Roland ran the back of his hand across his eyes. "The young ladies are very tired," he said, wearily. "It's time we took our leave."

"Come! I can see Lady Sarah is eager to enjoy some sport with you, Hawthorne." Sir Richard kissed the top of Sarah's head. "Damned fine filly this one," he murmured. "I don't wonder you're on fire to bed her."

Steeling himself against the unwise impulse to lunge at Sir Richard and thereby provide the man with the perfect excuse to fell him with an easy blow, Roland blinked at Sir Richard's yelp of pain.

"The bitch bit me!"

"I'll do more than bite you if you don't let us all leave," hissed Sarah. Her beautiful eyes were blazing. "If you were a man of any substance you'd realize your warped plans for revenge could hardly be satisfied by pitting yourself against a man who is so ill he can hardly stand up!"

Roland's fear intensified. "Stop, Sarah!" he begged. If they could suffer in silence just a little longer, if he could only lose consciousness, even if it was at the cost of his dignity, perhaps they could walk out of here relatively unscathed.

Sir Richard crossed his arms and directed an admiring look at Sarah. "The young lady has fair got my blood up, Hawthorne. However, to prove I am indeed a gentleman, first choice this evening is yours." He smiled. "Name the stakes. Shall it be the lovely, innocent and retiring Caro" - he asked, caressing her shoulder – "or this little filly, the fair and fiery Lady Sarah?"

Roland did not think he had uttered his horror but Sir Richard answered as if he had.

He chuckled. "It's merely a popular party game, old chap, which I've no doubt Lady Sarah has played countless times. Let me explain. Upon the roll of the dice an item of clothing from the chosen damsel is either removed, or replaced."

"The ladies do not wish to play," muttered Roland. His eyes were hurting from the light. "Gaming debts sent you into exile once before, sir; I assure you, your insistence on this route will send you to a place far worse."

"I did what I had to do ... for Venetia," snarled Sir Richard. "I sacrificed *everything* for Venetia." Violence lit his eyes. "And I paid the price, by God! These past seven years I have been paying the price as she haunts me from the grave. She was beyond pearls, that's what she told me. A string of pearls that cost a king's ransom is what she demanded. Yet when I risked everything to give her what she wanted, she prettily accepted the gift with the most half-hearted of favours" - Sir Richard's face contorted grotesquely as he hissed — "and then left me!" His eyes were pinpricks of malice as he looked at Roland. "Left me and returned to her husband."

So that was it. Relief kept Roland upright. He might have known money would ultimately guarantee their freedom.

"I cannot give you Venetia," he said, feeling the world closing in upon him, despite his sudden illumination as to what Sir Richard really wanted. "She was never mine to give ... but I can give you the pearls-"

"The pearls are mine by rights and I mean to claim them. This little entertainment is the interest upon what you already owe me."

Mrs Hawthorne clapped her hands. "Oh, this *is* sport." She quivered with excitement. "Do let us begin. There's the table, gentlemen, and there are the dice."

"I refuse to play." Roland eyed the die suspiciously. "Certainly, not with those."

"Always happy to oblige, Hawthorne. If you have them, we'll play with yours instead." Sir Richard pulled a delicate gilt chair into the centre of the room. "Lady Sarah, if you please?" With courtly exaggeration he assisted Sarah towards it.

She shrugged off his grasp and faced him with loathing. "Not only must Mr Hawthorne play with loaded dice, you can see he is seriously ill. If you force any of us you must know that your title will not protect you from the law."

"What a fearsome and tempestuous creature you must be between the sheets," he sneered. "Just like your gentleman friend's admirable predecessor." He turned to Roland. "I have to tell you, Hawthorne, I've bedded lusty wenches in my time but your Venetia put the most enthusiastic whores into the shade. Why do you look at me like that? Perhaps she did not provide the same excitement in the marital bed? Was she as great a disappointment to you ... as you were to her?"

"Oh dear! The table!" clucked Mrs Hollingsworth as it toppled over in Roland's haste to get his hands around his tormentor's throat. "Archie, won't you help poor Mr Hawthorne to his feet? Poor fellow's in his cups."

Nauseated, Roland suffered the grip of the young man's hands beneath his armpits. He was in no position to struggle, he realized, as he was set back onto his feet, only to stumble backwards as the world tilted once more on its axis. His inadequacy was compounded as Sarah, refusing to sit, taunted, "Perhaps, Sir Richard, you were a disappointment to *her*, since she so willingly returned to her husband once she'd tired of you."

Sir Richard's eyes flared. "Young Miss Hawthorne will suit my purposes just as well, though her retiring ways are not so pleasing to me." Lamplight glinted on the shaft of steel he pressed to Caro's throat. Roland and Sarah froze.

"Ah, finally you understand I will not be gainsaid." A voice of velvet in keeping with the charade. "Once more, Hawthorne, I ask you to make your choice. Remember, it's just a game. A game of chance, a roll of the dice, your luck against mine. Just tell me, who shall be the stakes? Your daughter?" He grinned. "Or this luscious wench?"

He gripped Sarah's shoulder with his free hand.

"*Still* you refuse to choose?" Sir Richard glared at him. "Perhaps I need to press a little harder."

Caro gasped and Roland had to close his eyes to the entreaty in her look.

Think! he exhorted himself. One wrong move and three lives could be in ruins.

"Please, father."

"Mr Hawthorne has too much honour to put *either* of us in your hands!" With dignity, Sarah relaxed in an attitude of defeat, sinking in the gilt chair set out for her. "If you must choose, choose me, though I warn you, you'll regret it!"

Roland gripped the back of the settee for support. "No, Sarah," he whispered. But what could he do? He was powerless. Emasculated. Defeated before the game had begun.

"That is against the rules of the game, my dear." Still smiling, Sir Richard removed the knife from Caro's throat. "Mr Hawthorne must make his choice." He looked at Roland enquiringly. "Or must I choose for him?"

Pressing the knife once more to Caro's throat, he drew her up from her seat. She made a strangled sound, like a trapped bird.

"There's something fitting to my breaking in Venetia's spawn though it's to be expected you'd place a higher value upon the very delectable Lady Sarah since your parentage of the sadly dispirited Miss Caro has always been in doubt."

"No!" It was all he could do to utter the word. He felt sweat crawling over his body, like an army of ants on his chilled, trembling frame.

Sir Richard cocked an eyebrow and his lips curled in a rictus of a smile. "No? Not Caro ...? Or no, you dispute my assertion?"

"I am her father," Roland managed, hoarsely, raising his head. "I will kill anyone who suggests otherwise." The entreaty he saw in Caro's eyes was agonising. He'd do anything to protect her. The doubts fed her regarding her parentage had led to this. Had led them all to this. He could not let her think he had forsaken her.

"The lovely Lady Sarah, then. Yes, an understandable choice. Knowing how you've lusted after her I can imagine what it will cost you to watch me arrive first at the finish line. So you've made your choice then. Lady Sarah ..." He paused, meaningfully. "Come,

Hawthorne, say it. You've chosen Lady Sarah as the spoils tonight. Is that right? Then say it!" Angrily, he jerked Caro's hair, the knife still at her neck. She began to cry.

"Yes ... Lady Sarah," gasped Roland, defeated, as he slumped over the back of the sofa, his head resting on his folded arms. *Stand up like a man*, he exhorted himself once more. But he could do no more than keep his flickering, light-sensitive eyes open for a few seconds at a time. The scene was reproach enough for his cowardice. Caro's whimpers contrasted with Sarah's admirable bravado were equally intolerable. Sir Richard was now fondling the dice as he stood beside the baize-topped card table set up near the fire.

"Garth!"

At a nod from Mr Hollingsworth the bullet-headed thug left his post at the door and pushed Sarah roughly back into her chair. Roland caught the flash of bravely concealed fear before she bowed her head.

So, she could no longer look at him? He didn't blame her. With difficulty, he raised himself at the rattle of dice.

"First throw is yours, Hawthorne." Sir Richard beckoned to him, then strode over to his side. "Let me help you, you're done in, old fellow." His voice was full of feigned concern. "That's right, steady does it. Got a head like a sore bear, have you? A nice warm fire will make you feel better. Isn't the lovely Lady Sarah a sight to behold?"

Roland cast her an imploring look. She looked like a queen on her throne with her haughty eyes and lips curled with disdain. Longing and despair slashed his insides as he feasted his eyes on her for as long as he could keep them open.

"Lady Sarah will appreciate your cooperation. Ah, luck appears to be on your side, which refutes your offensive charge that I am not a man of honour. Yours is the higher number."

"I forfeit," said Roland who was glad he could now see only throbbing pinpricks of light in front of his eyes. His overloaded senses were at breaking point. The best he could do was remain upright.

Dimly, he registered the heavy bulk of another of the brothel heavies just two feet from him.

"But not I," crowed Sir Richard in the next round. He circled Sarah, savouring her obvious loathing, and the terror she could not entirely hide. "Of course, I could simply request the young lady divests herself of her gown." He trailed a bony forefinger over Sarah's exposed throat, caressing her collar bone and closing his eyes in ecstasy, as he murmured, "Soft womanly flesh. But no, I am, and remain, a gentleman. If the lady would just point her toe I shall merely remove her dainty slipper."

Dropping heavily to his knees Sir Richard slipped off Sarah's shoe. Caressing her foot, he held it against his cheek, murmuring, "The anticipation is nearly killing me."

It did not surprise Roland to lose the next throw. He watched, his disgust and horror equal to his helplessness. As much as he struggled to remain clear headed, he wondered if losing consciousness would put an end to the nightmare for them all. What pleasure would Sir Richard gain if Roland were unable to witness it? This whole spectacle was designed purely to humiliate him.

Sir Richard eyed Sarah, lasciviously. "And now for the lady's stocking." He laughed as Roland was held back, this time by a chuckling Mr Hollingsworth.

On his knees again, Sir Richard held out Sarah's foot, as if parading it before them. Roland tried not to look but his gaze was drawn to the dainty white silk-clad leg before travelling to Sarah's face. Her brave attempt to mask her fear with contempt, and then the hope he saw when her glance locked briefly with his, was almost too much to bear.

He blinked open his eyes at the sound of Sarah's shocked whimper.

"The ribbons are a delight, don't you always think?" Sir Richard addressed Mr Hollingsworth in a matter-of-fact tone, as his arm disappeared up Sarah's skirts. "That join between silk stocking and flesh, just above the knee. I cannot help myself, but I must explore a little further–"

With a roar Roland tore himself away from his captor and hurled himself upon Sir Richard. "Blackguard!" he managed between gritted teeth.

Caught unawares, Sir Richard was thrown on his back. However, Garth and his compatriot exerted little effort to return both men to their feet.

Sir Richard quickly regained his composure. "So glad you appear to enjoy this as much as I had hoped," he said, smoothly, dusting himself down. "Hawthorne, you win the next toss. Congratulations! I await with anticipation your choice. What? You wish to have the lady's stocking *back*? I had thought to keep it as a souvenir, but" - he shrugged – "it is within the rules."

With trembling fingers Roland took the insubstantial garment Sir Richard withdrew from his pocket. He had never replaced a lady's stocking before. Of course he had undressed Venetia many times. She'd enjoyed all forms of bedroom sport. Dismayed, he reflected this may well have been one of the party games his late wife had enjoyed in company with Sir Richard and which her erstwhile lover was now enjoying at his expense.

No words were exchanged but Sarah pointed her foot obligingly so Roland could roll the stocking over it with clumsy, trembling fingers.

"You tie it," he whispered, leaving the slip of silk to fall slackly over her ankle. Not only did he feel incapable, physically, but honour dictated. The lady had suffered enough indignity. She'd not want to feel yet another man's hands climbing her leg. How she must despise him now. His manliness had been torn from him with as little effort as her stocking.

"I can't," she responded unsteadily. "Please ..." And she held out her leg again. A spasm engulfed her and he realised her fear was far greater than she displayed.

Feeling the contours beneath the smooth silk he eased up and over her calf was little consolation. His fingers were clumsy and tying the bow almost beyond his capabilities. Pausing in his difficult task, he glanced up at her face. "I'm so sorry," he whispered. He felt the light pressure of her hand on his head as he finished his task. An exoneration? A farewell to what they might have shared? Unable to stand he had to be helped to his feet.

"Douse him with cold water!" Mrs Hollingsworth's command echoed stridently through the room.

Blinking at the shock, Roland opened his eyes in response to Sarah's sudden cries. Until now she had been self controlled in her bravery. But now she sobbed as Sir Richard removed the pins that secured her hair and which now fell in a mass of thick, chestnut curls over her shoulders. It was glorious. Glossy, abundant, with a life of it's own. Roland's heart rejoiced at the vision of splendour, then shrivelled. Memories of this corrupt toad would forever mar whatever might have been between them. Roland had been stripped of his honour, and without honour his life was meaningless.

With another cry of helpless rage he lunged forward. A glint of silver caught his eye as his fists made contact with Sir Richard's skull.

And then the murky darkness that had punctuated the last hour or more enveloped him and he surrendered himself to the oblivion that so effectively extinguished his honour and dignity.

CHAPTER 16

SARAH AND CARO huddled together for warmth beneath the thin blanket. Neither spoke although Sarah knew sleep eluded Caro who so desperately needed it.

In the silence of the attic she soon became accustomed to the sounds of the house: the insistent scratching of mice, the muffled thumps and groans of its occupants plying their trade, and the muted sounds of the city.

After what seemed like hours she became aware of a new sound from behind the adjoining door. Muffled groans, but not like those others.

Joy banished her fears. Surely it must be Roland.

Though it felt like days, it had probably been only two hours since they'd been dragged up the stairs by Garth and locked into this hole of a room.

There was no light. Sarah had no idea how long it was before dawn, if they would be released or what their captors' plans were. Her greatest fear was reserved for Roland. He had been unconscious, blood trickling from a wound to his temple throwing into relief the pallor of his parchment skin as he'd been carted out of the room while they had all looked on. The indignity of it. To be humiliated before his own daughter and the woman he loved would be a near mortal wound to his pride.

The mood of the evening had quickly degenerated after Roland's departure. Mrs Hollingsworth clearly felt cheated of her sport and Sir Richard had become despondent. Slumping into a chair, apparently more in his cups than Sarah had suspected, he looked liverish as in answer to the brothel madam's question he'd muttered, "No, I haven't the faintest idea what we should do with 'em. Lock 'em up and we'll worry about it in the morning."

Sarah feared Sir Richard might consider the girls and Roland posed too much of a risk to be allowed their freedom.

Yet surely he would release them? Any petitions for Sir Richard to face justice would be dismissed as the manufactured grievances of a cuckolded husband towards his late wife's former lover.

Another, equally insidious thought intruded. If Sir Richard really were arrogant enough to believe he could get away with his crime, would he decide to prey upon the girls once more, now that Roland were out of the way? Or was it really only entertainment if Roland bore witness?

Sarah's ears were so busy monitoring Roland's laboured breathing that it was Caro who jerked upright at the faint scrape of a key in the lock. She gripped Sarah tighter as the door eased open on rusty hinges.

Someone moved stealthily towards them.

"Quiet! I've come to help you escape," came a breathless whisper. "If you have money and take me with you I know how it can be done."

"Miss Morecroft!" whispered Caro.

"Hush." The young woman raised her candle. In its dim glow she looked frightened. Wearing only a thin nightgown, her feet bare, she shivered. "There are ears everywhere."

Sarah rose from the bed. "Of course you want money." The softness of her voice did not hide her anger. "Isn't that behind this whole charade? You wanted revenge, Miss Morecroft – for your father's well-deserved banishment. I have read your diary."

The candle flickered and Miss Morecroft's dull countenance flamed. "Mr Hawthorne destroyed my father, but I wrote of my anger, not revenge. I'm as much a prisoner as you, thanks to the dreadful day

I met Archie Hollingsworth. Do you want me to help you? I assure you, there's no one else here who will."

"Yes, please," whimpered Caro, shivering beneath the blanket.

Shifting restlessly, apparently to get warm, Miss Morecroft continued in her frightened whisper. "I want ten pounds upon your safe deliverance so that I may buy respectable clothes." Her teeth chattered. "I'll need a reference, too, to secure a position. Do I have your word?"

"Respectable?" Sarah went on. Doubt had formed as to Miss Morecroft's role. "Surely you've been well rewarded for orchestrating the whole plan?"

"Well-rewarded? I've been ruined by a sham marriage. Duped into believing Archie's questions about Mr Hawthorne and his family was husbandly interest. Now, come. Dawn is nearly here and with it our only chance." Leaning across the bed she drew back the curtains.

"First we have to find Mr Hawthorne."

"There's no time."

"If Mrs Hollingsworth finds us gone, she's more likely to dispose of him in the Thames than provide him with the proper nursing he needs," argued Sarah. She glared at Miss Morecroft, ready to do battle. "I think he's in the adjoining room, only the door's locked. At least just try the key you used for this chamber."

"And if he's ill?" Miss Morecroft asked, looking in two minds as to whether to object as Sarah took the keys and candlestick, from her. "I'll not let *Mr Hawthorne* jeopardize our only chance."

Striding towards the adjoining door, Sarah turned to whisper angrily, "Do you know why your precious father was banished? Not because of his affair with Mr Hawthorne's wife, or that he gambled freely upon old Mr Hawthorne's generosity. No! It was because he put his men in the greatest danger on the battlefield through his ineptitude. It was only thanks to Mr Hawthorne that he wasn't court-martialled and shot!"

"Liar!" Miss Morecroft hissed. "All right, I'll take my chances, alone. Believe me, I'd not put it past madam to dispose of you with as much impunity as ... as the chickens whose necks she breaks for Sunday dinner."

Both froze at a new sound. Stealthy footfalls.

"We came as soon as we could," came a breathless whisper.

In the gloom Sarah could just make out the tawdry gold and mauve gown of the young girl who'd let them into the house.

"With stockings," came a deep, throaty voice which trembled on a chuckle. "I saw Her Fat Ladyship strip the sheets from the bed, so if leaping from the window was your plan, Miss Morecroft, you'll need these."

Raising her candle, Sarah stared with amazement at a tall, flame-haired woman with the most enormous pouter pigeon chest she'd ever seen. From her hands dangled a pile of variously coloured stockings.

"I can't countenance what Dicky's gone and done to you girls," she said, drawing her painted brows together disapprovingly, "so I'm donating the spoils he brings me."

"This is Queenie," whispered Kitty in hurried explanation, though her tone conveyed a certain reverence. Queenie was certainly impressive in her tight fitting gown of gold topped off by a matching turban sporting half a dozen peacock feathers. "She's Sir Richard's favourite—"

"His One and Only," Queenie corrected with a haughty toss of her head. "But Queenie's not one to abide an injustice, though there's also me job to consider, an all," she said, crossing the room to deposit the stockings on the bed. "They're all nicely knotted, too. Did it mesel' while I was passing the time waitin' fer Dicky to come to me. Serve him right for the humilatin' things he was doing downstairs." In another few strides she was back at the door. "Dicky was asleep last time I checked but I ain't taking any more risks. Wicked he might be, but he's me bread and butter. Come Kitty. You gotta consider yer own skin, too."

Sarah watched the door close behind them before turning to Miss Morecroft. "Why don't you start tying them to the bed post? It crossed my mind to wonder if the hay carter could be relied upon."

Miss Morecroft's scorn followed Sarah from the darkness as she struggled to locate the keyhole of the door to the adjoining room. "Very clever, Lady Sarah. Yes, he parks his wagon in the same spot every morning at dawn. But hurry, for if the key doesn't fit—"

"It does!" Pure, sweet relief surged through Sarah as she pushed open the door and raised the candle, her eyes drawn by movement to a pile of sacks in the corner. There was Roland, sweat-soaked and shivering, lying beneath a thin coverlet. His sunken eyes flickered the faintest recognition as she cast herself at his side and held one of his limp hands to her lips. He managed, hoarsely, "Are you alright?"

"Better than you, I'd wager," Sarah murmured, kissing his knuckles and stroking his lank hair back from his forehead. When she skimmed her hand over his sweat-soaked shirt, she shook her head. It was freezing outside and he had nothing warm or dry to wear. "Put your arms around my neck so I can help you up," she whispered. "Caro and Miss Morecroft are waiting in the adjoining room us. We're going out through the window."

He gave a weak laugh as he obeyed, and she managed to haul them both to their feet. "I'll go – in as much as I'm able – on one condition."

"There's no time for conditions," she said, struggling under his weight as he managed a few unsteady steps. "I will not leave you."

He stopped, panting with the effort of their progress and Sarah was dismayed by the heat from his burning forehead when she laid her hand upon it. "I need to rest," he rasped. "Sarah, I'm too ill. I'll ... just hinder you."

She'd have stamped her foot at his stubbornness were there not the need for silence. "I said I won't leave you," she repeated. "Freedom is just through that door."

"Sarah!"

"Roland, please!" she burst out, stopping when she saw his pallid face, limned with dawn light. Suddenly she was afraid. "Roland, you'll be well soon," she told him as he sagged against her. "You will!"

"Perhaps." With a ragged breath he drew himself upright again and managed to drag another footstep across the bare boards. His hand struggled to her cheek, touched it briefly, before falling away. "But swear you'll not sacrifice your freedom on my account."

"I'll promise, if only to urge you on. When this is over," Sarah panted, "you'll realize all that matters is that you love me" - with relief she reached the doorway and they collapsed against the frame — "and I love you."

He did not reply. His head was upraised, his eyes closed. He looked as if he'd lost consciousness on his feet. Then, with lips barely moving he managed faintly, "Love does not last."

Anger gave her the energy to drag him the final steps to the bed by the window. "Give me the chance to prove you wrong."

"I'd not be so cruel," he rasped as Caro rushed towards him.

"Papa!" she cried, joy turning to alarm as she helped him to the mattress where he crumpled.

The clank of harness and clopping of hooves entering the court-yard cut the morning air.

"Roland!" Sarah shook him. "The cart's below. You must get yourself to the windowsill."

Moaning, he struggled to follow her directions, his eyes vacant as he grasped the knotted rope of stockings Sarah thrust into his hands.

"Into the darkness," he managed between cracked lips. Weakly, he gripped Sarah's wrist. His eyes flickered open. "If I miss my mark, I hold you to your promise—" His voice was now so hoarse she could barely hear him — to ensure your safety before mine."

"I promise." Sarah knew it was the only way to secure his coopera-tion as she and the two girls helped him into position.

She looked down past his shoulder. It was as Miss Morecroft had predicted. The cart, laden high with hay, provided an ideal landing pad.

"I'm ready." His eyes flickered open for the briefest moment as Sarah gave him a gentle push.

To her relief he landed well before dragging himself to the side.

Caro quickly followed her father to the window sill before easing her way down the length of makeshift rope.

Tensely, Sarah waited for her to drop.

Grimly, Caro clung on.

"Caro, let go!" Sarah whispered, urgently. She could hear the early stirrings of the servants.

Frozen by fear, Caro stared up at her as purposeful footsteps sounded on the stairs at the end of the corridor.

"Caro!" urged Sarah, but still the girl did not release her grip.

The footsteps came closer. There was no choice. Leaning danger-ously far out of the window, Sarah prized open Caro's fingers and with a scream, Caro dropped the distance, landing safely amidst the hay.

"Your turn, Miss Morecroft! Hurry!" cried Sarah, running back to the door, her trembling fingers battling to fit the key into the lock as Mrs Hollingsworth's strident tones came from the other side.

"What's going on?" demanded the brothel madam, beating upon the door before managing to force it open a fraction. "Let me in!"

Sarah screamed when she realised she'd been too slow in turning the key, her weight insufficient against Mrs Hollingsworth's determined bulk. She swung round at the sound of more running footsteps, this time inside the room, gasping with relief as Miss Morecroft threw her own weight against the door and at last Sarah was able to grind the key, locking them in.

She'd earned them a reprieve but there'd be little time before Mrs Hollingsworth arrived with reinforcements in the stable yard.

"What the devil!" cried the carter, running towards his vehicle as the two girls hurled themselves into it from the window, Sarah scrambling from the box to take possession of the reins.

With an expert flick of the ribbons she coaxed the cart horse into movement, fending off the pursuing carter with a crack of the whip.

"SHE'S GONE."

Roland was hardly surprised by this. What did surprise him, however, was that Miss Morecroft – the real Sarah Morecroft – was bending over him, her familiar features arranged in a look of concern.

"Her father fetched her yesterday." Miss Morecroft set a tray before him, then lowered herself onto a chair by the side of the bed. "Eat your soup, sir. It's been some days-"

"Did Lady Sarah say if she'd return?" His throat was dry and his head ached. But his thoughts, at least, were lucid.

"No, sir. At least not that I heard. She'd been here four days. She couldn't stay longer."

Four days since they'd left the Hollingsworths? The sketchy details of their escape were not something he cared to dwell upon. Certainly not the indignity of being helped by two young women through an open window, although the image of Sarah driving a hay cart through the streets of London was one he would treasure. The carter had caught up with them soon enough and been easily bribed to take them to safety.

He stared at the steam rising from his dinner, unable to return his gaze to Miss Morecroft's face. She seemed content, however, to sit in silence and to help him when he struggled with his mug of water.

Five days since he'd banished Sarah. Barely four since she'd shown him how ill he had served her.

"The Hollingsworths," he murmured. "Are you one of them?"

He couldn't make her out. She looked like Godby but there was none of the mobility of feature which, in Godby's case, had always provided strong hints as to what he was thinking. This young woman had regarded the entire proceedings at the Hollingsworths with stony-faced detachment. And yet, she was here.

"I met Mr Hollingsworth aboard the *Mary Jane*. I did not know it at the time but he'd been soliciting girls from the Continent to work in his mother's establishment." With an ironic pursing of her lips she added, "Apparently there is a craze for French mademoiselles." She sighed as she twisted the wedding band she had moved onto her right hand. "When we were the only two washed ashore near a small Belgian village I thought Providence had entwined our fates. We were married by special license but soon I was living a nightmare. It was a sham marriage."

Although she told her story calmly, her eyes revealed the extent of her trauma.

"Perhaps it was better that way." He looked at her with sympathy before forcing down a spoonful of soup. Losing one's virtue to a Hollingsworth might be preferable to being legally bound to one.

"Yes," she agreed, mildly. "While I was incarcerated with Mrs Hollingsworth in London I had no idea Archie was at Hawthorndene preparing to entice Caro away."

Soup splashed onto the tray. He felt as weak as an infant, even eating was an effort. "What splendid story did he weave to make her go with him?" he asked. If Miss Morecroft were going to reveal every sordid detail, he wanted to know if Caro's dubious parentage were in the public domain.

"She did not go willingly, sir." Miss Morecroft looked at him, surprised, as she wiped up the spillage. "Surely you must have known she'd never leave you like that?"

Roland cast aside his napkin. Exhausted, he lay back against the pillows, unable to meet Miss Morecroft's eye. "I have not been a good father," he murmured. When she didn't reply he swallowed. He hadn't even asked. "Where *is* Caro?"

"Sleeping, sir. She's very fragile."

That was hardly to be wondered at. Roland closed his eyes. They were all fragile. What his darling Sarah must have endured, he could barely imagine. But his darling Sarah was gone now, recovering from her ordeal in the bosom of her family.

It was best she stay there. She would find it difficult to look upon him without reliving the past. His own inadequacy. A spasm of pain tore through him. He couldn't bring himself to ask Miss Morecroft the extent of Sarah's humiliation.

"You may take away the soup, Miss Morecroft," he said. He barely cared whether he ever ate again but of course there was Caro. He needed to be strong for her.

"Sir?"

"Yes, Miss Morecroft." Wearily he dragged his gaze to meet hers.

"I have a letter."

From an oilskin pouch she withdrew several folded sheets.

"My father wrote it after four of the little ones had died. When he felt the beginnings of fever he bade me bring him pen and ink." She handed him the brittle, sealed parchment. "He said it was the most important letter he'd ever written and I must guard it with my life."

Roland scanned the few lines. Tears burned his eyes.

Miss Morecroft twisted her hands in her lap. Turning in her chair, she fixed him with a wavering gaze. "I've done you a terrible disservice, sir," she began haltingly. "Not only for my part in what happened to you, and to Caro and Lady Sarah." She paused, struggling with the words. "I never knew, until recently, why my father was sent to India. And" - she swallowed – "I understand now he owed you his life."

Roland drew in a ragged breath. At least this time he was not the villain. He felt as if a great load had been lifted from his shoulders. "Your father was young and he lost his nerve under fire. I'd challenge any of his superiors who were so ready to make an example of him to prove they would not do as Godby under similar circumstances."

"Yet he blamed you for banishing him?" Miss Morecroft's lip trembled.

"He thought I was doing it for other reasons," said Roland, recalling that dreadful night he had discovered Venetia in bed with his foster brother. Roland and Venetia had been married only a month, and she was already pregnant with Caro. He'd not thought he could survive her betrayal.

"Are you able to ... forgive him, as he asks?"

"I only wish he was here to hear it from my own lips," muttered Roland. Taking refuge in brusqueness, he added, "You'll stay here, of course. This is your home now, Sarah."

To his amazement Miss Morecroft kissed his hand and burst into tears.

SUNLIGHT GLANCED OFF THE SNOW-CAPPED MOUNTAIN. ROLAND SAT back in his chair on the terrace of the Chalet and savoured the now familiar backdrop of the Swiss Alps that had helped calm his disordered spirits for nearly two months.

For the first few weeks he had missed his customary eggs, bacon and haddock. The strange foreign food would have been unappetizing, if he'd had much of an appetite. But then, it had been a long time since his appetites were of any consequence.

He'd taken Caro to this place on the advice of his physician who believed Caro was at grave risk of succumbing to her mother's emotional excesses. Though Caro had exhibited no such propensities Roland considered time away from Caro's critical, prying aunt as important as the need for a period of calm reflection for himself. Time, age and maturity had given him an understanding of what had angered and perplexed him before: Venetia's addiction to the poppy. To some extent, Lady Sarah's youthful and innocent desire for instant gratification had helped him put Venetia's desperate pleasure-loving into perspective. But while Sarah's natural sensitivity and generosity towards others tempered her impulses, Venetia's wild, untutored spirit had been allowed to develop at will, becoming warped in the process. Her father, addicted to drink and gaming, had lost his wits and his fortune through both.

Was it any wonder that Venetia's appetites were what they were? Or that she'd traded on her beauty, becoming venal and selfish in consequence?

Was it any wonder that Roland had failed miserably as a husband when he, himself, was so green, a slave to his own youthful desires, as yet untempered by the wisdom that came through age and experience?

He felt the rough parchment of Godby's letter in his coat pocket and the words chased themselves around his head.

'I make no apologies for what happened between Venetia and myself; from the moment I saw her, reason was beyond my power. Now I am older, and wiser, my heart breaks at the knowledge that my passion for Venetia destroyed your love for me which I have come to value so much higher. Forgive me.'

"Father, you'll catch your death!" Caro's admonition came upon a cloud of frosted air as she seated herself opposite him at the breakfast table.

Roland transferred his gaze from the magnificent, snow-covered Matterhorn, to his daughter's green eyes. It was nine o' clock in the morning. Caro rarely made her appearance before noon.

"Come," he said, rising. "Let's walk."

She tucked her gloved hand into the crook of his arm and they left the terrace, taking the snow-covered path Roland was in the habit of taking, alone.

And as they talked his soul, which had felt a dry and shrivelled thing only hours ago, began to grow and thrive. He felt hope for the future, both for them, and for the reforms he believed would one day improve the lives of all.

Lady Sarah ...

Sarah was one topic on which he dared not dwell. He acknowledged the great good she had wrought in his daughter, but that was as far as he was prepared to let his thoughts wander in that direction.

The nightmares that resulted from that ghastly evening at the Hollingsworth's were too brutal, too vivid to revisit willingly. Whenever his thoughts turned unexpectedly to Sarah his breath caught and his body burned with desire, only to be extinguished by shame.

Caro smiled up at him. The crisp air had put roses in her cheeks and he no longer doubted his wisdom in removing her from Larchfield's cloistering atmosphere and the carping of her aunt.

"You look so much better, Caro." He was uncertain if it was the right thing to say. He did not want to spoil her lightness of spirit by fostering unhealthy introspection.

"I am," she said, simply, adding after a silence, "I've been talking to a doctor of the mind. I realize how much worse things could have been for me but for your care and concern." Her eyes filled with tears. "But now *you* appear to be the brooding invalid."

He looked at her with amazement.

The gentlest of breezes loosened the snow from the branches of the fir trees. It fell like powder, and caught upon Caro's lashes so that he fancied she looked like a wood sprite when she turned her large eyes upon him once more. Her words cut him to the bone as she said, wistfully, "I wonder whatever happened to Lady Sarah."

"Lady Sarah." He could do no more than repeat her name with longing.

Caro glanced up at him quickly. "You were fond of her, weren't you, papa?"

Roland shot her a narrow look. What was this? For nearly two months Caro had shown little interest in her surroundings, had not uttered a word of her ordeal. Now she was dredging up the past and it was intruding uncomfortably on Roland's own blurred understanding of events after he had lost consciousness.

It was bad enough to have to remember his lack of heroism while he could still stand; unbearable to consider what might have happened after he had passed out, despite Miss Morecroft's reassurances.

"She was a fine young woman," he conceded, embarrassed.

"She saved our lives, papa."

At Caro's reproachful look he added, hastily, "I wrote acknowledging that. She is still with her father." Then – for Caro continued to look accusing, "A very long letter, thanking her for all she did for you, Caro."

"And *you*, Papa!"

Roland looked away. "I'm sure I thanked her very properly," he muttered, wanting to turn the subject. "Miss Morecroft tells me you were very brave."

"Brave! Lady Sarah was the brave one, for leaving her father once she had learned my likely whereabouts, and venturing alone to the Hollingsworths. Miss Morecroft – the real one - was only brave in taking a risk to escape. Her very life depended upon it. After Mr Hollingsworth grabbed me when he found me walking in the park, then pushed me into the coach and tied me up, I did nothing but quiver and cry." She bit her lip. "He made me write that letter, you know. You believed I went with him willingly, didn't you?"

"It would have been understandable if you had," he said, squeezing her hand, "considering the lies I thought he'd told you about me-" He broke off, realizing he had said too much.

"What lies?"

"It doesn't matter. Let's turn back, it's freezing."

But Caro wouldn't let him off so easily. After some moments in silence she said, softly, "You thought he'd told me you weren't my father."

"I am your father."

"I know."

The silence wasn't broken after that. The path took a circuitous route and they returned to the hotel just as luncheon's enticing aromas wafted out to greet them.

CHAPTER 17

S ARAH SAT STIFFLY in her crimson and gilt chair and stared at the guests enjoying this evening's charades. Once she, too, would have added her laughter to the peals which greeted Miss Emmeline Farquhar's racy charade but now she felt wrapped in a cocoon of misery and loneliness, disembodied from her old friends. They'd welcomed her back with a rapture born of her novelty, but as she remained withdrawn so too they had ceased to make an effort. Sometimes she almost felt a growing hostility. Perhaps they saw that she despised their thoughtless frivolity. Knowing the depth of pain that came from loving, she certainly despised the use of charades to so publicly mock the pain of a fellow house guest.

She slid her gaze across to Lady Stokes. On stage the attractive Lord Stokes, playing the Duke of Cumberland, was in an intimate clinch with Miss Emmeline Farquhar who played his mistress. Lady Stokes's jaw clenched with the effort of appearing to find the charade as amusing as everyone else. Clearly, she did not.

Sarah turned away in disgust as the audience broke into rapturous applause.

"And now for True or False!" Lord Stokes, tearing himself from the arms of his lady-love on stage addressed the audience. "The charade will first identify the three people chosen to take part in tonight's quiz. They will then have to answer questions put to them upon the roll of a dice."

"Lady Sarah? Are you alright?" Lord Giles, beside her, touched her arm. His frown was full of concern.

She smiled weakly. "I'm just a little weary." How could she admit that games involving the roll of a dice brought back terrible memories?

"Perhaps we could take a turn around the supper room?" he suggested, and although Sarah knew he had no ulterior motives, she shook her head. His admiration the past few days had been balm to her anguished soul after Roland's devastating letter but she had no intentions of pushing the boundaries of propriety. Who knew where a turn around the supper table could lead?

Another spasm of anguish gripped her as she reflected upon Roland's words. Indirectly, they were the reason she was here. At her father's admonition. It was he who had almost physically ripped her from Roland's side all those weeks ago and bundled her into his coach to take her home. But watching his daughter pine over Roland Hawthorne's silence had driven Lord Miles to the extremes of his limited forbearance.

"Worthless puppy if he can't appreciate a prize jewel like you, my love!" he'd fumed, forgetting that he had been strenuously against a possible match from the moment Sarah had finally hinted at her feelings for Roland.

"A girl with your wit and beauty mustn't squander her chances mouldering in the country with her cantankerous old Papa. Lady Mettling has invited you to spend the week at Middlebrook with a group of friends. You will write this moment and accept her kind invitation."

There had been a fierce battle between the strong-minded Lord Miles and his equally strong-minded daughter before Sarah had finally given in.

However the past few days only proved that she would have been far happier mouldering in the country with her cantankerous old Papa. The frenetic gaiety she'd once embraced seemed stupid and pointless. Though she tried to enter into the spirit she knew old friends and acquaintances whispered to one another that Lady Sarah was greatly changed – and not nearly so much fun.

To her confusion she heard several members of the audience cry out her name.

Lord Giles tapped her arm. He was smiling. "It's a shipwreck, can't you see?" he told her, indicating the badly painted backdrop meant to represent waves and Miss Hemmersly acting out a brave attempt at keeping her head above water. "They want you to go on stage."

Fear gripped her. Dear Lord, this couldn't be happening. "I don't think I can," she whispered honestly. Her legs felt weak and her head reeled.

"Mr Roger Burbank, you are also required," Lord Stokes called amidst general clapping and excitement. "Come, Lady Sarah, you're not known as a shrinking violet. It's all in the name of honest fun." He extended his arm and before Sarah knew it Lord Giles had pushed her forward and she was being helped onto the stage.

It was not the hostile grilling her overwrought nerves had envisioned. People were naturally curious about her ordeal and after a while she found it cathartic to answer questions like how cold had the water been and about the Belgian fishermen who had bravely swum out to rescue her.

"Many thanks for your brave answers," Lord Stokes told her at the end of her ten questions, indicating she could now rise her from her chair on the centre of the stage.

Smiling, Sarah inclined her head as she prepared to return to the audience amidst more applause.

"I ... have a question."

She turned at the interruption.

"Miss Bassingthwaite, why did you not speak up before?" Lord Stokes, still in his role as Master of Ceremonies stayed Sarah with a hand. "Lady Sarah, will you permit our shyest houseguest one final question?"

Frozen, Sarah stared at the girl, unable to answer. Millicent looked as plain in her blue round dress as she had the night Sarah had seen her at the London inn before walking into the trap laid for her by Archie Hollingsworth. There was a greenish tinge to her normally sallow complexion and her terror was apparent at commanding the attention of so many people.

Almost wearily, Sarah accepted her fate. It was clear enough. Lady Bassingthwaite had bullied her daughter into asking the question and Millicent, too frightened to disobey, had only now got up the courage to lay the foundations of a damning exposé. Naturally Millicent's veiled accusation would be given credence because of the kind of girl she was.

"What would you like to ask, Miss Bassingthwaite?" Lord Stokes prompted. His manner was expansive and congenial, like a master coaxing a nervous schoolroom miss. Sarah drew herself up proudly, smoothing down her sequin-encrusted crimson net skirts; a colour and picture she was sure the audience would always remember as Millicent blurted out, "It's my mother who wants to know, actually, and I am so sorry, Lady Sarah" — she swallowed, then stammered — "but she asks why you—"

She faltered, apparently unable to continue until Lord Stokes chivvied her in a friendly, encouraging fashion, "Lady Sarah is not an ogre, Miss Bassingthwaite. I'm sure she'd be delighted to answer your question."

Millicent swallowed and cast her eyes downwards as she continued in a voice that could barely carry across the room, but which certainly managed to be heard judging by the tumultuous response when she finally asked, "She wants to know why you were alone at the Crown and Anchor when you said you were being looked after at Larchfield and ... and why you then went unchaperoned to Sally Hollingsworth's address in Marylebone?"

CHAPTER 18

"WELL, YOU MIGHT have sent word more than two days ahead for there's been such a to-do getting the house prepared and matters just as you would like them Roland... Not that, inconvenience aside, it isn't wonderful to see you back again. And you, Caro, in *such* rude health. Really, I don't know what your father was thinking, assuming your heart was so tender it could not withstand a simple rejection. As if it isn't something most of us have to bear at least once in our lifetimes. My dear, there are far worthier gentlemen than Mr Hollingsworth and you'd do well to bear in mind what you have to offer a gentleman disposed to taking a wife. You may not be endowed with such a pretty face and figure as my Augusta and Harriet but, unlike my poor girls, you have a handsome dowry to entice the most discerning gentleman-"

"I hope we need not wait too long for refreshment, Cecily," Roland interrupted, stilling her words with a cursory peck on the cheek as he pushed his daughter out of her path. "It's been a long journey."

"I was hardly craning my neck out of the window for the first sign of your arrival, Roland," said Cecily, tartly, preceding him into to the drawing room and pulling on the embroidered bell rope. "Bessie knows to expect you. I'm sure if you can be patient a little longer we can all sit down and enjoy a pleasant chat while we wait for tea."

"So, Cecily, more than two months have elapsed, and yet your countenance and good humour remain quite unchanged," Roland marvelled with an irony completely undetected by his sister-in-law.

"I'm surprised, considering the trials I've had to endure since you left me so abruptly with the entire management of this house and estate upon my shoulders," she sniffed. "Thank goodness we found Miss Morecroft – and I mean poor Godby's daughter – lodging with Mr Hollingsworth's mother so she was able to take up her rightful post. I've a mind to call on the good widow when I'm in London and thank her for her care; though I think that son of hers needs talking to for allowing Caro's tears to overrule his judgment. I daresay he was flattered by Caro's attention." She ran a careworn hand across her brow. "That aside, Harriet and Augusta have been sorely trying. I've threatened to box their ears if they so much as mention Lady Sarah's name. You can't image the difficulty I've had explaining to them events in such a manner as will not damage their delicate sensibilities by putting ideas into their heads, or poisoning the high esteem in which they hold their cousin. Not that I intend ever referring to this again, Caro. What's done is done. You've learned your lesson and you've been lucky. You still have your reputation intact ... unlike that insinuating little baggage Lady Sarah, or whatever name she currently chooses to go by. Well, she's had her public come-uppance. The scandal! Exposed at Lady Mettling's house party for consorting with persons of ill repute!" she hissed before adding, complacently, "I daresay a nunnery might accept her if her father has deep enough pockets. Though it'll sit ill with her pleasure-loving disposition."

"Lady Sarah has been publicly shamed?"

"Oh, don't you start, Caro," said Cecily, irritated. "I've had enough to put up with without Harriet and Augusta snivelling at the news. I'd thought to instil in them a healthy dose of terror rather than touch their tender little hearts. It's exactly as I said. She was an insinuating little baggage, a trollop, and there's no kinder way to put it."

"How ... dare ... you?"

Shocked into silence, Cecily gaped at her brother-in-law. Then the gloating expression returned as she said, "You always fancied yourself in love with her, didn't you, Roland? Well, I hear she is no longer received in any respectable drawing room, and that only yesterday she'd been given the cut direct by Lady Jersey."

Hope flickered like a flame suddenly come to life in the cold cavernous regions of Roland' heart.

Lady Sarah needed rescuing.

He swallowed, his mouth suddenly dry as he recalled the dutiful, formal letter he had written her from Switzerland. His thanks for her bravery and subsequent care of him had sounded so trite. The words that followed were worse; a pompous-sounding death knell to all his hopes of what might have been: *It is my wish not to be distracted by life's frivolities so that I may devote my energy and passion towards furthering those worthy causes which remain the chief object of my life.'*

What he meant was that Sarah deserved to be happy and the kindest service he could render was to relinquish her.

What greater betrayal was there than to be discarded upon the roll of a dice? In the midst of the drama she had argued otherwise, but Roland knew that when normality returned, Sarah would come to despise him and his lack of heroism.

He looked beyond Cecily's shoulder. "Ah, Miss Morecroft," he greeted the serious, brown-haired young woman who entered the room flanked by her young charges, Augusta and Harriet. They were trying hard to contain their enthusiasm at seeing Caro.

"I trust you have not been overwhelmed by your duties." To his surprise he felt a pang as the little girls rushed to embrace his daughter. He'd missed his nieces.

"Not in the slightest," she said with her usual calm. "Harriet and Augusta have proved apt and diligent pupils while Mrs Hawthorne has been nothing but kindness itself."

Roland glanced from the demure governess in whose manner he could detect no irony, to Cecily whose lips were pursed in a prim, complacent little smile.

Good, it appeared he would not be required to arbitrate in order to keep a tenuous peace.

"Roland, where are you going?"

Roland had barely drained his tea cup before he was rising, inclining his head towards the three women.

"To London," he said, equably. "You've run the household so efficiently in my absence, Cecily, I've no doubt you'll not miss my company another three days or so."

⁂

"M'LADY?"

Sarah, reclining on the Gothic sofa in her friend's small drawing room, glanced up from her deep introspection of the dancing flames as her maid put her head around the door.

"A gentleman to see you."

James. Shame and embarrassment curdled in her belly. He'd written the moment he'd heard news of the uproar at Middlebrook.

She sighed. "Show him in."

Dear Lord, she'd never forget standing on the top step that led to the stage while the audience buzzed with excitement and Millicent wept, "I'm so sorry, Lady Sarah." Though if she really had been, and not such a wet-goose to boot, she'd hardly have continued in imploring tones, "Mother thought she recognised you at the inn and though I tried to stop her she went after the publican with some excuse and read the note you'd given him."

Drawing her green Pomona shawl more closely round her, Sarah dragged herself off the sofa, wishing she had the freedom to fly abroad and escape the nightmare her life had become.

After a cursory inspection of her appearance in the looking glass above the chiffoniere, and a weary adjustment to a flattened curl, she was ready.

She'd thought nothing had the power to rouse her from her from her lethargy, but the sound of his boots in the corridor outside the door made her feel suddenly ill. Not at what she'd done but at what he must be thinking.

She tensed, preparing herself for the moment James would thrust open the door and gaze upon her with reproach and disappointment.

"Gad's teeth, Sarah! You look like you've been sleeping in a haystack." Striding to the footstool she'd migrated to, he crouched down to grip her shoulder.

It was all she could do, not to cry. Instead, she took refuge in brittle pride. "I do not need a lecture from you, James," she said, turning away from him. "I hoped you would not come."

"That I'd give up on you at last?" he asked, rising and striding to the fire to warm his hands. "Don't think you can ruin yourself without more than a murmur from me." He twisted his head to look at her, dominating the room with his massive shoulders and red hair. But it was his look of puzzlement she found so hard to bear. Did he really think she was guilty, as charged?

"Say your piece and then leave me alone," she muttered, drawing her shawl close.

"Do you know what the gossips are saying? Not to mention the wags—? A house of ill repute in Marylebone, Sarah?" He shook his darling shaggy head. "Obviously there is some rational explanation. I, for one, do not believe you were enticed into the flesh trade. I'm sure most others who know you don't, either. So what I can't for the life of me fathom is why you don't defend yourself with the simple truth."

For a moment she considered confessing everything. But that would mean revealing too much: her rash stupidity in venturing forth alone, her subsequent humiliation and her undying loyalty to Roland. If James learned of Roland's role in all this and the passion he continued to inspire in her, he'd belittle it all with demands like why he wasn't here? He might even resort to anger and seek Roland out.

Well, Roland just needed time. His duty was to ensure Caro could survive without him before he came courting Sarah. And as Roland was doing all in his power to protect Caro, so must Sarah.

"I was looking for someone about whose safety I was concerned." She sighed. "I'm sorry James but I have vowed to say no more. The truth would only damage her reputation."

James narrowed his eyes at her, his disgust plain as he said slowly, "You believe it worthwhile to sacrifice your reputation for someone who remains silent in the face of your ruin?"

Sarah stared mutinously into the flames.

"It's that Hawthorne girl, isn't it?" he asked suddenly. "She ran away, or slipped up, and you went after her. That's it, isn't it? Now you're facing the music and she says nothing."

Sarah held herself rigid. She would remain silent.

"Good Lord, and her father, that damned Whig Hawthorne, the Devil rot him, is happy to let the wolves devour you with nary a murmur in case it hurts his darling daughter or reflects badly on him, more like it."

"James, please!" Finally roused, Sarah jumped up and gripped the lapels of his coat as she looked into his eyes. "Terrible things happened that night at this house in" — she swallowed — "in Marylebone. Mr Hawthorne took his daughter abroad to recover. You really must not judge what you can't understand—"

"I understand that knave Hawthorne is letting you suffer the consequences of his daughter's mistakes. What I'd like to know is, where is he when you really need him?"

Raw pain tore through her. She'd like to know, too. Wilting against James's chest misery settled upon her shoulders like a mantle.

James put his forefinger beneath Sarah's chin and raised her head to look at him. "Can't you see what you're doing?" he asked, more gently now. "To yourself? To those who love you? Your father was beyond comfort when he thought you dead. Now this! Sarah," he pleaded, "go back to Lord Miles, now. I'll escort you. We'll call the banns. Do what we'd all agreed was in everyone's best interests before your" — he exhaled on a disapproving grunt — "escapade under Hawthorne's roof." He gave her a bracing shake. "You know you'll be much happier at home with people who care for you than here" — he indicated the room with its common, ugly furniture — "accepting the charity of fawning little Mrs Hargreaves, hoping your dissolute friends will invite you back into the fold. They won't, you know."

"You're asking me to marry you?" she asked slowly, pulling out of his embrace to stand close to the fire. So it had come to this, after all.

"Well, no one else has offered, have they?" he asked, pointedly.

She didn't know whether to laugh or scream. Instead, she gave him a long, considering look. "Do you love me, James? Do you adore me? Does your heart beat faster when I enter the same room?"

"What nonsense you talk sometimes," he said, smiling down at her with fond exasperation. "You know it doesn't and nor would I want it to. It would be like—" He struggled for an analogy.

Sarah returned to her footstool where she waited with interest. James was not one to wax lyrical at the best of times and he did not disappoint her, now.

"I suppose it would be like having to mince around in diamond-spangled high-heeled slippers which pinched like the Devil." He patted the top of her head and Sarah was reminded of the fondness he had for his cocker spaniel, Bessie. "Give me a pair of comfortable leather slippers any day. Though, Sarah, you should do something about your hair. It's not like you to look so untidy."

She let out a hysteria-tinged laugh. "Well, how can I possibly say no to what must be the most romantic marriage proposal I've ever received?"

"Glad you think it's a good idea. I'm warming to it by the minute." Rubbing his hands vigorously before the fire he fixed her with one of his bluff, pleased-with-himself grins she remembered from childhood days after he'd winged a goose or shot a bulls-eye. "We'll deal well together, Sarah. No inconvenient passion and bruised hearts, eh?"

It was hard to hold back the tears. His generosity was so undeserved. She rose and crossed the carpet. Taking his wrists she gazed at him with affection. "That wasn't an outright yes. There's a caveat, James." She paused. "I cannot, in good conscience, agree to marry you when my heart is engaged elsewhere."

"Well, why didn't you say?" He sounded more put out than heartbroken.

Sarah hesitated. "Because I didn't think you'd approve. Papa doesn't, that's certain."

"Good God! Hawthorne?" he blustered. "After all that's happened and all he's done? Or rather not done since he's the one who should be fronting up with an offer, though Lord knows what your father would say!" He shook his head, scowling as he repeated Roland's name with derision. "Hawthorne! First he says nothing to defend you when he knows the truth, now he won't marry you when you're far and away more than the ungrateful blackguard ever deserved."

Sarah hedged. "James, perhaps he's not even heard the news. He's in Switzerland, still, I think."

"Well, you must tell him. Write to him. He deserves to know."

She hesitated, unsure whether to elaborate, then added reluctantly, "Before any of this drama at the Mettlings happened he wrote telling me he was disinclined ever to marry again as he wished to direct all his energies towards his political career."

"I told you — Damned Whig!" spat James, staring over her shoulder at the window as he digested her words. "Well, there's nothing more to be said, then. Regardless of your feelings for Hawthorne, the very man who should be rescuing you from this debacle, though I daresay your father would rather see a bullet through his heart than his ring on your finger, he's not here. And clearly, someone's got to save you for I'll not stand by and see you ruined."

Another surge of affection for her friend enveloped Sarah, but it was not love and it was so different from what she felt for Roland. She gazed at James, torn by shame and confusion. If she accepted him she'd be using him ruthlessly and shamelessly to save herself from a public disgrace which barred her from society forever. Yet without a timely marriage to save her, she'd never see another familiar drawing room or sip tea with a respectable matron again. The friends she'd once gossiped with would cross the road to avoid speaking with her. But worse than all that would be her father's hurt and humiliation. She didn't think she could do it to him.

"For Goodness sake, stop snivelling, Sarah." There was little sympathy in James's tone. "It's time to face the truth. Hawthorne doesn't look like he's about to play the gentleman, in which case you really don't have much choice for I can tell you now, I'll not see my dearest friend pay for a crime for which she's blameless." Picking an imaginary piece of lint from his coat sleeve he added, with a grin, "You'll make an excellent housekeeper and hostess at any rate and if you pay more attention to your hair than you obviously did today, you're a diamond of the first water."

HALF AN HOUR AFTER JAMES' MOMENTOUS VISIT, SARAH STOOD AT the window of the shabby drawing room wracked with indecision as to whether she was doing the right thing.

Though she wasn't sure she endorsed James's declaration that love was nothing but a load of codswallop invented to sell books and tickets to the theatre she had all but convinced herself that theirs would be a comfortable union. She'd had to remind herself it was she who had pursued Roland so if he held to his original stance that marriage was not on his agenda she had no one to blame but herself.

Swallowing past the great lump in her throat she traced his name on the fogged-up window pane.

Her father would be happy, James was pleased enough, so now there was only her inconvenient passion for Roland to overcome. Surely, after the dramas of the past few months, a comfortable arrangement such as marriage with James promised, was to be commended.

She wrinkled her nose at the faux Gothic furniture and tasteless artworks of Mrs. Hargreaves' drawing room. Suddenly she longed for the tasteful interiors of her childhood home. With a determined effort she banished the reflection that Larchfield had been just as beautiful.

"Darling Roland," she said to the stuffed hamster in its glass box upon a table near her, "where are you?"

She had attempted something with her untidy hair after James' criticism, but it still looked like a bird's nest.

The overloud rap on the door startled her and Betty Hargreaves's useless parlour maid put her head round. "Gentleman to see you, M'lady?"

Sarah looked enquiringly at her.

"Can't say as I remember his name, m'lady, but he didn't have red hair."

Life surged back, filling the aching void, sweeping away her lethargy and snapping Sarah's backbone and lazy posture to attention.

It had to be Roland. No one else would call on her.

"Keep him waiting," she ordered, flying to the door. "I'll be down in five minutes."

Heart beating furiously she doused herself with orange flower water, enlisted the maid's help to button her into her best gold flecked muslin, and swept her curls into the most stylish *à la Meduse* coiffure she could manage in the seconds available.

Surely this meant he had finally heard, or come to his senses or whatever the reason was for his silence? He'd only have to reflect on the eternal alchemy between them to realise he had no alternative.

Nerves jangling, she ran to the parlour. Her mind whirled with possibilities, but at the root of all was the knowledge that the only man she would ever love had returned. At the door she stopped to bite her lips and pinch colour into her cheeks, gathering her courage before signalling to the parlour maid to announce her.

"My dear Mr Hawthorne." She swept into the room with as much regal dignity as she could manage, extending her hand, smiling. "Welcome back."

He took her fingertips and bowed, but it did not escape her that his lips kissed the air, and his expression as he straightened was one she remembered well: wary, reluctant admiration, a throwback to the early days of her tenure at Larchfield.

"Lady Sarah," he had said, his smile strained, "I came the moment I heard news of your predicament."

Predicament? It sounded as if she'd contracted some nasty disease. Then it struck her that perhaps he truly believed her fall from grace was in more than name only. That it was something unconnected from the night at the Hollingsworths.

She dismissed the thought as nonsense saying earnestly as she ran her hands along the top of the Egyptian sofa, "I don't know what you've heard but I am guilty of nothing other than being a party to the crimes committed at the Hollingsworths."

When he didn't immediately answer, merely stared at her with a look she was unable to fathom, she grew afraid. She studied him, listening to the wind rattling the windows and the clock ticking. As usual he was turned out with his usual care and attention to detail. The cut of his russet coloured coat emphasised his broad shoulders and he wore a new pair of hessians with brown leather tassels. Though he did not exude quite his usual air of studied calm — frowning instead at the amber knob of his cane which he twisted in his hands — he'd managed to coax his cravat into an Oriental tie of utter perfection. Cosmo would have been green with envy. Calling on such irrelevancies was the only way she could stop herself from weeping, or throwing herself into his arms and asking him why he'd not come back to her sooner.

He advanced several steps more steps and stopped, putting his head on one side as he gazed at her. There was such sadness and sympathy in his expression she felt her lip tremble but instead of a smile, the lines of his face remained grim. He cleared his voice. "Sarah," he said, softly, "you know I don't believe you guilty of impropriety. I'd only just returned home when I heard you'd fallen victim to the gossips."

She waited for him to draw her into his arms. Her body ached for the closeness they'd once shared but she steeled herself against her old impulsiveness. She had to know he felt the same way she did.

He cleared his throat again. "When Mrs Hawthorne told me I came immediately." Sarah saw the derision in his eye as he glanced at their surroundings. "I've come to make you an offer."

She stared back at him. Shock and disappointment churned in her stomach. Where was the impassioned declaration of love, the hoarse avowals of his enduring passion, his confession of surrender to the feelings he realised he was unable to deny?

"An offer?" She cocked her head, devastation making her flippant. "To return to Larchfield as your governess?"

"Good God, Sarah, are you mad?" He sounded suddenly so much like the Roland she knew that she laughed, asking, "No, but I think you must be if you imagine I could be tempted by such an appalling proposal. It's even worse than James's offer only half an hour ago."

It had not been the right response. The clenching of his jaw and narrowing of his eyes told that. Realisation crashed through her brain. Lord, his pride was as damaged as hers. She said, quickly to ameliorate the damage, "Do you know how long I've waited for you, Roland?" How she wished she'd never spoken those flippant, thoughtless, *stupid* words. It was no time to indulge in wounded dignity. Roland had *almost* just asked her to marry him and she wanted Roland more than she'd wanted anything in her life.

But the damage had been done. Desperate, she tried another gambit, pretending she didn't notice his withdrawal, his clouded expression, the clenching of his jaw. "You came back to me, Roland, as I longed that you would. I did so hope you didn't mean what you'd said in your letter."

He managed a reluctant smile. "Of course I didn't mean it, though you surely understood what prompted me."

She looked enquiringly at him. Oh Lord, was his prickly pride really going to get in the way of all this? They'd come so far.

With a growl of exasperation he closed the distance between them only in as much as he gripped her elbows before releasing them in order to pace. "Good God, Sarah, of course you do. I lost any credible right to claim you as my wife the moment I opened my mouth and sacrificed you to Sir Richard."

"Roland!" She followed him to where he had taken refuge with an Egyptian armchair between them. Desperate to bridge the final distance, she whispered unsteadily, "If you believe that, you're only playing into Sir Richard's hands. Surely it's what *I* think that matters?" She reached out to touch him. Though he looked warily at her hand as she rested the flat of her palm against his chest he did not move away.

She craned her neck up to meet his anguished gaze. "Sir Richard set out to humiliate you. If that is how you feel, if it is humiliation that now prevents you from seeking what you want, then victory is his."

With a soft groan, Roland crushed her hand within both of his and brought it to his lips. "I've told myself the same thing, over and over," he whispered, his hot breath sending shivers of longing through her. "It's the knowledge of my weakness, my *undeservedness*, that's kept me from returning to you all those days and nights of wanting you so badly I thought I'd lose my mind."

For a brief moment she had dared hope, but his tortured expression stripped all that away. Too much still stood between them. She could see it in the rawness of his continued humiliation, his refusal to forgive himself. She had no words for the pain that sliced through her.

"Sarah, don't you see?" He clenched her hand so tightly it hurt. "I uttered the words that surrendered you to him, I made the choice to deliver you to horrors undreamt of. I have to live with that every day of my life."

"You were *forced*, Roland." She spoke through gritted teeth. "By knifepoint." She took a deep breath for courage and tentatively rested her head against his chest, melding her body against his, hoping to coax the loving softness from him for which she longed.

He averted his head, but stopped short of pushing her away.

"Roland, you came here to make me an offer—" She pressed herself closer, raising her head.

He looked down at her. There was longing in his expression but still he resisted the invitation implicit in her pleading eyes, her pouting mouth.

"Captain Fleming is a good man," he said, gruffly, setting her away from him. In ten years you're far more likely to still be happy in a steady, reliable alliance with a man you're fond of than you would with me."

"Nonsense!" she cried, reaching up to clasp her hands behind his neck. "You know I've loved you, wanted you since I first came to Larchfield." She was not yet ready to give up. If he could just accept that she did not share his fears. "You feel the same, I know you do." She raised her head, offered him her lips, but these gestures seemed only to increase his anguish and harden his resolve.

"Sarah," he ground out, "I owe you my life. Do you know how worthless that makes me feel after what I've done to you? Fleming has come to your rescue. If you love me, you must not hold me to the hasty and inferior offer I made you when I entered this room." A muscle worked at the corner of his mouth. Sighing, he ran his hand across his eyes. "If you marry Captain Fleming you'll please your father. It's a sensible match. He's open and honest and holds you in the greatest affection." He dropped his eyes, adding in tortured tones as he turned away from her, "I can only be a constant reminder of the horrors you do battle with every day."

A heavy, stifling lethargy crept upon her. He was resolved. Nothing she could do or say would change his mind. Dully, she asked, "Or is it that you cannot gaze at *me*, Roland, without being reminded of what I was in Sir Richard's hands? Perhaps it is not your humiliation that stands between us. Perhaps *I* am the constant reminder."

Defeated, she stepped back. It was like stepping out of the life embodied by all her dreams and hopes, and into another. One she didn't want, at all.

Silently, they stared at one another.

"I love you, Sarah." His voice was clear and direct, only the whiteness of his knuckles clenching the top of his cane betrayed the depth of his emotion. "But when a man more worthy than I is willing to offer you comfort, security and affection, I refuse to stake my claim." Bowing, he turned.

Sarah watched him through a sheen of tears. "I marry James in six weeks," she said, brokenly as his hand gripped the doorknob. "If you change your mind before then" — she exhaled on a shuddering breath — "I will be waiting."

✼

ROLAND STUMBLED INTO THE STREET. SELF DISGUST CLAWED AT HIM. How could he have imagined they had a future in view of all that had happened? Weaving his way through the traffic, He made blindly in the direction of St James. Passers-by jostled him, a dirty-faced boy in a greasy cap and coat too big for him tried to beg a penny. He was oblivious to everything but the pain that sliced through that treacherous, fallible organ, his heart.

"Have I got summat to tickle yer fancy!"

Roland stepped around the lightskirt who sought to detain him with an insinuating pout and thrust of her skinny bosom. Head down he continued towards Whites, his Club, intent upon burying his sorrows in a news-sheet.

An insistent tug of the sleeve made him look up in irritation. An instant later recognition dawned.

"Kitty!"

Smiling, she took his arm. "Right glad I am to see yer got yer colour back, sir. Thought you was bound for your eternity box, I did, and that's the truth!"

"It was a close thing."

"Yer still look as if you could do with a mite cheering up."

Garnering his wits and his manners, he smiled apologetically, in a strange way glad of the diversion. "I'm afraid I'm not in the market, Kitty," he said, adding quickly at her crestfallen look, "although if I were, I'd definitely court your kind offices." His gaze skimmed the length of her, from her glossy brown hair and bright eyes to the boots in need of mending which peeped from beneath her tawdry lilac gown. "So you've gone out on your own, have you? Escaped that evil den of vice and bondage?"

She frowned as she digested this, her hand still on his sleeve. "Didn't I tell you I signed a piece of paper wot gives Mrs Hollingsworth rights over me person 'til I've paid her back in full? That ain't fer another three years or more. After that she says she'll 'elp me set up on me own."

"Then you're not unhappy with the Hollingsworths?"

"Lord, I'd leave tomorrow if I weren't obliged to 'em!"

"Why don't you just leave, now?"

Kitty looked at Roland as if he were queer in the attic. "And get sent to Newmarket for me pains? The law 'ud be onto me in no time. Weren't you listening?"

"I daresay they've come to rely upon your trusting nature," Roland said, ironically.

"Young Mr Hollingsworth gives me special leave, s'long as I give him 'arf wot I earns in the street. The rest I gets to keep meself. The missus don't know, it's just his and my little arrangement and it ain't arf bad. I'll be able to set myself up right and proper, just like me friend, Queenie Featherlove, once I's paid me debt."

Kitty batted her eyelashes and squeezed his arm. "Come along, sir. Just for old times' sakes, eh?"

"And have half your earnings line young Mr Hollingsworth's pockets? Thank you, Kitty, but no."

"On the 'ouse, sir. It 'ud be a pleasure." She cocked her head and looked at him, coyly. "Ain't every day I gets to pleasure a gennulman o' me choice. Tells yer wot - there ain't many what are as 'andsome and obliging as yerself."

Roland gave her a wry smile. Then thrusting his hands into his pockets he withdrew, to Kitty's wide-eyed amazement, a pound note. "Why don't you give that to your friend Queenie Lovelyfeather or whatever her name is, for safe keeping on your behalf. If she's what you aspire to, she's obviously doing something right. If you don't trust her, then keep it in a safe place until you need it."

Kitty took the note from him and rubbed it against her cheek, eyes closed in rapture. "I ain't never had a pound note afore, sir," she breathed before letting out a regretful sigh. "Contrary to expectations, poor Queenie ain't in no position to 'elp me, sir, since you might be interested to know she's got fiddle-stick's end of the bargain with our old friend, Sir Richard. It might make yer feel better to know he ain't just into trickin' coves what's got money. Although 'es done plenty more of 'em than just you, sir, and that's the truth!"

Roland's first inclination was to wince at the name, his next was to ask, carefully, "Sir Richard did the dirty on a deal with your friend? How was that?"

"Oh, all sorts," said Kitty, warming to her theme. "Queenie's a perticular favorite with a lot of the fancy coves, but she's the only one Sir Richard'll see. They had some kind o' 'rangement, only he's gone an' diddled her ... feathered 'is nest at 'er expense, so she ain't about to set 'erself up, after all."

Sadly, Kitty handed back the pound note. "So it'll just line young Mr Hollingsworth's pocket, after all, sir and I ain't got nowhere safe to keep it."

Roland folded the note and put it back in his pocket, looking thoughtful. Then he took Kitty's arm and began leading her towards a dark, narrow laneway which led off the main thoroughfare.

"Perhaps poor Queenie can realize her ambitions, after all, Kitty," Roland said, smiling into her questioning brown eyes, "with you well rewarded in the process."

CHAPTER 19

"THE WHITE LUTESTRING is more appropriate, Caro, dear."

Mrs Hawthorne put down her needlework and leaned back in her armchair with a complacent little smile as she surveyed Caro's choice of gowns for her grand come-out ball in a few days' time.

"The ruby velvet is more becoming to my complexion," Caro protested as she caressed the gown's lustrous folds. It was draped, together with the white lutestring, over the arm of a chair in the drawing room of their London townhouse.

Though she had no intention of wearing scarlet, she was going to have to use all her wiles to avoid being forced to wear the white, which made her look even more sallow.

"Imagine wearing ruby velvet for a come-out ball! That sounds like something your mother would have done!"

Caro gritted her teeth as she gazed longingly at the dress in question. She thought it made her look more striking than she had ever looked.

She turned to her aunt. "*And* she'd have put everyone else in the shade! Insipid pastels make me look like I'm permanently suffering the ague," she grumbled, adding under her breath, "Sometimes I wonder if that's your intention." With a sigh she began to pace between the deep bay window and the fireplace then stopped to look out into the sunlit street. "Lady Sarah," she said defiantly, though with a wary look at her aunt, "says I need vibrant colours to ensure I'm noticed and that, surely, is the purpose of a coming-out ball."

Mrs Hawthorne dropped her cross-stitch and stared, open-mouthed. "How dare you mention the name of that disgraceful ... imposter?" she snapped. "If it were not bad enough that she impersonated a dead woman — or, at least, someone she thought was dead — in order to draw you girls dangerously under her influence, her recent disgrace has rendered her unacceptable to polite society. I doubt you will be seeing her at any *respectable* event this season."

Caro's eyes flashed. "Lady Sarah is a victim of injustice and the gossips. Since it is my understanding that the purpose of my come-out is to secure a husband, something I may do within six months, I believe I'm adult enough to speak as I choose."

This time Mrs Hawthorne's eyes flashed. The flowers adorning her bonnet swayed menacingly as she leant forward. "Don't answer back, young lady! You are not out, yet! Roland, what have you been teaching your child?" she asked, as the master of the house entered the room, looking for some mislaid article. "Once I pooh-poohed your fears she would turn out like Venetia. Now she is the spitting image!"

Roland sighed, pausing at the escritoire in which he had been rummaging. Cecily was clearly very angry and he had not the energy for tact.

"Caro is as far from being like Venetia as is possible – with regard to Venetia's venal points to which I presume you allude, my dear Cecily." He looked at her, a warning in his voice. "Nor have I ever feared she was in danger of inheriting her mother's less than commendable traits. The only difference between now and a year ago is that Caro understands her own mind." He nodded. "Please excuse me."

Gaining the sanctuary of his study he stood by the French doors that stood open to the gardens and remembered the times he'd gazed upon Sarah taking a walk with the children along the path that led to the woods.

He might not have been able to save her from her indignities at Sir

Richard's hands but at least he was no longer wallowing in the self disgusted lethargy that had plagued him during the months he had been in Switzerland with Caro.

After a lifetime spent fighting for justice for the disenfranchised, he was now fighting for justice for Sarah.

Revenge is a dish best served cold. He smiled. He had done his homework and laid his trap carefully. Sir Richard had acted with impunity for long enough; but he had not chosen his victims wisely.

Roland just wished Sarah would be around to witness the villain's impending fall from grace.

⚜

CARO WORE A CREAM DRESS WITH A RED VELVET SASH AND THREE rows of red roses around the hem. It was a small victory but a victory, nevertheless.

She stared at her reflection in amazement. Even Aunt Cecily had marvelled over her transformation. The old termagant didn't need to know that the brightness of her eyes and complexion had enjoyed a little help from Tincture of Roses and Olympian Dew.

Long-ago gifts from Sarah, and unappreciated at the time, they had come into their own, now. Nearly a year older, and a century wiser, Caro was determined to shine. It wasn't that she yearned for romance. In fact, right now she was decidedly wary of it although Mr Hollingsworth and Sir Richard were rooted firmly in her past. Having survived the ordeal she had been made stronger. She would never be a victim again.

She also intended to have her independence and follow her intellectual leanings – interests which hadn't been dampened by recent experiences. She remembered Lady Sarah's words: 'Marriage gives a woman status and independence the unmarried woman might never attain. A girl must just choose the right husband'.

Covering her face with her hands she reflected on the night at the Hollingsworths. She had forced herself to do so only through long training, yet she knew she had come through virtually unscathed compared with Lady Sarah. As if it weren't enough that Lady Sarah had suffered the indignities forced upon her by Sir Richard, she'd been recognised when visiting Caro's father at the inn where he'd stayed. She'd tried to learn more, but gossipy matrons did not readily divulge such details to innocents like Caro. Whatever was being said, Caro knew facts were unimportant compared with appearances. To be tainted by scandal was a crime in itself.

Twisting her hands together as she sat at her dressing table, while Mavis, her dresser arranged her hair, she reflected on her poor unhappy papa. He must have been distraught when Lady Sarah had accepted Captain Fleming.

"Do you approve, Miss Caro?" Mavis pushed in a final pin and Caro surveyed the elaborate but becoming hairstyle, smiling. Rose buds had been tucked throughout her shiny black curls. The effect was charming.

"It's lovely, thank you. That'll be all, Mavis. I need" - she hesitated, feeling such mixed feelings of excitement, anticipation and sorrow - "I need a moment or two to gather myself and then I'll be down."

It had been more than a month since her father's abortive trip to London to propose to Lady Sarah. His behaviour had been erratic in the interim. Sometimes he had seemed distant and morose. At others it was as if the old fires burned within and he spoke to her like an adult, almost a friend.

Now here he was smiling in the doorway, telling her she looked exquisite as he offered his arm to escort her to her coming-out ball.

"You do me credit," he said, as his eye swept from the curls that cascaded from her high crown, to the pearl-encrusted cream silk slippers that peeped from beneath the flounce of her evening dress. "Your mother would have been so proud of you."

"And Lady Sarah?"

He flinched but made a quick recover, saying smoothly, "She was a good mentor. Come," he added as if he didn't want to be drawn on the subject. "The carriage is waiting."

During a rare moment of quiet later that evening, Caro surveyed the well-dressed crowd. How wonderful it would have been for Caro and her father if Lady Sarah had accepted his marriage proposal. Her rejection had had far more significant consequences for her father's state of mind than mere disappointment. She bit her lip, pondering.

Only since she had recovered her old spirit following her ordeal had she understood the extent of her father's suffering.

Within the first hour her dance card was nearly full. None of her fears of six months ago had been founded. She had not been the ugly duckling, forced to sit out dance after dance. The sallow complexion, once marred by spots, had become white and translucent, her dark hair had not needed coaxing with sugar and tongs to achieve the fashionable look of the day. It had just the right amount of curl and bounce. And her gangly, awkward figure, once rail thin, had blossomed into a woman's body.

So it was easy to smile, to feel confident and almost happy this evening. Her father had told her in as many words how proud of her he was.

Still, something was missing.

She closed her eyes a second as she fluttered her fan in the midst of a conversation with a group of young ladies discussing the merits of feathers over artificial fruit as headwear embellishments.

Justice.

Although she and Lady Sarah and her father had survived their ordeal relatively unscathed, natural justice had been denied.

For the first time, Caro glimpsed the impulses which had driven her father his entire life. He could not bear injustice.

Philly Miniver pressed against her to compare dance cards. It seemed she, too, could not get over Caro's transformation yet she was not mean spirited. "What magic potion have you been taking, Caro? Or was it all those months in the Swiss Alps? Your dance card is almost full. Much fuller than mine. Perhaps Sir Richard will ask me to dance."

She simpered at a figure across the room.

"Sir Richard?" Caro's throat went dry.

"He's Papa's friend and ever so obliging. Mama simply dotes on him and he's always so attentive to me. I'll get his attention. Perhaps he'll ask us both to dance – *if* you have room! Caro, where are you going?"

"I've lost a pearl button. Excuse me!" Caro whipped around, just as Philly signalled across the room.

Escape! She had to get out of here before she fainted. Before she embarrassed them all. Her mind was racing. She had to think clearly; had to be calm.

There was a knot of people gathered in the doorway. It would be impossible to simply barge past them out of the room. She veered to the left, walking fast but as gracefully as she could before she sank against the wall near a luxuriant and partially concealing flower display. A green curtain served as a partition separating the saloon from a small alcove, affording her the opportunity to nestle partially into its velvet folds and gaze at the milling guests. Taking deep breaths, she fanned herself energetically, terrified she might succumb to that most feminine of maladies: the vapours. Never, however, had any female had more cause.

Sir Richard had moved gracefully over to speak to Philly. Her friend was looking coquettishly at him from over the top of her fan points.

Surely Philly couldn't find him attractive? Caro wondered as her stomach rose up in disgust.

He must be at least twenty years older than her. Tall, thin with an insinuating smile, he had confidence but the charm of a death adder. He was a slug, a leech sustaining himself on the spoils from the underbelly of society, sucking out goodness where he could while he paraded himself as a gentleman, ruining the lives of people like herself, like Lady Sarah, like her father. People who had no recourse.

Helpless...

She closed her eyes, her breathing rapid. Then with one final, sustaining breath, her backbone stiffened; slowly she straightened up against the wall.

Helpless?

She took another breath. This time she felt almost calm. She blinked a few times, slowly scanning the richly garbed guests until her gaze alighted once more upon Sir Richard.

He towered over Philly. His body was bent slightly over her in a stance which, to Caro in that moment, suggested an attitude of brutal vanquishment of the female sex as a whole. Anger and revulsion swept over her and, at the same time, an all-encompassing feeling of empowerment.

It was too easy to assume that because she was a young girl she was helpless.

No, there were ways, other ways than the law – or breaking the law - whereby justice could be served.

She sucked in a short, sharp breath and her heart gave a nervous flutter.

Helpless?

Only if she lacked courage. And if she hadn't learned courage from her father, she certainly had from Lady Sarah.

Justice for herself. Justice for Lady Sarah.

She closed her eyes and thought of her darling, devoted father.

Most importantly, she wanted justice for her father.

⚜

"HAWTHORNE!"

Roland, striding down the passageway in the direction of the music, stopped as the red-haired giant, James Fleming, advanced towards him across the crimson Aubusson carpet. A deep flush burned the captain's throat and cheeks which, had Roland not been such a keen observer, he might have assumed was embarrassment. However the hardening of Fleming's eyes and the clenching of his jaw quickly disabused him of that notion.

Whatever Fleming's reasons for speaking to him, Roland had not the slightest desire to pursue a conversation with Lady Sarah's intended, yet the fact that it suggested Sarah was here made his heart beat faster. He marshalled a smile. "Congratulations on your forthcoming nuptials. Lady Sarah is a remarkable woman," he managed with admirable fortitude.

"She is."

There was an awkward silence.

"I formed the greatest admiration for her character when she was a member of my household."

"An irony, then, that the stain upon her reputation was, indirectly, on your account."

"What?" Shocked, Roland could think of nothing else to say. He'd heard Sarah had been seen unaccompanied at a late hour and that some interfering matron had embellished this by suggesting all manner of outlandish hypotheses. Each time he'd enquired as to the exact nature of Lady Sarah's sins he'd received a different account. Certainly, he'd heard nothing which connected his name with hers.

"So you did not know, Hawthorne. I am glad to hear it, for your sake." Fleming's look was slightly less condemning. "Don't like your politics but didn't want to think too badly of you, if you weren't in the know. Lady Sarah's a mighty proud woman."

When he'd gathered his wits, Roland asked, "Why did Lady Sarah not tell me if my name were connected with hers, in the public domain?"

James grunted. "Seems she didn't want to exert undue pressure since you'd already sent her a letter outlining your thoughts on matrimony. And that's fair enough, Hawthorne. Only I wasn't going to see such a diamond of the first water end up an ape leader through no fault of her own." He sent Roland a challenging look. "Well, Hawthorne, I must return to Lady Sarah." He bowed. "I'm looking forward to rusticating in the country. London is a cruel place."

Still reeling, Roland returned his bow. "I wish you well, Captain," he managed. "You are a lucky man."

Captain Fleming turned on his heel with and shot him a look not without reproach. "Always been fond of the gel, and it didn't look as if anyone else was coming to her rescue," he said, pointedly.

ANOTHER TREMBLING PEACOCK FEATHER.

Sarah watched it atop the emerald green toque as the feather responded to the haughty toss of its wearer's head. Plucked eyebrows arched heavenward, Sarah's erstwhile acquaintance passed by without a greeting.

The cut direct. Stock standard treatment for those who had fallen from grace.

Except that Sarah was not a fallen woman. She had been painted as one but thanks to James's loyalty her disgrace would be relatively short-lived, although there were those who would never receive her.

Like the peacock feather a moment ago, Sarah could feel her mouth begin to tremble.

She must find James. This propensity to tears that plagued her lately was out of character and she despised herself for it.

She wished she had not begged James to escort her to tonight's ball. He'd been right when he told her she was positively courting such reactions as the trembling peacock feather, and that she ought to stay where she was, in the country, with her father. She wanted, though, so desperately to encounter Roland one last time before she married James next week. Even if she knew seeing Roland was courting even greater heartache.

The card room was to her left, the supper room at the far end. She hesitated, scanning the crowd. James had said he would procure her a glass of champagne.

Her heart gave a nervous flutter as she surveyed the crowd. In all her life she had never felt so alone.

With her head held high she began her regal progress down the length of the room. She could just spy James, semi obscured by a knot of gentleman.

She craned her head over a tiny voluble woman offering advice to a couple of gawkish girls, her staccato words like a volley of gunfire. Sarah almost smiled to hear her ... until amidst a group near James she saw him.

The bourgeoning smile vanished and her heart rate sped into dangerous territory.

"I beg your pardon." She vaguely registered spilling champagne upon a gentleman's sleeve but paid him no further heed as she negotiated the knots of chattering guests, all the while holding Roland in her sights.

He was not quite as tall as James, nor as broad shouldered. But where James was large and forceful and brash of manner, Roland was well proportioned, careful and reflective.

Advancing, she was conscious of the furtive glances in her direction and appreciated how Caro must feel as a fragile, vulnerable debutante. If possible her heart contracted even more. How was Caro faring, she wondered?

And then was able to see with her very own eyes, though what it was that distracted her gaze from Roland to the quivering girl in the far corner of the room she could not say.

Caro was alone, against the wall, one hand pressed against her chest, the other covering her mouth. She looked as if she were about to faint or, worse, be sick. Certainly, Sarah could see the waxy pallor of her skin from here.

Instinctively, Sarah glanced from Caro to the object upon whom Caro's gaze was fixed.

As she feared.

Sir Richard was engaged in intimate conversation with Philly Miniver in the far corner. His hooded eyes roved over her in a transparently speculative manner while Philly blushed and giggled, using her fan just as Sarah had taught her. Clearly, the young innocent was flattered. Sarah felt simply nauseated.

Caro clearly was.

Quickly, Sarah turned her footsteps in Caro's direction. She would be by her side within a couple of seconds. She would usher Caro into another room, soothe her, bolster her confidence. It was what Caro needed, but it was what Sarah needed also.

To be needed.

Her progress was interrupted by a couple of leisurely promenading dowagers and when Sarah glanced again at the curtained alcove Caro was gone.

She frowned. Then she saw her.

Caro was advancing upon Sir Richard, looking like an avenging Valkyrie. Three more footsteps and she'd be upon him, with consequences Sarah dared not think of just now.

Altering her trajectory, Sarah hurried past a footman bearing a tray of drinks, jostled a scowling scion of the aristocracy and nearly floored a club-footed colonel.

Her hand shot out and she grasped a scrap of lace.

"Caro!"

She pulled the girl from her studied path, her own grasp stronger, and her subject more pliant than she had expected.

Caro had been wearing that mulish look of old. The consequences did not usually augur well. She extracted her from the crowd, orchestrating the potentially risky manoeuvre with all the skill of a consummate society hostess. Caro rewarded her with a scowl. But at least they were now partly obscured by the curtained alcove.

"I didn't like the look in your eye as you were advancing upon Sir Richard." Sarah had not the time to formulate a more considered approach. Her words were blunt, her look direct. "It will do your reputation and our cause no good if you make a scene."

"Look at him!" hissed Caro. "Talking to Philly like he's the most eligible man in the room, and unless one of us shows him up for what he is, he will continue to ruin lives."

"But publicly condemning him is not the answer–"

"Credit me with some subtlety." Caro's tone was injured. "I was hardly about to rail at him like a Billingsgate fishwife."

"What, then, were you about to do?"

"Entice him."

"Entice him?"

"That's right." Caro's eyes narrowed. Her breathing came fast and shallow. "Entice him onto the balcony, alone. Then I was going to scream and succumb to the vapours, and when a large enough crowd was gathered I was going to accuse him of trying to ... to kiss me." She looked once more as if she were about to be sick before her expression became defiant.

"Caro..." Sarah was lost for words. Her young, awkward charge had altered a great deal since Sarah had arrived at Larchfield. The coal dark eyes shone with the fervour of old, but were set in a face that had matured and blossomed. Sarah had feared Caro's spirit had been extinguished by her experiences at the Hollingsworths. She needn't have worried.

She reached out and touched Caro's cheek. "You are an innocent, you do not know how dangerous this would be," she said softly. "Your reputation is your most valuable commodity. Nothing is worth endangering it."

"Justice?"

Sarah winced, feeling the familiar ache in the region of her heart. "Justice is never guaranteed," she said, softly.

"Clearly not, Lady Sarah, else Sir Richard would be in Newgate, not featuring on Philly's dance card." She made a noise of disgust before adding quietly, "And you'd be marrying Papa." She sighed. "But you're not and I am more than prepared to take a risk to avenge ourselves against Sir Richard."

Sarah frowned. "Caro, what happened that night at the Hollingsworths was something we are powerless to avenge. The risks we run in trying to prove the blackguardly behaviour of both Mr Hollingsworth and Sir Richard are too great to our own positions. And to your father's."

"But if I were to claim Sir Richard guilty of enticing me onto the balcony and trying to kiss me, Papa would have no choice but to challenge him to a duel."

So that was it. Sarah watched with dawning understanding as Caro warmed to her theme.

"Inaction is absolute anathema to Papa. He'll just wither away if he's denied recourse to justice." She hesitated, adding pointedly, "Papa will sacrifice his own happiness if he feels he doesn't deserve it."

Sarah knew this, but Caro's boldness had opened up new avenues of hope. It fizzed in her veins. Then she realised the futility of Caro's plan and the sudden excitement drained from her.

"Caro, do you know what lunacy your father considers duelling? Oh yes" — she interrupted the anticipated response — "he duelled my very own Papa in his hot-headed youth, but he is wiser now."

Caro opened her fan with an expert flick of the wrist and drew herself up tall. "I'm very sorry we are at odds, Lady Sarah, but I love my father and would do anything to give him back his sense of honour."

"You think I would not?" Sarah grasped her shoulder. "Your intentions are good, but you are too vulnerable—"

Caro swung away from her. "*Someone* has to take risks," she flared, marching into the centre of the room.

Sarah pulled her back. Caro was young with too much to lose; but Sarah had lost everything she held dear.

"It is a reckless, even stupid plan," she countered, her voice low as she tried to conceal themselves from general observation. Caro could only be hurt if seen associating with Sarah. "But if you promise me not to undertake it yourself, would you be satisfied if I did so?"

Turning with a slow smile, Caro touched Sarah's cheek with the tip of her fan. "I believe that would be as effective." There was a glint in her eye. "Perhaps Papa would win, as a result, even more than simply justice."

CHAPTER 20

"**Y**OU ARE NOT dancing this evening, Lady Sarah?"

Sarah ceased her regal progress across the saloon and turned at the familiar voice, heart hammering, her breath catching.

Caro, declaring herself proud to be seen with her old governess, had insisted Sarah deliver her to Philly and Mrs Hawthorne who were seated amongst a group of matrons and dowagers. Poor Philly. She'd blushed and stammered, terrified of acknowledging Sarah in front of Mrs Hawthorne who had clearly delighted in giving Sarah the cut direct.

Torn between humiliation and amusement, Sarah had left them and was by a large potted plant several feet away from joining James when Roland stepped into her path.

His eyes raked her with appreciation, his smile was confident. He seemed different, as if a great weight had fallen from his shoulders, and her heart soared with hope.

Bowing, he asked, "Might I persuade you to make an exception and stand up with me for the next waltz?"

She felt the blush creep from her bosom upwards. Unready to yield to her hopes, she inclined her head, warily.

How dashing he looked in evening clothes. His hair, thick and dark, swept back from his high forehead, but she thought she saw a touch of silver at the temples that hadn't been there before. It only distinguished him more.

"Your magnanimous gesture might promote the rights of fallen women," she said lightly, to hide her nervousness, "though you court society's displeasure."

"I take little account of the gossip mill, Lady Sarah." Offering her his arm as the orchestra struck up a Viennese Waltz, he led her onto the floor. "Mrs Hawthorne is watching and I am sure you'd relish the chance to demonstrate the grace with which this fine art form can be executed."

"I shall try to give satisfaction."

That his smile was colluding offered another beacon of hope. When his arm encircled her waist, Sarah wilted against him. "Embraced by society at last," she murmured as he raised her up and they began circling.

How commandingly he held her. She could indulge in all the adolescent daydreaming she chose and he'd navigate her surely to her destination. It seemed an eternity since she'd last danced in his arms. And under such different circumstances. She closed her eyes, surrendering to the rapture of the music and the familiar warmth and strength of Roland's body inches from hers. Dare she hope this was the precursor to an even closer union?

"Why did you not tell me the whole truth, Sarah?"

The intensity of his softly spoken words jolted her back to the present. Before she could answer he went on, "I knew you'd been seen alone and unchaperoned en route to a supposed assignation—" His look was heartbreakingly tender — "but tonight is the first I'd heard my name mentioned."

She clung to him as they navigated a tight turn, not trusting herself to speak. Out of the corner of her eye she caught James's disapproving look, saw Mrs Hawthorne fanning herself with a vigour unwarranted by the temperature. Beside her, Caro beamed.

Perhaps Roland saw James also for he went on, "I can only imagine you did not press me to do as honour dictated because you preferred

Captain Fleming, after all. If that is so, I am glad you are marrying the right man. You deserve only the best, Sarah, for I've not met a braver, more admirable woman."

"You know I don't prefer Captain Fleming," she whispered, stumbling as her vision blurred. Roland whisked her skilfully a few inches from the ground, averting disaster as he negotiated his own footwork, then set her down again and resumed the dance with all the finesse of a gifted athlete.

Sarah's heart lurched at the quizzical, wondering look in his eye. He loved her. Minutes ago she'd not dared hope. Now hope had taken root and was flourishing in the warmth of his gaze. So how could he continue to deny her? To deny himself? Was his honour really more important than his happiness? She recalled Caro's plan in a new light. Perhaps it was not so foolish.

He squeezed her hand and murmured with feeling, "How I long to repay you for all you have done for Caro and me."

She closed her eyes, tensing as she strove for courage. He declared his love and his admiration, yet the caveat was always the same. His honour prevented him. "Do you remember the last words I said before you left, Roland?" She heard the breathlessness in her voice.

He gazed down at her, silent a long moment. Then he said softly, "They gave me hope when all hope was lost."

The waltz was nearing the end. Desperation clawed at her. She couldn't let him walk away from her, yet again. She opened her mouth to speak but he shook his head, his eyes yearning, but — it broke her heart to acknowledge it, regretful— as he murmured, "Do you remember the last words *I* spoke to you?"

How could she forget? He'd sworn he'd not seek her out until he considered himself worthy of her. Well, time was running out.

Exhaling on a sob of frustration, she allowed him to navigate her towards the edge of the dance floor. Soon the waltz would be at an end.

Then what?

ROLAND STUDIED HER THROUGH NARROWED EYES AS SHE CLUNG TO

him, the music thrilling to an end. He tried to make sense of it. She should hate him. Loathe and despise him. The sight of him ought to excite disgust. He'd failed her. Time and again. Instead, she gazed up at him with such transparent yearning it was enough to make him weep with frustrated longing.

He must dampen this ridiculous feeling of elation that was sweeping good sense before it. Regardless of the outcome of this evening, marriage to Fleming ensured Sarah's happiness. James Fleming was a good man: loyal and worthy of her. Roland's past matrimonial credentials hardly bolstered his cause. That aside, the bluff, good natured James would be a far better anchor for his free spirited and headstrong beloved Sarah.

The knowledge that contact must soon be broken was almost more than he could bear. He thought of the entertainment to follow, the groundwork so carefully laid out. Later this evening would be a different matter, though the outcome was by no means assured. It would be foolish to get either of their hopes up.

But there she was, doing all in her power to convince him of her sincerity. Hadn't she already proved it? So much more than he deserved?

No. He must not weaken and take her somewhere secluded. It would be his undoing. He was entirely resolved to act only in Sarah's best interests. To take advantage of her misguided and incomprehensible tenderness would be an act of the greatest cruelty.

"What are you doing?" Sarah gasped the question as she was whisked off the dance floor and her arm was nearly dislodged from its socket as he dragged her across the room.

"Taking you somewhere secluded." He heard the urgency in his own voice, and didn't care. Dear Lord, he had no idea what he was doing, much less what he intended doing. All he knew was that this conversation could not start and end on a dance floor in the public domain.

"I know a private alcove, a balcony," she said, unresisting as he drew her along with him, delighting – it would appear - in the shocked expressions of those scions of respectability they passed. Certainly, the wicked gleam he saw in her eye when he glanced back, and the way the corners of her voluptuous mouth turned up, indicated she was delighting in something.

That's right, Roland remembered. Sarah knew the house better than he. Had attended balls here, before.

The French doors clicked shut behind them, and they were greeted by a blast of cold air. And she without a shawl.

In his arms she would feel no cold. He would make sure of that.

He wasted no time. Without roughness — but without undue gentleness, either, for the clock was racing — he had her against the wall. One hand steadied himself against the cold stone, beside her lovely face, the other gripped her shoulder, imprisoning her, before trailing down to encircle her waist. Her rapid breathing matched his, fuelled by the same energy. He was confident of that, now: desire.

Still he felt unable to act upon instinct: to thrust his body against hers and demand with a kiss, that she match him at all levels. Restraint was an integral part of his make up and right now, restraint was all-important. Any future they might have together depended on what happened in the next half an hour. Succumbing to his passion, now, was premature.

And yet, wasn't hope the wellspring of Sarah's charm and vibrancy? It had sustained her through so much. Despite all she'd endured she'd never lost hope. The way she was looking at him now proved that.

With just a trace of tentativeness Roland moved his face closer to hers.

"Sarah—" he began. It was just above a whisper. He could hardly trust himself to speak steadily. The look in those limpid hazel eyes nearly undid him. All that he could have hoped for was reflected in their fathomless depths. She smiled tentatively but the invitation in the way she melded into him was implicit.

"Why do you not despise me?" he whispered, his lips a hair's breadth from hers. Her warmth and the hammering of her heart against his chest nearly drove him crazy.

"Despise you?" She cupped his chin with her hand, her look impossibly tender. "When will you understand that you were as much a victim that night as I was. Stop blaming yourself. *I* don't."

He hesitated, loosening his grip around her waist, still unsure of the wisdom of this impulsive tryst.

"My darling Sarah, I want you more than I've ever wanted anything," he ground out, restraining himself from plundering her mouth as he would have Venetia's, "but I *must* give you this final chance to walk away."

Sarah stamped her foot. "For God's sake, Roland, was Venetia this patient? I've heard the gossip. The two of you couldn't keep your hands off one another. Is your reluctance towards me now a measure of your true feelings?"

Blood pounded in his ears. "I was twenty-one, an innocent boy enslaved by love but I *never* loved Venetia as I love you!"

"I'll say it again," she whispered, nuzzling him, brushing her lips across his, "If you want me, I'm yours."

The featherlight touch was more than he could bear. Groaning, he crushed her against him, bringing his mouth down hard upon hers, extinguishing her gasp of surprise as he plundered the velvet cavern with his tongue, seeking, exploring, tasting and wanting more. And still more.

The rapid beating of her heart through the silk of his striped waist-coat drove him mad with wanting. The softness of her chestnut curls, the contours of her delectable body were like fire to a power keg. But it was the enthusiasm of her unleashed passions that most fuelled the urgency within him; the base animal instincts he'd spent years beating into submission threatened to vanquish him.

Yet the beast could not be unleashed, for he had not yet won her honourably.

With a final groan he set her from him. For several seconds they simply gazed at one another, breathless and shaking.

"Sarah!"

Guiltily, they jerked around to face James upon the threshold.

Only the faintest uprising of his eyebrows indicated he suspected anything untoward.

"I've been looking everywhere for you," he said, smoothly. "I believe you promised me this dance."

"I'm sorry, James." She glanced towards Roland.

He saw the brightness of her eyes, the flush on her cheeks, noticed the faint breathlessness, and hoped Captain Fleming did not. "Mr Hawthorne and I were just—"

"Discussing Lady Sarah's future," Roland supplied, smoothly. "Perhaps we can continue our conversation during the next dance?" With a smile, he bowed himself out.

James turned to Sarah with a frown. "You'll catch your death out here," he said, taking her shoulder and propelling her indoors. "Gad, but I'm glad it was me who stumbled upon the two of you, which is not to say I condone your behaviour, Sarah. Reckless, as always!"

Sarah bit her lip.

Out in the passage, James turned, softening at her expression. "You bring your troubles upon your own shoulders, my dear girl." He sighed, draping an arm about her shoulders and giving her a bracing squeeze before setting her in the direction of the ballroom. "And I should remind you that you've already given Mr Hawthorne his chance. You are betrothed to me now, which gives me the right, I believe, to say I don't like to see you cosying up to him, alone. In fact, I won't have it."

"That's wounded male vanity, James, when you've made it clear you don't love me."

"Yes, but you're about to become my wife. The contract has been drawn up, the matter is settled and the kind of behaviour I was witness to just now is simply unacceptable. Hawthorne is merely taking advantage."

"I ... I just wish I were marrying a man who loves me," she said, bleakly, ignoring the interested looks of a couple of society matrons.

James continued to propel her towards the ballroom. "I hold you in the greatest affection. Isn't that enough?"

Sarah took a deep breath and turned, blocking his path. "James," she asked, gently, "would you be very disappointed if you *didn't* marry me?"

"Good God! Is that what all that was about on the balcony? Hawthorne's proposed at last? And you've accepted him?"

"No, he hasn't. James, please—" Sarah tugged at his sleeve to bring him back to her. His wounded pride was hard to bear.

"He's toying with you, Sarah. He's made it clear he has no intention

of being leg-shackled. Your admiration feeds his vanity. And he ..."
Flushing, James looked away.

Sarah waited.

"Truth is, Sarah," he said in a rush, his expression suddenly sympathetic as looked into her eyes and patted her shoulder, "the fellow has a *chère amie*."

Sarah blinked. "That's ridiculous," she said scornfully.

"Oh Sarah," he muttered, "I knew you'd take it like that. You might think it's a bag of moonshine and I'm trying to bamboozle you because I don't care for the fellow. Only I know this to be the truth." He hesitated, adding, "Though you're not to think *I'm* in the habit of frequenting bawdy houses—"

Relief made her gasp, "So that is where he was seen?"

The Hollingsworths! Someone must have observed him enter the brothel.

"No ... " James appeared to be weighing up his words. "Fact is, Lady Condon made it known. She was scandalized Hawthorne would carry his politics over the boundaries of what most people consider acceptable."

Sarah waited, still sceptical.

"Lady Condon visited her seamstress and was forced to pass the time of day with a ... female, clearly from the Cyprian corps who was being fitted for a modish ensemble." He sighed. "Hawthorne was with her, offering his considered opinion. He ... was financing her."

"She must have been a friend."

"She was no one Lady Condon had ever set eyes upon."

"A visitor from abroad?"

James looked at her with even greater sympathy. "I believe the violent orange hue of her glorious ringlets is not a colour favoured by the respectable. Besides," he added, "I saw Hawthorne with my own eyes lead a bit o' muslin into a dark alley off the Haymarket not three weeks ago."

Sarah shook her head as if to clear of it of doubt. James did not lie, yet there had to be some explanation. With dignity, she took the arm he offered as they continued their progress towards the ballroom.

"He's a dark horse," James persisted, oblivious to her feelings. "His wife was infamous. The betting book at White's is offering ten to one the daughter is going the way of her mother—"

Sarah swung round furiously, nearly knocking into a couple who had to sidestep past them. "How dare you slander Caro!" she flared. "Nor have you the right to cast slurs upon Mr Hawthorne's reputation on account of hearsay. If you want my opinion, the bit o' muslin he supposedly led away was a lass in distress whom he was offering assistance."

"Sarah, that's doing it too brown," said James, exasperated. "All right, I'm sorry I slandered Miss Hawthorne. I'd forgotten she was your charge for three months. But really, Hawthorne doesn't deserve your slavish defence. Now where are you going?"

She had to find Caro. She'd been away too long and Caro was inclined to rashness.

"To mend a tear in my skirt, James," she bit out.

Surely James's allegations couldn't be true, she told herself. Though what did a man plagued by loneliness do to ease his frustration? She didn't really know much about these things.

A cotillion was in progress as she entered through the double doors but it felt claustrophobic in the crowded ballroom. James had not gone after her. She knew he thought she was being ridiculous; that he didn't believe she'd end their betrothal so she could wed Mr Hawthorne. Well, he didn't believe Mr Hawthorne harboured those kinds of feelings. But he did. She knew he did.

She squared her shoulders. Marrying Roland Hawthorne was exactly what she intended doing. With a sigh she sagged against the wall near the supper room. That's if Roland could sink his pride or put a bullet through Sir Richard's head.

A footman bearing aloft a silver tray offered her a glass of champagne. She drank it too quickly, trying to find a reason for Roland's earlier behaviour. He'd surely not have kissed her like that if he was going to allow her to marry James? In which case, she thought, sudden excitement flaring within her, he must have come up with some plan to avenge himself against Sir Richard? That would account for the confidence she'd noted earlier.

Pushing herself back from the wall, she remembered the urgency of finding Caro. If Roland was forced into action against his better judg-ment he'd not thank his daughter for it.

Caro was no longer with Philly. When a thorough search of the card room, ballroom and ladies' dressing room did not yield the girl, she became anxious.

Interrupting James discussing his latest horseflesh with Colonel Marshall, Sarah asked if they'd seen her.

"Heading for the balcony not long ago," replied the colonel. "Couldn't believe me eyes when she was pointed out as Lady Venetia's gel. Already rivalling her mother in the looks department, and it'd appear Sir Richard's as taken with her as he was with the mother." He cleared his throat. "Beg pardon, Lady Sarah. Forgot you'd spent time under their roof."

Sarah hadn't waited for his apology. Almost running, she jostled her way through the crowd in the direction of the balcony.

Why had Caro not listened to her?

Because she thought Sarah had abandoned her with empty promises?

Perhaps an opportunity had afforded itself which, to the impulsive Caro, seemed too good to resist.

She heard voices on the other side of the door which led outside. With her hand on the doorknob, she glanced over her shoulder to ensure she was not being observed. She had almost pushed the door open by the time she registered the incredible sight in the ballroom behind her.

Roland was one of three gentlemen conversing in a knot in the middle of the room. Three gentlemen and one lady - if Kitty of the Hollingsworth nunnery could be called a lady.

Sarah froze.

Dressed in an elegant evening gown of lilac silk with roses upon the flounce, her dark hair curled at the front and drawn up in a modish topknot of ringlets, Kitty looked the epitome of the well-bred young lady she was obviously at pains to emulate. The three gentlemen were talking amongst themselves with the occasional nod of acknowledge-ment at Kitty who smiled expansively.

Kitty and Roland?

Sarah's amazement turned to confusion tinged with anger. Not even Roland would be brazen enough in his pursuit of egalitarianism to bring Kitty to a society ball. Especially not when his daughter was making her come-out.

Jealousy vied with common sense.

What was he playing at? And who was the Cyprian with the violent orange ringlets James had mentioned?

At that moment Roland glanced up and caught her eye.

Then, he smiled.

It was such a candid, warm, transparent smile Sarah was nearly undone. All her doubts and anxieties vanished upon the instant.

The gentle murmur of the room dulled to nothing, the moving throng of colour became a muted haze. Sarah was conscious only of the warmth reflected in his eyes, and the unbreakable bond between them. Seemingly physical, it spanned the distance from her heart as she stood upon the threshold of the balcony, to Roland, half a room away.

He raised his glass in a silent toast and his eyes crinkled in a smile. Slowly and clearly, he mouthed, "I love you."

Then Caro screamed.

CHAPTER 21

T HERE WAS LITTLE gratification in seeing Sir Richard pale and mute with shock as Sarah thrust open the double doors to the balcony.

Within seconds she became one of seemingly dozens of onlookers. Murmuring, they gaped at Caro who stood with her back against the stone balustrade, facing Sir Richard.

Caro was badly compromised. Sarah imagined Roland's devastation. His own daughter, compromised by Sir Richard? It would be more than he could bear. No man of honour or loving father could let this go, unchallenged.

She watched Caro remove her hands from her tear-stained face and open her mouth.

To condemn Sir Richard?

So she had gone ahead with her foolhardly plan, giving her father no recourse but to defend her reputation through pistol or sword, thereby regaining his manhood in the process.

Except that Roland had no need to regain his manhood. He had matters well under control.

Sarah did not need this. Not when happiness was so nearly within her grasp. Well, she was not prepared to stand by and watch Roland shot through the heart or forced into exile for taking honour to extremes.

"Caro," she cried, sweeping forward to envelop the girl in her arms so as to stifle the anticipated diatribe. "It was such a little spider."

She raised her eyes to Roland, who'd just appeared, as she crushed Caro's face against her shoulder. Then, as if unaware of the crowd of goggling onlookers that flanked him, explained, "Caro and I were taking the air when Sir Richard stepped onto the balcony ... just as a great, big, ugly spider suspended itself from the lintel. You *know* Caro's feelings about spiders. I went to find something with which to kill it."

Caro struggled within her grasp but Sarah was not about to release her. Not until Sir Richard was gone.

With a look of studied exasperation, she smiled at the man who had humiliated and ruined her, forcing down her nausea at the sight of his hooded eyes, wary and cold. How well she remembered them glinting with lascivious speculation, before he'd coldly condemned her to social isolation. "My apologies, Sir Richard" — she stroked Caro's hair — "you must have imagined you were walking in upon a couple of wild women." With a shaky laugh, she turned back to Caro.

How empowered she felt at the sight of his confused silence. By taking the offensive, Sarah had put him on the back foot.

Responding to Sarah's silent signal, Roland bowed him out, together with the remaining guests, then came to stand at her side. "What is the meaning of all this?" He sounded angry, but uncertain, also.

Caro wrenched herself free of Sarah's embrace and faced her old governess with blazing eyes.

"You ruined everything!" she hissed. "I thought you loved my father!"

"I love him too much for you to risk his life with your hare-brained scheme," Sarah said, her expression softening as she turned it upon Roland. Caro, fiery and impetuous, as ever, would thank her for it, later. "Now come, it's freezing out here."

"Gratified though I am by all this talk of love," said Roland, as they stepped into the warmth, "I would appreciate an explanation." He tilted Caro's head up with a finger beneath her chin, adding, "Though I shudder to think what your 'plan' involved."

He shepherded them into a deserted passage just off the ballroom. Old Masters stared down at them. Sarah moved to Roland's side, standing so close their bodies touched. A frisson of electricity charged through her reinforced by a surge of exultation as she felt Roland stiffen with similar awareness.

"Caro was concerned you were in the grip of a crisis of masculinity" — she was unable to resist stroking his sleeve — "resulting from your inability to defend us at the Hollingsworth's."

Roland glanced between the two women. "Caro is very perceptive," he said, "but it is not for her — or you, Sarah — to manufacture a situation whereby I can demonstrate my — er — manhood."

He sighed, the noise of muted gaiety just beyond the double doors. "I want justice as badly as you, but a public justice, more meaningful than that wrought at the end of a sword." He turned to his daughter. "Caro, if I were to demand satisfaction, what do you suppose might happen to me — and to the rest of you? Do you know what a crack shot Sir Richard is reckoned to be?"

"Such modesty," Sarah murmured. She was well aware of Roland's skill with a pistol.

Roland pulled out a snowy handkerchief and offered it to his snivelling daughter. "Now dry your tears," he said, gently, "and look at me. I have a request, but if you feel you're not strong enough to oblige me, I'll ask Lady Sarah."

They looked at him, enquiringly.

"I have brought a companion with me tonight who will entertain the audience with a piece that has been" - he slanted a smile in Sarah's direction – "carefully prepared. I had hoped, Caro, you might accompany her on the pianoforte."

Caro didn't immediately pick up the nuance. Her recent humiliation was too fresh.

But Sarah clapped her hands and exclaimed, "Why, Caro, you can play almost anything by sight and you've gained such confidence since that evening I instructed you in deportment." Gripping Roland's arm, she went on, "You may recall it. I had borrowed one of your late wife's gowns for the occasion."

To her surprise he seemed reluctant to meet her look as he murmured with feeling, "I remember it well."

"Only I believe I did such a clever job at pretending to be your late wife, you actually believed I *was* your late wife, returned from the dead."

Roland made a pretence of adjusting her hand upon his sleeve. "That kiss was for *you*," he said in a low voice, bending his head so his lips brushed her ear, "though it took me a while to admit it to myself."

She shivered at his touch, detaining him with a sly whisper, "Are you sure you didn't wish it *was* Venetia? It cannot have escaped you that my response was not exactly lacklustre."

He drew himself up and regarded her in silence. Then with quiet deliberation, he told her, "I've *never* wished you were Venetia. That was the evening" — he had difficulty uttering the words — "you broke through my defences and it was all over for me." He glanced at his daughter. "I was ashamed at how I scandalized and upset you, Caro," he said. "But that was the evening I realized I was unable to live without your governess."

Caro blushed. "I know."

Sarah's heart swelled and she nestled closer to Roland. They were only a few feet from the double doors that opened into the ballroom. Anyone might appear but she didn't care.

Roland leant down to cup her face in both his hands. His voice was soft but urgent as he said, "If this evening does not go as planned, Sarah, you are still betrothed to James."

"No, Roland—"

He stayed her protest with a finger to her lips.

"This song," Caro interrupted, frowning, oblivious now to her elders. "Papa, if you don't think it too difficult I'm prepared to court the embarrassment of a poor rendering."

He gave a short laugh. "Let me reassure you, Caro, your skill will not be under scrutiny." Then, as he pushed the doors open and they stepped across the threshold, he added, "I have worked very hard these

445

last weeks to ensure the audience's attention will be focused elsewhere."

Anticipation thrummed through Sarah's veins. What on earth could have inspired Roland with such expectation and fear of failure, in equal measure?

Since none of the guests this evening was inclined to engage her in conversation she sought out Kitty, who remained quietly within the ranks of the three gentlemen with whom Roland had been conversing, earlier.

"Kitty?"

Kitty's eyes widened. "Ssh, m'lady. I ain't s'posed to speak English."

Sarah took her arm and drew her aside.

"I'm s'posed to be a Polish princess," she said in response to Sarah's look of enquiry. "'Twere Mr Hawthorne wot said I could come." She gave a beatific smile as she clasped her hands to her scrawny chest. "Said was there anything I wanted above all else in the world and I told him, 'to go to a grand ball like a princess and see real diamonds, only I know the likes o' me wouldn't never see summat like that.' "

"You wanted to go to a ball more than be free of the Hollingsworths?" Sarah asked in amazement.

"That's what Mr Hawthorne asked, too. I told him, 'course I wanted that, only that weren't never going to happen while that piece of paper gave them such a hold on me."

Sarah smiled. "What did he say to that?"

"Said he reckoned he could find a man o' law who'd be able to look into that piece of paper and do a deal with the Hollingsworths what would release me shortly." Her eyes shone with excitement. "Fact is, he reckons his lawyer chap'll have it all organized within the next few days. Then he said he *wanted* me to come to this 'ere ball tonight *and* paid for me dress." Reverently, she touched the folds of her lilac skirts. As she returned her attention to Sarah, she added hastily, "Weren't in the way of payment, like, m'lady, as in I weren't required to do nuffink in return." Frowning, she added, "*My* fine gown weren't, leastaways."

"And your friend's finery was?" Despite James's allegations Sarah was not perturbed.

"Well, a bit of bartering went on, I guess—" Kitty shot Sarah a puzzled stare. "Mr Hawthorne told you already? He said it were to be a grand surprise. Me lips were buttoned 'pon pain 'o death."

"I was only guessing, Kitty. Just like my guess is that your friend is a striking redhead."

"That's right, I'd forgot you'd met Queenie, then, M'lady. Didn't think you'd 'ad the pleasure." Kitty smiled ingenuously. "She's the star attraction this evening and weren't to show herself 'til she steps out and" - she took a deep breath and frowned, memorizing the words "'strikes awe and admiration into the 'earts of all who behold 'er.' " She gave a decisive nod. "Oh, yes, and the fear o' God, too. That's quotin' Mr Hawthorne."

"Sarah—" It was James at her elbow. He bowed to Kitty.

"James, this is Princess-"

"Anna Pawlak," Kitty supplied quickly as Sarah explained, "I've been naming various personages to her this evening, though she speaks no English."

Before James could respond, Roland joined them. "I believe the entertainment is about to begin." He sounded calm, almost bored and Sarah struggled to stifle all signs of her almost unbearable excitement. What could he have up his sleeve?

James gave a long-suffering sigh. "Lord, I wonder what Lady Ponsonby has on the bill this evening: Miss Lavinia Longbotton swooning over her *Child Harolde* recitation?"

Roland gave Sarah a colluding look. "I think the evening promises something a little less insipid."

James's eyes narrowed. "Hawthorne, might I remind you that Lady Sarah and I are to be married within the sennight. I trust you weren't offended at not receiving an invitation—"

"Not at all," Roland reassured him. "I'd rather stoke the fires of Hell."

"Good Lord—"

Bowing, Roland turned to leave then checked himself. "My apologies, Fleming. That was discourteous. Nevertheless, I would ask to resume the subject of Lady Sarah's nuptials when tonight's entertainment has finished. Excuse me, Lady Ponsonby is signalling, for I've the duty of introducing tonight's guest of honour." His gaze caught and held Sarah's. Impulsively, he clasped her hand.

"Lady Sarah, my protégé, Miss Queenie Featherlove is performing a work, composed by me, in your honour." He hesitated and there was urgency in his tone as he added, "Listen closely, for it is my sincerest desire that her words find their way to your heart."

Before James could respond with justified outrage, he put out a hand to his worthy competitor.

"Captain Fleming," he said, "though I deplore your politics as you do mine, we do share a common interest: Lady Sarah's happiness. As one man of honour to another, may I be allowed a final opportunity to determine the lady's feelings with regard to myself?" He sent Sarah a heartfelt look. "At the conclusion of tonight's entertainment that will no longer seem so outrageous a request."

James responded with brittle pride. "I assure you, Lady Sarah's happiness is paramount. I doubt you can convince me you are the better man, Hawthorne. But if you can convince Lady Sarah—"

A hush fell upon the audience as Roland strode onto the dais. Then a surprised murmur rippled through the crowd.

"Good Lord!" breathed James.

"Heavens! I don't believe—" gasped a woman near Sarah.

Sarah couldn't help but silently agree. Queenie Featherlove was eye-catching, there was no doubt about that. Despite the costly accoutrements, including a spectacular string of pearls Sarah reckoned cost more than the diamonds worn by the duchess to her right, she made no secret of her trade. The way she thrust her bosom forward as she adjusted her plunging neckline, the turquoise feathers of her headdress swaying wildly, made no secret of her pride in it.

"Ladies and gentlemen," Miss Featherlove crooned in a throaty but carrying tone, her arms sweeping wide to embrace the audience, "it is my pleasure tonight to sing for you a song composed especially to honour a dear friend of mine—" She twisted her head as if searching for someone. When her gaze alighted upon Sir Richard she gave a dazzling smile.

"Sir Richard, you were not leaving, I trust? My song is for *you*."

Caught like a rabbit in a shaft of light, Sir Richard appeared to deliberate. His route to the open double doors was cut off as the interested crowd closed in.

A prostitute performing publicly in honour of a baronet? It was unprecedented. Not least cause for curiosity verging on scandal was the fact that Roland Hawthorne, an MP known for his radical egalitarianism, was promoting the woman and the entertainment.

Caro made her way to the piano, Sarah joining her to turn the pages. Like the rest of the crowd that evening, they were open-mouthed as Miss Featherlove named the personage she honoured. Then they smiled at one another.

"Better than swords?" whispered Sarah.

Caro nodded as she sank onto the stool and struck the first chord. "Better than swords," she concurred, softly.

Miss Featherlove inclined her head in response to the musical introduction before launching into her song in a fine, strong contralto, her peacock feathers trembling with emotion.

> *Dickie Byrd sat in an old fir tree,*
> *Gloating over his spoils, he rubbed his hands with glee,*
> *Laugh, Dickie Byrd, laugh, there's plenty more money.*

There was appreciable movement in the audience as people strained their necks to search out the hapless Sir Richard. From her elevated position to one side of the dais, Sarah could just see him, a lone figure scrutinized by the crowd. His hooded eyes roamed over Miss Featherlove before apparently seeking Roland, and his thin lips curled in a snarl as he ran a finger around his neck to loosen his cravat.

> *Dickie Byrd promised an equal half to me,*
> *"To feather your nest," he said tenderly.*
> *Laugh, Queenie, love, laugh,*
> *Together we'll have so much money.*

Sarah turned the pages, giving Caro's shoulder a reassuring squeeze as she glanced around the room. Some people appeared mesmerized, others distinctly uncomfortable. She guessed there were more than a few gentlemen who had sampled the charms of the inimitable Miss Featherlove.

The meaning of the song was quite clear and Sir Richard, publicly unmasked for his duplicity, was powerless to refute her musical allegations.

Miss Featherlove's massive bulk swayed in time to the tune, her loving glance never once leaving Sir Richard's pallid countenance.

> *Dickie Byrd said: "Use your charm," Queenie,*
> *Ferret out those secrets, enticingly,*
> *Then we can laugh, yes we can laugh, over all that money.*

He was powerless, thought Sarah with a thrill. Just as she had been powerless as his captive. Roland had engineered this situation to liberate her and to grant herself and Caro the satisfaction of seeing their tormentor publicly humiliated. Her heart swelled with love and gratitude.

And pride at Roland's ingenious endeavours.

> *The Duke of Lomar snuggled up to me,*
> *Lord Basil Swain and Harry Stokes said: "my dear Queenie,*
> *How you'd laugh, love,*
> *How you'd laugh,*
> *If you knew how we made our money."*

The murmurs grew and the three men named in Queenie's song, young blades well known for winning and losing fortunes upon the turn of a card, wiped their sweating brows and fingered their collective stocks as if they needed more air.

No one, however, looked as uncomfortable as Sir Richard whose compressed lips and narrowed eyes, as he fixed them upon Roland, made no secret of his loathing.

Sarah was glad of the protection her position on the dais afforded her.

Across the crowd her eyes locked with Roland's. Her heart turned a clumsy, lurching somersault before nestling cosily into position. A look of understanding passed between them. Though she was enjoying every minute of this, anticipation clawed at her. Soon Roland could declare himself, publicly.

Miss Featherlove raised her voice to be heard above the din, snatches of song plunging others into the mire of scandal.

No matter how much more of Sir Richard's villainy was revealed in this little ditty, Miss Featherlove's performance promised a scandal of such proportions he would never be received in respectable society, again.

Roland's focus shifted and Sarah's gaze darted back to Sir Richard. She half expected to see him bolt through the French doors which opened onto the terrace.

He was half way there already.

Then he hesitated. She saw him square his shoulders before he turned towards Miss Featherlove. In half a dozen strides he was up the stairs and onto the dais.

The songstress faltered only briefly as he approached her with angry deliberation. Sarah turned another page of music while Caro continued playing without a false note.

Only when Sir Richard put his hands to Miss Featherlove's throat did she falter. Caro stopped playing. The dowager to Sarah's right gasped.

"Release Miss Featherlove." Roland spoke quietly, but his voice reverberated in the sudden silence.

"I'd rather handle a snake," Sir Richard ground out, "but perhaps you forget, Hawthorne, that the necklace belongs to me."

With a cry, Queenie gripped the pearls as Sir Richard fumbled with the clasp.

A low excited hum rippled through the crowd.

"Legally, my late wife's property is my property," observed Roland, as he crossed the dais towards them. "You should have thought of that before you bestowed such a handsome gift upon Venetia."

Sir Richard's face contorted with rage. Roughly, he jerked Queenie within the circle of his arm. "I was exiled because of debts incurred procuring Venetia that ... tribute to my *enduring* admiration."

"You did more than admire her," said Roland, calmly. "You became her slave in the process. Do not blame me for that." Glancing between the audience and his adversary, he indicated the door with a flourish. "I think it's time to leave, Sir Richard."

Sir Richard's hands dropped from Queenie's throat. She took an unsteady step backwards.

"Pistols or swords, Hawthorne." Very deliberately the baronet flung down one black glove. It landed with a dull thud upon the stage at Roland's feet.

Sarah's heart lurched wildly and her knees went weak. No man of honour would refuse a challenge. Yet this was lunacy. And wasn't it what Roland had been striving to avoid?

To her surprise Roland smiled pityingly at Sir Richard.

"My point has already been proved. Why would I take up arms now that the whole world knows you for the villain you are?" Looking past Sir Richard, Roland found Sarah. In a moment he was at her side. She felt his comforting warmth through the thin fabric of her bead-encrusted muslin evening gown. Longing rippled through her but she fought the urge to sag against him. Let him deal with Sir Richard first.

"So you are a coward then, Hawthorne?" Sir Richard taunted. "Venetia said as much. How many times were you cuckolded?"

Fighting her indignation, Sarah pushed Caro back down onto her seat.

"My late wife's memory is not under discussion." Roland refused to be drawn.

It was clear Sir Richard's frustration was growing at the infertile ground upon which his taunts were falling. Yet Sarah was conscious of Roland's tenseness as he called on those reserves of restraint which had served him so well.

She was equally conscious of Caro's efforts to restrain herself and prayed the girl did not burst out with something inappropriate. Caro had grown in maturity but she was like a wound-up spring when her emotions were engaged.

Queenie, now standing half way between Roland and Sir Richard, fingered the pearls nervously. Hardly surprising, observed Sarah, in view of the way Sir Richard was eyeing them. Balefully. As if he would pounce any moment and rip them from around her neck.

The baronet scratched the side of his large, Roman nose. "Here's the bargain, Hawthorne. Return my necklace and I'll not mention the ... er ... compromising situation in which I found myself with your *dear* friend, the most delectable Lady Sarah in a certain house of ill repute."

Dear Lord, was she going to succumb to a fainting fit at the most inappropriate time of her life? Sarah closed her eyes as she swayed. She wondered how many in the audience would attribute the hot blush that crept up from her neckline as the stain of guilt. Not that it mattered, it would merely endorse what was already accepted as the truth.

Then she felt the wool of Roland's coat against her forearm and the surreptitious squeeze of her hand.

He was giving her strength and courage, just as she had given him the same that night at the Hollingsworths. She stifled a sob as he left her to return to Queenie.

"Miss Featherlove, I hope you'll forgive such an ungentlemanly act," he apologized, as his hands went to the nape of her neck to unclasp her necklace.

No. Sarah didn't quite say it. She was shocked, horrified. *It didn't matter*, she wanted to say to him. He must not cave in, publicly, on her account.

She saw Sir Richard's triumphant sneer as Roland held the pearl necklace like a delicate, sparkling spider's web, suspended between his hands.

But the victorious scorn was replaced with confusion, then frustrated outrage as Roland resumed his place at Sarah's side. Only it was not Sarah he addressed, but a blushing Caro.

"This belonged to your mother and is, by rights, yours now. Its history is not a happy one but its destiny is yours to decide."

Caro rose, slowly. Unable to speak, she stared, first at her father, then at the assembled guests. A movement from Sir Richard made her turn her head.

Admiringly, Sarah watched as Caro stood her ground for he looked in that moment as if he would wrest the necklace from her grasp if she dared take it.

Caro put out a tentative hand to touch the pearls then recoiled, as if stung. "No, Papa! I don't want them!"

Roland nodded.

"Sir Richard." He smiled as Sir Richard stepped forwards as if he expected Roland to relinquish them to him, after all.

"Perhaps, Sir Richard, you wish Lady Sarah to have the pearls as a token of atonement. It was, after all, on your orders that she was detained at the address to which she was directed" - he waited for the prurient murmur this inevitably created before continuing - "used as a pawn for vengeance against myself."

The murmuring grew in volume. Above the din Roland continued, "Lady Sarah should be honoured for her bravery that night." He shook his head, his expression one of disgust. "Instead, she has been pilloried, her reputation besmirched. She deserves far more than just those pearls, Sir Richard."

Sarah clasped her hands to her breast as she gazed about the room. She could almost believe she saw the scales falling from people's eyes. Even the way Mrs Hawthorne regarded her thoughtfully through narrowed eyes suggested she was reconsidering her opinion of her. Nevertheless, Sarah knew there were many other crimes for which she'd not forgive the former governess.

James, as if sensing her focus, transferred his fulminating stare from Sir Richard, to Sarah. The smile he sent her made her heart pound with joy and relief so that she nearly missed Roland's next words. James, like every other person in the room, now saw how things stood with her and Roland. And he condoned.

"Lady Sarah, unless you object, I would like to give these pearls to Miss Featherlove. They will fund a charitable project patronised by a certain Polish Princess in our midst tonight."

"Cor Blimey, sir," gasped Kitty, blushing fiercely as all eyes turned on her, "if that ain't arf rich!"

"No!"

Turning at Sir Richard's bellow of rage and gasps from the audience, Roland thrust the pearls at Queenie, sidestepping as Sir Richard barrelled towards him, manic desperation lighting his hooded eyes. Focusing on the pearls, Sir Richard altered his trajectory at the last moment.

There was barely enough time to act. Queenie screamed as her former lover, face contorted with malevolence, prepared to knock her off her feet and make off with the necklace. With a short, sharp upper thrust Roland sliced his fist into Sir Richard's jaw. Screaming with pain and rage, Sir Richard crashed to the ground.

"Can a member of the judiciary help our friend off the stage?" Roland asked.

A response came from several quarters accompanied by a smattering of applause as Sir Richard was picked up bodily and removed.

Roland inclined his head. "I look forward to furnishing a statement of events involving our friend's villainy, however I still have unfinished business with Lady Sarah."

He beckoned to her, his gaze full of love as she stepped towards him. Reaching out, he took both her hands and she caught her breath at the jolt of sensation which slammed through her at his touch.

Trembling, she smiled at him, her heart almost bursting with joy as they locked gazes and she witnessed the depth of his feeling for her.

"I denied you the pearls because of the evil with which they are associated," he said clearly, for all to hear, "but I want you to know you have *carte blanche* to choose whatever baubles take your fancy when we are wed."

Sarah intended more than *carte blanche* with regard to baubles. Roland was hers, now. Hers to love and cherish.

And to make her feel not only that she had met her match but that she was the luckiest woman on the planet.

"Caro, a final chord, if you will."

As relief and love surged through Sarah, she returned the kindling look in Roland's eye, squeezing his hands and longing for the crowds to disperse so they could be alone.

He had staked a great deal on this, she knew. And her answer, though she could not utter a word, was for all to see.

Caro obliged with an elegant few bars and Roland, flanked by Miss Featherlove and Sarah, drew them towards the centre of the stage.

Sarah gazed out across the sea of rapt faces, knowing she wore her heart on her sleeve and not caring. She wished her father could have witnessed Roland's performance. It would make him revise his assessment of him as a buttoned-up Puritan, she thought. And he'd have appreciated his showmanship.

Like actors on a stage, Roland raised the two women's hands in the air and, and to a final flourish of notes from Caro, they sank into a deep bow.

Rising, Roland brought Sarah's hand to his lips and kissed it extravagantly. "Ladies and gentlemen, the show is over," he said, loudly. "Thank you for coming here tonight."

❧

"AND THANK YOU, MY LOVE," HE MURMURED, HIS BREATH TICKLING Sarah's ear as she nestled against him, savouring his warmth as they watched the procession of carriages pass beneath their secluded balcony. "You were most obliging."

Sarah raised her hand to trace the watered silk of Roland's waistcoat. Wonderingly, she stroked his beloved forehead before cupping his strong jaw.

"Surely you knew, dearest Roland, I'd decided during my first days at Larchfield you would be my husband?"

"I hadn't realised your feelings went to quite those extremes," he said with a smile, "though you hinted to a certain fondness for my company. But marriage? What would a beautiful, confident young woman want with a damaged, taciturn fellow like me?"

It seemed he couldn't keep his hands off her, stroking first her cheek, and now, tenderly, her throat and collar bone. Tremors of love and excitement rippled through her.

"I saw the potential, my darling." Snuggling closer, she added, "I knew I could mould that damaged, taciturn fellow into the hero of my dreams." She gave a contented sigh. "And what a hero you turned out to be."

He looked down at her and the expression of bemusement on his lean, ascetic face, so much more handsome now that the lines of tension and worry had relaxed, amused her. She gave a short laugh. "Surely you must have been entirely confident of my answer?"

He brushed a tendril back from her face, his smile heart-stoppingly tender. "I certainly was not. Awaiting your response on stage was more terrifying than approaching your father."

"What?" She gasped, twisting out of his grasp. "My father has already given us his blessing?" Disbelief mingled with joy as she clasped her hands together. Her beloved, irascible father whose determination to enforce upon her an unpalatable marriage had had such wide-sweeping repercussions. Yet he had already sanctioned her one true love? She could hardly believe it.

"What's this?" asked Roland, touching her cheek. "You didn't cry just now when I told you I couldn't live without you."

"You needn't sound so wounded." Sarah laughed through her tears and hugged him tightly. "Once I'd decided to marry you I knew the hardest thing to reconcile would be Papa's displeasure. Especially" — she sent him a wry glance — "when I learned the two of you had been at each other like a couple of warring schoolboys."

"I suspect your father would take as much exception to that undignified description as I do." Roland drew himself up with exaggerated dignity. "He certainly took exception, initially, to my presumption."

Sarah shook her head, wonderingly. "I wish I could have been there. Did he throw anything?"

"I was a little concerned when he stoked the fire with such energy then didn't set down the poker as he addressed me." With a smile, Roland patted her hand which now rested against his lapel. "But after a couple of brandies during which I explained the situation, rather as I did on stage, his mood became much more sanguine."

"Oh, Roland," Sarah burst out with feeling, "I knew you'd win him over, just as you did me."

"Well, there were differences, but as regards timing, I hope you'll forgive my impatience." He cleared his throat, suddenly awkward. "I couldn't wait three weeks for the banns to be read, after all the time we've wasted."

Sarah's eyes lit up with joy. Standing on her toes she twined her arms around his neck. "You've arranged a special licence?"

Clasping her wrists so as to ease the stranglehold she had on him, he said, "Your father, in fact, offered to relieve me of the task, since I had so much to organise this evening." His sigh held relief as he added, "I'm glad you feel as I do, my darling. I was afraid you'd be disappointed at not preparing the event to your satisfaction. In about three hours, we'll be man and wife."

"Three hours!" Sarah cried, wrenching out of his arms, her hand fingering the simple gold cross at her throat.

"Sarah, what is it?" Drawing her back to him, Roland's look was a study in anguished confusion.

"Two things, Roland." She could see his suspense was agony and knew it was wicked to take advantage of the power she had over him. With an extravagant sigh she asked, "Don't you remember your promise?"

He seemed at a loss.

"On stage when you gave the pearls to Miss Featherlove you promised I could choose any jewels I liked." Maintaining her stricken look she went on, "Surely you don't imagine I can be married in just this simple gold cross?"

"Sarah, it's three o'clock in the morning." His brow still creased with concern, he added, "which is not to say I don't fully intend-"

Sarah laughed, and with a growl Roland snatched her back within the circle of his arms once he understood she was amusing herself at his expense. Narrowing his eyes he asked, "And the second thing?"

Sarah met his gaze with studied earnestness. There was no levity in her tone this time.

"I want a proper proposal, Roland." Only as she made the request did she realize how important it was to her. "Many men I've not loved have asked me to marry them." She swallowed. "James asked me, but he might has well have been buying a cow at market, and then you, Roland" — she reached up her hand to stroke his cheek, willing him to understand — "You began to propose when you came to see me that day, though it sounded as if you were being forced because duty required it of you."

Slowly Roland nodded. He understood. With a wry smile he said,

"And on stage I skipped the proposal assuming you'd make your feelings clear if you objected."

Sarah nodded.

Straightening to his full height, he drew her into the moonlight and for a long moment gazed down at her, as if the sight were to sustain him through all life's battles.

"Lady Sarah," he said, his voice soft and impassioned as he lowered himself on bended knee and looked up at her, "if I could be everything you ever wanted, I'd have no hesitation in asking you to make me the happiest man by agreeing to be my wife." Kissing her hand, his smile was wondering. "But if I let the fear of my shortcomings stand in the way of my happiness, I'd forever wonder what might have been. Sarah, words cannot express my admiration of your strength and courage" — there was a quaver in his voice — "and above all, your loyalty. Nor can you know the extent to which they've sustained me."

Sarah felt the great lump in her throat swell. Shocked by the depth of love and sincerity she saw in his eyes, she needed the catharsis of being in his arms once more, but he was not finished.

"You taught me never to give up hope and to you I credit my salvation. If you would do me the honour to be my wife, history would know no happier man."

"Oh, Roland!" cried Sarah, hurling herself at him as he rose, covering his face with kisses and catching him off balance so that he stumbled against the wall. "That was far and away the best proposal I've ever had. Yes! Of course I'll marry you!"

For an eternity they clung to one another, savouring the joy of deserving one another, equally and forever.

Finally, when they broke apart, Roland decided there was time enough to grant Sarah's first request, after all. She deserved to be married in something finer than her simple gold cross, and the grumbles of the nearby jeweller at being woken from his sleep were soon silenced by Roland's generous patronage.

When Sarah's gratitude far outweighed his expenditure Roland wondered how he ever could have compared her with Venetia.

And later, when he brought her back to Larchfield as his wife, he watched with loving pride as she greeted his two young nieces with kisses and hugs and cries of delight. Sarah even received Mrs Hawthorne with dignified kindness, though Roland suspected this had the opposite effect of soothing the delicate sensibilities of the former mistress of Larchfield. And he suspected Sarah knew very well it would, too.

As love for his new wife and hope for their future replaced the doubts and insecurities that had flourished in his once-barren heart, Roland no longer questioned his right to a second chance at happiness.

Sarah had made him see the world through her eyes. Happiness was the preserve of everyone, but only those who strove for it deserved it.

THE END

I REALLY HOPE YOU ENJOYED **LADY SARAH'S REDEMPTION.** THERE are several other books in the series so if you want to know about new releases or specials, here are some ways to stay connected:

- Sign up to my newsletter and get a free book here.
- Like me on Facebook here.
- Follow me on BookBub here.
- Visit my Website here.

And if you have a moment, you can help give the book greater discoverability and tell other romance readers why you enjoyed reading in as little as 11 words. I'd be so delighted if you considered leaving a review.

THANK YOU!
Beverley Oakley

LADY ROSE'S SECRET

THE DECEPTION

CHAPTER 1

London 1818

'WHAT CHOICE HAVE we but to give Lord Rampton the deeds to the plantation?' Rose sent her brother a withering look before focusing her contempt upon the comatose young woman upon the bed. 'There's nothing else with which to pay Helena's debt.'

Rose had never detested her sister-in-law more. Beautiful as ever, her dark hair undressed and spread out upon the pillow, Helena looked serene and innocent, her expression one of laudanum-induced contentment.

And as usual, Charles refused to accept that his wife's irresponsibility had plunged the family into deadly peril. Kneeling at her her side, he tenderly stroked Helena's hand, his mulish stare focused on the dome of St Paul's through the dirty windowpane rather than at his sister's flushed and angry face.

Outside, the rattling of carriages and shrieking of street vendors filtered into the room.

Rose stamped her foot. 'Listen to me, Charles! What are we going to do? Clearly, Helena is in no state to petition his lordship for clemency and I can't see you bargaining with him.'

A sheen of sweat bathed Charles's pallid brow, hinting at the pressure he was under but still he came up with the usual excuses. 'Helena's been unwell but she will soon recover her strength. She's clever. She'll know how to get out of this. We can delay tonight's dinner... play for time,' he muttered. Though still a young man, the lines around his mouth and the furrows across his brow were deeply etched.

He'd been handsome and carefree when he'd married Helena five years before, Rose reflected as she joined him on the threadbare rug, to reach beneath the bed for the blue glass vial, now empty, which had rolled there. Sighing, she held it out. 'This is what Helena promised never to touch again if you promised to take her to England.' She tapped the bottle with fingers noticeably more workworn than those of the West Indies beauty whose gambling and laudanum addictions threatened their futures. 'Well, *you* fulfilled your part of the bargain.' She rose to her feet. 'Perhaps it's just as well Helena can't attend Lord Rampton's dinner tonight. There's no telling how she might try to charm or cajole his lordship into reducing the debt or modifying the terms.'

Charles glanced up, as if shocked Rose could even suggest Helena might employ such tactics. 'You know that Helena will be deeply contrite when she wakes,' he muttered, causing Rose to swing round at the door with a harsh laugh.

'I've never before heard Helena apologise for anything she's ever done wrong,' she said. 'Anyway, Charles, Lord Rampton is expecting payment of the debt, if not tonight, then soon, so what shall we do? Perhaps I should accompany you. At least I can be relied upon to be decorous and obedient.'

Charles jerked up his head. 'You can't possibly go, Rose!' He looked more horrified than he had when he'd set eyes on his unconscious wife minutes before, and Rose almost laughed at the black humour of their predicament. Charles had status, Helena had beauty but Rose had wit and brains. Had she been the one orchestrating their precarious lives, she had no doubt they'd be in a vastly better situation. They'd certainly not be in danger of losing their only home.

'Surely, Charles, you don't subscribe to the notion that marriage confers some kind of magical status which I do not have, simply as your unmarried sister?' She'd said it with irony and in jest but he remained silent, stroking the face of the unconscious woman who'd held him in thrall since the moment she'd fluttered her eyelashes at him so many years before.

A surge of rage at her brother's weakness in allowing Helena to run roughshod over not just his life, but the lives of his two younger sisters, galvanised her resolve.

Helena would ruin them all if Rose did not act in their defence. Her mind raced over the possibilities as she hesitated by the door. 'Lord Rampton is due to set sail for the Continent before the week is up and our visit here is for less than three months.' Why could she not pretend to be Helena for that evening when she, of all of them, was most likely to broker a deal that would grant them time to come up with payment options?

Charles continued to look at her with that bovine obstinancy that had riled her since she was old enough to read faces. Nevertheless, she pushed on. 'Well, why can't I go in Helena's place? We'll have returned to the plantation before he's back in England. He'll never meet us in person again.' Her brother's failure to even articulate his opposition cemented her determination. Charles was weak and indecisive. Lord Rampton would almost certainly dictate terms that would be to their detriment and Charles would buckle. Suddenly her idea seemed their only salvation.

Decisively, she turned back from the door and crossed the floor, her tone wheedling as she stroked her brother's arm. 'It's true that *of course* I can perform no useful role as your unmarried sister, Charles, but why should you dine with Lord Rampton, alone, when at least *I* can get the measure of him? It's what we must do if we're to get the extension we need to repay Helena's debt.'

Charles didn't move but Rose could tell he was listening. No doubt he was hoping Helena would suddenly blink open her eyes and tell him what to do, just as she had since the moment they'd met.

'Time, Charles, is what we need,' Rose went on, her tone still soft and conciliatory. 'I'm certain poor Mama and Papa have a few relatives mouldering in the wings who could help with some funds but that wouldn't be enough to cover what Helen lost to Mr Babbage the other night. Now that Lord Rampton has taken over the debt from Babbage, he's quite within his rights to demand an immediate settlement.' She caressed his cheek. 'Don't you think I'd be far more successful playing on Lord Rampton's heartstrings than you?'

Rose could see Charles was wavering. His stubborn streak was always the final hurdle to overcome. To give in without a fight compromised the feeling that he was in charge, the young baronet, head of his household: his wife and two sisters.

She took a deep breath. 'If I went as Helena—'

'No! Good God, Rose, are you out of your mind?'

Rose drew herself up proudly, more determined than ever. Striving to remain calm, she countered, 'Lord Rampton has met none of us and Helena was in masquerade when she lost to this Lord Babbage who has —we don't know why—transferred the debt to his lordship. How's Lord Rampton to know the difference when it's just for one evening? I'm sure I could persuade him to alter the terms—'

'No, Rose.' Shrugging off her hand, Charles shook his head. 'As Helena's husband I'm responsible for her debts and as your brother I'm responsible for your welfare. It would not be right to expose you to this ... well, we don't know what kind of man Lord Rampton is. Ruthless. Calculating. Those are just some of the descriptions I've heard bandied about my club. I admit it's because of Helena we're in danger of losing the plantation but you had nothing to do with the sordid business that night.' He looked pained.

'With due respect, Charles,' Rose cut in sharply, 'I've had to contend with Helena's dangerous vices for the past five years and I think I can claim some credit for the fact that we still have a plantation!' She'd allowed her anger to get the better of her. Charles did not react well to anger. Changing tack, she added softly, 'I shan't disgrace you, I promise. I'll simply be there as Lady Chesterfield instead of Miss Chesterfield. It's not such a terribly wicked lie.'

※

'You will not attend Lord Rampton's dinner dressed like that!'

Edith, the loyal family retainer who had mothered the family for as long as Rose could remember, raked her charge with disapproving eyes before bundling Rose upstairs, pressing her down before her dressing-table. No further description was needed as to what she thought of Rose's drab grey velvet gown.

'It's the best I have,' argued Rose.

'And has been since you developed a chest and were out of short clothes. Miss Arabella! There you are! Tell me, what do you think of your sister's gown? Would you wear it in fine company?'

Arabella, combing out her long, white-gold hair as she perched on the edge of Rose's bed, regarded her gravely. 'Of course not, but Rose doesn't have any fine clothes. If I knew her ankles wouldn't show I'd lend her something of mine... which would still be preferable to that old rag she has on.'

Watching as Edith went about her task with deft fingers, smoothing her sister's glossy chestnut hair back from her high fore-head, coaxing the curls from a fashionably high top knot, she asked, 'Does this mean you plan on going about in fine company, after all, Rose? I thought you said the season was an expensive lot of nonsense and you wouldn't be caught dead at anyone's "drawing room"?'

'Your sister only says such things because there's no money to launch both of you, my girl. And does she look twenty-six with those fine eyes and glowing skin? Why, she'll always be a beauty.' Edith looked severely at her younger charge. 'Just bear in mind, Miss Arabella, that you have your sister to thank for the fact that you're to have a season at all.'

'Perhaps Rose could wear something of Helena's,' Arabella suggested, chastened.

'I couldn't possibly!'

'Well, you're exactly the same height as Helena and I'm sure she wouldn't mind, since you're going in her stead.'

Rose looked grim. 'That was not what I was worried about.' An image of Helena with her languid self-possession and love of finery flashed through her mind and for a moment the magnitude of what she was about to do threatened to engulf Rose. Could she carry it off? After all, compared with the worldly Helena she was a greenhorn, an unsophisticated Colonial. Cleverer than Helena, certainly, but by no means as self-assured in the company of men. Nor as beautiful. Without these attributes was she not as good as throwing herself to the lions and making fools of them all in the process?

She took a deep breath and cast all doubts from her mind. It was the only way. She had a role to play, and play it she would. To perfection.

'One of Helena's gowns,' she murmured, thoughtfully. Then, twisting her head to look at Arabella she said, wryly, 'You're right, dearest. Find me something... not too revealing. But don't tell Charles. Helena is still sleeping so I can't ask her, but it's for her benefit. Dear Lord,' she muttered, putting her hand to her chest and stroking the comforting drab grey velvet. It had been so long since she'd been in sophisticated company she'd never been told whether she had a cleavage worth showing, or not.

ASHLEY DELACROIX, VISCOUNT RAMPTON, EYED HIS DINNER GUEST appreciatively across the table. Babbage had not lied when he'd called Lady Chesterfield a beauty. His use of the term 'exotic' was, perhaps, a little off the mark. 'Classic English rose' was a more apt description; although perhaps Babbage had been referring to the young lady's unusually sun-kissed complexion and taste in attire, for the gown that barely clothed Lady Chesterfield this evening was considerably less modestly cut than the type of evening gown most English women favoured. Not that Rampton was complaining. It was always a pleasure to dine with a beautiful woman, especially one not too shy to display her ample charms to best advantage. It might explain, too, the reason for her husband's clear displeasure, although that could, just as likely, be due to the nature of the business which had brought them together.

Rampton raised his glass to his guests and fixed Lady Chesterfield with an appreciative look as he proposed the toast.

'To a pleasant evening and the satisfactory completion of our business.'

It was unlike him to mix business with pleasure. Boredom had been to blame. When his friend Babbage had sworn he would repay his loan to Rampton within the sennight, then reneged with the surprising excuse that he was reluctant to press the lady who owed him the necessary means to do so, Rampton had been unsympathetic. But when Babbage had elaborated upon the evening that he and the 'exotic' beauty had spent together, Rampton's curiosity had, despite himself, been aroused. To his surprise he'd found himself absolving Babbage of his debt by taking on Lady Chesterfield's debt in lieu. For no better reason than that he wanted to see for himself whether this apparently fascinating young woman would enthral him as much as the notoriously difficult-to-impress Babbage.

'I hope you are enjoying your visit to London, Lady Chesterfield,' he said, conversationally. 'My friend, Adrian Babbage—whom you will no doubt recall,' he added, his smile sly, 'tells me you have spent your life in the West Indies and this is your first visit to your father's homeland. You must still be adjusting to the climate.'

'I daresay I will not be here long enough to get used to it, Lord Rampton,' said Rose, coolly. She disliked the way her host's eyes travelled languorously from her décolletage to her face when he spoke. Certainly they were very fine eyes: a piercing blue, but the supercilious arch of the eyebrows disconcerted her. And while his unconcealed admiration was certainly balm to her self-confidence, there was something in their depths that hinted at a whole world of which she knew nothing.

She forced a smile. It was important that he should not suspect any discomfiture in her. Indeed, discomfiture was rare for Rose and it was highly disconcerting to suspect she wouldn't be feeling this uncomfortable had Lord Rampton not been such an exquisite nonpareil. Indeed, she could never remember having met a gentleman who exuded such potent magnetism—and who was aware of it, she thought grimly.

Thick dark hair swept back from high cheekbones while intense dark blue eyes glittered with unconcealed interest in her above his beautiful straight nose, a fine piece of physiognomy which she found herself admiring simply so she wouldn't be drawn by his mouth.

Yet she couldn't help herself. That mouth of his was the only part of him that seemed not constructed from marble, for it trembled just a little—from amusement? Although the suspicion that Lord Rampton found Rose or her predicament amusing should have outraged her, for a moment all she could think of was tracing those exquisitely shaped lips with her forefinger before touching her own experimentally against what seemed the only soft part of the man.

She jerked back. Where had such a thought come from? Blushing, she forced languor into her tone. She was, after all, playing Helena, the bored beauty.

'Once this unsavoury business has been attended to, and my sister —' she caught herself just in time, '—in-law launched, we will return home.'

Fighting the urge to slump and hide as much of herself as possible beneath the table Rose held herself proudly. Self-conscious though she felt in Helena's outrageously daring, diaphanous silver-and-white evening gown, she knew any attempts at appearing coy or modest would only look contrived and draw further attention to what she wished, heartily, was not quite so obviously on show. She must not look down and frighten herself with the sight of how much bosom was revealed, although the faint breeze that ruffled the curtains and caressed her bare skin was a constant reminder. Edith had assured her that although she looked every inch the seductress, she was not, actually, indecent. It was small consolation.

It was true that Rose was unaccustomed to male attention, and as a result by Lord Rampton's lazy, confident smile. Oh yes, he certainly looked like a man used to getting his own way.

Well, Rose knew how to get her own way too. And Success—no, survival—depended upon managing Lord Rampton in the same artful manner she managed her stubborn brother and her volatile, unpredictable sister-in-law. She must play the seductress, as naturally and consummately as Helena, who was the reason behind, and inspiration for, this whole charade.

Leaning slightly across the table, she contrived a faintly seductive pout, surprised at how easily it came ... and by how much she enjoyed the results.

Charles had tried, several times, to interject. Characteristically he had allowed himself to be quelled on each occasion by an impatient response from Lord Rampton. Rose felt vindicated. Of course she had had no choice but to have come this evening. Her brother was completely out of his depth.

And he looked it. But was he, Rose wondered, aware of the almost conspiratorial smiles that their host continued to direct at her? Her skin tingled.

Rose had always been surprised that Charles was not firmer with Helena on the subject of Helena's conduct and wardrobe, though until now she had never realized how much licence marriage gave one to behave as one chose, rather than as one ought.

Dropping her eyes beneath another of Lord Rampton's searing gazes Rose encountered her reflection in the highly polished silver epergne that formed the table centrepiece. Edith had worked wonders with her appearance. The plain creature she'd always thought herself had been transformed into a society beauty with her wide-set bright eyes, pert nose and creamy complexion the equal of Arabella's pale innocent charm and Helena's lush allure.

With the kind of confidence that now buoyed her she felt capable of anything. Even armed combat with Lord Rampton. Well, she had his measure. He was rich, bored, careless of others, no doubt having never suffered a moment's angst or deprivation in his entire life.

On reflection, the thought was not bolstering. Charity or leniency were not likely characteristics, nor had Rampton been given any good reason to extend either to the struggling Chesterfields.

She resisted the urge to slump in defeat as she acknowledged the size of the debt owed to this man which would suck the lifeblood out of even their marginal existence. What was Rose doing, dreaming of gilded futures when it was not too extreme to say a life in debtor's prison or the workhouse was a distinct possibility if she could not win over this man?

She took a deep, sustaining breath, flicking her tongue over dry lips. Lord Rampton, she realized, was waiting for her to broach the subject which had brought them to his dinner table.

'I realize, Lord Rampton, that you are owed rather a lot of money. Mr Babbage, however, indicated that ...'

. . .

The beautiful Lady Chesterfield's hesitation, and the sudden colour that flooded her cheeks piqued Rampton's curiosity. He waited for her to finish, recalling Babbage's colourful account of this young woman's conduct one wild night during the previous week. It was all the more intriguing for, while Lady Chesterfield, with her lustrous chestnut hair, pretty mouth and high cheekbones beneath intensely blue eyes was as beautiful as she had been painted, her demeanour did not accord with Babbage's description. In surprising contrast with her gown there had been lapses in her mien, indicating that Lady Chesterfield's confidence was not as iron-clad as she would have him believe.

'What did Mr Babbage say he was prepared to be, Lady Chesterfield?' Rampton prompted, unconcerned that, to his own ears, he sounded condescending. His efforts were rewarded as he watched the blush deepen and noted the difficulty she had in responding. He had not expected such sport when he'd asked the beautiful Lady Chesterfield and her lily-livered husband to dinner.

'Patient, Lord Rampton.'

'Ah, but there we differ, Lady Chesterfield. You see, Mr Babbage is a very patient man. At least, he is where beautiful women are concerned.' Rampton took a sip of his wine, savouring it, and the moment. 'I, on the other hand, am not.'

With amusement he observed the way her fingers clenched the stem of her wine glass and the obvious effort with which she forced herself to relax. She toyed with her glass before glancing at him over the rim, flirtation in her tone as she murmured, 'Mr Babbage is a gentleman.'

His lips curled at the implied rebuke. 'Whereas I am not?'

The seductive gleam that lit up her large blue eyes, and the curve of her mouth—shaped more like a rosebud than the full, sensuous look he generally preferred—went a long way towards explaining the effect this young woman had had on Rampton's erstwhile debtor. He felt a moment's exultation as he held her gaze. He could read collusion in their depths. Yes, he thought with satisfaction, with the Chesterfields as hard pressed for ready funds as rumour had it there would be no difficulty coming to some mutual agreement with the beautiful Lady Chesterfield whereby no money need be exchanged. Unconsciously he ran the tip of his tongue over his top lip as he returned a somewhat wolfish smile, gesturing to the footman who hovered at the sideboard to bring more wine. Here was the return on his investment this evening, considering the other diversions he had sacrificed.

'A gentleman?' repeated his lovely guest with evident amusement. 'I am forced to reserve judgement, Lord Rampton. Time alone will tell.'

It could be an entertaining season, thought Rampton, anticipation surging through his loins. Admittedly he already had a mistress but the relationship was on the wane. He was ready for fresh excitement and Lady Chesterfield was an exquisite-looking creature, long married and clearly disenchanted with her husband who had no doubt been chosen for her.

'Yes,' he considered. 'But Mr Babbage has no head for business. Which is why he is perpetually in debt and I am not. Nevertheless, Lady Chesterfield,' he inclined his head, smiling, ignoring Charles, 'I am confident that we can come to some arrangement.'

Yes, he was sure of it. He would not call in the debt. Once Lady Chesterfield had launched her sister-in-law, she and her husband would return to the West Indies. All that differed from the original plan was that, between now and then, he and Lady Chesterfield would have enjoyed a little more pleasure than either of them had anticipated. One only had to spend five minutes in their company to see that neither Sir Charles nor the lovely Lady Chesterfield were likely to object.

The time had come, he decided, to give his current mistress, the fiery, exquisite but no longer incomparable, Lady Barbery, her congé.

<hr />

'You missed a rum do at Baroness Esterhazy's this evening, Rampton.'

Hesitating on the threshold to the library, Rampton turned, narrowing his eyes in greeting. It was hard to tell whether his brother were foxed or not.

He waited as Felix was relieved of his outerwear by Lavery before preceding his brother into the library. 'I had dinner guests.'

'Important dinner guests for you to have refused the baroness's invitation.'

'I turned down three equally enticing invitations, I assure you, Felix.' Rampton's tone was dry as he went to the sideboard, asking carelessly, 'And did the baroness enjoy her evening?'

'Well, she did her best to appear unconcerned by your absence.' Felix waited while his brother poured them both a drink. 'But I wasn't fooled for a minute. Of course, at the first opportunity she holed me up in a dark corner to ask what you were doing.'

'Indeed?' Rampton handed his brother the tumbler half-full of amber liquid, then settled himself on the leather sofa, stretching his long legs in front of him to gain maximum benefit from the small coal fire that burned in the grate. He felt a little guilty that he had trouble visualizing the baroness's bounteous charms when she'd been out of his life for less than six months. She'd been replaced by Catherine Barbery, his very first lover, who had unexpectedly waltzed back into his life a few months ago.

Well, the sizzle had left that relationship, too. Catherine seemed as bored as he, however, being a gentleman, Rampton had thought to let her be the one to sever ties.

But if she didn't do it soon, Rampton would be forced to act, he reflected, conscious of a very potent surge of desire that made him cross and re-cross his legs. Since last night, all he could think of was Lady Chesterfield's fair and fragile beauty. And those eyes: clear and incisive, as if she knew exactly what was on his mind and was both intrigued and terrified. He must go about his wooing with care. So many of his mistresses had thrown themselves at him but Lady Chesterfield was an altogether different proposition. He was visited by the interesting thought that she might be sizing him up as her first conquest. Her lapses of self-confidence would attest to that. Also, five years married to that dandelion baronet who agreed with everything anyone said—if they said it with enough force or conviction—must mean poor Lady Chesterfield, who was clearly a spirited little thing, was panting for a forceful lover. Having been incarcerated in the West Indies most of her life she'd have little knowledge as to how to go about the whole business.

Amusement and anticipation flickered in his self-acknowledged carnal depths and he realised, unrepentant, that he was licking his lips, already relishing the sport to come. Indeed, there'd be much of that, and he was quite happy to lead the way.

'Come now, Rampton, don't assume that indifferent tone with me. Three months ago you were wild for the baroness.' Felix lowered himself into the wing chair opposite, his mouth curling in a boyish and far less cynical imitation of his brother's. 'I told her I had not the least idea what you were up to this evening but that I was there in your stead and hoped she could regard me with similar affection.' With a shrug, he added on a philosophical note, 'She was unmoved. Even flattery, far in excess of her merits, made no difference. And then the baron arrived, all husbandly solicitation, so that was the end of that. Such a shame you always fall for the married ones.'

Rampton gave a short laugh. This was not a topic he wished to entertain with his brother. 'I'd be a fool to do otherwise.'

'You can't shrug off your matrimonial duty for too much longer, surely?'

'I endured a tedious evening at Almack's last night, in case you had forgotten.' Almack's was bursting with debutantes at this time of year. Rampton decided not to add that he derived greater sport from the more comely chaperones than he did from their gauche young charges, fresh from the schoolroom.

Felix, however, was well aware of his elder brother's predilections, for he said, almost testily, 'You need a wife, not a mistress, Rampton. Soon you'll be considered even more ramshackle than our dissolute papa.'

The amused smile froze. Rampton drained his tumbler. 'Why, Felix, I do believe you are serious.' Collecting himself, he assumed a tone that was far more light-hearted than he felt as he pointed out, 'Ramshackle I would be indeed to saddle myself— and the rest of the family —with an unsuitable bride. I long ago learned that duty and pleasure are two very different matters. And matrimony, you would do well to remember the next time you find yourself in thrall to the latest goddess, does not fall within the latter category. Rest assured that in the meantime, unless some worthy contender for my affections drops from the sky into my lap, I intend to take my pleasure while I can.' Yawning, he added, 'I'm off to bed. Unlike some, I no longer have the advantage of youth.'

Felix pulled a face as he watched his brother rise. 'God forbid, I'd better make the most of the few good years left to me. Looking at you is like looking at myself in a mirror in five year's time, all craggy and going grey.' He grinned. 'But without the boyish charm. Little consolation that the women seem to find a viscount in his dotage a more enticing prospect than his younger, far handsomer brother.'

Rampton snorted as he headed for the door, tossing over his shoulder, 'I think my pocketbook accounts for that.'

'I understand your caution, Rampton.' Felix's tone grew serious. 'But are you so afraid of parson's mousetrap? Surely you'll confess to having been intrigued by just one unmarried miss tossed in your direction?'

Rampton turned slowly, forcing amusement to his lips. 'The short answer, little brother, is no.' He hesitated. 'I have never been in love and my desire is whipped up only when I am assured my quarry is safely unobtainable.'

'But don't you get fagged with Mama forever charging you with your neglect in securing the family line?'

'Mama will have to be satisfied another ten years for that is when I plan to retire quietly to the country and breed sheep,' he grinned, 'amongst other things. In ten years a pliant, suitable wife will fit nicely into my plans. So if these questions are on mama's behalf, you can tell her that the nursery will not need decorating for at least a decade.'

Felix looked unimpressed. 'You really are just like Papa. Still, it can't be too bad having all these designing mamas trying to entice you with their daughters. I wish I were so popular!' He sighed. 'At least you're more discerning and discreet than Papa and, lucky for you, it seems there's no shortage of pretty matrons panting for your attentions.'

Rampton shrugged as he stroked the doorknob. 'It's hardly surprising I'm not inclined to chase innocent virgins, given the astonishing number of bored, highly desirable married women who make plain their desire for a little dalliance with a viscount in his dotage—as you put it.'

Once again, his thoughts strayed to the enchanting Lady Chesterfield. The messages she had sent him that night might have been mixed but mutual attraction had charged the air. He couldn't wait until their next meeting.

Felix tossed back his drink, then rose to pour another, saying in falsely sympathetic tones, 'Poor Rampton, to be leg-shackled by such mistrust must be a terrible thing. As long as caution remains your mistress you'll never find a wife. Anyway, what are your plans for tomorrow that you have to be up with the birds?'

Rampton contemplated the question. 'My plans for tomorrow,' anticipation turned up the corners of his mouth, 'and perhaps those for the next few weeks, will be to mix a little business with pleasure.'

'But you said—'

'I never said,' Rampton grinned, 'that pleasure and duty were mutually exclusive. And it just so happens that tomorrow is one occasion when they are not.'

CHAPTER 2

ARABELLA LEANT BACK against the threadbare squabs of their hackney carriage, facing Rose, her eyes wide. Despite her new clothes she looked much more the schoolgirl than the debutante who must make a good marriage before Rose could return to her beloved island, having discharged her duty towards her little sister.

'You flirted with Lord Rampton? Just like Helena?' She giggled, ignoring Helena's darkling look. 'Rose, I can't imagine it. When you're with a gentleman you're always so ...' she floundered for the right word, 'prim.'

Helena was not in a similarly light-hearted frame of mind. Tossing her glossy dark head, her eyes flashed as she muttered, 'Well, when it came to my clothes, Rose was as careless of those as she was of my feelings regarding this ridiculous charade.'

'Edith noticed the tear in the skirt when she fetched it from your room. She made a beautiful job of mending it, didn't she?' responded Rose, smoothly. 'I believe you caught it on a rosebush during Mrs Caversham's card party the other week.'

Helena turned her head away from the two sisters on the seat opposite, her normally sensuous mouth a rigid line. She watched the handsome Park Lane residences pass before them.

'I daresay I'll never be allowed to forget that night,' she said, bitterly. 'I knew how it would be. Charles has never reprimanded me. With his experience of the world he understood that I was in an impossible position. Everyone had a wager. People would have assumed that Charles keeps me on short rations had I not kept up; or would even have accused me of putting myself above the rest if I had offered my excuses.'

'A shame you didn't know what fast company you were keeping, Helena,' remarked Rose. 'Or that you slipped out of the house and left Charles sleeping without asking his permission, for he'd have explained that gaming in England is very different from gaming at home, where people were a little more understanding of your ... vices.'

'Gambling is not a crime... unless an unmarried woman plays for stakes which can only be honoured by those upon whom she is dependent,' Helena muttered.

Rose forced back her anger. The implication was clear. When Helena married, her father had settled a modest sum upon her. When Rose's father had died he had been so deeply in debt there was no dowry to settle upon either her or Arabella. Unless Charles took care of them, or they could find husbands for whom fortune did not matter —a slim chance indeed—they were entirely at the mercy of their closest male relative, Charles, whose finances they knew little about, but who never seemed to reproach his feckless, beautiful wife.

'Yes, but back home you've been gambling with the same people since you were seven years old, when your father first encouraged you to place a wager. You've only ever gambled with friends. Until now.'

Rose was not going to concede anything. Helena had never been properly called to task for her behaviour. Charles had begged his sister not to labour the incident, despite its repercussions for the rest of the family, saying Helena was deeply upset and likely to dissolve into remorseful tears. Rose only wished she could see it.

'Did Lord Rampton laugh at you when you tried to flirt with him?' Helena asked, changing the subject.

'He flirted straight back at me,' Rose laughed, recalling the evening with a surprising jolt of pleasure.

'He would not have bothered if you'd been dressed the way you are now.'

All the pleasure drained out of Rose as she contemplated her drab apricot velvet walking-dress. Apricot was a colour that made her look horribly sallow. The dress had once belonged to her mother, who had been taller and, at the time she owned it, stouter. Rose, who was not naturally gifted with a needle, had made a gallant effort to remodel it, but it had never been a great success. Not that that had mattered ... until now. Their social life had been limited in the last few years of her father's declining health. Rose made few calls and rarely received them. Besides, it was not as if there had been suitors for whom she must make an effort.

Rose glanced at Helena and was disconcerted by an unexpected wave of envy. Despite wearing a sprigged muslin that was demure by her standards, Helena still managed to look striking. Like Rose the night before, Helena would have had no compunction about flirting with Lord Rampton.

No, she would not! Rose's momentary doubt as to whether Helena would have been the better candidate in persuading Lord Rampton to extend the terms of their loan was swept away by righteous conviction. Helena could persuade a man to do most things she wanted but Helena's voracious appetite would have had her setting out to make him her slave. Rose could even imagine Charles discovering his wife—Heaven forbid!—wrapped in Lord Rampton's arms in some dark corner, which of course Helena would find some way to justify.

Heat prickled Rose's skin and she crossed her legs, suddenly uncomfortable by the unfamiliar sensations raging through her body. She put it down to the fact that she couldn't bear Charles to have to suffer such disappointment. Charles loved Helena to distraction. Indeed, it was a good thing it was Rose who was trying to twist Lord Rampton round her little finger.

'I wish it would meet with some horrible accident,' said Arabella, referring to Rose's unbecoming dress. 'I'm always meaning to accidentally pour something dreadful on to it and quite ruin it. But then Rose has so few clothes.' Smiling, she added, 'Rose looked so beautiful wearing your white dress, Helena, and with her hair done so modishly. I couldn't believe it was her. Maybe you could lend her more of your clothes and then she could go about in society and find herself a rich husband. Isn't that what you've always said she should do?'

'Yes, but not in my clothes.' Helena shuddered. 'Anyway, you said yourself, my wardrobe is hardly compatible with the kind of figure darling Rose chooses to cut.' She glanced from her high-waisted, low-fronted sprigged muslin to Rose's prim, unfashionable gown. 'Rose looks every inch the spinster she is at such pains to present to the world. I wouldn't dream of insulting her by offering her the loan of my clothes.'

Anger silenced Rose as Arabella asked, 'But what about when Rose meets Lord Rampton again? She has to pretend to be you, and she can only do that if you lend her something from your wardrobe. It would be terrible if he discovered her deception.'

'Lord Rampton is about to set sail in search of far more engaging females than your sister.' Helena's clipped pronouncement shouldn't have excited the kind of emotion that assailed Rose—she knew it. She certainly was used to Helena's careless disregard, however it took a great deal of effort to remain on her seat and not lunge for Helena and slap her face. Rose closed her eyes for a moment and held her breath. Good Heavens, when had her temper nearly got the better of her? Rose was distinguished by her composure and good sense. She was the *antithesis* of Helena.

'Well, at least Rose managed to play for more time. She was very clever and clearly captivated the viscount.'

'He must be a kind man.' Helena smiled sweetly at Rose. 'No doubt he'd have been equally receptive to any petitioning female, whether she was an ape leader in drab apricot velvet or a diamond of the first water.' Ignoring Arabella's outraged gasp she added, 'Rose knows a dose of smelling-salts would have had me up to the mark in no time but clearly the chance to go about in company pretending to be a married woman proved too tempting to resist. But Rose had her chance.'

There had been just the tiniest pause before uttering the last sentence. Rose glared at Helena. It was just like her to drag up the past to bolster her case, rubbing Rose's nose in her failure to secure the one splendid marital chance Rose had ever been offered.

'Sir Hector was Father's best friend.' Rose's voice was tight. 'I had known him all my life. How could I possibly have thrown myself into his arms and felt joy at being his wife when he was more like a kindly old uncle?'

'He had the means to give you everything you wanted.'

'Is that why you set your cap at him after Rose rejected him?' Arabella looked uncharacteristically confrontational.

'Hush, Arabella,' Rose admonished, though touched that her docile little sister would take such a risk on her behalf. Five years ago the whispers were that Helena had indeed set her cap at Sir Hector before she'd married Charles with almost unseemly haste after Sir Hector's rejection. 'Why look! There's Aunt Alice waving to us from the upstairs casement,' she said, relieved that they were at their destination. 'At least, she looks so like Mama it must be Aunt Alice.'

'I DECLARE, IT'S LIKE SEEING MY DEAD SISTER WALK THROUGH THAT door!' With outstretched arms, Aunt Alice greeted Rose at the top of the portico steps before leading them into her fashionable townhouse. 'You must forgive me for being such a sentimental creature. I was always much more of a silly than Beatrice.' Dabbing at her eyes with a lace handkerchief, she ushered the girls towards a comfortable cluster of seats once they'd reached the over-decorated drawing room. 'And you are the exotic creature dear Charles married,' she added, turning to Helena who was ensconced on a blue and silver upholstered Egyptian sofa. 'I believe he'd been dangling after you since you were in short skirts. So now, Arabella, we need to find you a fine husband before the end of the season,' she gushed. 'Just see if we don't!'

Rose had never met her aunt, who'd waved Rose's parents off to their new life after her father had inherited the plantation shortly after gambling away his English estate.

'We are so grateful for your offer to launch Arabella,' said Rose.

'And Helena, of course, is dying for a Season. This is the first time she has left the island.'

'But what about you, my dear Rose?' asked Aunt Alice.

'Rose will look after Charles,' said Helena, with a complacent smile. 'They prefer a quiet life. Rose was telling me only the other week how much she preferred the idea of curling up with a good book than attending Lady Glenton's soirée tomorrow night. Isn't that so, Rose?'

Rose hesitated. 'I did say that,' she conceded, adding silently that it was only so Charles needn't feel so inadequate that he had not the funds to clothe both his sisters sufficiently, given his wife's extravagance.

'But my dear Rose, you are only in London this one Season. It may be your last chance to find a husband.' Aunt Alice's expression was almost comical in its distress.

'I do not want one, Aunt Alice.' Rose forced a smile. 'I couldn't bear to be away from the plantation for too long.' This, at least, was true. Rose had no intention of remaining in England which meant it would be unfair to spend money they did not have on a wardrobe for her. Arabella needed fine clothes to make a good match. The last thing on Rose's mind was attracting a husband when her heart longed for the heat and familiarity of her island home.

Her aunt regarded Rose as if she had just admitted to a penchant for robbing graves. 'Not want a husband?' she repeated. 'But, my dear, every woman needs a husband, whether they want one or not. I thought that was why you were in England.'

'That's why Arabella is in England, and why I am here, accompanying her.' Rose blushed, adding awkwardly, 'Did I not explain that in my letter?'

'Oh yes, you said Arabella was to be launched but that there were not the funds to launch you, also.' Aunt Alice cleared her throat. 'I realize you are quite a bit older, however, surely if the opportunity presented itself, you'd be amenable to the idea of marriage?'

'Rose declares she is too set in her ways,' said Arabella comfortably.

'She's right,' murmured Helena.

Aunt Alice's grey corkscrew curls bobbed about her ears as she looked from one girl to the next, seemingly at a loss for words. At last she managed, 'Ah, well, that's as may be, but some of us have been known to change our minds.'

The sound of loud clattering in the hallway followed by raised voices made them turn, but the new arrival passed by the drawing room, distance muting his heavy tread upon the stairway that led to the bedrooms on the upper floor.

Rose glanced across at Aunt Alice whose faced blanched and who was now holding her chest. She was surprised. Was that fear she saw cross her face? Almost instantly Aunt Alice dropped her hand and gave a girlish laugh, saying, 'With so much to be done, let us discuss wardrobes, and invitations this very instant.'

But Rose had not missed the momentary uncertainty before her aunt launched into a spirited discourse on the aforementioned topics, with occasional interjections from Helena and Arabella.

Rose looked on. Unexpectedly, she was assailed by such an all-consuming spasm of envy she wanted to shake herself. Helena was quite right. Rose could have contracted an alliance with the most eligible bachelor in the whole of the West Indies. Then all of them would have had wardrobes full of fine clothes.

Too late to turn back the clock. Five years ago Rose had not known that her father was virtually bankrupt, that the alternative to marriage was to be all but completely dependent upon Charles and the cold and beautiful Helena whom he'd married shortly afterwards with such unseemly haste.

'Oh dear, it's raining. And you girls had planned to go walking in the park.' Aunt Alice eyed the falling rain with concern. 'I'm sure it's just a shower. You'll have to stay until it's—'

Her sentence was cut short as the door burst open and an angry voice cried, 'Gad's teeth, Mama, will you look at what Riley's done to my hessians!'

Four pairs of startled eyes turned towards the door as a tall, dark youth of about twenty years strode into the room.

Ignoring the three girls, he made his way towards Aunt Alice and, turning to face her, stamped one boot upon the coffee table. Four china tea cups shuddered.

'I'm sorry, Oswald. I'll speak to him again.' Aunt Alice's voice wavered.

'You'll give him his notice, Mama, and that's final. He's already been warned once.'

'But, Oswald, I can't....'

Without waiting for her to finish, the young man removed his foot from the table, glared at the girls, then strode from the room.

Crimson, Aunt Alice stammered, 'I'm so sorry for the intrusion, my dears. That was my stepson, Oswald. Sometimes, when he gets in one of his moods ...' She trailed off before beginning a new sentence with pathetic eagerness, 'But most of the time he's quite charming.'

'I couldn't see anything wrong with his boots,' said Helena.

Aunt Alice shrugged helplessly. 'He likes them polished so he can see his reflection.'

Rose changed the subject and when a ray of sunshine lit up the room, declared brightly that now they had talked Aunt Alice's ear off it was time for the three of them to be on their way.

'It'll be lovely and fresh for a promenade in Hyde Park,' said Aunt Alice, as she accompanied them down the front steps to the pavement to wait for the carriage to be brought round. 'I declare, the three of you look as pretty as a picture.' She looked wistful. 'I remember the days when Beatrice and I used to promenade....'

A passing cooper's wagon drowned her words but as it took the turn it lurched into a ditch sending up a spray of muddy water before righting itself and continuing on its way.

'Rose! Your dress!' shrieked Aunt Alice.

Muddy droplets had disfigured the entire front of it. Dismayed, Rose said, 'I'll just stay in the carriage while Helena and Arabella take a stroll,' but her aunt wouldn't hear of it.

'You must borrow one of my pelisses,' she insisted. 'I have so many, I'll never miss it.'

After much resistance Rose eventually gave in and returned upstairs with her aunt to look through her wardrobe. When she presented herself to the girls her apricot velvet had all but disappeared beneath a smart white, fur-edged pelisse, with neat gold buttons from hem to neckline. In addition she carried over her arm three cast-off gowns, all the height of fashion.

'I so rarely go about these days, yet I can never resist when my dress-maker pays a visit,' Aunt Alice had assured her. Rose rather suspected that this was her aunt's way of dispensing charity but saw how much she'd offend her if she refused to at least take them home to try on.

'That's certainly an improvement,' Helena remarked, casting her eye over Rose as they took their seats in the carriage.

'White suits you,' said Arabella. 'You should wear it more often.'

Rose smiled. White was not a very practical colour, given the amount of time she spent overseeing their sugar plantation.

Now that the sun was shining so brilliantly the crowds were out in full force, promenading or driving through the park. The moment the girls were handed down they were caught up in the spirit of the specta-cle. Unconsciously they slowed their pace to match the languid saunter of the other promenaders.

Much of their conversation with Aunt Alice had been spent discussing the invitations she had received and from which they could, in turn, benefit. Helena had, at the time, appeared bored, but Rose noticed how her eyes lit up at the spectacle of the handsomely garbed crowd. She saw, too, the familiar glint of criticism and was not surprised when Helena, with a toss of her glossy dark head declared, 'English women have no style,' as she levelled an accusing look at Rose. 'If you had not insisted I wear my most missish gown so as not to scan-dalize your aunt, I'd have shown up these dull English ladies.'

Certainly, the gown she wore today was a great deal more respectable and modest than most of her clothes. Nevertheless her exotic looks did mark her out, Rose noticed, though Arabella certainly received her fair share of attention as she gazed about her, bright-eyed, fresh-complexioned, dimpling frequently in response to a doffed hat. What Rose did not notice were the admiring glances leveled at her.

She was so busy marvelling at the interest her companions were receiving that she failed to heed the gentlemen heading towards them, one of whom was directing a particularly wolfish smile in her direction. Instead, Rose was watching with growing concern the particularly seductive pout that Helena was concentrating upon some approaching stranger who was obviously not Charles. She raised her head, prepared to warn off the interloper with a frown.

'What an unexpected pleasure, Lady Chesterfield.'

Helena opened her mouth to speak, but her words were cut short as Rose blurted, much too hastily and with much too much enthusiasm in her attempt to block her, 'Why, Lord Rampton, what a pleasure, indeed! Lord Rampton, may I introduce to you my sister-in-law Miss Chesterfield and her sister, Miss Arabella. Rose and Arabella, pray meet Viscount Rampton, with whom we had the pleasure of dining several nights ago.'

Rose was aware that her furious blushes and rapid breathing might be misconstrued as Lord Rampton inclined his head before introducing his brother, Felix. What was vital at this point, however, was that Helena should play the role assigned to her.

'A pleasure, Lord Rampton.' Helena's voice was a modest murmur, and Rose watched, amazed, as her sister-in-law adopted the unlikely persona of a blushing innocent, her manner mimicking exactly that of Arabella who had not yet been to her first ball and who was often tongue-tied in the company of gentlemen.

'The pleasure is all mine,' murmured the handsome viscount, his amusement evident as his gaze rested on the transparently discomfited Rose before suggesting that fate obviously intended them to enjoy an afternoon's stroll together.

Whether by accident or design, Rose found herself in alarmingly close proximity to their recent host, while his lordship's brother, Felix, brought up the rear, flanked by Arabella and Helena.

'A happy coincidence to meet like this, Lady Chesterfield,' remarked Lord Rampton, lowering his voice which lent an unsettling degree of intimacy to their conversation. As an unmarried young woman, Rose was unused to such dealings with gentlemen, just as she was unused to the quickening of her pulse and unexpected self-consciousness. She felt heat burn her cheeks and a curious churning in the base of her stomach as she forced a half smile to her lips and stared straight ahead, taking the arm he offered.

Good Heavens! She almost leapt at the contact. She was worse than a schoolroom miss.

'Yet I couldn't help but notice that our sudden and unexpected appearance seemed to throw you into some confusion. Would it be rude to ask whether that was because you did not wish to see me again after the other night?'

'Of course not, sir!' Rose tried to channel her discomfiture into irritation. Naturally Lord Rampton surmised that it was for exactly the opposite reason. What a vain and arrogant gentleman. If he knew the real reason for her agitation he'd not be so smugly conceited. A glance at the self-confidence radiating from his beautiful blue gaze made her realize that a man of such consequence must be used to every other unmarried young lady setting her cap at him. Well, she was not one of them!

Managing an air of far greater confidence than she felt, she said, 'Since you were so kind in allowing more time to repay your debt, how could that be?' She cocked her head, proud of the way she managed to smile almost lazily up at him, just as she had seen Helena do a thousand times.

While she didn't like to admit how relieved she was to be wearing her Aunt Alice's fashionable white pelisse, teamed with a pair of pearl earrings that her aunt insisted had once belonged to her mother, she was amazed at the confidence her new fine clothes gave her.

'I feel mortified that your obligations towards me have placed you in such a difficult situation,' murmured Rampton, whose smile did nothing to bear out such a sentiment. 'Perhaps a hand or two at the card table could reverse matters?'

Rose cast him a narrow-eyed glance, tinged with doubt. It was difficult to know whether his tone of enquiry suggested that his offer might be one of gallantry, whereby he'd allow her to win thus settling the debt, or whether he was playing with her, enticing her to be as reckless and as daring as the Lady Chesterfield described by his friend, Babbage. She suspected it was the latter.

'I may be a gambler, Lord Rampton, but I am a principled one,' she declared, virtuously. 'I will not be returning to the gaming table until my debt is cleared.'

'I am sure your husband would be very relieved to hear that.'

'It was he who stipulated it.'

'Indeed? Then I am sure you would not dream of disobeying him and suffering the consequences of his displeasure.'

Rose bridled at his mocking tone. How dared he speak in such slighting, sarcastic tones about Charles? 'No, Lord Rampton, I would not dream of it.'

'Said like the most loyal and obedient of wives.' His tone was gently mocking.

'Besides,' muttered Rose, 'there will be little time for such an opportunity since I understand you are leaving within the week.'

'I've changed my plans, Lady Chesterfield.'

Rose nearly gasped aloud at his sardonic smile while his words struck terror into her heart.

His smile broadened as he placed his large hand over her fingertips which she'd been obliged by good manners to tuck into the crook of his arm. Was his amusement due to the fact he'd heard her small intake of breath? She certainly hoped he had not. Rose was a consummate actress and her role was to play the careless, self contained Helena. She could do it. She had to do it.

Lord Rampton lowered his head so that his striking eyes were on a level with hers, and said in conspiratorial tones, 'I'm a jaded bachelor, Lady Chesterfield, who has already sampled the wares across the waters.' He squeezed her fingers. 'The evening I spent with you and your husband made me realize that London offers greater diversions than I had thought.'

Dear Lord, what had she got herself into? Rose had no response though she understood his subtext perfectly. What she didn't understand—and certainly didn't like—was the tumultuous churning in her breast. Was it gratification, excitement or horror that Lord Rampton was making clear his interest in her?

But she was a married woman. Unobtainable. She didn't understand.

They walked on in silence, listening to the other three chattering and laughing behind them. Rose was struck by the unaccustomed girlish ring to Helena's laugh. She tried to force her mind from the implications of Lord Rampton's declaration. Of course, she must tell Charles immediately they returned, she decided. And with the next breath immediately decided that she certainly must *not*.

They had nearly completed their circuit. Rose indicated that the waiting carriage ahead of them was theirs and would transport them home directly.

'Sadly, if we are not to meet at the gaming table, we may see little of each other this Season,' said Lord Rampton.' In which case, we shall have to arrange some other venue to discuss our business dealings.'

Withdrawing her hand from the crook of his arm, Rose managed, 'I'm sure that won't be necessary.' No, it would be far too dangerous and besides, she was to all intents and purposes, a married woman. He couldn't possibly expect to further his acquaintance with her when Charles was in the shadows.

The pressure of Lord Rampton's fingers upon her own hand which she'd been in the process of clasping around her reticule made it suddenly difficult to breathe while the unexpected steel in his voice made clear the fact she'd spoken rashly.

'Indeed, Lady Chesterfield, I think it will. You do not deny that I have been unusually lenient in this matter.' The lively conversation behind them as they waited by the carriage reassured Rose that they could not be overheard. Or observed, for she feared she was trembling like some pitiful debutante caught in the glare of a powerful man's interest, and certainly not immune to his magnetism.

He gazed at her with undisguised interest. 'I am not usually so with my debtors. It's one of the reasons I am successful in my business dealings. However, most of my debtors are not so beautiful, nor so ...' he brought Rose's hand to his lips, 'desirable.'

Rose opened her mouth to speak but no words came. Her legs felt like jelly and her throat dry but it was not fear she felt. She was glad at the chance to step back as the jarvey let down the steps.

Undeterred, Lord Rampton moved closer. 'Call it my interest on the debt, Lady Chesterfield,' he murmured, his voice warning before becoming the consistency of rich treacle. 'I think my leniency entitles me to a little indulgence from you, do you not?'

Rose managed an uncertain smile. How should she react? Was such blatant familiarity accepted with equanimity by married women? She felt as if she were on another planet where all the social rules had changed. And yet, disconcerting though that was, she had never felt so ... alive.

As he swung round to greet the others, Lord Rampton's smile transformed into one of expansive good humour. 'Ladies ...' He bowed before handing first a blushing Arabella, followed by Helena, into the carriage. 'And Lady Chesterfield ...' his smile was half-conspiratorial, half-mocking as he assisted Rose, 'I await our next meeting with the most agreeable anticipation.'

Once settled in the carriage, Helena sent Rose a narrow-eyed look. 'So that was Lord Rampton.'

Rose realized that she had made a serious mistake in playing down the man's obvious attractiveness to Helena. Not even a blind woman would have been impervious to his charm.

'Now I understand why you've told me so little about him.' Helena's voice was cold.

Arabella's unawareness of the tension between the two women made her admiring declaration: 'He's so handsome!' sound a false note in the stony silence.

Rose was relieved that her sister had failed to register Helena's suspicion of Rose's motives. It gave her a moment in which to formulate a defence, while Arabella added, with a thoughtful frown, 'His brother was very charming, too—don't you think?'

Helena dismissed this with a toss of her head. 'Young master Felix? Why, he's just a greenhorn. But, my dear Rose,' her smile was curious, 'what I should like to know is why you would wish to hide from us the fact that Lord Rampton is such an attractive man? Generous, apparently; accommodating, certainly ... but not, we would be forgiven for thinking, in view of your description of him the other night, attractive. Surely that is a telling omission?' She paused, and Rose, already feeling the heat, knew she was fuelling Helena's enjoyment with her fiery blushes. 'I understood,' Helena went on, 'only that he had agreed to give you more time in which to honour your debt.'

'*Your* debt, since you seem to have forgotten, Helena.' Rose managed a scornful look before transferring her gaze to the passing street traffic.

'I beg your pardon. My debt,' Helena amended, unrepentantly. She paused, and a sly look crossed her lovely face before she added, disingenuously, 'Thank you so much for reminding me. I think it's time for me to pay Lord Rampton a call and make clear I am the one guilty of misdemeanour.'

'You mustn't!' Instantly Rose knew she'd made another grave miscalculation.

'Rose, darling.' The honeyed tone was at odds with the expression in Helena's almond-shaped, green eyes, narrow with speculation as she added, 'I believe you are quite taken with generous Lord Rampton.' She leaned across to pat Rose's knee and her voice dropped to a whisper. 'Just a word of caution: be careful. Without wishing to interfere, I don't think you realize what dangerous ground you're treading. Lord Rampton,' she uttered his name with relish, removing her hand from Rose's knee as she drew herself upright, 'is not the kind who likes to be deceived.'

'I thought he seemed very nice.' Arabella looked in puzzlement at the two women.

Rose hesitated. She did not want Arabella to be privy to the reasons for the undercurrents between her and Helena. Forging on, she responded with steely determination, 'Do not underrate me, Helena. I am not the young innocent you imagine.'

'I'm glad to hear it.' Helena feigned relief as she leaned back into the squabs. 'In which case, since dear, clever Rose is on a mission to undo the harm wicked Helena has wrought, I'm compelled to play the part you've assigned to me.' She gave a husky laugh, cleared her throat, then uttered a girlish trill. 'It'll be quite a novelty playing the unworldly schoolroom miss again.'

'If you ever knew how.' Stung into an uncharacteristically barbed response Rose was determined not to back down. 'You were not even out of the schoolroom before you were calculating how to make the most advantageous marriage possible.'

'Charles?' Helena's laugh was bitter. 'I was never in the schoolroom, Rose. You know Father's thoughts on education for females. He considered my beauty a lure for a duke at least! What use was education? But you insult me by implying that I was always motivated by avarice. When I was seventeen I was prepared to sacrifice everything for love! Yes! I'd have run away with nothing but the clothes I had on, but he who had no prospects was too proud to condemn me to a life which, he said, would be one of unending struggle. You didn't know that about me...that I was so selfless...did you? Now I'm married to your brother ...' Her eyes glittered with angry, unshed tears. 'So don't you accuse me of not making sacrifices!'

As the carriage negotiated a deep rut in the road the silence inside was tense. Rose bit her lip, repenting her earlier accusations. Helena was as unhappy with her lot as she was.

'Rose,' said Helena at last, the familiar mocking tone returning as she fixed Rose with a level look, 'this uncharacteristically madcap charade is, I assume, motivated by the desire to save us all ... and not, I trust, prompted by romantic folly?' Squeezing Arabella's shoulder in a motherly fashion, she went on, 'Perhaps you should talk some sense into your sister, my dear Arabella. She is taking a big gamble in her desire to be the confident woman of the world she imagines Lord Rampton would admire. And we all know that Rose is not a natural gambler.' She clicked her tongue. 'I fear what may happen if she pursues this dangerous charade.'

Arabella, out of her depth, remained silent.

'Lord Rampton and I have come to an arrangement, Helena,' Rose said, trying to sound more confident than she felt. 'It's only for ...' she steeled herself, 'a few weeks.'

'A few weeks! You told us all he was leaving by week's end.' A slow smile curved Helena's lips. 'Ah, but he is taken with you, Rose. He believes Lady Chesterfield can offer him diversions sufficient to make him want to stay.' She burst out laughing. 'What an interesting situation, and I, who have been bored for so long, am now enthralled.' Her eyes glittered above the steeple she made of her gloved hands. 'How will sweet Lady Rose play the dangerous Lord Rampton?' She looked thoughtful before adding, 'Meanwhile, I am only too happy to take my cue from Arabella so that I can convincingly play the ingenuous schoolroom miss.'

'You are?' It was all Rose could manage.

Helena leaned forward and tapped Rose playfully on the shoulder with her fan. 'Now that you have engaged the interest of London's most notorious rake, Rose, I shall have much more fun as an innocent with an eye to London's most eligible bachelors than I would as Charles's wife.' She sat back again. 'Perhaps he'll be at tonight's ball. If so, I shall enjoy watching you sink deeper into a mire of your own making.'

CHAPTER 3

ROSE PUT DOWN her stitching and gazed with pride at Arabella. It seemed Rose was not only the only one who'd secured the interest of a handsome, eligible gentleman—which, in itself was both good and bad though she didn't want to think about that right now.

After attending their first ball the previous night, Arabella had found herself admirer and as their visit to England was to secure a good match for her, Rose was delighted by her sister's success.

'He asked you to dance *three times?*' Helena repeated.

Rose, conscious of Helena's dampening effect on Arabella's previously high spirits, remarked with a smile, 'Viscount Yarrowby was obviously very charming, dearest.'

She knew Helena was chagrined; that she'd wanted to attend the ball the previous night but instead had had to nurse Charles, who had come down with a mild fever. Aunt Alice had chaperoned Arabella while Rose had hastily summoned an imaginary megrim herself and taken herself off to her bedchamber. She had no intention of nursing her brother, who was not a good invalid, when that was Helena's duty.

'He's lovely,' Arabella enthused, eyes shining as she held one of the blue drawing room cushions to her chest and executed a twirl in the middle of the room. 'He was so sweet and charming all evening. Of course, he couldn't take me into supper as Lady Belton had engaged him to take in Miss Mawks, but he was by my side the moment he'd executed his duties.'

Rose could see she was intoxicated by her success. And why shouldn't she be? Arabella exuded a fresh, ingenuous charm.

Her gaze strayed from her admiring appraisal of Arabella to Helena and a wave of trepidation engulfed her. Helena had always been, undeniably, the most beautiful of them all. She had spent her life being fêted and admired. Now, suddenly, she had been eclipsed. Not only by Arabella, but by Rose too.

Helena had promised not to expose her. But could she behave with malice towards Arabella?

Last night as neither Rose nor Helena had gone out in public, the charade over Rose's identity had not been an issue. But what of the next ball or masquerade? Aunt Alice had lent Rose sufficient items from her wardrobe so she could deport herself in reasonable style and Helena had agreed to play the debutante out of malicious interest, but what of Charles's reaction? And that of Aunt Alice?

Rose had come to England with no intention of entering into the social whirligig. So why did her heart now thunder at the possibility of venturing forth into society. Thunder—not from trepidation, but anticipation?

She was saved from having to explore the uncomfortable conclusion to these thoughts by Helena's dampening response, 'I believe Lord Yarrowby is quite a bit older than you.'

'What does that signify?' Arabella's eyes widened. 'Papa was twenty years older than Mama, don't forget. And Lord Yarrowby is only fifteen years older than me.'

'Oh, so you're well advanced with your calculations,' remarked Helena, apparently tiring of the conversation. She rose, her high heels clicking on the parquetry, her silk gown swishing around her ankles as she made her way towards the door. As she turned, her gaze travelled Arabella's length, as if assessing her worth.

Arabella's jaw dropped as she realized that Helena was mocking her, but the hurt look on her face only made her sister-in-law laugh. 'I was not insulting you, *ma chérie*,' she said, her tone more kindly now. 'Rather the contrary. It would have been simply too stupid of you not to have considered all matters pertaining to his eligibility. Ah, a letter!' she cried, gaily, snatching up the thick cream parchment sealed with wax as the maid entered with the morning's post. But her disappointment showed as she turned it over.

'Rose, your admirer,' she said, stonily, after she'd dismissed the maid. 'Although, by rights, any letter addressed to Lady Chesterfield should be opened by me. Well?' she demanded, when Rose merely stared at the missive as if she didn't know what she should do.

Rose would have told her to mind her own business had Arabella not also begged with childlike enthusiasm, 'Yes, do tell, Rose. Is Lord Rampton your new admirer?'

'Lord Rampton merely wishes to meet me this afternoon,' replied Rose evenly, once she had scanned it, folded up the paper and placed it in the pocket of her skirt. 'No doubt something to do with the arrangement we have over the debt.'

BUT AFTER BEING USHERED INTO LORD RAMPTON'S DRAWING ROOM, then spending several minutes engaged in trivial chatter about the appalling traffic conditions occasioned by that afternoon's wet and windy weather, Rose realized that her debt was far from Lord Rampton's mind as he eventually got down to the real reason for his request to her.

'I understand it was Miss Arabella's debut into society,' he said, conversationally, regarding Rose from above the rim of his cut-glass tumbler.

'Yes.' For some reason Rose was wary. With little experience of men she found being alone with one both disconcerting and exhilarating—or was that because of the man, himself? Her palms felt sweaty and her throat dry but she held her head high as she practised the self possession that had always served her well.

'She has a certain charming freshness,' he went on, seeming to observe her more acutely than the remark warranted. 'More sherry?' he asked, suddenly by her side, bending to relieve her of her half-empty glass.

Rose hoped that if she kept her eyes trained on the fire, and a polite but distant smile upon her lips, he would not notice the rapid rise and fall of her bosom and the heat that flamed in her cheeks.

'I couldn't help noticing that she appeared to catch the eye of Lord Yarrowby.' Surveying her with an assessing look as he returned to his seat, Lord Rampton raised his tumbler in salute, took a thoughtful sip, then smiled. It was an intimate smile, as if he had known her a long time, and was assured that each understood the relationship between them.

Rose felt both foolish and naïve. She should never have agreed to meet Lord Rampton, alone, though Edith had accompanied her here, allaying any suspicions Charles might have had. 'You were, perhaps, expecting Arabella to comport herself like a country bumpkin?' she asked, cautiously.

Lord Rampton's shout of laughter gave but short-lived relief.

'Having met the other women in her family the thought never crossed my mind.' His eyes twinkled.

Rose felt her defences crumble. No man had ever looked at her like that: with such unreserved admiration. Her pulse quickened. Nor would such a look ever have been likely to breach her defences, had it come from another man, she decided. Lord Rampton was utterly delectable. Never having lost her heart, or had it even slightly bruised, she'd not thought herself capable of thinking such a thing. But Lord Rampton, with his strong, angular face, his frank, direct gaze and the most beautiful mouth she had ever seen, threatened to turn her into a gushing, trembling ninnyhammer. Rose would have to exert all her poise and reserve to ensure she did not succumb to the invitation in his eyes.

When she continued to hold herself stiff and unyielding, he became businesslike. 'No, indeed, I'd wager that with your sister-in-law's refreshing want of airs and her pretty face she'll be the toast of the town. Which is all the more reason to warn you—'

Foreboding and confusion coursed through her. 'Warn me?' Rose repeated faintly, her hand going to the low neckline of the pretty pale-mauve voile Helena had surprisingly insisted she must borrow for her unchaperoned visit.

'Lord Yarrowby is a rake.' He stated it baldly, with relish.

'And Arabella danced with him but three times,' Rose replied. Clearly Lord Rampton had requested her company on false pretences. This would be the excuse she could use to show the strength she needed to leave. Now. Lord Rampton was dangerous territory. She must have as little to do with him as she could before discharging Helena's debt.

'If you ... summoned me here,' she emphasized the word with disdain, though her heart felt like breaking, 'simply to tell me that, then I think you have perhaps overestimated the depth of our acquaintance, sir.' She rose and looked around for a repository for her barely touched sherry.

She summoned up the necessary indignation to stare him down. Lord Yarrowby was a remarkable catch. Everyone said so, and if Lord Rampton wanted to pretend concern over Yarrowby's suitability merely to draw Rose into his lair... well, it was simply too much of a sacrifice to make—on either Arabella's or her behalf.

Drawing in a breath that she hoped would replenish the sensible side of her, she was surprised by his obvious dismay. Surely sh'd not strayed so far from propriety that he wouldn't understand by now that she did not take kindly to his subterfuge? His next words, however, had the effect of shocking her so much that she dropped back into her seat.

'I beg your pardon, madam. I had thought your apparent fondness for young Arabella betokened a certain regard for her personal happiness. I had not realized that you planned to honour your debt through her ... success.'

'Of course I intend no such thing!' Rose declared. 'Only I thought you had requested me to come here on the pretext of—' She stopped abruptly.

Lord Rampton watched her confusion with amusement. 'Yes?' he prompted, mildly.

She waved one hand through the air dismissively, then took another sustaining breath in order to gather her disordered wits. 'Naturally,' she said through clenched teeth, 'where my sister...er...sister-in-law is concerned it is of far greater importance to me that Lord Yarrowby should be a man of decency and honour than that he has a fortune and a title.'

'Bravo.' Her host congratulated her with heavy irony. 'Being somewhat tender-hearted myself I hoped to elicit such a declaration.'

'I am not completely shameless,' Rose muttered. 'You will get your money, as promised, my lord, and I shall ensure that my sister-in-law makes a match that will secure her future happiness which, I hope, will be free from financial hardship.' She rose. 'Good day.'

Lord Rampton shadowed her as she navigated her way around the furniture towards the door. She could almost feel the radiation from his body and she turned, supporting herself with one hand on the back of the club sofa, looking up to find his generously curved mouth smiling down at her, his deep-blue eyes sparkling with amusement.

'Lady Chesterfield,' he said, taking her hand, his voice filled with remorse, 'I have offended you. Hardly the action of a gentleman, especially when I have just accused Yarrowby—who is, I must tell you, a former friend—of lacking the qualities required to be called one.'

Rose had no choice but to surrender her hand, which he bent over with a flourish. A rush of sensation whooshed to her lower belly and she drew in her breath sharply. What had caused that? Surely not the mere touch of his lips upon her suddenly sensitised skin as he murmured, 'Pray, forgive me.'

'Perhaps I overreacted a trifle, Lord Rampton.' Rose slanted a sideways look towards him as she'd seen Helena do in the company of attractive men. 'You see, my sister-in-law is very dear to me and her happiness is paramount. I was horrified at the charge you just levelled at me.'

'In that case, Lady Chesterfield, all the more reason to heed my warning.'

'That Lord Yarrowby is a rake? But, my lord,' Rose smiled wickedly, 'I had not thought the charge such a terrible one. If we ladies were to be warned off every so-called rake in town, who would be left to marry?'

Instead of responding in like fashion to her flirtatious banter Lord

Ramtpon lowered his head even further. In fact, for one tantalizingly terrifying moment Rose thought he was going to actually brush his lips against hers and she stiffened, every fibre of her being on full alert.

She was still wondering whether she was disappointed or otherwise that he had not, when he added ominously, 'Most rakes, I am pleased to report, have more respect for their womenfolk. Now,' His tone was matter of fact as he straightened and saw Rose to the door, 'when shall I have the pleasure of furthering our acquaintance, Lady Chesterfield? Perhaps at Lady Pendleton's soirée tomorrow night? You have my promise – as a rake and a gentleman – that when next we meet, we shall concern ourselves with matters that are altogether more ...' the wolfish smile was in place as he supplied suggestively, 'diverting.'

HELENA SIGHED AS SHE TWIRLED A CUSHION TASSEL ROUND HER middle finger and gazed through the grimy windows at the church spire. 'I can't decide whether it's more fun being fêted as the unworldly virgin, or watching you grapple with the subtleties of experience. Come now, Rose,' she laughed her husky laugh, 'I've already pledged to play the part you've assigned to me.'

Too absorbed in her own dilemma as to whether it was pure folly to attend Lady Pendleton's soirée, Rose did not notice how bright her sister-in-law's eyes were, and how out of character was her enthusiasm for a plan from which she did not, apparently, benefit directly. She was relieved when Aunt Alice was announced.

'We were just discussing Lady Pendleton's masquerade tomorrow night, Mrs Withers,' said Helena, ignoring Rose's imploring look and small shake of the head. 'Happily Rose has agreed to accompany us.'

'Delightful!' Aunt Alice beamed as she settled herself.

'No, Helena, I was just saying I had decided not to accompany you,' Rose corrected her.

Helena, looking disappointed, turned an appealing gaze upon the older woman. 'Don't you think it wrong that Rose should deny herself the pleasures of the season when she has only this one chance to secure a husband, for all she insists she doesn't want one?'

'Indeed, yes! What is it, child?' asked her aunt directly, turning to Rose. 'Is it clothes?'

'Helena has kindly promised to lend me those.' Rose summoned inspiration for her excuse.

'Then what is it, dear? You're not ...' Aunt Alice's eyes widened as an idea dawned, 'afraid, are you?'

'Of ... men?' Rose shook her head in emphatic denial.

'Dear Rose thinks herself the equal of any man,' came a lazy-sounding voice from the doorway.

'My dear Charles, so good to see you!' Aunt Alice exclaimed as her nephew entered the room.

Taking a seat, Charles added, 'No, Rose continues to eschew the idea of marriage as she has not yet met a man she considers her equal.'

'Well, perhaps it is not quite right to consider ourselves equal to men, but it is most definitely a shame to allow fear to stand in the way of finding a good husband. How is the world to go on?' asked Aunt Alice with a definitive air, glancing about as if for corroboration.

'What wisdom, Mrs Withers,' said Helena with no hint of irony. 'The problem Rose has is that she can't go out without being involved in a terrible deception.'

In response to the obvious stupefaction of the others, she elaborated with an artful smile, 'All right, I confess, it was all my fault to begin with.'

'My dear Helena,' Charles interjected, but Helena cut him off, saying, quickly, 'Dear Aunt Alice—you don't mind if I call you that? No? And perhaps you, too, enjoy a little intrigue. Yes?' She glanced at Charles and Rose as if challenging them to interrupt before launching into her version of the truth. 'You see, it all began when Charles had an important meeting with a rich and influential gentleman—perhaps you know of him? Lord Rampton.'

'Indeed, I do.' Aunt Alice's tone was almost reverential. 'A dashing rake but the catch of the season, nonetheless.'

Helena nodded. 'However, I was indisposed, and as Charles could not go alone Rose had a wild idea that she would go in my place ...' she broke off, silence giving greater effect to her next words: 'masquerading as me!'

A small frown of incomprehension creased Aunt Alice's brow. 'I'm sure it would have been perfectly appropriate for her to have gone as herself with Charles as chaperone.'

'Of course it was,' Helena laughed. 'But Rose sometimes has these wild ideas and she doesn't think of the consequences until after she acts. Apparently she had nothing suitable of her own to wear, and it would seem that wearing my clothes filled her with some rather outrageous inspiration. Consequently,' she took a deep breath, 'it appears that Lord Rampton was quite taken with Rose, yet thinks she is ...' she looked around the room, her emerald eyes gleaming with amusement and finished with a staccato, 'me!'

Rose was fuming. Wouldn't Aunt Alice be shocked to learn that her niece by marriage was a gambler who had all but ruined the family, and that Rose's actions had been prompted to save the plantation and only home they had?

Revealing the bald facts was too much of a risk. Aunt Alice was a gossip and any suggestion that the Chesterfields were at the mercy of creditors would severely curtail Arabella's chances.

Rose smiled almost sheepishly at her aunt. 'Lord Rampton was supposed to be leaving for the Continent by the end of the week so it seemed a safe enough deception in view of the fact that I needed to petition him for a little extra time to meet a small debt we owe him.'

'You owe Lord Rampton money?'

Rose felt the heat in her cheeks. Unable to look her aunt in the face she murmured, 'Happily, he has given us until the end of the season. I couldn't have asked for more.'

Aunt Alice clicked her tongue and said, as if Rose were the guilty party, 'Just like your father, and yet he was adored by so many ...' She broke off, as if a thought had occurred to her. 'You say you owe Lord Rampton money? Why, I may just be able to help you. Meanwhile, perhaps all this deception is not such a wicked thing after all.'

Even Helena looked taken aback at this.

Obviously relishing the intrigue Aunt Alice continued, 'From what little I know of Lord Rampton, I gather he is only interested in married ladies...' She pursed her lips like a schoolgirl plotting a great surprise. 'Why, my dear Rose, I think you may have accidentally stumbled upon the only way to call Lord Rampton's bluff. So, as Arabella's chaperone tomorrow night and,' she directed a decidedly crafty glance at Helena, 'yours, Helena, I'll be able to assist in carrying off this perfectly wicked little charade while investigating other avenues for honouring this debt,' her blue eyes twinkled with excitement, 'if it is ever called in.'

CHAPTER 4

HAVING TAKEN LEAVE of two satyrs and a wood nymph, Rampton fingered the cutlass at his belt, slung low upon his hips, and scanned the crowd.

For a moment he regretted his choice of costume. With one eye covered by a black leather eye-patch it was even more difficult to find her amongst the sea of elaborately costumed guests. Surely, if Lady Chesterfield saw him first she would make her presence known?

A frisson of concern tempered his confidence. She'd been angered by what she considered his underhand tactics in luring her to his drawing room the other night.

With a sigh of moral righteousness he drew himself up. Of course he had to warn Lady Chesterfield of the danger Yarrowby posed to her young sister-in-law, even if it had provided a convenient excuse to see her again.

As for the debt, well, he'd much rather absolve her from that in return for her sensual charms though she seemed not as forthcoming with those as he'd been led to believe. He tested the blade of his weapon. Something did not sit right with the picture that Babbage had painted, though outwardly Lady Chesterfield lived up to every detail of his glowing description.

'One of the few villains here, I see.' Glancing down at the owner of the husky voice which had intruded upon his reverie, he smiled at the exquisite Helen of Troy who now swept a pair of stunning emerald eyes from his boots upwards, pausing as they encountered the triangle of chest revealed by the open linen shirt. The young woman tilted her face up to his. 'Most gentlemen, I note, have chosen to parade as their favourite hero.' The full lips curved into a slight smile as she purred, 'I, however, have always found villains much more exciting.'

Rampton returned her admiring look.

'As bold as you are beautiful, fair Helen of Troy,' he said gallantly, bowing over her outstretched hand. 'However, villain that I am, I adhere stringently to convention by never pursuing conversations with beautiful women to whom I have not been properly introduced.'

'We have been introduced, my lord,' the young woman said pertly, adding in response to his enquiring look, 'The other day in the park. You were with my sister-in-law—'

'Forgive me, Miss Chesterfield.' He cut her off, emphasizing her maiden title, 'but as you are a foreigner and apparently unaware of appropriate behaviour for debutantes in this town I feel it my duty to escort you back to your chaperone. Please lead the way.'

Her look of outrage made him smile, however he had no intention of fostering false hopes. The young Miss Chesterfield was undeniably an exquisite creature. To judge by her knowing eyes she was of the kind who would singe a thousand admirers who worshipped at her flame before waltzing off with the prize catch of the season.

And that was not him.

No, Rampton was far more interested in her exquisite sister-in-law, the strangely alluring and quixotic Lady Chesterfield. The brazen beauty at his elbow, now looking more sulky than sultry, was just the one to assist him.

'Allow me to escort you back to your party. Ah, Lady Chesterfield.' He bowed, gratified by the faint blush that bloomed in the young woman's cheeks. Unless she were a master of deception she appeared genuinely discomfited by his presence. 'Your sister-in-law became separated from your group and lost in the crowd. Fortunately, I was on hand to return her,' he swept Helen of Troy a disapproving glance, adding, 'before any damage was done.'

Rose managed a slightly shaken smile, despite amusement at Helena's obvious chagrin, but for all that, she was seriously discomposed. Not just by Lord Rampton's sudden appearance—and what a fine figure he cut in his pirate's rig-out. Nor by the wonderfully disconcerting fact that he looked positively delighted to see her, but by the discovery that he clearly disapproved of young women wandering off alone without their chaperones.

'Thank you, my lord.' Rose directed a chastening frown at Helena, adding reprovingly, 'Take care, next time, my dear. You are no longer a colonial hoyden amongst familiar society.'

As soon as Rampton had left, after claiming a waltz later in the evening from Rose, Lord Yarrowby appeared. Dimpling, Arabella graciously acceded to his request, before gushing excitedly, 'He wants to wait for the waltz. Like Lord Rampton. Oh, Rose, imagine! If we take the fancies of Lord Yarrowby and Lord Rampton, Helena can gamble to her heart's content.'

Helena, directing a singularly unimpressed look at her sister-in-law as Charles returned to her side, placed a graceful hand upon her husband's sleeve and coldly indicated that she wished him to lead her on to the dance floor.

'What Arabella says is entirely true,' declared Aunt Alice when Helena and Charles were out of hearing. 'Two perfect matches! How I wish your mother were here to have seen it.'

The pang of unease that assailed Rose was not prompted by her own behaviour. She glanced at Arabella, who was gazing happily in the direction of her new admirer. Before Rose voiced concern regarding Yarrowby she must investigate whether there was truth in Lord Rampton's allegations. And she must do so before Arabella's feelings progressed beyond youthful adulation.

Yet how could Lord Yarrowby be guilty as charged by Lord Rampton when she had heard not a whisper against him? Dressed as Julius Caesar, a laurel wreath topping his golden curls, Lord Yarrowby looked handsome and boyish, despite his more than thirty years. Rose watched as he turned and perceived Arabella's eyes on him, his own crinkling in response. His extravagant bow caused a blushing Arabella to turn away to collect her disordered wits. The face she presented to her sister shone with excitement.

It was too early to voice caution. Lord Rampton's summons the other afternoon had been nothing more than a ruse to see how willingly Rose would go to him—and believe him. Rampton was clearly conscious of his power over women.

It was time to take him to task.

Thus, when Rose found herself in that gentleman's arms on the dance floor, questioning him about Yarrowby was one way to alleviate the self-consciousness she felt at being in such close proximity, to counter the light-headed sensations that threatened to turn her into a fool, for the aroma of bergamot-scented soap, leather and fresh sweat were a powerfully erotic combination.

Watching an ecstatic Arabella whirl past in Lord Yarrowby's embrace, Rose remarked, 'I can't believe Lord Yarrowby is as bad as you say. He appears such a good-natured gentleman.'

Rampton, executing a tight manoeuvre past a couple who had stumbled, pressed Rose more tightly against his chest. For one wild moment she was possessed by the idea of touching her lips to the triangle of bare flesh revealed by his open pirate's shirt—pretending it an accident, of course— just to see what a man's bare skin actually felt like. Indeed, daring and excitement thrummed through her and she immediately berated herself for missing her opportunity as he resumed the former steady rhythm of the dancing and remarked, conversationally, 'Far more good natured than I am, I daresay.'

'But the other day you said—'

He cut her off. 'With respect, my dear Lady Chesterfield, this is neither the time nor the place. Now,' he finished briskly, as the music slowed to a finish, 'perhaps you would care to admire our host's fine collection of Old Masters.'

A tantalizing offer she dare not accept. 'I can't possibly leave Aunt Alice on her own....'

'Your Aunt Alice looks very pleasantly diverted by that notorious gossip, Lady Rodham. She'll keep her entertained for hours. Now, if that's the best excuse you can come up with ...' Caging her hand on his arm, he led her off the dance floor as if he would countenance no refusal.

And why not? Rose thought, fearful and excited as she followed him, uncertain as to what she felt about the liberties he might take.

Heart pounding, she justified her lack of resistance. What could be the harm in taking a married woman to view a collection of old paintings in a house filled with hundreds of people?

Nevertheless, when they found themselves in the annexe Rose was concerned to discover no evidence of any of the hundreds of guests who had thronged the ballroom as her lack of experience was brought home to her. She was an inexperienced, unmarried woman with a reputation to protect, after all.

She turned to leave but his grip on her upper arm was firm and, as he drew her almost languidly back to him, she felt her defences crumble amidst a myriad of other emotions, not least self-condemnation.

This lasted little more than a second. Now was no time to act the coy maiden. There was Lord Rampton's good will to retain, and the knowledge that discovery would render her a fool, not to mention endangering their good standing with the gentleman to whom they owed so much.

'Lady Chesterfield. Ah, but must I call you that? It is so... matronly.' Placing one finger under her chin he tilted her head so that she was gazing into his eyes, hooded as they lingered on her face.

'You may call me...Lady Rose, if you wish,' whispered Rose as her insides turned to jelly, a sensation accompanied by all the other hallmarks of what she increasingly realised denoted melting desire. Helena was Lady Chesterfield to all who'd been introduced to her since they'd arrived in London while Rose was often referred to by her Christian name.

She closed her eyes while she felt herself enslaved by sensation. His proximity was driving her wild. Heat prickled the surface of her skin and she was conscious of her ragged breathing. She sucked in air sharply at the disconcerting feeling of her nipples puckering beneath her stays, opening her eyes in time to see his beautifully shaped lips moving closer towards hers.

Sense prevailed. She stepped backwards and out of his grasp, affecting a polite, amused smile as she wandered over to stand before one of the paintings. She was a single young woman. Yes, she was mad with desire right now but she also had no desire to be married. Should someone who knew or discovered her real identity walk into this room to find them kissing her reputation would be compromised and his lordship would be under an obligation to marry her.

It was as simple as that.

Oh, but how she longed to feel his arms around her and his lips pressed to hers. Never in all her twenty-six years had she felt like this.

'Although I daresay you can call a woman who owes you a thousand pounds anything you like,' she responded, relieved to have managed to effect a mantle of cool experience. 'I have always admired Lely, haven't you?'

'I must confess to a preference for Van Dyck.' Dropping the intimate tone he appeared at her side to study the painting that had caught her apparent interest. 'A noble calling, don't you think? Committing the world as you see it to canvas, and preserving it for posterity.' He pointed to a portrait. 'The Duchess of Conway. Warts and all. To have painted her as a beauty would have made a mockery of the artist's talent. My brother paints, you know.' He fixed Rose with an appraising look. 'I feel sure that if I asked him he would paint your portrait.'

'And why would you do that, my lord?'

'Because, my dear Lady Rose,' Lord Rampton extended a hand towards her and gently traced the line of her cheek with his forefinger, his words dripping with suggestiveness, 'apart from the fact that such a painting would add to your husband's consequence, it would mean I could spend a great deal more time with you.'

'Cousin Helena!'

Startled by the youth who stepped in front of her, blocking her progress, Helena's momentary confusion was replaced by derision as recognition dawned.

'Master Oswald, I did not recognize you. A common highwayman.' With a curt nod she made to brush past Aunt Alice's stepson, adding, 'And I am not your cousin Helena.' The lad was a spoilt brat, at least three years her junior, and here he was trying to play the swaggering sophisticate. She did not appreciate such forwardness.

Unless it came from a real man like—she licked her lips and felt desire tingling her nerve-endings at the thought of him—Lord Rampton.

'Ah yes, Mama told me! Nevertheless, you are married to my cousin, Charles.' Oswald took a step backwards, impeding her progress. 'Perhaps you would honour me'—slate-grey eyes glittered at her through the slits of his mask—'with the next dance?'

'I wouldn't dance with a highwayman if my life depended upon it.' Removing his gloved hand from her arm, Helena made no attempt to mask her distaste, but after a couple of steps she faltered, discovering to her dismay and irritation that her husband had disappeared, and there was no sign, either, of her sisters-in-law or Aunt Alice. Or, regrettably, his lordship.

'The lady is abandoned?' Oswald's voice sounded in her ear. 'Perhaps, indeed, it is an opportune moment for a dance. Ah, a waltz. Not too daring, I trust?'

He was a good dancer, she allowed him that after he had led her on to the dance floor. After several more glasses of champagne, Oswald didn't seem quite so insufferable, especially as he was so fulsome in his admiration of her.

Obviously he enjoyed talking about himself, like most puffed-up popinjays, and it amused Helena enormously when he suddenly burst out, irritated, 'What you are looking at?'

Raising her head to look into his eyes, she broke into a peal of laughter. 'My reflection in your hessians!'

Oswald, who had been about to respond angrily at the slight, found himself, instead, steadying Helena as she swayed on her feet. 'It would appear the lady is foxed. Come, Cousin Helena, we must find somewhere where you can sit down.'

With little show of gratitude she accepted the orgeat he procured for her as he led her to a small sofa in a secluded annexe between the card room and the ballroom.

'I'd rather have what you're having,' she complained.

'And I'd rather return you to the company at large without besmirching my reputation.'

She hiccupped. 'Your reputation is nothing to be proud of, if what your dear mama says is true.'

'Oh ho, tales from home.' Oswald sounded more amused than angry. 'Incidentally, she's not my mother. She's some addle-brained fool my senile old father married before he jumped ship for the Far East, and now I'm stuck with her until Papa gets called up. Sadly, his Maker appears to be in no hurry.'

'Just as I'm stuck with that addle-headed fool I married until he slips off this mortal coil.' Helena studied the trompe l'oeil on the ceiling while Oswald regarded her with greater interest.

'So the novelty of becoming Lady Chesterfield has lost its lustre ...' He moved a little closer. 'You realize, madam, that there are other avenues for disillusioned married women to pursue?'

'It wasn't my idea not to be Lady Chesterfield,' said Helena petulantly, slapping away Oswald's hand which he had insinuated on to her thigh. 'Your cousin Rose hatched the ridiculous notion that she could do a better job than I of petitioning Lord Rampton for a little favour.' She gave another hiccup. 'Now he's decided not to go to the Continent after all and I'm stuck playing the innocent virgin. I'm sure your mama has exacted the promise of silence from you under pain of death.'

The champagne was having its effect and Oswald's persistent questioning soon ferreted out the details his mother had omitted.

Helena smoothed the silky folds of her diaphanous gown. 'Your mother hinted that she knows how to lay hands on the funds to repay Lord Rampton. I think we're just waiting for someone to die ... though she said she's prepared to lend an advance if that takes too long—'

'Oh, she is, is she?'

'Well, it seems only fair, since your stepmama inherited a fortune while nothing went to Charles and Rose's mama—'

'Because of their late father's faro habit, I believe,' Oswald interjected drily.

'Anyway,' Helena bit back defensively, 'Aunt Alice has no children, for you don't count.'

'Though she has reared me since I was ten years old.' Oswald smiled. 'So Mama is aiding and abetting this wild charade with her usual childish enthusiasm.'

'Yes, although she doesn't quite know the size of the debt owed to Lord Rampton. She just thinks Rose has lost her head to him. Which of course she has. And while I don't care a fig about Rose's reputation, I do care about securing the funds.' She hesitated, then added, 'Charles says if Rose can find a way of absolving us of the debt, he'll buy me a diamond collar.'

The corners of Oswald's thin mouth curled up. 'A diamond collar,' he said, as if much impressed.

'Yes, a diamond collar,' repeated Helena, avarice making her eyes sparkle.

'Well, my dear, I would hate to stand between you and a diamond collar.' His gaze strayed from her face to her décolletage, then back again. He scratched his pointed chin, appearing to ponder the matter. 'In effect, you want to dash your sister-in-law's chances of making good out of this so-called ridiculous charade and win yourself a diamond collar.'

'Yes, and I can't decide which is more important to me.'

Daringly, Oswald plucked at the sheer fabric of Helena's costume, as if to smooth it, and gave a low chuckle. The lovely Helen of Troy was clearly lost in a reverie of sparkling diamonds and heady revenge. Putting his lips to her pretty, seashell ear, he murmured, 'Have you not considered that both might be possible?'

❦

ROSE RETURNED TO FIND AUNT ALICE DEEP IN CONVERSATION WITH Lady Rodham.

'Where's Arabella?' she asked.

The women jerked their heads up almost guiltily.

'She's in safe hands, dancing with Yarrowby,' Aunt Alice reassured her.

'Dancing with Lord Yarrowby—again?' The concern in Rose's voice caused the women to break off their enthusiastically resumed conversation.

'She's made a fine impression on him.' Aunt Alice looked smug.

Rose glanced across the floor and saw Arabella, a fairylike creature in palest pink, supported like a fragile flower in Lord Yarrowby's embrace as he waltzed her around the room.

'We really know very little about Lord Yarrowby, Aunt Alice,' Rose cautioned. 'He appears charming, but ...'

'Only son, set to inherit a vast fortune, and a title that goes back to Henry the Eighth's time. Like Rampton, he'd be a catch of the season. What else do you need to know, my girl?' asked the Lady Rodham. 'A simple lass from the West Indies would struggle to do better.'

'Yes, but what about other ... well, you know ... other associations?' Rose floundered.

'Ay, there've been mistresses. Noble women and dancing girls, alike. What of it?'

Rose felt embarrassed for reacting like the cloistered colonial she was. Of course, many married men of their rank kept mistresses; it wasn't as if Lord Yarrowby had a wife as well.

'Miss Celia Baxter was the most notorious,' Lady Rodham said thoughtfully. 'An opera dancer. Dark-haired, round, ripe and pretty. I saw her at Covent Garden the night London was buzzing over the famous altercation between Rampton and Yarrowby.'

Rose concealed her distress. 'Altercation?'

'Yarrowby was set upon by Lord Rampton in Regent's Park, of all places. In the middle of the afternoon. Quite a scandal it caused, I need not tell you! Pistols at dawn—now that wouldn't have raised an eyebrow. But common street brawling!'

Aunt Alice ventured a surreptitious glance at her niece before quizzing her friend in what was clearly intended to be a tone of no more than casual interest, 'I am shocked. I had heard only good reports of Lord Rampton.'

'Men are brutish by nature.' Lady Rodham made a noise of disgust. 'I'll wager it was over nothing and certainly nothing I'd be worried about if I was planning to throw my daughter Rampton's way.'

'Yes, but what about Lord Yarrowby?' Rose asked with an anxious glance at the gentleman in question, who was now leading Arabella towards them. The thought of Lord Rampton being driven by strong passions for a woman made it hard to breathe.

'A charming man,' Lady Rodham assured her without qualification. What does it matter if their quarrel was over some common little opera dancer? If Yarrowby stole her from Rampton, I'm sure Rampton had fixed his interest elsewhere within a day or two. That's men for you.'

'Your Lord Rampton has a long and shady past,' Helena said brightly, as she swept up to Rose. 'There was even a rumour that he locked one of his mistresses in his tower for seven days before the fair lady's husband discovered her whereabouts. There was a duel over that little scandal, too.'

'Spurious gossip-mongering,' Rose muttered, though her voice lacked conviction. Of course Helena would blithely say the first thing that came to her if she knew it would rattle Rose. She did not like the tumultuous feelings that overcame her, however, when Lady Rodham replied, 'What your sister-in-law says is perfectly true, my dear. Not that it has done his lordship's reputation any harm.'

'Ah, Oswald,' said Aunt Alice, forestalling Rose's reply. 'I'm sure Rose would be delighted to partner you in this set.'

With an ironic bow to Helena, Oswald offered Rose his arm, brushing suggestively against his raven-haired cousin before putting out his hand to steady her.

'Forgive me, Cousin Helena,' he apologized, his eyes raking her salaciously.

Helena tossed her head, only to catch the yearning look her husband sent her from where he was engaged in conversation a few feet away. As Charles took a step towards her Helena lanced him with a look of contempt before feigning sudden interest in Aunt Alice's description of her new bonnet. Tiring quickly of the discussion, and having successfully deflected Charles, she allowed her eyes to stray across the ballroom thronged with exquisitely garbed, rich and titled people who knew not a care in the world while she, Helena ...

Oh, but she was wasted on a sugar plantation far from the world's real excitement with a husband who was as exciting as a yam supper. And how Helena detested yams, though Rose claimed she missed the food of their island home.

Well, Rose was welcome to the West Indies—and Helena fully intended that's exactly where her sister-in-law would be returning. As for herself... Helena was still working on the conundrum as to how she could engineer remaining in England. Certainly for longer than the remaining several months scheduled.

It was in the midst of such ruminations, as she affected the right facial movements in response to Aunt Alice's puerile chatter, that the glimpse of a familiar sardonic leer sent Helena's heart free-falling.

She spun round, her heart plummeting all the way to her slippers as, with a laugh, the object of her horrified fascination excused himself from his portly companion, a clergyman, and stepped into clearer focus. For a moment Helena thought she might faint.

There he was.

William the Conqueror.

She sucked air into her lungs. Conqueror, indeed! After all these years.

She didn't know whether to be filled with joy or fury. Her vision blurred and she had to blink several times.

Geoffrey Albright stood alone by a stone plinth, broader and even more handsome than she remembered. His light-brown hair was a little longer than he used to wear it but his look was just as she remembered: confident, tinged with arrogance, as he surveyed the crowd.

He turned, shock and recognition flaring in the depths of his cool grey gaze when he met her look. Geoffrey Albright, the man she loved and hated in equal measure, was right here in this ballroom, exuding all the familiar dash and heady danger he had all those years ago.

Helena sucked in air as she gripped Rose to steady herself. And as her world spun out of control she swore that *someone* would pay for all she had sacrificed.

CHAPTER 5

'Y OU'RE WHAT?' Rampton looked at his brother as if Felix
had just announced a trip to Outer Mongolia.

'I said I'm spending a few days in Kent. With the Kenilworths.' Felix helped himself to more kippers at the sideboard.
Returning to his seat, he smiled blandly at his brother. 'I take it you've
no objection?'

'You've declined their last three invitations. I don't know why you
suddenly choose to accept now. How long will you be out of town?'

Felix grinned. 'You must have noticed that sweet Cecily is no
longer a child. I actually failed to recognize her at Lady March's
masquerade.'

'You realize, of course, that if you accept this invitation, you'll be
expected to have offered for sweet Cecily before the Season's over.'
Rampton didn't know why he suddenly felt so angry. No, of course that
wasn't true, he amended as he poured himself more coffee. He'd
assumed Felix would be on hand to paint Lady Chesterfield's portrait
and the fact he'd have to wait until his brother had returned from his
jaunt to the country was more than Rampton's already-tried patience
could endure.

Felix scarcely paused as he shovelled the food into his mouth. 'No,

I won't,' he mumbled between mouthfuls. 'Your problem, Rampton, is that you think that when you're handsome and titled, everyone is setting their cap at you. Sweet Cecily could do far better than me, and she knows it. But the glint in her eye told me she'd enjoy my little visit just as much as I would and for exactly the same reasons.' He dabbed delicately at his lips with his napkin and offered his brother a saccharine smile. 'Who knows, perhaps I will offer for her before the Season's over. I certainly don't want to wind up a miserable old bachelor like you. Anyway,' he added, 'I don't know when it's ever been of any concern of yours what I do.' He fixed his brother with a studious look. 'Why, what other plans had you in mind for me?'

'I had hoped you might feel inclined to do a bit of dabbling in oils for a few days.'

'As a matter of fact, the very idea had struck me,' Felix said, rising. 'I intend to preserve the fair Miss Cecily's foxy prettiness for posterity. I suspect her mama will be much too taken with the idea of her daughter's immortalization to object to the many hours we shall necessarily be closeted together.' From the doorway he asked, 'Whose portrait had you in mind that I should paint?'

Rampton shrugged, as if it were of no consequence. 'Obviously you're not going to be here, so it doesn't matter,' he said, rising also and following his brother out of the door.

'Perhaps the fair Helen of Troy whom I saw you manhandle at the masquerade?'

Rampton managed to sound cool though the thought that he'd been blatantly targeted by a calculating debutante was terrifying in the extreme. 'The shameless young woman positively threw herself at me.'

Felix made a pretence of being scandalized. 'No! And don't tell me. She isn't even married? Mark my words, Rampton, you'll get your fingers burned one of these days. However, I'll paint the fair Lady Chesterfield's portrait—as I assume that's what you want—when I return from the Kenilworths.'

Rampton frowned. 'No discussion over remuneration? Why do you accept so readily?'

Felix raised an eyebrow. 'Because, Rampton, your exploits are legion, and I am filled with envy and humility. And it just occurs to me that I have never properly seen you in action.'

Rampton allowed the corners of his mouth to turn up but he remained silent as he contemplated the very delicious idea of being closeted alone with Lady Chesterfield for hours at a time. He was not about to admit the extent to which he'd been affected.

The little chit knew exactly what she was doing and was enjoying this game of cat and mouse, he thought with irritation. Quite clearly, the lacklustre Lord Chesterfield was as exciting as a wet rag and she'd singled out Rampton for more than just the benefits of absolving herself of her debt. The fact she'd chosen to pursue him using blushing innocence as her bait, was a novel change, he supposed, to the jaded sophistication employed by most married women. But it did mean the chase was a little more drawn-out than he'd have liked.

His reverie was broken by Felix's laugh. 'Just make sure you're discreet when you finally succeed in bedding this fair creature with whom I can see you're entirely obsessed.'

'Oh, I don't think her husband is a concern."

'It's not her husband I was referring to," Felix said over his shoulder from half way up the stairs to his quarters. 'Jealous adversaries of the female variety can be far more dangerous.'

'Oh, you mean the baroness?'

'She's not the only one. I mean, Rampton, you're the catch of the season." Felix grinned. 'Just be careful.'

WHEN ROSE RECEIVED A HASTILY SCRAWLED NOTE FROM HER AUNT Alice after she'd dressed herself for the morning she had no idea as to the reason for the peremptory summons. Especially knowing her aunt was laid up in bed with a nasty head cold.

Alice was certainly playing the invalid to the hilt when Rose was announced. She was propped up in bed on pillows, a scented flannel upon her brow but her eyes were bright and her voice eager. Indicating a chair at her side she gushed, 'My dear girl, I am so glad you came so promptly. Now, tell me, what communication have you had with your father's family since he died?'

Rose tried to think. 'Why, none,' she replied. 'That is ... not since the condolences.'

'Ah.' Alice smiled knowingly. 'Do you perhaps recall your father's Aunt Gwendolyn? An older half-sister of his mother?'

Rose looked blank, though she had an inkling as to where this was heading.

Aunt Alice sat up straighter, the sudden exertion causing a fit of coughing. Waving aside the glass of water Rose offered her she said, 'My dear, I've just heard the most wonderful news.'

'Yes?' Rose suspected that what Alice considered wonderful involved a corpse or two.

'Lady Rodham came to visit me last night. She mentioned the death of the son of a dear friend of hers, a certain Obediah Pike. At first I didn't take much notice, but the name sounded familiar. It wasn't until this morning that it struck me. Obediah was the only child of your father's Aunt Gwendolyn. Well,' Aunt Alice wrapped her shawl more tightly round her, warming to her theme, 'I had one of my lads make enquiries first thing, and I was right!' Falling back into the pillows, her expression was full of expectation as she searched her niece's face.

'Well?' she demanded in response to Rose's silence. 'Say something!'

Rose hesitated. 'Poor Mr Pike,' she said, lamely.

'Yes, yes, and pity his mother too,' Alice said impatiently. 'The thing is, it won't be long before Gwendolyn starts thinking about her heirs, now that her only son is dead and she an invalid. She never was very close to her natural brother and sister, but was quite attached to your father at one time. My dear Rose,' she rubbed her hands together, 'the time has come to pay your Great-Aunt Gwendolyn a visit. But first I'll take you to my dressmaker!'

Rose chewed her thumb nail and contemplated the possibilities an unexpected windfall—whether it was from Great-Aunt Gwendolyn's quarter, or elsewhere— suggested.

If she were able to repay Lord Rampton's debt she'd have no reason to see him again. It was a dampening thought. The intensity with which he'd gazed into her eyes had quite clearly conveyed his interest in her. As for herself, simply conjuring up his image was enough to make her breath come fast and shallow and her body react in all manner of unexpected ways. She fanned herself with the book Aunt Alice had just asked her to read to her as she tried to master her emotions using her usual ally, common sense. Clearly, she must have misinterpreted his lordship. She was a married woman as far as he was concerned so there could obviously be no deeper association between them than existed now.

But it was disquieting to know what a slave she was becoming to her feelings for him. No, she decided, clearing her voice to begin a novel titled *Sense and Sensibility*, which surely preached the virtues she must uphold, there could be no future with the handsome viscount for so many reasons, meaning she should limit any contact she had with him.

That meant accompanying Aunt Alice to visit her Great-Aunt Gwendolyn with the hope the old lady would see fit to remember her fondness for Rose's father through a bequest to his all-but impoverished family. A bequest that would enable them to pay Helena's debt which would therefore remove the need to ever have dealings with Lord Rampton again.

This was a more dampening thought than any Rose had entertained to date.

❧

SITTING IN FRONT OF A SMALL FIRE IN THE DRAWING ROOM, Charles laid down the law. Reluctantly, Rose agreed that accompanying everyone to Almack's after dinner was unwise, telling herself for the thousandth time that she must avoid opportunities that would only inflame her dangerous infatuation with the gentleman to whom they owed so much. At Lord Rampton's dinner which was to precede the outing to Almacks, she need only respond when spoken to directly, and allow Charles to speak whenever possible on her behalf.

Aunt Alice had nearly secured the funds that would enable them all to sail honourably home after Arabella had contracted a suitable match, he told them. Therefore Rose had no further reason to court the good offices of Lord Rampton.

Rose glanced across at her brother, who was still talking, his tone now fearful. 'But, why has Lord Rampton invited us to dine? You don't think he's changed his mind and is going to call in the debt *immediately*, do you?'

'I expect we'll just have to wait until the turbot in chive sauce to find out, darling.' Helena's voice drifted across the room from where she sat playing cards. As usual, her sarcasm seemed not to faze Charles.

Raking his fingers through his thin pale hair he addressed Rose, who sat opposite him, with contrived firmness. 'Now, you're to behave yourself, Rose. Your conduct last time we dined with Rampton was scandalous and deeply embarrassing.'

'Well, I for one wouldn't miss it for the world,' interjected Helena. Rose bit her lip and forced herself to remain silent. She was usually good at wheedling her brother into doing things for which he had no enthusiasm, but she recognized that, in this matter, the least said the better. He could dig his heels in at any moment and state categorically that she should not be allowed to go. And the sad truth was that she couldn't bear that to happen, having decided that tonight's dinner must be the last time she enjoyed Lord Rampton's company.

'Watching Rose at the masquerade, anyone would think she was quite a woman of the world,' Helena added, appearing at her husband's side and resting a hand on his shoulder. 'With vast experience of men.'

Rose quelled the impulse to defend herself. 'Are you still put out that he rejected the advances of the fair Helen of Troy by bringing you back to your chaperone so smartly?'

'I was simply put out at being treated like a silly little debutante— all on account of your silly little deception,' Helena said, coolly.

If Rose felt angered by her sister-in-law's remark then, she was able to enjoy a sense of victory later that evening as their host gazed at her across the table with blatant admiration.

'You're not missing anything, Lady Chesterfield, if you elect not to accompany the rest of your family to Almack's.' Lord Rampton's tone was intimate; and of course Rose should have been embarrassed by the fact that he had eyes only for her and that dinner, as on the first occasion on which they had met, was almost a tête-à-tête between them. Charles was again rendered virtually mute by a mixture of awe and helpless indignation, while Helena contributed little because it seemed she was playing the debutante to the hilt.

Yes, Rose should have felt embarrassed. Instead, she felt exultant.

'Its reputation is quite undeserved.' Rampton's eyes were once more drawn to Rose as he added, 'I have never understood the lengths the public will go to be admitted. Desire will have people do extraordinary things.' His voice was like a caress. Rose plucked at the neckline of the gown Helena had lent her and wondered whether the others noticed the viscount's interest. It certainly could not have escaped Helena's attention.

'I'm told the strongest refreshment served is orgeat,' she said. 'Not even champagne punch. And that Lady Jersey and the other patronesses wield enormous power.'

'A mere whiff of scandal will have one banned from their hallowed precincts,' said Helena. 'Which is enough to destroy anyone who has social pretensions. Still,' she added, virtuously, 'scandal is only dangerous to those careless enough to get caught.'

Rampton gave a short laugh. 'Hypocrisy is alive and well, Miss Chesterfield.' He rubbed his jaw and added, with a disarmingly frank look at Rose, 'Alas, subterfuge is often the only defence when one is a slave to duty and one's family's dynastic ambitions.'

Rose felt herself blush to the roots of her hair. Of course he could know nothing of her own deception. Nevertheless, it was a wounding remark to make in any husband's hearing, and Rose sent an anxious glance across to Charles. It appeared that he'd not registered Rampton's words. He was gazing at Helena whose sharp eyes followed the exchange between Rose and Rampton.

'Phew!' Charles whistled once they were back in their carriage, relaxing into the squabs with apparent relief before glaring at Rose. 'This is madness! Why on earth do we persist with this ridiculous charade? When will Aunt Alice tell us whether we have the money to pay the man, or not? If we don't, I'd rather come clean with his lordship and to hell with the consequences.'

'It certainly was none of my idea,' Helena pointed out, self-righteously. 'But darling Rose swears her stalling tactics are necessary to give Aunt Alice time to lay her hands on the necessary funds, and that scandal and humiliation are in store for all of us if her fraud should be revealed.'

Rose didn't enter into the argument, only pushed aside the curtain to look into the darkened streets. The back of her neck prickled with a mixture of guilt and desire. Of course she should never have got themselves into such a mess, but revealing the truth was too dangerous and had the potential to cause a scandal that would damage Arabella's chances.

She had always prided herself on her sense of duty, yet nothing now seemed important when compared with the pleasure of Lord Rampton's company. It wasn't just that he was handsome and exuded a magnetism she'd never encountered before. No, for the first time she knew what it was like to be fêted as a beautiful and desirable woman, just as Helena was constantly feted. And the feeling was irresistible.

She listened as the rain beat loudly on the carriage roof and felt the carriage jerk as the horses responded to the coachman's whip. Not only was she in love, she relished the freedom that her disguise as a married woman gave her. Longing tugged at her heart and she closed her eyes, despair curdling in her stomach as she reflected upon Lord Rampton's obvious desire: a desire she had no choice but to resist.

She was glad when the others deposited her at their town house before going out again to spend the rest of the evening at Almack's. She must wean herself off this dangerous man who made her feel things she should not, and want things she knew she could never have. Her heart was not important. As long as they repaid Rampton his debt they could return to their plantation after seeing Arabella contract a wonderful match....

Yarrowby?

She felt a moment's discomfort at the thought of Lord Rampton's warning but she rallied at the memory of Lady Rodham's description of two young men fighting in Regent's Park. Rampton and Yarrowby had clashed over a woman. Clearly, rivalry was at the root of Lord Rampton's caution. And all over a common opera-dancer or actress.

'Miss Rose, you have a visitor.' Edith stood in the doorway, her grey hair hanging down her shoulder in one heavy plait, a thick shawl wrapped about her shoulders.

Rose put down the book she was reading and glanced, surprised, at the clock. 'It's nearly ten o clock.'

'It's Lord Rampton.' Closing the door quietly behind her, Edith crossed the room. 'Fortunately no one else saw him.' She spoke softly. 'I was able to leave him to wait in the library while I enquired as to whether you were receiving visitors at this late hour.'

Rose felt the colour flood her face. Lord Rampton? Did gentlemen really visit married ladies at such a late hour? But then, if no one but Edith and seen him....

She tossed the book to the floor, sat up straight. 'Oh, Edith,' she whispered urgently. 'What shall I do?'

'Do you want to see him or not?'

'Oh yes!' Embarrassed by such a heartfelt and spontaneous admission, she added, 'Well ... I daresay I shouldn't, should I? I mean ... what would Charles say?'

'We would never tell Sir Charles,' declared Edith, as if Rose were mad. Her pale eyes shone. 'And what harm could there be in receiving a gentleman caller? I would be near by if you needed me.'

Rose blinked. Could Edith, who had always been such a stickler for proprieties, be encouraging her to do something which would cause any self-respecting mama to die of shame? Or would it? That is, if it were never made public? It did not require much persuasion.

'Lord Rampton is greatly taken with you, Miss Rose. He is not here on account of the debt he is owed.' Edith gripped her wrists, her meaning never clearer. She'd devoted her life to Rose and her siblings and was as vigilant as any designing mama. 'Make the most of your chance, Miss Rose.' The urgency in her tone infused Rose with daring. 'It does not knock at your door every day. You are unmarried and he is in need of a wife.'

Shocked and excited by Edith's approval, while ignoring the inherent conflict created by her deception, Rose tilted up her chin and took a deep breath. Then, like a woman of the world who was used to such requests, and not the green girl she really was, she said, 'Yes, tell him to come.'

The wave of anticipation that flooded her as he was announced was nearly overwhelming but she managed to retain her composure with the observation that she'd discussed Byron with him over his dinner table, calmly and intelligently, not two hours since. Now he faced her, tall and broad-shouldered, his eyes impossible to read. He had come seeking her out. Her and her alone.

Not that his first words indicated this. 'I see you are unaccompanied, Lady Chesterfield,' he remarked casually, as if this surprised him.

'You know very well that I'm alone.' Her voice was low as she watched him carefully. Why had he come? What did he want? 'We discussed this evening's plans over your dinner table.'

'Ah yes,' he said in a low voice, taking a step forward and standing just a little to the right of the fire so that he did not block her heat. Not that there was any need for such a gesture. Rose's temperature was rising rapidly.

His eyes held hers and a smile curled the corners of his lips. This time Rose had no response. Her heart thudded so painfully she wondered whether he could hear it. She schooled herself to remain still, not to squirm with embarrassment or appear too eager. Nor to turn him away with a lack of enthusiasm.

'I looked in at Almack's briefly.' He remained standing a few feet from her, his hands clasped behind his back. 'In case you had chosen to accompany your family, after all. When I saw you had not I was concerned ...' His voice trailed away and his intensely blue eyes bored into hers before he added softly, 'that you might be lonely.'

Still Rose made no rejoinder. It was hard enough just forcing herself to breathe. Every nerve ending was like a taut violin string, heat prickled the surface of her skin and the most unbearable longing threatened to turn her into a fool. No, she had no choice but to wait, then act accordingly.

'Come here,' he said, softly, and Rose felt her body answer the summons before her mind had time to fully comprehend. Before she had registered what she was doing she had closed the distance between them and was abandoning good sense with the breath that left her body in a whoosh as she raised her lips to meet his.

There were no gentle preliminaries. Hot and demanding, his mouth covered hers as he cupped her face, almost drinking her in and she, seemingly boneless, wilted in his embracem her arms twining behind his neck.

His lips were soft and warm, a contrast to the faint roughness of stubble upon his jaw that grazed her skin. The sensation was inflammatory, his touch searing as he growled, 'I've looked forward to this moment since I first laid eyes on you,' before resuming his passionate assault, his hands roaming over her body, cupping her bottom as he drew her against him.

Dear Lord, it was terrifying, and it was wicked and oh, so exhilarating. She was an innocent. Inexperienced. She knew she should be shocked by the liberties and the jutting angles of his masculinity but her body answered with equal ardour as she tightened her grip and her tongue tangled with his in a dance of seduction that could have no happy resolution—but she could take what he offered, now, and she'd have that to sustain her for the rest of her days.

She squirmed at the disconcerting feeling of molten liquid pooling in her lower belly but she only pressed herself closer for in the drawing room she was still mistress of her own destiny and her reputation was preserved. She could show him how much she desired him but when he released her, here it would end.

'You are wicked, my lord,' she told him, kissing his ear, running her palms over the roughness of his angular cheekbones and revelling in his caresses, arching into him as he contoured her body without shame.

'And you are a minx, Lady Rose,' he muttered against her throat, drawing back at the sound of heavy footsteps in the passage, and adding, just before Edith made her presence known, 'but don't you think you've got the better of me.'

Rose widened her eyes and smiled into his face, still only inches from hers. 'Time will tell, my lord,' she said, with emphasised coquetry. She sighed as she stepped backwards and out of his embrace. 'I am mindful of the fact I am deeply in your debt.'

He reached out one hand to stroke her jawline. 'Yes, you would indeed do well to bear that in mind,' he murmured. 'I am growing impatient to call in that damned debt.'

CHAPTER 6

ROSE WAS STILL awake and churning with excitement over her wicked encounter when she heard the others return home. At the top of the stairs Arabella's voice sounded sleepy as she bade everyone good night but Helena's was sharp and Rose wasn't sure if it her words were intended to be heard as she said, near Rose's door, 'When are you going to take your sister to task and demand that she have nothing more to do with Lord Rampton? He's dangerous.'

'You think it wise to expose the charade at this juncture?' Charles sounded nervous, as well he might, and Rose cringed at the knowledge that she'd forced it upon all of them, without real thought for the consequences.

Helena sighed. 'No, I'll continue to play the innocent virgin but Rose is out of her depth. Do you not see how she turns into a blushing fool the moment he looks at her? As soon as Aunt Alice secures these funds she's promised I think it's time to send Rose out of London and far from this danger she's courting.'

Rose jerked into a sitting position, her pulses racing as terror and dismay skittered through her. *Send her away?* The idea of never again seeing Lord Rampton when this evening had only reinforced how deep her feelings were for him was intolerable.

Yes, he *was* dangerous but Rose could manage the situation. There were only a few weeks until they'd be returning to the West Indies. *Please*, she found herself exhorting the fates, just allow her this once opportunity to discover what love really was all about and then she'd meekly accompany Charles and Helena home and never complain again.

With such pining thoughts chasing away the practicalities which normally occupied Rose, it was difficult, the next morning, to concentrate as her Aunt Alice expounded upon the possibilities inherent in a recently-received invitation from their fabulously wealthy Great-Aunt Gwendolyn.

'She wishes you to call on her,' Aunt Alice told her as they took a turn about the rose bushes. 'She's very ill, you know. The end is expected daily.'

Rose stopped and stared at her aunt. 'But—' she began.

'Yes, yes, I didn't waste time, my dear.' Aunt Alice beamed. 'And nor did she. This could make all the difference to your prospects, you know, Rose, if Lord Rampton considers a sizeable marriage portion a necessary part of the settlement.' She floundered for a second. 'Which is not to suggest that I doubt your ability to entrance him of your own accord.'

This was something Rose had not considered and she drew in a quick breath. If Rose came with a dowry, would Lord Rampton exhibit the same interest in her? Helena had said he was only interested in married women as if that precluded any possibility of him being a genuine suitor for Rose—under any circumstances. Could that be true?

They resumed walking. 'In all good conscience,' sighed Rose, gathering her wits, 'I can't visit Aunt Gwendolyn like some blood-sucking relative.' However, it was hard to concentrate on the conversation when her mind kept running over how Lord Rampton would react if he discovered he'd been deceived. Then she counselled herself, all that really mattered as far as Lord Rampton was concerned was that he was paid the money he was owed. And that was what Rose was intent on doing.

'My dear, Rose,' he aunt was saying, patiently, 'your Aunt Gwendolyn is, if nothing else, pragmatic. Her fortune must be left to someone and she has little love for the *other* blood-sucking relatives who are suddenly offering their condolences.'

At Rose's continued silence she persisted, 'So, you will call on your Great-Aunt Gwendolyn soon? The poor soul would so enjoy the company. She is quite bereft.'

Rose was soon to discover this a lie on both counts.

'I don't know how many times I told that lazy good-for-nothing boy of mine that whist would be the death of him,' pronounced Aunt Gwendolyn in what Rose discovered was the old woman's characteristic hiss, and not the vestiges of a bad throat. 'Gaming! Were I prime minister it would be outlawed and punishable by transportation.' She drew in a laboured breath, exhaling on an even more venomous hiss. 'He was raking it in when his heart gave out and he landed with his nose in the middle of his pile of coin. Obediah never knew how to deport himself!'

'I'm so sorry,' Rose said in tones that she hoped sounded passably sympathetic. Not that the wizened old face which peeped from the starched frills of Great-Aunt Gwendolyn's white lace bonnet appeared in need of cosseting or sympathy.

'So.' She gave Rose a beady look, her eyes travelling from the top of the curling feather that adorned Rose's bonnet to the tips of her slippers. 'I see you favour your father. Now there was a notable rake, to be sure!' There was admiration in her tone. 'Broke a dozen hearts and kicked up a lot of dust before he married your mother—for love!' She made a noise indicating disgust. 'Worst mistake either of them ever made. He needed someone strong to keep his dangerous impulses in check. Not some whining, puling beauty who'd be the death of him. Make no mistake about that! Were you to have favoured her I'd have given you short shrift for sitting at my bedside with only one thing on your mind: my fortune.'

'With respect, ma'am, Aunt Alice insisted that I came. I have as little desire to be sitting at your bedside as you do to be entertaining me.'

'Miss Alice Wentworth! Addle-headed muttonhead who runs

around in terror of that stepson of hers. Oswald! Now there's a nasty piece of goods. If the whisperings I've heard are true he should be sent packing to the Peninsula or transported.'

'Aunt Alice has been very good to me.'

The old woman shrugged and her small black eyes seemed to sink into the folds of her wrinkled flesh. 'Perhaps more so than you might suppose.' Her eyes flashed. 'The irony is I'll never see the reaction of those grasping relatives upon finding they'd been passed over in favour of the daughter of my disgraced half-nephew, eh? A girl who only turned up at my deathbed to inveigle her way into a fortune.' She pursed her lips and watched for Rose's reaction.

'Why would you do anything so addle-headed?' Rose knew she was being tested. 'When I am nothing to you?'

'Except the vehicle of my malicious pleasure.' The old woman gave a gusty sigh and turned her head. 'But you're not the first to whom I've intimated such intentions.' When Rose did not respond she swivelled a sidelong glance at her. 'I'm tired,' she said, petulantly. 'It's time for you to go, young lady. Rose? That was your name, wasn't it?'

⚜

AT LAST. RAMPTON FELT SATISFACTION COURSE THROUGH HIM AS HE raked his eyes over lovely Lady Chesterfield...*his* Lady Rose...whom he'd just ushered into Felix's studio. His brother was to do the preliminary sketch of his subject in his artist's studio, a quaint circular room on the second floor of the tower.

It had not been easy. The lady really was determined to make him sweat over this protracted courtship, for she'd declined his offer to be painted twice until he'd approached her husband and stated, baldly, that his brother, a noted portraitist, had a week only in which to render her likeness; that her good fortune would inspire envy amongst the ton, inferring that this could only be a good thing.

Rampton increasingly got the impression that there was little of substance in the relationship between Sir Charles and the intoxicating little minx that was making Rampton's life hell.

Fortunately Sir Charles had waved one of his long-fingered, ineffectual hands in the air and muttered something about being honoured, whereupon Rampton had fixed a time, there and then.

Now she was here and he was aware of his urgency to have her almost as if it were a living thing co-existing within himself. If he couldn't orchestrate the necessary solitude so that he could begin to make the most of the few short weeks left to them he thought he'd go mad.

Watching the play of emotions across her mobile features, Rampton considered how unlike she was from the worldly women whose company he usually sought. His brother, a short distance away, was mixing paints but he'd already been coached on what signals indicated he must leave them to it—and not return.

'What an inspirational view,' said the young woman, impressing him by her artless tone as she went to the large windows. *Ha! As if she didn't know what game they were playing.* 'I know your brother shall do a famous job in painting me.'

A stab of jealousy surprised Rampton. Wishing he were the one wielding a paintbrush, he replied, 'He'll have me to answer to if he fails to capture your perfection.'

Her shy laugh touched him, surprisingly, with something beyond the baseness of his intentions. Impulsively he moved towards her, hesitating at the last moment, for clearly she was not priming herself for passion. Good God, he was on the verge of asking permission for a kiss. When had he ever felt the need to ask permission? It was why he associated only with married women. The rules were established. Each knew exactly where they stood with one another. Conversation was sophisticated and entertaining and expectations not unrealistic.

Mind you, there had been surprising exceptions, the most recent being Catherine Barbery, whom he'd always considered the most aloof and detached of his paramours. She'd exhibited an uncharacteristic show of jealousy when he had – with great tact and predictability, he'd thought at the time – severed their relationship the evening after he'd met Lady Chesterfield.

He was ashamed to recall that her tears had elicited in him a strong desire to put as much distance as possible between them.

The flicker of surprise in Lady Chesterfield's clear blue gaze as she realized what he was after, followed quickly by delight, nudged at some unrealised tenderness within him. She was enchanting. A quixotic mixture of intelligence, strength and disarming naivety. Standing before her in the tower room he imagined himself the knight in shining armour who must once have stood at these very windows, wielding bow and arrow to protect his fair lady.

When was the last time he had thought like that? Had he ever? Certainly not in relation to the dozen or more beauties he'd taken as his mistress since he had graduated from the schoolroom. Rampton had not ever considered himself ready to pledge himself to a single woman and what he felt now was decidedly uncharacteristic.

'I prefer what's inside the tower room to the view outside,' he said, savouring the clean, fresh scent of orange blossom water as he enfolded her in his arms.

Her face tilted upwards. Gently he kissed the tip of her nose, preparing to signal to his brother to leave them ... before the sounds of approaching girlish chatter made him freeze. Surely not?

Lady Chesterfield stepped back, her expression regretful as she ran her hand across his cheek and he said, through gritted teeth, 'Do not tell me, madam, that you have come with an army of attendants.'

The door was thrown open before she could answer and there was the admittedly beautiful but dangerously forward Miss Chesterfield, whose intimate smile only served to highlight why he was so wary of designing debutantes.

'I'm told you can see the dome of St Paul's. Ah, Lord Rampton, Mr Felix...' This was delivered in a breathy gasp as Felix stepped forward while Rampton quickly dropped Lady Chesterfield's hands and felt his rising frustration assume monumental proportions.

'Mr Felix, how clever you must be to paint my sister-in-law. How many sittings do you think you'll need?'

'Three,' said Felix at the same time as his brother nominated 'five', adding with a laugh, 'Although Lady Casterton needed seven to get the proportions of her monstrous nose right.'

'Well, Rose has a little nose – too little, really, for the proportions of her face,' said the young woman with a guileless smile, 'so I'm sure it won't take as long.'

Rampton felt his protective instincts rise to the fore. 'Perhaps you are envious, Miss Chesterfield, if you feel the need to criticize. Lady Chesterfield could not be improved upon. However,' he continued, softening, 'I'm sure if you asked my dear brother nicely enough he would paint your likeness, too.'

'I doubt that brothers are so appreciative of their sisters' likenesses staring down at them from the breakfast parlour wall,' responded the young woman with a sigh.

Briskly, Rampton said, 'If it is to be finished before the charming Chesterfields leave England Felix will have to work hard—without interruptions.' With a meaningful look at Lady Chesterfield, he bowed over her hand, adding, 'Madam, what about Thursday, in the morning when the light is best, for your next sitting?'

Two days from now. It seemed to Rampton an eternity before he could spend time alone with her. In the meantime, though, he might manage an intimate moment's conversation or two at Catherine Barbery's ball, an entertainment for which he had little enthusiasm but which he'd felt obliged to agree to attend.

He levelled a challenging look at Helena and Arabella. 'My mother intends calling on me on Thursday. She has been quizzing me tirelessly about the West Indies and indicated that she wished to meet Lady Chesterfield most particularly.' He frowned at Helena. 'I understand you young ladies are committed to a dancing lesson.'

'As is my dear sister-in-law,' said Helena sweetly.

'Then it's just as well that she is already such an exquisite dancer.' He sent a colluding look towards his alluring Lady Rose, 'So, Thursday morning it is.'

'Thursday morning I have made other arrangements,' said Felix, testily, when he finally put down his charcoal having rendered a preliminary sketch after their visitors had gone.

Rampton grinned. 'Perfect.'

'OH, LOOK! A PARCEL!' REMOVING HER BONNET AS THE THREE GIRLS entered the drawing room, Arabella darted towards the low table on which the small, beautifully wrapped item lay.

'It's addressed to Lady Chesterfield.' Edith's tone was uncertain as Arabella handed the cigar-shaped box to her sister-in-law, who frowned as she scanned the accompanying card before thrusting the parcel at Rose.

'A paean to Lady Chesterfield's fiery tresses,' she said with disgust, 'which would suggest it was not intended for *this* Lady Chesterfield.'

Heart thumping, Rose lifted the lid, then gasped as she beheld the magnificent gift: a diamond necklace composed of alternating flower-heads and entwined oval links.

'Oh Rose, I've never seen anything so beautiful. Why, no man would give such a gift if he didn't intend to make an offer,' gabbled Arabella, who immediately put her hand to her mouth, blushing. 'But of course, Lord Rampton doesn't know he's free to make an offer. Why, you must tell him—'

Edith cut in sharply, 'Miss Rose will not be accepting the gift.'

One look at Edith's grim look stayed Rose's objection, but it was Helena who said, frowning, 'I believe I've seen it before.'

All eyes turned upon her as she reached for the priceless article and studied it carefully. 'I don't believe it's paste, either,' she gasped. 'But why...?' she shook her head and Rose, desperate to know what she was alluding to, asked, 'Are you sure? Where have you seen it?'

Slowly Helena handed it back, still frowning. 'You are very fortunate to have won the esteem of such a gentleman, Rose. You will indeed make all our fortunes.' Suddenly she smiled. 'As for where I've seen it, I believe it was displayed in the window of a jewellery shop. Yes, I'm sure of it.' She turned to Edith. 'And why must Rose not wear it? It is but a trinket compared with what Lord Rampton is owed, yet it would offend him if his gesture were refused ... and Rose seems willing to go to any lengths to please our esteemed friend.'

Edith's voice was tight. 'I will not see Miss Rose compromised over this.'

In the tense silence Rose caressed the intricately fashioned gift while her insides churned. Was Lord Rampton in the habit of such generosity? Could he really admire her so greatly as to believe her worthy of such extravagance? She knew the answer already. Lord Rampton considered her favours worthy of such extravagance, but Edith was right. She'd gone too far already and it was time to focus on Aunt Alice's avenues of repayment. However much her own body yearned for Lord Rampton's caresses and her mind considered the risks worth taking, she could not compromise herself and thus her family.

'You are harsh, Edith, when no Chesterfield woman has received anything as fine as this,' Helena complained, fingering the thin gold chain around her neck.

The argument that followed was short and decisive. 'Miss Rose will not have her reputation besmirched in order to repay *your* debt, my lady,' Edith said, pointedly.

But it seemed that Helena was not too chagrined to make her own generous offer to Rose later that evening when visiting her in her dressing room.

'After all, you're on a mission to repair the damage I've caused so I must support you,' Helena said, offering Rose the diaphanous gold-and-green silk and net gown she'd not yet worn. 'Charles has said how important it is to keep Lord Rampton on side while Aunt Alice secures the funds to repay him.'

Rose took the gown Helena proffered and stroked the lustrous fabric while she waged an internal war between wanting to accept the loan while at the same time wondering at Helena's motives.

'You don't trust me, do you?' Helena asked after a silence. 'You can't believe I'd lend you my most fashionable gown and meekly accept the role you conferred upon me while you masquerade as me the entire season.'

Rose sat down on the bed, the gown across her knees. 'No.'

Helena never acted charitably without an ulterior motive. Helena hated Rose. Rose had known this deep within her since the day Helena had become Charles's wife. She wasn't certain why. Surely it wasn't that she was jealous of Rose. Helena was far more beautiful than Rose and Charles doted on Helena, lavishing clothes, jewellery and attention upon his wife while barely catering to Rose and Arabella's needs.

'Perhaps it would appear more in character if I told you I'm enjoying being Charles's sister far more than being his wife.' Helena's voice was cold. 'As his unmarried sister I can flutter my eyelashes at every eligible gentleman who takes my fancy and know I'm driving Charles mad with jealousy.'

The syrupy sweetness of her smile stuck in Rose's craw. Her first instinct was to leap up, grip Helena's shoulders and shake her, demanding that she speak of Charles with respect. Taking a deep breath, she straightened. 'Charles married you, Helena, despite the whispers that were circulating about you,' she said in a low voice. It took all her self control to maintain her composure. 'You owe him everything.' With difficulty she swallowed. 'Charles loves you more than anyone ever will.'

Helena's eyes blazed. 'What is that worth when everything I ever wanted has been torn from me?' Her bosom heaved. 'What does it feel like to love Lord Rampton? Well, I loved a man a thousand times more than that, and those whispers, as you so lightly refer to them, became the rumours that were fanned by *you*, Rose.'

Her words were like a slap in the face. Rose had no idea what she was talking about; only that Helena's sense of injustice was very real. In a faint voice, she said, 'I don't know what you mean. I never meant to cause you any harm—'

'It no longer matters.' Angrily, Helena pushed the garment into Rose's hands before marching to the door. She turned. 'I married Charles and must make the best of things. A woman's lot is to make the best of things, isn't it?' Her eyes glittered while her mouth twisted in a smile. 'So you must wear a gown that does you justice so *you* can make the best of things. You need to keep our dear Lord Rampton sweet so that my little debt doesn't ruin us all. I'm counting on you, Rose.'

Rose bit her lip, her mind churning over the identify of the gentleman to whom Helena referred. Had she really been responsible for rumours which had ruined Helena's happiness? If so, she'd had no idea about it at the time.

'Helena, I'm sorry if—'

Helena raised her hand for silence. 'It's in the past, Rose,' she ground out. 'But just remember this, every woman must pay for her happiness. It is our punishment.'

WITH DISQUIET ROSE DONNED HELENA'S GOLD-AND-GREEN SILK FOR the ball that evening before Edith arrived to fashion Rose's thick chestnut-coloured hair into the graceful, flattering style which had won her such approval lately. Why had she never realized the difference clothes and hair made to a woman?

But inevitably this reflection was tainted by the thought that life would soon be very different once she was back in the West Indies. Tainted also by reflections over what Helena had said, though she tried hard to dismiss that as she did most of what Helena said in order to make everyone else feel they were responsible for the bad hand she obviously felt life had dealt her.

No, Rose knew that when they returned to the plantation hard work would take precedence over all. As her mind turned to the next few weeks, the familiar knot of worry lodged in her throat. What was to be done about the debt to Lord Rampton?

Not for one moment could she happily assume her great-aunt would leave her a groat.

Lord Rampton himself refused to discuss the matter. She had tried to broach it on the dance floor but he just laughed that deep, sardonic laugh of his and changed the subject. Then he tightened his grip on her.

It left her confused. He seemed to be reading from a subtext she couldn't quite understand, though increasingly the thought of tomorrow's sitting to Mr Felix terrified and excited her. The wanton longings of her body reminded her she must be careful and that she should take comfort in the knowledge that Lord Rampton's brother and mother would be in attendance. Whatever happened, preserving her reputation and good name was just as important as repaying Helena's debt.

LATER THAT NIGHT, WITH JUST AN HOUR BEFORE THEY WERE DUE TO depart for Lady Barbery's ball-assembly, Rose met Helena in the passage. Her exotic sister-in-law looked like an exquisite bird of paradise, dressed in celestial blue lutestring with gold trimmings and for a brief moment Rose was filled with envy. Helena never suffered pangs of guilt or momentary loss of countenance. Why, at this very moment, Rose's insides were churning with fear and indecision as to how she would best negotiate her dealings with Lord Rampton while Helena looked as fresh as a gardenia.

'Why aren't you wearing the necklace Lord Rampton gave you?' Helena's tone was sharp as her eyes skimmed Rose from head to toe. There was no approval in her look.

'You heard Edith. What she said was true.'

'Do you think Edith knows more about the rules of society than you—or I?'

She touched the modest chain that hung at Rose's throat. 'I would never have lent you such a beautiful gown if I'd known you'd insult it with such an inferior jewel. Who gave you that?'

Before Rose could express her anger – for Helena knew perfectly well that Charles had given the gold chain to her – her sister-in-law gripped her arm.

'Come!' She dragged Rose up the passage to her own room and pushed her on to the bed before rummaging in the drawer of her dressing-table. Rose heard her muttering under her breath before she turned, brandishing a velvet pouch. 'For one terrible moment I thought Charles might have found it. There!' she said, triumphantly as out of the pouch tumbled an exquisite confection of gems linked by a gold chain.

'Where did you get this?'

'It was given to me.'

'Charles...?'

'Of course not!' Helena's tone was impatient. 'You're not the only one to have admirers.'

'You should never have accepted it!' Anger replaced Rose's fear.

Helena tossed her head and began to pace the room. 'I wish you and your loyal retainers didn't share such outmoded scruples,' she said, before conceding with a sigh, 'Of course I can't. If I could, you'd no doubt insist I sell it to repay Lord Rampton... though it wouldn't go far.' She put her hands on her hips. 'An irony, isn't it, that the most valuable jewels I possess I cannot wear because of my husband who should be the one to gratify all my desires.'

Suddenly she was brandishing the velvet-lined box that had arrived earlier in the day, saying, 'If you don't wear it, I will!'

Rose reared back in anger. 'You heard Edith, how can I possibly wear a gift that—?' but Helena cut her off, her tone bitter. 'Oh yes, you have too much honour to accept a token which is nothing to the giver but by insulting him you risk us retaining a roof over our heads. What if Lord Ramton calls in his debt now? Come, Rose, I know you can manage to tread that delicate line between making him want you and making him despise you.' Helena's nostrils flared and she lowered her voice. 'You had the chance to salvage all our fortune's once. Don't throw away the opportunity *again*.'

Rose heaved in a breath. This argument had its roots in past history. It was hard not to scream her defence. Instead, she said in as controlled a tone as she could manage, 'I will not have you accuse me of ruining all our lives once more, just as I supposedly did when I refused Sir Hector's offer all those years ago.' Rose thrust the necklace at Helena.

'Don't be ridiculous!' Helena snapped. 'Do you think I blame you for refusing to sacrifice the rest of your life because your brother is too pathetic to provide properly for the rest of us? This is different. It's a piece of jewellery, a token of someone's esteem.'

'A married woman ought not accept gifts from admirers.'

'The woman Lord Rampton admires is not married.'

Rose gasped and Helena laughed, saying bitterly. 'Look at us. You've been given a gift that you can flaunt to the world to remind them that we Chesterfields are people of substance. If you don't wear your diamonds, then I shall wear my gems.'

'Of course you can't! What would Charles say?'

'Do you think me such a fool?' Helena snorted. 'Of course I can't possibly wear the thing, and this—' again, she touched the simple thin gold chain at her neck, 'is all I have to set off my gown.' Her bosom rose beneath her tight, lace-edged bodice. 'All I'll ever have,' she said, bitterly. 'Oh, I know you think I'm extravagant with my silks and laces, but at least I can make the most of my youth with some beautiful things, and I'm fortunate to have such a skilful seamstress ... but beautiful jewels will always be beyond my reach. You, however, can wear this tonight. Put it on after Edith has finished attending to you and tell Charles you borrowed it from Aunt Alice. It will raise the tone of your ensemble and surely put our family on a better footing in the eyes of the ton.' Her shoulders slumped as she ran the back of her hand across the tassel fringing the faded curtains. 'While it is common knowledge that Arabella comes with little enough of a dowry we don't want to be distinguished by our penury.' Rallying, she draped the diamonds around Rose's throat and fastened the clasp.

Rose turned to the cheval mirror and trembled at the sight that met her. The glittering diamonds set off her ensemble more exquisitely than she could ever have foreseen. The string of stones nestling against the creaminess of Rose's throat became an object of fire and brilliance and Rose felt the confidence of a queen course through her veins.

'Show Lord Rampton what you're made of.' Helena's whisper tickled her ear. 'You are worthy of his attentions as a proud and beautiful woman ... not a supplicant who depends on his benevolence.'

৩৯৩

In the large marble-tiled hallway of Lord and Lady Barbery's London residence the Chesterfields were relieved of their outer wear, before mounting the stairs to the saloon, a magnificent room of stately proportions, decorated in rose and gilt and illuminated by hundreds of wax candles.

When Rose almost immediately spied Lord Rampton beneath a candle sconce on the other side of the room deep in conversation with several soberly dressed gentlemen, her hand went unconsciously to her throat. Bolstered by the confidence of how well she looked, she was able to curtsy and smile with the regal possession of a queen when the viscount acknowledged her with a gracious half-bow.

Compliments rolled off lips while coupes of champagne were procured—and anything else, it seemed, that could be desired—as the three Chesterfield women made their progression through the room.

Charles grew weary of being complimented upon his 'wife' and plagued by enquiries as to whether the affections of his 'sister' had yet been engaged. He'd told more than half a dozen interested gentlemen that she was on the verge of allying herself with a neighbouring landowner in the West Indies. In truth, he greatly feared that he might receive an offer for Helena before the season was over and heartily wished for an end to the charade, if only it could be brought about without the need for embarrassing revelations or discovery. Rose, who had never shown any desire to expand her horizons in fashionable circles, was a changed creature. He would have had to be blind not to have noticed her improvement in looks and the excitement she created wherever she went, he thought sourly, wishing she'd simply come to London to contract a decent marriage. With both his sisters off his hands he and Helena could have returned to the plantation, Helena's taste for society would have been satisfied and she would surely have shown her gratitude by becoming, henceforth, the docile, loving and accepting wife he had always desired her to be.

Rose drifted from conversation to conversation, wending her way into the heart of the company and steadily closer to Lord Rampton. It was like a game. She knew he was acutely conscious of her. Several times she caught him watching her out of the corner of his eye. Instead of directly accosting her, however, it appeared they were destined literally to bump into one another.

But all her pleasure in the evening was about to come to an abrupt halt.

When several knots of revellers still separated them, Rose was surprised to be addressed in the familiar clipped tones of Lady Barbery, to whom she'd been introduced at the masquerade earlier in the week.

Rose turned, the icy glare directed at her very different from the gracious charm the lady had bestowed upon her when last they met.

And as Lady Barbery clawed at the diamonds at Rose's throat, her shrill words sent Rose reeling into a vortex of horror.

For no one had ever called her a thief before.

CHAPTER 7

MUTE WITH EMBARRASSMENT, Rose was unable to reply to Lady Barbery's angry questioning as she backed into a corner, the blood pounding behind her eyes as she clutched the diamonds at her throat. 'It was a gift,' she managed, glad the gentleman closest to her appeared to be deaf and was addressing his companions in stentorian tones, which drowned out Lady Barbery.

Lady Barbery's nostrils flared. 'A thief *and* a liar!'

'Dear Lady Barbery, what appears to be the trouble?'

Rose froze at his nearness. Lord Rampton's quiet, authoritative tone was music to her ears.

'That woman,' Lady Barbery's words suggested Rose was beneath contempt, 'is wearing the diamond necklace given to me by my own husband... *my* diamond necklace which went missing three days ago.'

'Perhaps it is a copy,' murmured Lord Rampton. 'Imitation is, as you know, the sincerest form of flattery.'

'And, pray, tell me, my dear Rampton, where is the craftsman who can fashion my necklace down to the last diamond in less than three days? Without the original to work from?' Lady Barbery sounded in no mood to be mollified.

The only advantage of being in this horrendous situation was that

Lord Rampton was pressed tightly against Rose's side, a barrier to those who would have shown the prurient interest that would spell death to the Chesterfield's social aspirations.

'It would appear someone has played a very cruel or wicked joke on Lady Chesterfield.' Lord Rampton gave Rose's hand a surreptitious and reassuring squeeze. 'For I was in her drawing room when she received the gift from an unknown admirer.'

Rose and Lady Barbery gasped and the viscount went on, 'Perhaps we're looking for a light-fingered anonymous admirer who did not foresee the consequences of his actions and sought to impress Lady Chesterfield with his devotion. Perhaps the necklace changed hands several times before it was legitimately bought.'

'Someone must be called to account!'

'Someone will be.'

Rose was as admiring of the viscount's resolute tone as his hostess appeared to be. Lady Barbery placed an elegantly gloved hand upon his forearm and purred, 'You'll discover the thief, Rampton, won't you? If someone is wanting to make mischief, it is in all our interests to learn why.'

'Of course,' Rampton murmured. 'Meanwhile, I suggest discretion is our ally. Lady Chesterfield can return the necklace in the morning while you will be civil to her for the sake of appearances.'

Who was the intended victim? Rampton wondered a little while later, as he gripped the railings of the small balcony off Lady Barbery's private rooms and gazed into the darkness. That was his first question, before asking the perhaps more obvious question: who was the perpetrator, and for what reason?

Someone wanted to make mischief but at whose expense? That of Lady Barbery or Lady Chesterfield?

'You were most gallant this evening, Lord Rampton.'

Startled by the low, husky voice, he turned, unable to place it as that of one of his female friends, while his companion went on as she advanced towards him, 'Lady Chesterfield is fortunate to once more find a protector who will defend her.'

Rampton summoned a quelling look to match his tone. 'What the devil are you doing out here, Miss Chesterfield, alone with me? Go back downstairs at once!'

'No need to act like an agitated mother hen.' Her amusement was evident. 'I'm not a child.'

'You are not yet presented.' Dear God, the last thing he wanted was to be compromised over his dear Lady Rose's sister-in-law.

'Where I come from debutantes are not as protected as their sisters in England.'

'You know well enough that if anyone should find us—'

'You may well find yourself having to make an offer to marry me,' his bold companion supplied sweetly. 'Have no fear on that score, my lord. I've no intention of marrying an Englishman when I am simply counting the days until I return to the West Indies.'

Rampton stopped just short of placing his hands on her shoulders and pushing her away. If he were caught even touching her he hated to think of the possible consequences. 'Good. And that's where you're going not soon enough, Miss Chesterfield. I have *no* desire to be accused of ruining some gently reared young debutante and thus saddled with a wife as a matter of honour,' he muttered.

Discomposed by her chuckle and proximity, he stepped back adding, 'And pray explain yourself. Are you implicating your sister-in-law in the theft of Lady Barbery's necklace? A bit rich, I think, don't you?'

Miss Chesterfield's eyes widened as she shook her head and the dark, glossy curls that framed her face bounced at the level of her high cheekbones.

'Of course she didn't steal it. Not like a cat burglar, creeping into this house in the middle of the night, or a common light-fingered thief who snatched it from Lady Barbery's neck when she wasn't looking?' The girl laughed again: a deep-throated, sensuous noise which Rampton found hard to reconcile with the debutante by his side.

'It's one of my sister-in-law's famous little games. Her way of relieving boredom.' Miss Chesterfield gave an eloquent shrug. 'You must know by now how she simply loves to play games. Of course, she means no harm and would have returned it to its rightful owner in good time but my sister-in-law considers the West Indies a virtual prison. She's too delicate for the harsh climate and she despises her husband; so she's developed her own ways of amusing herself. Of course, poor Charles is at his wits' end, and will be so grateful that you've saved her from yet another scandal.'

Rampton put up his hand to stop her going on. Her poisonous prattle was nothing but lies, of course!

She dropped her eyes demurely. 'At the masquerade the other night she was with her cousin, Oswald, a nasty piece of work, let me tell you!' She shuddered. 'But they are in many ways of the same mould. I heard her dare Oswald to steal Lady Barbery's necklace—'

Rampton snorted. 'And parade the stolen gems without discovery?'

The girl shrugged. 'That was not the point. Lady Chesterfield's dare that Oswald could steal it was matched by his speculation that Lady Chesterfield would wear it ... and be championed.'

Rampton gave a harsh laugh. Her claim was outrageous.

Miss Chesterfield raised one eyebrow and stared back at him, daring him to refute her story. 'Each time, my sister-in-law goes just that little bit further. It's like a disease and poor Charles can do nothing about it, short of locking her up.'

'You certainly are no friend of hers.'

'You think I don't speak the truth?' She shrugged. 'Dear Lady Chesterfield hasn't got this far in life without being a gifted liar, a consummate actress. After living such a limited social existence as we did in the West Indies her exploits are known and, to an extent, tolerated, but now she has a new audience. A multitude of new admirers.' After a long pause, she added in a whisper, 'Poor Charles.'

'Poor Charles, indeed,' Rampton echoed, straightening and indicating the double doors that opened in to the rooms behind the balcony. 'Not only does he have the exploits of his wife to contend with, but his sister seems happy enough to excite the gossips also. It's time to leave, Miss Chesterfield.' Gripping her elbow, he steered her into Lady Barbery's boudoir, which was in darkness. 'Alone.'

Anger quickly replaced her surprise as she jerked her head up. For a minute he almost thought she was going to stamp her foot.

'It's been a pleasure, Miss Chesterfield.' He bowed, and was relieved, when he straightened, to find she had gone.

He turned back to the railings, thoughts of Lady Chesterfield churning in his mind. Lady Chesterfield ... masterminding the theft of Catherine's diamond necklace so that he would champion her? He rolled his shoulders as if his perfectly cut coat were too tight, and balled his fists.

That couldn't be true!

Yet, regardless, she certainly knew how to tantalize a man, upping the ante with each innocent visit. Had he misread the signs? Each time she'd seemed to be holding him at bay, but was she really trying to convey to him that she was tired of waiting; that it was time for him to be more masterful?

Rampton was not a man who liked to be kept waiting too long, either. He exhaled into the crisp air, making a noise that was part sigh, part growl of anticipation. Regardless of the truth of Miss Chesterfield's poisonous assertion, it was time Rampton took matters more boldly into his own hands.

He shifted position, unable to shed the heady desire he felt at the thought. What sweet relief it would be to finally tear off Lady Rose's clothes and tumble her on his expansive carved four-poster designed for such nefarious activities located in his tower room.

Lady Rose was clearly panting for his tender—or not so tender—ministrations.

And she'd been kept waiting long enough.

⚜

WHEN ROSE SAW HELENA EMERGE FROM THE PASSAGEWAY INTO THE ballroom she found the courage to launch into the throng of revellers and accost her sister-in-law, pulling her into a secluded corner.

'It was you, wasn't it?' she accused, fingering the hated jewellery at her throat which Lord Rampton had advised her to wear in order to save face. 'I don't know how you did it but you found a way to spirit this out of Lady Barbery's possession and around my neck in order to damn me in everyone's eyes.' She was nearly in tears and Helena's superciliously raised eyebrows did nothing to soothe her disordered nerves.

'Pray, calm yourself, my dear Rose, and do not accuse me of under-hand dealings. Yes, it came into my possession but I've no idea where from. Perhaps Lady Barbery herself sent it.' With a self righteous smoothing of her powder blue sash, she went on, 'Never fear, your lovely Lord Rampton will get to the bottom of the matter. But tell me, do you really think I came to London to be dressed as an innocent while you parade around in the clothes Charles bought for *me*? Yet have I even once stamped my foot and told you I will no longer coun-tenance the charade you forced me into?'

Rose shook her head and said hotly, 'No, because *you* suggested I continue with the charade.' She exhaled on a sigh. 'I concede that I acted rashly by masquerading as you in the first place, and I'm sorry for it, but your actions tonight could have had me facing the hangman's noose. Do you not realise that?'

Helena clicked her tongue. 'Lord Rampton championed you, Rose. That's all that's important. And now we know how deep his feelings go, you can redouble your efforts to ensnare his delectable Lordship. I'd say this was a very happy state of affairs and you should be thanking me for insisting you wear a necklace that came anonymously rather than accusing me of stealing it. Why, the idea is preposterous!'

Rose glared at her. 'I'm not accusing you of stealing it but I am certain you know more than you're admitting. Furthermore,' she added, lowering her voice, 'as a supposedly married woman Lord Rampton is hardly about to offer for me. Oh, yes, I know you think I should play my hand. After all, a rich husband would benefit us all. And you say I should thank you for achieving tonight's outcome whereby he's championed me, but,' she drew herself up proudly, 'what joy would there be in a union with a man I'd tricked into marriage? You should know that as well as I, Helena.'

She'd struck a nerve. Tossing back the last of her champagne Helena looked at her with loathing. 'I did not trick Charles into marriage,' she hissed. 'He'd been panting for me since long before I was out of short skirts. If you want the truth, I was forced into marriage with him when the man I loved left me. Yes, that man I told you about the carriage. The man I'd have cut off my right hand to be with if we could have survived on passion alone. But that's a long-ago story. Let me just warn you now, my dear Rose, that I intend that you redress all the past ills you've visited upon the family—namely me. You *will* marry Lord Rampton and it won't be hard to achieve. I've seen the way his eyes follow you... the lust that consumes him.' She paused, snatching up another coupe of champagne from another passing waiter. 'Yes, Arabella will receive an offer from Lord Yarrowby within the next six weeks, and you will ensnare your handsome Lord Rampton and somehow your good fortune will aid Charles and therefore me for I am weary of living in penury.' Raising one eyebrow she contoured the tip of Rose's breast with her fan and leant into her. 'You've kissed him, haven't you?' Her voice was low, sending fear and excited longing up Rose's spine. It mingled with the disquiet Rose felt at Helena's reference to the untested Lord Yarrowby and was swept away by shame when Helena whispered, 'And it made you want more, didn't it?'

Fiercely, Rose shook her head while she reined in her temper. 'Honour dictates that I repay what is owed him, as promised, and Aunt Gwendolyn has all but promised—'

'Great-Aunt Gwendolyn likes to play games and the only assurance you have that we will not all be forced to live like paupers is to play on the feelings of your handsome viscount.' Helena twirled the stem of her glass as she contemplated Rose over its rim. 'It is your duty. My hands are tied for I am already married to a man who has not the funds to pay the lease on our shabby little London abode for more than two months, but you, Rose, have a duty to ensure that you and your pretty little sister make the matches that will liberate us all.' She gave a short laugh. 'I am limited by the narrow sphere to which you relegated me, Rose, but you can be sure that I, too, will be doing all I can to achieve the happy outcome we all deserve.'

CHAPTER 8

R AMPTON PACED THE tower room and watched the road, his agitation fuelled by frustrated desire.

In the three days since Catherine Barbery's ball-assembly his enquiries had given vastly different perceptions of Lady Chesterfield. Of course, she'd been in England for barely two weeks, but a member of his club who had spent time in the West Indies had some interesting *on-dits* about the enigmatic beauty. While these had made Rampton feel a dupe, they'd fuelled the fires of his desire.

Lady Chesterfield, from most accounts, had a decided penchant for money, mischief... and men.

To think that he'd truly believed *he* was going to be her first conquest.

When she'd come to her last sitting to Felix the previous day—with her maid in tow, God dammit!— the gleam in her eye had hinted that she was as eager as Rampton was to graduate to the next stage of their relationship.

She'd just been playing with him, he realised, now, asking him with that wicked, colluding glint in her eye, how investigations were proceeding into the theft of Lady Barbery's necklace? Did the woman think him a grinning dweedlenap making small talk while her maid sat demurely in the corner. Or did she really want him to tie up the maid and bundle the wretched servant in the antechamber so he could ravish the object of his lustful desires upon the hearthrug?

The thought had crossed his mind but the maid looked like she'd be a force to reckon with and Lady Rose had simply simpered and made polite conversation over the rim of her tea cup.

Now, though, Rampton had reasonable grounds for thinking that his waiting was at an end. There was only so much cat and mouse a man could take and the surprised look the confounded woman had levelled at him when he'd told her so under his breath as he'd farewelled her during her last visit had been followed up by a colluding squeeze of his fingertips.

In the meantime, Rampton had appeased his former mistress with the sop that the theft of her jewels was just one of a curious spate being investigated at higher levels. It was entirely possible, he'd suggested, that sensitive documents in the possession of Catherine Barbery's husband, who held an important government position, were the real target while the theft of Lady Barbery's jewels merely a ruse to deflect attention. It was fortuitous that news of another diamond necklace theft had come to his ears since Lady Barbery's ball.

Waiting for Lady Rose now, Rampton realized how tense he was when the ribbon of dust in the distance which heralded an approaching carriage made him literally sag with relief.

At last. So she hadn't reneged and made a fool of him.

Felix was in the opposite tower, now, mixing his paints, and would soon usher Lady Rose to her seat for her final sitting. Casting his eye over the masculine appointments of his bedchamber Rampton focused his attention upon the panel behind the large, baronial four-poster in which he and his forebears had been born. The panel hid a secret staircase that connected each floor with the courtyard outside as well as a passageway to the opposite tower. It had been constructed during the time of the dissolution of the monasteries several centuries earlier, when the family had been devoutly Catholic. Many Catholic priests had sought refuge in the darkness before making their escape but now, in safer times, its use was limited to pursuits of a far more frivolous kind. He gave a low laugh. Lady Rose, he felt sure, would be keen to view such a curiosity.

Running his hand across his freshly shaven jaw in anticipation of the fact his waiting was nearly at an end, he felt himself harden as the blood surged to his extremities. No woman had ever affected him like this one. Lady Rose was fascinating. Intriguing. And damnably playful.

Fascinated and horrified in equal measure by the rapid tattoo in his chest cavity, he realised he wanted her like he'd never wanted anything in his life.

***

WITH DIFFICULTY, ROSE HAD SUCCEEDED IN DISPENSING WITH Edith's services, slipping out of the house when Helena and Charles had taken Arabella to the Bullock's Museum. To avoid the outing, she'd pleaded a megrim and although Helena had looked at her with scepticism, her sister-in-law said nothing. No, Helena must have no idea that Rose intended seeing Lord Rampton, alone, even though she'd condone it since she clearly felt Rose owed them all a glittering marriage to a moneyed peer.

Well, Rose knew very well the repercussions would not be worth it. She wanted his love, not his angry scorn, which is what would be inevitable should he find himself tricked.

No, today she intended to visit Lord Rampton on her own terms.

Felix would be wielding his paintbrush, acting as chaperone, but she felt sure Lord Rampton would somehow engineer a few stolen moments where she could melt in his embrace and revel in the kisses he rained upon her. It seemed an age ago that he'd come to see her in her drawing room and made clear his desire.

She tried to breathe evenly, but couldn't. Ever since Helena had spoken of 'wanting more' the phrase had assumed monumental proportions. The truth was, Rose wasn't entirely sure what that entailed. She was keenly aware of the extraordinary sensations whipped up by his kisses that made her feel breathless and out of control. But surely a final bout of passionate kissing would alleviate that? Yes, she was risking her reputation in calling upon an unmarried gentleman but he'd have as little desire to be caught if it resulted in being leg-shackled to her. Lord Rampton, she'd heard around the traps, was most definitely *not* in the market for a wife.

There, Rose had determined that this secret visit to Lord Rampton, ostensibly for a painting session, would cauterise her feelings for the dangerous viscount.

A few stolen moments of passion would satisfy her cravings, forever, and there would be an end to it.

However, Rose had no idea *quite* how much she was anticipating her rendezvous with his lordship until disappointment threatened to undo her after Felix greeted her warmly, adding, 'Can't imagine where Rampton's got to.' He led Rose to her chair where he began to arrange the folds of her gown while Rose simply felt sick with the deepest sense of loss.

As Felix moved an arm here, and tucked a lock of hair behind her ear, she wished with an intensity that frightened her, that he was his brother.

Felix returned to his easel and, picking up his paintbrush, continued, unaware of the pain his words caused, 'There was some business with the overseer. They're out on the estate but I think Rampton was unsure whether he'd be back in time to see you.'

'Oh,' was all Rose could manage, thinking of the lengths to which she had gone to orchestrate this clandestine meeting with Rampton.

Felix's tone was conversational. 'I hear you set sail in a little under four weeks.'

'A great loss, I'm sure you'll agree,' came a familiar drawl and Lord Rampton strode in.

As usual, he dominated the room, his broad shoulders filling out his perfectly cut riding-coat, his buckskin breeches tucked into highly polished hessians. He bowed deeply to Rose, taking her hand in his, caressing the sensitive skin with his lips. It was a blatantly provocative gesture and, embarrassed, Rose darted a look at Felix who was pretending great interest in mixing the burnt umber on his palette.

Lord Rampton stepped back and took up position at his brother's shoulder. 'A rose,' he murmured, transferring his gaze from the almost completed portrait to Rose who reclined on the velvet-draped chair.

Rose licked dry lips and fiddled with the tassel of her shawl. 'You have the most fascinating home, my lord. I've heard tales it was used to hide Catholic priests in fear of their lives.'

His eyes crinkled with amusement. 'I'll show you the secret passageway, if you like.'

'Very much.'

This seemed to please the viscount who, after peering over his brother's shoulder, remarked with a sigh, 'Fine work, Felix.' He glanced warmly at Rose, adding, 'I hope you do not take it amiss, little brother, when I say that no painting could do justice to her exquisite beauty.'

'The inevitable passing of time will ensure Lady Rose is always remembered as the great beauty she is, and will no doubt, remain,' Felix murmured, gallantly.

'And what a terrible loss that you'll be leaving England's shores so soon—though perhaps you'll be a more frequent visitor if you could only taste more of its delights.' Lord Rampton's voice was like molten caramel and Rose felt the heat burn her cheeks while she forced herself not to meet his gaze.

She cleared her throat. 'I shall have to make the most of those delights while I am here for I cannot see myself returning.'

She glanced at Rampton when he made some noise between impatience and humour.

Well, she was equally impatient for Felix to finish so that she and Rampton could be alone. Five minutes. No, fifteen. That was all she craved. Surely it was not such a great sin to want a handsome man to make her feel beautiful and desired? It was not as if either were otherwise attached.

Just as long as he did not discover her charade.

She put her hand to her décolletage which was rising and falling rapidly as she grew increasingly nervous over what would happen in the next few minutes.

No, Lord Rampton would not discover her charade and Rose would get her taste of passion but emerge with her honour intact, regardless.

This would be between her and Rampton alone.

As Great-aunt Gwendolyn had reiterated her intention to favour Rose with her fortune, Rose could therefore pay Rampton's debt honourably. She would not be trading favours or compromising herself.

The knowledge was liberating.

After what seemed an eternity Felix, with a great show of deliberation, put down his paintbrush and stepped back from his work, pronouncing his labours at an end.

Rampton seized Rose's hand to whisk her out of her chair and they crowded behind the portrait to admire his brother's work. Felix was grinning with well-deserved pride, for the portrait did Rose justice, highlighting her fragile paleness, imbuing her with a shining innocence that was far from wifely but strangely true to life.

Rampton pulled the velvet bell-rope and a footman entered with a silver tray bearing a bottle of vintage champagne and three crystal coupes.

'We must celebrate!' Pouring out the frothing liquid, he handed Felix and Rose a glass each.

Rose felt deliriously happy. Regardless of where the portrait would hang, Lord Rampton had considered her worth the time and trouble to convey her likeness onto canvas.

She didn't know if honour required that Charles pay for it or whether Lord Rampton intended to keep it for himself, and right now she didn't care. She just wanted to feel Lord Rampton's arms around her.

Another bottle of fizz was poured to general light-heartedness during which Rampton caught her round the waist and declared her the beauty of the day, then Felix made his excuses and left.

Rose exhaled on an enormous sigh of relief while her heart beat even more wildly. She glanced up from beneath her lashes at the handsome viscount. The room was quiet and shadowed and Rampton was looking at her with longing. At last, she and the man she desired were alone.

'I'm honoured, Lord Rampton.' Rose felt ridiculously lightheaded. She nodded towards the painting. 'And you have been patience itself.'

Slowly he moved to her side, his body so close but not quite touching, until his hand closed around the glass in her hand. He set it down on a little table beside the window and she could feel his breath on her brow as he bent his head. 'I have been patient, haven't I?'

The deep timbre and intent of his words resonated through her and she trembled as he pulled her within the circle of his arm. Cupping her chin, he tilted up her face and kissed her gently on the lips.

Fear and anticipation flooded her, but also the need to state her position. Her voice wavered as she whispered, 'I mean, patient with regard to my repaying my debt to you.'

She felt him stiffen.

'My dear, I assure you, I have no intention of hounding you for such a trifle.' His eyebrows arched over his blue eyes as if in faint censure for spoiling the moment. 'Now, where were we?'

The pressure of his lips on hers increased, pushing away the faint concern she felt at his words. She could not let him think she'd trade ... *so much* ... for what she owed him. She opened her mouth to speak and the tip of his tongue which had contoured her lower lip, plunged in, deepening the kiss.

Rose gasped, feeling her legs buckle as he caught her fully in his arms, pulling her against him. There was no mistaking his desire but what frightened Rose was the force of hers. Her head spun with wicked, unbidden thoughts while unfamiliar, intoxicating sensations coursed through her body, making her skin prickle and causing her to push her breasts against his seeking hands.

What was she doing? She'd plunged into dangerous territory. Uncharted territory.

'Not here,' she protested, her voice a thread of sound as she pushed him away.

Clear-headedness had returned. She blinked up at him as she pulled out of his embrace, straightening her clothing while he stared at her, his expression quizzical.

Rose swallowed as desperation and mortification threatened to consume her. Lord Rampton was a consummate rake in the habit of seducing married women. Yes, she knew that. And, when she came here, she knew she was opening the flood gates to something potentially sinful.

But now common sense had the upper hand. She could not potentially destroy herself over a few stolen moments of passion.

Rose was unmarried and the kisses they'd shared were the extent of her experience of men.

As he continued to stare quixotically at her, waiting for her to speak, a thousand conflicting voices squabbled inside her head.

Lord Rampton offered a forbidden, sensuous slice of life she could never know as the innocent virgin she was destined to remain.

Yet, no one knew she was here. She could take the greatest risk of her life and hope she got away with it.

She closed her eyes and squeezed her hands into fists. She *wanted* to know what it was like to be with a man she desired but a lifetime of obedience stood in her way. Rose might be bold, but she was not *that* much of a risk-taker.

The silence lengthened. 'You like playing games, don't you, Lady Rose.' The warmth had gone from his tone.

With a desperate gasp, Rose covered her face with her hands and confessed the truth. 'I've never...been with a man before, Lord Rampton! I'm...sorry!'

There! She'd just killed whatever might have been and now his anger at being duped would come raining down on her. Well, she deserved it.

His response—to her astonishment—was very different.

Suddenly she was enfolded in a very warm and loving embrace. As Lord Rampton kissed the top of her head, he was actually chuckling.

'I knew there had to be something at play, my dear Lady Rose. Oh, my! So, this is your first dalliance behind your husband's back, eh? My, my, I should have guessed!'

Rose sucked in a breath. That was not what she'd meant to imply, but when Lord Rampton took her hand, saying in robust tones, 'I think it's time to show you the secret passageway,' she felt relieved that he'd accepted so readily that she was out of bounds.

CHAPTER 9

R AMPTON LED HER down the stairs feeling like the cat
that's swallowed the cream.

What a little vixen she was, always turning the tables
when he least expected it. Did she really expect him to believe that?
Did she imagine Rampton hadn't heard the rumours surrounding Lord
Chesterfield's wife. Babbage, for a start, had thought he was in for a
very well-rewarded evening until Lady Chesterfield—Rampton's very
own Lady Rose—had fled at the final moment. Chagrin as much as loss
of face had led him to insist on her debt being honoured, which is
when Rampton had stepped up.

Now, Lady Rose followed him down the stairs and out of the house
towards the tower, willingly, her footsteps light, almost happy, he
thought, while he felt in physical pain at having had to truncate so
abruptly their earlier passionate proceedings.

Still, it would be even more worth it when he finally tumbled her
on the feather mattress.

She clung to his arm like a little lamb. Or, rather, like a woman
filled with excitement at the prospect of what a real man could offer
her. Not some ninnyhammer like her milksop husband.

He glanced down at her as they reached the final landing, his gaze lingering on the décolletage of her virginal white gown. A vision burst into his head of her naked, writhing beneath him, eyes vacant with lust, skin flushed and covered with the moist sheen of their love-making labours.

He couldn't wait to show her the pleasures she'd missed out on her whole life. Indeed, she'd not want to leave his bed until she was forced to do so in order to return to her island home. Her husband would not object for he clearly didn't know what to do with her. And, of course, turning a blind eye would conveniently take care of the debt he owed Lord Rampton.

Breathlessly, she asked, 'Tell me some of the legends about the heroic Delacroix men.'

He laughed, his mood expansive. 'Ah, so many of them. But not all Delacroix were men of honour.'

'Unlike you, my lord?'

He smiled at the irony in her tone. 'You flatter me, madam.' He hoped his look was not too salacious. An English rose. He had said it before, but how apt was the description, for in the summer sunshine, her bonnet tied demurely under her pretty little chin, she was like a piece of Dresden china but in his bed where he'd have her in less than two minutes she'd be transformed into the goddess of his lustful imaginings. How would her breasts feel when freed of their confines? Would they be pert? Or ripe? It didn't matter. He was so hard he could barely walk. He tried to swallow. Normally he didn't like surprises but he was looking forward to this one. Would she be like an unleashed wild animal when her clothes were off—like Catherine Barbery? He shuddered. Now was not the time to make comparisons, but to focus all his expertise on this exquisite woman who'd kept him waiting so long.

Clearly she was an accomplished coquette, regardless of whether her claims about not having had a lover were true. Good God, she'd kept him on the barest thread for longer than any mistress of his had. Two thousand pounds and she was his. Indeed, he'd have absolved her of twice the amount and believed he'd got a bargain.

At the foot of the tower just across the courtyard he lifted the latch and pushed open the door. It gave way, protesting on rusty hinges and they stepped into the gloom. Closing the door behind them, they were plunged into darkness and immediately he felt her pull away.

'I don't think ...' she began, but her coyness seemed unnecessary now they'd come this far. He laughed again.

'My male vanity is wounded. I'd have imagined you'd draw closer to me for protection.'

SUDDENY, ROSE WAS AWARE OF WARNING BELLS RINGING IN HER head. Where was he leading her? Had he mistaken her meaning, earlier.

'I'm sorry.' Rose chided herself for being foolish. Lord Rampton was taking her, at her request, to see the hidden passageway. Hadn't he already proved he was a gentleman of honour by pulling away at her first display of reluctance?

'If you're afraid of the dark we'll open the door to the outside and let in the light. I'd thought to give you a sense of the authentic. Remember, these Catholic priests made their escape in the dead of night, their lives hanging by a thread.'

He pushed open the door to let through a weak shaft of sunlight; then, taking Rose's hand, he led her up the spiral stairs.

'What's in there?' Rose asked as they reached a room on the next level.

'You are impatient,' said Lord Rampton as if something amused him. 'It's nothing but a room full of dust sheets. It's the room on the next level that's of interest.'

'Where does the secret tunnel lead?'

'From behind the bed down a back staircase and under the court-yard to the park beyond.'

'From the bed,' Rose repeated faintly. She should not be allowing a gentleman to lead her alone and into the dark, to an unknown destina-tion. Her years of training, her innate common sense, should have her pulling her hand out of his and stumbling back down the stairs and into the sunshine.

She thought she'd made herself clear.

And yet, she was torn. Torn between wanting to please him and to please herself, and knowing what danger she was courting.

They were not there yet. The destination to which he was propelling her. There was still time to save face. To save her reputation.

'You did say you wanted to see the secret passageway.'

Was that the faintest note of exasperation she heard? She hated not knowing what to do.

'Yes, of course.' She was finding it hard to breathe. Whether it was because of the many stairs or caused by his nearness, she had no idea. And now she was on the second landing and Lord Rampton was throwing open the doorway to a sumptuously decorated room. His bedchamber! In horror, she took in the intimate details: the dressing-table on which was laid out his brushes and combs, the shaving-stand, the brocade banyan draped casually across the end of the bed. And what a bed it was! Exquisitely carved with a headboard depicting a hunting scene, there was nothing fainthearted about the rest of it. Instead of the conventional brocade counterpane it was covered by what appeared to be an enormous bear skin.

'And the secret passage begins...?' she said, hoping her voice didn't tremble as much as she feared it did.

'One has to climb onto the bed in order to access it, my love.'

Rose jerked her head up at the endearment that was both music to her ears and the death knell to her previous good intentions to end this now.

Lord Rampton closed the door behind them, catching her to him so suddenly that she stumbled and fell into his arms.

'Please—' she began, but his mouth, hot with desire, drowned out anything else she might have said.

For a split second she thought to push him away but her simmering desire so clearly answered his own. It combusted into desperate passion and the pulsing desire to push the boundaries of her sensual experience meant resistance wilted before it was even born.

His arms were strong and tight around her, and she sagged against him, another attempt at protest dying upon her lips as he lifted her and carried her to the bed.

She'd never felt a man move above her as he did now, covering her with his body and kissing her eyes, her nose and throat. In mere moments, of course, she'd return her two feet to the floor and profess her desire to end matters there. Yes, that's what she'd do....

Dear Lord, what was he doing? All thoughts of acting upon her good intentions evaporated as she gave herself up to these new sensations which threatened to drown her in a surfeit of pleasure. He'd somehow managed to undo the back of her dress and now his mouth was hot upon her exposed breast. What started as a cry of objection became a cry of pleasure as molten desire coursed through her, making her surely the most willing captive that ever existed.

'You are exquisite, Lady Rose,' he murmured as he kissed the hollow of her throat.

Opening her eyes, she was reassured by the intensity of his smile. He wanted her because his feelings were real. She wasn't just another conquest. He *desired* her...

Common sense returned.

What a fool she was! Would she really compromise her whole future for a few moments of stolen passion?

Struggling out from beneath him, she made an ineffectual attempt at restoring modesty, pulling her skirts back over her knees. How many women had been brought to ruin by such naivety?

But with a deep chuckle and, as if she had no more strength than a butterfly, he whisked her up into his arms and pushed her onto her back once more. 'You've tried my patience long enough, you little minx, though I'll admit your merry little dance has nearly killed me with the need to have you.'

Unable to move, she watched him remove his boots, then his coat and waistcoat. Her mouth dropped open as he fumbled with his breeches, revealing lean, muscled white flanks dusted with fine dark hair beneath his shirt.

Only when he raised his eyes to hers did self-preservation kick in and she jerked herself into a sitting position.

His laugh drowned her gasp as he threw her back onto the bed whereupon he had her clothes off in record time and was now lying above her, his body a warm, sensuous cage. One in which she would have been quite happy to flounder in captivity if there were not her future to think about.

Yes, she wanted him, but not like this. The realization flashed through her mind that she had never known quite what the joining of a man and woman entailed as she caught sight of his rampant manhood which terrified and excited her in equal measure. Her body seemed to pulse with the desire to receive him while her mind railed against such sinfulness.

What kind of woman was she? Terror and mortification gripped her. She managed to twist her head away and with a gasp forced out, 'Please—!'

It was an ill chosen protest, for of course he interpreted it as a plea for more of the delights he was showing her.

'You are a delightful enigma, Lady Chesterfield,' he rasped, between hot kisses. 'I don't think I've ever wanted anything more in my life.' He paused a moment to brush a lock of hair back from her face. She could feel her heart hammering. Surely he could feel it too. He would attribute it to desire, not panic, and she had only herself to blame.

She opened her mouth to speak. To tell him the truth, but a contradiction of emotions rendered her mute. Her body was willing him to continue his pleasuring, while her mind railed at her wickedness. She had been a fool. A naïve, innocent little fool, but would she ever experience such pleasure again? She was unlikely to have another chance at love. Why should she not simply succumb to enjoyment ... just for once?

It was not worth the risk.

Lord Rampton's voice, husky with passion, made her pause. 'I wanted you from the moment I met you, my love.' He kissed her lips as he cupped her face. 'No woman has stirred my senses as you have.'

They were words she longed to hear but a lifetime of training dictated that she should make her escape.

Now he was creating even more wicked sensations, and the words she'd been trained to say would not come. Her desire for this man was stronger than anything she had yet experienced.

His mouth was upon hers again and his kisses were working their magic. His clever hands were seeking out her most sensitive parts, gently massaging the tops of her thighs with feather-light strokes which only seemed to stoke her need for more, his explorations moving into the most forbidden territory, making her gasp. She was out of control. Drowning... in hot, sensuous pleasure.

It was terrifying and it was exhilarating.

It was sinful.

She should galvanize every ounce of restraint in order to extricate herself from his irresistible embrace, but where was her will? She'd never known what love and desire were until now. Arching her body, she heard the ecstasy in her groan as if from someone far away. He moved above her, the wild, irresistible scent of him filling her nostrils, the mastery of his mouth working its magic as he suckled her breasts, kissed her lips. She skimmed his smooth, hard flanks and felt more insistently the pulsing of her womb as his manhood pressed against her belly.

It was madness but she'd do it. Give herself to this man for this one time only, yes, take the chance for it would be the only chance of love she'd ever get and she had a lifetime of loneliness to fill with the sustaining memory of these burning few short moments.

She stilled as she felt him position himself at her entrance. Trembling, she sucked in a shuddering breath as she prepared herself. She was ready to do this. With this one man only for she...

Loved him.

Loved him for making her feel what no other man on earth had ever made her feel. Loved the humour deep beneath his ironic, masterful façade.

He tilted his head and his words came out as a soft rasp. 'What did you say?'

Surely she'd not spoken of her love aloud? She opened her eyes to see his fleeting confusion but she shook her head, arching against him, not wanting to lose the moment now that she had steeled herself to receive him.

His breath was coming fast and shallow. Lust glazed his expression, twisting his lips into a wicked, colluding smile as he ground out, 'My God, Lady Rose, but you are–'

On the periphery of her consciousness, Rose registered the heavy footsteps upon the stair, growing louder as they approached. She tensed, momentarily, then cast concern from her mind as she shifted beneath this man she loved in order to accommodate him, blind to all but their mutual desire.

A grave error she now realised as she heard the door being wrenched open on creaking hinges, before gasping at the cry of rage that echoed through the room. 'What in God's name is this?'

She felt Lord Rampton's momentary shock before he pulled back and rolled off her, drawing her into his embrace to cover their nakedness. He needed almost no time to collect himself before he was demanding of the interloper in a low, accusing growl, 'I might ask you the same question, bursting into my bedchamber like this.'

She was impressed at Lord Rampton's ability, even under such duress, to play the cool, affronted party. Trembling, she ventured a quick look over his shoulder and saw Charles upon the threshold, his normally pale and placid face suffused with outrage.

Advancing to the centre of the bearskin rug that carpeted the floor, he stabbed a finger in their direction, struggling to force out his words. 'What are you doing?'

Rose buried her face in Lord Rampton's chest, her body burning with shame as she tried to soak up all the warmth of that moment, for it would be a cold place she was going to be living in, soon, she realised.

His lordship did not flinch as he continued to shield her. Her brother was visibly shaking. Charles's rages were few but unpredictable, so when he hissed, 'If I'd thought to bring a pistol I'd shoot you through the heart,' she exhaled in relief, silently endorsing Lord Rampton's rejoinder which he uttered in a tone of unconcern, 'I'm relieved at your lack of foresight,' before he added, 'Your wife might have taken exception to such overexcitement—though I would suggest a little more excitement in the marriage bed might not have seen her here.'

'Wife?' expostulated Charles, his pale face mottled purple with rage.

Rose swallowed and pressed her forehead against Lord Rampton's warm, hard chest, dread and weary acceptance swamping her as she felt his arms tighten when she tried to withdraw.

Charles could have only one response to this and the silence seemed an eternity as she awaited the inevitable unmasking. Waited for the moment when her hopes and dreams would be reduced to cinders and she was exposed for the fraud she was.

'That's not my wife.'

She groaned softly as she felt Lord Rampton stiffen in shock at Charles's next words: 'That's my sister!'

CHAPTER 10

'MISS CHESTERFIELD.' *Miss* Chesterfield. The name should have provoked rage. Instead, Rampton was dismayed by a surge of feeling that was so far from rage as to render him no better than a slavering schoolboy when contemplating coming face to face with his adolescent obsession.

'Show her in,' he said, struggling for the self-possession that had always been second nature to him and tossing aside the reading matter that had failed to engage his attention for the past hour.

So, she had come to state her terms.

Having been caught well and truly in *flagrante delicto*, he accepted he had no one but himself to blame. Experience with women had tuned his antennae finely when it came to sensing all manner of ruses calculated to inveigle him into matrimony. But Lady Chesterfield —*Miss* Chesterfield, as it turned out—had hoist him on his own petard.

Yes, she had bested him and he was willing to take his medicine but he was also conscious of doing what was within his power to save face.

Adopting his stoniest expression, he faced the door while he waited for her to enter, the events of the past week flashing through his mind. For twenty-four hours after she'd been hauled off by her brother,

Rampton had paced his study like a caged lion, fuelling his anger with the multiple lies and untruths she'd fed him as he tried to relive exactly the moment at which he should have become aware of her deception. Any half-intelligent man would have sensed that not all was as it seemed at the very outset, he told himself.

Initially, he'd waited, cynically, for *Miss* Chesterfield to call and negotiate the terms of his matrimonial incarceration. He had practised all manner of snide and ironic responses, while his anticipation at seeing her again had grown steadily more unbearable.

He wanted only to tell her what he thought of her.

So he assumed.

But she had not come, and that had been worse.

After three days he'd snapped. Arriving unannounced, he'd confronted a pale and patently uncomfortable Sir Charles in his study and dictated the terms of a marriage contract. He was a man of honour and he had compromised a lady. She was the clear victor in their final round. She had more than just pinked him. Now he must pay the price.

Rampton had been prepared for a rambling defence from Sir Charles of his sister's behaviour. And, if Sir Charles were in a robust mood, perhaps a healthy lashing of recrimination for Rampton.

But when the young baronet said only that his sister did not wish to marry him, Rampton was at last moved to anger.

'Doing it too brown, sir!' he declared. 'She masterminded that little scene so that I'd have no choice but to suffer her joy as she leg-shackled me to her triumphant progress to the altar!'

Sir Charles, looking white around the gills, said miserably, 'My sister has made me tell you, expressly, my lord, that she has no intention of holding you to marriage. That, in fact, she does not desire it and she has in place a plan whereby you will be paid your debt, in full.'

The last part of this sentence didn't register, initially. *'Does not desire it?'*

He could not believe it. It was all part of the charade. There was a trick involved somewhere, though right now he could not see it.

Not want to marry him?

Why, every unmarried female participating in the social whirligig was there with only one thing on their minds. Most of them saw waltzing off with *him* as the ultimate feather in their caps.

Not want to marry him? When she'd gone to such pains to ensnare him? Furthermore, she *intended repaying the loan?* Was the idea of intimate relations with him *so* abhorrent?

Preposterous!

He would not believe it.

Then he realised that this was all part of the charade. Of course, she wanted marriage. She just wanted it to look as if she were unwilling.

And now the damnably alluring, deceiving Miss Chesterfield stood before him. She looked proud and defiant, that strange combination of strength and fragility piercing his armour, dissipating his anger and whipping up the desire to enfold her in his arms. Except that the look in her eye warned him to have a care.

'My brother conveyed to you my feelings about the idea of matrimony with you, my lord?'

He was silent while he tried to make sense of her mood. Her beautiful mouth was compressed, her breathing shallow, while her eyes bored into him with something that felt uncomfortably like recrimination.

Or, at least as if she had no desire to stand before him.

Nothing could have been more calculated to drive Rampton to fury. The longing to hold her tenderly was replaced by an overwhelming urge to shake—no, kiss—some sense into her.

He reined in his anger. 'A pity, then, that you took matters to such extremes. Lady Barbery's diamond necklace? Was that to ascertain the level of my affections? You were testing me, weren't you, Miss Chesterfield? To see how easily I would dispense with common sense in order to come to your rescue?' Rampton snorted. 'A bold risk, but it paid off.'

She had been staring at her boots, still having refused his offer of a chair, but she raised her eyes at this. 'My sister-in-law ... Helena ... said she thought she recognised Lady Barbery's necklace in a parcel that arrived from an unknown admirer. I know nothing more than that.'

He saw her attempts at appearing discomposed: the slight tremble of her hand as it went to the thin gold chain she wore round her neck. He was not taken in.

She said, 'My Lord, do you not think it possible that Lady Barbery herself was behind this malicious act, designed to make me appear the culprit? I believe she was very upset when you gave her her congé ... is that not the term?'

'Pah!' Rampton swung to face the window and balled his fists. The thought had occurred to him at the time but it had since been buried by Miss Rose Chesterfield's far greater treachery: her devious husband-hunting methods, which had caught him like a fool. He turned back to her. 'Catherine and I parted amicably enough, though I'll concede she may have felt ill will towards you, having usurped her in my affections.'

She inclined her head. 'Then the theft of her necklace remains a mystery. It must have been motivated by jealousy but since no harm was done and I shall be returning to the West Indies next week there is perhaps no longer the imperative to solve it.'

'Good God, are you out of your mind?' The expletive was out before he could stop himself. He had not expected this. Without thought he acted on his overriding instinct which was to keep her here. She was so very appealing in her guise of distress and he had grudgingly to admit that he was finding this interview more diverting than he'd expected.

Trying to maintain his composure he asked through gritted teeth, 'Can you really suppose I am so devoid of honour that I would not insist on marriage between us?'

'My virtue remains intact, my lord, and my brother is the only witness to my want of propriety.' She raised her chin proudly. 'You remain a free man.'

He wanted to seize her, hold her tight her in his arms and—well, once again kiss some sense into her.

Then he realized this was exactly what she intended he should do, so he restrained himself in order to call her bluff. Miss Chesterfield might be devilishly disarming, but she had used the vilest trickery in her attempt to lure him to the altar and he'd be damned if he'd be saddled with such a cunning female for the rest of his days.

No, he would go to his club, take up where he left off before he ever met her, and banish her from his mind.

He had fully intended to do the honourable thing, but if she were going to play games in order to boost the terms of a proposed settlement then she would find that she had sorely miscalculated.

His mind ran over his alternatives. He would leave her dangling for a few days. Of course, she had no intention of simply sailing back to her island home. That declaration, too, was part of the act. She wanted to marry him. That was what this was all about. Had been since the day she'd met him. And to tell the truth, he'd got used to the idea during the past seven days. He'd even come to like the notion.

But, first he'd call her bluff. She would not fleece him into the bargain. He would marry Miss Chesterfield on *his* terms.

Before he'd formulated the right response she'd bowed, saying, 'Good day to you, my lord. My apologies for giving the impression that I tricked you, however I stand by everything I said. We no longer have anything to discuss.'

Looking at the space she'd occupied just before the door closed behind her, Rampton was conscious of a sickening, sinking feeling.

Like the sands slipping through an hourglass that measured happiness.

But then he galvanised himself with the comforting thought that Miss Chesterfield was simply one of many designing females who'd sought to wed him. She'd be back.

He'd just call her bluff in the meantime.

BUT THE DAYS PASSED AND HE HEARD NOTHING.

His anger grew. What was she playing at?

He'd hoped the rallying company of a few chosen male friends and a visit to the opera would restore his spirits. Of course, it wouldn't be long before Sir Charles and his sister would resume their assault upon him in order to persuade him to settle a ridiculous sum upon his dowerless and shameless bride-to-be. He'd be generous, but he wouldn't be taken for a fool.

His spirits rallied as he realised this waiting game must yet be part of her elaborate charade to fleece him of the grandest marriage settlement that could be bled from him. No doubt it would entail a handsome living for her brother and sister-in-law and a dowry for the youngest Miss Chesterfield.

So each day he went to his club.

And each evening he waited in vain for some word or message from her.

When, after seven days, she still had not come, he returned to pacing his study like a caged lion, his anger increasing, while he mulled over what to do.

Of course, he had no choice but to marry the wench he'd defiled—well, nearly. Compounding his certainty that she intended to milk him royally was the fact that Town was now buzzing with the titillating story of Miss Chesterfield's daring charade and the fact Rampton had compromised her.

He was sickened. Some of his more respectable acquaintances snubbed him. No doubt they believed the rumours that he'd failed to behave like a gentleman.

He wondered if her lily-livered brother had spread the scandal, prepared to destroy his sister's reputation in the sly knowledge that honour would prompt the duped viscount not only to make Miss Chesterfield a viscountess but to pull strings and make possible a handsome sinecure to replenish the fortune he'd lost.

One day, across the desk in his library, Felix shook his head and said in a tone of exasperation, 'I don't know what has got into you, Rampton, but if she has a fine head of chestnut curls and flashing blue eyes you'd better hasten to the docks because she sails on tonight's tide.' Savouring his after-dinner brandy, his brother added, thoughtfully, 'Thought, meself, that you'd already made her an offer she couldn't refuse.'

If Rampton imagined he'd harboured only fury towards Miss Chesterfield, he realized in that moment he'd been deluding himself.

Irritation, anger, severe provocation—all the emotions against which he'd been battling for more than two weeks—were swept away by dismay.

Clearly, his feelings were written all over his face for, with raised eyebrows, Felix gave a surprised laugh. 'Don't tell me you didn't know?'

Rampton shook his head.

'Well, don't that beat all? I was surprised you'd let her go, knowing how your feelings had got in the way this time. I say, Rampton, where are you going?'

Rampton had risen with such force that he'd knocked over his chair. Now he turned on Felix as if his brother himself were responsible for the current dire state of affairs.

'Where did you hear this? Why did you not tell me before?' he asked grimly.

'Good Lord, Rampton, the girl's free to do as she chooses. If she's already turned you down don't you think it a little on the brutish side to chase after her and drag her off the boat?'

'Brutish?' He snorted. 'I'm sure it's no more than she expects, playing her clever little games and waiting for me to come running.'

'Which – might I point out? – is exactly what you are proposing.'

Rampton glared. 'Don't you grin at me like that, little brother, unless you're after a hiding. You always were dashed provoking.'

'Not, it would appear, as provoking as the lady in question.'

CATCHING SIGHT OF HER, ALONE ON THE DOCKS, OVERSEEING THE stowing of her luggage, was like receiving a veritable knee in the solar plexus. After riding like the wind, now that Rampton had her in his sights he could afford to relax and feast his eyes on her a little while he tried to make sense of why he really was doing this.

It was dusk. A brisk wind tossed some escaped chestnut strands from beneath her bonnet and whipped her cloak and dress around her ankles. There was no sign of her brother, but she appeared entirely in charge of the situation, directing several porters who were carrying her trunks up the gangway.

'Mind your step,' she said, as one of them stumbled. 'Those are my worldly goods. Take care of them.'

Rampton focused on her rosebud lips and her pert little nose as she dispensed orders with all the confidence of one who was used to running a large estate. Another justification for making her his wife, he thought, pleased, for it went beyond his simple lust for her.

He stepped forward and raised his voice above the stiff breeze. 'I'd have thought you'd take better care of your reputation, Miss Chesterfield. What, in God's name, are you doing?' Rampton had to steel himself against the overpowering desire to approach her from behind and either whisk her, struggling, into his arms, or to press her against his chest and crush all resistance from her.

He nodded to the porters who'd momentarily put down Rose's trunk, 'Carry it to my carriage. The lady will not be sailing, after all.'

'How dare you—'

'How dare *you* make off like a thief in the night with no word to me, Miss Chesterfield?'

She drew herself up indignantly. 'What concern is it of yours whether I stay or leave, my lord? No! Do not take that trunk over to that carriage,' she said, crisply. 'Despite what this gentleman says I *will* be sailing.'

Rampton gripped her wrist and jerked her round to face him. Blinking she stumbled and he was finally able to hold her.

'I forbid it!'

'You are in no position to forbid anything, my lord,' she ground out. 'What becomes of me is none of your concern. My reputation is ruined but that was not your fault.'

'Have you no concern for your sister, then?' Surprising himself with such creative logic, he went on, 'You once had me believe that Arabella's happiness was of more account than your own.'

'You know it is!' She seemed close to tears. 'I am entirely at fault and I deserve everything that will no doubt be meted out to me for conceiving this outrageous deception.'

He was astonished to see her tears. *Was* this play acting?

'Truly, my lord, I had no more thought when I took on Helena's identity than to salvage a situation which might see us lose our home.' She shuddered and he put his hands on her shoulders to look at her.

Properly, this time. And suddenly he didn't see her as a conniving wench. He believed her.

'I simply wanted to play for more time in which to repay our debt to you when Helena was unable to meet you.' She bit her lip as she looked up at him with tear-filled eyes. 'I never imagined I would fall in love with you. And then I realised how much you would hate me if you discovered my charade.'

The sincerity in her limpid gaze found their mark, lacerating every doubt he'd harboured towards her. Suddenly his greatest challenge was to persuade her to stay and marry him.

He enfolded her in his arms, his beleaguered brain running through artful arguments while his heart thundered its encouragement. 'What is to become of poor Arabella if you just leave? What chance does she have of a good marriage if you turn tail and run, given the rumours regarding your scandalous behaviour?'

She bowed her head and he went on, 'You're condemning her to social pariah status if you simply leave her here. Or are you forcing the poor innocent to return home with you?'

She shook her head. 'Aunt Alice has said she'll look after her. Arabella's kind nature and her loveliness will compensate for my deficiencies. I have released you from your obligation.'

For the first time, there was no warring within Rampton's heart. His heart and his mind were one and he knew he was on course for discovering the happy union his own beleaguered parents had never found.

He gripped both her wrists and brought his face down to hers. 'If I asked you to marry me because I truly believe I couldn't live without you, and if I swore an oath that my greatest mission would be to make you happy, would that make you stay?' The ardour that injected his question surprised him. But then, he'd been consumed by it since he'd first met her.

ROSE'S FIRST INSTINCT WAS TO QUESTION WHETHER SHE HAD HEARD him correctly. Lord Rampton had asked her, for the second time, to marry him? Not just asked as if out of duty, but begged, the force of his feelings revealed not just in his emphatic tone but by the raw longing in his expression.

It was beyond her wildest imaginings.

She opened her mouth to respond. To bare her own heart and tell him she had never believed such happiness possible; that she had never sought to trick him. But as she did so a nearby shout demanded their attention.

'Lord Rampton! Good morning to you.' Her brother's head emerged from below decks where he'd been inspecting Rose's cabin, an uncertain smile of welcome on his face.

Rose saw there was no similar warmth on Helena's face though there was a certain sly satisfaction as she murmured with a smile, 'Lord Rampton, what a surprise.'

Helena might well have been referring to the fact that Lord Rampton had not relinquished his hold on Rose.

He saluted them both, squeezed Rose closer and announced in expansive tones, 'It may come as a greater surprise to you that Rose has just agreed to become my wife.'

The smile he directed at Helena was so imbued with pleasure and goodwill that Rose could not doubt that his decision to wed her stemmed from desire, pure and simple.

'Isn't that right, my love?'

It must have been the dazed expression that caused him to laugh out loud and kiss her quickly upon the lips before releasing her to the expected gestures of congratulation from her family.

'How very clever of you, my dear Rose,' her sister-in-law murmured as she touched her lips to Rose's cheek. 'And it is what I directed you to do. I can't tell you how worried I've been that you'd let this one get away. Just make sure you are not greedy with the benefits.' Her breath tickled Rose's ear. 'And that you remember those who facilitated your good fortune.'

'I'm afraid you'll be sailing without her,' said Rampton, stepping forward to reclaim his intended. He seemed unable to wipe the grin from his face.

'Rose was to travel alone,' Charles said, casting a troubled look at Helena. 'Our plans have changed, for we intend to remain some while longer in England. I had hoped to,' he looked nervous, 'find a means of securing the funds we need to repay you. We have expectations that an aunt of—'

Rampton cut him off. 'No need to lose sleep over such a trifle. This marriage obviously negates the debt.' He looked warmly at Rose. 'Though I hesitate to call it a trifle when it was the means of bringing your sister into my orbit.'

Rose felt as if *she* were in a different orbit. Lord Rampton ... holding her as if he could not bear to let her go? Speaking as if their marriage were the most marvellous outcome?

Raising his hand to halt Charles's sputtering gratitude, Rampton went on, 'Let us return to town and tell Arabella and Felix the happy news.'

'Expect Arabella's congratulations to be more muted than you might have expected,' Helena said. As always, she managed to find a way to dampen Rose's happiness. 'Arabella is nursing a broken heart.'

'Yarrowby?'

Rose felt as much as saw Rampton's relief. All he said, though, was,' My commiserations. Perhaps my alliance with her sister may aid her future prospects.'

Rose's heart leapt. Might Rampton really be generous to her family even after having been so thoroughly duped? She realized that any prospective suitor for Arabella would have withdrawn on account of the scandal Rose had caused. Indeed, her misery of the past week had been as much due to her guilt over Arabella's injured prospects as in accepting that Rampton was lost to her.

He'd insisted on 'honouring his obligations', as he'd put it the first time he'd proposed marriage terms, but Rose would rather a loveless spinsterhood than marriage to a man she knew would not have *chosen* to wed her.

Now her world had been turned upside down and Rampton was discussing the legalities of their union, declaring his intention to get a special licence so that they could be married without delay. 'After that, I think a protracted bridal tour sounds in order. The world needs to know this is a love match.'

A love match. Rose existed in a state of euphoria that nothing Helena could say, and not even Arabella's unhappiness, could dampen.

· · ·

SADLY, RAMPTON'S MOTHER PUT AN END TO THEIR PLANNING A protracted bridal tour by pleading a severe chest ailment that, she insisted, was mortal but the wedding ceremony was held at St Mary's three days later with a sprinkling of well-wishers.

Rose had never been more nervous in her life. The last thing she'd expected when she set out from the West Indies was a glittering match.

And while a glittering match was all very well, it was the man himself who set her pulses racing. Each time she glanced at him she had to pinch herself to realize that the fairy tale had come true.

THE CONSEQUENCES

CHAPTER 11

EXCEPT THAT IT wasn't all a fairy tale.

Scandal was inevitable.

But it need not be attached to her name indefinitely. She would see to that. The gossip-mongers who asserted that the new Lady Rampton had deceived her husband into marriage would search in vain for signs that all was not well between them. He himself had called it a love match.

She smiled at her new husband and her heart leapt as she saw her pleasure reflected in the gaze he returned as they stepped out of the church, now man and wife. Tenderly, he caressed her cheek as she rested it briefly against his shoulder.

'Try not to over-exert yourself at the wedding breakfast,' he whispered. Tipping her face up towards his, he added with his characteristic wolfish grin: 'You'll need all your reserves for tonight.'

Helena was the first to offer her congratulations after the ceremony, mustering an impressive display of sincerity as she kissed Rose. She was radiant in primrose silk, her dark hair caught up in an ivory comb in a simple style that accentuated her high cheekbones and dark, smouldering eyes.

'Brother-in-law,' she said, eyes dancing, holding out her hands, forcing Rampton to walk forward and take them. 'May your impulsive gamble on a wicked Chesterfield pay off.' It was a bold and familiar speech ameliorated fortunately by Rampton's obvious delight in his unexpected and hasty marriage.

'Congratulations are due to my clever wife for realizing before I did what a crotchety old bachelor like myself really needed,' he said.

Proudly, he led Rose across the threshold and into the vast marble-floored hallway of her new London home. The household servants stood in two ordered lines from the foot of the sweeping staircase.

Having introduced them to the new Lady Rampton, the newly-weds preceded the guests into the saloon, where the sumptuous wedding breakfast was laid out.

'I didn't think you had it in you, Rose. You have triumphed.'

Helena had not wasted an opportunity. Finding Rose alone for the moment, the silken tones hid the unkind insinuation.

'My good fortune is all due to you, my dear Helena,' Rose responded. 'It was, after all, you who sent Charles looking for me the day the painting was finished, was it not? You wanted this marriage at any cost. And I am not sorry, so you have my thanks.'

'I am always so conscious of your shining halo, my dear Rose, I had not anticipated that he would find you so compromised.' Helena's smile did not reach her eyes. 'A lucky thing for you that Lord Rampton is an honourable man, otherwise you'd be languishing, a lonely and maligned spinster in the West Indies for the rest of your days.'

'I'd have had company when Charles finally brought you home.' It was an effort to sound brighter than she felt. Helena could be depended upon to find her most vulnerable places. 'Tell me, Helena, what really keeps you in England? It wasn't the debt, was it? You'd have found some way of brushing that under the carpet, or otherwise appeasing Lord Rampton.' Rose was pleased to see that this found its mark.

A shadow crossed Helena's face before she resumed smoothly, 'What does it matter why I persuaded Charles to allow me a few more weeks here. Besides, we just received news that our overseer appears to be doing a better job than Charles, or you, ever did. The plantation is prospering and now that you've landed yourself such a catch, Rose, I no longer have to *pretend* to be someone I'm not. My enjoyment has just begun. Besides, if I play my cards right Charles might find his way to furnishing *me* with a diamond necklace.'

'Ah...Like Lady Barbery's?'

'Exactly. Only I don't mean one that's been stolen, my dear Rose. *What* a perplexing mystery that was.'

It was wrong to feel such vitriol for anyone on this most joyous of occasions. Five years of training enabled Rose to say with reasonable equanimity, 'You achieved nothing, Helena. Rampton knows I am innocent.'

Helena's eyes widened with mock concern. 'Rose, you surely didn't imagine that my insistence that you should wear the necklace—though I admit, I was uncertain as to its origins—was prompted by malice? *You know* I just wanted to test Lord Rampton, and see how he'd champion you if indeed there were something havey-cavey about the gift.'

'Well, he passed the test with flying colours.' Rose met Helena's stony gaze with one of her own. 'And there is not the slightest doubt how much he *wanted* this marriage.'

Helena skimmed her gloved hand the length of Rose's forearm, feigning affection. 'No doubt at all,' she agreed. 'Of course, marrying your viscount was the easy part.' She drew back and her smile faded as she added, almost as if it were a vow, 'And may you be as happy, Rose, as *I've* been the past five years.'

Before her spirits had quite plummeted to her toes, Rose was relieved to see Rampton advancing, wearing the well-satisfied smile that filled her with happiness and banished her fears regarding their future together. Helena had not seen him. She was still eyeing Rose with a distinct lack of felicity. It was this which enabled Rose to feel charitable. She must remember, she told herself, that dissatisfaction was not a crime and nor had Helena committed anything beyond achieving, in fact, Rose's happiness. Helena's discontent with Charles did not mean she was a disloyal wife in more than thought, and if she could find happiness as the feted Lady Chesterfield in London's drawing rooms, Rose would be glad.

'Rampton ... darling.' What power Rose felt to purr those words and have her husband respond—in front of her jealous sister-in-law.

'My clever wife has brought me to heel, Helena, and long before time, too. Now, my dear ...' He put an arm around Rose's waist and was about to draw her away before good manners intervened as he glanced at Helena's empty hand. 'Shall I fetch you an orgeat, in case you've developed a taste for the sickly liquid, sister-in-law?' He smiled wickedly. 'Or should it be champagne? I keep forgetting that you are the worldly, married Lady Chesterfield.'

'Just as long as you remember that dear Rose is your innocent and unworldly wife.' Helena's eyes glittered, but her laugh was mirthless. 'Though for someone so innocent and unworldly she has done a fine job achieving what a great deal more designing misses have failed to achieve, I must say.'

⚜

RAMPTON ASSIGNED HIS HOUSEKEEPER, MRS HOPKINS, TO SHOW Rose the house of which she was now mistress. The wedding had been conducted in such haste that Rose had only seen the entertaining rooms.

Now, while Rampton was ensconced in his library with his man of business, preparing to leave for Larchwood, his country estate, a few days later, Rose trailed after Mrs Hopkins as the venerable retainer flung open the doors to Rose's private apartments.

Her bedchamber was decorated in green and gold. Once sumptuous, it now had a faded charm about it.

'This used to be her ladyship's room, but his lordship says it is to be redecorated to your liking.' Mrs Hopkins did not look encouraged by the prospect.

Rose was about to ask what her ladyship, languishing, apparently on the point of death in the country just now, might have to say about that, but then thought better of it. Mrs Hopkins looked as if she might enjoy explaining the point.

Rose's trunks had been unpacked. Her nightdress, in sheerest lawn and exquisitely embroidered, lay upon the bolster, her gowns and underclothes had been folded and put away. Upon the rosewood dressing-table her bottles and brushes were neatly arranged. Staring into her new bedchamber Rose felt like a stranger imposing upon another's hospitality. It had all been so unexpected.

The chill of it made her tremble and she had to grip the carved post of her new bed while she tried to comfort herself with the thought that this must be what every new bride felt like.

Certainly, the warmth of her husband's reception and his surprising equanimity towards their marriage had chased away most of her fears. She felt assured of his support and, surprisingly, his love. Surely she could not have mistaken the force of his ardour or misinterpreted his patent desire for her.

But what of the servants?

Mrs Hopkins, cold and erect, nodded stiffly as Rose dismissed her. Was she one enemy in a houseful of hornets? Did the minions downstairs make malicious remarks about their mistress's dubious claims to her new title? Had they heard the rumours surrounding the new Lady Rampton's wicked deception? Did they know she had been implicated by Lady Barbery in the theft of that lady's diamond necklace?

As Edith had decided to remain with the still heartbroken Arabella, a plain, sour-faced young girl called Beth had been assigned as Rose's lady's maid. Though Rose would rather have had Edith as an ally in her new home she feared for Arabella's welfare with Helena as her protector. Her younger sister's happiness was now Rose's chief concern. Once the scandal Rose had created had subsided – as Rampton had assured her it soon would with him by her side – she hoped the girl would be settled before too long. Helena was quite capable of forcing an unpalatable alliance upon Arabella if there were advantages for her and Charles.

'What does my lady wish to wear for dinner?' Beth's tone was courteous but, as she awaited instruction. Rose saw no warmth, no desire to do more than simply her job.

She was disappointed. Having the respect of one's lady's maid was important to bridge the divide between upstairs and downstairs. Rose would have hired a girl herself, except that Rampton's mother had assigned Beth to Rose specifically after hearing that Rose's old nurse would not join her in her new home. Rose wondered whether the act had been kindly motivated, or the opposite. Judging by her new maid's sharp features and thin mouth, young Beth had an uncertain temperament.

'Whatever you think most suitable.' It would be a test to see how competent the girl was.

While Beth laid out her clothes Rose walked over to her dressing table. She looked well. Her blue eyes were bright beneath their dark, arched brows. Her gleaming chestnut hair, released from the pins and coils which Edith had used to create a regal and lovely style fit for her wedding now shone in fine ripples over her shoulders, and her bare skin gleamed. It was better to look like the cat that had swallowed the cream, rather than something the cat had dragged in. And if she were already branded a scheming fortune hunter, well, it was better to be considered anyone's match than a poor, dispirited creature.

'An apt choice,' she remarked, with more than a hint of irony when she saw that Beth had laid out the most daring and revealing of all the gowns she'd had made in such haste during the three days available: a low-cut confection of deep-red silk.

Although these were not the words he used, Rampton's greeting as he stood awaiting her in the dining room went something along the same lines. But there was a sly gleam in his eye which banished any suggestion of disapproval.

'You're quite at liberty to tell me to change my dress,' Rose responded as she slid into her seat at the opposite end of the table, 'if you think it sends the wrong message to the servants.'

'I was thinking what a fine choice it was.' Tension crackled between them. He felt it as much as she, she could tell, as they locked glances.

When the wine was poured and the footman had retreated to his silent post by the sideboard, Rampton raised his glass. As he was about to make his toast, a light breeze stirred the curtains and caressed the flesh exposed by Rose's evening gown. She shivered.

'My dear, you're cold,' said Rampton, beckoning to the footman to close the window.

'No, please. Keep it open,' said Rose. Her reaction had been prompted by memories of that first fateful dinner with Lord Rampton when she had deceived him into thinking she was Helena. What a novel experience it had been pretending to be a married woman.

And now she was married.

'What is it?' Rampton was looking at her anxiously.

Realizing that she was frowning, Rose forced a smile. 'I was remembering how I sat here only a few weeks ago ...' She nibbled the inside of her lip. 'And how much I enjoyed deceiving you.' Despite her sly smile, doubt still gnawed at her. 'I never expected to marry you.' She glanced across at him, wanting his reassurance.

'Just as long as you enjoy the marriage part as much as you enjoyed the deception.' To Rose's surprise Rampton rose to his feet. Advancing upon her while the first course was growing cold, he said, 'You really are not quite the thing, are you, my dear?' His voice was solicitous for the benefit of the servants. His eyes, however, danced wickedly as they travelled from Rose's surprised face to her décolletage. 'That nervous headache has laid you low once more, hasn't it, dearest?'

The temerity, Rose thought with delicious wickedness as he concocted the lie for the benefit of the servants, struggling to hide her delight as he murmured, 'Allow me to escort you to your bedchamber. I'll have something sent up to your room, later. In fact, I'm not at all hungry, myself.'

Not risking an objection he caged her hand upon his arm before she had answered, and led her from the table. 'That will be all,' he dismissed the servants, turning as they reached the doorway.

At the foot of the staircase he lowered his face and with complete disregard for whoever might be watching, kissed her thoroughly upon the lips. 'I've had enough of charades,' he declared, as he swept her into his arms and mounted the stairs, 'including the pretence to enjoy dinner when I've only one thing on my mind.'

CHAPTER 12

ROSE WASN'T SURE whether she was sorry or otherwise that the Dowager Lady Rampton was not present to observe her son's obvious self-satisfaction—and satisfaction with his new wife—at breakfast the following morning.

Any qualms she'd had regarding her ability to please her husband in the bedroom as his legal wife, as opposed to the woman he'd obviously intended to take for his mistress, had not been realized.

Not only were they not realized, they were well and truly quashed.

She'd woken to find him looking down at her, admiration and desire brightening his gaze.

'Do you know,' he'd said, running an appreciative hand along the curves of her body as she lay on her side, 'that you are the first woman I've woken up next to who has filled me with the insatiable desire to repeat in every detail the events of the past eight hours.' Collapsing on his back and looking ruefully at the ceiling, he murmured, 'But I must not be a brute. You're an innocent and must be feeling very tender.'

'Yes,' agreed Rose, reaching across to kiss him on his beautifully shaped mouth. 'Very tender towards you, my love.'

She squealed as he flipped her onto her back.

'You must know the penalties for your trickery include a great deal of close contact with the man you set out to deceive,' he chuckled, straddling her.

Rose's face must have revealed her feelings for he stilled, his hands which had been gently massaging her breasts shimmying up and behind her neck. He rolled onto his side beside her and pulled her against him.

'You're a clever woman for knowing before I did exactly what I needed, dear heart,' he reassured her, kissing her neck, tenderly, while his other hand strayed over her belly, then downwards.

'Surely a man who has no intention of being leg-shackled has good reasons for not wanting a wife,' she responded. 'Helena tells me you tire quickly of your mistresses.'

'A good friend, isn't she?' he responded drily. With a sigh, he conceded between kisses, 'My thirst for novelty does not reflect well on me, I'll admit.'

'Will you take a mistress when you tire of me?' She cupped his face. 'After all, albeit unwittingly—or at least for noble reasons—I deceived you, Rampton. What happens after the novelty of having a wife wears off?'

Raising himself on one elbow he looked down at her, his expression serious. With his forefinger, he gently traced the contours of her nose and cheeks as he said in a low murmur which resonated with sincerity, 'The reason I have not wanted a wife before now is that I truly believe that wives and mistresses are not a happy mix.'

Rose bit her lip and felt a surge of hope at his tone. Conviction burned in the depths of his eyes and the expression he focused upon her sent tendrils of the deepest love and communion curling about her heart.

He kissed each eye in turn, almost reverently, before resuming. 'My father found it exhausting while my mother became a bitter creature obsessed with finding endorsement of her charms as a result of the disregard she received at home.' Stroking her cheek, he added, 'To tell you the truth, I'm delighted that I was led into a union which I heartily believe will satisfy me on all levels. Now, are *you* satisfied?' With a wicked grin he seized her by the hips and raised her so that she was lying the length of him. 'No, there's no need to tell me in so many words. Actions will do just as well.'

And as Rose was entirely satisfied with his response to her fears and the fact that she could not have desired any man more than her husband, she lowered her lips to kiss his nipples, succumbing to the languorous sensation of his hands rhythmically stroking her lower back and buttocks in the prelude to more of the delicious sensations to which she'd been initiated the previous night.

RAMPTON SHOWED EVERY SIGN OF BEING ENTIRELY SATISFIED WITH his new wife. Unfortunately, Rose's meeting with her mother-in-law in the country the following week suggested that her every fear about this lady's feelings towards her were right on the mark. She was glad to be bolstered by having Rampton at her side, making clear his obvious pleasure in his sudden and unexpectedly changed circumstances.

'So glad your health has improved, Mama,' he remarked, as he kissed her powdered cheek.

The newlyweds had travelled together by carriage, breaking their journey for the night at an inn some hours away, arriving at Larchwood around noon the following day. The dowager viscountess received them at the top of the shallow stone steps of Rampton's magnificent home and had, with a great show of fondness embraced Rampton, and with a great deal of reserve, stooped to plant a cool kiss upon her daughter-in-law's brow.

'Rampton never told me you were so small,' she said in greeting, turning to lead them into the house.

'I'm sure I never neglected to mention any one of her many virtues,' said Rampton, smoothly, giving Rose's hand a reassuring squeeze.

He reassured her again when he put his head around the door of her dressing-room where she was seated in front of her looking-glass in her own sumptuous apartments a little later.

'Mama may appear a gorgon, and I'll admit she'll need time to come round. Just remember, my love, no woman would ever have been good enough for her son. Soon she won't be able to help loving you.'

It didn't take long for Rose to be quite certain that loving her daughter-in-law was something his mother would never do. Not only was Rose inferior in birth and address to the wife Lady Rampton had desired for her son, she was clearly a fortune hunter with a past mired in deceit and scandal.

Rampton, too, was made privy to her feelings as he and Rose took tea with her in the drawing room later that afternoon.

'I had more refusals than acceptances, I wasn't sure whether to cancel the whole thing,' the dowager said as she recounted her difficulty in making up a party of ten, which was to serve as Rose's introduction into local society.

Rampton reached for a spiced biscuit. 'Lord and Lady Albright?'

'They accepted, yes.'

'What about Geoffrey?'

'He returned from London yesterday, so he has been included,' his mother replied, referring to the Albrights' son.

'You were not obliged, Mother,' Rampton said in clipped tones, before asking, 'The Colonel and Mrs Carstairs?'

'Declined, I'm afraid. As expected. The trouble is,' his mother went on, refilling his teacup, 'half the county have drawn their own conclusions about such a hastily conducted marriage.' She took up her own dainty teacup and added, over its rim, 'You must have expected this.'

There was an awkward silence. Rose, out of the corner of her eye, saw her husband tense.

'How could there not be?' Rose said, smiling. Rampton had been about to defend her, but she must not pit him against his mother. She had not lived five years in the same household with Helena without learning how to defuse a potentially explosive situation. 'Our courtship was highly irregular and I'd be surprised if I were not branded a scheming fortune hunter.'

'Who vehemently opposed the notion of marriage to me until I wore her down,' added Rampton, with a bolstering smile at Rose.

The dowager sniffed. 'Rampton never could resist a pretty face.' She glanced up at the enormous portrait that hung above the fireplace.

It was of the dowager, painted when she was a young girl. She had been beautiful, if the artist were to be believed, and had obviously been conscious of it, judging by the complacent little smile. She was smiling at Rose just like that now. Only youthful complacency had, with age, turned to malevolent smugness.

'At least you don't disgrace the family line with your appearance, though that's hardly the first consideration.'

'The first Lady Rampton was mistress to Charles II,' explained Rampton, smiling at Rose. 'Nor can it be forgotten that my own dear mama had the honour of turning down our good King George.'

'Rampton, this is not a competition,' said his mother with almost grotesque playfulness. But when she turned her gaze once more upon Rose her eyes were cold and her words held a warning. 'Rose, I've no doubt, is well aware of her obligations. She knows she'll have to tread warily to avoid being branded the scheming fortune hunter she has just described herself.'

❁❀❁

RAMPTON WAS CLEARLY PLEASED BY ROSE'S ENTHUSIASM FOR GOING riding that afternoon.

'Another surprise. I did not know that you could ride,' he said as they wandered over to the stables.

'How do you suppose I oversee the estate back at home?'

'Your home is here now.' Stopping by the stables he took her wrists, bringing them up to kiss the back of her hands. 'Everything happened so suddenly, my darling, and I freely admit I was hoist by my own petard and, for a time, felt distinctly aggrieved, but I would not have wanted it to be any different. I needed to be shown what I really wanted. You have no regrets?'

The husky tone of his voice made her insides cleave. She hesitated. Of course she had regrets. How much better if Rampton could have fallen in love with her as plain little Miss Chesterfield and there had been no subterfuge. Scandal was unpleasant and damaging. But neither of them had any choice but to wait for it to subside, as Rampton had assured her it would. He'd been endlessly reassuring since the fateful afternoon he'd waylaid her at the docks.

'No regrets,' she reassured him quickly in response to his frown. Then, changing the subject she added, 'I hope you don't plan to mount me on some docile little mare with absolutely no spirit.'

'That's exactly what I plan to do. Until I've satisfied myself you're not going to break your neck within a month of marriage I'll decide what's best for you.'

Rose dropped her voice to a murmur and said, provocatively, 'Perhaps the neighbours would think that a little drastic in order to rid yourself of the wife you were forced to marry in haste.'

'Madam, if we were not in public your inflammatory suggestion might be met by a sturdier response.' Smiling wickedly as the groom led a docile grey mare across the yard, he gave Rose's bottom a small spank.

She was not expecting it and blushed as the groom raised his eyebrows at her squeal.

"Fraid she's the littlest, most docile one we 'ave, miss. But if you's afraid of 'orses—' he said, misinterpreting her response.

'No need to worry, Briggs,' replied Rampton, leading Rose across the cobbles. 'I believe it was you who once remarked I'd as sure a touch with the ladies as I have with the horses. Now Rose, as you can see, this is the horse. Over here is what's called a mounting block. I shall assist you to get on to this creature's back but you mustn't scream. It only looks a long way down.'

Ignoring Brigg's mumbled response and fierce reddening and his wife's indignation, Rampton encircled her waist.

'In answer to your previous question, my love,' he murmured, his breath tickling her ear, 'the neighbours will soon be in no doubt as to exactly why I was so eager to wed you, my little vixen.' He glanced behind to make sure he was unobserved, then skimmed Rose's shapely contours before hoisting her on to the horse. 'Because I can't keep my hands off you.'

She had a better seat than most, he was forced to admit. And he did not mind telling her she looked extremely fetching in her severely cut dark-blue velvet habit and her high crowned riding hat with its curling feather.

Unexpectedly he found himself hoping they would be observed by all and sundry as they traversed the country lanes and tracks. Rose would certainly be seen to advantage here and he was just as anxious to dispel any speculation that this had not been a marriage of his choosing.

To think he had nearly thrown away this chance of happiness.

Away from the house and Lady Rampton's cold disapproval, Rose's high spirits returned. As soon as they were out of sight of the grounds, trotting sedately along a bridle path that ran through the woods, Rampton dismounted and, holding his arms up to receive her, told her there was something he must show her.

Rose glanced around as his arms tightened about her.

'What do you wish to show me?' she asked, for she could see nothing but lush foliage and tall trees.

'How much I adore you,' he replied. His voice held no irony, only a deep sincerity that left her in no doubt that she must be the luckiest woman on the planet. A feeling that intensified as he brought his head down and his mouth fixed upon hers in a kiss that stoked up once more the intense, lustful feelings that always left her gasping and also disbelieving she could be so lucky.

Breathing heavily, once they broke apart, Rampton traced her cheek with his fingertips. His eyes were dark with emotion. 'Don't allow Mama to wound you, Rose,' he told her with an earnestness that made her heart full. 'You'll win her round. A duke's daughter would have received little warmer welcome. It's just the way she is.'

Rose appreciated his attempts to make her feel better. She squeezed his hand and allowed him to help her remount. 'Thank you,' she said, although she knew family relations would be a great deal easier had her past been blameless.

Once through the wood they reached open country where they gave their horses their heads and enjoyed an exhilarating gallop.

By the time they headed for home Rose was feeling a great deal better. That is, until there came an uncomfortable and somewhat perplexing encounter along the way.

'I say, the bridegroom returns.' From around a bend in the rutted lane appeared a tall young man on horseback. Judging by his attire and the way his hair was curled Rose could tell he was a Corinthian. Rose was conscious of her husband stiffening in the saddle.

'And you, Geoffrey, I hear, managed to slither free of your obligations.'

Rose hid her surprise. It was not often Rampton failed to dress up his disapproval with jest.

'Not without honour, my dear Rampton,' replied the young man with a graceful bow from the waist, smiling, despite his hostile reception. 'If your own wife were not herself such a beauty you might well have benefited from my advice on such matters.' He nodded at Rose, adding, 'No disrespect intended, Lady Rampton. Your husband and I are old friends.' He paused. 'But as he appears to have forgotten his manners allow me to introduce myself. Your neighbour, Geoffrey Albright, at your service.' He gave another half-bow in the saddle, his eyes lingering on Rose.

With a curt nod, Rampton prepared to move on. 'Good day to you, Geoffrey. I believe we expect the pleasure of your company at dinner.'

'You must dislike him very much,' Rose remarked glancing back at the young man's departing figure. 'Your reception somewhat belied his assertion that you are old friends. How long have you known one another?'

'All our lives.'

WITH THE LAST-MINUTE CANCELLATION OF MR AND MRS BRIERLY the dinner party was reduced to eight. Rose learnt this by arriving at the drawing room just before the event in time to hear the dowager mutter, 'I don't see why you appear so surprised, let alone put out, Rampton. Frankly, I'm surprised the Brierlys are the only ones to have offered their apologies at the last minute. It's only because the rest of them thrive on salacious gossip that they can't bear to refuse an invitation to see the woman who has— Ah, Rose, there you are,' she broke off as she noticed Rose framed in the doorway. Lady Rampton did not even blush.

'The woman who has stolen my heart,' said Rampton, softly, warningly. Sweeping his mother with cold eyes, he moved to Rose and put an arm about her shoulders. 'Rose is the woman I love and that is the reason I married her.' He looked as though he was making an effort to keep his anger in check and Rose was half-afraid, half-gratified by the expressions that flitted across the dowager's face: surprise, indignation and ... apprehension. No doubt she knew she had gone too far.

'Rose, my love, shall we greet our guests?'

Despite Rampton's earlier chilly reception of his old companion, Geoffrey, he was cordial as he greeted him now, this time in company with the young man's parents.

Although Geoffrey's starched shirt points weren't so high as entirely to obscure his cheekbones, it was apparent by his elaborately tied cravat that Mr Albright aspired to high fashion. He was handsome in an affected way, but Rose far preferred her husband's understated elegance.

'I hadn't thought to see you returned so soon, Geoffrey.' The dowager Lady Rampton greeted the young man with a certain reserve. 'Rumour had it you'd be gone another month.'

'That's why it was just a rumour,' he replied, smiling as he bent over her hand. 'They're simply buzzing around me at the moment.'

'Yes, aren't they,' she replied drily, and again Rose wondered at his crime, if that was what it was.

Then the dowager was smiling almost coyly as she quizzed him on his latest exploits. Obviously his crimes did not really matter. People would never snub him by declining his dinner invitations. He was a man.

A man who certainly knew how to charm for not a minute after his frosty reception he was enjoying a tete a tete with his hostess who seemed to be murmuring in a decidedly intimate manner and whose reference to the West Indies had Rose twisting back from her stilted conversation with Geoffrey's unforthcoming step-father.

'You look absolutely gorgeous, darling.'

Rampton's murmured praise as he brushed past her enabled Rose to muster a dazzling smile. She had won over her husband against the odds. Now she must do the same with the neighbours she decided, as they all seated themselves.

Taking comfort in her appearance was a novelty. In the West Indies she had barely made the effort to dress her hair in anything but the most rudimentary twist, nor had she worried about complexion enhancers. What was the point when she owned no fine clothes? Or when there was no one who held the least interest for her?

But while it bolstered her confidence to be so openly admired by her husband and at least several of the gentlemen there, she wished she'd not been seated next to Geoffrey whose bold and piercing looks made her distinctly uncomfortable.

'Lady Rampton, it is an honour to meet one of the ravishing Chesterfields at last,' he said, turning to address Rose now that his neighbour had been engaged by the gentleman on her other side. 'I believe the three of you have taken London by storm this season.'

Glancing up from spearing her pigeon breast, Rose had half antici-pated the predictable gallant admiration, but his gaze was peculiarly intense, frankly appraising, and distinctly unnerving. She licked dry lips, uncertain how to answer, but certainly wary of appearing too cool, or too encouraging. Certainly not until she knew better what kind of man Geoffrey Albright was. She was saved from having to respond when he asked, unexpectedly, 'Do you suppose we have met before?'

She drew back, startled. 'I've only been in the country a couple of months.'

Geoffrey leaned a little closer. His long, contemplative silence was unsettling. At last he said, with a little laugh, 'Perhaps in another life, madam. I am sure that in another life we were once ...' he drew back, his gaze flicking over her as if she were a prime article, 'very close.'

Before Rose could voice her indignation Geoffrey resumed, 'I hear you sat to your brother-in-law, a noted portraitist.'

'I hear you've been out of the neighbourhood,' responded Rose, coolly, though she was churning with disquiet inside.

'Just in the neighbouring county, staying with friends.' His smile was bland before he turned the conversation back to her. 'Of course, all the talk was of the unexpected speed of your nuptials. You can imagine how many fair noses were put out of joint when it was learned that the beautiful but obscure Lady Chesterfield—I beg your pardon, Miss Chesterfield—had no sooner stepped ashore from the colonies than she'd snared one of the country's most eligible and elusive bachelors. So, ma'am, having known Rampton all my life, and of his resistance to marriage, you understand why I have been excessively keen to meet you.'

'It's as well, then, that you're such close neighbours, since I'd hate to think you might have travelled a great distance only to be disappointed,' said Rose, leaning aside so she could be served from a platter of beef.

'I would not have been disappointed had you been cross-eyed and hare-lipped. It was my curiosity that needed satisfying.' Geoffrey's eyes reminded her in that moment of those of a well-fed cat, confident of itself and its quarry. 'Rampton's idea of the perfect wife is a plain, docile girl who will leave him to his own devices,' Geoffrey went on, cruelly. 'From what I have heard, you are far from docile, and you most certainly are not plain. Already you've led him quite a dance.'

Rose acknowledged his words with the barest of smiles, forbearing to reply as she picked up her knife and fork. She felt embarrassed and trapped. Mr Albright, senior, on her other side, was deep in conversation with Rampton's mother. Glancing across the table she caught her husband's eye, and he, reading the desperation he saw there, went so far as to breach good manners by leaning across the table to say, 'I believe you've been a guest of the Huntingdons this past fortnight, Geoffrey. Weren't you supposed to stay a month?'

Geoffrey gave a careless shrug but a faint blush belied his assumed indifference. 'A week would have been sufficient in such dull company,' he said. 'Naturally I had no desire to cause offence, so I invented the excuse that Mama was poorly and wanted me home. If you've heard anything other then it's been invented.'

'Ah.' Rampton, nodded, as if satisfied that he had just been furnished with the real reason while a wisp of memory curled around Rose's brain as she tried to recall if she'd seen Geoffrey Albright before.

'Knowing you, Geoffrey, as I do, I was unable to give credence to the rumours that have been circulating. I see you've been admiring my new bride.' Rampton changed the subject. 'I had to act quickly to secure her consent before she set sail for the West Indies. She was on the point of embarking, in fact, when I waylaid her,' he sent Rose a smouldering look, careless of the interest of the rest of the table, 'and finally overcame her resistance to the idea.'

When the guests had left and they were alone Rose looked up from her dressing-table and asked, 'Does Geoffrey Albright have a sister whose aspirations towards marriage with you I might have blighted?'

Rampton, stroking her shoulders, looked perplexed. 'He has no sister.'

'Well, he certainly made it plain that his attendance here was more in the nature of a visit to the zoo to see what sort of creature I really was than a genuine desire for our society.' She bit her lip, watching him in the looking-glass, close to tears. 'I wonder how many others felt the same?'

'Geoffrey—my friend as you erroneously term him—would not have been invited here at all if I had had anything to do with the guest list.' Rampton leant down and put his cheek against hers, smiling at her reflection. 'Rest assured that you were mightily admired tonight. By Geoffrey too, who, I must warn you, is very much in the petticoat line. I do not care for his society but for some reason my mother has had a fondness for him since we were brats together.'

'Were you not even friends as schoolboys?'

'Age and proximity were all we had in common.' Rampton gave a grim laugh. 'You'll have heard, no doubt, several sly references to his recent house visit to Colonel and Mrs Huntingdon. They have a son and two daughters, the younger a pretty enough creature, just out of the school-room but too giddy, it was thought, to unleash on society this year. In usual fashion it seems Geoffrey played fast and loose with the young girl and she, knowing no better, her head doubtless turned by his pretty compliments, has become in consequence the talk of the town, to her detriment.'

'You mean he's compromised her reputation and won't behave in good part?'

'My dear, the man is married with an invalid wife. Not that you'd know it from the way he comports himself about the countryside like a gay young blade.'

He drew Rose up to stand beside him and continued, as he led her to the bed, 'But no, Geoffrey prefers to brag about his involvement with Miss Huntingdon, suggesting it was she who led him into all sorts of disgraceful scrapes.'

He had Rose trapped against the bed. Leisurely he began to nuzzle her neck while loosening her silk peignoir. Beth had performed her duties and been dismissed for the night.

'A wife!' Rose was shocked. She arched against him. 'He never mentioned her during our conversation and I quizzed him all about his family.' For once she felt little answering response to Rampton's obvious desire. All her plans of dazzling the company and gainsaying the gossips who said she'd trapped her husband lay in ruins. If Geoffrey, with his obvious penchant for female company, could make her feel this unworthy, how would she fare when confronted with the more virtuous element of her neighbours?

'Yes, scandalizing, isn't it?' Rampton sounded amused. The palm of his hand was now travelling in gentle circular strokes from her shoulder, moving down to her breast. 'I blame his pea-goose of a mother,' he went on, conversationally. 'She dotes on him. Takes his part and always has done, whatever mischief he's engaged upon.'

Rampton bent to nibble Rose's earlobe, both hands being now engaged upon their journey of discovery. Normally Rose would have been in thrall. Now all she could think of were Geoffrey's insults and hurtful insinuations. Rampton had sat across the table and observed the conversation, yet he had no idea just how insulting Geoffrey had been.

Tonight's dinner with its declined invitations and Geoffrey's brazen curiosity, and his cruelty in dealing in home truths, made Rose realize how compromised she really was. And how much it affected Rampton's standing in the community.

'He's been horribly indulged by his stepfather, too. His mother was a poor widow and Geoffrey just an infant when she married Albright. She believes her precious Geoffrey was inveigled into marriage. But the girl's a simpleton. A very comely simpleton, I grant you. Geoffrey was loath to do his duty until forced.'

Rose pulled away again and closed her eyes. His words scorched her soul. Perhaps Rampton would think her in the throes of ecstasy. But for that moment she could not bear his touch.

She sighed softly. 'Unlike you were forced to do your duty?'

She felt Rampton draw back in surprise. His expression was quizzical. And uncertain. He must have felt her reserve.

'My duty?' he began. His hands dropped from her shoulders. 'My duty, my dear?' he repeated, his head cocked on one side. 'Do you consider this a duty?'

Shaking her head, she exhaled on a sob. 'Of course not. But please, Rampton, I'm very tired tonight...'

She knew she should say more. Rampton had been so understanding and used every opportunity to reassure her that her place in his heart was secure. Good lord, it was more than a bride who'd married for love could have expected.

Married for love? As she lay in bed, alone, that night the phrase kept returning, until she finally acknowledged the truth of those words.

Love was the basis for her union with Rampton, not deceit, and she was only harming herself and what they had if she kept harking back to it.

She shivered beneath the counterpane of her large, empty four-poster in the private apartments she'd been assigned. How foolish of her to have elected to 'give him his privacy', thinking space apart would be good for them, and how much she wanted to go to him.

But she didn't think she'd know how to find his quarters in the dark.

Berating herself for thinking no further than her foolish insecurities she tossed and turned until daylight when she would have sought him out immediately had sleep not finally claimed her.

CHAPTER 13

ROSE'S GUILT COMPOUNDED her unhappiness when she found that her husband had left on an unscheduled trip at dawn the following morning.

'A man needs his freedom,' her mother-in-law said, looking up from her tatting. Rose had seen the malicious gleam in her eye as she informed her that Rampton had ridden to town and she had no idea when he might be back.

'It must be at least four hours on horseback. Perhaps longer. He must mean to spend the night. And you only just married. Still, it cannot be said he has not done his duty by you when all's said and done.'

Duty. That is what Rampton had talked of last night, before he had kissed her cheek and left her. She had clung to him for a moment. She wanted to rest her cheek against his chest and cry her heart out; she wanted him to reassure her—again, in view of Geoffrey's unkindness—that he had married her not out of duty but plain desire. She had been too self-absorbed to see that he had wanted the same reassurance. And now he was gone, before she could tell him so.

SINCE RAMPTON WAS NOT REVELLING IN HIS WIFE'S WARM EMBRACE that morning he'd decided on his usual dawn ride. It was only as he was dressing that the remembering of a neglected piece of business prompted him into changing his plans and making a day trip to London.

It had been a piece of perversity not to slide into bed beside Rose and inform her, he knew. The truth was that he was chagrined. Last night Rose had clearly not desired him.

It had been less than two weeks since they had wed and they had shared a bed every night. He'd thought his desire would run its course, but its trajectory was ever upward. He grimaced. He could feel a certain piece of his anatomy taking the same course at the mere thought of her.

But last night Rose had not felt the same lustful desires she previously had and the knowledge had sent him off like a schoolboy full of pique.

Catherine Barbery, his most longstanding mistress, had once declared it was impossible to desire one's husband. 'Desire implies excitement, and who can be excited at the prospect of duty?' she had asked.

Catherine had been twenty-seven to his twenty years when he'd met her. Married to the wealthy banker, Claude Barbery for ten years at the time, she was famous for her fiery and often indiscreet amours. Within five years she'd provided her elderly husband with three sons and had then embarked upon a life of self-gratification, unchallenged by Barbery who was content to spend much of his time with his own mistress of thirty years.

Rampton had been just a callow, untried youth just down from Cambridge when Catherine had first cast her lures.

This bold, adventurous and unconventional woman had proved a voracious lover and had shaped his ideas on love. She'd been the one to end his first romance, introducing him to her bosom friend. 'A year is a long time and you are only twenty-one, my love. We've taught one another as much as we can. The excitement has lost its lustre and now it's time to move on.' Then she added, with great prescience, 'I think you will like Annabelle.'

But Rampton's association with Catherine did not end there. They remained friends and the romance had been rekindled the previous year.

Then Rampton had met Rose.

Catherine had not been happy. 'I could be reconciled if your marriage were contracted on dynastic or pecuniary grounds but it revolts me to see this foisted upon you as an obligation,' she'd flared.

'Honour, not duty, my dear.' He'd tried not to be riled.

'Same thing. The girl should have known better but if she is enceinte then I know a very discreet gentleman just off Harley Street who'll take care of her. Neither of you should be forced into a marriage you'd never have contracted willingly.'

Rampton had replied with spirit, 'I married a virgin... on the novel grounds of love.'

Having Rose cleave to him, and knowing that they were bound until death was immensely satisfying.

Yes, satisfying. She made him feel whole.

Last night he'd wanted her to tell him she felt the same. He'd ceased his amatory explorations, held her away from him and bluntly asked her if she considered this a duty.

He'd laid the groundwork; all she needed to do was deny it and sink, boneless into his very responsive arms. Instead she had been unable to meet his eye. When he'd indicated he was going to bed she'd clung to him, and tears had glistened in her eyes. But then she had released him and turned away.

Restlessly, Rampton turned the page of the periodical on the table before him at his club.

It was only after last night's dinner that she had behaved differently. And for the very first time.

Which was when Rampton had abandoned her.

Turning another page of the periodical in front of him, realising he hadn't taken in a word, Rampton realised what a cad he was. Just when Rose needed reassuring over her role as his wife and hostess he'd disappeared. That blackguard, Geoffrey, playing on her vulnerabilities, probably to spite Rampton, was largely to blame for her downcast spirits but Rampton had been too absorbed in himself that he'd been unable to see what was right in front of his nose.

At this point Rampton's thoughts were interrupted by a heavy-set elderly gentleman stumbling against his chair.

As he stopped to apologize Rampton could not but be struck by his deeply tanned complexion. He was about to murmur that it was quite all right when the gentleman, obviously recognizing him, declared, 'It's Lord Rampton, ain't I right? Lucky man who's just married the incomparable Miss Chesterfield. I'd not the nerve to approach you directly when you were pointed out to me before, but since I've literally stumbled upon you ...'

He held out his hand, white teeth brilliant, like his snowy hair, a dazzling contrast with his leathery complexion.

'Sir Hector Stokes,' he introduced himself. 'Knew your wife back in the West Indies. Known her since she was born, in fact, and, what's more, had the dubious honour of being declined by her nigh on five years ago.' He chuckled. 'Thought that'd surprise ye. Yessir, I'd like to think she was in good, safe hands now. Couldn't be worse off than with that brother of hers whom she all but wet-nursed, and got little thanks for it. So ... married last week, I hear.' He shook his head. 'And me only off the boat on Tuesday. Not that she'd have had me for all the fancy palaces I could have bought her, if she'd have let me. Ay, when I hear she set her cap at you it makes my blood fair boil. My Rose never set her cap at anyone. If ever there was a goddess of virtue, 'twas Miss Chesterfield.'

Rampton, as much astonished by the revelation of this character's identity as by his speech, was about to invite him to sit when they were accosted by his new brother-in-law.

'Good Lord, Sir Hector, is it really you?' Sir Charles asked, a smile lighting up his normally hangdog expression. 'Why, it must be five years. Surely you've not been in England all this time?'

'Just stepped off the boat Tuesday last, as I was telling Lord Rampton. Been adventuring since I last saw you. Spice Islands, Americas. Nothing like travel to mend a heart and fire up the constitution.'

Rampton pressed his new acquaintance to take some brandy with him. He was disappointed when, instead, he found himself alone in the company of his brother-in-law.

'Back in town already, Rampton? Then perhaps you've heard the news. I don't know whether to be pleased for Rose or indignant.'

It was clear Charles was enjoying Rampton's suspense, however as Rampton responded with merely a slight raising of one eyebrow, Charles said, 'She's just been left a sizeable legacy from a great-aunt. Or half great-aunt. Fact is, I didn't even know Aunt Gwendolyn existed until I heard that Rose had struck up an acquaintanceship with her a month or two ago.'

Dutifully, Rampton congratulated him.

'Oh, I won't see a penny of it for her house and an annuity has been willed to Rose, so of course you'll benefit, Rampton.' He grunted, shifting uncomfortably when he seemed to become aware of the churlishness of his tone. 'Fact is, Rose was counting on this some weeks ago, so she could repay you without obligation. Not that she didn't want to marry you, of course,' he added, hastily. 'Still,' he shrugged, 'life works in mysterious ways and you've been very generous to us, don't think I don't appreciate it. Now all that's needed is a marriage offer from Yarrowby to settle Arabella and then I can take Helena back to the plantation where I know she'd be so much happier.'

Rampton raised one eyebrow. 'Has Rose not passed on my cautions to you regarding Yarrowby?' he asked.

'Cautions?' Charles looked blank before he went, 'Not that it matters, I daresay, since Yarrowby who looked set to offer last week in fact has suddenly disappeared without a word. So if it's cautions regarding the fellow's address, I'd say he could learn some manners about what it is to let down a hopeful young maiden. I found Arabella in tears twice yesterday and I can't tell you how wearisome it is to live in a household of discontented women.'

Rampton stood up, bowing his intention to depart. 'I'm sorry Yarrowby has departed but you might like to quiz Rose on what I have to say about his suitability as a suitor. Good evening, Charles.'

ROSE HAD LEFT HER MOTHER-IN-LAW'S COMPANY TO RESTORE HER spirits, so the last thing she needed as she rode out and inhaled the crisp morning air, gazing out over the beautiful hills and valleys which her husband owned, was to see Mr Albright, also on horseback, hailing her.

"Morning, Mr Albright,' she said, with a decided lack of pleasure as he brought his mount abreast of hers.

'Surveying your newly acquired estates, madam?' he remarked in that outrageously direct way of his; so insulting.

'I had no idea it was so beautiful.'

'Then I hope you will remain in the country to enjoy it rather than rushing back to town at the first opportunity.' His tone was insinuating. 'I was looking forward to furthering our acquaintance ... now that we are such close neighbours.'

Rose tried to look as unwelcoming as she could. He was sticking by her side like a leech.

'Your husband and I used to fish off that stone bridge over there whenever we could get out of our lessons early,' Geoffrey said, pointing. 'Not that that was often, for our tutor took fiendish delight in setting us Latin translation which took for ever to finish.'

'You had lessons together?'

'Evidently Lady Rampton felt her son wanted in the way of playmates. As we were both roughly the same age and had no siblings she proposed to my mother that I should take my lessons with Rampton. I daresay I can thank him for opportunities which might not otherwise have come my way.'

'And what use have you made of them, Mr Albright?'

At her arch look and tone he roared with laughter and then responded, as if he genuinely thought she'd been making a joke, 'Absolutely right, Lady Rampton, I've never done a scrap of good since the day I was born. I am the despair of my poor parents. They even sent me off to the West Indies for a short time, you know. Alas, our paths did not cross, Lady Rampton. Perhaps you'd have seen that the wayward youth I once was needed the strictest of overseers, not some indulgent – and somewhat drink-sodden – brother of my mother.' His eyes gleamed at Rose as he assessed the effect his words had on her.

Rose frowned, recalling her father mentioning some lazy ne'er-do-well relative of some acquaintance. Perhaps it had been Geoffrey.

When at last she was rid of him she stopped in at the kitchens to supervise dinner. Little matter that the dowager would consider it a gross violation, but Rose wanted not only to see the way things were run and, if possible, make improvements. She knew how to run an estate and, after all, she was the new Lady Rampton and her husband had given her carte blanche. Following a heated but, she hoped, profitable exchange with the cook she spent the rest of the afternoon exploring the house. She was determined to acquit herself more than creditably as wife and hostess and was not afraid of hard work.

Just before retiring to her apartments to change she was handed two letters: one from her Aunt Alice and one from a man of the law of whom she'd never heard.

⚜

RAMPTON HAD BARELY DRAWN BREATH, CHANGED HIS COAT AND sponged the dust from his face before going in search of Rose. He'd behaved like an immature schoolboy, misinterpreting her strained behaviour after her first dinner party in her new home. Then he'd rushed off without a word, giving his mother more ammunition against his new wife. The last thing he wanted!

He found her in her private sitting room, white-faced and trembling.

'My great-aunt Gwendolyn has died,' she told him.

He looked at the cream wafer she waved distractedly before her, and then at her face. Her eyes were blank with shock.

Having galloped as if the devil was after him he'd hoped for a warmer welcome than this. Still, he was in the wrong. He'd left her when she needed him.

And, by the look of her, she needed him now.

'My commiserations,' he said, as he put a comforting arm around Rose who was standing in the centre of the room. 'When is her funeral? I daresay you're obliged to attend?'

'It would be the least I can do, considering she has just left me a rather fine address in Mayfair, and an annuity for its upkeep.'

It was more, much more, than he had expected. He also had expected Rose to be delighted. He led her to the window seat and sat beside her. Clearly she was in shock. This woman must have meant a great deal to her, after all. He murmured, 'That was magnanimous of her.'

'No!' Rose shook off his arm and buried her face in her hands. 'Why did she choose to die now? Everyone said she was a vindictive old woman. And so she was. To die now ... not three weeks ago!' The wafer which had conveyed the news, now a crushed ball, was flung across the room. Rose stood up and began to pace, hands at her throat, her breathing laboured. 'Don't you see?' she continued. 'If she had given some indication of her intentions earlier I would never have been forced to continue my deception. I could have paid our debt to you – honourably.'

Seeing his dismay, she twined her arms around his neck.

'Oh, my darling, I have no regrets at marrying you!" she assured him. 'My only regret is that Aunt Gwendolyn's beneficence, had it come earlier, could have avoided all this scandal!'

Relief filtered through his core. He looked down at her fondly. 'If you'd been in a position to repay Helena's debt, honourably, chances are I'd not be married to you now.' The familiar desire she evoked and which had found no outlet last night, snaked through him. He toyed with the bow that secured the front of her dress and dipped his hand into her bodice, making her gasp when he gently pinched her nipple.

'Perhaps I know a way of making you feel better about it all, my love,' he growled.

Rose bit her lip and clearly tried to look disapproving, though her smile won out. 'Oh, Rampton, it sounds very appealing but what of the servants? And your mother? It's true that I was not close to Great-aunt Gwendolyn but what will people think if we disappear to the bedroom within minutes of me learning of her death?'

'For someone so cunning, you surely are displaying a decided lack of imagination, my darling,' Rampton murmured. 'Why, you are distraught, naturally! And I intend to comfort you!'

610

With a quick glance to reassure him they were alone, Rampton whisked her into his arms and bore her up the stairs and along the corridor to his bedchamber.

She clung to him while his mind raced with the desire to feel her naked beneath him, to stoke her passions into feelings that echoed his and thus reassure him that her desires for him were mutual.

Dumping her on the bed, he kept his eyes on her as she tore off his coat and hessians, then, looming over her before climbing onto the bed he asked, 'Do you want me?'

Wordlessly, she nodded, rolling onto her stomach so he could undo the buttons of her gown. Her trembles of sensation as he slid his hands across her satiny skin added to his need for her, but he wanted the reassurances of her words, too.

He felt her swallow convulsively as he kissed her throat, his hand reaching for the hem of her chemise, raising it, slowly, as he trailed his fingertips the length of her limb, across her heated thigh.

Still she said nothing, just mutely allowed him the liberty of his exploration. The moistness between her legs should have delighted him, as testimony that she desired this as much as he but there was something hollow in the act.

With a sigh she received him, moving with him, slowly at first, matching his pace, and all the while he stared into her face, waiting for a sign that he was the only man who could satisfy her until his thoughts became mindlessly concentrated on his own pleasure.

His climax coincided with the dinner gong. He had no idea if he'd satisfied his young wife for she immediately slid to the floor and reached for her gown, pulling it over her head and turning so he could do up the buttons. 'Beth will be looking for me.' Her breathing was fast and shallow and he wondered if it was from their exertions or her fear of possible consequences when she added, 'and we can't have your mother waiting.'

He looked over his shoulder as he put on his hessians. 'Pleasing my mother is more important than pleasing me?' He'd said it half in jest but she bit her lip as she hesitated, half way to the door. 'You know I'd do anything to please you, Rampton darling, but your mother has the potential to make my life very ... uncomfortable.'

Her hand lingered on the door knob and she was clearly waiting for some rejoinder. She looked ill at ease and Rampton, who'd thought taking her to bed would be the answer to all his troubled feelings, could only sigh and shake his head.

'Only if you let her, my dear,' he said, not bothering to hide his exasperation. 'Now run along or you'll keep Beth waiting, too, and we can't have that, can we?'

As she turned, he called her back. 'I expect you'll wish to make arrangements for your earliest possible departure. Tomorrow morning? That should see you there in good time.'

She looked confused. And hurt. Though why that should be Rampton had no idea.

'I'll sell it, Rampton. The property might be willed to me, but the proceeds are yours, by rights. The debt—'

He waved a hand dismissively through the air. 'Does everything hark back to that goddamned debt? Do what you wish with your new address, my dear. Give it to the orphans' asylum for all I care. The house and whatever proceeds it may reap you are yours and of no interest to me.'

Of course, his mother had a different view. Smiling grimly, she said, 'This will go down well with those neighbours who might have attributed baser motives to the way in which you went about persuading Rampton into marriage.'

'Mother!' Rampton rose to his feet, fiercely protective of Rose who extended her arm towards him saying in mollifying terms, 'If it's the truth, as I'm sure it is, you must not blame your mother for saying what I need to guard myself again. Yes,' she smiled at the dowager, 'my inheritance will help to redress many of the wrongs for which I must take responsibility.'

'It seems you have a more sensible head on your shoulders than I'd thought,' said the other woman. 'But now, tell me, I'm curious as to why you said nothing about knowing Mr Albright in the West Indies all those years ago.'

Rampton, surprised, jerked his head around at Rose who was looking blank. Then she shook her head. 'I've never met him before, though he seemed to think he knew me,' she said, slowly.

The dowager frowned. 'You say you don't know Geoffrey?'

'She certainly has no reason to like him,' Rampton muttered.

❧

AN UNCHARACTERISTIC CONFUSION OF SPIRITS MADE RAMPTON restless as Fanshawe, his valet, brushed his russet superfine coat in preparation for dinner.

Was it true that if Rose had received her bequest from her late Great-Aunt Gwendolyn she'd have continued to resist Rampton? The question chased itself round his brain.

Had the old woman died a few weeks earlier, as Rose had stated so plainly, she'd have had financial independence.

Freedom to choose her husband?

But *of course* she'd have chosen him. She'd made that clear on any number of occasions.

'Are you satisfied with the construction of your cravat, sir?'

Rampton studied his reflection and then the anxious expression of his valet. 'Perfectly satisfied.'

He drew himself up. Whisking Rose off to bed before they'd properly discussed matters had been a mistake, he realised. The problem was that he was utterly mad with lust for his new wife yet his poor darling was facing so much that was new and unknown.

Naturally, though, she'd have wished a bequest that might have swept away the scandal attached to her publicly revealed charade and compromised reputation followed by their hasty marriage had come earlier.

Still, there could be no mistaking Rose's physical responses to him. This, Fenton found to be enormously gratifying.

Catherine Barbery was jealously stirring up trouble with her response to Rampton after he'd proudly told her to what lengths Rose had gone to in order *not* to force him to honour his matrimonial obligations.

She'd actually claimed that such behaviour must indicate Rose's heart had belonged to another.

What would Catherine know? After all, he was certain, now, that it was Catherine who'd sent her diamond necklace to Rose and then claimed Rose had stolen it.

Catherine, he decided, was not to be trusted. She seemed determined to sow trouble.

After declaring himself satisfied with his appearance, Rampton went in search of Rose, but found only his mother in the darkened drawing room. The light gave her a headache, she said. He could not remember a time she she'd embraced the sunlight and the outdoors. Or when she'd truly smiled.

'Your new wife has taken herself off for a walk,' she greeted him, detaining him when he would have gone after her, with, 'Sit, Rampton, we need to talk.'

Stifling a groan, Rampton lowered himself onto a leather armchair far from the fire and looked enquiringly at her. 'I trust you have not inveigled me into conversation merely to bring to light some other defect of my new wife,' he muttered.

His mother shook her head. 'To be truthful, she is not the woman I'd have chosen for you but she is agreeable enough. I find I'm not so disposed to dislike her as I'd supposed.'

Rampton chuckled, despite himself. 'You are lavish with your praise, mother. Small wonder I've grown up so accepting and forgiving of the foibles of those around me.'

She ignored his irony. 'I took tea with Mrs Albright this morning and she told me something quite extraordinary.'

Rampton cocked an eyebrow, ready to pounce in defence of Rose, if necessary. Mrs Albright was a gossip. Still, he was glad his mother chose to share the rumours that might be circulating about his wife if only to be in a better position to quash them.

'Rampton, you remember five years ago when Geoffrey returned home after a year in the West Indies helping his uncle—Mrs Albright's brother—manage the sugar plantation?'

Rampton nodded.

'Do you recall that his mother was at her wits' end because he was so changed? So wild?'

'That's right. I believe I suggested he might be a poppy-eater. And barely had he been here a month than he got that poor simpleton into trouble and was forced to do the honourable thing. He's been nursing a grudge ever since.' He wondered what relevance any of this had to Rose. Perhaps it didn't.

His mother clicked her tongue. 'It turns out that Mrs Albright believes Geoffrey's anguish was on account of a young woman in the West Indies. A very beautiful young woman who captured Geoffrey's heart. He was very bitter over the affair. Of course, Geoffrey won't talk about it other than to say that this young woman returned his love but refused his marriage offer because he hadn't sufficient funds to keep her in the style to which she intended to become accustomed.'

Rampton had an inkling as to where this was going. 'You're suggesting it might be Rose?' He shook his head, groaning inwardly. More false rumours to have to counter. 'Nonsense, it could have been anyone. And Rose denied ever meeting him.'

His mother picked up her tatting with a sigh. 'Yes, she did deny it. Yet Rose did seem very uncomfortable about being in his company.'

Smiling, Rampton rose. 'Well, I'll just have to ask my darling wife myself—in case her memory has subsequently returned,' he said, brightly.

He already had his hand on the doorknob when Rose appeared upon the threshold. The faint scent of the orange blossom water she liked to wear seemed to power directly from his olfactory senses through to his loins and it was all he could do not to run his hands all over her. Instead, he stepped back to allow her to pass by then followed her into the room, asking, 'Rose, mother is curious to know if you perhaps recall having met Mr Albright since you were distant neighbours at roughly the same time in the West Indies.'

She gasped. 'I've never met him,' she said quickly. 'And if you'll pardon my rudeness, I'm glad of it. He seems a most unpleasant young man and I make no apology for saying so.'

Rampton put his hand on her shoulder to calm her. 'I'm sorry if he upset you, my dear. And that's quite all right. Mama was just curious, that's all.' Over the top of Rose's head he levelled an 'I told you so' look and was about to suggest they take a turn around the roses when the dowager called Rose to her side, asking, 'Since you must be worn out after your walk, Rose, I wonder if you'd be good enough to help me untangle these skeins of thread.'

Rampton's chagrin only reinforced how obsessed he was with the beautiful woman he was so glad was his wife.

⚜

ROSE TOSSED AND TURNED IN BED THAT NIGHT AS SHE WENT OVER the events of the past twenty-four hours. She'd made a grave miscalculation in the way she'd delivered the news of her bequest and that this had been compounded by her lack of interest in her husband when he'd whisked her off to bed in the middle of the afternoon. But the ominous presence of Rampton's mother was a great inhibitor, especially when she strongly suspected Beth was furnishing the dowager with intimate details of Rose's conduct.

Eleven o' clock. Rampton should have come to her by now if he was going to at all. He'd been kept up attending to business affairs and had promised to join her later.

With thundering heart Rose slipped out of bed and wrapped a shawl around her shoulders. If Rampton had misinterpreted her distress then he needed reassuring as to exactly where her affections lay.

Her tumultuous emotions had certainly not abated by the time she reached his bedchamber where the sound of his even breathing indicated that he was not being kept awake by the same pangs of doubt and worry that besieged her.

She wasn't sure whether coming here was a mistake or not, but she had to show him honestly what was in her heart. Perhaps a distant approach might have been better, but wasn't that a device a scheming huntress employed prior to the wedding vows? No, Rose was determined to show Rampton that she found him the most irresistible gentleman she'd ever encountered.

'Rose, is everything all right?'

His voice was thick with sleep and surprise as he struggled onto his elbows, but she snuggled into the crook of his arm and, wrapping her ankle round his while nibbling his earlobe, made it quite clear her intentions had nothing to do with needing his assistance. Except in the bedroom department, for he'd unleashed a healthy dose of lust she'd had no idea existed in her deepest recesses.

'I only want to show how much I love you,' she whispered, nuzzling his neck, 'and that I'm sorry if it seemed, before, that I didn't.'

'Oh, Rose.' All the relief for which she could have hoped was invested in those two words as he crushed her against his breast. 'And I'm sorry for being a cad and not realising how difficult it must be for you to enter a new life where everything is so strange. I was going to come to you earlier but it was so late I feared you'd consider me a selfish cad.'

His touch was reworking the familiar magic that she was coming to desire with ever-greater intensity. Her heart skittered and sensation prickled the surface of her skin. Oh, what joy it was to see him similarly affected. His breathing was becoming more rapid and she could feel the growing evidence of his desire pressing into her stomach.

Soon he would make love to her again and she'd welcome it but first she must tell him more. 'Do you understand that I feel, keenly, the loss of pride and dignity in being foisted upon you as a dowerless, indebted damsel mired in scandal?' She made no objection when he rolled her on top of him and wrapped his legs around her hips in a shocking reversal of the position to which she'd become accustomed. Just when she thought she knew everything. Warming to her theme she tensed her thigh muscles around his hips as she went on in a whisper that grew increasingly hoarse, 'An independent fortune would have changed all that. It would have given me social standing and respect. Everyone would have congratulated you on a fine match, including your mother, no doubt.'

'You don't need anyone's congratulations but mine, dear heart,' he muttered huskily, gripping her bottom and rocking her gently so that, inch by inch, she slid closer to where he wanted her. In the dim light of the candle she'd placed upon the chest of drawers beside the bed he could see her eyes glaze over with the heady sensations that were fast engulfing him before she threw her head back, gasping as he entered her.

His last coherent thought was that Rose could come and apologise to him any time.

⚜

THEY DIDN'T DISCUSS ROSE'S INHERITANCE BEFORE ROSE LEFT FOR London, though he'd made clear the asset was hers. Rose wished he'd relented in his decision to go on horseback, if only to save her having to endure the next few hours with the lacklustre Beth but he'd said he had some business to attend to and would join her, later.

Beth's sickly pallor and sour expression advertised her disgust at repeating the tiresome journey so soon, as eloquently as words. It was clear she had no love for her mistress and as the hours stretched Rose determined she'd find a way to give the girl her notice, hopefully without offending the dowager.

Rose's only entertainment was in imparting the information that the recent rains had raised the level of the river so high that only yesterday morning the mail coach, while trying to ford it, had been overturned and several passengers swept away to their deaths.

'I fear, also, that the Mayfair house is in some disrepair,' she informed Beth, smiling. 'I'm told the servants' quarters leak. And, regrettably, there's been a rat plague. However, with your able assistance we'll soon put matters to rights, won't we, Beth?'

She settled back into the squabs with a satisfied smile. Beth rarely showed pleasure or enthusiasm, but she certainly didn't disappoint when it came to exhibiting fear and distaste.

At last they arrived in London. Rose was thrilled at the opportunity to be once again reunited with Arabella. Unfortunately that necessarily entailed Helena's company, but the barely contained outrage with which Helena congratulated her on her inheritance was almost worth it. Goodness, but she could be a spiteful piece of goods, Rose berated herself, as she took a seat opposite her sister-in-law and began to regale her with an account of the wondrous size, location and fixtures and fittings of her new Mayfair residence which she had just returned from viewing for the first time.

Of course, Helena was doing her best to hide her true feelings, though her politely enquiring tone gave her away. Helena was never politely enquiring when she was addressing Rose. And her eyes glittered as she marvelled, 'So, Rose, barely a moment after gaining a rich and titled husband, fortune smiles upon you yet again. If you didn't so obviously deserve it we'd all feel positively spiteful.'

Rose was not surprised when, later, Arabella deluged her with a torrent of tears.

'I can't endure another moment of Helena's company,' she wept, throwing herself upon Rose's shoulder when they were alone in Arabella's bedchamber.

Rose soothed her. 'There's still plenty more entertainment to be had before Helena and Charles take the ship back.'

'But then I'll have to go with them.'

Rose held her at arm's length and surveyed her sister. 'You'll be snapped up before then, my pretty,' she reassured her.

Arabella hiccuped and threw herself on her bed. 'Helena says no man of any consequence would look at me with less than six hundred a year.'

'Your nice Lord Yarrowby did.'

The words were immediately regretted. Rose knew Arabella was nursing a broken heart, although neither had spoken about Arabella's previous admirer's defection. Guiltily, Rose realised she'd taken the coward's path when she'd failed to address the conflict between their views regarding Yarrowby's potential as a suitable husband and Rampton's low opinion of the man.

'Perhaps it's for the best,' she now said, taking a seat on the bed beside her and stroking her sister's disordered hair. 'To tell you the truth, Rampton doesn't care for the fellow and in fact positively warned me to ensure you had nothing to do with him.'

Arabella turned her wide-eyed look upon her sister before biting her lip. 'Oh, Rose, I know I shouldn't say anything, but Lord Yarrowby has told me all about Lord Rampton's jealousy of him.'

'Indeed?' Rose didn't try to hide her scepticism.

Innocently, Arabella went on, 'There was a lady they both were very fond of, only she preferred Lord Yarrowby.'

'Is that so?' Rose decided it was time to change the subject, but regretted bringing up Helena's name for it almost caused Arabella another bout of tears.

'Helena says he was only toying with me and that he left because I had no dowry and—'

The guilty way she bit off the last word made Rose suspect what other soothing reassurances Helena must have had for Arabella.

'Because your sister scandalized respectable society?' With heavy heart Rose pulled Arabella to her feet, saying in a falsely jolly tone, 'What do you say to our shopping for some new gloves to go with your pink sarsanet? You know I can afford it, now. Come. It'll take your mind off your troubles.'

A shopping expedition would be a tonic and help to while away the hours until Rampton arrived to fetch her, as arranged. Her guilt over her role in damaging Arabella's prospects had led her to come up with what she believed would be a grand plan regarding the disposal of her house, but she wasn't sure if Rampton would share her enthusiasm.

Several hours later the young ladies were back with their booty: two pairs of gloves and a shawl each. Clearly, Arabella was just as miserable as she'd been before.

At last Rampton arrived. Rose caught her breath as he entered the room, marvelling at the fact he was her husband and at his power to make her heart miss a beat. Each time he entered her orbit she had to pinch herself to remind herself she was the woman he'd chosen to ally himself with.

Supressing a thrill as her thoughts strayed to the previous night, she jerked her head round to Helena who had risen gracefully from her seat by the window.

'My lord—I mean, Rampton,' purred Helena as she clasped Rampton's hands between her own.

Despite every attempt to keep it at bay, jealousy rose in Rose's throat like bile, although she managed, cheerfully, 'Good afternoon, Rampton. The house isn't in nearly as much disrepair as I had been led to believe. I'm told it'll fetch quite a sum.'

Rampton smiled. 'Good fortune has certainly smiled upon you, my dear. What does Helena think of it?'

'The house, Rampton... or Rose's good fortune?' With a coy smile,

Helena answered the question herself. 'She has been fortunate in her marriage to you, my lord, but it would appear you are not the only slave to her charms. Aunt Gwendolyn must have loved Rose very much to have made such a generous bequest. I believe they met only once. Before we arrived in England we never knew that dear Great-Aunt Gwendolyn existed. But Rose worked very hard to find favour with the old lady. Darling Rose is not all she appears, as you've discovered only too well.'

'BUT RAMPTON, YOU SAID I COULD DO WHAT I WISHED REGARDING the house.' With clenched fists Rose stared at him across the few feet of Aubusson carpet in her sitting room as she persisted with her argument. 'Now that I have been so fortunate in marrying such a wonderful, generous husband, I want to provide Arabella with a dowry.' She glanced from her husband's stony face to her clasped fingers and realised they were on the edges of an argument. It wasn't a pleasant thought.

'So that Yarrowby will come sniffing around her ankles again?'

'Well, yes. Arabella's broken-hearted.'

'She'll be more than that if he weds her.'

Rose was unexpectedly spurred to anger. 'You have no right to interfere with her happiness.'

'You have no right to ruin it.'

'I've heard nothing to discount Yarrowby as entirely suitable, eminently eligible.'

Rose was not expecting the thunderous look in her husband's eye as he said, quietly, 'Except my warnings.'

She looked appealingly at him, but he had turned away. His voice sounded very distant as he stared across the gardens. 'I understand Arabella must be provided for and, as you know, I am not an ungenerous man. What does disappoint me, however, is that you appear to have completely disregarded all the cautions I've voiced regarding my aversion to Yarrowby. Quite simply, I will not countenance a match between your sister and that man.' She saw his fingers clench as he added, 'I really do not feel it necessary to elaborate. My strictures on the matter should be sufficient.'

Riled, Rose turned with a whoosh of skirts, muttering under her breath, 'Your injured pride, more like it. 'I know you hate Yarrowby because ...'

The expression on his face as he swung round to face her made the words die on her lips. 'Take care, my dear.' His voice was low. Dangerous.

Rose had not thought it possible. Was he warning her that his altercation with Yarrowby over the opera dancer who had been snatched from him was forbidden territory?

Anger made her incautious. 'I will not be dictated to like this.'

'Then you should have been more careful in who you led to the altar,' came the viperish rejoinder.

Rose gasped. 'Do not blame me, my lord, for forcing your hand. You virtually dragged me off the gangplank.'

'Honour dictates that a gentleman offers marriage to the lady whose virtue he has stolen.'

'My virtue was not stolen.'

'Your brother put it about that it was.'

Rose was seething. 'You were adamant that honour was not your motive. Now, during our first argument, you say it was? What kind of a marriage does that make it?'

He drew a laboured breath and muttered, 'Society would have turned on you like a pack of baying hounds.'

'I was on my way back to the West Indies where such consequences did not matter.'

Miserably, Rose watched her husband fasten the cufflinks with slow, deliberate movements.

He was only partly dressed. Tight-fitting breeches moulded his well-muscled legs. He stood more than a head taller than she in his stockinged feet. His shirt was undone to the waist and his dark hair was tousled, as if he had spent the day in manual labour and had not yet attended to his appearance.

To Rose he had never appeared more desirable. Or more unattainable. This was their first real argument and she wasn't sure how they'd reached this point. Because she'd accused him of dictating to her without offering a reason for his seemingly unreasonable strictures?

Her feathers were severely ruffled but more, she wanted to reach out to him, to bridge the gulf with an olive branch.

But he was not looking at her so did not see the softening of her features as these thoughts flitted through her mind. As she was on the verge of moving forward he gave a grunt of irritation as the second stud continued to fight his best efforts. Then he said, crisply, meeting her eye, 'Of course, I should not be surprised—or allow myself to feel disappointed – that you completely misinterpret my concern over Yarrowby's suitability for your sister. Like my reasons for marrying you, you attributed the basest of motivations.'

She gasped, before defending herself. 'Likewise, my lord, I'd thank you not to attribute the basest of motives to my actions. Entrapment was not my plan.'

Confrontation did not come easily to Rose. She did not want to risk angering the man she loved; but in the desire to elicit more than coldness, she squared her shoulders. 'Whatever the truth, the fact is that we're bound to one another—*for life*.'

'I had no idea I was quite so repugnant to you, madam.'

She saw that he had conquered the cuff link.

Now, she had to conquer him.

This was their first argument. A silly altercation that stemmed from the fact that Rampton was not used to being defied—only she could not put it into such words.

Feeling helpless, she bit her lip to steady its trembling. She would not let him see her weep. His hand was on the doorknob. In a moment he would be gone and she'd be left nursing the fear of what came after anger and rejection. Could he really be the kind who'd trawl for more diverting company if his wife denied him what he wanted?

She didn't think so, but just then she wasn't prepared to take the chance.

'Stop.' Hearing the hysteria in the single word Rose struggled to compose herself, even as she told herself she was over-reacting. 'You are too harsh, my lord. We have argued and I am sorry. I am not igno-rant of my duties.'

He looked at her strangely. 'You are angry with me because you think me unreasonable yet you would entice me with your body?' He shook his head. 'I have no desire to force my attentions upon a wife who refuses to accept my judgement.'

She felt her mouth drop open but before she could rail at his arrogance he had bowed curtly and exited the room.

CHAPTER 14

S tanding amidst the revelry of a riotous ball-assembly, Rose wished she'd not accepted Helena's invitation to attend Lady Jeffrey's ball without first appeasing Rampton.

However, since Helena's note had arrived shortly after their argument saying that Arabella needed her and hoped very much to see her that night, Rose had simply informed Rampton she going out for the evening.

The company was far more louche than she'd expected. At the centre of a noisy gathering, Rose spied a clearly inebriated young lady who sat untidily in the centre of the dance floor with the remains of a smoking chandelier strewn around her.

A bevy of swains, one of whom had just tossed her high in the air as a finale to a very lively polka, were swatting the singe marks on her dress.

'Geoffrey, see if you can toss Rose into a chandelier and make her laugh,' cried Helena, welcoming a newcomer into their midst. 'You must lead her in the next dance. Poor Rose is having a fit of the dismals, as you can see.'

Geoffrey bowed. His full mouth curved into an apologetic smile, which he directed first at Rose, then at Helena, as he answered, 'I don't think Lady Rampton cares for my company.'

Rose knew her expression revealed the embarrassment the truth of this remark caused her but before she could reply Geoffrey said, 'If I promise to be on my best behaviour and don't throw you into the chandelier would you partner me in the next waltz?'

Despite her aversion, Rose had no choice but to accept his offer, and several minutes later Geoffrey led her on to the floor as the orchestra began to play. Almost at once she noticed her husband on the other side of the room. She had not expected him at Lady Jeffrey's ball. She faltered and immediately Geoffrey was all solicitousness.

'Are you well, Lady Rampton?' he asked, pausing while she regained her balance and her composure.

He would think she had had too much to drink.

But she had not had enough. Certainly not enough to dull the pain of the memory of parting from Rampton on such appalling terms.

She was about to pull out of Geoffrey's embrace and go straight to him when she suddenly saw him lead another woman on to the dance floor.

When she saw who the woman was she averted her head quickly, and in the process gripped Geoffrey a little more tightly than she meant to. She had no desire to meet Lady Barbery face to face.

'It's all right, I'll hold you,' Geoffrey murmured. 'I know how quickly the bubbles in champagne go to one's head.' The words sounded frighteningly intimate as his breath tickled her ear. Rose tried to pull away, apologizing as she trod on his foot.

'Relax, my dear Lady Rampton, and I'll steer you in the right direction.'

Again Rose tried to push him away but the champagne must have made greater inroads into her coordination than she had thought. She stumbled again and this time he had to clasp her tightly to him to prevent her from sprawling across the floor.

She gasped and flushed as he laughed, 'I beg your pardon, madam. Pray, I am not trying to take liberties, I assure you.'

'No, of course not... I'm being very foolish, I realize,' she managed to say as he executed a few more surprisingly graceful turns with her around the room.

'Not at all,' he murmured, reassuringly.

She found that if she just relaxed and let him hold her then she was coordinated enough not to make too much of a fool of herself and thus become the focus of critical attention.

Soon Geoffrey was leading her off the dance floor, his arm about her waist.

He murmured in her ear, 'Lady Rampton, permit me to escort you home.'

Rose pulled away from him, but he clasped her all the more tightly as Helena swept up to them, saying, 'You must go with him, Rose. There's no need to worry about appearances.'

'I must go to Rampton,' Rose argued but Helena smiled and shook her head. 'It was in fact Rampton who just told me he thought you should go home. Clearly, dearest, you're foxed.'

'I think I should see my husband,' Rose protested weakly, trying once more to pull away, but Helena merely steered her, with Geoffrey, towards the door saying, 'You are hardly in a fit state to speak to your husband, believe me.'

❧

WITH ROSE TAKEN CARE OF FOR THE MEANTIME, HELENA WAS ready to tackle Charles, fixing a smile upon her face as she turned at the sound of his concerned voice, and reassuring him, 'My dear, Rose is in perfectly good hands. You know that Rampton and Mr Albright are neighbours and boyhood friends. It's hardly as if Rose will be accused of cuckolding her husband within a month of snatching London's most desirable catch from beneath the noses of every designing debutante.'

She leaned into him, skimming his cheek with a fleeting caress before gaily suggesting he might lead her onto the dance floor.

Charles's concerns evaporated upon the instant, as she knew they would. Charles was so very easy to manage. And so was Oswald, she decided, smiling across at the scowling boy she condescendingly called her little step-brother. Oh yes, he was mad for her but he'd do her bidding. All she had to do was crook her little finger.

It was Rose who posed the greatest problem, Helena decided as she pondered her means of achieving the happiness she deserved. She forced herself to sink deeper into Charles's embrace on the dance floor. He could refuse her nothing—and would refrain from asking difficult questions—if she was sweet and plaint with him.

Yes, all Helena wanted was the same degree of happiness Rose had gained through Helena's machinations. And, later, as she twined herself in Geoffrey's arms while he rained passionate kisses upon her in a small antechamber behind the dance floor, once he'd returned from depositing Rose home, Helena was even more determined upon it.

⚜

WITH A HEADACHE FIT TO SPLIT LIKE AN OVERRIPE MELON ROSE WAS in no mood for Helena's excessive good cheer the following morning when she burst into the drawing room where Rose was languishing.

Nor for her suggestion for riding in Rotten Row. 'Arabella is very keen to be seen, you know, and she has made an assignation with her young man.' She looked at Rose meaningfully. 'You don't want to be accused of nipping that little romance in the bud. It would be a fine catch.'

At that moment Arabella appeared on the threshold looking exceptionally modish in a rust-coloured riding-habit and a dashing hat adorned with a single curling feather.

'I've no intention of nipping any little romance in the bud, but don't expect me to accompany you,' said Rose, cradling her head in her arms with eyes closed as she sagged into the corner of the chaise longue.

'Oh Rose, darling Rose, does that mean you'll agree...? I mean, that you'll make sure Charles will agree?' With a whoop of joy Arabella swooped upon her sister and began showering her with childish kisses. 'Why, he was so cast down telling me that he was sure it was no good even offering, because of some silly argument he and Rampton once had—' She broke off, blushing at the realization they were no longer alone.

'Helena and I were just leaving,' she said, hurriedly, as they went out through the door Rampton had just entered.

'I have the most ghastly head, Rampton,' Rose muttered, feeling at a distinct disadvantage as she found herself staring up at her husband. His look was inscrutable. Rose tried to sharpen her wits. Eventually she gave up. It was painful even to focus. She closed her eyes and asked, 'Sorry, Rampton—did you ask a question?'

Rampton sighed and looked disapproving as he folded his arms and leaned against the mantelpiece. 'My dear, I have no objection to you enjoying yourself. However, would it be too much to ask that you comport yourself with the decorum your position demands?'

Rose glared at him. How dare he speak to her like that? 'I had one glass of champagne too many,' she said, in clipped tones, adding with heavy sarcasm, 'Pray forgive me.'

Ignoring her, he asked, 'And what is it that Arabella fears I may not agree to? The moment she realized I might have overheard her she scuttled out of the room like a frightened rabbit. It was most unlike her.'

Rose twiddled with the tassel on the cushion. She'd been unsure how Rampton would take the news and realized she'd been somewhat compromised by her sister this morning.

'Arabella is very much in love, and apparently the object of her affections approached her last night to ask if she would object if he applied to Charles for her hand.'

Rampton raised his eyebrows superciliously and Rose's heart sank. She could tell he already suspected who it was and that he was not happy.

'So Yarrowby has come back, just as I predicted, now that there's a handsome dowry in the offing?'

'Apparently his uncle was very ill and he had no time to leave a message, and then his cousin from France was over and he was required to dance attendance on her ...' Rose realized that she didn't sound very convincing. She finished crossly, 'Rampton, you've given me no good reason to warn her off Yarrowby. You say he's a brute but you've hardly behaved like a gentleman in this matter, either. Arabella is very much in love. It will break her heart—'

'He'll do worse than that.'

Rose sat up straight and glared at him. 'You're so unforgiving! What happened between you was years ago. Why, it's a great opportunity for Arabella... and Arabella's sweet nature will tame him, if that's your concern. Besides, it's not for you to give or withhold your consent.' She took a deep breath, ready to field his anger.

Instead, he looked at her strangely. 'My dear, I had not realized quite how ambitious you really were.'

'A fine marriage for Arabella will set her up for life.'

'And bring her untold misery for the rest of it. Do you wish that for her?'

'You don't know that!'

Quietly Rampton set down the tinder box he'd been toying with and looked at his wife through narrowed eyes. 'Yarrowby is an inveterate philanderer. He only wants Arabella because she's an ingenuous debutante with a pretty face who won't make a scene when he strays—and who now suddenly has a respectable fortune to tide him over when the cards don't go his way.'

Rose closed her eyes, haunted by the image of Arabella pleading with her to say a good word to Charles on Yarrowby's behalf. Rampton called him a philanderer but her investigations suggested that Rampton had had more mistresses than Yarrowby.

'Do you think he'd offer if she had nothing in the way of dowry?' Rampton went on.

Rose bridled. 'So, now you're suggesting that if Lord Yarrowby's suit is accepted I'll be responsible for delivering my own sister to the wolves, since I'm the one providing the dowry.'

'In effect, yes.'

'Yarrowby's quarrel with you was a long time ago. I'm sure he's changed... grown up.' Rose persisted with her argument, more out of pique at her husband's dogged disapproval than anything else.

'Men such as Yarrowby don't change just because they marry a good woman... or because they've grown up.' Rampton put down the box and took a few steps. 'You'll be doing Arabella no favours if you allow this match to go ahead.'

Rose sighed. She wished her head would stop throbbing so that she could form coherent thought and discuss this properly with Rampton. All she was conscious of just now was that he was being unreasonably obstinate and taking the matter personally.

'Rose.' The tone of his voice made her raise her head to look at him. His beautiful blue eyes kindled with anger. 'For once, just trust me.' He paused. 'It will be a marriage made in hell. Believe me, I know what I'm talking about.'

Rose opened her mouth to speak but Rampton shook his head. 'If you trust me, Rose, you'll make sure this marriage does not go ahead.'

When Arabella rushed into her bedchamber later that day, dragging aside the thick curtains and letting in the offensive summer glare whilst declaring in effervescent tones, 'Oh, Rose, I had the most marvellous morning,' Rose had not the heart to check her high spirits.

'I'm so pleased to hear it, dearest,' she said, dragging herself up to rest against the pillows. Her headache should have long since abated but her exchange with Rampton had done nothing to hasten her recovery. The image of his smouldering eyes and his warning regarding the purgatory of an unhappy marriage were not the sort of thing to send one into an easy sleep.

Now Arabella was babbling on about Yarrowby and how he intended to call on Charles, and had Rose had a chance to speak to their brother?

'Not yet.'

'You don't think there'll be any difficulty, do you?' Arabella settled herself on the end of the bed, her look so troubled that Rose couldn't help but say reassuringly, 'No, dear,' before adding dutifully, 'but we do want to make sure that Lord Yarrowby is the kind of man who would make you happy. I mean ...' She hesitated, before adding, 'I mean, he has only become so attached of late since ... since—'

'Oh Rose, you're not going to suggest he's a fortune hunter are you?' Arabella's laugh was light with relief. 'Why, Yarrowby was afraid that others might accuse him so. But that's not the reason he's returned, at all. You remember how attentive he was at the beginning of the season? And then his uncle was so ill and he thought his sister had delivered his letter, only—'

'Yes, yes, I know,' Rose interrupted. She ran the back of her hand across her eyes, swung her legs over the side of the bed and stood rather shakily. 'I'm sure you're right, dear. Now, if you don't mind, I'll just call Beth to help me ready myself for this evening.'

In answer to the concern she read in her sister's eyes she explained shamefacedly, 'I'm afraid I still have a touch of the headache from last night.'

Having summarily dismissed Arabella, whose high spirits refused to be dampened even by her sister's cautionary tone, Rose suffered herself to be ministered to by Beth's less than deft fingers while she pondered her dilemma.

What could she do? She did not want to anger her husband. Yet he'd not made a case compelling enough against Yarrowby to disqualify him as a desirable suitor.

She sighed. She must sound out Aunt Alice and see if she could dredge up further details about the quarrel between the two men. There must have been more to it than she believed.

THE SEASON WAS WINDING DOWN. IN ANOTHER MONTH HELENA would board the *Sara Jane* with Charles. In the meantime Rose observed her desperate pursuit of pleasure. Her sister-in-law had formed her own coterie of admirers and, while her behaviour was not exactly scandalous, neither was she a model of decorum.

Rose had decided to delay her return to Larchwood, feeling that her presence in London was necessary for Arabella's benefit. Any day now Yarrowby would offer for her, and then Rose would have a gargantuan task ahead of her in seeing to the wedding preparations.

Aunt Alice had obligingly found out all she could from various acquaintances what she could about Lord Yarrowby. And to Rose's relief – and disappointment – the worst that could be dug up was that fisticuffs session with her own husband in Hyde Park ... over a common opera singer.

At Arabella's insistence, Rose had told Rampton she believed Yarrowby was not as sincere a suitor as she'd thought him and Rampton's relief had been palpable. They'd not discussed the matter, since.

Meanwhile, Rose and Rampton dealt well enough together. Certainly, he'd abandoned her bed the first few days after their removal to London, spending his evenings at his club and returning in the early hours of the morning. However, in the second week, there was a normalising of their previous relations and their love-making was intense and almost satisfying to Rose.

Yet, something was not quite right. Rose couldn't put her finger on it and wished Rampton hadn't invited her family to live with them for their final few weeks.

She'd been thrilled at his generosity at the time, but now she suspected their continual presence was the reason he was so often out at his club.

So, when he put his head around the door as she'd just finished dressing one evening, she welcomed him warmly.

'Darling, how do I look?' She fingered the diamonds he'd given her and that set off her gold net ball gown so well, and he nodded approvingly.

'They do, indeed, do you justice but I believe you'd look even better without them.'

She laughed and swatted away his hand as he caressed her throat. 'You know we haven't time.'

'Alas, there never seems to be an opportunity with your family turning up whenever I round a corner.' He sighed. 'No, no, don't take it amiss. I don't regret the offer, but I'll be glad when Arabella is snatched up by some worthy suitor and Helena and Charles return home.' He stood behind Rose and gently clasped her shoulders, staring at their reflection in the mirror. 'Thank god, Yarrowby proved as faithless and as worthless as I warned you he was,' he muttered. 'I believe the far worthier Mr George Sanderling might prove a contender. He spoke warmly of Arabella to me at my club last night.'

Rose sucked in a breath. She had to tell him, even though Arabella had sworn Rose to secrecy, begging that she not divulge the fact that Yarrowby was still a contender until their union was all but cemented.

Initially, Rose had said she couldn't keep secrets from Rampton but Arabella had wept so fiercely, a week before, claiming that Yarrowby believed Rampton would do anything to slander him in order to prevent them being married when their argument was on such specious grounds, that she'd relented.

Now, she put her hand over her husband's and gave it a squeeze. 'Rampton, dearest, I'm sorry to say it when I know it irks you, but Arabella's heart still belongs to Yarrowby.'

'The word 'irk' is a very mild descriptor of the way I feel about Yarrowby.'

Nevertheless, Rose felt heartened by his smile, albeit grim. She licked her lips and summoned her courage. 'In fact, I suspect...they are meeting secretly...' she faltered at the flare in his eye.

'If you suspected that, why did you not say something to me?'

'Rampton, please, don't be cross—'

'I'm not cross. I'm furious!' He gripped her shoulders and turned her to face him. 'Rose, when Arabella had no dowry Yarrowby was not a serious suitor. Surely you're not *both* taken in by him? I told you before what kind of man he is. Arrogant. Brutish. And *worse*.'

Rose felt her loyalties torn asunder and came down on the side of her sister's happiness. 'Rampton, I know there's bad blood between you and Yarrowby over that quarrel you had several years ago.'

'How little you must think of me if you truly believe that is the *only* reason for my opposition.' His look was stony. 'I told you weeks ago—no, when I very first met you—that she should stay away from Yarrowby. When it appeared the man was no longer sniffing around, I didn't think I had to say more. But now you're telling me they're meeting in *secret*?'

'Rampton, you've had plenty of time to furnish me with the truth. Weeks, in fact.'

'And why would I do that if I believed Yarrowby was no longer a contender?' he muttered, beginning to pace.

Rose bit her lip, torn between apology and chagrin. 'Well, Rampton, why don't you furnish Charles with the full details so he's *fully* cognisant of Lord Yarroby's black nature. You're very coy about the truth with me, though it seems you like putting me in my place.'

He stopped and glared, as if he couldn't believe what she'd said. 'Putting you in your place? I'm accusing Yarrowby of being such a man. It's rich to hear it from you, Rose.'

Maybe she had gone too far. Trying to keep her voice light, she said, 'Well, I'm sure you'd *like* to put me in my place for tricking you into marriage, just as like to put me in my place the moment I oppose you.'

She turned back to the looking glass and her task of combing out her long, rippling hair. Out of the corner of her eye she saw her husband freeze.

'You accuse me of being puffed up with pride and nursing grudges?' His voice was low and dangerous. 'What of *your* true nature, Rose? What do I really know of you?'

Shame burned her at the truth of his words. 'Well, I am your wife, Rampton, and for all your insinuations as regards my character I will endeavour to be a dutiful one.'

'Oh, don't give me the whole duty spiel, Rose,' he muttered, raking his fingers through his hair. 'I just would have liked some honesty over this Yarrowby matter.' He went to the door, sending her a jaded look over his shoulder as he opened it. 'After all, it's not the first time you've deceived me.'

CHAPTER 15

L IKE GILDED PEACOCKS the guests at Lord Yarrowby's lavish entertainment promenaded across the lawns of the grand house in which he would soon ensconce the visount's intended. His unexpected offer was the subject on the lips of many of his guests that night, although Charles had only given his consent that morning. Lord Yarrowby's long-planned fireworks spectacle coincided well with the news of his impending nuptials.

Helena, watching the setting sun from the balcony, felt it was setting upon her dreams. Time was running out. Charles would remove her from England within the fortnight and she had not yet discovered a way to stay, though she was closer than she had been since Rose's wedding. Rose had married money and Rampton had been generous to his new wife's impecunious relatives, though not yet generous enough.

Irritation bubbled within her as her mind roamed over the few avenues open to her.

'Any glittering baubles you see here with which you'd like to adorn your swanlike neck?'

Flinching at the familiar voice of her cousin by marriage, she cast a baleful eye over the crowd. 'Even if you were clever enough to do it so that no one could lay the crime at my door, Oswald, you'd probably mistake the real thing for paste.'

'I hear that it was not paste that adorned your lovely sister-in-law's neck when she ventured out wearing the stolen necklace belonging to her intended's erstwhile lover.' Oswald looked enquiring as he lounged against the wall at right angles to her. 'I also heard Lady Barbery's ire only brought our star-crossed lovers closer. Married, no less! Does that please you, Helena?' He moved closer, gripping the balcony railing so their hands nearly touched.

Helena heaved in a breath and stared into the darkness. 'I worked hard to orchestrate that marriage. I used my cunning to understand how far Rampton would go to champion Rose and it is due to me, alone, that she made her match in heaven. But how have I been rewarded?' She turned to face him. 'I came to England, Charles' wife and as poor as a church mouse. It appears I shall leave the same way while Rose and Arabella remain here, drowning in wealth and admiration.'

Oswald scratched his nose. '*You* stole Lady Barbery's necklace?'

Helena was genuinely amused. 'I like the fact you believe I did, but no. Rose received the necklace from an anonymous admirer, and was forbidden to wear it, however I recognised it as that belonging to Lady Barbery. I'd seen her wearing it the week before, in fact—"

'Indeed, you would notice what the rest of us would consider trifles.'

Helena gave a mirthless laugh. 'A diamond necklace is hardly a trifle. Nor were Lady Barbery's actions. As you may or may not know, Lady Barbery was Rampton's mistress before he married Rose and it occurred to me that the anonymous giver was the lady herself. So, I insisted Rose wear the necklace...and you know the rest.'

Helena was intrigued by the fascination on his fox-like face until, losing interest, she snapped, 'It's rude to stare.'

'I had no idea you despised your sister-in-law quite so much.' Oswald grinned. 'Why, I believe you despise her more than I despise my addle-headed step-mother.'

Helena felt the bitterness rise up her gullet. She feared she might drown in it. 'Rose condemned me to this life I despise. For five years

I've lived in penury in a barren prison with a feeble husband whose attentions I must at least pretend to endure if he's not to sulk like the pathetic child he is and make my existence even more hateful.'

Oswald clicked his tongue. 'Poor Helena. And you at the height of your beauty. Is there nothing I can do to ease this terrible burden of yours?'

She slapped away his hand, catching sight of Rose on the path just below. Her sister-in-law appeared the picture of self satisfied smugness as she fingered the handsome diamond necklace Rampton had given her for her wedding. A Rampton heirloom. Meanwhile, the best Helena had received from Charles was an all but worthless gold chain.

Following the direction of Helena's disconsolate gaze, Oswald chuckled. 'Nothing so desirable as the unobtainable, is there?'

'Unobtainable?'

'Word is that Rampton is unfashionably mad for his wife. I hardly think he'll slip between the sheets at a crook of your little finger.'

'Mad for his wife?' Helena repeated, ignoring his other insinuation for though she'd once desired it her interests had been very definitely swayed in a different direction. 'There's trouble in Paradise according to her maid.'

As they watched Rampton join his wife, the pair nevertheless looked the picture of marital harmony.

'So, you want a necklace like the one your sister-in-law is wearing,' Oswald remarked.

'A gentleman would have observed by now that I am surely dying of thirst,' Helena said, turning to go inside. Oswald could not help her. He was simply revelling in her distress. 'You have not even offered me refreshment.'

'I had thought to offer you something else.' He put his head on one side. 'Any jewel your heart desires. Rubies? Diamonds? You only need to name it.'

Helena snorted. 'Much good that would do me when I could never wear it.'

Oswald gave an exasperated sigh. 'I'm in thrall to your beauty and your cunning, Helena, but you're not being terribly clever right now. I could procure diamonds you could take back to your little island home. Or ...' he paused. 'You could sell them.'

Helena stopped and smiled. 'I want two. One to keep, and another which Rampton will find in his wife's possession.' The tossed her head. 'But I hardly think you can manage that.'

'Well, *I* have nothing against Cousin Rose.'

Impatiently, she swung back to Oswald. 'Rose leads a charmed life. Look at her tonight, dripping with jewels while I have only this.' It had become a compulsive gesture to finger the gold chain around her neck when she watched others parade their jewels as if such wealth were nothing. 'My husband will never have the funds to do justice to my worth. But Rose,' she pointed to her sister-in-law weaving leisurely through the crowd, smiling at her husband beside her, 'Rose has her heart's desire, all thanks to me ... and I can't bear it.'

When Oswald took her hand between both of his and brought it up to kiss, she did not pull it away. Oswald wanted to perform some act that would please her. He'd fail, like all the other men in her life but he'd be expected to be rewarded for his efforts. She smiled. 'My dear Oswald, what a lovely gesture. You can't imagine how grateful I would be with a diamond collar...or two.'

'Very grateful? I would hope so for the risks are enormous.'

She allowed him a few seconds in which to soak in the promise of her warm, fragrant cheek which she pressed briefly against his neck. Then she laughed, making clear she had no confidence in him, whatsoever. Nevertheless, she quickly twined one hand up behind the back of his head while the other trailed from his breastbone to his thigh. 'If you could manage that, I would think my cousin Oswald the cleverest man in all England.'

WITH PLEASANT SMILES GLUED IN PLACE THERE WAS NOTHING TO indicate to the casual observer that Lord and Lady Rampton were anything but the most content of newlyweds.

'Have you seen how happy Arabella has been since his offer?' Rose bit her lip, anxiously, despite her question. It had all been so sudden.

'She didn't look very happy yesterday,' Rampton remarked mildly. 'I found her in tears in the drawing room.'

'Yes, because Edith wants to return to the West Indies with Helena. They were both torn. Edith has been with us since before Arabella was born. But Edith's family is there....'

'Arabella says you've promised to find someone to attend her?'

Rose nodded.

'Who? Beth?'

Rose rolled her eyes and Rampton chuckled. 'Dismiss her if you dislike her. You'll not offend Mama. But haven't any of the other girls volunteered to attend Arabella? Weren't you going to ask them?'

Rose sighed. 'I spoke to them all this afternoon. No one wants to go. Arabella is such a sweet-tempered girl. And for some of them it would have constituted a very real elevation in position.'

After a moment's silence Rampton said, 'Don't lose too much sleep over it, my dear. This wedding will never take place.'

Rose gritted her teeth as they passed a throng of revellers, 'Your arrogance astonishes me. You might hate him but my sister happens to love him. And to me, that counts for much, much more.'

Rampton gripped her upper arm as he steered her along a more private path. 'You shall have your proof. As for your remark regarding my arrogance, I find it wounding. I had warned you on several occasions that he was an undesirable suitor. Little did I know matters were proceeding behind my back until the betrothal was all but announced. Since, however, you need proof of Yarrowby's unsuitability, I am arranging it.' He frowned down at her. 'To think, Rose, that when I warned you the first time I barely even knew you.'

'That was simply an excuse to entice me to be alone with you.'

Rampton gave a wry smile at the memory. 'That may have been part of the reason,' he admitted. 'But do you think even I would besmirch the good name of an acquaintance for such ulterior motives?'

Rose, who was feeling increasingly uncomfortable and beleaguered for her part in Arabella's impending nuptials, shrugged. 'Your reasons for hating him are personal.'

He lifted one eyebrow disdainfully. 'Give me credit for some finer feelings, Rose.'

'I do,' she whispered, her voice heavy with irony. 'You displayed them to me only last night.'

Referring to it made her blush. Despite their difference of opinion the previous day, he'd still come to her bed. Their love-making had been fuelled by lust and anger though from a physical point of view it had been satisfactory in its culmination. She studied the half moons of her fingernails and felt the weight of her unhappiness upon her shoulders. All satisfaction had quickly drained from her when Rampton had rolled off the bed and left, instead of nuzzling close as he used to do.

She felt she was in the wrong. But so was he.

Fireworks lit the dark sky. The crowd murmured their anticipation for the next burst but Rose had no heart for the entertainment. She raised her head and said, 'I've been told Celia Baxter was the opera dancer who was your mistress before Yarrowby took her over.'

'Yes, she was, but, dear God, Rose, do you seriously think I would stand in the way of your sister's happiness because of personal animosity?'

He seemed to withdraw, though he had not moved. 'The reason for our altercation, I assure you, went far deeper than *Celia Baxter?*'

'That's not what everyone believes.'

'Including you, it would appear. How terribly sad, Rose, that you would honestly have so little respect for my integrity that you believe me capable of such pettiness?'

'What else was I to believe? You gave me no other explanation.'

Rampton looked at her a moment then began striding away so that Rose had to hurry to catch up with him. She could not let this argument go unresolved.

'What was I supposed to think, Rampton?' she demanded, moving in front to block his path. 'You simply told me he was unsuitable. You made insinuations but said I either had to accept your edict or find out for myself.'

Rampton barely allowed his progress to be checked. As he walked around her he said, 'I assumed I'd found myself a wife who would value the judgement of her husband.'

'So you are now suggesting that the real reasons are so terrible they could not be revealed to my innocent little ears. And now poor

Arabella is to pay for my lack of faith in you? Is this a lesson in morality, Rampton? That a good wife will simply obey her husband without question because he tells her she should?'

'Arabella will pay no price, my love.' Rampton's tone matched Rose's scorn with irony. 'I've told you. She will not wed Yarrowby.'

Rose gave a strangled laugh. 'I see. Then why are we here?' Struggling to keep up with him she indicated Yarrowby's great mansion and the peacock-and-guest-strewn lawns with a sweep of her arm.

'Come, my love.' He took Rose's hand and laid it upon his arm. 'Your sister is beckoning to us.'

Rose glanced across the lawn and saw, to her dismay, that Arabella, radiant with happiness and flanked by Charles and Helena, was waiting for them.

'I see. Ever the knight to the rescue,' Rose murmured, stifling her anger. 'You know best … '

'Yes,' Rampton said, conversationally, smiling as the distance between them and Arabella closed. 'I predict that very soon Arabella will lose her heart to another.'

'Oh, you do, do you? And who might this be?'

'My brother. Good evening, Arabella.' He greeted her with an extravagant bow. 'I believe Felix is to paint your portrait.' With an indulgent look at Rose, he added, 'It seems that painting your beautiful sister has whetted his appetite.'

Arabella dimpled. 'I will be the envy of the ton and, like Rose's portrait, I hope it will be a happy reminder to my husband of his good choice in a wife.'

CHAPTER 16

ROSE PACED THE Aubusson carpet and pondered her dilemma. Arabella had left not two minutes before—breezed out would have been the more appropriate description—on her way to Mayfair to sit to Felix. Clearly she was thoroughly enjoying the sessions and, while Rose had wanted to warn Arabella against Felix, Rampton's caution carried weight. Arabella was old enough to make up her own mind, he'd said. Unless Rose had a very strong case for Arabella marrying Yarrowby, rather than for Arabella making a match to please herself, Rose could rest assured that Felix was not a young man to undermine Rose's good work merely for the pleasure of it.

Now the reason for Rose's diminished spirits stood before her: a downcast girl whose enthusiasm and dedication to her work, good humour and surprising skill in arranging a complex coiffure had deeply impressed Rose. She had thought of employing Polly for herself and to find Beth some other employment, however Polly appeared to have formed a fondness for Arabella. Rose had thought the girl would be delighted to attend Arabella after her wedding but was now surprised by her obvious aversion to the idea.

'But Polly, not only would your wages be greatly increased, your position would be far superior. If you stayed here it might take years before you became a personal dresser.'

'That's as may be, ma'am, but I don't wish to leave.'

Rose had always thought Polly mild to the point of timidity. Frustrated, she demanded, 'Why is it that no one wishes to accompany my sister? Has Arabella been unkind? Is she not as sweet and mild-mannered to the servants as she is to her family?'

Polly had dropped her chin on to her chest. This unusually sharp demand from her mistress caused her to jerk her head up and bite her lip.

'It ain't Miss Arabella, my lady. Lord knows, she's the sweetest mistress and I'd have danced for joy at the prospect o' accompanying her anywhere else.' She took a deep breath, struggling. Then at last she blurted out, 'But it's the master I ain't so fond of.'

For a moment Rose thought she was alluding to Rampton. Then realization dawned. 'You mean Viscount Yarrowby?'

Polly nodded.

There was silence. Rose stared out of the window miserably as comprehension dawned. At last she asked, 'And why has no one said anything?'

'Weren't our place, ma'am. And Miss Arabella's been so 'appy in love.'

Deep dismay was now replacing Rose's misery. It seeped through her bones. More insinuations. This time she had to discover something substantial.

'Did it not occur to anyone that Arabella might be saved heartache herself—considering you all felt Lord Yarrowby was not an employer whom any of you would wish to work for?'

Polly didn't answer. Her narrow shoulders slumped even further. At last, as the silence stretched into seeming eternity, she said in a small voice, 'We talked about it, ma'am but ... but then we decided that what great lords do to servants and what they do to fine-bred ladies surely ain't the same thing. So we decided that, since Miss Arabella found him so to her liking, and her being a great lady and no common serving lass, he'd most likely be good to her.'

Rose digested this in silence for some moments. After a while she said, 'So, Lord Yarrowby chooses to take his pleasures in the servants' attic?' Distractedly she nibbled the tip of her forefinger. It was not a good reflection on the man's character. Unfortunately, so many men did indeed take advantage of their staff. It was not as if Lord Yarrowby were the only one.

When Polly still did not answer Rose said, more sharply this time, 'So you're telling me that Lord Yarrowby made advances to the servants?' She sighed. What should she do?

She moved to the window, her tone half apologetic as she turned, saying, 'I'm afraid, Polly, that it is not only in Lord Yarrowby's residence that such things happen—'

'Well, it don't 'appen here!' Polly interrupted fiercely.

'I am relieved to hear that,' said Rose with a wry smile. 'Nevertheless, it is, sadly, a well-established double standard that the way gentlemen cavort with obliging kitchen maids is not the way they deal with womenfolk of their own class.'

'Well, it ain't as if Jenny were that obliging,' Polly muttered under her breath.

Rose, about to continue her exoneration of Lord Yarrowby, stopped short. 'What did you say?'

Colour flooded the girl's peaky little face. Eventually Polly raised a pair of defiant eyes. 'I'm trustin' you 'eard me first time, ma'am, as I don't care to repeat it.' Gone was the timid little creature with whom Rose was so familiar. 'Jenny was my friend. I knew 'er 'cause we came from the same village and she's sister to the master's man, Fanshawe. Anyway, Jenny were a good, honest girl and, what's more, about to be married. But she were too pretty by 'alf and my lord Yarrowby didn't like that she objected when he tried to kiss her.' The slumped shoulders rose and the voice became more resolute. 'One day he chanced upon her, alone, in the scullery. It were late at night and she 'ad just one or two more things to finish up. Everyone else was abed 'cause otherwise we'd 'ave 'eard her screamin'.' There was a long, uncomfortable pause. 'Well, 'course, once she was... spoiled... and, what's more, 'aving a baby, she couldn't marry Johnny. Oh, he wanted to, but she were set on that point.'

Rose's chill deepened as Polly recounted her story. Of course, there was no proof that Jenny had been telling the truth, she told herself. She didn't even know what kind of a girl Jenny really was. She asked, 'Was Lord Yarrowby accused of the crime? I mean... it's only Jenny's word....'

Polly looked first confused, then affronted and Rose, despite the fact that she could not accept slander with no evidence, felt deeply ashamed. 'No, it ain't! Anyway, 'sides from the fact that Jenny ain't no liar, there was bruises on her arms, and blood on her dress, and, what's more, Rafferty, the butler, saw Lord Yarrowby sneakin' up the back stairs minutes before he came down and found Jenny all hurt and cryin'.'

Rose didn't need any more convincing. Added to her distress at Polly's tale was the fact that Rampton had known of Yarrowby's crime all along.

'I'm sorry, Polly,' she said, truly humble. 'I had no idea of this. I think ... perhaps... my husband knew something.' Then, realizing that this sounded more like an accusation she was about to rephrase her sentence when Polly broke in, "Course he did. Fanshawe's been valet to my lord since the master came back from Eton, and Jenny's 'is sister. The master's bin supporting Jenny and the young 'un nigh on three years.'

'But... but why was Lord Yarrowby able to get away with such a crime?'

Polly's look made Rose squirm with embarrassment as the inequality of their respective situations was brought home to her. Great men like Lord Yarrowby were not brought to justice for raping mere kitchen maids.

Not three minutes after Rose had dismissed Polly, Rampton strode, unannounced, into the drawing room.

The pale and drawn countenance his wife raised to his face, coupled with the fact that he had passed Polly in the corridor left Rampton in no doubt that Rose was now in complete possession of the facts. It had not been a certainty that one of the girls would volunteer the story. In fact, Rampton would not have been surprised if shame had kept their lips sealed.

'Did you mean to make a fool of me, Rampton?' Rose's tone was bitter. 'Or should I be apologizing for having misjudged you?'

Rampton shot her an ironic smile as he leant against the mantelpiece. 'When I explain you can rest easy that I am indeed the base scoundrel your miscalculations forced you to wed.'

Before Rose could raise an objection he went on, 'First of all, my dear, how would you have explained to Arabella that the man she professes herself to be madly in love with is, in fact, not just a philanderer, but a brute of the first order?'

She was silent.

'Could you have found the right words to explain it to her? Would Arabella in fact have understood? It is my understanding that the mysteries of life are a somewhat neglected part of the education of a young, unmarried female.'

'Yarrowby should have been brought to justice,' Rose declared, hotly. 'Then Arabella would never have found herself in such a situation.'

'Of course, my dear,' Rampton agreed, admiring the gold-and-enamel snuffbox he withdrew from his coat pocket. 'Unfortunately, justice is not always served—most often not served in such situations. I think you know that.'

'But how could Yarrowby have the audacity to offer for Arabella, your own sister-in-law, when he knew you were acquainted with his crime?'

'Yarrowby is a conceited villain. But he didn't know—' He stopped abruptly before adding, 'He has a child, you know. But he doesn't know that I know that. He doesn't in fact believe that what he did was a crime, much less that it'll ever be laid at his door. He thought he was quite safe in offering for Arabella.'

'She'll be heartbroken when she discovers the truth. Why did you allow the romance to progress ... when you knew all along? It'll be so much harder for her, now.'

Rampton made a noise of frustration. 'If you recall, Rose, my warnings were dismissed while you allowed the romance to flourish behind my back. I'd thought I'd be saved from having to reveal the particulars, once you acted on my well-meaning advice.'

'But you knew I settled a sum of money from the Mayfair residence for her dowry.'

'As you were within your rights to do, for I'd have done it, otherwise. However, I'd have done a more thorough job of vetting all suitors.'

Rose, feeling swamped with despair, went to the window. 'So what do you plan to do now? Confront Yarrowby and make him withdraw his offer?'

'A man cannot withdraw his offer without risking a breach of contract.' Rampton studied the snuffbox in his hands. 'Catherine gave me this,' he said, opening the lid and trailing a finger over the engraving. 'You may be surprised to learn that lust is not the only motivation for taking a mistress. There is companionship... often mutual benefits in a wide range of matters. I was instrumental in her husband's promotion, incidentally.' Rampton closed the lid, pocketed the gilt box and directed his wife a level look. 'And, of course, there has to be trust. That,' he finished pointedly, 'as much as anything else, is what this was all about.'

He looked at his watch. 'My dear, we must get ready for Lady Gunther's alfresco party.' The flint in his deep blue eyes belied the easy tone. 'I'm sorry that you assumed you'd married a petty tyrant.'

'Naturally I shall withdraw the offer of the house,' murmured Rose.

'So now you wish us both to appear tyrants.' He gave a mirthless laugh. 'Do you really want to deprive poor Arabella of any shoulders to cry on? Now, when is the contract to be signed? Tomorrow?' Rampton appeared to be thinking. 'You must remind Charles that you meant merely to offer the newlyweds the loan of the Mayfair house but that Arabella won't come into possession of any proceeds until she's twenty-one.' He chuckled. 'That should get Yarrowby's back up.'

'Arabella will be crushed. It's not what was promised.' Though Rose had no wish, now, to see the marriage go ahead, she felt unbearably compromised.

'Of course it is! Besides, Yarrowby is a man of great fortune.'

Rose, still sickened by her interview with Polly, felt close to tears. 'How shall I explain it to Arabella? She's just out of the schoolroom. I don't think she'd even understand what ... what Yarrowby is actually guilty of.'

'I'm not sure I'd tell her what she hasn't the wisdom to even begin to understand.'

How reasonable he sounded. Rose wanted to throw herself into his arms and beg his forgiveness.

She felt ill, both in body and spirit. As she reached up a hand to stroke his, he pulled away and began to pace, muttering, 'Far better to *show* Arabella Yarrowby's less pleasant side: the real reason, in fact, behind his interest.'

Staring into the grate, he went on, 'If Yarrowby is after Arabella because he loves her, why should it concern him whether the pecuniary benefits brought by this chit of a girl land in his lap next month, or in three years' time? He'll be devilish put out ' – thoughtfully he rubbed his chin with his forefinger – 'while Arabella will have no choice but to alter her mind and feelings when her erstwhile adoring swain turns ticklish over a few pence.'

❦

RAMPTON HAD BEEN DETERMINED TO SHOW THE WORLD THAT HE'D not only made a love match but that he was not a man who made hasty decisions he soon regretted. And nor was he.

He'd married Rose because he loved her with all the love of which he'd been capable. He still loved her. More than he believed possible.

Nevertheless, as he gazed at the moon and heard the babble of chatter all around him at Lady Gunther's alfresco the following evening, he felt deeply concerned by the mire in which he and Rose seemed currently to be flailing.

He had married in haste but only as he was so certain he'd not repent at leisure. Now, while he admitted he'd been wrong in waiting so long to unmask Yarrowby, he was also disappointed in Rose.

As he bowed in acknowledgement of Lady Barbery's greeting – a suggestive *moué* as she slid her eyes over him – he again wondered who was the mischief maker. He could imagine Helena concocting a story to make Rose appear the villain.

As he watched Rose make her way through the crowd towards him, a guileless smile upon her lovely face, his jaded reflections fell away.

Male pride must answer for much of his current turmoil, he decided. Rose had a burden to bear and the scandal surrounding her deception would have been mitigated had she been an heiress. No one could have branded her the scheming fortune hunter his mother, among others, did.

And he should have told her the truth about Yarrowby much earlier.

As she reached his side a great weight seemed to fall from his shoulders.

From the moment he had laid eyes upon Rose she had intoxicated him. As ever, when she was near, he was overwhelmed by the desire to whisk her away from those with whom he must share her and revel in the sensual delights he had only truly enjoyed with her.

When Rose complained that he was crushing her as he led her through the crowds he realized that it was his excuse to get close to her.

BUT ROSE HAD NO OBJECTION TO BEING CRUSHED AGAINST HER husband's side. The physical proximity overpowered her with a desire to block out all the world but themselves. She was furious with him but after much soul-searching she acknowledged the guilt she bore in the whole, ghastly Yarrowby affair.

As Rampton would not want gossip that suggested disharmony between them, Rose decided that this evening was a wonderful opportunity to flirt with her handsome husband. They'd both acknowledged their culpability, though not in so many words.

Yes, they were both to blame but now they must make amends.

It started as a game; and she was surprised at the alacrity with which he joined in.

Soon she was dimpling when he made a remark, laughing at his witticisms, and on one occasion pretending to brush a crumb from the corner of his mouth.

The more she threw herself into her role the easier she found it to be in charity with him, her heart soaring at his unreserved responses.

It was wonderful to engage in light-hearted banter, to press against this man who still thrilled her with such clear signs that he desired her. For tonight she could see, clearly, that he did. And she felt the answering call like an ache at the very core of her.

They were a popular couple that evening, always part of a group. Even the most jaded observer must have seen that Lord and Lady Rampton were mad for each other.

The moment they found themselves alone, however, Rose's laughter faded to concern as Rampton gripped her arm and hustled her down an ill-lit path.

'What—' she began to ask as he pushed her against the sturdy trunk of an elm tree; but her question was cut short as his mouth covered hers, and his strong arms caught her to him.

She returned his kiss with relief and enthusiasm, revelling in the feel of him pressed against her. He smelled good: of snuff and sandalwood and brandy. Twining her fingers through the short dark hair at the nape of his neck as she sagged into him, she felt her troubles drain away.

'I thought you were doing such a good job play-acting in front of the guests here tonight that I'd set you a more difficult task,' he said, smiling through narrowed eyes as he set her away from him after their passionate trysting.

'Did I pass?'

He chuckled. 'I'm not registering any complaints.'

'That was not the whole-hearted endorsement I was hoping for.' Rose insinuated herself into his arms once more and tilted her face up to his. 'Am I allowed to try again?' She raised her face to his and closed her eyes in anticipation of more kisses.

'Rose!'

Rose stiffened in his arms as she heard her brother's voice.

'Ignore it,' whispered Rampton, his arms tightening.

'I think he's seen us. Perhaps Arabella is in trouble.'

With a grunt of irritation Rampton released her and within a moment Charles was beside them.

'Have you seen Helena?'

Sounding distinctly acidic, Rampton replied, 'Being fêted by her admirers. She's certainly not here.'

Helena gave the lie to his statement by appearing at that moment, effervescent with excitement and too much champagne punch.

'What a dreadful squeeze!' She hiccuped, then laughed unashamedly. 'My husband doesn't know how to keep me in good order, does he?' she asked, looking directly at Rampton. 'Not the way you manage Rose.'

Rose was about to retort when she was addressed by Yarrowby bringing up the rear, a radiant Arabella clinging to his arm.

'Where's Oswald?' Helena asked abruptly. 'He assured me he was going to be here.'

She pouted when Rose said she had no idea, then immediately berated her husband. 'It's a poor escort who can't even see that his wife's glass is empty?'

'Do you really think—' Charles began, before her answering look obviously decided him against arguing. The moment he'd gone, Helena made her excuses— something about a torn dress—and dashed off in the opposite direction.

'The picture of marital harmony,' remarked Rampton, drily.

Arabella blushed and Yarrowby, bending over his betrothed's hand, murmured, 'Your connection is by marriage only, my dear. Your virtue shines like a halo.'

Rose, nauseated by this remark, murmured to Rampton, 'I'm going to find Helena. It's unwise to leave her like this in such a mood.'

He nodded and Rose left the group, sick at the thought of what she was going to have to eventually tell Arabella.

Beneath a weeping willow Rose was startled when a hand was laid on her arm and a familiar, but unwelcome, voice, said softly, "All alone? Why is your errant husband not at your side?'

Rose gasped. 'Geoffrey?'

She wished Geoffrey Albright hadn't discovered her in such a remote part of the garden. There was no one within sight. Or, fortunately, hearing.

"I fear Lady Chesterfield may have lost her way,' she said curtly as she pulled away and scanned the gloom, which was lit by only a couple of lanterns.

'Then let us hope she does not take fright easily. I was accosted by bats during my lonely perambulation to the bottom of the garden.'

'Bats? Surely you have friends—'

'Many,' he assured her. 'But one does not always choose to remain with one's friends ... or one's husband,' he added, pointedly.

Somehow Geoffrey did not seem the kind of gentleman to choose the solitude of the country—much less the bottom of the garden—over more ostentatious pleasures.

'Then I'd hate to intrude. If you will excuse me—'

'Of course,' said Geoffrey with a smile, taking her hand and pressing a kiss to her reluctant flesh. 'I trust I will see you soon at Larchwood. Now, I suggest you try down that path for your lovely sister-in-law. I see a lantern twinkling through the trees and I believe I heard voices carried on the breeze just a few minutes ago.'

But Rose was unsuccessful since Helena had no intention of being found.

'Not the prettiest,' Oswald told her, relaxing against the back of a wooden bench in a secluded rose arbour. 'It's not as if you're choosing it to keep... It'll be keeping you.' He laughed at his own poor joke.

'Surely I could wear it just once.' Wistfully, Helena fingered the chain around her neck.

'Good God, no!' Oswald exclaimed. 'It'll be out of your hands by mid morning or else I'm for Newgate. And I don't intend going alone.' He watched as Helena unconsciously caressed her own neck, her eyes glittering in the darkness.

'What do you intend doing with your newfound fortune?' He smiled slyly. 'Improving the slaves' quarters?'

'You don't suppose I'll be going home with Charles, do you?' she asked scornfully, not realizing he was teasing her.

'The proceeds from just one, or rather, two, diamond necklaces won't keep you in style for long, you know,' he reminded her. 'Certainly not in the style to which you'll quickly become accustomed.'

After a moment's hesitation Helena said, without any attempt at cajolement, 'Why, then you'll get me another.'

Oswald laughed. 'No, I won't. You don't suppose I'm prepared to risk my neck out of habit, just to please you.'

'I'm paying you handsomely for it,' she reminded him, sharply.

'Ah, yes, I was just meditating as to whether your barely controlled anticipation was for owning the necklace, or the reward you were contemplating for my benefit.' Slyly he extended his arm around her neck and dipped his hand into her bodice. 'Perhaps I should ask for a down payment immediately. I'm about to take a great risk for you, after all.'

She swatted him away. 'Next time I'll slap your face,' she retorted.

'No, Helena...' Oswald nuzzled her ear lobe and his fingers caressed her creamy neck, 'next time you'll be writhing beneath me, begging for more.'

She struggled free, glaring. 'The bargain is definitely weighted in your favour.' She shuddered. 'Procure me three necklaces. I need five thousand pounds' worth, Oswald, or this is as close to me as you'll ever get.'

Effectively checked, it was his turn to glare. Then he said smoothly, 'It makes no difference. Two are as easy to obtain as one. But my dear, surely I deserve to know what you intend? Do you really mean to leave your husband?'

Helena snapped a thin twig beneath her fingers. 'He's broken all his promises. He said that as soon as he got his baronetcy we'd return to England and he'd buy back the old family estate, and we'd come to Town every season and he'd buy me all the jewels and clothes I desired.' She sniffed. 'But it was all lies.'

Oswald put his hand on his hips. 'Since you've made it clear that you have no interest in how I procure your heart's desire, I think it's time to offer you my apologies, madam, and ascertain the whereabouts of our hostess's quarters. My guess is that the ladies flaunt paste while the real thing languishes under lock and key.'

CHAPTER 17

R OSE CLOSED HER eyes and sank back into the pillows with a deep sigh. At least there had been no tearful recriminations. Arabella had simply bowed her pretty head and whispered that of course she understood her sister must obey her husband. And no, of course she didn't resent Rampton, either, since he had obviously compelling financial commitments himself which she did not understand. After all, it wasn't as if the promise of a great house in one of London's most fashionable quarters were being withdrawn. What was three years, after all? There had been a slight misunderstanding; however she was certain—quite confident—that Yarrowby would be perfectly obliging when he visited Charles that afternoon with regard to drawing up what had hitherto been only a verbal agreement.

In her usual good-natured fashion Arabella had tripped out of Rose's bedroom on her way to her sitting for Felix, turning with a smile to announce her excitement at presenting her finished portrait to her husband-to-be, then adding after a thoughtful pause, 'Why Rose, I do believe Felix is almost as charming as Rampton.'

Matters had not reached so much of an impasse with Rampton, either, that Rose needed to despair. She stretched, luxuriating in the

memory of last night. For many hours during the course of the evening at Lady Gunther's alfresco party they had acted the parts of happy lovers. Each had obviously felt sufficiently negligent in respect of the other that they felt the need to atone. Certainly, when they had returned home it had been a natural progression into the bedchamber where proceedings had been ... well, far from unpleasant.

She caressed the empty space at her side, imagining it still warm from when he had left not so long ago for a morning canter with Charles in the park. She was glad she didn't have to be involved in that encounter.

After she'd washed and dressed in a lace-edged morning gown of twilled lemon silk she was halfway down the stairs to the breakfast room when a sound on the landing above made her glance up. The door to Helena's room clicked shut but Rose had seen enough of the peaked white face with its large, staring eyes above purple smudges to realize that something was amiss.

Laudanum, again? she wondered, and her previous high spirits drained away.

Quickly Rose retraced her footsteps. After a cursory knock she let herself into Helena's bedchamber. There was a scrambling noise.

'Helena?'

The room was in shocking disorder. Clothes lay scattered over the bed, across chairs, and Helena was nowhere to be seen.

A daintily shod foot stirred beneath the silk dressing-screen.

Rose advanced, her heart thumping, imagining Helena collapsed on the floor, but when she put her head around the screen Rose merely saw her sister-in-law on her knees, bundling a green silk dress into a bag.

Helena looked up and focused blearily on Rose. Rose glanced around for the tell-tale little blue bottle.

'Helena?' She crouched down, not at all sure of her reception. 'You don't seem at all the thing. Are you unwell?'

Helena's dark hair hung lankly down the sides of her face; and although she slurred her words her explanation was coherent enough for Rose to deduce that she had done something last night of which Charles would definitely not approve.

Surprisingly, too, Helena seemed frightened. The last time her sister-in-law had behaved so abominably she had carried it off with bravado. Never once had she apologized, even though she had put their very existence in peril.

Anger replaced Rose's sympathy. 'What was it this time, Helena? Loo? Vingt-et-un? Whist?' Her voice was harsh.

'What does it matter?' sighed Helena. 'All I know is that I've lost a lot of money, which somehow I must repay if Charles isn't to discover it.'

'Well, I'm glad you're concerned enough this time to worry about doing the right thing.'

The irony was lost on Helena who continued bundling another lovely gown into the drawstring bag.

Rose reached forward. It was Helena's diaphanous gown which had outraged Charles when Rose had worn it to meet Lord Rampton for the first time. Following the dress went Helena's small jewellery case, rattling with the meagre contents that Rose knew she scorned so much.

'You're not...' Rose clasped her sister-in-law by the shoulder and drew face close. 'Helena, whatever you've done Charles will forgive you. Stop it. Come downstairs with me. We'll have a soothing restorative and you can tell me your troubles.'

Helena's expression made clear what small comfort that would be. With calm deliberation she packed another gown into the bag.

'Where will you go? Where were you planning to go?' Rose amended. As long as she was able to do anything about it Helena was not going anywhere. Rose was fond enough of her brother to realize his devastation—not to mention how injured he would be by the ensuing scandal—should Helena abandon him.

'Nothing would give me greater pleasure than to leave Charles, and you know it.' There was a feverish flush to Helena's cheeks and the pupils of her eyes were like pinpricks. 'But I have nowhere to go... except home with him to the West Indies. Nevertheless,' she added, stuffing one last shawl into the bag and pulling the drawstring tight, 'my immediate mission is to the pawnbroker's.'

'The pawnbroker's?'

'Unless you have a hundred guineas you'd like to advance me before tomorrow.'

Rose was checked. To begin with, she did not have anything like that sum. Rampton did not keep her short of pin money, but a hundred guineas was a different matter. Secondly, she had little doubt that that would be the last she would ever see of it if she lent it to Helena. And besides, it would do Helena good to settle her own debts.

'You've not done this before, have you, Helena?'

'I heard of a pawnbroker's in conversation. It's not far. I mean to go there' – she looked at Rose as if daring her to challenge her as she stood up -'this very minute.'

Rose was torn between persuading her to make a clean breast of things to Charles, and allowing her to continue her mission. She decided upon the latter course.

If Helena were forced to give up some of her most precious possessions which could, of course, be redeemed at a later date, she might be less inclined in future to make wagers she couldn't afford to lose.

'Arabella's taken the carriage.'

'I think a hackney might be a little more discreet, Rose.' After jamming a black bonnet into the bag, Helena headed for the stairs.

Rose wondered what to do. Tell Charles? No, Charles had put up with enough. They all had. It was only right that Helena should atone for her misdemeanours.

Once in the street Rose hailed a passing hackney. Snatching the bag from Helena, she withdrew the veiled black bonnet and stuffed it on her sister-in-law's head.

'So devious,' marvelled Helena as the vehicle drew up. 'I always thought that was where I excelled. But then...' she sighed, 'you are the illustrious Lady Rampton and I am merely impoverished Lady Chesterfield.'

Rose uttered a mirthless laugh. 'Such loyalty, Helena,' she said as she helped her sister-in-law on to the lowered steps. For some reason her high spirits had returned. Rampton loved her and Helena was doing the right thing by Charles.

The door slammed and Helena leant out, reaching out her hands.

'Bear me company, Rose,' she pleaded. 'I know you're not dressed for it, but you can stay in the carriage. Please!'

Rose began to protest. She had told no one she was leaving the house.

'It's only round the corner. We'll be back in ten minutes and no one will be any the wiser.'

No, thought Rose, just as she was weakening. Helena could do this on her own. She needed to. For all their sakes.

'Please, Rose!' Helena began to cry as she fumbled for the door to try and let herself out. 'I cannot do it alone. I don't have your courage, Rose. Come... please? You may scold me all you like during the journey.'

'That's a rare treat and hard to pass up.' Relenting at last, Rose settled herself opposite.

'You're always scolding me, anyway,' said Helena, sourly.

'Only because you've not shown my brother the loyalty he deserves from his wife. Anyway, what have you done this time that you must resort to all this cloak and dagger?'

'I'm not telling you. But as for Charles, I have not one ounce of guilt. He promised me the moon and anything else I desired if I'd marry him.' Helena tossed her head.

'You knew Charles had been in love with you since you were in short skirts. And you knew he wasn't in funds. It's only because Sir Hector wouldn't have you that you crooked your little finger at my brother. Though I can't imagine why, since clearly a great fortune was your chief requirement.' Rose remembered the whispers that were circulating at the time. She'd been astonished when Helena accepted Charles with such alacrity.

'Well! Sir Hector made it brutally clear you were the only woman for him. And, Rose, you hardly advanced my case after you rejected him when it would have meant so little to you, and so much to me.' Helena's look was black. 'You couldn't have done better than Sir Hector. He was so rich! Richer even, than Rampton.' She glowered out of the window.

'But not nearly as charming.' Rose smiled.

A faint twitch of the shoulder and turn of the head indicated Helena's scorn. 'What does that signify? You can't tell me you love him.' Before Rose could open her mouth to deny this, she added, 'Well, you can't tell me you love him any more than you loved poor jilted Sir Hector.'

Forcing herself to remain calm, Rose asked, levelly. 'What makes you say that?'

'Why, you and Sir Hector seemed as thick as thieves—until he asked you to marry him. You were always together. I've never seen you laugh with Rampton like you used to laugh with Sir Hector.'

Helena had obviously been too wrapped up in herself to have noticed that last night Rose and Rampton had laughed like lovers. Poor Sir Hector. She'd felt terrible when she'd realised his feelings towards her were not paternal. Nevertheless, the truth was that now she was happier than she could remember. A warm glow suffused her.

Arabella's future bridegroom—whoever that might be—was another hurdle to jump, but at least Rose and Rampton had apologized to one another and were of one mind in ensuring the marriage to Yarrowby would not go ahead.

Returning to Helena's remark she defended herself, 'You know very well the reason was because I had known Sir Hector such a long time and had supposed him Papa's friend—and mine.' She thought of his unexpected kiss, and shivered.

Not long afterwards Helena and Charles had married and everyone had said how lucky Charles was. Helena was famed for her beauty... and her numerous admirers, too many to recall.

There had been one, though, who lodged in her mind. Rose frowned, trying to remember the man Helena had alluded to on several occasions. She had never met him but word was that he had swept Helena off her feet... before sweeping suddenly out of her life.

She gave Helena an appraising look. 'Had I married Sir Hector the material gains would have made me as content as you are now with Charles. You were too impatient, Helena. You should have waited for your heart to mend after you were jilted.'

Helena's green eyes glittered. 'I jilted *him*. Granted he was dashing, but with few prospects. His pay wouldn't have kept me in silk stockings. We quarrelled and when I realized my mistake he had gone.' She muttered, 'Lord knows why I imagined I could live with Charles.'

'Well, you'll just have to make the best of it,' said Rose, adding, as the hackney drew up in a most insalubrious-looking neighbourhood, 'and I'm glad to see you've started.'

Helena stared, horrified, out of the window. 'Perhaps we don't need to go through with this. I think just fifty would do.'

Rose laughed. 'What, you think I have that in my reticule at this moment?' She shook her head. 'You must think Rampton even more generous than he is.'

'And is he?' asked Helena, a greedy light in her eye.

'Generous?' Rose gave a soft, husky laugh. 'Very!' As Helena looked on the verge of tears, Rose relented. 'Wait...' and Helena, rising from the seat, turned.

'The white gown is a favourite and I know you'd planned to wear it on Friday. Don't give that one to the pawnbroker. I'll pay the equivalent of what he would.'

Helena clutched the bag more tightly to her bosom and said in a strangled voice, 'Thank you, Rose, but no! Now wait here, I won't be but two minutes.' She glanced with distaste at the street urchins who had gathered, shooing them away as she held her handkerchief to her nose.

Wearing a look of utter tragedy, Helena put a dainty foot upon the step. One hand went shakily to her chest while the other gripped the door frame. She turned to Rose as she stepped down, saying proudly, 'Charles will not be disgraced by his wife on this occasion.'

It was a performance worthy of Shakespeare, thought Rose, before leaping forward as Helena's speech was cut short by her strangled cry. Relieved, she saw that her sister-in-law's fall had been arrested by the attentive jarvey.

'Got any burnt fevvers?' he asked, smirking as he cradled Helena in his arms.

'Put her in the carriage!' Rose snapped. 'That's right. Let her lie across the back seat.' Tossing off her own bonnet she replaced it with Helena's black veiled piece and seized the bag.

'Stay here,' she commanded the jarvey as she arranged the veil over her face. 'I daresay I can trust you with the lady. Here,' she rummaged in her reticule for her smelling salts, 'wave this under her nose. I shan't be long. Oh, and here's something for your trouble.' The man's eyes glittered at the sight of the coin; even more as she added, 'There'll be another of those if you stay here... and remain discreet about this.'

Although what was indiscreet about a lady swapping bonnets and taking a stuffed bag into a pawnshop? Many ladies of quality found themselves under the hatches and resorted to such temporary means of delivering themselves from pecuniary embarrassment.

When Rose saw how the eyes of the wizened old man who emerged from the musty shop interior lit up she nearly turned on her heel and fled, but the thought of Helena languishing in the carriage, unable to complete the necessary errand herself, spurred her on.

A warm current of fetid air made her nostrils quiver as the old man leaned forward to finger the items she passed across to him.

'Ain't everyday quality comes visitin' my premises, for all the 'and-some terms I'd be prepared to offer ... knowin', naturally, 'ow as you'd be back in a twinklin' to redeem all yer pretty things.' He gave an insinuating chuckle. 'I'm sure a fine lady like you'd only needs to smile nicely at her gent'mun and—'

'Just tell me what sum you are prepared to advance me,' Rose cut him off as the old man fingered the diaphanous dress lovingly.

'No stains or damage. A dress of the first stare, as you young ladies would say, eh?' He gave another wheezy laugh, setting aside the dress and opening the clasp of the jewel box with shaking fingers. 'Not much 'ere,' he said. His tone was accusing as he held up first a pair of paste earrings, then a thin gold chain.

Bargaining complete, Rose was relieved to be out of there. Perhaps Helena had been expecting more, but Rose had done her best.

THE SATISFACTION ROSE gained from her endeavours on Helena's behalf were short-lived. Helena had retired to bed to nurse a nervous headache and Rose was about to change when Rampton entered her dressing-room after a cursory knock. One glance at his grim countenance and Rose immediately dismissed Beth.

'What's the matter?'

'As expected, Charles isn't very happy at the new state of affairs...' He broke off, eyeing with distaste the black bonnet she was removing. 'Not one of your most becoming, I must say,' he said before resuming, 'for of course he will bear the brunt of Yarrowby's displeasure. I told him new information had come to light which suggested the fellow might not make an ideal husband.'

Rose sat down at her dressing-table and ran a hand across her forehead. She too now had a nervous headache. She wanted to unburden herself of the events of this morning but had promised Helena to keep the visit to the pawnbroker secret.

'He'll only judge me harshly,' Helena had said. 'And I intend to approach Charles first and then redeem what I can so that no one will be the wiser.'

So, Rose made no remark upon the bonnet and listened as Rampton said, 'Arabella will probably want to retreat to the country for a little to nurse her wounded heart while this whole business blows over.'

'For goodness' sake, keep your voice down,' urged Rose. He had paused by the door which he had left half-open.

He looked at her for a moment before shaking his head as if to clear it. 'Sorry, my dear. Of course it would not do for the servants to hear of Arabella's disappointment before she does.'

'Rampton ...' Rose stopped him as he was about to leave. He levelled such an enquiring look at her that she almost did not have the courage to ask, 'Is something else the matter? Apart from Arabella, I mean?'

There was a pause before a flicker of warmth returned to his expression.

'Just the pressure of business which, after all, is why I'm in town – and to facilitate the pleasure of my new wife,' he added, with a brief caress of her cheek. But there was not sufficient humour in his tone to reassure Rose.

Rose twined an arm behind his neck and pulled his head down. 'If something is troubling you, my darling, you must tell me,' she murmured against his lips. Sighing, she gave herself up to the pleasure of feeling his strong heartbeat against her straining breasts as his arms wrapped themselves around her and he pulled her against him. Taken unawares, she tightened her grip and ran the tip of her tongue across the seam of his lips, inviting entry. She'd not anticipated her answering reactions would be so strong. Or his.

'Little vixen,' he muttered against her mouth, before crushing her closer so she could feel the full force of his desire.

'How so?' she gasped, when her response had begun as mere coquetry.

'You know very well.' Busily his fingers worked at the pins in her coiffure until her hair suddenly tumbled down to her waist and he was burying his face in its rippling tresses as he scooped her up.

'Where are you taking me?' she whispered as she clung to him. Her heart hammered with excitement and her limbs felt boneless with desire.

'Somewhere more comfortable and where we won't be interrupted,' he growled and she saw the glint of wicked suggestiveness in his eye before her next words were cut short by his mouth upon hers the moment the door to her bedchamber closed behind them. Raw need powered through her as he tossed her onto her bed before caging her with his large, well-built body. She arched her neck for kissing, shivering at the trail he blazed along her throat while he deftly removed her shoes and stroked her the length of her highly sensitised thighs.

She closed her eyes and gloried in the attention, bringing her mind back to conscious thought only when he asked, 'You have no objection?'

'Only to your obeying the dinner gong,' she whispered.

'And believe me, you're going to have such an appetite by the time I've finished with you,' he promised. His eyes bored briefly into hers before his mouth reclaimed hers in a fresh assault that swept away all but her deepest longings to be possessed by the only man who'd ever stirred in her such feelings.

LUST CAN ASSUAGE DOUBTS BUT NOT DISMISS ALTOGETHER THE lingering uncertainties. Rampton acknowledged this as he gazed down at his lovely wife, her hair spread out upon the pillow, licking her lips like the cat who had swallowed the cream.

But he resisted the impulse to quiz Rose on the matter that had cast him into such gloom before their unexpected coupling. No, her enthusiasm and now her serene gaze made him decide otherwise. How could she be guilty of the wrongdoing alluded to by his unsavoury companion this morning?

Rampton's own impending visit in response would prove her innocence although he'd arrived in Rose's dressing room determined to charge her with the allegations that had been made against her.

He'd been passing St Paul's Cathedral, returning from his unpleasant meeting with Charles while happily dwelling on the pleasures he'd enjoyed in his wife's arms the previous night, when he'd been hailed by the stepson of Rose's Aunt Alice, a man Rampton knew only vaguely.

'What brings you to these parts? Business, or the need to repent?' the young blood asked, bounding down the steps, brushing his dark hair back from his high brow.

There was something so out of place and unacceptably familiar about the question and its delivery that Rampton could not help but repulse him with a frown.

'My apologies, sir, but I'm late for an appointment,' he said, continuing to walk.

Despite Rampton's lack of encouragement the young man took no offence. 'How did you enjoy last night's squeeze? Cousin Rose had the right idea, seeking the solitude of the bottom of the garden.' He matched his footsteps to Rampton's.

'I turn down here.' Abruptly, Rampton changed direction while his companion, limpet-like, turned with him, saying, 'Lady Biddle warned Rose she would take cold, for there is a pond, quite marshy, at the bottom of the garden. It's why the entertainment is held on higher ground. And of course Rose couldn't see a thing, it was so dark. At least, I couldn't.'

'Keeping a close eye on her, were you? I had no idea you held her in such affection.' Rampton's tone was dry. As was his throat. He knew some slander was about to issue from this uncousinly cousin's mouth, and he did not want to hear it.

He would not entertain the idea of Rose's guilt, neither in the instance of Catherine's necklace, or now. Rose would not knowingly flaunt a stolen piece merely to win some extreme response from him, as Helena had suggested. And now she had all the jewels she could desire.

Oswald eyed him speculatively and Rampton steeled himself, not realizing until now how much he wanted Rose to be above suspicion, beyond slander.

'Your neighbour, Mr Albright—' Undoubtedly Oswald's abrupt pause was designed to centre tension on the name. 'I believe you've been acquainted with Mr Albright since you were boys together, my lord?'

Silent, Rampton continued walking. The greasy looking fellow's manner suggested blackmail but there would be no proof. The necklace incident had taught him that. Rose had enemies. He was now very sure of it.

Disgusted, Rampton stopped to lean against the half-timbered wall of the house that abutted the narrow lane. Geoffrey Albright? Rose claimed she held him in the greatest aversion. She claimed she'd never met him before his mother's dinner and Rampton believed her.

Then why was he now experiencing this stomach-churning discomfort?

Oswald clapped a hand upon his shoulder, frowning with feigned concern before saying brightly, 'Mr Albright, I'm pleased to report, looked after Rose's interests when she became lost for quite some time at the bottom of the garden. Miss Arabella was distraught and you could not be found.' He cocked his head. 'Have no fear, my lord, for my cousin and Mr Albright knew one another in the West Indies, don't you know? They were once quite close. Or perhaps Rose neglected to mention that.' He clicked his tongue. 'A touch of the ague, perhaps, my lord? You don't look at all the thing. Perhaps we should step into this chophouse and partake of a nuncheon. It's past the hour but I've not eaten and—'

'I'd as leif dine with a toad as with you, sir.'

Rather than be offended Oswald grinned. Thumbs in his gaudy waistcoat pocket he looked as if he might even crow with triumph. 'No, well, now you mention it, I haven't the time to be dawdling, either. Pleasant chatting to you, Rampton. Oh yes, I forgot to mention ...'

With his malicious lizard eyes flicking over Rampton Oswald had proceeded to spew forth an inventory of Rose's recent exploits such as would see her deported to the Colonies at the very least, before finishing with a cheerful, 'So sorry time was too pressing for you to partake of a pot of ale with me, Rampton, though if you'd care to put your head in at the Merry Mermaid about four...?'

Now, as Rampton gazed appreciatively at his wife's pale, slender limbs and tried to concentrate on her chatter, he weighed up whether to pass on the nature of Oswald's insinuations before he departed to meet the villain who, her cousin maintained, was in possession of several diamond necklaces which had gone missing the previous night. Oswald's involvement, the odious creature claimed, was in the name of protecting the family reputation – albeit with handsome recompense from Rampton.

'So, Rampton, darling, I know Arabella is going to be heartbroken but if necessary...I mean, if Yarrowby doesn't withdraw his offer...I'll have Polly speak to her.' Rose smiled up at him, tracing the fleur de lys design of the counterpane with her fingertips while she shifted her hips, sending another spiral of desire powering through him. 'That way she can't say it was merely hearsay.'

Merely hearsay. Suddenly Rampton was decided. He would not quiz Rose about her cousin's allegations since that was merely hearsay, too. She might interpret his questions as doubt about her innocence and he had no desire to churn up the waters between them when he so badly wanted their union to continue on the passionate, satisfying path it had taken after the several false turns that had proved just how wretched disharmony with his wife made him.

⚜

OUTSIDE, ON THE PAVEMENT, RAMPTON WAS SURPRISED TO HEAR HIS name called.

'Rampton! Please, step up and explain to Arabella that it is all for the best.' Rampton, who'd decided to walk to his assignation rather than take a hackney, was startled to see Helena leaning out of his carriage. 'I couldn't take her to the house like this,' she went on, indicating the weeping Arabella beside her when he'd opened the carriage door.

Her tone was not characterized by the sensitivity and sympathy that Rampton felt was better suited to poor Arabella's plight.

'Your heart will mend,' he said gently, indicating with a nod to Helena to change places once he was inside so that he could sit beside the young girl. Arabella gave a wail and put her head on his shoulder.

'Never,' she wept. 'He was so cold!'

'Ah, Arabella ...' Rampton felt like a cad. How had it come to this?

Because he'd wanted Rose to accept his judgement on Yarrowby. 'If there was anything I could do...'

Arabella scanned his face with feverish hopefulness. Turning his head away, he muttered, 'You can do better than Yarrowby,' prompting the strangled response, 'I love him!'

The words came muffled from the shoulder of Rampton's coat. He wondered vaguely what Fanshawe would have to say about it. He would no doubt consider the sit of a coat's shoulders of more importance than a weeping damsel in distress. He certainly wouldn't have any sympathy should he know that the damsel was shedding tears over his own sister's violator.

'Well, it appears he does not reciprocate the intensity of your feelings, dearest,' said Helena, 'since he's done a complete turnaround, and all on account of a bit of petty accounting over an old house. Come, we've all suffered disappointments.'

This, as no sympathy could, finally elicited a more robust response. 'Yes, but only when your calculations are disappointed. Not your heart, Helena, for you don't have one—so don't start prosing on to me.'

Even Helena looked startled for a second. She made a quick recovery. 'You underestimate me, darling. My heart beats every bit as passionately as yours, I assure you.' She exchanged a wry glance with Rampton.

Wiping her face with the back of her hand, Arabella removed herself from Rampton's shoulder. 'Yes, but you've only ever loved what you can't have. You've never loved Charles.'

After assisting Arabella from the carriage, feeling a complete cad as he watched the quiet dignity with which she suffered herself to be led by Helena up the steps to their lodgings, Rampton set his coachman in the direction of his unsavoury destination.

IF OSWALD INTENDED TO PLAY ON THE VAIN HOPE THAT RAMPTON did not trust his wife, Rampton wondered if money was his only motive. Certainly he'd be disappointed on that score since Rampton would need irrefutable proof that Rose was behind whatever nefarious dealings he was about to become acquainted with. He was convinced he would find none. Mind churning, he ducked his head to enter the dim, musty shop.

It would not be a crime if Rose had pawned the several pieces of valuable jewellery he'd given her since their marriage, though he'd be surprised. He'd gained the impression she was mindful of expense and proud of her efforts in keeping the family's head above water amidst the financial difficulties created by her profligate father.

The woman had pride in spade-loads. She'd gone to extraordinary lengths to absolve herself of the debt she owed him—without forcing him to the altar. True, he wished she'd shown a little more unfettered delight at the prospect of snaring London's most desirable catch, but she was more than satisfied with her lot, now.

With pleasure he thought of their recent encounters and wished he had not been so surly with Rose this morning, but that damned black bonnet had unnerved him. Once he'd laid this matter to rest he would buy Rose something to reflect his true sentiments, in case his words sounded clumsy and inadequate. Diamonds, he thought, as he ventured further into the unsavoury premises, wrinkling his nose at the smell of mouldering goods.

He would buy her diamonds.

Then he would take her to the bedroom and show her how much he loved her. *Really* loved her.

Brushing past a pole offering up layers of discoloured petticoats, Rampton looked with distaste at the rheumy-eyed old man behind the counter who nearly dropped the silver teapot he had been polishing.

'I ain't got nothing to 'ide,' the pawnbroker whined. 'Not every day that Quality graces my 'umble abode but if it's about the necklace I never cheated the young lady, not a penny of what 'twas worth. 'Pon my honour.'

Rampton stared. What on earth was the old man getting in such high dudgeon over? His hands were shaking and it wasn't because of his age.

'Which young lady?'

'Mighty fine looking woman in a yellow silk gown.' Scratching his head, the old man asked suspiciously, 'She weren't my lady's maid wot pinched your missus's necklace, were she?'

Beth sounding like Quality? 'May I see the necklace?' Rampton heard the curtness in his tone at the same time he told himself it was nonsense to be concerned.

'Indeed you may, sir.' The old man rummaged through a drawer, and then the treasure was produced: a magnificent emerald and diamond heirloom which, held up, cast its dingy surroundings into unappetizing relief.

Rampton studied it carefully. It was not paste. Nor was it a piece with which he was familiar, but its value could not be disputed. Lady Chawdrey's? Rumours had begun circulating of a series of daring thefts. A kernel of doubt spawned in his entrails.

'Was this all the young lady had to barter?'

'Some clothes also.'

Rampton still clung to the hope that Rose was nothing more than an innocent pawn in a plot to smear her. Somehow the devious cousin was behind this, though Rampton had no idea why, or what his motive was.

Except that his fears which he'd anticipated would prove groundless took on a different dimension the moment the old man produced the dress that Rose had worn to her first dinner with him.

He shook his head to clear it, forcing alternative solutions to the fore while he reached for the dress, the better to study it. Was it possible it could have been copied in order to lay the blame at Rose's door. Perhaps the same person who sought to blacken Rose's name through the incident of Lady Barbery's necklace was behind this?

For he was certain Rose was not. Certainly not until he asked the question, 'Could you describe in particular detail the young woman who pawned the necklace?' and received a precise description of his wife, right down to the tiny mole beneath her right eye.

He took a hackney home. He didn't want his shock and

despair to be on display to the world but in the dim, musty interior he closed his eyes and rested his pounding head against the squabs while his mind screamed for answers.

Why?

What had possessed Rose to come to a place like this and pawn a valuable piece of jewellery that didn't belong to her? It wasn't as if she had no fine jewellery of her own. Or that she was married to a penny-pinching tyrant.

It was inexplicable. He felt his nerves tauten at the prospect of challenging her. She'd claimed Lady Barbery's necklace had come from an anonymous admirer—and he'd believed her. She'd claimed she'd never met Geoffrey Albright in the West Indies—and he'd believed her. Would she claim innocence once again? When there was irrefutable evidence of her involvement? He didn't think he could bear it. His heart seemed to lurch to his stomach as the jarvey opened the carriage door once they'd draw up up outside his townhouse. If she would only confess he would be able to hush up the incident and, just as importantly, he would help her.

If she would only confess.

Once again, Rampton regretted his generosity in housing all of Rose's relatives when he entered the drawing room to find Helena busy at her stitching.

'Was that Dr Horne's carriage I saw leaving just now?' he asked and was surprised when Helena replied, 'Charles called him on Rose's account.'

Rampton looked at her enquiringly. 'I hope she is not unwell.'

Helena shrugged. 'A megrim. Nothing serious,' she said lightly, as her needle stabbed at the tapestry. She glanced up. 'Arabella, however, is deeply upset, as you know and Rose thought a change of scene might be in order. She suggested that if business held you up in town Mr Albright might go as their escort. You remember they knew each other in the West Indies?'

'I do. However Mr Albright will not be escorting them.'

Helena inclined her head. 'Dr Horne also said that if you wished to see him he'd be at home this afternoon, but not to discuss Rose's condition with her for fear of upsetting her more than necessary.'

'Upsetting her? Is Rose upset?'

'Yes.' Helena sighed and looked up. 'Rampton, Dr Horne is concerned about Rose.' She struggled to choose her words. 'When Rose gets these terrible megrims she does strange things. Things she wouldn't normally do and which she either denies having done, or has genuinely forgotten about. I think I mentioned it once before, if you recall. At Lady Barbery's ball-assembly.'

Rampton watched a couple of children playing at fisticuffs in the park while his confusion deepened. He did not believe Helena's sympathy was genuine. Nor did he, in his heart of hearts, believe Rose capable of all the misdeeds of which she was accused. Something didn't add up.

He turned. 'If Rose is upset it must be over something other than her husband.' He sent Helena a studied look. 'She was very happy last night.' He paused, adding, 'And this afternoon. Perhaps you can shed some light on her state of mind.'

Helena shrugged. 'Rose has never been fond of me so I was hardly surprised when she rejected my offer to accompany her on a carriage ride this morning. What was surprising was that Arabella had wanted to go, only Rose was quite snappish to her, too.' Helena met his look, candidly. 'That's when I discussed the matter with Charles. He's obviously had to deal with his sister on occasions like this in the West Indies and so he summoned Dr Horne. He attended Rose several times just after we arrived. She seemed so much better for a while but she's been acting decided oddly, of late. Haven't you noticed?'

It was too much to take in. No, he did not believe Rose had stolen Lady Chawdrey's necklace, or to whomever it belonged. And no, he did not believe she had ulterior motives in suggesting Geoffrey Albright accompany her back to Larchfield. Most of all he did not believe her powerful responses to him in the bedroom both last night and earlier today were anything but genuine.

He *could* not believe it.

'Perhaps the country air will do her good. Rose and Arabella can leave for Larchwood in the morning,' he muttered. 'Jeremy and Hobson can go as outriders. That'll be sufficient escort.'

Ignoring Helena's outstretched arm, her mouth pursed in false sympathy, he made for the door. He longed to hold Rose and quiz her himself about her activities, but right now he lacked the courage. He needed to go to his own quarters, mull over everything he had learned and try to deduce what the devil was really going on. If that failed to provide clarification, he'd talk to Rose.

CHAPTER 19

'Y ES, YOU'LL LEAVE tomorrow.'
He'd twisted his mind in knots trying to come up with a motive for her actions and then he'd visited Dr Horne who'd said 'in these cases' the motive was simply the attention, even if that were in the form of anger. He said the general recommendation was that patients be removed to a quiet location to calm their over-excited minds.

Rose was not one to get over-excited, Rampton had immediately thought, before remembering the passionate heights the two of them had recently scaled. Did that count?

Now, the sight of the yellow silk morning gown, the bonnet still lying at the end of the divan, hardened his heart, despite the latitude he was determined to show her.

Her languid, welcoming smile had almost undone him as he'd put his head around the door but he steeled himself to be business-like. Dr Horne had said that if Rose took responsibility for her actions it would be a great leap forward. Dr Horne had said a great many other things that had thrown his entire world into turmoil but he couldn't dwell on those right now.

'My dear.' He tried not to let his fondness for her cloud his purpose. She looked so very lovely, draped upon the bed. How he wished to close the distance between them and have her rest her head upon his shoulder. Then he would gently ask her about the two necklaces: Lady Barbery's and Lady Chawdrey's. He'd also ask her about Geoffrey and why she'd lied when she insisted she'd never met him before his mother's dinner. Instead he said, with commendable self control, 'You are at liberty to petition me for funds if you find yourself short.'

She blanched. 'So you know about the visit to the pawnbroker? I promised Helena I wouldn't tell you.'

'Helena?'

'Yes, I went on her account.'

His heart tumbled to his boots in sheer relief. Sinking on to the bed he took her hand and brought it to his lips. 'Did you not think it prudent to ask her where such a valuable necklace came from? When it clearly did not belong to her?'

His voice was only as reproachful as was needed to remind her that she should be more careful in future. He watched the play of emotions across her delicate features while she struggled for an answer. God, she was beautiful. Once she had confessed he looked forward to a long and leisurely afternoon luxuriating in her arms. He'd forgive her anything.

Frowning slightly, she asked, 'What necklace?'

He stared. The silence stretched as he waited for her to see that lies did not sit well with him. Did she honestly think he'd be quizzing her about it if he did not know? Dropping her hand he rose and went to the window. Turning, he asked, carefully, 'You admit visiting a pawnbroker's this morning. Why? To redeem some worthless trinkets when you know I am not ungenerous.' He answered his own question. 'No, to pawn a valuable necklace that did not belong to you. I have the evidence.'

She continued to look blank. 'It was on Helena's behalf I went. I just took some clothes and jewellery. The sum total was less than five pounds.'

Turning away Rampton steeled himself to face the truth. Rose had pawned a necklace that did not belong to her, and now lied about it. His mind raced. Was she unhappy? Last night and today would suggest otherwise. But Rose was a good actress. No. He dismissed the idea. She'd not give herself to him if she were trying to obtain sufficient resources to get away. The idea was preposterous and certainly did not fit with all he knew of her.

He stopped, mid-thought. What, exactly, did he know of her? She'd deceived him into marriage, for a start.

Was her motive money? He thought of the Mayfair house and realized the difficulty of procuring immediate funds. However, the only reason she'd need money was if she intended to leave him. A bitter thought, indeed!

Rose and Geoffrey Albright? He could not countenance it. Rose actively disliked the man. But then, she'd not mentioned the fact they'd known one another before. His mind trawled for possibilities. If Rose had learned that Rampton was the close neighbour of the man she had loved in the West Indies, could she have...?

No, she could not have been so calculating that she'd put out a lure to Rampton on the chance he'd bite just so she'd be closer to her old lover. He was reading conspiracies into everything.

He tried to calm his disordered thoughts with a deep breath. First he needed to ascertain whether the owner of the necklace he'd retrieved from the pawnbroker's was indeed Lady Chawdry. Then he needed to discover what Rose was planning to do with the proceeds. He would have to hire someone very discreet to follow her every move for the next few weeks – if only to confirm that she was not guilty of any wrongdoing.

He did not know how he managed to say, so calmly, as he turned back to her, 'The doctor says your health would be much improved with some country air.'

'My health!' exclaimed Rose. 'Why, all I have is a slight megrim. Besides, Dr Horne said nothing to me about it.'

Despite her look of injured surprise, he pressed on. 'I think it best to follow the doctor's orders, Rose. I've arranged for you to leave first thing in the morning.'

Surely, he couldn't dispatch her to the country so summarily without some explanation? Having made her excuses at dinner, Rose waited in her bedchamber.

Even the most hard-hearted man, believing his wife guilty of some dreadful crime, would want to confront her with it. All she could think of was that Helena had intimated she'd pawned a valuable necklace. Perhaps Charles had asked after one of her trinkets and Helena had balked at telling the truth.

Ten o' clock chimed. Rose changed into a filmy nightgown, dabbed a little Olympian Dew beneath her eyes to make them sparkle and arranged her hair. One hour stretched into two. Cold forced her to cover the diaphanous nightgown with a shawl, but the effect she strove to achieve was still the same: a beautiful woman who, once her innocence was established, was too desirable to resist.

When she put her hand on the doorknob her heart was hammering. Foolish! she chided herself. Last night they had talked like old friends, after which had followed hours of delicious intimacy. Only a few hours before, their desire had again escalated into incendiary love-making followed by an amicable leave-taking. Galvanized by the memory, she quietly turned the knob and pushed open the door to the library.

They had their backs to her. No wonder they did not notice her, she thought briefly and bitterly as she saw how entranced they were with one another. Helena, dressed in white like an exotic gardenia, the patina of her olive skin soft and dewy – just as Rose imagined her look —had her head tilted to one side as she gazed at Rampton. And Rampton? One hand lightly cradled one of hers; as if he were on the verge of clasping her round the waist and pulling her to him.

As he half-turned, Rose saw in his eyes a look she had never seen: hunger and yearning.

Fighting back the tears she turned away. How long had this been going on? Was he a man of such appetites that one woman wasn't enough for him? Had Helena finally worked her way under his guard and issued an ultimatum? Was that was why he was sending her to the country?

RAMPTON TORE HIS TROUBLED GAZE FROM HELENA. HE THOUGHT he'd heard a footfall in the passage outside.

'Did Rose confess?' Helena recalled his attention.

Taking a few steps back, he winced at Helena's brutal phraseology. The moment he'd entered the library with her he realized it had been a mistake. If Dr Horne's earnest advice regarding Rose's mental condition had not been bad enough, Helena's feigned concern was enough to tip him over the edge.

'I must go to bed,' he said, abruptly, turning.

She stopped him with a hand on his sleeve and yearning gripped him. If only it were Rose, detaining him with a heartfelt plea for forgiveness; even a cry for help at the demons that tormented her.

'I warned you at Lady Barbery's of Rose's dangerous impulses, if you recall, but love knows no reason.' She traced the contour of his arm before taking his hand. 'Rose was never quite the same after Geoffrey left so abruptly from the West Indies. But when I quizzed her about it she said the subject was closed and never to be reopened. I think seeing him in England was a very great shock. And I'm sure discovering he was your neighbour and old friend must have been an even greater one.'

'Good night, Helena,' he muttered, unclasping her fingers and making for the door. 'I've had quite enough sympathy for one day, thank you.'

'WHAT TOOK YOU SO LONG?' THE ASPERITY OF HELENA'S TONE WAS at odds with the air of serenity she had projected for the benefit of her legion of admirers promenading in the park.

For an instant Oswald was checked. But then, laughing as he reached down to help her into the phaeton beside him, he said, 'I have what you want, dear heart, though I'd venture the bargain will be mine. At least, I'll not be saddled with a shrew for a *lifetime*.' He winked salaciously. 'How charming to see you, too.'

Pulling from his pocket a roll of bank notes he grinned at her gasp. 'Might I remind you it was no mean feat. Twice I thought I was in trouble and it was only luck that stymied the one factor I'd not taken into account—Lady Hocking's puling pug. There it was, yapping at me, fit to burst just as I was sneaking out of my lady's dressing-room with her gems in my hands. Then suddenly it had a seizure or some such thing. The old dragon or chatelaine of the jewel box had been on the point of investigating more extensively and was sure to discover me hidden amongst my lady's dresses, but when she saw the animal in a swoon it was she who had an attack of the vapours before rushing off to find the hartshorn or burnt feathers with which to revive my lady's precious pug.'

Oswald grinned at the memory. The rush of adrenaline had made it fine sport—not that he hadn't been close to having a seizure himself at the time. But Helena had not the sense of humour that made her want to enjoy the details with him. She just wanted the money.

'What a wondrous clever plan it was,' she said, 'to have doubled my reward by blighting Rose into the bargain. So Rampton paid up for you to keep mum over his wife's grave misdemeanours and now my honest brother-in-law is anonymously posting back the goods to Lady Chaw-drey. Poor Rampton will be feeling very pinched in the pocket. What did he say when you told him about Geoffrey?'

Oswald grinned. 'Not very much. It was lucky that his neighbour spent time in the West Indies and that you ran into Mr Albright, what's more. Still, it was an evil tale that I was loath to put about. It's one thing to thieve valuables from a fat old trout who'd lief as not realize they'd gone missing until the next season. But to destroy a man's faith in his wife's virtue. That's a grubby thing to do. It nearly broke my heart to see how easily Rampton swallowed the tale. Still, you don't think he'll find out, do you?'

Helena's smile was serene as she smoothed the skirts of her dashing coquelicot pelisse.

'Dr Horne was an absolute darling. He earnestly verified every little symptom I suggested.' She giggled. 'He blushes when I so much as look his way so it pleased him to corroborate my story that Rose has been suffering from a rare disorder of the mind. Indeed, he was assiduous in advising Rampton of various avenues he might pursue.' With a look of moral rectitude she skimmed the length of the feather that adorned her handsomely trimmed headdress, adding, 'Of course, it's Rampton just desserts since he only made a play for Rose because he thought she was married.'

'Such fitting consequences to please one as virtuous as yourself.' Oswald, leaning back in the phaeton, was pleased this made her cross. 'Still, I'm sorry to see it end this way for them. Seems that old grudge of yours won't be satisfied until she's packed off to Bedlam.' He yawned as he studied his fingernails. 'And all on the basis of your lies completely swallowed by the husband who might have loved her.'

'Oh, very prosy,' sneered Helena. 'Anyway, you're up to your neck in manufacturing evidence. How did that fence of yours perform?'

'The hunchback?' Oswald's momentary sympathy for Rose was quickly replaced by his delight in the success of his little project. 'Worthy of Drury Lane from what I can gather. With magnificent conviction, he identified the purveyor of stolen goods as none other than our good Lord Rampton's lovely, troubled wife and obligingly whipped out her gown that you packed at the very bottom of the bag. There was not the shadow of a doubt in poor Rampton's mind that would prompt him to question whether in fact it was a con job. Obviously you did fine work sewing the jewels into the bodice of your gown—'

'Yes, and she was on the verge of whisking it out of my hands and paying me for it as she knew it was a favourite!' Helena snorted.

'She's very much nicer than you are,' Oswald returned, reaching across to snatch the bank notes out of her hands and replying with raised eyebrows to her look of fury, 'You don't imagine I'm fool enough to hand them over before I've received my reward, do you, my dear Helena?'

The insinuating thigh that rubbed against hers caused Helena to look sidelong at him with distaste. 'You know very well you have not fulfilled your side of the bargain and that I need four thousand to set me up so I might leave Charles. The money from Rampton and three diamond necklaces which need to be disposed of are not enough.' She smiled. 'I think perhaps a few mementoes from Lady Rampton's armoury of gems will suffice but as I can easily persuade Rose to hand those over I don't think you'll have done enough to enjoy my favours.'

Dimpling at the thunderous expression on his face she said lightly, 'Yes, I suspected you might be capable of violence if I tried to renege.' She tapped him playfully on his knee with her fan. 'I only dared suggest it because we're in a public place.' As she stroked the point of her fan slowly up his thigh, her smile cloying, the thunderous look on Oswald's face dissipated. 'Dearest Oswald,' she sighed, 'you're so predictable.'

THREE DAYS IN THE COUNTRY WITH NO WORD FROM HER HUSBAND was as much as Rose needed to persuade herself that her deepest fears were confirmed.

Rampton's moods had been erratic since they'd returned to London.

Where Helena had been waiting.

Of course, the idea that Rampton's feelings did not reciprocate her own hadn't occurred to her until she'd wandered listlessly about for several days with nothing but her increasing fears and doubts for company. She'd returned to thinking of his change in attitude since she'd inherited Aunt Gwendolyn's house.

Perhaps this wasn't entirely due to the Yarrowby affair. His anger with her at failing to heed his warnings suggested a man who liked to exert his own authority.

If Rose had dissatisfied him how easy would it then be to succumb to one of Helena's lures?

Rose knew Helena had no wish to return to the West Indies. Was she therefore making a play for Rose's husband? Rampton was conveniently under the same roof while Rose was ... three hours away in the country.

At whose instigation had the doctor been summoned before he'd suggested all manner of ailments from which Rose might be suffering. Helena's? Or, God forbid, Rampton's? This afternoon Rose had dismissed a clearly concerned Dr Marsh – her mother-in-law's physician – with bright and energetic denials of any symptoms of ill health ... and a deep foreboding.

No, it didn't make sense. Rampton's banishment of her had occurred too suddenly. They'd reconciled. Not hours beforehand they'd made love.

Which Rose had initiated. The uncomfortable thought kept intruding on her perambulations as her mind cast about for some plausible reason behind Rampton's change of heart. Something had happened, she thought wearily, that had convinced her husband that she had deceived him again.

After her third walk that day, with no catharsis from the fresh tears she had shed, Rose opened the door of the drawing room to the unsettling spectacle of Arabella and Felix with their backs to her, standing surprisingly close to one another. For a second Rose imagined she had disturbed a lovers' tryst; but their faces were guileless and welcoming as they turned to greet her. Arabella moved forward to take Rose's hands, thus revealing two paintings leaning against the wall beneath the window.

'Felix, it's splendid!' cried Rose after a quick recovery. 'Arabella must be so pleased!' The sight of her own portrait beside it brought a pang of memory. It had not been many weeks since the fateful sitting which had precipitated her unexpected and hasty marriage. Yet had her husband already had tired of her? A spurt of anger bolstered her reserves. Whatever the problem was, she'd get to the bottom of it. She had to or else she was condemned to the same misery Helena complained of and for which she'd perhaps sought Rampton's assistance to alleviate.

'It's much too good for Yarrowby, don't you think?' Arabella dimpled at Felix.

'I'll take it,' offered Felix, with a sly grin. 'It's a fine advertisement of my skills. When I've tired of the social whirligig, and my impatient brother has put me out to grass on a paltry allowance, I'll have to find some means of keeping my future wife in silk stockings.'

'You must be nice to Rose because when she becomes a well-established society matron you might need her patronage,' Arabella teased.

Looking embarrassed as Rose mumbled some excuse about seeing to dinner before leaving, Arabella lowered her voice as she stepped closer to Felix. 'Surely the rumours aren't true?' Then, more robustly, 'How could Rose have anything to do with Lady Chawdrey's missing diamond necklaces when she is languishing up here... while your brother does nothing to gainsay the gossips who like nothing better than to say the rift between Lord and Lady Rampton came even sooner than expected.'

Felix looked admiring. 'I say, you are quite the little information monger. I thought you'd been drowning your sorrows in this ignorant backwater and quite oblivious to what's going on in town.'

She dimpled. 'I have friends who keep me in gossip.' A shadow crossed her face. 'At first I was only interested in hearing what Lord Yarrowby was up to but then everything else started to get interesting. And really, Lord Yarrowby is terribly old and has silver in his hair and perhaps he'd have left me a widow for a very long time.'

'Repeating the litany of comforts you've managed to come up with?' Felix grinned before frowning, 'I thought he was my brother's age.'

'Oh, he is,' said Arabella blithely. 'He's very old, too, which is why I'm surprised he still wants to be a young buck and send his wife to the country so he can gallivant around town with the ladies.'

Forgetting himself, Felix put a comforting arm around Arabella's shoulders. 'I can't understand what the devil is the matter with Rampton, but although that might have been in character once, I do believe he's changed.'

Arabella chewed her lip. 'I think Helena's got something to do with it,' she said. 'I think she's made up stories which your brother has wanted to believe.'

'Not without evidence,' said Felix. 'Rampton can be deuced vexing but he's not a nodcock and he wanted this marriage. His enthusiasm was decidedly out of character as was his sanguine attitude towards being duped.' He shook his head, pulling Arabella closer as he stared thoughtfully at the two paintings. 'Something decidedly havey-cavey is going on, Bella, and it's time we found out what.'

'FELIX!'

There was more surprise than warmth in the inflection of Rampton's voice. His brother, radiating his usual robust good health and general bonhomie reminded Rampton—who felt both smug and wistful at the thought—of a reincarnation of a much younger version of himself. It seemed a long time since he had walked into a room and thrown himself down upon a chair with such abandonment and obvious satisfaction with life.

Rose had been less than a week in the country and he felt as though the sun had gone out of his life.

'Fanshawe said you weren't going out tonight.' Felix raked his fingers through his dark curls. 'And since I've just returned from discharging – most assiduously, I might add – your parting command, I thought you might like to hear how things are faring at home.'

There was a secretive smile on his face as he assessed the shine of his hessians, his long legs stretched out in front of the fire.

Rampton was glad he had his face averted. When he turned, bearing two glasses of brandy, one of which he offered his brother, he had schooled his features into more ordered lines.

'Mother's well, I trust.'

'Oh, you know ... same as usual.' Raised eyebrows and a glimpse of the whites of his eyes indicated what did not need to be said. 'She'd certainly have been more content had you chosen the younger Chesterfield sister for a wife.'

Rampton took a swallow of the amber liquid. The burning sensation was welcome. 'And how is Arabella bearing up?' he asked. 'Not driving mother to distraction with her moping?'

'Moping? Oh, yes, of course, Yarrowby.' Felix took a gulp and wiped his mouth with the back of his hand. An even more wicked glint appeared in his eye. 'As I've been following your instructions to the letter I've not allowed Arabella to spare him a thought the past couple of days. Poor Rose is missing you, though.'

'I understand the doctor saw her yesterday.'

'Can't imagine why. She's the picture of good health, though she'll run herself into the ground if she's not careful. You'll be impressed with the changes she's made. New cook, for one thing.'

Rampton decided he didn't like this tack. Rose, in good spirits, when she ought to have more reason to be pining even than Arabella. But then, Geoffrey Albright was right next door.

He banished the thought. There was no substance to it. The odious Oswald had planted the idea in his head.

But then, so had Helena. And his thoughts kept to returning to why Rose should lie about having met Geoffrey in the West Indies? Why deny that they have ever known one another when too many accounts corroborated the fact they had? For the week Rose had been at Larchwood, Rampton had left no stone unturned in his attempts to prove Rose was entirely innocent of wrong-doing.

It weighed heavily on his shoulders that he could find nothing to exonerate her.

Faithlessness was one matter but then there was the felony. The theft of Lady Chawdrey's necklace lay conclusively at Rose's door and now that several other valuable baubles had been reported missing at events attended by Rose he'd been told that Catherine Barbery was running around dredging up the evening she'd discovered Rose wearing her own diamond collar.

Why, it smacked of lunacy. He ran the back of his hand across his eyes. If Rose had only trusted him with the truth. He recalled the guileless look in her eye as she denied knowing anything about the necklace she'd pawned when the evidence was irrefutable.

As for Geoffrey, he still couldn't reconcile the idea of Rose harbouring a secret tendre for the unworthy Geoffrey.

Flooded with resolve to visit Rose at Larchwood, he refilled his brandy. He'd sent Rose away partly in order to protect her from the gossips. Perhaps another theft while she was gone would deflect interest in the whisper that she was somehow responsible. Of course she wasn't! Rampton had kept her close by his side at each of these entertainments. The only opportunity would have been if she'd visited the ladies retiring rooms...

Another thought intruded.

Oswald. The odious Oswald had been quicker than Helena to mire his wife in suspicion. Wasn't it equally possible Oswald was behind those suspicions? Did he have a secret motive for blackening Rose's name? He'd already gone over this avenue but somehow he must have missed something. Hearing Felix discuss Rose made his heart cleave with frustrated longing for her.

'What did you say, Felix?' He jerked his head round to attend to his brother while his spirits soared at the thought of seeing Rose again and going through everything that might exonerate her.

'I said, if you weren't the elder I'd be charging you with a similar mission to the one I've just undertaken.' He grinned. 'Different sister, though, if you take my drift. Anyway, I suggested Arabella come back to town which she thought a jolly idea.' He hesitated. 'Told me some unbelievable *on dits*, though—' His blue eyes bored into Rampton's. 'About the West Indies and Albright and—'

The ugly fears which had swamped Rampton earlier returned with a vengeance. He clenched his hands so tightly that his glass was in danger of splintering. Breathing heavily, he said, 'I don't wish to discuss it!'

Felix blinked. Rampton appeared surprisingly agitated. Could it possibly be true that his brother had decreed Rose's removal to the country to give him free rein in London with Helena—only to have Geoffrey Albright throw a spanner in the works, as suggested by Arabella who was highly suspicious of Helena's involvement with their neighbour. Who'd have believed that Rampton's old friend had played fast and loose with Rampton's own scheming sister-in-law all those years before in the West Indies?

Disappointed, Felix returned to the safe contemplation of his boots and the merry fire beyond. He was sure Rose was innocent of any wrongdoing despite everything Lady Barbery and the gossips were saying, though what the devil Rampton was about in sending her away, he had no idea. Rampton should be championing Rose. Rampton's next remark, however, went some way towards restoring his faith. 'As you can imagine, I've been worried about Rose—'

'Can't imagine why,' said Felix. 'She's as hale and hearty as I've ever seen her.' Her presence at Larchfield had made his visit home much pleasanter than usual.' Well, perhaps Arabella's company was largely responsible for that... and the fact that he couldn't wait to return.

'What did the doctor say?' Rampton shot him a piercing look. How much did Felix know? he wondered. The gossips were apparently having a field day with Rose's propensity for bold risk-taking, if Catherine were to be believed. His five minutes in her company the previous evening had decided him they must never be alone again. He'd nearly throttled the woman with her inane prattle about the deep water he'd got himself into with this hasty marriage against which she'd so strenuously warned him.

'He was very encouraging about his patient's general good health.' Felix felt it necessary to sound heartening; Rampton was looking very long-mouthed about all this. 'I'm sure you'll find her blooming, and quite anxious to see you again.'

'You think so!' Rampton was embarrassed to hear the echo of his own hopefulness. He chewed his lip contemplatively. It was difficult to know what to feel at this. Rose had behaved so reprehensibly and refused to take responsibility for her actions while she blithely deceived him on so many counts. Could she be suffering some disorder of the brain? Did he want this to be the case so he'd not have to suffer the pangs of wondering what deficiency there was in him that she'd resort to thievery and, God forbid, adultery. No, there was no suggestion of adultery! He could forgive her anything but that.

Felix leant forwards. 'I say, you wouldn't have a spot of Spanish bran, would you?'

With a grunt, Rampton shifted in his seat. He was never comfortable these days; he ached to hold Rose again.

He rose abruptly. 'I'm going to Larchfield,' he said in answer to Felix's look of surprise. If Rose wouldn't volunteer her role in Lady Chawdrey's stolen necklace he'd shame her into it.

After that...?

He disliked the unfamiliar churning in his breast; the accompanying churnings somewhat lower were far more familiar.

Shrugging into his greatcoat after ordering his carriage, he considered how great must be her crimes before he could no longer forgive his wife.

CHAPTER 20

'Y OU HAVE THE money?' Helena's breath felt like the caress of a feather against Oswald's cheek as she leaned into him. A waltz was playing and couples milled nearby but Helena and Oswald were hidden from view in a small curtained alcove with a large, obtrusive pot plant placed near its entrance.

In the dim light, the blush of her anticipation descended to her décolletage, swallowed up by a froth of lace. He'd once been fool enough to mistake the signs for sexual desire.

Just as he had thought to do her bidding only once.

But Helena was only interested in the fruit of his labour—not the desire of his loins.

'Mmm,' he murmured, taking advantage of their seclusion to caress her breast. Let her think he wasn't on to her game, he thought, and take his rewards while he could.

'Where is it?

Did she not have the finesse to at least pretend? Or was he that repulsive to her?

'I have it,' he murmured reassuringly, dropping a line of kisses down her neck.

She pushed him away, irritated. 'You can't imagine I'd reward you before you prove you've discharged my request?'

The flint he recognized in her eye sent his senses into complete revolt. What was he? An errand boy? One so beneath contempt that she couldn't bear that he should even touch her? When the terms of their bargain went so far beyond that?

With an effort he reined in his uncertain temper. It would serve no purpose to draw attention to themselves. But as he faced her down he realized that Helena had as much intention of honouring their agreement as she did of returning to the West Indies with her husband.

He caught her to him, roughly covering her mouth with his.

'You're hurting me!'

He enjoyed the way she wriggled against him, furious yet afraid to scream. Her outrage as he ran his hands all over her, then pushed against her, making her all too aware of his arousal, was almost worth it.

'Enjoying yourself, Helena?' he panted. 'You like it rough? You certainly aren't afraid to dish it out, are you?' His hands, filled with bank notes, thrust into her bodice.

'There's your money,' he grunted.

'Get away from me!' she hissed, finally freeing herself. Swinging back after she'd feverishly counted the bills, she burst out, 'That's not nearly the agreed sum.'

'And this is the closest I've got to being rewarded.' His eyes blazed. 'Do you take me for a fool, Helena?'

'You'll be rewarded when you've fulfilled the terms of our agreement—'

'Three times I have thieved for you. Granted, it was a lark the first time and the thought of my just reward creamed the deal. But,' he gripped her shoulder and shook her, 'do you really imagine I'll be satisfied with smouldering looks and empty promises?'

'You'll get your rewards when—'

'When what? I've set you up like the bloody Queen of Sheba... only then you'll be far too good for me!'

'I just need—'

She was too stupid to see the signs. All she cared about was the money.

❦

HELENA'S SECOND INTIMATE ENCOUNTER WAS FAR MORE PLEASING TO her although her reaction was just as fiery.

'How dare you act so indiscreetly!' she demanded after being whisked from the saloon on to a balcony and into a passionate embrace.

'Because you're irresistible,' came the smooth rejoinder. 'Virgin or virago, you're equally irresistible... says the only one who's in a position to judge.'

Helena snorted. 'Don't sound so smug. If you hadn't cast me a lure I couldn't resist I'd not be married to Charles. Do you know how many times I've damned you to hell?'

'As many times as I have you?'

Leaning with her back against the railing for support she covered her eyes with her hands.

'This is madness, Geoffrey,' she whispered. 'I should hate you for what you've done to me. Instead...' She left the sentence hanging.

Geoffrey's low, mocking laughter came in place of the comfort for which she'd hoped. 'You're making the most of your revenge, Helena. After that—imagine it—domestic bliss!' He paused. 'Though I doubt domesticity will suit you.'

Helena shrugged. 'You and I are destined to be together.'

'Rather rich, coming from the woman who refused to run away with me?'

'I was seventeen and you were penniless!'

'I was a man on the make. You had no faith.'

'My father was pushing me to marry.' Helena's defence was spirited. 'I had not the luxury of refusing all offers while you got your life in order, but how long did you wait after we quarrelled? Why, the very next night I packed a bag and went to find you, only you had gone. Anyway, you quickly saddled yourself with a replacement.'

'Through threats and coercion after that simpleton threw herself at me! Not even the son that was supposed to be the sweetener. Still-born!' He swung round adding bitterly, 'Three stillborn sons! Can you imagine what that does to a man?' Geoffrey's thin lip curled. Discontented, he didn't look nearly as desirable, Helena thought.

She sniffed. 'Well, my life hardly went to plan either.'

'No! You just set your cap at Sir Hector, probably the one man in the world who didn't find you as irresistible as I—'

He stopped abruptly as the door was pushed open several inches. There was loud chattering, then the conversation was broken by the intruder's abrupt suggestion of 'punch first'. The door closed.

'Enough of trysting! Champagne punch, my lovely?' Geoffrey proffered his arm and with a demure nod of acquiescence Helena placed her gloved hand upon it.

'Champagne punch to celebrate. Oswald was difficult. However, we will have enough ... when the final cache of jewels is delivered to us,' she sniggered, 'by the ever-obliging Rose, thanks to her loyal little maid.'

'You're sure you trust the girl?'

'She's as avaricious a dollard as is required. Besides, Beth cannot read.' After outlining the plan that promised her freedom, Helena added, 'Beth is motivated by the sizeable bounty I've already advanced for merely delivering the missive. With the doubling of the amount upon completion, I doubt she'll disappoint. She's a greedy simpleton.'

Geoffrey laughed. 'Pity the woman who tries to thwart you, dearest,' he said. 'I'll warrant the wench is motivated much more by fear of you than by material gain.'

⚜

DRESSING HAD NOT BEEN SUCH A TIME OF TENSION FOR A LONG while. First Rose discarded the coquelicot that Beth had laid out for her. No, white was much more in keeping with the image she wished to present. Then the expectation that had sustained her drained away and she sagged over her dressing-table. What was the point?

One glance at Rampton's cold look when he'd materialized so unexpectedly in the Larchfield drawing room told her she had no hope of rekindling the passion they'd once shared. Perhaps the purpose of his visit was to inform her of his liaison with Helena.

'Are you all right, my lady? Would you like a vinaigrette?' Beth was unusually solicitous but Rose waved her away saying, 'Just help me dress. I'll wear the primrose silk.'

Rampton was waiting to escort her in to dinner. Assiduous in his duties as husband, there was more concern than warmth in his smile. Nor was there opportunity for frank speech with his mother in attendance.

'Rampton, your wife has been busy,' the dowager told him tightly, as the first course was cleared away, 'showing us up. She's met all the tenants, inspected their living conditions, and plans to start a school so the girls can learn their letters and a little sewing.' She raised an eyebrow. 'Giving them ideas above their station and setting them up for disappointment.'

'It's only one morning a week,' protested Rose. 'Obviously the girls have to work, too. But for those who can set aside the time, and see value in it.' She blushed and looked defensive, 'I think it's helpful.'

'It would perhaps be more helpful if you kept your husband close.'

The clatter of a knife shifting position as it was carried away sounded in the tense silence. Rose stood abruptly. 'I have a megrim,' she whispered.

Instantly Rampton was at her side. She felt his hand clasp her elbow, the touch sending a sharp pain of longing to her heart.

'Mama's words were unpardonable,' he muttered as he thrust open the door to her dressing-room, closing it behind them once Beth had scuttled through.

Her legs felt boneless as she sank on to the divan. Watching him carefully she could see the struggle it took him to face her, calmly.

'Why did you deceive me?'

His words lanced her. She swallowed, turning her head away. Had the old anger returned so soon? Helena had warned he'd never truly forgive her for forcing him into marriage.

'I never intended matters to get out of hand as they did.' The words rasped painfully through dry lips.

Closing the distance between them he gripped her shoulders, bringing his face close to hers.

'Did you not trust me enough to tell me the truth? You pawned a valuable necklace, Rose. I have the evidence.'

She gasped, rearing up, angrily. 'I might have trapped you into marriage, Rampton, but I swear I'm telling the truth when I assure you that is the extent of my crimes.' Foul play was afoot. Her name had been blackened by enemies, she saw exactly how it was. Rampton had been deceived—but this not time, not by her.

'Helena—'

'Enough!' His lip curled as he put her away from him and made for the door.

Rose could not believe it. He was ready to believe Helena above herself? Why, because she'd trapped him? Lured him with that extraordinarily potent allure of hers so that Rampton's enslavement made him insensible to what he surely must know in his heart of hearts: that Rose was innocent.

Already his hand was on the doorknob when Rose asked, her words sounding amazingly bold to her own ears, 'Rampton, why did you send me away to the country ... without a word of explanation?'

There, let him crush her with an avowal of his passion for Helena. At least it would clear the air.

For a moment he said nothing. Rooted to the spot with his eyes fixed on a painting on the wall, it was a moment before he met her look.

She had expected contrition, sympathy and relief at this opportunity to unburden himself.

Instead his eyes smouldered; but not in the manner she wanted. She trembled. How frighteningly devoid of warmth they were. She was unaware she was holding her breath. Unaware of all but the slow, deliberate approach of her husband.

What would he do to her? What did he want to do to her? Certainly passion kindled in the depths of his eyes – but not passion of a loving nature. She held her ground, refusing to move as her fear grew. She would not put her arms out to ward him off. Or to hold him, which was her first instinct.

His eyes bored into hers. Lightly, he traced a line from her shoulder, down over her right breast. She caught her breath, desire making her light-headed. She dared not speak, much less breathe, lest she spoil it. He did desire her! She felt the joy physically expand her lungs.

And then disappointment sucked the air from them at his next words.

'Confess, Rose,' he whispered, his tone ominous as he gripped her wrists. 'Confess so that I might forgive you.'

She shook off his hand while her thoughts roiled angrily round her head. *Confess so you can be with Helena, conscience-free?* So this is what it had come to. She swallowed painfully. 'You will never make me,' she muttered.

CHAPTER 21

IN THE MORNING the letter was waiting for her. He must have entered her bedroom while she was sleeping for there it was, propped up on her dressing-table, the beautiful, formal script a chilling foretaste, she knew, of its contents.

'Later, Beth.' Rose waved the maid out of the room. She had seen the letter the moment her maid woke her with a copper jug of warm water.

Hastily wrapping a Pomona green silk shawl about her shoulders, Rose sat down at her dressing-table and, with trembling hands, tore open the wafer.

Dear Madam...

She needed to read no further to understand that this was not a love letter.

In just a few sentences Rampton set out the proposed course of both their futures. Futures which held no place for them as a couple. Lust, he wrote, had obviously set the tone for their relationship which, following their marriage, had become poisoned by its descent into greater deception and disillusionment. The prevailing situation, characterized by lack of love and mutual respect now made their union intolerable to him and so he was offering her an option that, he felt, promised greater future happiness to both. With the money contained in the wooden box beneath the letter, Rose could resume her life in the West Indies. Rampton would be free to spend his time unencumbered in England for the next few months or until such time as he could stomach the idea of joining her in order that she might produce the required heir.

If she left with Beth this morning there was just time for her to reach Southampton where her ship was to draw anchor. He'd procured her a passage and he would appreciate it if she were discreet about her departure.

'M'lady?'

When Rose did not respond, Beth obviously felt no compunction in imposing her presence upon her mistress, tidying the bottles on her dressing-table, collecting the pins from the floor.

Rose continued to stare unseeing over the top of the looking-glass and through the window. Only when Beth began laying out her prim-rose twilled silk morning gown was she galvanized into action.

'My blue travelling dress, if you please.'

'Are we going somewhere, my lady?'

Rose might have expected more concern in her tone, knowing how much her maid hated travelling, but her future yawned bleak and empty before her.

Once she was dressed she dragged herself to the door, fearful of coming across a member of the household, as if the shame of her eviction was written upon her face.

'Rose, you missed breakfast and Rampton left early this morning.' Arabella smiled her greeting from the bottom of the stairs. 'Urgent business. He said he didn't want to disturb you. What's happened?' She frowned as she took in Rose's travelling attire.

'I'm leaving,' Rose announced, brandishing Rampton's letter as Arabella followed her into her room. 'Rampton has decreed it.'

'I don't believe it. You're over-reacting.' Arabella looked perplexed. 'You can't just go... without confronting Rampton.'

'How can I when he's made himself absent. Clearly, he intended me to receive this letter before he returned. He wants to speak to me as much as I want to speak to him.'

Arabella gasped. 'No!'

'Oh, Bella, you're such a romantic.' Rose gave a short, pained laugh. 'You didn't really think this was a match made in heaven? That we both fell in love with one another, despite the inauspicious beginning?'

'Then you don't love him?'

Trailing over to the window Rose stared miserably across the sweeping lawns. 'Would it make you feel better if I said I didn't?' she asked. 'He gave me a thousand pounds to go away. With a thousand pounds I can make huge improvements to the plantation ... and to tell you the truth, there is no other place that I would rather be just now.' Seeing that Beth was now securing her trunk, she picked up her reticule and went to the doorway. 'Send my regards to my mother-in-law. You might remind Rampton that I was ever the obedient wife. Rawlings is waiting with the carriage. Rampton apparently ordered it so I'll at least go in comfort.'

Arabella tried to bar her way. 'This is nonsense, Rose. I don't believe it. You're acting with too much haste. You must at least challenge Rampton.'

Rose pushed past her. 'If Helena has decided Rampton is the only man who can make her happy I don't stand a chance.'

'Helena? No, Rose. Something's not right.'

'I know what I saw and my eyes did not deceive me. If Rampton is so easily lured, then I don't want him, anyway!'

A DEEP SCOWL BLACKENED SIR HECTOR'S ALREADY BRONZED complexion, causing the captain of the Mariah to wonder whether his esteemed client considered he'd been cheated.

'The goods arrived in prime condition, I assure you, Sir Hector—'

'Excuse me!' Elbowing his way out of the saloon of the Pelican with uncharacteristic lack of courtesy, Sir Hector bore his portly form down the front steps with the agility of a man half his age.

'Miss Rose! I say!'

Rose turned, quelling the urge to hurl herself into her old friend's arms.

Rising from his bow, Sir Hector cast a puzzled look at her trunk, which several porters had set down while they waited, then at the tall-masted ship towards which Rose was clearly headed.

'I'm sailing on the Mariah,' said Rose, swallowing past the lump in her throat.

'Since it will be some hours before the tides favour her departure might I request the pleasure of your company, Miss Rose?'

It was indeed a pleasure to enjoy the company of a man not disposed to judge her harshly. After a bottle of Madeira had washed down a hearty meal of jugged hare and pigeon pie Rose was ready to pour out her heart for a sympathetic hearing.

Sir Hector, however, was more sceptical than sympathetic.

'Dispatched you by letter?' Lacing his hands over his stomach, he shook his head. 'Sounds deuced queer, if you ask me. Not at all Lord Rampton's usual modus operandi, surely?'

Rose wiped her eyes as the servant cleared the table.

'So you love this fellow you've led such a dance, eh?'

'As I've never loved anyone,' Rose replied with a sniff, before explaining the circumstances that had given rise to her scandalous behaviour, followed by her suspicions regarding Helena and Rampton.

'I might have known Helena was behind the trouble,' Sir Hector harrumphed. 'Always eyeing out the advantage.'

'And now she's cast Rampton a lure he couldn't resist and that's why he's sent me away.'

She looked indignant as Sir Hector chortled at the apparent ludicrousness of her deepest fears. 'Maybe she did, but it's Mr Albright she's carrying on with. I happened upon them by chance in the Serpentine Walk at Vauxhall Gardens on Thursday last and it would appear she's as susceptible to his charms now as she was when he swept her off her feet six years ago.'

Rose nearly fell out of her chair. 'Helena and Geoffrey Albright!?'

Nodding, Sir Hector rose. 'I'd be investigating this letter a little more closely before I did anything hasty, Miss Rose. Now, my dear,' he stooped to kiss her forehead, 'there's nothing more I'd love than to see you safely back to town but I have urgent business to attend to and you have your maid. Besides which, I'd hate to intrude on the fond reconciliation.' With a heartening squeeze of her hand he sent her on her way, adding, 'If I wasn't so sure you'll find nothing more than a simple misunderstanding and a vengeful sister-in-law behind your troubles I'd be first to step into the role of gallant hero. But Miss Rose, your gallant hero awaits. Go to him now and see what he thinks about what I've said.'

Emboldened by her resolve to confront Rampton directly, Rose, on Sir Hector's arm, swept out of the inn and commanded that her trunk be retrieved and her passage cancelled. What had she been thinking? A week in the country with Rampton's brooding, critical mother had sapped her of her normal fight. Without Rampton's belief in her she'd found herself longing for the familiarity of her island home. But is that where she wanted to be?

Sir Hector had quizzed her directly on the subject and it was only then that she'd realised with utter conviction that she wanted Rampton to love her and that it was up to her to get him back.

ROSE HAD LEFT HIM?

Rampton poured himself another brandy and stared at his wife's portrait. There was the hint of amusement in her eyes. Her mouth looked ready to break into a smile. As if she were secretly laughing at ·him behind the composed expression.

Was that what she was doing now? Laughing at him as she sailed into the sunset with Geoffrey Albright? That's what she'd told him in the letter she'd written.

Crumpling the cold-hearted missive she'd penned before she'd absconded during the night, he hurled it at the wall.

'Rampton, I thought at least you'd be with your wife if you hadn't the courtesy to dine with your mother.'

Rampton stared at her. No, he didn't have the heart to tell her.

No one seemed to have noticed her absence, yet for the house had been in an uproar when he returned from his dawn ride. Arabella had become hysterical after the warm milk Beth had brought her in her bedchamber.

Rampton hadn't enquired further. To be told she was still pining for Yarrowby would have been too galling, not to mention uncomfortable.

Rampton had immediately gone in search of Rose, only to be informed she'd not been seen all day. Fortunately Arabella's condition had improved but it was just before dinner than he'd found Rose's letter, tucked beneath the turn-down of his bed.

'Rose is... resting. Is there anything else I can do for you, Mother?' His tone was as frosty as hers.

'I'm looking for my emerald necklace. I lent it to Rose for Mr and Mrs Lake's dinner last week.'

'Have you asked her maid?'

'No one seems to have seen her. And if Rose is as indisposed as she would have one believe I felt it discourteous to knock and disturb her.'

'Well, I don't have your necklace, Mother,' said Rampton, irritably while his thoughts revolved around Rose's no-doubt dreadful legacy. As he watched his mother depart he felt dismay spurt its poison into the fibres of his being.

Trying to compose an inventory of the family jewels, Rampton made his way to the dowager's dressing-room and set upon the task of uncovering the full extent of his runaway wife's misdemeanours.

THE CLOSER TO LONDON ROSE TRAVELLED, THE BRIGHTER HER spirits. By contrast Beth looked increasingly long-mouthed until Rose asked in exasperation, 'Were you hoping to set sail with me to the West Indies, Beth, and never see your family again?'

'It's just I were to meet someone at the docks, m'lady and now I dunno how I'll be paid.'

Rose looked at her curiously. 'You'll be paid as you always are. By me, at the end of the month.'

'You're going back to London, m'lady?'

'That's right.' Rose envisaged, with a surprising degree of relish, the confrontation that lay in store. 'I'm very much looking forward to my chat with Lady Chesterfield.'

The way she said it appeared to frighten the girl. 'You're going to see Lady Chesterfield?' Beth gasped. 'Oh no, ma'am, you ain't takin' me with yer.'

Rose stared at her maid. Beth's normally dull brown eyes gleamed in her sallow face. Fear lent her bovine features rare animation. Like a mirage taking shape and substance, suddenly everything made sense.

For a moment shock rendered her silent. Helena had recruited Beth to help blacken Rose's reputation in her husband's eyes. All the time Beth had pretended to serve her she had in fact been acting for Helena.

Rose's hands shook and she tried to school her features into impassive lines as she sought for a motive.

Why?

Another insidious thought intruded. She'd believed Rampton had sent her away so he could be with Helena. If she'd believed he was being untrue, what other lies must he have been fed to think the same of her?

Oh, God, she thought, shivering with fear and dismay. The sooner she could be at her husband's side the sooner they could sort out this tangled web of lies.

But first she must find Helena.

The carriage bumped uncomfortably over the rutted roads. London would soon be reached. So, too, she desperately hoped, would a reconciliation between her and her husband, once Helena's part in the conspiracy to part Rose from Rampton had been explained. In the meantime she needed to find out from Beth as much as she could. She took a deep breath and strove for icy calm. 'So Lady Chesterfield paid you to place the letter on my dressing-table yesterday morning?'

Beth looked mutinous. 'I ain't saying nuffink.'

'And Lady Chesterfield intends running away with that ne'er do well, Mr Albright?'

'Dunno, ma'am, only I don't want to never see Lady Chesterfield again if she knows that you knows everyfink, now. Please,' begged the girl, 'if you're not going on that boat just take me back to Lord Rampton's 'ouse so I can get me fings and do a runner.'

Rose pounced. 'Lady Chesterfield is not at Bruton Street? Has she gone already?' Fear that Helena might have neatly slipped away without being called to account for the damage she had caused Rose made her grip Beth's arms and shake her. 'Where is Lady Chesterfield going? What do you know of her plans?'

'I dunno, m'lady.' Beth looked close to tears. 'Only that she's bin visiting Mr Albright at a 'ouse in Marylebone. Aitken Street—number nine, I reckon—so you go and sort it out wiv 'er but leave me out of it for I don't know nuffink!'

Before Rose could stop her Beth had thrust open the carriage door and thrown herself on to the road. They were not travelling fast and as Rose pulled back the curtain she saw that the girl had regained her footing without apparent injury and was covering the adjacent corn-field with surprising speed.

CHAPTER 22

R AMPTON CONTEMPLATED THE unsavoury truth. Rose had known what she was about. Just like the necklace she'd pawned, the family heirlooms were valuable stones in unremarkable settings. Having dismissed Fanshawe, Rampton was dressed only in his silk banyan when Arabella and Felix burst in upon the briefest of knocks.

'Most men find more honourable methods of disposing of their wives when they tire of them!'

The angry blaze in his brother's eye was so at odds with his normally placid demeanour that Rampton was momentarily speechless. Felix advanced a few steps and, to Rampton's incredulity, put up his fists, saying, 'If you weren't my brother I'd have no compunction in dropping you this instant!'

'Welcome home, Felix. I'm glad that brotherly love prevails.' To his further surprise, Arabella, who looked pale and wan, appeared fully to endorse Felix's threat of violence. 'Would you mind,' he asked, 'explaining to me the reason for this uncharacteristic, and certainly unwarranted, attack?'

'Unwarranted?' Felix made a noise of disgust. 'Unwarranted? Because my sympathies lie with my sister-in-law rather than my brother?'

Rampton blinked. 'I'd have thought I was particularly deserving of your sympathies at this moment. You are, I assume, aware that my wife has left me?'

It was the first time he had said the words. How remote from reality they sounded.

'Left you! Why, you sent her away with as much compunction as you would discard an old coat that no longer pleased you. Like so many of your mistresses.'

'I would like you to find one of my former mistresses who considers herself discarded in such an uncaring fashion,' Rampton was stung into defending himself. 'But I find the charge as regards my wife a bit rich since she has just run off with Albright ... taking, I might add, a king's ransom's worth of our mother's jewellery.'

He felt only transitory satisfaction at the dismay and confusion that replaced their anger.

'It can't be true!' Arabella was the first to break the silence. 'She has left Larchwood yes, but only because you sent her away. Back to the West Indies!'

'I did no such thing!' Rampton glared at Arabella. 'What else did Rose tell you? That I am an unfeeling, nay, violent husband? That she can no longer tolerate my mistresses? That I have refused her every comfort? Failed to indulge her at every turn?' With superhuman effort he reined in his temper. 'I have not so much as looked at another woman since I married your sister!'

He looked witheringly at each distraught face. 'I wrote a letter sending her away? Show me! She went of her own volition... to be with her lover. Here is the letter she wrote to *me*!' He thrust the crumpled piece of parchment covered in Rose's handwriting at Felix.

'I can't believe it,' Felix said, putting a comforting arm around the now weeping Arabella. 'Albright? They hardly know one another.'

'They never met in the West Indies?' Rampton barked the question at Arabella.

Arabella looked downcast. 'But it was Helena, not Rose, who caught Geoffrey's fancy.'

'How would you know? You were only a child, still in the school-room?'

'I know my sister!' Arabella cried. 'She's incapable of such deception.'

'She deceived me into making her my wife.'

They jumped as the clock in the landing chimed the hour. Rampton went on, 'Are you now going to tell me she has never been seen in Geoffrey Albright's company during the past few weeks? Pray, cast your mind back to Lady Barbery's ball. And Lady Chawdrey's. A little too much champagne punch and she was throwing herself into his arms. If you don't believe me, then *read* it!'

Felix held the letter to the light and murmured Rose's words of shame and regret at her decision to elope with Geoffrey, adding that she was taking nothing from Rampton that was not due to her.

'Nothing, except the family jewels,' muttered Rampton.

Soberly, Felix handed his brother back the letter. 'It doesn't make sense. To everyone else you appeared the love match of the season.'

'It doesn't make sense, because why would Rose tell me she loved her husband, despite the fact he was sending her away?' asked Arabella, fiercely. 'I saw the letter you wrote her.'

'The letter *I* wrote her?' Rampton harrumphed. 'Did you read it?'

Arabella bit her lip as she shook her head. 'Why would Rose lie about that? And I refuse to believe she wrote that letter to you.'

'Well, my dear,' countered Rampton, 'what do you propose? That I saddle Chestnut and ride post haste to the docks to fetch my runaway wife – who has probably already departed – and prove this is all a lie, and that she is somehow the wronged party?'

'Yes!' came the unanimous rejoinder.

'And I shall follow in the carriage!' declared Arabella.

'Before Mother discovers her jewels have gone,' suggested Felix.

A RELENTLESS DRIZZLE MADE THE ROADS SLIPPERY BUT THEY PRESSED on. Not to the docks but to London following information that a carriage had been sighted on the London road, answering the description of the one Rose had taken.

It was not until they reached the first post house, where they procured fresh horses and stopped for a hurried breakfast, that Rampton and Felix were able to exchange a few words.

'That little maid of hers went with her. I'll wager anything it's she who's taken Mother's jewellery,' Felix asserted as the publican's daughter removed the lid from a platter of calf's liver and bacon. 'Probably wrote the letter, too, to hide her part in it. Which she has conveniently taken with her.'

Rampton raised his head from his pot of ale and levelled a long, hard look at his brother. 'You're really championing that sister-in-law of yours, aren't you?'

Felix met his stare, confidently. 'You don't have much faith in your wife, do you? Or her sister, since you don't give much credence to what Arabella says about the state Rose was in when she left.' He shrugged and added between mouthfuls, 'Why, she's mad for you!'

'Then why has she left?'

Felix shrugged. 'A woman used to taking charge of her own life might consider disgrace and ignominy a fair price for her freedom if the alternative were a loveless marriage.'

The knuckles which held Rampton's mug handle turned white. 'A loveless marriage,' he repeated in a whisper and Felix said hurriedly, 'I'm not pretending I know anything about your marriage but—'

'You obviously know nothing about it, otherwise you would sympathize with the number of times I've been deceived.' Waving away the hovering publican's daughter who had made to remove several finished dishes he went on, 'I'm not talking about the kind of love that every greenhorn experiences half a dozen times in his life; I mean the anguish of loving one woman, one's wife... despite everything.'

⁂

'WHAT DO YOU MEAN, SHE WAS SIGHTED ON THE LONDON ROAD?'

Helena swung round, her skirts frothing at her ankles, her high heeled shoes clicking across the floorboards of the shabbily furnished little room as she advanced towards the fireplace. Her voice shook.

Geoffrey snorted. 'I thought it a ridiculous plan in the first place and we couldn't trust that little maid of hers to carry it out properly.' His voice sounded bored, disembodied in the gloom of the wing chair in which he was ensconced. He didn't even look up from the book he was reading; merely puffed on his cigarillo with irritating indifference.

'We needed the attention to be on her rather than on us,' Helena persisted in defence of the letter she had insisted Geoffrey should write, copying Rampton's hand. 'Rose might well have not questioned that it was written by her husband, taken the money and sailed away. By the time Rampton discovers the truth—if he does—we'll be long gone.' She forced a smile. 'And rich.'

'But we'd have been a great deal safer if we'd simply taken the jewels without going to such lengths to blacken your sister-in-law's name into the bargain.' Geoffrey sighed. 'If Rose hasn't gone to the docks then she's coming to London to win back her husband.'

'Not even Rose is that stupid,' Helena spat, going to the window and wiping at the grimy pane for despite her bold words she felt a tendril of discomfort. 'We've covered every contingency.'

'Well, if she's smelled a rat and elicits Rampton's sympathies we're in trouble.' Geoffrey's head appeared from the wing of the chair. 'Jeremiah was to have met Beth at the docks to pay her off but if the girl's taken everything and fled we'll have to cut our losses and head for the coast.'

Helena closed the curtains at the window with a violent tug. 'The coast is where Rose should be at this moment. You're sure Jeremiah knew what he was looking for when he reported that she'd turned south on the London Road? Oh Geoffrey,' she burst out in sudden agitation, 'what can we do when we don't even know where Rose is headed?'

'I daresay we should leave.' Geoffrey rose. He glanced at the shabbily furnished little room and advanced, gripping Helena by the shoulders and pulling her against him. She felt his erection straining against her stomach and, with a grunt of irritation, pushed out of his embrace.

Geoffrey snorted. 'You never had a sense of occasion, did you, Helena?'

'I hardly think now is an appropriate time for what you appear to have in mind, Geoffrey.'

'How do you know what I have in mind?' His hands spanned her neck before he began caressing it, twining his fingers into her hair. Despite her anger, Helena shivered as he touched his lips to her ear.

'You probably mistake the motivation for my desire, also,' he murmured.

She stilled, silent and suddenly afraid as his hands moved over her body, caressing her breasts, moulding her buttocks, while she tried to make sense of his words.

Jerking her against him with sudden violence, his voice held an edge to it she'd not heard before. 'You've accused Rose of lying but you're the worst.'

'I've never lied to you!' She jerked her head up to see him shaking his head.

'All those weeks when I forced myself to withdraw at the pinnacle of the act, only to discover you were barren, Helena, darling,' he rasped.

One hand was upon the back of her head while his other squeezed her buttocks, kneading them roughly.

She tried to use disdain to mask her fear. 'I thought you'd be only too delighted not to be saddled with a brood of brats. We'll enjoy our gains with no complications. Stop it, Geoffrey!'

His hand was hiking up her skirt and she struggled to pull away.

'Not this time, Helena,' he muttered. 'For once I'm in charge.'

Frightened, she ground out, 'I know where everything is hidden. The jewels, the money... You need me—'

'I want a *son!*' His breath rasped in her ear. 'Three stillborn sons my wife has presented me and all these weeks you've pretended that's what we'd have together. A family of boys. We'd start anew. Disappear to the Continent. Does Charles know what you did? Why you've not presented him with the son he, too, longs for? Of course not!'

'If you want to blame anyone, then blame yourself!' Helena gasped, for he was pressing her so hard against the wall she was finding it hard to breathe. Suddenly she was very frightened. 'Everything that happened to me was because of you, Geoffrey!'

'You sent me packing!' he snarled. 'You knew I'd have done anything for you—'

'We had an argument. When I looked for you so I could apologise, you'd gone.'

'You've never apologised to anyone in your life.'

His face, black with anger, was filling her vision. His breath was hot on her skin, moist now from her growing fear. Raising her knee, suddenly, she connected with his groin, wriggling out of his arms as he crumpled to the floor with a howl of agony.

JUST DESSERTS

CHAPTER 23

T HE COLD SWEAT of fear made Rose shiver, despite her warm pelisse, as she looked up at the dark house in the afternoon light.

For five years Rose had lived with Helena's volatile temper. She knew her sister-in-law's capacity for vengeance, her spitefulness and her devious nature, but surely forging the letter purportedly from her husband was worse than anything she'd done before. Now the time had come for Helena to be called to account.

But this house? Is this where Geoffrey lived? She'd not taken him into account.

Rose's nerve nearly failed as the hackney drew to a halt and she heard the jarvey prepare to descend. She closed her eyes while her heart hammered. How would she approach Helena? How would she make her not only confess, but come with her to confess to Rampton?

Her thoughts were interrupted when a panicked voice hissed, 'Rose! I don't believe it, but thank God you've come!'

Before Rose could protest, the carriage door was flung open and Helena had grasped her by the wrist and was hustling her up the steps and indoors, crying, 'Rose, you have to help me!'

In the gloomy passage, Rose took stock. The peeling wallpaper and dust lent the dwelling an unsavoury aspect and she wrinkled her nose at the smell of damp. This was not where Rose had expected to find Helena.

'Beth told you what we'd done, didn't she? Where is she?' Helena's voice was thick with fear. As she put aside the heavy veil of her black bonnet her eyes glittered in the small amount of light that filtered in from outside.

'Gone!' said Rose, harshly, gaining courage from the knowledge Helena had set out to ruin her life. 'And now you're coming with me to tell Rampton that you wrote that letter. I put the pieces together after I realised Beth's involvement and how you must have been using her to spy on me.'

Helena dropped Rose's grasp and stepped backwards with a tinkling laugh. 'You really know nothing, do you?' She sounded incredulous. 'Beth isn't with you?'

In the gloom Helena's rapid breathing indicated her agitation. She sounded as if she were speaking her thoughts aloud. 'No, obviously Beth is cleverer than I thought. Or perhaps it's just that her sense of self-preservation is more well-honed than I'd expected. As for me, if you don't help me get out of this house before Geoffrey returns you may as well prepare my eternity box.'

'Don't be ridiculous!' Rose snapped. 'You're lucky I've said nothing about this or you'd be so mired in scandal you'd never be received again. It's Charles I care about, not you.'

In the dim light Rose saw Helena's mouth drop open. 'You really came alone, Rose, without telling anyone?' Her surprise seemed genuine. Gathering her concealing black shawl more tightly around her, she shook her head. 'You really don't know what people are saying?' she asked, adding under her voice: 'Fortune favours me, after all. Now Rose, I know you don't want me to elope with Geoffrey though you've never thought me good enough for your brother.' Her smile was one that Rose knew well. She waited for the inevitable bargaining or wheedling and was not surprised when Helena said, 'What would you say if I told you I've realized the error of my ways and I need you to help me?'

'Help you!' Rose gave a strangled laugh. 'You're asking for my help after everything you've done to damn me in the eyes of my husband? If you'd had your way I'd be on a boat bound for the West Indies.'

Helena gave a dismissive wave as if this were of no account. 'Rampton would have intercepted you. You know he would have!'

'I don't know anything except you've been telling Rampton lies about me.'

'And when Rampton discovered the truth—which he would have in good time—he'd be so beside himself with remorse for doubting you that you'd want to shower me with gratitude... only I'd be long gone.' Helena laughed again, impulsively pulling Rose to her and saying with apparent sincerity, 'I'm so glad to see you, though. Now that you put it like that, I can't tell you how terribly guilty I feel about what I've done—'

'You don't know what remorse is, Helena! You wrote the letter and you were behind the stolen necklace, too, weren't you?'

'What stolen necklace?'

'Lady Barbery's.' Rose heaved in a breath as Helena dropped her hand. 'You made Rampton think I'd stolen it, didn't you?'

Helena's laugh was spontaneous. 'I thought you were clever enough to deduce the truth of that long ago.' She put her head on one side. 'You really are very credulous, Rose. Surely it was apparent Lady Barbery was behind that? Do you recall when the parcel first arrived addressed to Lady Chesterfield and I naturally assumed it was for me? Do you remember my surprise when you opened it?'

Rose nodded, her suspicions far from allayed.

'Well, I recognised it as Lady Barbery's and of course it made perfect sense that she would act so maliciously since she was Rampton's mistress until you entered the scene. But yes, I suppose I did play on Rampton's suspicions.'

Rose drew herself up. 'So much so that he sent me to Larchfield.'

'Well, you obviously didn't do a very good job defending yourself.'

Rose felt like throttling her. 'I didn't know what I was defending myself *against*. But worst of all was the letter. You forged his hand so that I would believe he was banishing me to the West Indies,' Rose finished, hotly. 'Meanwhile, everything you've done is so that you can run away with Geoffrey, isn't it?' She threw a glance at their insalubrious surroundings and added, 'Though what you think will sustain you both, when Geoffrey is clearly as impecunious as you, I don't know.'

Helena gave a supercilious sniff. 'Geoffrey's gone to fetch a hackney. He'll be returning any moment to pick me up, only the problem is,' she sounded remarkably calm as she went on, 'I've changed my mind about eloping with him since I greatly fear he intends to kill me.'

Rose blinked. Curtailing the heated response she'd intended, she muttered, 'It's a shame you didn't consider his character before you embarked upon this bold and wicked course of action, then, isn't it?'

The blaze in Helena's eyes was at odds with the calm in her voice. 'You think me disloyal and inconstant, but the fact is this isn't the first time Geoffrey's asked me to elope. I refused him when I was seventeen and I've regretted it ever since. Well, until now, that is.'

Rose gripped Helena's shoulders and put her face close. 'Do you know that you will be forever barred from polite society if you go with Geoffrey? Not to mention that Charles will never get over it. Please, Helena, if you've no further wish to associate with Geoffrey then what choice do you have but to return with me to confess to Rampton? Charles would forgive you, for if you come with me now I swear I'll say nothing about Geoffrey.'

The sound of a hackney carriage pulling up in the street outside made Helena gasp and pull away. 'Oh God, I thought I had more time!' She sounded truly panicked. 'Now it's too late! What will we do? Where can we flee? He'll hunt me down.'

'Well, why didn't you think of that before?' Rose muttered, her own palms sweating as for the first time she wondered what involvement Geoffrey had in Helena's plans to discredit her. She felt a tug and turned to see Helena untying the ribbons of her bonnet.

'Rose! Please, change clothes with me. My cloak, my bonnet.' Already she was divesting herself of these garments, forcing them into Rose's resisting hands. 'Nobody wants to kill you, do they? You'll be safe. But hear me out.'

Untying the ribbons of Rose's bonnet and whipping it off her head, she hissed, 'The reason Geoffrey wants to kill me is he believes I betrayed him. We were lovers, you see, only we argued and he left. Yes,

yes, I understand you'll have no great sympathy for me when I tell you that the reason I was so desperate to marry Sir Hector was because I was going to have Geoffrey's child.'

Shock and disgust made Rose drop her hands though she listened as her sister-in-law went on, 'Then I heard you'd said terrible things to Sir Hector to put him off me.' Bitterness overlaid the panic in her voice. 'So I had no choice but to consult Madame Dubrovsky.'

Rose shuddered at the mention of the back-alley abortionist who'd caused the death of many desperate and ignorant women in the neighbourhood.

Almost ripping Rose's cloak from her shoulders, Helena continued, 'After that I could never have children. That's why Charles and I have never...' she shrugged and gave a short laugh, 'been blessed. But over the years I've begun to see it as indeed a blessing. I never...' Her voice broke as she staggered back against the wall and covered her face with her hands. 'I never thought...' she wept, 'that having a child, a son, would mean so much to Geoffrey. I assumed Geoffrey suspected, or even knew the truth, within a short time of us being together but when I revealed everything that had happened...' she took another heaving breath, 'I thought he was going to kill me.'

The sound of Geoffrey's voice telling the jarvey to wait came clearly through the partly opened window. Helena was now dressed in Rose's hat and cloak, but Rose had refused to tie the ribbons of the bonnet Helena had placed on her head.

'Help me, I beg you!' whispered Helena before, to Rose's amazement, she flung herself at her feet to kiss the hem of her skirt. 'If you don't believe me, look at this!' she cried, twisting her head so that for the first time the left side of her face came into full view. A large purple bruise was beginning to form under her eye. On closer inspection Rose saw traces of blood from a small gash.

'You are asking me to go with the man who did that to you?' Rose asked, incredulous, taking Helena's wrist and pulling her to her feet. 'Let us both flee from here!' The last thing Rose wanted was to see Helena jump into a carriage alone with Geoffrey and escape.

'There's no other way out of the house. Geoffrey's barred the door and lower window and he paid a man to guard the back to prevent me getting away. I'm surprised you made it in here at all.' Helena's quick deft fingers tied the ribbons of the thick veiled bonnet beneath Rose's chin and buttoned her cloak. 'All I'm asking is for you to buy me a little time, Rose. If you love your brother like you say you do, you know that preventing me from going with Geoffrey is the greatest service you can render him. Truly, I've repented. Geoffrey's not the man I thought he was and if you go with him now to put him off the scent I promise to confess all to Rampton and be the meek and obliging wife Charles has always wanted... but only if you help me now!'

'You had better be telling the truth, Helena,' Rose muttered as her sister-in-law pushed her towards the door. 'Go to Rampton, now, and tell him everything. I won't be long after you. When Geoffrey realises it's me he's eloping with he'll quickly set me down.'

Geoffrey's low growl from the other side of the door drowned out Helena's reply. The grating sound as he fumbled with the lock echoed the fear that reverberated through Rose, though she was certain she could handle Geoffrey if she had to.

She pulled down the veil as Helena seized her by the wrist, calling out to Geoffrey in a falsely reassuring tone, 'I'm ready, my love.'

Thrusting a small drawstring bag into Rose's hand, she pushed her on to the front step.

IT WAS MID AFTERNOON BY THE TIME RAMPTON ARRIVED AT HIS London townhouse, only to be told that her ladyship was not at home.

Disappointment choked him. He'd allowed himself to be swayed by Felix's determined assurance that this was where Rose would be waiting for him, together with a full accounting of all the misunderstandings and manufactured evidence his brother claimed lay at the heart of their estrangement.

'However, her maid came in a short while ago. When I questioned her she appeared greatly agitated and seemed to have no inkling as to her mistresses's whereabouts. Decidedly odd, my lord, and I'm only telling you since I thought your lordship might be interested.'

'Very interested, Whibble. I want Beth brought to me immediately.'

'Very good, my lord.'

Rampton and Felix were in the library when the girl was delivered, clearly reluctant.

'Found her slipping out the back way, sir, and had to run to apprehend her when she failed to respond to orders.' Whibble looked with distaste at the sullen creature. Her mutinous gaze was fixed upon the floor.

'Where's Lady Rampton and why did you not obey Whibble when he called you?'

When Beth mumbled something about being turned off halfway between Larchfield and London Rampton glanced at his brother. Felix looked smug, as if Beth's answer already exonerated Rose, before interjecting smoothly, 'Really, Beth, I can't believe her ladyship would be so unfeeling as to turn you off in a muddy field, no matter how great her distaste for your company.'

Beth said nothing, though she squirmed when Rampton said, 'You must tell us if there's anything you're owed. Fortunately you were able to collect your things.' He indicated the small bag she carried.

'Yes, sir. If that's all, sir?' Beth clutched more tightly the drawstring bag from which protruded a grubby apron. Felix darted a horrified look at his brother as she sidled towards the door but Rampton had no intention of allowing her to leave yet.

'Just one thing, more, Beth.'

Like a frozen rabbit she hesitated on the threshold. 'Yes, sir?'

'I believe my wife entrusted you with some of her jewellery which may have escaped your attention. Please just ensure it's not in that bag of yours.'

Beth's eyes widened. Slack-jawed she whispered, 'Here?'

'You don't mind, surely?'

She reddened, gripped the door handle, hesitated, then said in strangled tones, "Twere Lady Chesterfield wot said I must take the pieces. I never asked for nuffink only she said she'd slice me throat if I didn't do what she said and I'd be well rewarded if I did. Wot could I do, sir?'

Felix sounded disarmingly sympathetic as he encouraged Beth to elaborate on what else Lady Chesterfield had instructed her to do until his brother cut in.

'You could have informed Lady Rampton of the evil intended her. She'd have rewarded you for seeing to her best interests.' Drily, he added, 'I wonder what else you may have done to further her best interests. Delivered an important letter from me, perhaps?' His tone was at odds with the churning in his breast: the beginnings of a tremendous tide of self recrimination. For the moment, though, he had to remain calm and discover everything he could.

Beth clearly decided she'd had enough. Clasping the bag to her chest she thrust her small frame through the door and bolted down the passageway.

She collided with Whibble, who was bringing refreshment, so it wasn't long before she was back in the library and facing a far less sympathetic hearing.

'I think the most pressing questions we need answered are Lady Rampton's whereabouts and Miss Helena's motive in soliciting your help, Beth.' Rampton looked up from studying the instep of his shoe. 'If you've stolen Lady Rampton's jewellery, Beth,' he went on, acidly, 'you could be looking at the end of a noose. However if you were coerced by somebody you could expect a great deal of leniency.'

Beth dropped the bag, which made a dull thud as it landed at her feet. She looked terrified. 'When Lady Chesterfield told me there were things that she was happy to pay me to keep an eye out for, there seemed no harm in it,' she whispered, staring at the bag. 'Lady Chesterfield wanted to know Lady Rampton's habits and where she liked to go, so what 'arm was there in tellin' her that? 'Twere only at the end when that other gennulman got involved that me nerves started to jitter.'

With a triumphant look at his brother, Felix asked, 'Which gentleman was that?'

'Only met 'im once, and it were enough, handsome and nice though he seemed at first. Don't rightly know 'is real name except that maybe Lady Chesterfield called him Geoffrey once, if I recall rightly. It were 'im wot said if I failed to do me job right and see that Lady Rampton got the letter an' if I didn't get the jewels he'd slice me neck from the rest o' me.' Beth took a step back from the bag and said on a dramatic sob, 'So there you 'ave the truth, me lord. If you don't send me to Newgate it'll be just the same if I meet this other feller.'

Rampton scratched his chin in an attempt to cover the extent of his agitation. How could he have been so blind? God, how utterly he had failed Rose by believing all these manufactured lies about her. Overlaying his remorse was his desperation to find her and beg her forgiveness. She must feel utterly abandoned by him.

But where was she? This was his most pressing question, but when he asked it, Beth's answer was terrifying.

'Gone to Mr Albright's to find Lady Chesterfield and try and make her 'splain to you that it were Lady Chesterfield wot wrote that letter.'

Rampton leapt to his feet. 'Does she not know the danger? Why did she not come here first?' he asked, adding, 'Dammit! She truly believed what was in that letter and didn't have the faith in me to confront me directly.'

'Her ladyship don't know about any of them jewels that were stole or that it were her name put about as though she were a criminal.' Beth sounded as though she was recounting nothing more than a matter of fact. 'I s'pose she thought it safe enough to visit Lady Chesterfield and her gennelmun.'

Felix rephrased Beth's words slowly, as if his brother were an imbecile. 'Rose has no idea of the lengths Helena and Geoffrey have gone to in order to blacken her name?'

'Or to what lengths they are likely to go in order to keep her quiet and the rest of the world ignorant,' muttered Rampton, struck with fresh horror as he contemplated the peril his wife faced.

CHAPTER 24

A UNT ALICE PUT her hands to the lace trimming of her voluminous gown and repeated in accents of horror, 'Helena...? Eloping with Geoffrey Albright? Oh my! Poor Charles!'

'It's Rose I'm worried about.' Arabella strove for calmness, clinging to the newel post in her aunt's lobby and wishing she didn't have to raise her voice about such a sensitive matter since her aunt appeared dumbstruck on the landing a few steps above her. 'Helena has done some very wicked things in Rose's name and is no doubt attempting to flee the country as we speak, but we have no idea where to find Rose.'

'Geoffrey Albright?'

Arabella turned as Oswald sloped into the room. 'Geoffrey Albright?' He repeated the name in disgusted tones.

Arabella was about to make some dismissive remark in the hopes he'd go away when she was struck by his growing fury as he muttered, 'God in Heaven, so she's planned everything in order to elope with *Geoffrey Albright!*'

Arabella stepped back, frightened, as in a blinding flash, it all made sense. How often had she seen her cousin conversing with Helena, usually in dark corners? She'd thought nothing of it at the time but... She drew in a sharp breath. Dear Lord, if Oswald had something to do with the plot in which her sister was mired, he needed to tell them now.

'Cousin Rose is not the only one in danger,' Oswald snarled as he headed towards the door, reluctantly turning as his step-mother cried out, ineffectually, and Arabella pushed in front of him, saying urgently, 'Wait for me! You'll have a much greater chance of getting Geoffrey to talk to you if you take me!'

⚜

THERE WAS NOTHING ROSE COULD DO, IF SHE DID HAVE SECOND thoughts. Pushed out of the door by Helena, Geoffrey quickly hustled her into the hackney and it didn't take long to see he was in a black mood.

Squeezing herself into the corner, she told herself she was in no danger. What could Geoffrey do when he found he'd been duped? He'd hardly hurl Rose through the door to risk death beneath the wheels in the middle of a London street?

'Still angry with me?' Moving forward, he touched her face through the veil. 'Vanity, Helena. Or is this your silent reproach?' His breathing was heavy and his voice filled with emotion. 'Ironic, isn't it?' he went on when he received no response, 'Now that we are on the point of fulfilling our childish dreams we find that the love we once pledged would last forever has leg-shackled us to one another until death. I'm sorry for your accident but you deceived me, Helena. Certainly, your cunning has achieved the wealth that's now to set us up. But,' his voice grew harsher and he leaned forward and gripped her knee, 'had I known that your confidence sprang from the fact you knew there would be no issue from our congress, I'd not have considered it a fair bargain.'

Rose knew the danger in answering, but she croaked, 'Your wife—'

He snorted with derision. 'I've been trying to sire an heir on Daisy for six years! But you, Helena, are so clever. Stupidly, I assumed you'd avoided producing an heir by that milksop husband through intent.'

Rose felt the anger rise on her brother's behalf and prayed for some opportunity she could seize for flight, as Beth had done hours earlier.

Helena had not been lying when she said she feared Geoffrey. Oh, dear Lord, how had she allowed herself to be here and what good would it achieve?

'For God's sake, Helena, answer me!' Lunging forward, he grasped her forearms. 'Don't you realize we're tied to one another, more surely than if we were married? We have thieved and deceived... you have blackened your sister-in-law in the eyes of her husband to achieve all this. If we are caught we face the noose for our misdemeanours.'

Rose gasped, struggling in his grip as his hands felt their way insinuatingly over her body.

'My God,' he whispered, drawing back in shock before reaching over and wrenching the hat and veil from her head. 'Lady Rampton!' Cupping her chin he dragged her face to within an inch of his, which was black with rage.

Rose flinched, fearing he was going to strike her.

'What the devil? Where's Helena?' His voice was a terrifying whisper. Before she could reply he pounced on the bag at her feet and snatched it up, fumbling with the drawstring.

The discovery of its contents did nothing to improve his temper. With a blood-curdling howl he dashed it against the window and turned on Rose.

'Rocks, by God!' he screamed. 'So you were a party to Helena's deception all the time!' He shook her so hard her brain rattled. 'Where is she? Are you both so stupid you thought you could hoodwink me? Did you plan to jump out of the carriage before I discovered?'

Rose cowered into the corner while the old carriage rocked and lumbered over the uneven cobblestones. She whispered, 'I knew nothing until I arrived at the house less than half an hour ago and Helena pushed me out of the front door so that she could escape because you'd hit her.'

'Innocent Rose,' he sneered. 'Doing what was best to help Helena. Why come to my house if you were looking for an ally?'

'Beth said you and Helena were eloping.' Rose clasped her hands to stop them trembling. 'That's all I knew. I was suspicious about the letter and wanted the truth from Helena.'

'Where is Beth?'

'She jumped out of the carriage before I reached your house.'

Geoffrey let out a crack of laughter. Shaking his head at Rose he muttered, 'Aren't we the fools in this madcap charade for allowing Helena to manipulate us into achieving exactly what she wants, while we wear the consequences? It's a good thing you're not Helena at this moment for I can't answer for what I'd do to you.'

Rose drew in her breath on a sob. Slowly she tried to reach for the door handle but Geoffrey dashed it away.

'Not so fast, Lady Rampton. You've not yet paid your dues.' He chuckled. 'You're going to help me find some valuable trinkets that are going to fund my escape – and retirement – and hopefully my revenge.'

Rose bit her lip. In the last couple of minutes she'd realised there was far more going on than she'd understood before she'd blithely confronted Helena. Clearly Helena and Geoffrey were complicit in some dangerous game involving thievery and who knows what other skulduggery. And now she was alone in a carriage with a vengeful Geoffrey Albright who'd never liked her.

'What have you done?' she whispered.

After a considered look, he said, 'You do know that Beth stole a quantity of jewellery from Rampton's mother's dressing—room to coincide with your departure?'

Rose stifled the gasp that would only amuse Geoffrey as he went on, 'And that she sewed Lady Chawdrey's missing diamond necklace into the lining of the gown you obligingly pawned on her behalf so that when Rampton redeemed it he had overwhelming proof of your thievery and deception?'

This time Rose did gasp. 'Helena cannot get away with this! I went to your house to find her so she'd confess to Rampton that she'd written that letter.'

'Actually, I wrote that letter, and the one he received purportedly from you, but I confess, I was not happy about doing it.'

'A letter from *me*? Why did you do it?' Rose challenged.

Geoffrey pushed back his carefully coiffed curls. His nostrils flared. 'To make Helena happy. She was determined to have her little revenge upon you for wrecking her liaison with Sir Hector after I'd sailed out of her life not weeks before.'

Rose, who had been slumped against the window, jerked upright in anger. 'Would she see me hang?' she hissed. Shaking her head, she added, 'Sir Hector saw through her from the start. It's a pity Charles never did.'

'Or you,' Geoffrey added. 'Come to that, neither did I.' He seemed to rally. 'It's time to find Helena and I think I know where she's headed for all she was so cunning in trying to keep her own little insurance policy secret from me.'

'I want to find my husband first.'

Geoffrey shook his head. 'Rampton can wait. We must reach Hampstead Heath before Helena slips out of the country, laughing, while you and I contemplate the hangman's noose.'

***

RAMPTON BALKED AT THE UNAPPETIZING SMELL OF BOILED CABBAGE though it wasn't that which accounted for the nausea which made him clap his handkerchief to his nose.

Droplets of blood beneath the mantelpiece attested to the violence perpetrated in Geoffrey's house, as did a damp, blood-stained handkerchief, not yet dry.

'Where would they have taken her?' Felix asked, looking blankly at his brother.

'God only knows,' snapped Rampton, crouching to pick up Rose's bonnet, squashed and battered, from the floor by the sofa. What a fool he'd been. Rose's guilt had seemed incontrovertible, yet he had been duped. And not just once. He considered himself an intelligent man yet he'd blindly accepted what was presented to him. Now, as he took in the dank, gloomy house he gathered Geoffrey had leased for his romantic trysts with Helena, he cursed himself for a fool. He put the blood-stained handkerchief to his cheek. Rose's blood? Had she been injured? Remorse and pain tore through him. If Rose had been harmed he would never forgive himself.

He opened his mouth to speak then stilled as Felix raised his hand for silence. A stealthy tread sounded in the passageway. Rampton straightened and slid into the shadows as the doorknob turned, and the door opened slowly.

A figure appeared upon the threshold. Seizing his arm and twisting it up behind his back, Rampton thrust him into the room while Felix leapt from behind.

Arabella, following in the wake of the now apprehended Oswald, screamed before letting out her breath in a relieved gasp. 'Rampton! Have you found Rose?'

'I'm more interested in whether you've found Helena,' growled Oswald, casting a black look at Rampton as he rubbed his mauled arm.

Rampton regarded him contemptuously while waiting for his heart rate to steady. He'd been ready to give Geoffrey Albright everything he deserved. 'Helena seems to have acquired a multitude of enemies for good reason, but at this moment my wife's safety is of greatest concern.'

Oswald exhaled on a hiss. 'Arabella tells me Helena formed an inappropriate alliance with your neighbour, Albright, six years ago in the West Indies. Now they have vanished with more than four thousand pounds worth of the baubles I was foolish enough to be inveigled into procuring for Helena. Do you think I'm more concerned for your wife, or for my neck?'

Rampton contemplated the slimy character. 'So your role was in the thefts and placing the evidence so it implicated Rose. What else are you guilty of? Forging those letters?'

The righteous anger in Oswald's eyes pierced the gloom. 'I know nothing of any letters,' he muttered as his gaze traversed the room. With quivering nostrils, he suggested, 'Forged letters are a useful device for facilitating a lovers' flight, are they not? Well, Helena's not going to get away with her evil deeds. I have as much to charge her with as you do, my lord.' He laughed, a bitter sound though tinged with pride. 'Ah, but it was devious. She was devious. Helena, that is. A woman after my own heart and now she's *gone*. Gone with that scoundrel, Geoffrey who just sat back, waiting to reap the rewards of *my* labour.'

Rampton wished he did not have to ask the question that painted him as the credulous fool he so keenly felt himself at that moment.

When he was reunited with his darling girl he'd make it clear he'd spend the rest of his days atoning for his lack of faith. Fear sliced through these thoughts. He had to find her first.

'Tell me what Helena did for her ill-gotten gains. It might help piece together where Rose actually is.'

Oswald chuckled. 'The clothes Rose pawned on Helena's behalf...? Rose did not know Lady Chawdrey's necklace was sewn into the lining. The pawnbroker was paid handsomely for his well-rehearsed act.'

Arabella rushed forward to shake Oswald, crying, 'How have you the effrontery to confess such crimes which could send you to Newgate, Cousin Oswald?'

He put her away from him and Felix moved in, smoothly, to hold her against his side.

Oswald glared. 'Only Helena could send me there for only she knows the energies I expended on her behalf.' His cocky banter was replaced by a menacing energy. 'She has all the fruits of my labours and my only reward is telling you just how black her heart really is.'

Impatiently, Rampton moved to the door. 'I'm more concerned with Rose's safety than Helena's black heart. Where in God's name could she be?'

'Have you asked that little maid of hers?'

'Beth is locked up at Bruton Street,' muttered Rampton, shoving the tell-tale blood-stained handkerchief into his pocket. 'She'd have told us anything to lessen the sentence she's facing.' He opened the door but Felix blocked his way, saying with sudden excitement, 'Not if she knows other secrets and there were any chance of escape. Remember, Beth was in league with Helena. Helena used many avenues to gain the funds she needed—'

'Poor Charles doesn't even know she's gone!' interrupted Arabella. 'We must return to the house to tell him, gently.'

'We must return to the house,' said Rampton, pursuing his brother's line of thought, 'to discover from Beth what it is she has neglected to tell us.'

ROSE STRUGGLED TO KEEP UP THE RELENTLESS PACE GEOFFREY HAD set. The length of cord that attached her wrist to his waist chafed painfully.

Her energy was flagging and her slippers were wet through and torn. 'You can't have trusted each other very much,' she managed between gasps as they toiled through a thicket of gorse, 'if Helena hid from you the ill-gotten gains that were supposed to buy your freedom.'

She felt the chill through to her bones and glanced fearfully at her surroundings, deserted in the gathering twilight. What was Geoffrey planning? She'd felt frightened in the carriage but had believed she would be freed eventually. Geoffrey had no use for her, after all, she'd reassured herself. He'd be leaving England on the next packet. He had no choice but to flee, but he'd not harm Rose, surely?

But then he'd bound her wrists with rope and dragged her out of the carriage to this deserted expanse of countryside.

'I could say we trusted each other about as much as Rampton trusted you after you deceived him into marriage,' muttered Geoffrey.

Rose turned her head from his unkind grin as he went on, 'Desire and trust don't go hand in hand, surely you know that? Cousin Oswald was thieving for Helena on both our accounts, though of course Oswald didn't know it. If it made Helena feel safer to store some of the booty where no one would find it, why should I care when what we each know binds us to one another as surely as marriage binds man and wife?'

Pausing to catch their breaths in a clearing, Rose glanced at Geoffrey's hard profile. She supposed some would consider him a handsome man but loose living was taking its toll while Helena, ten years his junior, was still an exquisite creature.

Bitterly Rose contemplated how easily Helena had persuaded her to go with Geoffrey so that she could skip away, free from the men who desired and had thieved for her, while she claimed the booty.

Would Helena seek greener pastures with the jewels Geoffrey was convinced she'd hidden somewhere near by? Choking down her rage at the sister-in-law who'd gone to such lengths to ruin her life, she whispered, 'If you find her, what will you do?'

'I shall remind Helena that she needs my protection.' Geoffrey's look was ugly.

'When my husband finds *me* all the wickedness you and Helena perpetrated in my name will be revealed.'

'Which is why you're such a threat, my dear Lady Rampton," growled Geoffrey, swinging round, 'since we need time to leave this country without you revealing all.'

Cursing her stupid bravado as Geoffrey gripped her chin and tilted her face upwards, Rose gulped, 'I'll keep your secret.' She was shaking so much she could barely get the words out. Geoffrey was volatile. She knew him only enough to be certain he'd have little compunction in doing what was required to save his own skin.

'You'll have to, but the only way to ensure that,' said Geoffrey, contouring her face without tenderness, before tapping her nose lightly as if she were a child, 'is to bind you securely to a tree in the midst of the thicket we've just come through and leave a note which, we must hope, will be delivered at the appropriate time.' His lip curled. 'While I have no particular wish to see harm come to you, my safety is more important to me than yours.'

Panicked, she glanced at the trees and thick gorse behind them. How would anyone ever find her, if Geoffrey bound her as he threatened? Rampton would believe she'd left him. Why should he send out a search party, much less look for her here? With Geoffrey and Helena neatly executing their evil plot he would forever think her guilty of their crimes.

Weakly, she began, 'Rampton will—' but Geoffrey cut her off. 'Rampton believes you a liar and a thief, my dear.' He stroked her hair. 'You're a pretty thing that caught his fancy but your allure quickly palled when he discovered the depths of your wicked soul.' He laughed. 'Poor Rose. Even Dr Horne innocently gave credence to Helena's diagnosis of your illness of the mind... of the lapses, where a pretty jewel was too hard to resist and telling the truth beyond your capacity.'

Rose sucked in her breath sharply and twisted her head away from his loathsome touch. Dear Lord, what had they *not* stooped to? And at her expense. She'd had no idea Helena hated her quite so much. All these years she must have bottled it up, waiting for a chance to have her wicked revenge on the sister-in-law she held responsible for her own blighted happiness.

Her breath misted in front of her. A bird startled into flight made her cry out but there was not another soul upon the heath to hear her. In the faint mist the trees looked like ghostly spectres of doom. If Geoffrey bound her leaving her helpless in such a remote spot, Rampton might never learn the truth. The forlorn desperation that her life not be cut short here was like a flickering flame, faint but strong enough to sustain her; but more than her safety, Rose wanted her husband to believe in her honesty.

She felt the rope tug as Geoffrey turned back to the thicket but she stood her ground. New strength surged through her. She'd not give in without a fight. Someone might help her. Someone could possibly be round the next tree, out of sight. Opening her mouth, she was about to utter a shriek when, from the corner of her eye a slight movement caught her attention. She drew in her breath, hope giving her the strength to remain calm as she extended her arm and pointed down the hill.

'I think,' she managed crisply, 'you might want to attend to other matters, first.'

She watched the play of emotions cross Geoffrey's face as he looked in the direction she indicated.

In the far distance, near a copse of trees, Helena was wielding a large shovel with surprising expertise. A small pile of dirt rose from beside the hole she was creating.

Geoffrey measured his response. 'How observant, Lady Rampton, though congratulations are due to me, also, for my hunch has paid off. You see, I followed her one night after a particularly heated argument.' He pushed back his handsome curls from his sweating forehead, his delight apparent as he added, 'Let's discover Helena's intentions and who's included in her little plan, shall we?'

Stealthily, Geoffrey bore Rose along with him as he descended the hill, approaching Helena from behind. The pain from Rose's cold, torn feet was nothing compared with her fears for her own future. Helena was ruthless. Rose doubted she'd countenance anything that might jeopardize her escape with the jewels.

And Rose was the greatest threat of all.

Above the horizon Rose could see the moon, as if caught in the tree tops. Soon darkness would be upon them. Geoffrey and Helena would have their booty and Rose would be the inconvenient witness. She drew in a shuddering breath and cast about for some means of escape as Geoffrey bore her relentlessly onwards.

'Not a word,' he hissed, 'or you'll be sorry.'

Rose wasn't about to do anything to try his already ragged temper. Obediently she followed, despite her fear and the pain of every footstep. In the distance she could see Helena, the folds of her coquelicot pelisse spread about her as she knelt with their back to them.

Stealthily they continued, halting a few feet away. Geoffrey regarded his erstwhile lover with a mixture of amusement and anger and Rose stiffened in anticipation of the response as Geoffrey's clipped tones sheared the silence. 'Well, prepared, as ever, my love, and just in time to make the evening's tide.'

It was clear that Helena had not expected to see him. Stifling her gasp as she swung round, she assumed the air of having intended Geoffrey to be a party to her escape plan as she straightened, indicating Rose and saying, 'What possessed you to bring her along? Couldn't you have dispatched her?'

Geoffrey shrugged. 'Couldn't find an opportunity. I thought we could tie her up hidden in the trees so we'd be unhindered.'

Helena's small white teeth glinted in a parody of a smile. She put her head to one side, as if contemplating the matter and with sinking heart, Rose knew that in Helena's mind there was nothing to contemplate. Helena would go to almost any lengths to ensure her silence, for Helena's crimes were sufficient to send her to Newgate.

Gulping down her terror Rose squared her shoulders and said with an assurance she was far from feeling, 'Rampton will come before you can harm me.' In truth, Rampton had never felt further from her.

'Rampton! Little loyalty he's shown you when you were mad for him from the start, which is so unlike you, my dear.' With a toss of her head, Helena sliced the shovel she'd retrieved from a clump of bushes into the damp earth as she went on, 'Now you're learning what pain really is; the pain of separation and of love gone wrong. I hope you're suffering!'

She looked beautiful, her dark eyes glittering with a mixture of malice and self pity, her raven hair half tumbling from its coiffure. Rose could understand Geoffrey's enslavement. She'd lived with Charles and Helena long enough to have observed the pattern Helena used to exert her power. It had been like living with an unrelenting tide of cloying sweetness interspersed with cutting scorn and wheedling requests.

'Not as much as you will be when Rampton learns of your villainy and that I was never once untrue,' Rose bit back, trying to block from her mind the very great threat that she faced. Her heart cried out to Rampton. He'd been so cold the last few times she'd seen him but if he only knew the truth, would he not love her again?

Memories of the closeness they'd shared descended upon her like a comforting caress before the chill of fear tore away the warmth.

'So confident, Rose, but I'm always one step ahead. Granted, Rampton may learn of my villainy if I have not time to dispose properly of your remains, but when he does it will be too late.' She swung round to Geoffrey, her voice hard. 'We must get rid of her.'

It was small consolation that Geoffrey visibly blanched. 'Theft is one thing, Helena, but murder—'

'Both carry a death sentence.'

Rose closed her eyes as she forced strength into her legs to prevent them buckling. Geoffrey's arguments would carry no weight when Helena was the stronger force.

'Tie me to a tree,' pleaded Rose. 'You only need a few hours before you're on a boat bound for France. No one will find you. You'll have all the money you need.'

Helena drew herself up like a cobra about to strike. 'For as long as I can remember, Rose, you've been my nemesis, for all that I've been the daring one, the beautiful one.'

Rose flinched at the venom in her hissed judgement, blinking with disbelief as Helena went on, 'You hated me enough to condemn me to the worst fate imaginable, damning me in Sir Hector's eyes after Geoffrey left me.'

'Leave it, Helena!' The note of warning in Geoffrey's voice gave

Rose hope. He was just behind her and though he was not about to release her, Rose knew he could at least see reason. 'We had a bitter fight, if you recall, and you told me never to show my face again. You have only yourself to blame.'

Helena dismissed this with a snort of derision before warming to her theme of highlighting Rose's role in her own downfall. 'Because of you, Rose, I was forced to marry Charles. Charles!' She spat her husband's name with more hatred than Rose had ever heard. 'He had not the means to support a wife when he could barely feed his sisters, but did you warn me?' Helena's grip on the shovel tightened while her eyes narrowed. 'Even when you were dowdy Miss Chesterfield in your drab clothes with your hair pulled back I heard the men whisper their interest, but you were too stupid to see how you could benefit us all. Why should I show you any clemency when your inaction ensured that we all remained stuck on that island, condemned to a poverty-stricken existence? When I was destined for so much more?'

'You blame me for all that?' Rose gasped. 'So much so that you would see me die?'

'It's what you deserve for killing *my* hopes and dreams!' Helena's voice rose as she took a step back, readying herself. Poison and vitriol radiated from every pore as she raised the shovel, its steel edge as well-honed as a fine blade, deadly and merciless when wielded with the force of so much hatred.

Rose jerked back but the ropes that bound her hands tautened as Geoffrey pulled her in the other direction. To save her? Or better position her? She was imprisoned regardless as her vision wavered and her legs buckled, the sound of fear thundering in her ears.

So this was how it would end. Here, in a remote part of Hampstead Heath with her grave already half-dug. A great sob rose in her throat and she tensed in anticipation of the blow, closing her eyes to Helena's face, twisted with malice, as the blade, sharp and deadly, swished through the air in line with her neck. Her shriek seemed not to come from her as her mind raced through all that had led to this: Helena's determination that Rose should pay for her perceived sins by sacrificing her happiness, and when that was not enough, her life.

There was not even the consolation that Rampton knew the truth;

that Rose was blameless in all but assuming the role of a married woman. For that, though, he had long ago forgiven her.

Helena and Geoffrey were about to make off with the family jewels, which Rampton and the rest of the world assumed she had stolen. Not only was she now condemned to death, she was condemned to being a party to a multitude of crimes of which she was innocent yet Rampton would forever consider her a thief and a sinner. The fear thundered in her ears like cannon-fire.

'No!'

All the desperation and despair at the injustice of such a brutal, heinous act resonated from the one word. The anguished plea for clemency echoed in the void left by the flight of rational thought as she was reduced to a cornered animal facing slaughter. She didn't want to die. Where was Rampton? Where was her husband? He'd forsaken her, believing every vile lie that had been disseminated yet she still loved him. Perhaps if he knew the truth he'd love her too.

'No!'

The cry continued to resonate in the chill evening air, its desperate hollow timbre sounding eerily like it belonged to a creature from another world. Going to another world, she thought as she was pushed to the ground, the air knocked from her lungs, her last conscious thought that she'd accept even a loveless existence only life was too precious to be condemned to eternity with a reputation she didn't deserve burnt into the memories of all those who spoke her name.

Shock, blackness. She thought she was dead. She thought she was still screaming but she was trapped beneath a body in a coquelicot gown and the scream had taken on a different dimension: shrieks of pain interspersed with disbelieving howls of rage.

Choking on the acrid smell of gunpowder, Rose struggled beneath the weight of a body slumped over her own.

Helena?

'In God's name!'

She turned her bewildered face to Geoffrey, raising her hands to see them sticky with blood. Not hers? Geoffrey must have....

But Geoffrey's face was a mask of horror as he bent over Rose to reach Helena now writhing beside her. Helena had uttered the cry. It came in staccato gasps of horror as she held her hands to her wounded head.

'What has happened to me?' Her hysteria grew as her bloodied hands revealed part of the answer.

'Rose!'

A masculine voice sounded from a short distance away. Familiar and comforting. Filled with heartfelt emotion.

Rose transferred her shocked gaze from the grisly sight of Helena's mutilated face, to the direction in which Geoffrey now stared as he stood up, rapidly fumbling with the knot that bound him to Rose; preparing for his own flight though Rose in that moment had eyes only for her husband.

And all the fear, shock and horror of the past few hours was replaced by joy at seeing him bounding down the hill, tucking his pistol inside his coat before opening his arms to claim his wife.

CHAPTER 25

ROSE AWOKE TO the sounds of birds singing and a lively chorus of frogs and insects. Stretching luxuriously on the blanket her husband had laid out for their picnic beside the river, she rolled against his side. Although she could not see his face she knew he still slept. His breathing was deep and even, yet even in sleep, in the middle of an innocent afternoon, he held her as though he'd never let her go. As he had every night since he'd eliminated the greatest threat to Rose's health and happiness. It was as if he couldn't keep her close enough.

Tremors of comforting warmth crept over her as he stirred, turning to stroke her hair.

'It'll be the last time we can do this,' she murmured, gazing at the hazy blue sky, conscious that the season was changing and their long rambles by the riverside would come to an end. Rampton, too, would inevitably become less attached to her as familiarity reduced the novelty of their reborn love, she acknowledged in the deepest recesses of her mind.

'What do you mean *the last time?*'

He was awake now. Leaning over her so he could look into her face he demanded, 'How can you say anything will be "for the last time"? '

His voice was a low, demanding growl while his hands caressed the contours of her cheeks, nose and eyes as if committing them to memory. 'Has everything we've been through not proved how tenuous happiness is... how careful we must be to safeguard it?' His breathing was heavy, as if he'd been offended by her suggestion.

'I was talking about the weather making this sort of thing no longer possible.' Rose laughed and reached up to kiss him, pulling him back down beside her. She felt him relax with a slow, satisfied sigh as they both stared up at the sky, holding hands like the lovers they were.

There was gentle amusement in his voice overlaid with conviction as he warmed to his theme. 'If we feel like trysting amidst the pouring rain, we should do it. Time is too short to allow convention to prevent us squeezing every last drop of enjoyment from life.'

Bringing his hand to her cheek, Rose sighed. 'That was obviously Helena's philosophy, but look where it landed her.'

With great reluctance Rampton helped her to her feet. 'Exactly where she deserves,' he said, plucking the leaves from Rose's hair before wrapping his arms about her from behind. 'And she should consider herself lucky to escape the hangman's noose.'

'I'm not sure that life with Charles in the West Indies bearing those terrible scars would have been her preferred option.' Rose shivered, remembering the horror of seeing the blade slice the air in line with her neck.

'It was your life, or Helena's,' he reminded her as he began to wind her hair back into some semblance of respectability. 'Thank God Beth was induced to reveal the exact point where Helena had buried the jewels, and that I got there in time though a pistol was the last weapon I'd have chosen to use.'

'Because of the damage you've caused Helena?'

'Because of its lack of accuracy. I had only to trust to the fates to save you when I had no other avenue open to me. Now, stay still.' As he laced her gown, Rose was aware of his shudder as he performed the task of her lady's maid. Briefly he pressed his cheek to the hollow between her shoulder and cheek. 'I don't know how I could have lived with myself if something had happened to you, my darling.'

Hearing the catch in his voice, Rose reached up her arm to caress his soft, springy curls and closed her eyes. This was by no means the first of such avowals but they still had the power to stir her in ways she'd not believed possible. How sweet love was. And she and Rampton had a lifetime together in which to enjoy it.

Edith now fulfilled Beth's role, except when Rose and Rampton slipped away for afternoon pleasure jaunts like this one. It seemed they could not get enough of one another.

She thought he'd straighten and resume the task at hand which was to prepare themselves to return to Larchfield for the vicar's visit, which the dowager had organised. Instead, shivers of longing radiated through her as his soft murmur tickled her cheek. 'You think it won't always be like this?' The gentle pressure of his hand, which had grasped one of hers, increased. 'It won't, my darling, I promise you. It will only get better. I shall only grow to love you more. You must believe it.'

Rose turned in his embrace and twined her arms about his neck. She stared into his face. 'Then I will believe it,' she whispered, with a surge of that now-familiar emotion, joy. 'I'm sorry Charles could not have found similar happiness.' She thought of him with sadness, bearing his grievously disfigured wife back to their island home aboard the *The Emily*.

'If Charles had shown her a firm hand from the outset, I doubt her behaviour would have got so out of hand.'

Rose ignored the criticism. 'Poor Charles. He'll forgive Helena anything. But it will be a life sentence for Helena.'

Rampton's arms tightened about her and she saw the fervour in his eyes as they locked gazes. 'My life sentence is one I have yet to earn, my sweeting.' Briefly, he caressed her cheek, his look tinged with remorse. 'I needed forgiveness for believing what was offered to me as irrefutable proof... though I wasn't sure whether you would grant it to me.' He sent her a meaningful look and Rose blushed. She could not deny the thrill of power she had felt when Rampton had gone down on bended knee and kissed the hem of her skirt, pledging his love and begging her forgiveness while Helena lay screaming in Geoffrey's arms. For all his faults, Geoffrey had not left her, although that was probably more due to the fact he'd been unable to slip the cord that bound him to Rose before Rampton had arrived.

Of course Rose had given her forgiveness without reserve. She knew that her husband, having already been deceived by Rose, was not to know she was blameless when all the evidence pointed to her.

They strolled back in leisurely fashion to Larchfield, pausing at the edge of the park to gaze at the beautiful stone house with its mullioned windows peeping through its cloak of ivy as the sun dipped behind the hill.

A nightingale began its evening tune and Rose shivered with pleasure.

Rampton squeezed her hand. 'Mother has offered you her diamond and ruby choker to wear to Felix and Arabella's wedding.' There was amusement in his tone, for Rose had declared that her mother-in-law would never fully trust her until Rose had supplied the nursery with at least half a dozen sons. 'Perhaps you should wear it when you pay your last respects to Geoffrey and Oswald in prison.'

Rose shuddered. 'I never want to see Geoffrey Albright again. The person I feel saddest for is Aunt Alice.'

Rampton's response was robust. 'Aunt Alice has never slept so peacefully since Oswald was incarcerated. She told me so.'

As Rose's mouth dropped open Rampton seized the advantage, stooping to brush her lips with his own. As always the familiar sensations of earthy satisfaction and all-consuming happiness swamped Rose as her wonderful husband murmured, 'I'd say we've all been given our just rewards. Wouldn't you?'

THE END

I really hope you enjoyed reading the three books that make up **Scandalous.** If you want to know about new releases or specials, here are some ways to stay connected:

- Join my newsletter and get a free book here: https://dl.bookfunnel.com/pvokkjfp2z
- Like me on Facebook here.
- Follow me on BookBub here.
- Visit my Website here.

And if you have a moment, you can help other romance readers by telling them why you enjoyed reading in just a few words. I'd be so delighted if you considered leaving a review.

OTHER BOOKS BY THE AUTHOR

Do you enjoy intrigue-filled romances with unexpected plot twists?

Beverley Oakley's **Daughters of Sin** series follows the intertwining lives and sibling rivalry of Lord Partington's two nobly born - and two illegitimate - daughters as they compete for love during several London Seasons.

With Hetty and Araminta both falling for men on opposing sides of a dastardly plot that is being investigated by Stephen Cranborne, a secret agent in the Foreign Office, there's lashings of skullduggery and intrigue bound up in the central romance.

What Readers are Saying About the Series:

"...lies, misdeeds, treachery, and romance. What an impressive story! Ms. Oakley has a unique way of telling her stories, bringing unknown heroes/ heroines into the spotlight, as they navigate a world of espionage, and intrigue, all while trying to survive and find their HEA. Magnificent and mesmerizing!" ~ **Amazon reader**

"Oh my! What a great read. The characters were extraordinary and believable. I couldn't put it down..."

"This is a good story of misalignments and couples trying to make the best of bad situations. Twists and turns abound as this impossible romance blossoms and you really cheer for this couple as things work themselves out."

"It's refreshing to read a Regency that doesn't remind me of others, and I found the heroine to be very relatable. It's also nice to get an older female lead, and I really enjoyed the family dynamics."

"Talk about risqué! Keep the fans close to cool you off. A tale of lust and love that is sure to curl your toes."

Books in the Series...

Book 1: Her Gilded Prison
Book 2: Dangerous Gentlemen
Book 3: The Mysterious Governess
Book 4: Beyond Rubies
Book 5: Lady Unveiled-The Cuckold Conspiracy
Below is the order of the books:
Book 1: Her Gilded Prison
Book 2: Dangerous Gentlemen
Book 3: The Mysterious Governess
Book 4: Beyond Rubies
Book 5: Lady Unveiled: The Cuckold Conspiracy

You can get the first three stories in the Daughters of Sin Box Set

Or the entire Box Set.

ABOUT THE AUTHOR

Beverley Oakley is an Australian author who grew up in the African mountain kingdom of Lesotho, married a Norwegian bush pilot she met in Botswana's Okavango Delta, and started writing historical romances to amuse herself in the 12 countries she's lived as a 'trailing spouse' (in between working as an airborne geophysical survey operator, a teacher of English as a Second Language, and writing for her former newspaper).

Her *Scandalous Miss Brightwell* series was nominated **Best Historical Romance** by the *Australian Romance Readers Association*. She is also the author of the popular *Daughters of Sin* series, a Regency-era 'Dynasty-style' family saga laced with scandal and intrigue.

Under her real name Beverley Eikli, she writes Africa-set romantic suspense, and psychological historical romances. *The Reluctant Bride* won Choc-Lit's **Search for an Australian Star** competition which provided the Australian launch of her UK publisher, while her Regency tale of redemption *The Maid of Milan* was shortlisted in the *Top Ten Reads of 2014* at the **UK Festival of Romance**.

Beverley lives north of Melbourne (overlooking a fabulous Gothic lunatic asylum) with the same gorgeous Norwegian husband, two daughters and a rambunctious Rhodesian Ridgeback.

You can read more at www.beverleyoakley.com

Please get in touch here:
www.beverleyoakley.com
beverley.oakley@gmail.com

www.ingramcontent.com/pod-product-compliance
Lightning Source LLC
Chambersburg PA
CBHW021927110726
47901CB00003B/739